T0004394

# ALSO BY ANNE BISHOP

# THE QUEEN'S WEAPONS

A BLACK JEWELS NOVEL

## Anne Bishop

ACE
New York

ACE
Published by Berkley
An imprint of Penguin Random House LLC
penguinrandomhouse.com

ISBN: 9781984806666

Ace hardcover edition / March 2021
Ace mass-market edition / February 2022

Printed in the United States of America
1   3   5   7   9   10   8   6   4   2

Book design by Alison Cnockaert

*For Merri Lee and Michael*

# JEWELS

WHITE
YELLOW
TIGER EYE
ROSE
SUMMER-SKY
PURPLE DUSK
OPAL*
GREEN
SAPPHIRE
RED
GRAY
EBON-GRAY
BLACK

*Opal is the dividing line between lighter and darker Jewels because it can be either.

When making the Offering to the Darkness, a person can descend a maximum of three ranks from his/her Birthright Jewel.

Example: Birthright White could descend to Rose.

Note: The "Sc" in the names Scelt and Sceltie is pronounced "Sh."

# BLOOD HIERARCHY / CASTES

## Males

**landen**—non-Blood of any race

**Blood male**—a general term for all males of the Blood; also refers to any Blood male who doesn't wear Jewels

**Warlord**—a Jeweled male equal in status to a witch

**Prince**—a Jeweled male equal in status to a Priestess or a Healer

**Warlord Prince**—a dangerous, extremely aggressive Jeweled male; in status, slightly lower than a Queen

## Females

**landen**—non-Blood of any race

**Blood female**—a general term for all females of the Blood; mostly refers to any Blood female who doesn't wear Jewels

**witch**—a Blood female who wears Jewels but isn't one of the other hierarchical levels; also refers to any Jeweled female

**Healer**—a witch who heals physical wounds and illnesses; equal in status to a Priestess or a Prince

**Priestess**—a witch who cares for altars, sanctuaries, and Dark Altars; witnesses handfasts and marriages; performs offerings; equal in status to a Healer or a Prince

**Black Widow**—a witch who heals the mind; weaves the tangled webs of dreams and visions; is trained in illusions and poisons

**Queen**—a witch who rules the Blood; is considered to be the land's heart and the Blood's moral center; as such, she is the focal point of their society

# PROLOGUE

———◈———

Tersa drooped on the stool in front of her worktable. Her brown hands trembled as she pushed her tangled black hair away from her face. Her gold eyes, dulled by fatigue, stared at the latest tangled web of dreams and visions that she had woven in an effort to understand the uneasiness that kept scratching at her. It would go away for days, sometimes weeks, and then it would return. Scratching and scratching. Daring her to remember a life best forgotten for everyone's sake. For her own sake most of all.

With this latest web, she could almost see . . . *something*. But the truth of it eluded her, as so many things eluded her. Simple things. Ordinary things. Some days her body and most of her mind were present in Halaway, the village where she lived. Some days she looked at the decorated cakes in the bakery window and *saw* cakes. Then there were other days when she saw fragmented memories of other windows, other cakes full of sharpness and pain and screams.

Perhaps the cakes had held those things. Perhaps not. Sometimes it was difficult to tell one thing from another because she was a broken Black Widow—and a shattered crystal chalice.

The breaking had been done *to* her, the savage rape destroying her potential and turning her into another witch whose power had been broken by a man's spear. But the shattering that had fragmented her mind and left her forever wandering the roads in the Twisted Kingdom? That had been *her* choice in order to regain the Hourglass's Craft. She had done it in order to *see*, to give warning and hope to her boy and the winged boy.

So many years had passed since the night when she had told Daemon Sadi and Lucivar Yaslana that Witch was coming. So much had happened—joy and pain, sorrow and celebration.

And now . . .

Tersa closed her eyes and let herself slide away from the border between sanity and the Twisted Kingdom. There was often clarity in madness.

She followed a familiar road, stopping when the road began to fragment into paths that might hold the answer— or might hold some terrible memory. As she stood before those paths, knowing she could lose her way and never find the road back to the border, back to her boy, she wondered if all the pain and sorrow, if all the prices that had been paid, had been for nothing.

*I am Tersa the Weaver, Tersa the Liar, Tersa the Fool.* She spoke the words she'd said once before, sent those words into the Darkness on a braided thread of power and madness.

A midnight voice, rising from deep in the psychic abyss that was part of the Darkness, replied, *Not a liar, and not a fool.*

*Something's coming, but I cannot see.* She wondered if her ability with the Black Widow's Craft, the ability she'd paid for with her sanity, was fading. Failing.

*Even if you can hear the sound of a man's feet marching on the road, can you see him when he's still on the other side of a hill?* Witch asked.

She considered that for a moment. *Not until he reaches the crest of the hill and becomes visible.*

*Well, then?*

Tersa looked at the fragmented paths that would fragment into more paths that would fragment into even more paths. So easy to get lost in the fragments, where yesterday might be tomorrow. So hard to remain close to the border and its noisy, everyday living.

But her boy needed her. The winged boy needed her. Even the girl, the assassin, needed her.

*You will help the boy?*

*I will help him.*

Turning away before she couldn't resist the lure of following just one of the fragmented paths, Tersa began the climb back to the border of the Twisted Kingdom.

She opened her eyes and grabbed the edge of the worktable as she swayed on the stool, adjusting to the harsh return to the tangible world. As soon as she felt steady enough, she disposed of the tangled web and cleaned the wooden frame that had anchored all the threads of spider silk. Then she locked her tools and supplies in their trunk before tidying up her worktable. When everything was in order, she left the workroom she'd created in the attic of the cottage she shared with the Mikal boy, locking the door before going downstairs.

Because of the vision in this tangled web, she'd heard the warning sound of footsteps, but it wasn't time yet to see. She had to believe there would be enough time to see.

That night, Tersa dreamed she was standing in a place full of mist and stone—a place with a chasm that held an enormous web of power that spiraled down, down, down into the Darkness. As she stood there, feeling the weight of that place pressing on her skin, Witch whispered, *Keep watch, Sister. Listen for those approaching footsteps.*

*What will you do?* Tersa asked.

*I will make sure that, when the time comes, all the weapons are honed for war.*

# PART ONE

***

## Weapons Forged

# ONE

Using Craft, Daemonar Yaslana called in a ball of twine and then considered the puzzle in front of him. After adjusting a couple of pieces for a better fit, he began lashing together the fallen branches he and his cousin had gathered for this harebrained, idiotic, get-their-asses-kicked-for-this idea—an idea that sounded intriguing enough that he might have tried it on his own at another time if he'd been able to talk Jaenelle Saetien out of building a raft today and testing it on the river.

It was a warm summer day, and floating on a raft sounded like fun, but there were rapids downriver and a waterfall. Testing himself against those things on a raft made out of branches and twine appealed to him. After all, he was an Eyrien Warlord Prince, and until he was old enough to test his strength and skill by making the Blood Run, this could be considered practice. Right?

That almost sounded like a reasonable explanation for doing this. He'd have to remember it if—okay, *when*—his father found out about this adventure. And he'd have to figure out a suitable reason why he wasn't alone on the raft. Maybe Auntie J. could help with that—if she didn't give him a whack upside the head before his father had a chance to do it.

Jaenelle Saetien set the next load of branches beside the ones he'd laid out. Then she sighed. "Why can't we just use

Craft to hold the branches together? Tying them is going to take *forever.*"

"You afraid we're going to get caught before we get this thing in the water?" he asked, lashing two more branches together.

"Maybe."

He looked at her. Jaenelle Saetien SaDiablo had the straight black hair and gold eyes of all the long-lived races, but her skin was a lighter, sun-kissed brown and her delicately pointed ears were a sign that some of her bloodline had come from the Dea al Mon, a race of warriors often called the Children of the Wood. She was smart, usually sweet in a feisty kind of way, and she sometimes had more backbone than sense.

Then again, so did he or he wouldn't be out here helping her build a raft that most likely would break apart when they hit the rapids and waterfall.

*"Your father takes calculated risks, not foolish ones,"* his grandfather had said once. *"He measures risk against his own strength and skill, as well as the strength and skill of the people with him. As you get older, he'll expect you to do the same."*

"There is a difference between taking a calculated risk and a foolish one," Daemonar said, echoing words that lingered in his memory. "We take the time to make this ride a calculated risk, or we walk away."

She wouldn't walk away. Not completely. If he insisted on walking away today, she'd test a raft and a river at another time in another place without him, and that was unacceptable. She was family, and it was his duty and privilege to honor, cherish, and protect.

"But . . ."

"What are you going to say to our fathers if either of us gets hurt because you were impatient?" he asked.

She sat back on her heels and sighed. "That's hitting below the belt."

That was where truth, when it was inconvenient, usually hit.

Jaenelle Saetien might want to try things that were risky, but she would yield if *he* would get in trouble because of *her* actions. Well, she would yield most of the time, unless the impulse to *do* something overwhelmed every bit of common sense that should warn her about how her father would react to a particular scheme.

She was the daughter of the Warlord Prince of Dhemlan, and even though she loved her father, sometimes being the daughter of a powerful man was a burden. Daemonar understood that kind of burden. He was the son of the Warlord Prince of Askavi—the feared Demon Prince of Askavi. Those two men were not only brothers united by family and their service to a Queen unlike any other in the history of the Blood, they were also the most powerful, and dangerous, men in the entire Realm of Kaeleer.

But they were still men, and fathers, and if their children felt a reckless need to explore what could be done with Craft, that inclination must have been inherited from them. Right?

He'd point that out if he had a chance to argue his reasoning for doing this harebrained adventure before his uncle or father killed him flatter than dead.

Jaenelle Saetien sighed again. Then she shrugged, accepting the need to put in the work before having fun, and began helping him piece the branches together to provide the snuggest fit, using Craft to trim them to the best shape while he wrapped power from his Green Birthright Jewel around the twine to make it stronger without making it thicker.

Finally satisfied that the raft was the best one they could make, he secured the last branch. "I guess we're ready."

Daemonar looked at Jaenelle Saetien. She looked at him. And they grinned.

He wore a Green Jewel. She wore an extraordinary Birthright Jewel called Twilight's Dawn, which had a range of Rose to Green power. It had been a gift from Witch, the Queen of Ebon Askavi, the living myth. Auntie J. no longer walked among the living, but she was still his

Queen. Would always be his Queen. And that was a secret known only to the other men who also still served her—his father and uncle.

Now Jaenelle Saetien tapped into the Green strength in her Jewel to help him float the raft on air and guide it to the water. He steadied the raft until she stepped on it and had her balance. Then he got on behind her, his legs spread in a fighting stance, his dark membranous wings opened halfway to help them keep the raft balanced. Calling in the last branch they'd collected and hadn't used, he pushed off from the bank, dropped the branch, and settled his hands on his cousin's waist.

"This is wonderful!" Jaenelle Saetien said as they floated down the river.

Daemonar scanned the river and the banks, watching one for debris that could snag the raft and upend it and the other for any Eyrien who might have spotted them and sent word to his father on a psychic communication thread.

He felt the change in the river, saw the white water and boulders seconds before Jaenelle Saetien said, "Uh-oh."

He wrapped an arm around her waist and closed a fist around some of her tunic, wishing she had worn something with a belt. Easier to hold on to someone if they wore a belt. He'd remember that for next time.

"Here we go," he said as they hit the rapids.

He leaned this way and that way, using his whole body to steer the raft around the boulders as best he could.

*Not easy,* he thought, exhilarated by the challenge. *Not easy, but, sweet Darkness, this is fun.*

He saw sky ahead of them and mist from the waterfall. One more tight passage and—

He leaned one way. Missing her cue for the first time, Jaenelle Saetien leaned the other way. Instead of skimming past a boulder, they hit with enough force that it took all the skill he had to keep the raft from flipping and tossing them onto the boulders or into fast-moving water.

They hit another boulder and spun—and the raft began

breaking under them, the twine snapping from the strain, despite the coating of Green power.

"Hang on!" he shouted, wrapping both arms around her as the raft reached the end of the rapids and shot over the falls.

They rode the raft down partway. Then the last of the Green power he'd used on the twine burned out, and what was left of the raft fell apart.

Should they go down ahead of all those branches or behind them? Ahead, they'd have all that wood coming at them, and even if he shaped a shield around them, one of them could receive a nasty knock on the head if they surfaced right in front of one of the heavier branches.

Behind, then.

Daemonar spread his wings, pumping hard to get some height—or at least delay the plunge into the pool below long enough for the branches to move downriver.

Jaenelle Saetien was younger than his sister, Titian, but the girls were about the same size. He hadn't considered either of them large, but, Hell's fire, it was everything he could do to hold that weight—and he wouldn't be able to hold her much longer.

Judging the distance to the water, Daemonar created a Green bubble shield around them and folded his wings.

Jaenelle Saetien screamed as they fell.

*Hold . . . ,* he began on a psychic thread.

No time. They hit the water and went down like a stone halfway to the bottom of the pool before the buoyancy of the bubble shield popped them back to the surface. They rolled a bit in the Craft-made bubble before he eliminated the shield and they went under a second time.

"You okay?" he asked when they surfaced.

She tipped her head back and whooped, a sound full of the joy he also felt. "That was wonderful! Daemonar, let's . . ."

"Hell's fire," he muttered when he spotted movement on the riverbank.

"What?" Treading water, she looked in the same direction. "Uh-oh."

"Yeah. Uh-oh."

Lucivar Yaslana, the Warlord Prince of Askavi, stood on the bank, watching them. He didn't shout, didn't make a come-here motion with his hand. He just watched them.

That could not be good.

"Come on," Daemonar said. "We'd better not keep him waiting."

They swam to the bank, fighting the current with every stroke. Well, *he* fought the current, aiming for the ground where his father waited. Jaenelle Saetien either wasn't strong enough or wasn't trying hard enough to reach stern judgment, so the river floated her away from her uncle. Lucivar paced her, letting her struggle—more than necessary, in Daemonar's opinion—until she finally reached the river's edge.

Lucivar reached down and pulled her up to the bank.

Daemonar let the current take him to that spot on the bank. When Lucivar reached down, he accepted his father's hand, unable to decipher the look in those gold eyes. His father had a volatile temper, even by Eyrien standards. It should have been in evidence and wasn't—and that was a worry.

"It was my fault, Uncle Lucivar," Jaenelle Saetien said. "It was my idea to build the raft."

"I figured that." Lucivar looked them over. Satisfied that there were no apparent injuries, he studied the river and said mildly, "Listen carefully, witchling. If you ever test that river and waterfall again—or any river or waterfall anywhere in Askavi—without my permission, you will be banned from Askavi for a year. All of Askavi, including my home. Do you understand me?"

Daemonar's jaw dropped, and he imagined his expression matched Jaenelle Saetien's. No visits *for a year*?

"But . . . ," Jaenelle Saetien began.

"Do. You. Understand?"

Oh, Hell's fire. *There* was the heat of temper under the mildness.

"Yes, sir," she replied.

"Then let's get you home and into dry clothes." Lucivar wrapped them both in Red shields and took them with him when he caught the Red Wind, one of those psychic roads in the Darkness, and headed back to the Yaslana eyrie.

The Winds were connected to the power in the Jewels the Blood wore. The darker the Wind, the faster you traveled. Traveling on the Red, which Daemonar couldn't have used on his own since the Red was darker than his Green, they arrived at the eyrie too fast. He wasn't ready for the reckoning that had to be coming.

When they arrived at the eyrie, Lucivar handed Jaenelle Saetien over to Daemonar's mother, Marian, then looked at him.

"Get cleaned up. I'll be waiting for you in my study."

"Yes, sir." Nothing else he could say.

"Do I want to know what the two of you were doing?" Marian asked.

"No, Auntie Marian, you really don't," Jaenelle Saetien replied.

"I want to know," Andulvar said, joining them in the large front room.

*I'll tell you later,* Daemonar said on a psychic spear thread.

He smelled like the river, which wasn't a bad smell at all, but because he'd be closed in a room with his father and wasn't sure what kind of discussion they were going to have, Daemonar took a fast shower before getting dressed and reporting to his father's study.

He usually liked the room in the family eyrie where his father took care of the business of ruling Ebon Rih, the valley that lived in the shadow of the mountain called Ebon Askavi. Also known as the Keep, Ebon Askavi held a vast library, was the repository for the Blood's history, a sanctuary for the darkest-Jeweled Blood—and the private lair of Witch.

He often did his schoolwork in his father's study, sitting quietly while Lord Rothvar, Lucivar's second-in-command, reported on the Blood and landen villages in the valley or received orders for the other Eyriens who protected Ebon Rih. The men knew he listened, and he knew anything they considered private was discussed on a psychic communication thread. He also knew that when Lucivar, who had trouble reading, asked him to read a document out loud, it was as much to give him a glimpse at what it meant to be a leader as it was to help his father.

Maybe someday, if he proved worthy, he would be the one ruling Ebon Rih while Lucivar took care of holding the lines of Blood law and honor throughout the rest of Askavi.

Since he couldn't measure how much trouble he was in while standing outside the door, Daemonar knocked, waited for permission to enter, and went in.

Lucivar wasn't sitting behind the desk; he leaned against it and gave the boy a careful study before shaking his head. "Tell me all of it."

Daemonar told him all of it, from the first glimmer of the idea to building the raft. He even threw in the words about the difference between calculated risks and foolish ones—and heard his father snort in an effort to suppress a laugh.

Still no sign of anger or disappointment or anything except . . . amusement?

"Hold out your arms," Lucivar said.

Daemonar obeyed and said nothing while Lucivar ran his hands over shoulders and arms before moving around to examine back muscles.

"You are going to be hurting sore by tomorrow, boyo," Lucivar said. "You don't have the muscles or the strength yet to carry that much weight safely."

"I wouldn't have dropped her," he replied defensively.

"No, you would have gone down with her, because that's who you are." Lucivar came around again and looked Daemonar in the eyes. "Smarter to use Craft and the reservoir of power in your Jewels to lift something that's too heavy to lift otherwise. So I guess those are the Craft lessons we'll be working on this week."

Lucivar's hands rested on the boy's shoulders, and the strength and power Daemonar felt in those hands reminded him that he had a lot of growing up to do.

"Did you have fun challenging the rapids?" Lucivar asked, that mild tone still a worry to the boy.

"Yes, sir." Daemonar grinned. Couldn't help it.

"Then I guess another thing you need to learn is how to build a better raft."

He studied his father. "You're not angry."

Lucivar stepped back to lean against the desk again. "Well, I can't get pissy about you and Jaenelle Saetien doing the same thing your aunt Jaenelle and I did. Only we rode those rapids and went over that waterfall on a raft built out of nothing but kindling and Craft. Twice."

"Twice?" Daemonar's voice rose to the point of cracking. "Hell's fire! Doing it once was a dumb-ass thing to do but . . ." He stopped and considered who he was talking to. "I mean . . ."

"It was a dumb-ass idea. Both times. But I imagine I did it for the same reason you did. That sparkle in the eyes that warns you that she's going to try this with or without you, and the thought of her doing it without whatever skill and strength you can give . . ."

"No." Daemonar shook his head. "We couldn't do that."

Lucivar smiled. "No, we couldn't do that. But sometimes that means drawing a line and being willing to fight someone you love into the ground if that's the only way to protect them." He looked away, seemed to be seeing something that wasn't in the room. "Jaenelle Saetien reminds me of Jaenelle Angelline in a lot of ways, but they aren't the same. When it came to Craft and spells and the use of power, my sister was brilliant and could do things no one else in the entire history of the Blood had done. Things no one else will ever do again. Her ideas didn't always work, but she wasn't impetuous or careless. Jaenelle Saetien is a child in a way that Jaenelle Angelline never could be, because your cousin is growing up safe under her father's protection."

"So are we. Growing up safe." Uncle Daemon wasn't the only Warlord Prince who took care of his family.

Lucivar laughed softly, then sobered. "Yeah, you are safe, and I don't know if you'll ever appreciate how much that means to me and your uncle. You'll carry your own scars. That's part of growing up. But you won't carry the kind that Daemon and I carry. You won't have to live with those kinds of scars."

Serious talk. "Would you tell me about those scars?"

Something about the look in Lucivar's eyes made him wonder what line he'd just crossed.

"That's campfire talk," Lucivar finally said. "Private talk. But not until you're older." He pushed away from the desk. "I need to go to Dhemlan. Better your uncle Daemon hear about this adventure from me than from someone else since I know what to say to smooth it over."

He and his sister, Titian, and his younger brother, Andulvar, were protected in their father's house, but outside the eyrie . . .

"You should talk to Titian." The words were out before he considered if he was protecting his sister or betraying a trust. But talk of scars and growing up made him think this wasn't something he should keep to himself any longer.

"Later," Lucivar said, heading for the door. "I'll be back before your bedtimes if Titian wants to talk."

"No, sir." Daemonar hesitated when his father turned to face him—an Ebon-gray Warlord Prince responding to the sound of a challenge issued by a Green-Jeweled Warlord Prince. Then he stepped up to the line. "You should talk to her before you go to Dhemlan."

A crackling silence as the Warlord Prince of Ebon Rih studied him.

"It's that important?" Lucivar finally asked.

Was it? Titian had been excited and happy about her secret, but lately she'd been unhappy and afraid of what

Lucivar and Marian would say when they found out. "Yes, sir. I think it is."

"All right." Lucivar walked out of the study.

Daemonar bent at the waist and braced his hands on his thighs. Challenging a male as strong and as powerful as his father was a messy way to commit suicide, and even a son couldn't count on getting away with a challenge without paying a harsh price.

But he had gotten away with it. Sure, he'd argued with his father plenty of times and had even sassed him on occasion, but what was overlooked in a boy—up to a point, anyway—wasn't tolerated in a youth, especially one who wore a dark Jewel. Even though he was years and years away from that day, the closer he came to being considered an adult, the more dangerous it became to test the temper of the Ebon-gray.

*It will be all right,* Daemonar thought as he left the study and went into the kitchen to see what his mother might have for a snack. *Father will know what to do for Titian.*

Spotting his daughter at the far end of the play yard, where a stream filled a small pool before continuing down the mountain, Lucivar considered all the messages—intentional and unintentional—that he'd picked up from Daemonar.

What had been said that had pushed Daemonar to draw a line? A small one, sure, but this was different from their usual pissing contests. The boy knew something about Titian, something that hadn't been shared with him or Marian.

The boy wasn't looking to get his sister in trouble in order to draw attention away from his own dumb-ass choice. The demand that he talk to the girl now was . . . protective. Concerned.

Titian was his quiet little witchling, a gentle contrast to her brothers. Why was Daemonar concerned about her?

Lucivar wasn't trying to approach with any stealth, but Titian was so focused on the paper in front of her, she didn't realize he was there until his shadow fell over her. Then she gasped, closed the pad of paper, and hunched in on herself as if she'd been caught doing something shameful.

Going down on one knee beside her, Lucivar wondered about the misery he saw in her face.

"What are you doing, witchling?" he asked quietly. "Will you show me?"

"It's not Eyrien," she mumbled, glancing up at him.

The tears that filled her eyes ripped his heart. "Okay."

She opened the pad of paper and looked away from him.

Lucivar frowned at the half-finished drawing of the pool and the flowers Marian had planted to bring some color to a spot they all enjoyed in the summer.

"I'm sorry, witchling. I don't understand why this makes you unhappy. I think you've captured the pool and your mother's flowers pretty well. I'm not an expert about such things, but I can see the difference in the flowers and—"

"A real Eyrien wouldn't want to draw *flowers*," Titian said.

He ruthlessly leashed the fury rising in him before she sensed it.

Now he knew why Daemonar had pushed at him.

Scars.

The boy had known about the drawings and hadn't tattled on his sister—and why should he?—but now he needed someone else to know about the hurt. Which meant the hurt was recent.

Lucivar snorted, a dismissive sound. "Whoever said that doesn't know much about Eyriens."

Her startled look made him tighten the leash on his temper until it hurt. So. Another *Eyrien* had slid that needle of doubt into his daughter's heart.

He ran a hand down her braided black hair. "Listen to me, Titian. Are you listening?" He waited for her nod. "In Terreille, Eyrien girls from the aristo families were the only ones who were given drawing lessons and music lessons, because it was assumed that they would serve in the courts and be companions to the Queens. Some of the boys received lessons, too, but they mostly used the skills they learned to make sketches of the hunting camps or the killing fields as a kind of record of the men and the battles. I can't tell you what the girls usually drew because I never had much to do with them."

"We're aristo," Titian said in a small voice.

"We certainly are, which is something your uncle Daemon takes pains to remind me of from time to time." A finger under her chin brought her head up until she looked at him. "Since you want to draw, why are you unhappy?"

"Because you would be disappointed in me when you found out."

She couldn't have stunned him more if she'd smacked him with a rock. It took him a moment to find his voice. "Witchling, the only way you could disappoint me is if you allowed someone's meanness to push you away from doing something you love. If you don't feel strong enough to meet that meanness on your own, you come to me and I will back you all the way."

Suddenly his arms were full of a girl doing her best to squeeze the breath out of him.

"Thank you, Papa."

He didn't see that he'd done anything to deserve thanks, but he cuddled her and let her sniffle until her feelings settled. His were churning with a fury that needed an outlet, but he'd deal with that later.

"I'm heading out to see your uncle Daemon," he said. "Would you let me show him your drawings?"

Titian hesitated, then eased out of his arms and handed him the pad. "You'll bring it back?"

"I will bring it back." He hesitated. Andulvar was too young for that adventure on the river, but why hadn't Titian been invited? "Jaenelle Saetien and Daemonar are back. Did they tell you they were going to the river?"

Titian nodded. "Daemonar said he didn't think I'd have fun helping Jaenelle Saetien today, but he promised he'd take me to the river another day so that I could draw the waterfall."

He and his firstborn were going to have a little chat about sharing information within the family. "Maybe we can all go there some afternoon soon. Your mother and I can make up a hamper and we can have a picnic by the river."

She gave him that shy but sunny smile—the smile that said she still believed her papa could fix anything.

"Come on." He vanished the drawing pad and led her back to the eyrie. "Unless your mother caught them in time, your brothers will have everything out of the cold box and half the food in the pantry spread over the kitchen in search of a proper snack. You might as well lay claim to your share."

She might be gentle and a little shy, but when they walked into the kitchen, she wasn't afraid to tussle with her cousin or her brothers in order to get what she wanted. As far as he was concerned, that was a first step to her learning that she could also hold her own against the meanness of outsiders.

"No," Marian said, tapping the kitchen table. "These are the choices for a snack. Pick from what's on the table or wait until dinner."

Daemonar, Jaenelle Saetien, and Andulvar looked away from the cake cooling on the counter.

"But . . . ," Jaenelle Saetien began.

Marian tapped the table again. "What's here or nothing." She watched Lucivar and Titian enter the kitchen. She knew that look on her husband's face, but she supervised the tussle of who got what, and she noticed how Daemonar didn't look at his father or sister—and how he fended off his cousin and little brother but let Titian claim the second piece of his favorite treat.

When everyone had made their snack choices, she put a Purple Dusk shield around the cake before walking down the corridor to the laundry room. Considering the Jewels

Daemonar and Jaenelle Saetien wore, a Purple Dusk shield wasn't any kind of barrier, but *breaking* that shield to get a treat they'd already been told they couldn't have would have brought Lucivar's wrath down on their heads.

Lucivar walked into the laundry room moments after she did. After centuries of marriage, she still felt that flutter in the belly when she saw him, still remembered how he'd refused to see her as "just a hearth witch" and had pushed her to find her own strength and stand up for herself—and for him. Being the second-most-powerful man in Kaeleer, he needed someone who could love him without reservations. Someone who could also accept being loved by a man like him.

The Warlord Prince of Askavi. The Demon Prince of Askavi. Their lives had changed when he'd accepted the need to take control of the whole Territory of Askavi instead of just ruling Ebon Rih. She'd never had many friends, even among the Eyriens. Witches from aristo Rihlander families—the other race that lived in Askavi—didn't have any common ground with a witch whose inclinations leaned toward domestic skills like cooking and keeping a house, and every generation of that short-lived race speculated about why Lucivar Yaslana had married—and stayed married to—someone like her. Outside of Nurian, the Eyrien Healer, the only other Eyrien woman living in the eyries nearby was Dorian, Lord Endar's wife. There was nothing *wrong* with Dorian, although the woman seemed dissatisfied with nothing and everything of late, but Marian never felt quite comfortable being around her because she had the same name as Marian's mother, and memories of her life before Witch saved her and brought her to Kaeleer weren't something she could set aside.

It wasn't easy being the wife of the ruler of a Territory, but the man . . . Oh, the man more than made up for any troubles that came with his title.

"Since neither of them needed a Healer, I gather Daemonar and Jaenelle Saetien's adventure was successful?"

Lucivar huffed out a low laugh. "If that's the measuring stick, then it was successful."

*Oh, dear.* "Do I want to know?"

"No, you really don't, but I'll tell you when I get back if they don't tell you first. As it is, I need to go to Dhemlan and explain this adventure to Daemon."

Marian braced a hand on one of the laundry tubs and reminded herself that any day that didn't end with one of her children testing boundaries to the point of needing a Healer . . . was most likely a day when the children were visiting their aunt and uncle and she didn't hear about whatever it was until much later.

"And Titian?"

Lucivar stepped closer. "She's fine. She's inherited some of her mother's talents but expresses them in a different way."

Now, that was intriguing.

"I have to go." Lucivar's voice sounded low, a little rough. But the kiss he gave her was warm and full of promise. "I may not make it back for dinner, but I'll be back tonight."

"And we'll talk?"

He gave her the lazy, arrogant smile that always meant trouble. "Sure."

He went out the side door to catch the Winds and ride the Ebon-gray Web to SaDiablo Hall in Dhemlan. She went back to the kitchen to see if there was anything left to put away and was surprised to find Daemonar combining the remaining food into a covered dish to go into the cold box.

He gave her a measuring look that reminded her that he wasn't a boy anymore—that he was, in so many ways, his father's son.

"Did Father tell you?" Daemonar asked.

"He left that to you," she replied.

Another measuring look. Then Daemonar took a clean plate out of the cupboards, selected some of the food he'd been about to store, and set the plate in front of her before fetching glasses of water for both of them.

So she sat and ate and listened while her firstborn told her everything.


Lucivar dropped from the Ebon-gray Wind to the stone landing web in front of SaDiablo Hall. Built thousands of years ago by Saetan Daemon SaDiablo to be his family's seat, it was an imposing structure of gray stone, with so many wings, rooms, interior courtyards, and gardens the place could be its own village—was, in fact, the main source of income and employment for the adjoining village of Halaway, despite there being only three members of the family in residence.

The Hall was also testimony to the differences between his life and Daemon's.

His eyrie had as many rooms as a modest mansion, but it was still small enough that Marian took care of the housekeeping and cooking, with help from him and the children. Occasionally she had "helpers" from Riada, the closest Blood village in Ebon Rih, but those were youngsters who wanted to learn hearth Craft from Marian Yaslana—or who were willing to trade time doing chores in exchange for lessons in weaving since Marian was becoming known as a "loom artist."

For many years, he'd had one home to look after and the valley of Ebon Rih to rule. He also had a Dhemlan estate that had vineyards and made wine, but he didn't oversee it directly any more than he oversaw the town house in Amdarh, despite having use of one side of the building.

Even now, with him ruling all of Askavi, his home and work were fairly straightforward.

Daemon's life was so much more complicated.

The Hall, which was Daemon Sadi's primary residence, employed close to two hundred people to take care of the building, cook the meals, work in the stables, and tend the grounds and all the gardens, both the exterior gardens and the interior courtyards that provided light and greenery to bedrooms, sitting rooms, workrooms, and all the other rooms that the massive structure contained.

Besides dealing with the senior staff at the Hall—which, considering the personalities of the senior staff, was sufficiently challenging—Daemon also dealt with the town house and its staff, the family estates in Dhemlan, an estate that was run as a self-sufficient school for half-Blood children, and a school on the Isle of Scelt that trained and educated kindred Scelties. He also owned or co-owned several businesses throughout the Realm of Kaeleer, as well as a few farms and businesses he still supported in Dena Nehele and Shalador Nehele in the Realm of Terreille. Added to that, Daemon took care of the SaDiablo family's vast wealth, working with his personal man of business and the firm that had been managing some portion of that wealth since Saetan had hired them centuries ago.

That much responsibility might have overwhelmed a lot of men, but Daemon actually enjoyed the work, the challenges of business. They were almost a way for him to relax from the duties of being the Warlord Prince of Dhemlan and dealing with the Dhemlan Queens as well as the Queens who ruled Kaeleer's other Territories.

They were almost a way for him to rest from the duties of being the High Lord of Hell—a title Daemon had shouldered after Saetan went to the final death. A title, a truth, and a secret that was only known to a few who were among the living. Sadi would give his daughter as much time to grow up as he could before that title cast a shadow over her life. That was a choice Lucivar understood, seeing the shadow his title of Demon Prince now cast on his own children.

Added to the complications of Daemon's life was the fact that Daemon Sadi had been damaged by a savagely abusive childhood and centuries of being used as a pleasure slave, and his brilliant mind had been broken and repaired three times, the last time leaving him fragile in a way that also made him extremely dangerous to the whole damn Realm.

But Sadi was Lucivar's brother. He loved the man and would stand with him against anyone—except their Queen.

A psychic probe at the level of the Red told him that Daemon was home and Surreal SaDiablo, Daemon's Gray-Jeweled partner and second-in-command, was not.

Officially, Surreal was Daemon's wife, and Sadi gave her everything a wife was entitled to have from a husband, including his body. They loved each other but had never been in love with each other, and that had made the difference when mistakes made on both sides had led to Surreal seeing the full truth about the man she had married and developing a bone-deep fear of some aspects of Daemon's temper—and it had led Daemon into the cascading self-destruction that had ended with him splintering his mind almost beyond repair.

Daemon asking for help that should have been impossible, from a Queen who almost everyone believed no longer existed in any of the Realms, had saved all of them. Witch had intervened and repaired Daemon's mind, as she had done twice before. But everything has a price, and having the Queen who was the love of Daemon's life return, even as a presence without flesh, changed Sadi's relationship with Surreal.

Daemon still referred to Surreal as his wife. Lucivar couldn't. Once things had settled down and the routines that were set up to keep Daemon sane were in place, Lucivar discovered there were some lines he couldn't cross. He loved Surreal like a sister, would defend her against anyone but Daemon, but he saw the differences in Daemon's relationship with Surreal compared to his relationship with and feelings for Marian.

He and Marian had a marriage—a commitment to each other—in the truest sense of the word. Daemon and Surreal had a partnership that included sex and raising their daughter. But in Surreal's presence, Daemon couldn't be everything he was, and the acknowledgment that some distance was required to keep her safe—and keep her fear of him at bay—had stained everything they were to each other for the past few years.

Lucivar shook his head. No point rubbing up against rough stone until you hurt.

The door opened before he had a chance to knock. Beale, the Red-Jeweled Warlord who worked as the Hall's butler, studied him for a moment before stepping aside.

Beale was one of the people Daemon had entrusted with telling him his control was slipping and he needed some solitary time to regain his balance. Lucivar was another who had accepted that responsibility. It wasn't unusual for him to show up at the Hall for a meal or a quick visit, but that first meeting between butler and brother always held an unspoken question about the man who was the High Lord of Hell as well as the Warlord Prince of Dhemlan—and who, at his most lethal, was known as the Sadist.

"Prince Sadi is working in his study," Beale said. "Should I have coffee brought in?"

"Hell's fire, no," Lucivar replied. "I'd rather he wasn't completely sober when I explain this." He shook his head at Beale's momentary look of alarm. "The children are fine, and this is nothing you haven't heard before. Same story, different father."

"I see. Perhaps I should talk to Mrs. Beale about making something . . . fortifying . . . for the Prince's dinner. You'll be staying for dinner?"

It was phrased as a question, but it wasn't.

"I was hoping to get home for the children's bedtimes."

"An early dinner, then. Since the Prince already requested that the meal be kept simple, it shouldn't be an imposition."

Lucivar bared his teeth in what could be mistaken as a smile. Beale recognized the warning and wasn't impressed. Of course, the man was married to Mrs. Beale, who was the cook at the Hall. She was an excellent cook. She was also a large woman who wore a Yellow Jewel and tended to bring her well-honed meat cleaver to any discussion.

"Fine," Lucivar said. "Please thank Mrs. Beale for accommodating me."

"It will be a pleasure."

Shaking his head, Lucivar went to the study, gave the door a quick rap with his knuckles, and walked in. "Hello, Bastard."

Daemon looked up from a stack of papers and started to smile. Then that beautiful face went completely blank.

"They're fine." Wondering how many times he would have to say that today, Lucivar walked up to the large blackwood desk, filled a snifter to the brim with brandy, and set it in front of Daemon. "You're going to want to slug a good bit of that down before we talk."

Daemon looked at the brandy, then at him. "But the children are fine?"

Lucivar filled another snifter and settled in the specially designed chair Daemon had made to accommodate an Eyrien's wings and still provide armrests. "Oh, yeah, old son, they are just fine. And if Father was still around, he'd be laughing himself silly right about now."

"That doesn't sound good." Daemon took a long swallow of brandy. He breathed out a resigned sigh. "Tell me."

The delay had been enough to give Lucivar the measure of his brother's mental and emotional health. A jagged feel to Daemon's psychic scent meant trouble. Since he wasn't picking up anything like that, he went ahead.

"My son, your daughter, on a raft made of branches and twine, riding rapids and going over a waterfall."

Daemon's hand trembled. He set the snifter on the desk before covering his face with his hands. Then he spread his fingers enough to peer at Lucivar and said, "Why?"

"Because it's the sort of thing those two would find challenging and fun."

Daemon groaned and rubbed his face briskly before sagging in his chair. "What did you say when you caught them? I'm assuming you caught them?"

"Not much I could say, since Jaenelle Angelline and I built a raft out of kindling and Craft and rode those same rapids and went over that same waterfall." A beat of silence. "Twice."

Daemon stared at him. He *looked* like he was trying to say words, so Lucivar drank brandy and waited.

"Why do it twice?" Daemon finally said.

"Because it was a wicked bitch of a ride—and it was fun. And because Jaenelle had given me that look and that smile—you remember those?—and said, 'Lucivar, I have a wonderful idea; you're going to hate it a lot.'" He shrugged. "We were well shielded."

Daemon drank the brandy like it was water, then took a shuddering breath. That much brandy might make him a little light-headed for a minute or two, but wearing Jewels as dark as the Black or Ebon-gray meant they both burned up alcohol as fast as they burned up food, and even getting a bit tipsy required serious effort.

In fact, the only time they had managed to get stupid drunk since they began wearing the Ebon-gray and Black was on a pub crawl with Jaenelle Angelline. That night—and what they had done—became tilted and fuzzy after Jaenelle started making a drink called a gravedigger.

"What did Father say?" Daemon asked.

"He would have said plenty if I hadn't told him that the only reason he was angry was because he was jealous that Jaenelle invited me to test the raft instead of him."

Daemon wheezed.

Lucivar watched his brother. This was going better than he'd hoped. "Father tossed me out of his study—this exact room, in fact—and never spoke of it again. Didn't allow *anyone* to speak of it again." He drank some brandy and waited until Daemon's face was almost its usual golden brown color. "That's why we never told him that we tried it again a couple of years later after Jaenelle had perfected blending small objects with Craft to create a raft—or a pallet if you were out in the wild and needed to move someone who was injured."

Daemon leaned forward, placed his tightly locked hands on the desk, and said, "So our Lady built another raft out of kindling and Craft and the two of you did that asinine stunt again?"

Lucivar snorted. "Not much point doing the same thing again. That last raft was made out of twigs, leaves, and Craft—and shaped to have a bow. Made it easier to maneuver in the rapids."

"You are a heartless prick," Daemon snarled. "Is telling me that story supposed to make me feel better?"

"Doesn't it?"

Daemon's answer was succinct and very unflattering.

"For what it's worth, I don't think I took a breath from the moment I saw them go over the falls until they surfaced in the pool below," Lucivar said.

"Why would they even think to do this?"

"Because we—meaning you and me—had children who are, in every sense, *our* children."

Daemon closed his gold eyes. "Mother Night."

"And may the Darkness be merciful."

"How is young Andulvar doing?" Daemon said after a moment. "Staying out of trouble?"

"As much as any Eyrien boy that age stays out of trouble."

"Which means he's no trouble at all when he's asleep." Daemon shook his head and smiled. "Beron has a supporting role in a new play that will be opening in Amdarh soon. If Marian wants to get away from trouble, I would be happy to stand as her escort for an evening at the theater."

"I'll let her know and have her make the arrangements with you. She could use an evening for herself." He would attend the theater with his darling hearth witch or go to musicals or whatever else Marian wanted to attend, but Daemon would discuss the play and the actors and the costumes and sets and all the other things that would interest

Marian but had no interest for him. Well, Lord Beron, being Daemon's legal ward, was of interest to him, but that wasn't the same thing.

"And your cuddly witchling? How is she?"

Nerves danced under Lucivar's skin. He pushed out of the chair, set the snifter on the desk, and began to pace.

Daemon came around the desk, immediately on alert. "Prick?"

"Something I want to show you."

"All right."

Lucivar called in the drawing pad and handed it to Daemon as he passed the desk. He needed to move, couldn't quite look at his brother as Daemon examined the drawings and sketches on each page.

"Titian drew these?" Daemon asked.

Lucivar nodded.

"This upsets you?"

"No, it doesn't upset me!" Lucivar whirled toward the desk and Daemon. So tempting to aim some of the fury churning inside him at a man strong enough to meet it. But his hot fury would be met by Daemon's cold rage, and that rage could freeze blood. Literally.

He gripped the back of his neck, trying to ease some tension. "I just found out about her drawings before I headed out to see you. She'd been hiding them from us. From me more than Marian. Someone told her a true Eyrien wouldn't be drawing flowers, and she was afraid I'd be disappointed in her." That stung more than anything else.

He inhaled warm air—and exhaled in a room that had turned so cold he could see his breath.

Daemon held up a hand. A few moments later, the room returned to its normal temperature—but the brandy left in the snifters had frozen solid.

"My apologies," Daemon said.

"No need. It took my mind off destroying your furniture to work off some temper."

"I could ask Beale to find something in the attics that you could rip to shreds."

Daemon would do it, and that made him smile. "Save it for another time."

"Do you know who said that about true Eyriens?" Daemon asked too softly.

Lucivar shook his head. Better if he didn't know. Much better for everyone if Daemon didn't know. Besides, he'd have a pretty good idea of who had said it the next time Daemonar scrapped with someone. But . . . "How do I fix this, Bastard? I don't know a damn thing about art, but if my girl wants to draw flowers or wolf pups or rocks or . . ."

"Nudes?" Daemon suggested.

"Not at her age," Lucivar snapped. Seeing Daemon's smile, he blew out a breath and began pacing again. "The point is, if she wants to draw, how do I help her?"

"Does she know you're showing me her work?"

Lucivar nodded.

Daemon looked through the drawings again, then fingered the paper. "Would you allow an indulgent uncle to handle this?"

"How?"

"A gift of better paper and a set of colored pencils. Not so much that she might think we had expectations she couldn't meet but enough to let her know we want to encourage her interest and she has our support."

Lucivar felt the tension easing out of his neck and shoulders. "An instructor?" He wasn't sure where to find one. Were there any artists in Ebon Rih? Would he trust anyone with a sensitive child who was the daughter of the Demon Prince? *His* sensitive child? Wouldn't more verbal needles inserted in a vulnerable heart be a subtle way to attack the man?

"Let her play and explore on her own for a while," Daemon replied. "If she wants a teacher, give her a chance to ask."

It might take her a while to work up to it, but if Titian wanted something, she would ask.

Daemon closed the pad and handed it to Lucivar. "How early is that early dinner we're having?"

"I don't know. I didn't ask."

"Sometimes, Prick, you're as useful as a boot full of piss."

Lucivar laughed. "I'll ask Beale how much time you have to deal with more of those papers."

Daemon looked at his desk, then headed for the door. "Forget the papers. Holt can scold me in the morning while he pulls out the paperwork and contracts he needs to have me look at first. Let's take a walk."

Lord Holt *would* scold his employer in the morning. That was one of the things that made him a valuable secretary. Like their father, Daemon needed people around him who didn't fear him. Standing so deep in the abyss, having so much power and so much potential for destruction, could leave a man feeling isolated and lonely. And that, as their family's history had made clear, could lead to mistakes that would have repercussions for centuries.

Having confirmed the time that dinner would be served, they went out for a walk, happy to be in each other's company.

Surreal dropped from the Green Wind close to the house she owned in Halaway and had once shared with Rainier, a Dharo Warlord Prince who had been Daemon's secretary for decades. Before that, Rainier had served in the Second Circle of Witch's court, so he'd been trusted on many levels. For her, he'd been a friend and companion, but never a lover. During all the years they had lived together, she had never asked about his lovers or liaisons and he had never asked about hers.

And they had never spoken of the attraction they had both felt for the beautiful, dangerous man who was fiercely in love with Jaenelle Angelline and wore her wedding ring.

So many things remained unspoken where Daemon Sadi was concerned.

Pulling back from thoughts that wouldn't do her any good, Surreal gave the house a quick psychic probe to determine who was home. Confirming that the only people currently in residence were the staff, she went around to the kitchen door and knocked. The cooks came and went, as did the maids and personal servants, but the butler and housekeeper worked for her, not her current tenants. That assured her that her property was not mistreated. It only took a minute's chat with the butler and housekeeper to confirm that the current staff also wasn't being mistreated in any way.

If informing a potential tenant that they were renting a house from Sadi's second-in-command didn't seem like sufficient warning about the consequences of randy behavior that wasn't consensual, mentioning that she was a highly paid assassin whose mother had been the Queen of the Harpies and had taught her daughter what to do with a knife usually did the trick.

Of course, some potential tenants bolted a minute after learning that about her.

Unfortunately for them, she gave their names to the Province Queens on her next visit to their territories, just in case some fool thought that what couldn't be seen wouldn't have a price.

Wanting to postpone her return to the Hall a little longer, Surreal walked to the village's bookshop and browsed the new selection of books.

The Hall might be the family seat, but it didn't feel like a home. Not to her. It was too big, too imposing, too full of people who were neither friends nor family in a way that allowed her to simply be herself. The town house in Amdarh, which was Dhemlan's capital, suited her—a small house in a large city. The Hall suited Daemon, giving him the breathing room he needed to be away from people who might be overwhelmed by his sexual heat and respond in a way that put them, and everyone else, in danger.

And Jaenelle Saetien? A child between. The estate offered her space to ride and walk and explore, either on her own or with a Sceltie or two for company, or with Mikal, who lived with Tersa and was Daemon's ward. The girl enjoyed physical activities and the protected independence that came from being able to go to the village without an adult in tow. But she also enjoyed the theater and the parks and the shops that were in Amdarh, even if she had less independence in a city that size. She enjoyed mingling with girls from other aristo families when they gathered for some event.

Fortunately, the movement between one residence and the other wasn't unusual. Sometimes Daemon came with them. Sometimes she planned the time in Amdarh to coincide with his staying at the Keep. Either way, her goal never changed—to keep her daughter safe and let her grow up without the scars that had marked her life, and Daemon's life . . . and Jaenelle Angelline's life.

In that, she and Daemon were united.

After purchasing two books, Surreal walked to a dining house. She didn't offer an explanation for why she was dining out instead of going to the Hall, and no one asked. Everyone in the village knew that Jaenelle Saetien was visiting her cousins in Ebon Rih, and Surreal often had dinner in Halaway, alone, during those times—or when Sadi was also not in residence.

He was there, at the Hall. She could feel the presence of the Black. That dark power ran under the whole village as well as the SaDiablo estate, both a comfort and warning to Halaway's residents.

Funny how she hadn't been as aware of it during the years she'd lived in the village.

When she was a child, she'd had a crush on Daemon Sadi, who already was a young man when she met him and had been a pleasure slave for centuries by then. She'd had a girl's romantic notion of what it would be like to be with him. As a young whore, whose training he had financed because that was the only kind of help she would accept from him at the time, she'd gotten drunk one night and made a mistake that had provoked him into showing her what sex wrapped in cold rage could feel like. That was the night she had brushed against the side of his temper the rest of the Blood called the Sadist.

Then there was the night when Saetan Daemon SaDiablo, Prince of the Darkness and High Lord of Hell, had gone to his final death and become a whisper in the Darkness. She and Daemon came together as a way of dealing with a painful loss. If she hadn't gotten pregnant that night, maybe they would have become lovers, maybe not. But because Daemon had been taken from his father at so young an age, and because of what had happened to him after that, he couldn't tolerate her leaving with his child. So she agreed to marry him, and at the time, she'd believed her reasons to be sound.

A mistake. They were good as partners, good as friends. She'd had plenty of time to think about the night that had damaged their marriage and almost destroyed Sadi, and she could admit now, to herself, anyway, that she should have declined when he invited her to play, should have retreated to her room and closed the door. That might have bruised his feelings a bit, but he would have shaken off that particular edge of desire by morning, and her refusal wouldn't have changed things between them. Not like her accepting the invitation had done.

That invitation hadn't been about sex, as fabulous and terrifying as the sex had been. Not really. Not at the core. That's what she finally realized after years of struggling to understand why she'd run away instead of confronting Daemon the next morning. She'd run in order to survive, because that night what Daemon had really offered was to be a husband to her in the same way he had been with Jaenelle, offering everything, holding back nothing. And Daemon holding back nothing . . .

She'd run from him, and she'd run from the truth, was still running in some ways because she was afraid of what would happen to the family, to Dhemlan, to the whole damn Realm if she spoke the truth.

She didn't want to be a wife in the same way Jaenelle

Angelline had been. *Couldn't* be a wife in that way. Not to the High Lord of Hell or the Sadist. Sadi's partner and lover? The Warlord Prince of Dhemlan's second-in-command? Yes, she could be those things, enjoyed being those things. That woman could aim a crossbow at a man and establish boundaries without hurt or harm. Sadi hadn't expected his second-in-command or his friend to accept everything he was. But a woman who was his wife in the fullest sense of the word? Oh, yes. He would expect her to accept all of him.

After all, his first wife had done exactly that.

He didn't want to cause her pain. If she asked to end the marriage, he would let her go. And then? All the women who romanticized what it would be like to be with Daemon, who thought it would be wonderful and exciting to be surrounded by his sexual heat but didn't understand what it would feel like to be surrounded by it day after day after day, who hadn't any notion of *everything* he was . . . They would swarm around him, an irritation that would fray his control until the leashes that held his temper and the Sadist in check snapped.

The slaughter would be horrific.

For everyone's sake, she couldn't leave Sadi without the protection of having a wife. But sometimes—often, lately—she wished Jaenelle Angelline hadn't made being Sadi's wife look so damn easy.

Daemon felt Surreal's return to the Hall a few minutes before he felt the departure of the Ebon-gray.

Dhemlans, Eyriens, and Hayllians were the three long-lived races, their life spans measured in thousands of years. Too many years. While generations of other races bloomed and faded like summer flowers, the long-lived grew slowly—spurts of growth followed by long plateaus before reaching the next level of maturity. But races that measured their lives in centuries also needed more time to let go of words or actions that had caused a wound.

On the surface, Lucivar behaved toward Surreal as he'd always done, with a mix of caution for the Gray-Jeweled witch who was a highly skilled assassin and a willingness to fight her into the ground if that was what had to be done. But under the surface, Lucivar was still pissed off that Surreal's choice to suffer in silence when she'd been overwhelmed by her husband's sexual heat instead of talking to someone—*anyone*—had led to Daemon making mistakes that had resulted in his coming too close to shattering his mind again and sliding into the Twisted Kingdom.

There had been hurt on both sides, and if Surreal had talked to him after he'd made the mistake of allowing the Sadist to play as lover, their lives and marriage might have been very different. But they all knew if someone had told him outright that he would have to endure hideous pain for months and almost lose his sanity in order to bring Witch back into his life in any way, he would have done it without a second thought, would have embraced that pain and paid any price.

Not a body he could touch or hold or physically love. Not anymore. But the embrace of mind to mind, to be seen and accepted for everything he was in all his terrible glory, whether he was Daemon Sadi or the High Lord of Hell or the Sadist . . . That had saved him and continued to save him. Jaenelle Angelline, his Queen and the love of his life, might use those different labels to acknowledge aspects of who he was, but she saw no distinction. Sometimes he was more of one thing than the other, but for her he was always Daemon. Just like Saetan had been Saetan, whether he was going by the title of High Lord or Steward of the Dark Court . . . or father.

It hadn't been her intention, but Surreal's choices had brought Witch back to Daemon, and for that alone, he had been willing to work hard at being a good husband. A careful husband. Staying connected with the living and working on his marriage had been part of the bargain he'd made with Witch in order to spend time with her at the Keep, where her Self, using the enormous reservoir of power still at her command, could create a shadow of the dream that had lived within flesh.

So he worked on his marriage—or his partnership, as Lucivar called it—with Surreal, and Lucivar worked to let go of the kernel of anger that the Eyrien still felt toward Surreal.

Returning to his suite of rooms in the family wing of the Hall, Daemon took a quick shower and dressed in fresh clothes—his usual black trousers and white silk shirt. He debated for a moment about adding the black jacket, then decided that would look too formal, too official. He wasn't looking for a report from his second-in-command; he was offering to spend the evening with his wife, doing whatever she wanted to do.

As he styled his thick black hair, he noticed the first threads of silver at the temples. At nineteen hundred years old, he was a little young for his hair to start changing color, but if he ended up with the silver wings at the temples that his father had, well, he wasn't going to kick about that. Besides, his face, while still beautiful, looked mature now, but it was unlined except for faint lines at the eyes. Laugh lines. Couldn't kick about acquiring those either.

He studied himself in the mirror over the dresser. Gold wedding ring on his left hand. Black-Jeweled ring on his right hand. Thinking about the woman in the adjoining bedroom, he vanished the pendant that held his Black, replacing it with his Birthright Red. Less intimidating.

Finally he took stock of the leashes—the self-control and self-discipline—that controlled his temper, power, sexual heat . . . and the Sadist. Everything was quietly leashed, comfortably leashed. He couldn't tighten those leashes anymore to the point of harming himself. A barrier formed from Witch's power made certain of that.

Since she'd been away for several days, Surreal might not mind the sexual heat that, even leashed, could overwhelm a woman and make her desperate for a lover's attention.

Only one way to find out.

He knocked on the door between their rooms and waited for her invitation.

She had taken off the matching jacket but still wore the long dress—a simple design in a rich shade of green that looked marvelous with her light brown skin, gold-green eyes, and black hair pulled up with decorative combs to reveal her delicately pointed ears.

"I saw Lucivar as he was heading home," Surreal said. "Official visit or family visit? Or . . ." She paled. "Hell's fire, Sadi. The children?"

"They're fine. Lucivar probably aged a decade by witnessing it, but they had a thrilling adventure riding rapids and going over a waterfall."

She plunked down on the small sofa in the sitting area of her room. "Mother Night."

Crossing the room, Daemon sank to his knees in front of her and removed her shoes. "Breathe, darling. Just breathe."

"Did you when he told you?"

Daemon huffed out a laugh. "Eventually." His hands moved up her legs, massaging her calves. "If they had been in any real danger, Lucivar would have intervened."

"And if he's not around the next time they get an idea?"

"Then this experience has taught them how to protect themselves." His hands moved higher, his fingertips lightly caressing her outer thighs from knees to hips and back again. Then that teasing butterfly caress moved to the tops of her thighs as he watched her face and read the look in her eyes. When he shifted from sitting on his heels to an upright position, she opened her legs to accommodate him.

He stroked her inner thighs, coming close to the juncture but not touching—not because he was playing with her, but because he was waiting for her invitation.

She leaned forward. One hand fisted in his shirt and pulled him toward her. "Sadi."

When there was barely a whisper of space between his lips and hers, he resisted the pull and said, "Yes?" A question. A requirement.

"Yes." *Damn you.*

He heard the unspoken sentiment, but when his thumb stroked the damp silk and lace of her panties and she gasped, he closed his mouth over hers and let his kiss fill her with the heat of his desire and need. He gave her what her body and emotions told him she wanted—and he loved her until she was too sated to want more.

# TWO

Surreal woke at first light and looked at the man sleeping beside her. Maybe still sleeping. His awareness of her was such that he usually woke before she did, sensing some change in her body or her breathing or her psychic scent.

Daemon never fully relaxed anymore when he slept with her. Hadn't fully relaxed in her bed in years. Just like he wouldn't go beyond the first indication that he was willing to have sex until she said *yes*. Not an unspoken agreement either. She had to say it. Even when she initiated that particular dance, she had to tell him she wanted him.

She knew why he did it, but Hell's fire, who would have thought Daemon Sadi would turn into milquetoast in bed, always asking permission, always assessing her reaction to see if what he was doing pleased her? Remembering the thrilling edge that used to be part of his lovemaking, the difference between the man who *should* be coming to her bed and the man who *was* coming to her bed grated.

"Problem?" Daemon asked. His deep voice with its sexual purr made all kinds of promises that wouldn't be fulfilled.

Maybe she could persuade him to give her a little of the old lover again.

She reached under the covers and closed her hand around his cock. Already hard and ready to be ridden.

Fisting one hand in his hair just hard enough to sting, she kept working him with her other hand as she gave him a hard kiss, her tongue tangling with his.

Breaking the kiss, she straddled him. "Yes?" she asked, leaning over him but holding his head down to keep him from kissing her.

"Yes."

She positioned herself over his cock, eased down just enough for him to feel her opening. Teasing. Tormenting.

"Yes?" she asked sweetly.

*"Yes,"* he snarled, his gold eyes glazing with a hint of temper.

She sheathed him and rode him—and thought she saw, and felt, a glimmer of the man he used to be.

Daemon tucked into his breakfast with enthusiasm—and wondered what had come over Surreal that morning. It was the first time in a long time that she'd seemed to enjoy being with him instead of being overwhelmed by his sexual heat or disappointed in the careful sex he offered.

"What are your plans for the day?" he asked, slicing into a piece of steak.

"Nothing I can't change as long as Holt isn't allowed to scold me for not handing over reports and paperwork," she replied. "Why?"

"I'm on a hunt. Care to join me?"

She set down her knife and fork, and he saw the Dea al Mon side of her nature shining in her gold-green eyes. Surreal did love a hunt.

"What are we hunting?" she asked.

"Art supplies and artists."

She blinked. Then she picked up her utensils and resumed eating. "When people talk about critics killing an artist, they don't mean that literally." She paused. "Usually. So who are we hunting down and why? Garish colors? Poor design?"

"If that were the case, it would be shortsighted of me to make a kill and have the artist end up in Hell. One doesn't acquire talent by becoming demon-dead, not if it wasn't there when the person walked among the living." Considering the artwork he displayed in the Hall located in the Dark Realm as a kindness to someone fulfilling a dream before becoming a whisper in the Darkness, he *knew* being dead didn't unleash any latent talents.

He told her about Titian's interest in art and Lucivar's desire to encourage the girl—and his offer to help.

"The art supplies are easy," Surreal said. "You can find those in Amdarh."

*You,* not *we.*

Daemon swallowed disappointment along with his coffee.

"However, I did cross paths with a couple of artists who might be able to offer some advice," Surreal continued. "One of them is on my list of things to discuss with you. She expressed an interest in teaching art at the school we run for half-Blood children. I gather a relationship of long duration has ended recently, and she wants to get away from the city where they had lived and make a fresh start."

"Are there any available cottages or row houses at the school?"

She shook her head. "I checked on my way home. But there are a couple of cottages in the village itself that are available. One is in good condition. The other would need some work, but it has a small building at the back of the garden that I think would work as an artist's studio. Big windows. Lots of light. I think we should look at the cottages and talk to the artist before you choose the art supplies."

Daemon smiled. An adventure they could share before his heat became too uncomfortable for her to tolerate and they needed to go their own ways. Again. "Yes. Let's do that."


Daemonar and Jaenelle Saetien strolled down Riada's main street. At least, he hoped they looked like two youngsters who were checking out the shops.

"Why did you want me to walk around the village with

you?" Jaenelle Saetien asked. "Are we going to *do* something?"

She would wander around the countryside for hours, finding all kinds of things that caught her interest whether it was here or at the Hall. But she needed some kind of goal in order to hold her attention when walking around a village.

"You're my blind," Daemonar replied, nodding to Lord Zaranar when the Eyrien warrior stepped out of a shop across the street.

"I'm your what?" Jaenelle Saetien said too loudly.

"Hush. Don't make a fuss. A blind is a way hunters can disguise their presence and not alarm their prey."

She thought about that. "So you're hunting?"

"I am."

"Who? Why?"

"Someone hurt Titian, and I want to have a little chat with that person without my father or Rothvar figuring out who it was."

She stopped and stared at him. "Who hurt Titian?"

She was only one-quarter Dea al Mon, but she was a scrapper—and her loyalty to family was as fierce as his own.

"I'll deal with the who," he replied. "That's why you and I are walking around Riada this morning, looking in shop windows and ending up at the bakery, where we'll buy pieces of fudge cake drizzled with chocolate sauce."

"My payment for being a blind?"

"Sure." Also something his father could verify if the question arose about what they'd been doing in the village.

"We could go to the bookshop," Jaenelle Saetien said. "I've read all the books I brought with me."

"I'll pay for the fudge cake, but I'm not buying a book," Daemonar said, drawing a line on how much he was willing to spend for her help.

"I didn't ask you to." Her voice turned snippy. "I have my own money."

"All right, then. But let's go to the variety shop instead. They have some books there." Just not as many. Best to avoid bookshop temptation if they wanted enough time to eat a piece of fudge cake before they had to head back to the eyrie. His mother expected them home for the midday meal, and being late would spark his father's temper, something he didn't want to do since he had important things to discuss with Lucivar.

They headed for the variety shop that lived up to its name by having a little of this and some of that—and never the same this and that from one month to the next. He had a better chance of finding his quarry there than in the bookshop since she claimed books were dull—a recent change of opinion—but was always looking for something to buy, despite having limited spending money. He'd helped her out a couple of times to spare her the embarrassment of admitting that she couldn't afford the item she'd placed on the counter, but he wouldn't do that again. He saw no reason to help someone who was mean to his sister.

As luck would have it, his quarry and her "court" were coming out of the variety shop as he and Jaenelle Saetien approached it.

"Why don't you go in and look for a book?" Daemonar suggested quietly. "This won't take long."

Jaenelle Saetien nodded to Orian and the handful of Rihlander girls who were with her and went inside the shop.

"Daemonar." Orian's smile seemed genuine, but there was a look of expectation in her eyes that he didn't like—as if she wanted confirmation that her words to Titian had hit their mark.

"Orian," he replied. He nodded to the other girls. "Ladies."

"It's *Lady* Orian." She tapped a finger next to her Birthright Summer-sky Jewel. "A Queen is not addressed so informally in public, even by a friend."

"If we're playing that game, you should address *me* as *Prince* Daemonar—or Prince Yaslana, since I outrank you."

"It's not a game," she snapped. When she spotted Lord Tamnar and her brother, Alanar, across the street, she reined in her temper. "You shouldn't be disrespectful to a Queen."

"Respect goes both ways," he replied, well aware of the two Eyrien Warlords who were watching them. They weren't moving toward him to intervene. Not yet.

Orian gave him a sharp smile. "How is Titian? I hope she took my advice to heart."

*Bitch.* All right, then. Like to like. "You mean the advice that a *true* Eyrien wouldn't draw flowers?" He bared his teeth in a smile as he gave her hair, with its natural curl, a pointed look. "Well, I guess you would know about not being true Eyrien."

The other girls gasped at the insult. Orian looked like he'd stuck a knife in her and twisted the blade.

Good.

He stepped closer to Orian, aware that Tamnar and Alanar were crossing the street and he had only moments left to deliver his message. "I don't care if you're a girl. I don't care if you're a Queen. If you jab at my sister again, I will bloody you."

He took a step back and looked at the two Eyrien Warlords, who were his friends. "Tamnar. Alanar."

"Daemonar," Tamnar said. He eyed the girls. "Ladies." Then he focused on Daemonar and asked on a psychic spear thread, *Problem?*

*No, no problem,* he replied. *I think the message was understood.*

He swung around the girls, who scrambled to get out of his way, and walked into the shop. He wasn't surprised to find Jaenelle Saetien hovering near the door instead of looking at books, but he wondered if she'd intended to try to help him or pull him off Orian if it had ended up a physical fight.

"The books are that way," he said, pointing to the corner of the shop that held the shelves.

"What you said to Orian about not being true Eyrien," she said quietly. "That was mean."

"She deserved it."

Jaenelle Saetien hesitated. "Uncle Lucivar wouldn't have said it."

"True." *But Uncle Daemon would have.*

He wasn't going to get away with this clean, not with Tamnar and Alanar having witnessed his collision with Orian. Alanar wasn't that much older than him, but Tamnar had made the Blood Run, the first important rite of passage for an Eyrien male, and was on the cusp of making the Offering to the Darkness. Since he was considered an adult and would be held accountable if he said nothing, *he* would report the incident to Rothvar and let Lucivar's second-in-command decide if the Warlord Prince of Ebon Rih needed to be informed.

So be it.

Despite the limited selection, Jaenelle Saetien found two books of interest, and he found one for himself. By the time they walked out of the shop, Orian and her "court" weren't in sight. Neither were Tamnar and Alanar. He suspected the Warlords were now escorting the girls to wherever they wanted to go.

He hoped it wasn't the bakery.

"I think we should split a piece of fudge cake," Jaenelle Saetien said as they walked into the bakery.

"Why?"

"And I think we should pool our money and buy a full cake and a jar of the chocolate sauce and take it home for the sweet."

Even if she'd already made something for the after-meal sweet, his mother would appreciate the gesture. "All right."

He would have let Jaenelle Saetien have more than her share as thanks for her help, but she carefully cut the piece of cake in half—and she was just as careful to pay for half the treat they were bringing home to Marian.


Arriving home a few minutes before the midday meal, Lucivar looked at the fudge cake and jar of sauce on the kitchen counter and said, "Well, everything has a price."

"What trouble are those two trying to buy their way out

of with that?" Marian asked, tipping her head toward the cake and sauce.

He wasn't sure how to answer that. "I'll deal with it."

"Lucivar?" She laid a hand on his arm and studied his face. "You don't disapprove of whatever Daemonar and Jaenelle Saetien did."

"What he did." He hesitated. "I'm not sure. I can't say I wouldn't have done the same." But not in the same way, and it was his firstborn's method of retaliation that gave him an uneasy twitch.

At Daemonar's age, he'd been fighting to survive in the Eyrien hunting camps, but he wouldn't have slapped at a Queen in any way, regardless of what she'd said or done. But after he'd gotten the first taste of pain that the Queens in Askavi Terreille inflicted on men just because they could hurt anyone under their control? He would have savaged the bitch as lesson and warning.

He *had* savaged the bitches, and the stories of that savagery were one reason why he had been so feared. Was still so feared.

"He didn't come home bloody," Marian said with a sigh. "I guess that's something."

"I'm going to wash up." Lucivar gave her a light kiss. "Don't worry about it. Nothing but feelings were hurt."

As he reached the archway that separated the kitchen from the large front room, Marian said, "Sometimes those are the hurts that take the longest to heal."

He looked back at her. "Yeah, I know."

Nothing was said during the midday meal. Maybe that meant no one had told his father about the chat he'd had with Orian.

That kernel of hope was crushed as soon as the meal ended and Lucivar looked him in the eyes and said, "My study. Now."

Wondering what had been said, and if he'd be dealing with his father as his father or as the Warlord Prince of

Ebon Rih, Daemonar followed Lucivar into the study—
and wasn't sure what to think when Lucivar took one of
the seats in front of the large blackwood desk instead of
sitting behind it.

He settled in the other seat and tried to look curious and
attentive, as if he had no idea why he'd been called into the
study. No idea at all. "Sir?"

Lucivar said nothing for a piece of forever. Then, "Endar and Dorian came to Kaeleer with their children during
the last service fair, same as Jillian and Nurian. Same as
many of the Eyriens who live around Ebon Rih. Everyone
who came to those fairs was hoping for a chance at a new
life, a better life. In Endar's case, it was also to protect a
daughter who was a Queen—and whose hair made it obvious that there was another race besides Eyrien somewhere
in her bloodline.

"You've known Orian since you were both toddlers.
You've played together, gone to school together. From what
I could tell, you've always gotten along. And yet, today, you
gave her a verbal punch in front of her friends. Why?"

Daemonar stared at the floor between his feet and
clamped his hands over his knees to keep from fidgeting.
He couldn't lie, and he couldn't slide around a direct question. "Orian said something mean to Titian, so I said something mean to her so she would know how much it hurt."

"You said it in front of Orian's friends."

"So did she," Daemonar snapped, meeting his father
look for look. "Titian had done a drawing for Mother, and
she was so happy until Orian . . ." He stumbled, not sure
what Titian had told their father.

"Until Orian said a true Eyrien wouldn't draw flowers?"
Lucivar said.

He nodded. "Titian likes to draw. She really likes to
draw. But after Orian said that, she didn't want anyone to
know about her drawings because . . ." Deep breath, in and
out. "Because she was afraid you and Mother would be
ashamed of her. She *cried.*"

He watched Lucivar's eyes glaze, felt the fury rising

from the Ebon-gray to brush against the killing edge. Then he watched his father leash that fury and step back from that edge. That gave him the courage to say the rest.

"If I slapped at Orian to let her know she couldn't get away with being mean to my sister, then that's between us, that's between . . . children. But you're more than Titian's father, and if you had confronted Orian, it would be seen as an Ebon-gray Warlord Prince calling a Queen to task for her behavior. That would stick in Orian's craw a lot longer than an insult from me because all the Eyrien males would take notice of *that*."

"Did you say anything else?" Lucivar asked.

"I told her if she jabbed at my sister again, I would bloody her."

Lucivar studied him. "Would you do that?"

"Yes." No one was allowed to hurt his sister or his brother or his mother—or his father. Not while he could stand and fight.

Lucivar blew out a breath. "All right. Just keep in mind that you and Orian will be living around each other for a lot of years. That will be easier to do if you can remain friendly, or at least civil, with each other."

"Forgive and forget?" Daemonar said.

Oh, such a queer look in his father's eyes.

"Forgive, certainly. Eventually. Especially if your uncle finds a way to erase the hurt Titian feels right now. Forget?" Lucivar shook his head. "What Orian said might have been nothing more than showing off to her friends or experiencing a momentary need to feel powerful by making someone else feel small. Or this could be an indication of who she is at her core —something that wasn't apparent when she was younger. No matter the reason, what she does and says from now on will be weighed in the balance when she becomes old enough to establish an official court. And I need to talk to the Riada Queen about working with Orian and teaching her what it means to be a Queen."

Lucivar stood, an indication their discussion was over.

"There's something else," Daemonar said.

"Oh?"

He wiped suddenly sweaty hands on his thighs. "I would like you to speak to the Queen on behalf of a Brother in the court." No need to specify which Queen. For the men in their family, there was only one.

"Oh?" Lucivar sat.

"You and Uncle Daemon go to the Keep every month and spend time with Auntie J., but whenever I need to talk to her, I still have to try to reach the Misty Place, and it's so deep in the abyss, I can't stay long. That's not fair. She's my Queen too. Why can't I go to the Keep to visit and talk to her? I won't pester her. And I won't go there when Uncle Daemon is there because that's his healing time. But now that I'm not the only one to see her . . ." He hesitated, remembering that he'd kept that secret from his father for a long time before Witch had made her presence known to Lucivar and Daemon.

Lucivar pushed out of the chair. "I'll think about it."

That wasn't a firm *yes*, but it wasn't a *no*.

Daemonar stood. "Thank you, sir."

Lucivar snorted. "Sure. Come on, boyo. We have things to do."

As his father rested a hand on his shoulder and led him out of the study, Daemonar said, "What things?"

"Well, I need to talk to Rothvar and the other men as well as the Queen of Riada. You need to keep your cousin out of trouble for the rest of the day."

He had to find enough things for Jaenelle Saetien to do to keep her from coming up with another wonderful idea? Hell's fire. "Oh."

"Yeah. Oh. And don't think I don't know I have the better deal, no matter what Rothvar has to report."

His father was not wrong.


Lady Cambrya was a moderately successful artist who was currently living in her sister's guest room while she sorted out where she wanted to go and what she wanted to do.

While the paintings she showed them were pleasant, Daemon wouldn't have purchased them for any of the family residences. It was Cambrya's other work that intrigued him.

She had taken some of her drawings and traced them as outlines, allowing someone else to fill in the shapes with colors. She'd taken a dozen of those drawings to a printer and had paid to have copies made that she'd intended to sell at harvest fairs. She'd also created an artist's primer for youngsters interested in art whose families couldn't afford private instruction. She'd been gathering her courage to approach publishing houses to see about marketing the primer when the Warlord who had been her longtime partner severed their relationship and demanded that she leave the town house they had shared for decades.

Since his name was on the lease, she'd had no choice but to get out as quickly as she could with the possessions that had mattered the most—namely, her art and these potential pieces of work.

As Daemon knew well, relationships could be thorny, and there could have been reasons why her partner had made this choice after being with her for so many years. It wasn't his business as the Warlord Prince of Dhemlan to interfere with the personal lives of the people he ruled—unless someone crossed a line and made it his business. Still, there was nothing of the bitch about Cambrya and nothing in her psychic scent that scraped his temper. So he wanted to know about the man. Even if it was none of his business as the ruler of Dhemlan, whom he did business with on behalf of the family was quite a different matter.

Aware that Cambrya was struggling against the effects of his leashed sexual heat, Daemon studied the line drawings and the artist's primer, letting Surreal tell the woman about the school and what they could offer if she accepted an instructor's position. He acted like he wasn't giving the conversation more than his nominal attention, but he was very aware of the woman's emotions. Excitement. Hope. Relief. And a need for some distance from the part of her life that had just ended.

Silence.

He looked at Surreal. She looked at him.

*I think the school would benefit from having her as an instructor,* Surreal said. *And Cambrya would benefit by being there—and perhaps she would find a special friend.*

*Oh, Hell's fire.* It took everything he had in him to keep a straight face. Decades ago, one Sceltie—*one*—came to the school with a boy named Yuli. There had been Scelties at that school ever since. Most of them happily herded everyone, children and teachers alike, but there was usually one that was looking for a poor human who would receive that Sceltie's undivided attention.

Then again, Cambrya might benefit from having a special friend.

"The position is yours if you want it," Daemon said. "Lady Surreal can show you the available cottages in the village. If either of them suits you, we will expedite repairs so that you can settle in as quickly as possible."

"I'm sure either place would be satisfactory," Cambrya said quickly.

Wounded. As if she needed to apologize for anything that she wanted for herself or for anything that might inconvenience someone else.

He heard that under the words—and he knew Surreal heard it too. That, more than the woman's artistic ability, was probably the reason Surreal wanted to offer Cambrya the job at the school.

"I'd like to purchase four sets of these line drawings," he said. "I'd also like to borrow this primer. My niece is interested in drawing. I'd like to see how she would use it. If it does what I think it will, you and I can talk about having copies printed."

"I don't know what to say." Cambrya blinked back tears. "This is more than I'd hoped for when Lady Surreal contacted me."

*No,* Daemon thought, seeing a kind of gratitude—and hunger—in her eyes that could turn into a terrible—and lethal—mistake. *Don't.*

He was up and moving before either woman could react. *I'll be outside,* he told Surreal. *Can you finish this?*

*Of course.*

Daemon walked out of the house. For centuries, he'd used the sexual heat that was an inherent part of being a Warlord Prince as a weapon against the bitches who had used him and tried to control him. Now that the heat had matured to its full potency, it was a damned inconvenience—and the price he paid for wearing the Black. The cold, glorious Black.

With the help of his Queen, he'd developed ways to lessen the impact of the heat on the people who worked at the Hall and the family's town house in Amdarh, had found ways to lessen the discomfort it caused Surreal— mostly by living apart from her some of the time, even when they were both in residence at the Hall. But dealing with other women who might not realize that the heat was *not* an invitation for any kind of intimacy always strained the leash on his temper—and put an edge on everything he was.

He felt the Sadist waking, felt a dangerous edge to the undercurrent of desire to spend more time with his wife, and knew that wouldn't be possible. He didn't go to her bed when desire had that edge. To keep her safe. To keep her fear of him quiet enough that they could live together.

He heard the door open and close behind him and turned just enough to look at Surreal and measure her fear as she walked toward him. There was some, but the woman who had backbone and sass, the witch who was his second-in-command, had that fear under control.

"I'll return tomorrow and take Cambrya over to the school and show her the cottages." She held up a package wrapped in brown paper. "And I have the sets of drawings and the primer you wanted."

He nodded. "Surreal . . ."

"No." She stepped close to him and lightly touched his face. "Let's stay at the town house tonight. It's closer than going back to the Hall. Stay with me, Sadi."

"I can't tighten the leashes any tighter than they are. I can't promise you'll be safe in the way you want, and need, to be safe." He hated that she feared him even when simple precautions would keep her safe, but that, too, was the price he paid for being who and what he was.

"I know. But I'd still like you to stay with me tonight. Can't we try?"

She wanted him to stay with her, to be her lover tonight. He wasn't picking up anything in her psychic scent that said otherwise.

Then he brushed his lips against hers and felt her shiver. There was fear, but it was mixed with a spike of anticipation and desire. And something else he couldn't quite name.

"We can try."

Lucivar spent his first hour at the Keep reviewing the week's business with Karla, the demon-dead Gray-Jeweled Black Widow Queen who was now the Warlord Prince of Askavi's administrative second-in-command. Askavi's Province Queens would have chafed at dealing with Marian—and his darling wife would have been unhappy and uncomfortable dealing with them. But Karla had ruled the Territory of Glacia, had been in the First Circle of the Dark Court at Ebon Askavi—and had been one of Witch's closest friends. Any Province Queen who sat down with *her* knew she wouldn't be intimidated by their bloodlines and wouldn't be wary of their power because she had known a Queen who had *power*.

Still knew that Queen.

"I heard your boy slapped at a young Queen," Karla said once they had reviewed the decisions she had made on his behalf.

Lucivar sighed. "Yeah, he did." He should have known she would have heard about that. *How* she knew? That he couldn't say. But very little happened in Ebon Rih that *wasn't* known by the residents of the Keep.

"Did she deserve it?"

"She said something that made his sister cry. As far as he was concerned, that was reason enough."

Her smile was sharp and in no way friendly.

He didn't move, but he saw that smile and prepared himself for battle. Ebon-gray could, and would, win against Gray, but Karla wasn't someone he wanted as an adversary—and not someone he wanted aiming any kind of dagger at his boy.

"Just as well he was the one who tangled with her since they're the same age or close enough not to matter," Karla said. "Any one of the boyos in the First Circle would have done the same. Hell's fire, *all* of them would have shown up to explain, in their polite and lethal way, that the next time she acted the bitch, they would give *her* a reason to cry. And then they would have done it."

Interesting. He hadn't thought of it in those terms, but Karla was right. He'd known those Warlords and Warlord Princes when they were on the cusp of becoming men. Given a reason, they could have, and would have, committed a devastating social execution without spilling a single drop of blood.

Karla's smile sharpened a little more. "Unlike her brother, who can be bossy and overbearing because he's her brother and she has to put up with him, you have to encourage Titian to stand up and fight her own battles—and learn how to get up again after she's bloodied."

Lucivar snarled at her, not because he disagreed but because he didn't like that she was right.

"Of course, knowing her father is standing right behind her, ready to step up and protect her if she needs him, will help her grow a backbone."

"You don't think that will keep her dependent?"

"About as dependent as your wife," Karla said sweetly.

Which meant not at all. Being dependent was very different from depending on someone, and he depended on Marian as much as she depended on him.

"Well, the boy's actions are something I need to discuss with the Queen." He pushed out of the chair.

"Daemonar is his father's son," Karla said. "And his uncle's nephew."

That, more than anything, was the reason he needed to talk to Witch.

He walked through the corridors until he reached the ornate metal gate that separated the Queen's private rooms from the rest of the Keep. He stayed away from the Queen's bedroom and the adjoining Consort's suite. Those rooms had become Daemon's territory. But the sitting room across from those rooms had become the place where someone could have an audience with the Queen who shouldn't exist—and yet did.

The body had died decades ago after a long and love-filled life, but the Self—the mind, heart, personality, and power—that was Jaenelle Angelline, and Witch, had remained in a deep part of the abyss she called the Misty Place. There, for decades, she had been a hope, a dream, a song in the Darkness for those who still needed her. For Daemon most of all.

But she'd been more than that for his boy because she'd understood the young Warlord Prince had not had enough time with her when she'd walked among the living and needed more from the Queen whose will was, and would always be, his life.

Lucivar entered the sitting room and waited. She would feel his presence. Whether she chose to respond, well, that was always her choice.

"Is this a social call?" Witch asked.

He turned toward the voice and watched Craft and will and power create a shadow—an almost-tangible illusion of the Self that had lived within the flesh of the extraordinary Queen who had been the living myth, dreams made flesh.

Not all the dreamers had been human. While most of her body looked human, her golden hair was more like fur, and her hands had retractable cat's claws. There was a small spiral horn on her forehead and a fawn's tail at the base of her spine. The legs changed below the knees and ended in a delicate horse's hooves. And she had the delicately pointed ears of the Dea al Mon.

But the ancient sapphire eyes were the same in this form as when her body had been completely human and she had walked among the living. Those eyes had looked at everything he was and seen him clearly, reshaping the violence in him into a weapon that fit her hand—and showing him that being with a Queen could be fun.

Hell's fire, they'd had fun.

"I need to talk to you about Daemonar," he said.

Those eyes stared at him. Stared right through him. "I am not taking sides in any of your squabbles."

He snorted. "Since when?"

The feral sound she made would have scared a full-grown Arcerian cat. Lucivar felt impressed—and wary.

He made a placating gesture—and hoped she let him keep all his fingers. "All right, you never actually took sides when he went to the Misty Place to complain about me. You just helped him adjust his thinking."

"I can help adjust *your* thinking," she said.

He sighed and pressed a hand against the back of his neck to ease tension he hadn't known was there. He'd always enjoyed these pissing contests, but that wasn't why he was here tonight.

"I really need to talk to you," he said quietly. "Start again?"

"Daemonar is all right?" Witch asked.

"He's fine. He tangled with Orian. That's one of the things I want to talk about."

"Orian is the young Eyrien Queen?" She frowned.

As he explained what had happened, he watched her. Jaenelle Angelline had been a powerful Queen and could be dangerous when her temper turned cold. Witch was the feral side of Jaenelle's temper—and far more dangerous.

"What bothers you about what he did?" she asked in her midnight voice.

He'd stayed still for as long as he could. Now he paced, needing the movement. "If Daemonar had gone after Orian as soon as he'd heard what she'd said to Titian . . . Well, he inherited his temper from me, so it would be hard for me to fault him for that. But he waited, Cat." So easy to fall back into calling her by the nickname he'd given her. A spitting little cat. At the time, he hadn't known how close he'd been to the truth of it. "He waited to see if Titian would shrug it off or handle it on her own. But she didn't fight. The words wounded her to the point where she hid her drawings from Marian and me—even hid the fact that she *was* drawing because she was afraid we would be ashamed of her, would be disappointed in her."

His fists clenched. His dark membranous wings flared out to their full span and resettled. His temper was rising hot and ready to burn.

Witch waited quietly, watching him.

If he struck at her, his hand would go through the illusion. If she struck at him, her claws would leave him bleeding. An almost-tangible shadow of her Self meant exactly that—touch only went one way.

"What bothers you about what he did?" she asked again. "That he used words instead of his fists?"

"Yeah, that bothers me. Using words . . . That's more like something Daemon would do."

The room chilled, a warning that any criticism of Daemon Sadi had best be said carefully.

He wasn't trying to criticize his brother; he just needed her to understand so that she would agree to what he wanted from her.

"The boy drew a hard line, and he used the same kind of verbal meanness to punish Orian as she had used on Titian, calculating the amount of hurt his words would cause. Daemon might have done the same, but even when he was young, Sadi had intuitive knowledge about his prey and knew if a verbal warning was sufficient or if he needed to slide in that knife and twist in order to pay a debt. He knew

when to draw a soft line and when to gut someone. Daemonar is a blunt blade and hasn't acquired that skill yet."

The room warmed back to its previous temperature.
"Go on," Witch said.

Lucivar resumed pacing. "He's already a strong Warlord Prince. He's going to be dealing with Queens all his
life, and that means he'll be doing it for centuries. If he
reaches his full potential—and I will do everything I can
to train him so that he will reach it—he will wear the Gray,
and there won't be many, if any, Queens strong enough to
stand up to him. He needs to learn how to deal with
Queens and how to deliver a warning when a Queen's behavior has crossed a line. He needs to learn how someone
with his potential strength can take a stand without gutting
the opposition—at least initially."

"So you want . . . ?"

"I want you to train him." Lucivar looked into those
sapphire eyes. "You're his Queen. Your will is his life—
and it always will be. Help me shape him into the man he
should be. Hold the leash. Give him the guidance he
needs."

She walked over to the windows and looked out at the
terraced gardens that she had helped create when she became the Queen of Ebon Askavi.

"What you're asking takes time, Lucivar."

Someone else might have been implying she didn't
want to give that time. He knew the woman, and the
Queen—and his sister—better than that.

"I know. That brings me to making a request on behalf
of another Brother in the court."

She turned to look at him, her eyebrows rising. He noticed she didn't correct him and say there was no longer a
court, even if it was an unofficial one now.

"I'm asking, for myself and for my Brother in the court,
that you permit Daemonar to visit you here at the Keep
instead of him having to go to the Misty Place in order to
ask for advice. I understand why you did it that way when
he was the only one, and his Self was meeting your Self

there. But it's different now. You're allowing Daemon and me to be with you here, so why not him? And it would be safer for him." Lucivar waited a beat. "He promised not to pester you."

"And you believe him?"

"Of course not. But you're more than capable of sending him home if he gets underfoot." He looked down. "Or under hoof."

Jaenelle huffed out a laugh. Then she sobered. "How will you explain this?"

He gave her the lazy, arrogant smile that always meant trouble. "I'm the Warlord Prince of Askavi. The Demon Prince. I don't have to explain anything."

"And what are you, as a husband, going to say to your wife?"

"Oh. Well. I'll tell Marian, of course. But as far as anyone else is concerned, Daemonar is receiving private instruction. If everyone assumes the instruction is being given by Karla, I have no trouble letting them assume that."

"In that case, I'd better define the boundaries with Prince Daemonar sooner rather than later."

Lucivar walked up to her and wished he could touch her, hold her. Saetan had waited thousands of years for this Queen to be born. So had Andulvar, Prothvar, and Mephis. Even supporting one another, the loneliness must have been crushing at times, but they'd endured it in order to be there to serve her. And now she was doing much the same thing— enduring the loneliness of almost being connected to the living in order to support those who needed her.

"I made the choice, Lucivar," Witch said. "I understood the price I would have to pay."

*Did you?* he wondered. "Thank you, Lady." He stepped back and bowed, a Warlord Prince showing respect and fealty to his Queen.

When he reached the door of the sitting room, she said, "If he does become a pest, it will be your ass that will have bruises in the shape of hoofprints."

He grinned at her. "I wouldn't expect it to be any other way."

"Wake up, boyo."

Daemonar's wings flared and his back arched, lifting his chest high enough for him to brace himself on his forearms. "Huh? What?" Why was he sleeping on the floor? And why did his mother sound like Auntie J.?

He blinked. Not his bedroom. Not his family's eyrie. And yet a familiar place.

Why was he in the Misty Place? He hadn't been trying to reach Witch's lair, which probably meant he was in a *lot* of trouble.

He just wished he was awake enough to remember *why* he was in trouble.

He climbed to his feet and rubbed sleep from his eyes. "Auntie J.?"

That was when his brain finally engaged and he realized he was wearing nothing but his underpants—a compromise between wearing pajama bottoms like his younger brother and being naked at night like his father. He'd put two and two together and realized his father slept naked in order to easily have sex with his mother. That might not be the only reason, but it was definitely one of the reasons. While he was curious about what sex felt like when you were a man compared to the explorations he did with himself, he was having trouble wrapping his brain around the fact that his father did those . . . things . . . with his mother, even though he knew those things were the reason Marian had gotten pregnant and had Andulvar. Well, had him and Titian, too, but he didn't remember those times, so they didn't count.

"We're going to discuss the rules and set some boundaries."

"Rules? Boundaries?"

She looked amused. Or pissed. He really wished he was

more awake. He wondered if that would make a difference, since he had no idea what she was talking about. Then . . . a glimmer of possibility thunked into his brain.

"I heard about your encounter with Lady Orian," Witch said.

Hell's fire! "Oh."

"If she had made that remark to anyone but Titian, would you have said what you said?"

He opened his mouth, intending to assure her that he wouldn't have been that mean if it had been anyone else. But he stopped and thought and finally said, "Yes. If she'd hurt someone else as much as she hurt Titian, I would have slapped at her the same way."

Witch nodded. "To the best of your knowledge, was that the first time Orian had been verbally mean to someone?"

"Yes."

"Then that is not the way you, being a Warlord Prince, should have handled it. A Queen who hurts people by word or deed is a danger to everyone. While there will be times when you have to be the one to draw the line and fight, in this case, you should have had a private word with Orian, or reported her misconduct to Lord Rothvar—or Lady Karla if you didn't want to approach another Eyrien."

His temper heated, but he resisted the desire to argue. She was the Queen. *His* Queen. She wasn't inviting him to debate his behavior. She had made a statement.

When he offered no argument in his defense, she nodded again—and looked pleased.

"Lucivar has asked that you receive some private training in dealing with Queens and their courts. He's concerned about your response to Orian because you are already a strong Warlord Prince and you will grow up to be a powerful man."

"My father didn't receive that kind of training." Training sounded bad. It sounded like he was going to be strapped in by rules that would hamstring his ability to protect people he loved.

"Until he reached the age for his Birthright Ceremony, your father had had your grandfather teaching him the rules that apply to Warlord Princes as well as the Blood's moral code. Those lessons are the core of Lucivar Yaslana, and he has lived by those rules and that code all his life, even when holding on to Saetan's lessons cost him dearly. However, the pain and suffering he endured as a slave in Terreille changed him. The core held, and still holds, but it is clothed in savagery quickly unleashed. That is who he is. He wants your education about Queens and courts to be a different experience."

Witch walked up to him and put her hands on his shoulders. He felt the weight of flesh on flesh, felt the warmth—and wished he could hug her the way he used to when he was young and took such things for granted.

"That is why you will come to the Keep for one hour twice a week from now on to receive that private training . . . with me. There will be forty minutes of focused training. The last twenty minutes will be set aside for you to ask questions or discuss anything you choose."

Her hands squeezed his shoulders. A light touch, but he felt the prick of her claws.

"Understand me, boyo. This is *private* training, and you will not talk about it, brag about it, allude to it in any way with anyone except your parents and your uncle. My presence at the Keep . . ."

"I know, Auntie." Maybe he didn't see it quite the way she did, but he understood enough about his uncle Daemon to know how the Black would respond if there was a flood of aristo families showing up at the Keep, demanding that *their* sons receive private training with Witch. As if the Queen was some commodity to be used.

"You and Lucivar fix the time and days when these lessons will be held, and we'll begin, starting with an alternate way to let a Queen know she's crossed a line and behaved badly."

"Thank you, Lady."

Her lips twitched. She released his shoulders and stepped back. "Time for you to go, boyo."

Daemonar lifted his head from his pillow.

His bedroom. His family's eyrie. But he *had* been in the Misty Place, and Auntie J. *had* said she was going to train him in how to deal with Queens and courts.

He got up and poured a glass of water from the carafe that sat on the table near the window.

He didn't think for a moment that Auntie J.'s lessons would be easy. The most powerful Warlord Princes in Kaeleer had served in her court, and the standards for serving in that court would have been high.

Lucivar had helped build the core and the bones of who he was. Witch would shape the flesh of who he would become.

Looking forward to discussing this with his father in the morning, Daemonar drank the water and went back to bed. Because he was excited about the future, it took him an extra minute to fall asleep.

# THREE

```
            ✦
 ━━━━━━━━━━━━━━━━━━━━━
```

Surreal quickly dressed in what she thought of as one of her second-in-command outfits: pale green shirt, green waistcoat a few shades deeper, dark trousers with a matching summer-weight coat. She brushed her black hair and used Craft to secure the decorative combs that held the hair away from her face—and revealed the delicately pointed ears.

Then she stared in the mirror and thought, *Fool. Have you learned nothing? Why do you keep trying to prove that the line you know you can't cross doesn't exist? Why do you keep pretending you can handle him when temper mixed with sex turns dangerous? Is it stubbornness? Left-over professional pride from your years as one of the highest-paid whores in Terreille? Why do this to yourself and to him? Why?*

He'd warned her that he wasn't calm enough for her to feel safe having sex with him, but she had insisted and he had obliged, using his mouth and hand to bring her to a swift climax before he walked out of her bedroom and spent the night in his own room behind Black shields and locks to keep her out.

All she'd done last night was prove he knew her better than she knew herself. At least she could show him that she wasn't going to run away again. She had enough spine—and pride—to do that.

Surreal rushed down the stairs, handing the coat to Helton on her way to the town house's breakfast room. She paused at the door long enough to use a psychic tendril to confirm that Daemon was in the breakfast room. Then she walked in.

No warmth or welcome in Daemon's eyes, but she hadn't expected any.

Her nerves danced. Who watched her? Sadi? Or the Sadist? His eyes weren't glazed in the chilling way that was distinctive of the Sadist, but Daemon was definitely in a predatory mood—and his heat was becoming too potent again to be around him in a place the size of the town house. Ignoring her physical response and discomfort, she filled her plate, then sat across from him. After the footman poured her coffee, she thanked the man and told him to leave, giving him the escape that she couldn't give herself.

"I'll take Cambrya to the school this morning so that she can look around and meet the staff, and then show her the available cottages." She took a bite of her omelet. Chewed. Swallowed. "Are you going to pick up the art supplies and then go on to Ebon Rih?"

"I am." A clipped reply.

"Will you be staying at the Keep for a day or two?" She kept her voice matter-of-fact—just a second-in-command confirming their schedules in case she needed to reach him.

"Yes."

Last night had unsettled him and sharpened his temper—and no one in Kaeleer could afford to have Daemon Sadi unsettled for long. Even after all these years, his mind was still healing; his sanity was still fragile. If he fell into the Twisted Kingdom, he would inflict devastation on the Realm and on the Blood.

She couldn't help him mend what had been broken, so his spending time at the Keep was best for all of them.

"When you're ready to return to the Hall, Jaenelle Saetien should come home with you. She's had her turn at visiting."

He nodded.

She couldn't say he was eating with any enthusiasm, but at least he was eating.

She selected one of the iced cinnamon rolls and took a bite. Still warm . . . and delicious. "Hell's fire, these are good." She reached across the table and held it out to him—and hoped her hand wouldn't shake. "Taste this."

His eyes never left hers as he leaned forward enough to take a bite. He chewed. Swallowed. And relaxed enough to take a cinnamon roll for himself. "Those are good."

As she told him her schedule for the next couple of days, she watched him finish most of the food on his plate.

Having eaten her fill, she pushed away from the table and walked around to his side. She gave him a soft kiss that made no demands, then eased back. "Try not to get your brother into too much trouble while you're in Ebon Rih."

"That's like expecting water not to be wet."

She grinned. "Then you'd better pick up some fudge for Marian before you leave town."

There was some warmth in his eyes when she stepped away. "An apology before the fact?"

"Absolutely."

His quiet laugh soothed her. When she left the town house a few minutes later, she almost believed there was a way to mend things between them.


Daemon walked into the art supply shop, saw the way the two shopkeepers—a Blood male and female—almost drooled at the sight of him, and felt his temper sharpen until he stood a heartbeat away from the killing edge. He smiled at them—a cold, cruel smile—and watched lust and greedy anticipation change to fear.

Good. It would annoy Lady Zhara, the Queen of Amdarh, if he splattered these people over the walls—or worse, much worse, if he let the Sadist off the leash to play with them.

"I'm looking for some art supplies for my niece," he said.

"Of course, Prince," the man said. "I can show you—"

"No, I'll show him," the woman said.

*Or I can show you something you'll remember for the rest of your blighted existence, because once I'm done with your bodies, I will make sure I see you in Hell—and then we can have a proper chat.*

"Art supplies for a beginner?" a young voice said. "I can show you, Prince Sadi. I have a list."

Daemon turned toward the girl standing in the aisle, holding up a piece of paper. About Titian's age. Sweet smile. Determined smile.

As he breathed in, he sent a tendril of power toward her and caught her psychic scent.

A Queen. He'd seen her before, but where . . . ?

Then he remembered being introduced to Zhara's granddaughter a few years ago. "Lady Zoela." He gave her the small nod of respect that a Warlord Prince of his rank would offer to any Queen who wasn't his own.

She came forward and kept her eyes on his. She was too young to be affected by his sexual heat. The guard who trailed behind her wasn't that lucky. The heat washed over him, and Daemon was aware of the man's efforts not to sink to his knees under the weight of unwelcome lust. Then the guard pulled back his shoulders and looked at Daemon, silently acknowledging that he might die in that shop trying to protect the young Queen.

"Want me to show you?" Zoela asked. "I'm just starting drawing lessons, so I have a list of the supplies I'm supposed to purchase. Grandmother said I was old enough to make the selections, so I'm here on my own." She looked back at the guard and grinned. "Well, not by myself on my own, but I'm making my own choices—unless I ask for advice."

She delighted everything in him. Wherever she'd been in the shop, she had felt him rising to the killing edge and had come forward—a young Purple Dusk–Jeweled Queen determined to do what she could to quiet that rage.

The guards assigned to her must weep with exhaustion

at the end of the day, trying to keep up with, corral, and protect her while she followed her instincts and did her best to embrace the people in her grandmother's city.

Zoela stepped closer, grabbed his hand, and tugged him down an aisle. "I'll show you."

"Thank you, Lady." What else could he say? She was practicing her lessons in how to be a proper Queen, and it was part of his duties as a Warlord Prince to respond correctly and allow her to have that practice. So he really didn't have any choice but to follow her.

It occurred to him that Jaenelle Angelline must have run over his father in much the same way when she'd been an equivalent age.

And it occurred to him that he should talk to Zhara about introducing Zoela to Jaenelle Saetien. Knowing his daughter's sense of adventure and having this glimpse of Zoela, he would offer to pay the bonus he was sure would be required to have any guards accept *that* escort duty.

"What is your niece's name?" Zoela asked.

"Titian."

"That's a lovely name. My friends call me Zoey." She looked up at him and smiled—and Daemon wished he could leash his heat tighter and spare the guard that much discomfort. The man didn't need to waste energy fighting against unwanted sexual desire.

Zoela consulted her list, then turned him and her guard into pack mules while she explained which kind of paper was used with charcoal and which was used for pencils and why one should have a sketch pad of less expensive paper for practice and experimenting and . . . and . . . and . . .

"Lady Zoela." He wedged the words into her explanations. Did the child never take a breath? "I appreciate the advice, but Titian is just starting to explore drawing pictures. I don't want to scare her with all of this."

"My friends call me Zoey." She looked at him, all innocent sincerity. "Aren't we friends?"

Hell's fire, Mother Night, and may the Darkness be merciful. Zhara was going to kick his ass for not holding to a formal line—and rightly so. But . . . "Of course we're friends. You're helping me choose all these wonderful supplies, aren't you? But, Zoey? Titian is learning on her own, so which of all these art supplies do you think I should give her first? Right now all she's using is inexpensive paper and a couple of pencils."

"No colors?"

Daemon shook his head. Then he used Craft to set the supplies on air and relieve his arm muscles.

"It's not as much fun without colors." Frowning, Zoey consulted her list again, then pointed out the supplies Titian absolutely had to have. Then . . . "Maybe she would like watercolors?"

"Maybe as a Winsol gift?" he countered.

She grinned.

The guard sighed.

"Since we're friends, maybe you could do me a favor?" Daemon called in one set of the line drawings he'd acquired from Cambrya. "I'd like to know if someone would enjoy adding colors to an existing drawing." He gave her half of the set and then vanished the rest. "See what you think about coloring in a picture when you don't want to do your own drawings."

She beamed at him. "Should I send you a report?"

Aahhh . . . "That would be appreciated."

"Lady, I believe we have everything on your list," the guard said. His tone came close to pleading. "At least for today."

"Yes, you're right," Zoey replied. "And you're getting tired." She led the way to the counter at the front of the shop, where the shopkeepers had been smart enough to remain.

Daemon added a couple more sets of colored pencils and sharpeners to his stack of supplies, floating the whole lot in front of him while the guard continued to play pack mule.

"May the Darkness have mercy on me when she's old enough to have her own court," he said in a quiet voice.

"May the Darkness have mercy on me *now*," the guard replied.

They looked at each other, then looked away, fighting not to laugh because then they would have to explain *why* they were laughing.

After paying for his purchases and saying good-bye to Zoey and her guard, Daemon caught the Black Wind and headed for Ebon Askavi. He looked forward to telling Witch about a young Dhemlan Queen who, in a few more centuries, was going to give him trouble of the best kind.

After informing Draca of his arrival, Daemon retreated to the Consort's suite. While he waited for Witch to appear, he used Craft to heat the water in a mug before adding a tea ball filled with a blend of mint leaves. He didn't need the healing brew Witch and Karla had created specifically for him—a sedative that was strong enough to relax him and smooth out the savage edges whenever he arrived at the Keep too close to losing control. He wouldn't need to smooth out those edges if there was an enemy to fight. All that power and temper would have a target. Since it didn't, he needed to be here, with his Queen. And sometimes he needed to be sedated for a few hours.

Outside these rooms, he would have fought against being so vulnerable. Even at the Hall, he wouldn't use anything that diminished his awareness of his surroundings and the presence of potential enemies. But here he was protected in all ways.

"Something changed," Witch said, walking into his bedroom from her adjoining suite. She could have simply appeared in front of him—and sometimes did—but more often she walked into the room as if she were still flesh and not a shadow. "Considering how the Black rippled through the abyss a few hours ago, I didn't expect you to arrive here this calm."

"I wasn't calm a few hours ago," he admitted. Then he smiled because just hearing her voice lightened his heart.

"But I ran into a young Dhemlan Queen who has a way of crushing edges of temper with happy enthusiasm. She reminded me of you."

"Oh? And who is this edge crusher?"

"Zoela. Lady Zhara's granddaughter." Daemon laughed softly. "One moment I'm ready to kill the shopkeepers for the way they were looking at me, and the next I'm being buried under art supplies for Titian. Zoey, as she is known to her friends, of which I am now one, is taking drawing lessons and was on her own to buy the supplies on her list. Not by herself on her own, since she did have a guard with her—poor man—but she was there without any other adult supervision."

"Sounds like neither of you had adult supervision."

"Smart-ass." He sipped his tea and called in all the art supplies, using Craft to spread them out and float them on air above his bed. He also called in the sets of line drawings and the artist's primer. "I gave her half a set of these line drawings and asked her to let me know if children would enjoy coloring the pictures. She's going to send me a report."

The only way to describe the look on Witch's face was horrified amusement. "Oh, Hell's fire, Daemon. You really are still an innocent in some ways."

Well, that was just insulting. "Am not."

"You gave a young Queen permission to send you reports about things she feels are important enough that you should be aware of them."

"One report. One. About these line drawings."

Her smile turned the bones in his legs to jelly—and not in a good way.

"Zoey would show her reports to Zhara before sending them," he said.

"Why would she if you didn't specify that Zhara had to review the reports before sending them to you?"

"Because . . ." He recalled what he'd said in the shop. It wasn't much. Zoey hadn't given him a chance to say much. "I just assumed . . ."

"That a young Queen who reminded you of me wouldn't happily grab the initiative now that she's been invited to correspond directly with the Warlord Prince of Dhemlan?"

When she put it *that* way . . . "I did hold firm about the watercolors."

She sat on air, braced her elbows on her knees, and rested her face in her hands—and looked like she anticipated being told a really good story. "How?"

"I suggested the watercolors should be kept for a Winsol gift."

She sat up and said in a young voice, "'But, Grandmother, it would be lovely to learn how to use watercolors. Prince Sadi is giving his niece a set of watercolors for Winsol, and she's my age.'"

"I didn't . . ." He set the mug on the serving tray before he dropped it.

Witch's silvery, velvet-coated laugh filled the room. "Face it, boyo. You were outmaneuvered."

"She's a . . . child."

"A child whose grandmother is a strong woman and a strong Queen. When it comes to teaching another Queen what it means to rule part of a Territory and the people who live under her hand, you couldn't ask for a better role model than Zhara. And now you've had a taste of what it will be like to deal with the next generation of Queens. The good ones, at any rate."

"I was thinking I should arrange an introduction between Jaenelle Saetien and Zoey. I don't think they've crossed paths yet."

"Mix up the activities," Witch said. "If Zoey rides, take them for a ride in one of the parks the next time you're all in Amdarh. The next day's activity should be an art gallery or a bookshop—some quieter activity that matches Zoey's other interests."

Daemon nodded, but he watched his Queen. She wasn't making an idle suggestion. "Because . . . ?"

"Because a Queen needs a court, and friendships make up the core of a strong First Circle. Whether the girls are just friendly or become close friends, whether Jaenelle Saetien has any interest in serving in a court, even for a little while, Zoey will need men and women in her First Circle who have similar interests and others who have distinct skills that can be brought into the mix."

"Do you think Jaenelle Saetien would want to serve in a court? Isn't it too early to think of these things?"

"Daemon." Witch gave him a warm smile. "In the end, you'll have no say in your daughter's choices. Maybe she'll serve in a court. Maybe she won't have any interest in doing so. Maybe she'll be friends with Zoey. Maybe she won't. Not your choice or decision, Prince. You're providing an opportunity. The rest is up to them." She paused. "Is there a stout lock on your study door?"

"Yeeesss."

"Then you'll be fine."

Oh, that didn't sound good.

"Your father survived this, and he had the entire coven living with him."

That sounded worse—and he did not want to think about it. "Which art supplies do you think I should give to Titian to let her know everyone in the family supports her interest in drawing? Right now she's been using a pencil and cheap paper."

Witch stood and walked over to the bed. "It would be more fun with colors." Using Craft, she sorted the supplies into packages. "Start with the colored pencils. You can give her the charcoal another time, and then the pastels." A beat of silence. "And, of course, the watercolors for Winsol."

He sighed, but he couldn't say he minded.

"Speaking of children, how are Beron and Mikal?" Witch asked.

He and Jaenelle Angelline had become Beron's and Mikal's legal guardians after Sylvia died and made the transformation to demon-dead—and married Saetan. Jaenelle had made sure Beron had been allowed to go to drama school and train to be an actor, despite his grandfather's objections. She'd also arranged for Mikal to live with

Tersa, an arrangement that had suited everyone over the years. He was still the boys' legal guardian, but Witch didn't ask about them often. His time at the Keep was usually spent in the continued healing of his mind and the quiet draining of some of the Black's reservoir of power to keep him sane and steady. It was not a time for her to show interest in other males, even boys he loved.

"Beron's doing well," Daemon said. "He doesn't always win the second male lead when he auditions for a play, but he's happy to take a small role, so he's seldom unemployed. And unlike many young men, regardless of their occupation, he doesn't spend everything he earns, so he can weather the idle times." He shrugged. "He shows up at the town house at least once a week for a meal. That works well for everyone. He keeps in touch with me, per his agreement with me, but I also hear about him through Helton—a fact that Beron uses as a roundabout way of telling me things without telling me things. That way I know which young Lady he's currently escorting around the town without him having to make a formal statement of interest—and without me showing up in Amdarh to ask a few pointed questions about something someone else mentioned."

"Aristos can be such gossipmongers," Witch said primly.

Daemon choked on a laugh. Lady Perzha, the former Queen of Little Weeble, had said much the same thing. Still said much the same thing. Having Witch and Perzha agree on something was a little terrifying—and a bit like trying to reason with a rockslide instead of getting out of the way.

"Mikal is growing into a fine young man, into adolescence now and thinking about his future," Daemon continued. "Depending on the day, he wants to be a butler, since he feels that, while I may own the Hall, Beale is the real power there."

Witch laughed. "He's not wrong."

"Or he wants to be some kind of court administrator, either a secretary like Holt or a Steward, because they also control the day-to-day running of things and people. Or he wants to design and run a hotel for kindred horses so they don't have to stay in stables with the ordinary horses when they have a reason to deal with humans on an official level. Or maybe it was for all the kindred since he naturally would include Scelties if he was accommodating horses. He was vague about that part."

It was so gratifying to see her standing there looking flummoxed.

Then he realized why she'd brought up the boys. "Any other young men you would like to discuss?" he asked sweetly.

Flummoxed changed to suspicious—as well it should, since she also used that particular tone of voice to good effect.

"Daemonar will be coming for private lessons twice a week from now on. Lucivar requested it after the boy had words with the young Eyrien Queen."

The sweetness now had a chill and an edge as the Sadist purred, "Now, why did he do that?" Did Lucivar know the bitch must have been the one who had hurt Titian? Daemonar wouldn't have gone after the girl otherwise.

"Not your fight, Prince," Witch warned.

"Not my fight?" He smiled a brutally gentle smile. "When the sun shines in Hell."

"Not your fight," she said again. "Daemonar's response was more than adequate, and anything you and Lucivar did now would be out of line. But Daemonar's response is the reason Lucivar wants him to have that training—with me. In the sitting room right across the corridor from our suites, since it would be too much of a risk for the boy to stay in the Misty Place long enough to receive lessons. He's not strong enough, or mature enough, to survive that."

Daemon looked toward the door to give himself time to quiet his temper and the Sadist. The Queen's suite, including the sitting room connected to her bedroom, was private, out-of-bounds to everyone but the Queen's triangle of Steward, Master of the Guard, and Consort—or those who were invited. But there had been sitting rooms within this area of the Keep where the First Circle could gather with the Queen to relax or discuss any concerns.

She was asking him to tolerate the presence of another male. Here. Spending time with his Queen. *Asking* for his agreement, not telling him he had to swallow this decision even if he choked on it. That difference gave him room to think about who had made this request.

Lucivar. Asking his Queen for help with his son.

"Sometimes Daemonar's lessons will coincide with your being here for solitary rest," Witch said. "I'll make sure he doesn't disturb you, but you'll have to tolerate his presence for that hour."

Could he do it for his brother, for his nephew?

Daemon took a deep breath and let it out slowly.

Not just another male. Not even family, which was important to him. A young Brother in the court. Someone who also needed their Queen.

He looked into her sapphire eyes and relaxed his hold on the leashes that held his temper, his power, his sexual heat—and the Sadist. Even when she'd walked among the living, a part of her had stood too deep in the abyss to be influenced—or frightened—by any aspect of who or what he was.

"If I have trouble with him being here, I will tell you."

Witch smiled. "Good. Then we're agreed?"

He nodded, then asked too softly, "Are you sure it's not my fight?"

"I'm sure." She gave his arm a thumping pat. "Besides, you already have a young Queen to deal with."

Yes. He did. Not the same, though.

"Maybe you should suggest that Titian write to Zoey and let her know how she likes working with the colored pencils," Witch said. "That way you won't have to be the go-between."

She rested a hand against his face. He turned his head just enough to kiss her palm. He felt nothing, but his lips—and heart—still knew exactly where her skin would be, and he wondered if she felt his touch even if he couldn't feel her.

"My apologies, Prince. I undid all the good Lady Zoela achieved."

"No, you didn't. She was just a respite in a jagged day."

"Then give yourself some quiet time. In the evening, we'll drain some of the reservoir in the Black."

He nodded. "I'll see Titian tomorrow."

She didn't kiss him. She never did when she was with him here. That was an intimacy that would have wounded his wife. Even if Surreal never knew why, she would have sensed a difference in him. As long as he could separate wife and lover from Queen, as long as he knew without any doubt that it wasn't possible for the Queen to be the lover again, he could stay connected to the living and stay married—and faithful to his wife.

Witch walked into her bedroom. The door shut behind her.

Daemon vanished the art supplies and settled into a chair by the window, letting the immense power of his Queen quiet his mind and heart.

# FOUR

◈

---

I don't want to go!" Sitting beside the pool at the far end of the play yard, Titian pulled her knees to her chest and wrapped her arms around them.

Jaenelle Saetien sat back on her heels, hooked her black hair behind her delicately pointed ears, and tried to puzzle out her cousin's behavior. Titian didn't like adventure the way she did, which she didn't mind because that was Titian, and they did have fun together. And she could talk to this cousin and say things she couldn't say to anyone else.

"We're just going to run some errands for Auntie Marian and pick up the things she needs at the market," she said. "It won't take long. I'm not allowed to go by myself, and Daemonar and Andulvar are at the communal eyrie doing their weapons training." If she'd known Titian was just going to sit there doing nothing, she would have joined the boys in order to do *something*.

But maybe not. Her cousin looked so unhappy, so maybe having someone there was helpful even if Titian didn't want to talk about . . . whatever . . . and Jaenelle Saetien couldn't figure out anything that would make this better. Kind of like one of the Scelties curling up with her when she felt sad and just wanted company.

She could be a Sceltie. But not as bossy.

Maybe not as bossy.

Her ability to stay quiet lasted another minute. "Are you worried that we'll run into Orian and her friends? They won't say anything mean." Not after Daemonar promised to bloody the girl if she jabbed at his sister again.

"I just don't want to go down to Riada." The words were close to a wail.

Sighing, Jaenelle Saetien returned to the eyrie and found Auntie Marian in the kitchen. "Titian doesn't want to go to Riada, but I could go. I go to Halaway on my own all the time." Well, on her own with a Sceltie as escort.

"That's Halaway," Marian replied. "I'm not giving you permission to break your father's and your uncle's rules about you going to Riada on your own. And you and Titian aren't quite old enough to stay here on your own."

"But . . ." She felt the familiar dark power a moment before someone knocked on the eyrie's front door. "Papa's here!"

She ran to the front door as her papa walked into the eyrie. She flung herself at him and hugged him as hard as she could.

"Witch-child?" He returned her hug for a moment before he eased her back enough to look at her. "What's wrong?"

"It's Titian. Can you help her, Papa?"

He didn't answer. He simply led her back to the kitchen archway, where Auntie Marian waited.

"Lucivar and some of his men left early this morning," Marian said. "A Province Queen requested his assistance. The girls were going to run some errands for me in the village, but Titian . . ." She looked at the glass doors that led to the play yard.

"Why don't you and Jaenelle Saetien go down to Riada and take care of your errands?" Daemon suggested. "I'll stay here with Titian."

She wasn't sure what message passed between the adults, but Auntie Marian nodded and said, "We won't be long."

As she and Auntie Marian walked out of the eyrie, Jaenelle Saetien wondered if by asking her papa to help, she was somehow saying Uncle Lucivar *couldn't* fix this.

Since Jaenelle Saetien's Jewel was unique and, therefore, easy to locate, Daemon waited until his daughter and Marian dropped from the Winds and he could feel their presence in Riada. Then he turned his attention to the girl sitting at the far end of the yard.

Of all the children in their family, Titian was the quiet child, the one content to sit and think or daydream; the one who wondered about so many things but often wasn't bold enough to ask questions or look for answers. Not yet, anyway.

And she was the one, right now, who was deeply wounded by another girl's cutting remark and needed protection and help. It didn't matter that another child might have shrugged off the remark as unimportant—or shrugged off the person, letting any connection fade. It didn't matter that this whole thing had boiled up from a moment that was childish and petty. For Warlord Princes, the promise to "honor, cherish, and protect" was a serious vow. For him and Lucivar—and Daemonar—the reason for the wound didn't matter anymore. That verbal wound striking Titian so deep, for whatever reason, *did* matter.

The fact that a Queen had delivered that wound mattered beyond family. He and Lucivar remembered too well how many men had died because of Queens hurling insults at one another until they insisted that a battle was the only way for them, and their courts, to recover lost status.

A Queen needed time to grow up and make mistakes like any other child, but deliberate meanness couldn't be overlooked or excused because of the girl's age. Anyone who thought otherwise hadn't seen what had happened to the Blood in Terreille.

Daemon opened the glass doors and walked the length of the play yard until he reached the small pool.

"Hello, witchling."

"Uncle Daemon." She smiled, but he read misery and dullness in her eyes. And some measure of fear.

No wonder this was tearing at Lucivar's heart. He was just surprised his brother hadn't sent Orian to Hell yet—living or dead.

After putting a thin shield over his trousers to avoid grass stains, and the subsequent scold from his valet, Daemon sat down next to Titian.

"Your father showed me some of your drawings. I thought they were excellent, especially since you're self-taught."

She didn't look at him, but he could *feel* her listening.

"I like to draw," she said in a voice so soft, he had to strain to hear her. "But . . ."

"No buts." Daemon bumped his arm against hers—his right arm, which carried the four white scars Witch had given him as remembrance and reminder. "You like to draw. But I think this was . . . private. Maybe so your brothers wouldn't tease you about it?"

"They wouldn't have teased me." Titian frowned. "Well, Andulvar might have, but Daemonar would have thumped him if he did."

That was not surprising. "Being private," he continued, "you probably didn't think much about what you used to create your drawings because you were exploring and not quite ready to show your work to other people." One finger to her chin, bringing her head up as a command to look at him. "After seeing your drawings, I did think about it."

Releasing her, Daemon called in the pads of paper and a decorative box that held one set of colored pencils, the sharpener, and the eraser. "An artist should have the proper tools."

"Oh." That was all she said as she examined the pencils and then the different kinds of paper. After carefully setting everything to one side, she threw her arms around his neck. "Thank you, Uncle Daemon. Thank you!" Then she sat back. "But I'm not an artist."

"Yes, you are." A simple statement said with all the

conviction he could put in his voice without using a spell to influence her into believing him.

"What if I can't be a good artist?"

"You would still have fun drawing pictures." Not the answer she wanted—or needed. He took one of her hands in his. "Witchling . . . can I tell you a secret?"

Titian blinked. "Okay."

"It's something your father and I would have told you when you were older, something none of the other children know yet."

"Okay."

*Careful, old son. Don't become a burden on a young heart.* "Your grandfather was the High Lord of Hell, and he ruled the Dark Realm for a very long time. When he went to the final death and became a whisper in the Darkness, I became the High Lord. I rule the Realm of the dead."

Her eyes looked huge. "But you're not dead."

"Neither was he when he first began to rule Hell."

She appeared to be thinking very hard, but he had no idea *what* she was thinking.

"That's the secret?" she finally said.

Daemon nodded. "Someday everyone will know, but not now. Not yet."

"But Papa knows?"

"Yes. So does your mother and your aunt Surreal. And a few other grown-ups. Very few."

"Because people would think you were scary if they knew?"

He expected they would do more than *think* he was scary. "Yes."

She nodded. "Some of the Queens and Ladies who come to visit think Papa is scary because he's called the Demon Prince now. But the people in Riada don't call him that. It's important to have a place where people don't think you're scary."

*What does this child think about when she's on her*

*own? And how big a heart does a person need to understand that truth at so young an age?*

"Yes. It's important." He waited a few moments. "The reason I'm telling you now is because I see the Blood who make the transformation to demon-dead and come to Hell. Some are there for a short time. Some stay a long time. Often they linger because they have unfinished business—something they ignored or put aside while they were living. Many times, sadly, it's something that would have given them joy while they were alive. Like playing a musical instrument—or drawing."

He was no longer holding her hand. She was holding his.

"Some of them have talent, and their sketches and paintings are exquisite enough to have been shown in galleries. Some . . . Let's just say there is joy in the discovery of making an idea tangible."

"You hang their pictures on the walls, just like the good ones, don't you?"

His face heated, and he hoped he wasn't blushing. "I do. There is a gallery at the Hall in Hell where work is displayed. Anyone who wants to is allowed to hang pictures there, whether the work is brilliant or awful, whether it's charcoal sketches or oil paintings or pencil drawings. For a while, these people can share something that is important to them." He brushed her hair away from her face. "Don't wait, Titian. Whether this is a hobby you'll enjoy throughout your life or something more, don't wait. And don't let some girl who is probably envious of your talent stop you. Don't let her win."

"Envious?"

"Darling, Queens learn a variety of social skills, including drawing, music, and dancing. That doesn't mean they have any talent for those activities or continue doing them a minute beyond what is necessary. I think Orian jabbed at you because she couldn't produce a drawing as good as yours, and she attacked so that you wouldn't want to draw anymore."

She didn't say anything.

"And saying flowers aren't a proper subject for an Eyrien to draw is a barrel full of crap."

She gasped at his crudity. "Uncle Daemon!"

"You know who Andulvar Yaslana was, don't you?"

"The first Demon Prince. He was the founder of our bloodline and a great Eyrien warrior. As good as Papa." She thought for a moment. "Almost as good."

Daemon bit back a smile. "That's the one. A fierce warrior who wore Ebon-gray Jewels, just like your papa. And he ruled Askavi before your papa took over ruling the whole Territory. Sometime soon, I'll stay an extra day when I'm at the Keep, and you and I will talk to Geoffrey, the historian/librarian, about some pencil drawings Andulvar did. They are very old, and fragile, so they can't leave the private part of the library, but Geoffrey will show them to us. I will give you three guesses about the subject matter of some of those sketches."

"Flowers?" Titian guessed.

"Flowers. Now, who, with any honesty, would say that Andulvar Yaslana was not a true Eyrien?"

She'd had enough, maybe even more than she could absorb for now, but he had one more thing.

He called in the artist's primer. "If you could do me a favor? I'm considering helping an artist get this primer published so that youngsters have some instruction in how to draw objects. Could you try out some of the instructions and examples and let me know if it would be helpful?"

She took the primer and carefully set it with her new supplies. "I can do that."

Deciding to leave talk about Zoey for another day, Daemon said, "Would you show me your drawings again?"

She called in her drawing pad, and they reviewed the drawings one by one. Some places he recognized from the times he'd gone to some spot or other that Lucivar enjoyed. Some flowers he recognized from the years when he and Jaenelle Angelline spent time at the cabin near Riada. He pointed out techniques she had used for shading that he'd seen in other artists' work and promised to take her to one of the art galleries in Amdarh the next time she came to visit.

When he sensed Marian and Jaenelle Saetien's return, he rose and helped Titian to her feet. He almost offered to help her carry the art supplies, but the way she hugged them made him think she wouldn't surrender them to anyone easily.

By the time they walked into the front room, everyone except Lucivar had returned, and Marian had started preparing the midday meal.

"Uh-uh," he said when Daemonar and young Andulvar crowded round to see Titian's presents. "Those are for your sister's art. These are for you." He called in a set of the line drawings, another set of colored pencils, and another sharpener.

Young Andulvar was mildly interested in the line drawings. Daemonar wasn't interested at all. And Jaenelle Saetien? A swirl of emotions dominated by her relief that he had fixed things and Titian looked happier.

"Wash up," Marian called.

The girls went to Titian's room to store her supplies. Young Andulvar headed for a bathroom to wash his hands sufficiently that his mother would let him sit at the table.

Daemonar studied Daemon. He studied the boy in turn.

"Did the Lady tell you about the lessons?" Daemonar asked.

"She told me."

"You're okay with that?"

Careful. Cautious. This wasn't a boy asking his uncle; this was a Green-Jeweled Warlord Prince asking the Black.

"There are times when I won't be able to interact with you," Daemon said.

"I know. Your healing time is private."

"Healing time" sounded so benign. Maybe someday it would be. "Yes, it is. But being that it's you, I can accept the presence of another male in that part of the Keep." He hoped that was true.

The boy didn't ask about the time Lucivar spent at the Keep, although most of that time was spent with Karla, reviewing the business of ruling Askavi.

"We should wash up," Daemonar said. "If Mother won't let Papa sit down until he washes his hands, I don't think she'll bend that rule for you."

Daemon laughed. "I *know* she won't bend that rule. You go on."

He walked into the kitchen. Marian put down the platter of sliced meats and looked at him, a question in her eyes.

He kissed her cheek and smiled. "She'll be fine. I have some thoughts for a couple of outings, both here in Ebon Rih and in Amdarh. In the meantime, Titian is helping me with a project related to art."

"Helping her uncle." Marian nodded. "That changes things, doesn't it?"

"It does." He washed his hands at the kitchen sink and accepted the towel she handed him. He looked at the table and the various dishes. A simple meal by Marian's standards. "Can I . . . ?"

"No one fills a plate until everyone is seated," she said sternly. "And don't think giving me that but-I'm-starving look will make any difference. I have male children. I am immune to that look."

"You are so strict."

"Always." Then she laughed. And because he was family, she tossed him in with her ravenous horde and let him battle for his share of the food.

There were questions Jaenelle Saetien wanted to ask, things she wanted to know, but she didn't want Papa to think she was being a brat and fanning about because she was special and thought she could ignore any rules that didn't suit her. But her teachers and the other grown-ups in Halaway *had* treated her like she was special because she wore Twilight's Dawn, and all her friends—except Mikal, but he was part of the family and didn't count in the same way—had thought she was special.

Or maybe they hadn't dared tell her that her Birthright Jewel *didn't* make her special. Except Mikal, who didn't hesitate to call her on it. He didn't *say* she was fanning about. Not anymore. He'd just point at her, then stick his butt out and wiggle it.

She'd been a brat and had told Morghann to do a wrong thing when the Sceltie had been very young. It hadn't seemed like such a bad thing at the time, but now that she was a little older, she understood how much trouble a person could cause when she let selfishness rule over kindness. The younger Scelties who were now living at the Hall played with her and kept her company, but went to Papa for training and teaching. Or they went to Holt or Beale to understand about human things. Or they went to Morghann, who taught some of the Scelties how to be a special friend when she wasn't being Papa's special friend. But they didn't want to learn from her because she had told Morghann to do a wrong thing.

She was sorry about breaking trust with the Scelties, but more than that, she sometimes worried that her being a brat during that time was the reason Papa had become so ill and still needed to go for special healing at the Keep twice a month and stay in the sealed suite of rooms at the Hall a couple of days each week.

She loved her mother, but she adored Papa, and she tried very hard not to be a brat or cause trouble or talk about things that would upset him and make him ill again.

Making the raft and going over the waterfall *might* be considered trouble, but Papa didn't know about that, and Uncle Lucivar hadn't seemed all that concerned—and the reason for *that* made her upset and wasn't something she could talk about until she got home and could tell Mikal what she'd learned.

"Something on your mind, witch-child?"

They were riding the Winds in a small Coach, and Papa

had allowed her to sit in the other driver's seat instead of in the back, which was wonderful, except Papa tended to ask questions, and even small fibs could have consequences.

But she didn't want him to think she was being a brat.

"Titian is really happy with the pencils and art paper you bought for her," she said.

"I'm glad. Lucivar and I are hoping that our encouragement will negate one person's unkind remark."

"And the boys liked the drawings they can fill in with color."

He laughed softly. "I'm not sure about that, but the line was drawn between what is hers and what is theirs."

She found a loose thread and pulled it—and started unraveling the hem of her shirt until Papa made a snipping motion with his fingers and used Craft to cut the thread.

"What's on your mind, witch-child?"

His deep voice was still quiet, still pleasant, but the question was no longer an invitation; it was a command to speak.

"How come you never bought drawing stuff for me?" she asked in a small voice.

"You, my darling, have never been shy about telling me when you were interested in something. I didn't always agree with you pursuing a particular thing, usually because I didn't think you were old enough. And sometimes you decided you weren't interested enough in a thing to follow the rules that were part of the deal. I simply assumed that if you were interested in learning to draw, or play a musical instrument, or do any number of activities, you would have pounced on me when I was working in my study and told me all about it."

"I don't pounce on you."

He burst out laughing.

She didn't think it was *that* funny.

He finally stopped laughing and cleared his throat. "Yes. Well. If you are interested in trying your hand at drawing, we can visit the art supply shop in Amdarh when we're in the city later this week and pick up what you would need. If you would like to have an instructor, I will find one. If you would like to invite your friends in Halaway to join you for drawing lessons, I will arrange it. However, if I do arrange for an instructor to provide drawing lessons for any children who are interested, those classes will continue whether you give up on drawing or not. And I will insist that you give the lessons a try for the full measure of a season, and not give up after your first attempt simply because the cat you drew looks like a sausage with ears."

He gave her a pointed look softened by a smile—a reminder that she often gave up on things if she couldn't do them perfectly on the first try. Some things. Other things she worked hard to learn. And some things Papa insisted she learn, like basic Protocol and the proper way to do Craft. Papa gave her those lessons and didn't allow *anyone* to interrupt their time together, but he wouldn't let her . . . embellish . . . a spell or alter the way she used Craft to do something until she could show him that she could do the thing the ordinary, *proper* way. And Protocol was just *booooorrrrring*. But those lessons had started as soon as she'd acquired her Birthright Jewel, and it was the same thing over and over and over.

She grumbled sometimes, but Papa's answer was always the same: *Among the Blood, Protocol isn't about following a bunch of tedious rules. Protocol is about survival. Protocol is the way those with less power can survive dealing with the Blood who wear darker Jewels. Without it, there would be slaughter.*

Maybe she would ask Uncle Lucivar if the Blood would kill one another if they didn't have a bunch of stupid rules. No, she'd ask Daemonar if *he* had to learn Protocol. They didn't have to do boring lessons whenever she visited; they did things like sparring and exploring and learning about plants and animals. So maybe, if Uncle Lucivar didn't think things like Protocol were important, she could talk Papa into dropping the boring stuff for lessons that were more interesting.

He was always willing to add lessons, but dropping lessons? Not so much. Not at all, really, until she fulfilled her side of the agreement for having the lessons.

Not knowing what to say about the art lessons, she said nothing.

After a while, Papa called in a set of the line drawings and a decorative box similar to the one he gave Titian. "You could start with these and see if art in some form appeals to you—and also let me know if you think it would appeal to other children. I'm considering giving assistance to the artist who made these in order to have more sets printed."

When she'd seen them at the eyrie, she'd thought the drawings looked boring, like something to do on a rainy afternoon if you couldn't find anything else to do. But helping Papa decide on a business matter made the drawings and pencils much more interesting. "I can do that."

He smiled. "Thank you."

She hesitated and wondered if her question would touch dangerous territory. "Did the Lady in the Mist like to draw?"

She'd been named for Papa's father and his Queen, and ever since she ran into trouble for acting like she was special, she'd wondered about how she compared to the most powerful witch in the history of the Blood—and often worried that she was found wanting, especially after what she'd overheard during this visit with her cousins.

It took forever before he replied, but he sounded thoughtful, not upset, when he finally said, "She did. All the Queens who lived at the Hall during that time took drawing, music, and dance lessons. These were considered necessary social skills and restful activities that balanced the Craft lessons and the training required of Queens in order to rule well. The Lady often did charcoal sketches when she had some free time or when the coven gathered and they all decided to spend an afternoon talking and sketching. Some of her drawings were quite good. Others . . . She would laugh when she was done and twist up the paper to use as kindling. Out of all the Queens who ruled during those years, only Lady Kalush, the Queen of Nharkhava, was a gifted watercolor artist. We have a couple of her paintings on display at the Hall."

Did she want to learn to draw now that she knew Papa's Queen had taken drawing lessons? Wouldn't that be another way she'd be competing against someone great and powerful? Besides, drawing meant sitting still.

"I met a young witch about your age," Papa said. "Lady Zoela, who is Lady Zhara's granddaughter. She helped me select the art supplies for Titian, and it occurred to me that you might enjoy her company. I could inquire about Zoela coming with us for an outing when we're in Amdarh."

"To do drawings?" She wasn't sure how much fun it would be to spend an afternoon with Zoela if they were going to sit and do drawings.

"I was thinking more along the lines of a ride in the park, if Zoela rides."

Oh. Maybe this girl *would* be interesting. And *us* meant Papa would be doing something with them and not just chaperoning. "That sounds good."

They didn't speak for a while. She was just happy to be with him, even if he had to give lots of his attention to guiding the Coach because they were riding the Black Wind.

"So," he finally said, "what did you do on this visit? Anything interesting?"

"We didn't do much. Nothing different." Which was pretty much true, except for that one thing.

He made a sound, like he'd choked on a laugh. "Were the 'not much' and 'nothing different' before or after you and Daemonar built a raft and went over a waterfall? Because I truly hope that *was* different from what you usually do."

Uncle Lucivar must have blabbed. "We've never done that before."

Oddly enough, Papa didn't seem to find that reassuring—but he did smile.

Lucivar walked around the family room, tidying up. Marian had gone—alone—to the eyrie's heated pool. Normally, he would have joined her, but he knew by the change in her physical scent and her psychic scent that her moontime was about to start, and his presence this evening bothered her.

That explained some of her emotions after Daemon and Jaenelle Saetien headed home, but he suspected it was bad timing on Daemonar's part—and the subject that was on the boy's mind—that had pushed his darling hearth witch too far.

*"I guess Uncle Daemon and Auntie Surreal have sex, since they're married."*

*"Yes, they have sex."*

*"So he puts his cock inside her?"* Not really a question, more just wanting confirmation.

*"Yes."*

*"But not from behind like the wolves mate."*

*From the kitchen archway, where she'd been standing when she'd overheard them, Marian had shouted, "Dinner!"*

Yeah, bad timing on the boy's part.

As they had taken their seats, Marian had snapped at him in front of the children—something she'd never done before—and didn't even realize it. The boys, however, sat at the table, stunned, while Titian silently slipped into her seat beside Daemonar.

It had been a long few days, and they were all feeling raw to various degrees because of the children's conflict with Orian, so Lucivar had let it pass without challenge.

He looked around the family room. Everything was back in place except the line drawings and box of colored pencils Daemon had brought for the boys to balance his gift to Titian.

Andulvar had colored in a few parts of one drawing before losing interest. Daemonar hadn't shown even that much interest. He'd sat with Titian as she looked at the artist's primer and quietly told him what each lesson demonstrated. The boy would absorb some of the information, but mostly what he'd absorbed was his sister's excitement and pleasure.

Lucivar looked through the drawings. Was there too much detail for youngsters Andulvar's age, especially when you didn't know what the picture was supposed to look like? Although this one . . .

A quick psychic scan of the eyrie told him Marian was still in the heated pool, the boys were in Andulvar's room, Titian was in her room—and there were no other demands on him this evening.

He settled in a chair and called in the hinged lap desk that his father had given him for Winsol years ago. Made of fine wood by a master carpenter, the top lifted to reveal storage compartments for paper and pens, as well as wax sticks and official and personal seals. He didn't use it often when he was home. He didn't see any reason to spoil being outside by bringing out paperwork. But the lap desk came in handy when he was visiting the villages in Ebon Rih and reviewing reports from the Eyrien guard camps and mountain settlements, or needed a flat surface for some reason.

After putting a shield over the wood, he set one of the drawings on the lap desk, selected a couple of pencils in shades of green, and starting filling in spaces. He let his mind drift, absorbed in the colors giving shape to something stark, like the green buds on trees after the barren wood of winter.

A movement at the doorway had him looking up. Titian hesitated, then hurried over to join him. She was dressed in the top and knee-length pants she wore as summer pajamas, which made him wonder how long he'd been sitting there and . . .

Marian was in their bedroom. Had her moontime started enough for her to notice it?

"Something on your mind, witchling?" he asked.

Instead of answering, she used Craft to kneel on air before sitting back on her heels. Standing—or sitting—on air as if it were solid ground wasn't a bit of Craft that was second nature to her yet, but she was steady. Even so, he created a shield and slipped it under her to catch her if she wobbled and fell.

She studied the part of the drawing he'd filled in, then studied the green pencils. Scrunching her face in fierce concentration, she pointed to part of the drawing. "How did you get that shade of green? None of the pencils are that shade."

He held up the pencil in his hand, then used it to point at another one. "I used this pencil and that one and smudged the colors together."

"Why?"

He handed her the pencil to let her hold the two shades of green side by side. "Because that's how I see the leaves on the trees around that pool we visit on warm summer days." He looked at the pads on the fingers of his left hand, now stained green from his color smudging, and called in a handkerchief. As he rubbed the color off his fingers, Titian gasped.

"Papa! You can't use a handkerchief for that. It might stain it, and you can't blow your nose on a handkerchief with stains." She called in a cloth and handed it to him. "Mother gave me a couple of old diapers to use as art rags."

He vanished the handkerchief and accepted the diaper, scrubbing more color off his fingers. Then his curiosity got the better of him. "If it's clean, why would it matter if the handkerchief was stained?"

"Because you're the Warlord Prince of Ebon Rih and Askavi."

Apparently, that was supposed to be sufficient explanation.

"Come on, witchling. Time for bed." Lucivar slipped the drawing into the lap desk's compartment for papers before vanishing the desk. The pencils and the rest of the drawings were put on a shelf set aside for the children's games. He escorted Titian to her room and tucked her in before checking on the boys. Andulvar was asleep in bed, which meant Daemonar had hauled his younger brother off the floor before going to his own room.

At Daemonar's bedroom, Lucivar tapped on the door before opening it just enough to look in. The boy was propped on his side in bed, reading.

"A few more minutes to finish this chapter?" Daemonar asked.

"A few more minutes," Lucivar agreed. He started to close the door.

"Papa?"

He leaned in—and waited, noting the worry in the boy's eyes. "Son?"

"Mother smells different."

Ah, Hell's fire. "Your mother is fine. You just picked up the scent of moon's blood. There are rules about men dealing with women during that time—and women include mothers. We'll talk about the rules in the morning."

Relief flowed from the boy. "All right."

Lucivar closed the door and headed for his and Marian's bedroom, thinking, *May the Darkness have mercy on her. And on us until she gets used to having two Warlord Princes who are driven to fuss over her.*

Marian was already in bed, maybe even asleep, but she had left a candle-light on low so he could see while he undressed. As soon as he settled in bed, she turned to him, the arm around his waist holding him tight while she rested her head on his shoulder.

"I was a bitch," she said. "I'm sorry."

"Not a bitch, just a bit bitchy." He turned his head and kissed her forehead. "Want to tell me what I did to piss you off?"

"It wasn't you." She sighed. "I had . . . words . . . with Dorian today when I went to the market."

"Since I wasn't informed of a brawl on Riada's main street, I assume you both kept it to words," Lucivar said mildly.

"Why would you think we would brawl?" Marian demanded.

"The last time you had *words* with someone, you and Roxie were tearing into each other—and I, who was just trying to be helpful and rescue you, almost got my balls kicked into my throat and then got slugged in the face."

"Well, I didn't know it was you, did I? I felt someone grab me from behind, and I did exactly what you had taught me to do." She sniffed. "And that was a long time ago, before we were married, and you shouldn't be remembering it."

As if he was going to forget it. He'd dodged the kick in the balls and most of Marian's roundhouse punch after he'd separated the women, but the bruise on his face had still hurt like a wicked bitch.

She wouldn't have gotten past his guard if he'd thought for a moment that she would try to hit him. He loved her dearly, but he'd never made that mistaken assumption again, because his hearth witch could be damn feisty when she was riled.

"You had words with Dorian," he said. "About . . . ?"

Her fingers dug into his ribs, making him glad she kept her nails short. Even so, he gently pried her fingers off his side and held on to her hand.

"She was offended that Daemonar had insulted Orian in public in front of her friends, and she insisted that he should not only apologize in public but make some amends."

"Like . . . ?"

"She said he should be Orian's escort for some dance or other such event—as if our boy is old enough to be doing that. As if that *girl* is old enough to be *thinking* about things like that." She pushed up, struggling out of his hold, and narrowed her eyes at him. "And don't you think for one moment that Daemonar should oblige either of them in order to soothe Dorian and restore peace in the Eyrien community, because I will loose the hounds of Hell on Riada before I allow that to happen."

Well . . . shit. If anyone else had said it, he'd think it was a figure of speech, but if Marian Yaslana asked the High Lord of Hell for a couple of Hell hounds in order to cause all sorts of problems, Daemon wouldn't refuse to help her.

Even as the High Lord, Daemon might be obliging enough to give his brother a warning about what was coming, but Marian was special to him, so he might not do anything beyond keeping her safe while she . . . did whatever she would do with the hounds.

He really hoped this was part of her moontime moodies, and his gentle wife would return in the morning, having forgotten all about Hell's carnivorous flora and fauna.

"Okay, Daemonar isn't going to be obliging—and neither am I," Lucivar said. "Did Dorian say anything about the comments that were made to Titian, since that's what started this?"

"Oh, yes. But *Orian's* remarks were just teasing, were harmless. They were an observation that had been kindly meant, but Titian took the words the wrong way because she's too sensitive and then acted hurt to get her brother to take her side."

His hand was in her hair and closing into a fist to hold her in place. Marian let out a startled gasp.

"Listen to me, Marian. Are you listening?"

"Y-yes."

"I know you don't feel friendly toward Dorian, but up until this clash between Orian and Titian, you've gotten along with her well enough. Or is there something you haven't told me because you didn't want Endar's family to be tossed back to Terreille—or end up in Hell?"

He felt her heart beating a fast rhythm as she realized he was worried.

"There's nothing," she said. "This all bubbled up because of things said by the children."

"Then we'll handle it. But I want your word that you will never tell Daemon what Dorian said about Orian just teasing and Titian being too sensitive."

"You have my word, but . . . why?"

Lucivar tried to relax his fist and release her, but he

couldn't. "Right now Daemon has a better idea than we do of how deeply those words hurt our girl. And the fact that those words were said by a young Queen? Bitches who inflicted wounds, whether they used knives or whips or words, were the kinds of females the Sadist hunted. Especially if they were Queens. If it comes down to that, I would rather have Orian meet my war blade for a clean death than have her destroyed by the Sadist."

"Mother Night, Lucivar." Marian searched his eyes. "You're serious?"

"Yes, I'm serious. And you might want to avoid mentioning Hell hounds being set loose in Riada, even as a jest."

He'd unnerved her. Might as well shake her the rest of the way. "Your firstborn caught the scent of moon's blood this evening."

She tried to pull away from him. He managed to open his hand and release her.

"No." She shook her head. "No."

"Yeah. Seemed better to tell you instead of letting you stumble into that change of attitude in the morning."

"But . . . he'll start fussing."

"Yes, he will." Lucivar gave her that lazy, arrogant smile. "And because you snapped at me at dinner and scared him, you'll have to let him fuss in order to reassure him that you're all right otherwise." Not giving her time to chew on that, he said, "Do you know of any reason why I couldn't use a clean handkerchief just because it has a stain?"

She looked at him as if he'd lost his mind. "Hell's fire, Lucivar. You're the Warlord Prince of Askavi. You can't be pulling out a stained handkerchief in front of the Province Queens!"

Had to be a female thing. But just in case it wasn't, he was *not* going to put the question to Daemon. "Okay. I just wondered." He gave her a light kiss and extinguished the candlelight. "Go to sleep, Marian."

"Is there something I should know about a stained handkerchief?"

He closed his eyes. "Not a thing. Go to sleep."

"What kind of stain?"

"A no-kind of stain."

"Are you sure?"

"Woman, will you let me sleep?" Exasperated, he created a ball of witchlight and floated it above the bed in order to glare at her—and caught her smiling at him.

# FIVE

The next morning, Lucivar left his eyrie while the children were having breakfast. Lord Endar's household wouldn't be up and about earlier than his, but he had a quick stop to make before he confronted Dorian and her daughter.

He flew down to Riada and knocked on the door of the Queen's residence at an hour of the day that should have had her court bristling at the interruption in their Lady's private time.

She'd been expecting him, had even anticipated what he'd come to ask—or officially request, since she ruled Riada but was under his hand. He listened to her proposal and agreed with how she wanted to approach a problem that involved Eyriens but would have a serious impact on the Rihland people for generations if the problem wasn't corrected now. Then he flew to Endar's eyrie to deliver the terms by which a young Queen would be allowed to continue residing in Askavi.

Endar and Dorian's son, Alanar, answered the door. Lucivar figured the only reason the boy still held half a pastry in one hand was that he already had so much food crammed into his mouth, he couldn't fit another crumb in and still breathe.

"Prz," Alanar said, adding a quick bow to help with the meaning of the sound.

"Chew," Lucivar said. "Swallow. *Then* you can fly. If you hit a pocket of air with your mouth stuffed like that, you'll choke." Or spew it out, creating a very unpleasant sort of rain for the people below him.

The boy eased past him and went outside.

Shaking his head and wondering how often his own boys stuffed themselves that way when he wasn't home and they weren't under Marian's watchful eyes, Lucivar closed the door and stepped farther into the eyrie's front room. Unlike the front room in his home, which was un-cluttered because he used it as a workout space in bad weather, this one held benches and tables—an arrange-ment that suggested a waiting area for people requesting an audience.

There were privileges to being a Queen, just as there were privileges attached to being a Warlord Prince. But those privileges came with a price, and if the price wasn't paid . . .

Endar hurried toward him. "Prince? Did we have a meeting?"

"No, we didn't. I'm here to speak to Ladies Dorian and Orian. You should stay and hear this so that you know the lines that are being drawn."

Endar's brown skin took on a gray hue. "Lines?"

Having come from Askavi Terreille, Endar would have heard the stories about how—and why—Lucivar had earned the reputation of being volatile and savage. And Endar had seen what happened here in Ebon Rih when Lu-civar had stood alone on a killing field against the follow-ers of another Warlord Prince. That the Demon Prince was in his home so early in the morning talking about drawing lines would be enough to frighten any sane man.

"Your wife and daughter, Lord Endar."

"They're still—"

"Now."

He knew Endar had sent the message on a psychic thread. He knew the man had conveyed the urgency of the command. But it seemed Orian—or her mother—decided to keep him waiting as a way to test the status of a Queen against the power and temper of the Warlord Prince who ruled the land where they lived.

Endar was sweating by the time woman and girl made their appearance. Lucivar just waited.

"Prince Yaslana," Dorian said, "how unexpected."

Meaning, *How rude of you to show up so early.*

Lucivar waited.

"But it's a delightful surprise," Orian added.

The disrespectful undertone in her voice scraped at his temper and made it hard for him to remember that she and Daemonar were the same age, which meant the girl was riding the rough air and long years of adolescent emotions. But that disrespectful undertone being directed toward an Ebon-gray Warlord Prince also made it easy for him to remember what it had been like when the Queens in Terreille had thought they could get away with anything just because they were Queens.

Lucivar waited, assessing the females as members of the Eyrien community—and as adversaries. He kept his temper leashed, but when he finally spoke, his voice was sharp enough to sting—a tone every Eyrien warrior who worked for him recognized as a warning that, if challenged, his temper wouldn't stay leashed, and his response would be brutal and bloody. "When I say *now*, I don't mean after you're done primping—or until you've delayed long enough to test me."

The look in Dorian's eyes confirmed that that was exactly what she'd been trying to do—test how far he would yield because her daughter was a Queen. The look of anticipation in Orian's eyes made him wonder if the girl had been tainted to the point that she was already beyond saving. But he remembered the bright-eyed toddler she had been, and he wasn't willing to give up on her, although he didn't think she would thank him for the restrictions he was about to place on her life—or the indelicate ways he was prepared to assure her obedience.

If the only way to shake her out of whatever belief was

taking root was to scare the shit out of her now, so be it. "When I say *now*, I mean *now*, and you will do well to remember that in the future. I am the Warlord Prince of Ebon Rih. I am the Demon Prince of Askavi. For the sake of every other person living in Askavi, and especially here in Ebon Rih, whether they are landen or Blood, I will not allow you to test me again."

"If this is about Titian being . . . ," Orian began.

"It's not about Titian. Not anymore. The wounds you inflicted will heal or scar as they will, and there is nothing you can do about that." He stared at her until she squirmed. "This is about you, Orian, and what kind of Queen you will be. This is about whether or not you will survive. If you follow the path you seem to be on right now, of thinking that a Queen can do and be anything she pleases, then you won't be looking at forming a court when you come of age. At best, you'll be looking at exile or, more likely, execution. If you are what your behavior of the past few days suggests you are, then I will be meeting you on a killing field—and I will destroy you in order to protect everyone else."

"Prince, please," Endar begged.

He heard fear in the father's voice. He saw shock in the mother's eyes—and in the daughter's.

"You will report to the Queen of Riada every afternoon from now on," Lucivar said. "You will be given lessons in Protocol since your behavior this morning tells me that you have not received that necessary part of your education—or have been told, for some reason, that those rules don't apply to Queens." He ignored Dorian's outraged gasp at the insult, which confirmed the truth of his words. "You will also receive the training necessary to understand your responsibilities and duties as a Queen. You will accompany Riada's Queen whenever she desires your presence in order to observe how a court works—even if that means canceling your own plans. The only days you will be excused from the training are the first three days of your moontime. If you lie even once because you're feeling pissy or defiant, and claim your moon's blood started when it hasn't, I will haul you down to Riada to face whatever discipline the Lady's court demands—and I will be here every time after that to make sure you're being honest."

"That's insulting," Dorian snapped. "You would humiliate a Queen?"

"I'm informing her—and you—of the consequences of a lie. If she's humiliated, it's because she made a bad choice and has to pay the price."

"You're calling my wife's and my daughter's honor into question," Endar said, sounding as if he'd received a gut wound.

"Yes. I am." Lucivar regretted hurting the man, but he'd come here to keep what was said private in order to spare Endar and his family from being isolated from the other Eyriens—because no one wanted to be on the wrong side of a line drawn by the Demon Prince.

"What about *your* son?" Dorian said. "What about what *he* said to a Queen?"

"He said nothing to a Queen. He insulted Orian in the same way she had insulted Titian, matching hurt for hurt. But he, too, is going to receive additional training because of this incident." He focused on Orian. "You're dismissed."

"But . . . ," the girl protested.

*"You're dismissed."*

"Orian, do as you're told," Endar said.

Lucivar waited until Orian left the front room. Then he put an aural shield around the room because he suspected the girl would try to listen to them. When that was done, he turned to Dorian. "I haven't had a quarrel with you until now. I would prefer not to have one because you don't want to enter into a fight with me. You really don't. Whatever ambition you're planting on the back of your daughter being a Queen, tear it out by the roots, Dorian. Tear it out now, for her sake. Or have you forgotten what it was like to live in Terreille?"

"I've forgotten nothing," Dorian snapped. Then her eyes filled with tears. "What's wrong with wanting better for your children? What's wrong with wanting Orian to be someone people will respect and deem important?"

"She's a Queen," Lucivar replied. "She's already important. Whether she'll be respected will depend on whether or not she's a good Queen. I won't let a bitch hold so much as one man or an acre of land. Not in Askavi." He looked at Endar. "Orian is expected in Riada after the midday meal. You should make sure she gets there."

"If that is all, Prince?" Dorian spat out the words.

He released the aural shield and waited until the woman left the room before turning toward the door.

Endar looked miserable. "Could I have done something?"

Lucivar started to shrug off the question, then paused to consider. "Orian is centuries away from forming a court. Why this sudden need for the girl to be important? What's scraping your wife's heart, Endar?"

"I don't know." Endar sighed. "I think she's disappointed in me, in my being a teacher. Eyriens always considered it demeaning work unless a man was so physically damaged in battle that he could no longer fight."

"That was in Terreille. This is Ebon Rih in Kaeleer." He studied the man who'd had to work hard to improve his own education in order to teach the Eyrien children. "Has anyone said that to you? Implied that your work wasn't valued in the Eyrien community?" *Anyone besides your wife?*

"No, but it's hard to shake off generations of beliefs. What was a relief to Dorian when our children were younger now seems a source of embarrassment to her. Maybe that's why she's become obsessed with what Orian will be able to do once she's old enough to establish her court—and is always talking about how the girl should be setting up an unofficial court now."

"Unless Orian is befriending the Eyrien youngsters who live around Doun, her unofficial court would be made up of Rihlanders, and that court will change every few years as those girls grow up and look toward serving in official courts or following other adult pursuits."

Endar hesitated. "I think Dorian expects Daemonar to join Orian's court when she forms one and feels he should be eager to escort his Queen around the village now."

Oh, his boy would be thrilled if he could escort his Queen around the village. But Witch wasn't going to stroll around Riada, and whether he spent some time serving in another court or not, Daemonar would never consider any other Queen to be *his* Queen and have his absolute loyalty. Knowing that, Lucivar considered his words carefully. "They're growing up and taking separate roads. Orian shouldn't think of Daemonar as anything more than a childhood friend she used to play with. If she, or Dorian, thinks he'll be more, she's setting herself up for disappointment." *Or worse.*

Endar made a sad sound. "I figured Orian put an arrow through the heart of that friendship the moment I heard what she'd said to Titian. Daemonar wouldn't remain friends with someone who did that. Not even a girl who was a Queen."

"Keep trying to find out what's wrong with Dorian. If she keeps pushing, she and Orian are both heading into rough winds and jagged canyons. And if you need help, ask me."

As he flew to the communal eyrie to do a bit of sparring and review the day's tasks with Rothvar, Lucivar wondered about the reason for this change in Dorian's behavior.

Since he maintained a psychic web that kept him quietly aware of everyone within the boundaries of the SaDiablo estate, Daemon felt Jaenelle Saetien's continued agitation long before she reached his study, and resigned himself to an unpleasant afternoon.

His own fault for allowing his daughter's emotions to adjust the day's plans—not only his plans but also those of the Province Queen whom he'd intended to see that afternoon. Now he would have to see the woman before she headed out for her own evening commitments.

Lucivar wouldn't have let a child's emotions get in the way of scheduled lessons. Lucivar would have let the child sulk or grumble or wheedle or cry or shout and be angry. What he wouldn't have done was let the child reschedule the lessons because she had to do something terribly important but wouldn't tell him what it was. He would have sat there, waiting for the storm to pass, and *then* turned the hourglass that indicated the length of the lesson. And if another lesson followed that? So be it, and whatever plans the child had made with friends were either postponed or forfeit. End of discussion.

It was lowering to admit it, but Jaenelle Saetien seemed to thrive better in the Yaslana household than she did with him at the Hall. Then again, she was only there for a week when she went to visit. The Darkness only knew how much she would clash with Lucivar if she stayed longer. Since he and Lucivar set up rules for the children that applied to both households, maybe it was the way they upheld the rules that made a difference?

Living at the Hall was different from living at the eyrie. Different in size, different in the way they lived. Sometimes Daemon wondered if Jaenelle Saetien would be better off living in Amdarh with Surreal, except Surreal traveled so much as his second-in-command, visiting the family estates as well as checking in with Dhemlan's District Queens and Province Queens. He needed to stay at the Hall most of the time for everyone's safety. That meant he took responsibility for Jaenelle Saetien's education, whether it was overseeing what she was learning at the school in Halaway or giving her lessons in Craft and Protocol.

He suspected her lessons in Craft and Protocol were going to be a problem today.

Something had happened shortly before he and Jaenelle Saetien left Lucivar's eyrie to return to the Hall, something she didn't want to tell him about. Something more than the things they *had* discussed on the way home. But that *something* had been the source of her growing unhappiness last night and had turned into agitation this morning, so he'd given her time to think about it or work through it. Gave her every opportunity to talk to him about it.

Now that agitation was going to bump up against the rescheduled lesson time, and he couldn't make further adjustments to the day. But how could he deny her the space to regain her emotional balance when he required the same thing? How could he say her feelings weren't as important as scheduled lessons because her feelings wouldn't put the Blood in danger if she lost control?

And what would he be teaching her if he buckled under her drama and emotions instead of insisting that she fulfill her tasks within the family, even if those tasks were simply showing up for her lessons?

As Jaenelle Saetien flung the door open and rushed into his study, Daemon looked at the clock on the corner of his desk and said mildly, "You're late, witch-child."

"Mikal's here, and I really, really need to go out riding with him," she said, sounding breathless.

"You really, really need to stay here so that we can do your Craft and Protocol lessons," he countered.

"Papa! This is *important*."

Daemon hesitated—and cursed himself for the hesitation.

After he'd been taken away from his father immediately after his Birthright Ceremony, nothing he'd wanted or needed had been important. Now everything in him wanted his daughter to have what was important to her. But giving her everything she believed was important at a particular moment was as bad for her as being given nothing—and he fought that inner battle almost daily because she was just a little older than he had been when Dorothea had put a Ring of Obedience on him and . . .

He shoved those thoughts away. He couldn't allow memories of his life at that age to color his decisions about Jaenelle Saetien's life and what she *needed* rather than wanted.

"Why can't you talk to Mikal for a few minutes here?"

he asked. "Or ask him to come in after his ride and talk to you after your lessons?"

"Because I *can't*." Her voice turned wheedling. "We'll just take a short ride, and I can have my lessons after that. *Please*, Papa."

Knowing how long she could stretch out a short ride, he said, "Let's see your schedule."

"What?"

"Your schedule," he repeated patiently. "That thing you and I work out each week so that we both know when your required appointments, which include lessons, are going to take place, as well as the social invitations you chose to accept and what you need to do in preparation for those invitations."

"I don't know where it is," she mumbled.

Daemon doubted that was true, but he called in his copy of her schedule and turned it around so that she could read it. He pointed to the lessons that had been crossed out that morning and written in for the afternoon.

For now, actually.

Then he pointed to the outing she had arranged before she had gone to Ebon Rih. "You and your friends are sup-posed to see a play in the village this afternoon. It starts at a specific time. When we spoke this morning, you asked me to adjust your lesson time so that you would still be able to change clothes, meet your friends, and arrive at the theater before the play started."

"I know, but talking to Mikal is *important*."

"Important enough to give up going to the play?"

She stared at him. "I can get to the play on time!"

"Your lessons take two hours, witch-child. We do this three times a week. You know this. You'll be home from the play in time for dinner. Mikal can join us, and you can talk to him then."

"I need to talk to him *now*."

She wasn't going to listen to him, so he accepted that she was going to experience the emotional equivalent of skinned knees. "Very well. Your Craft lesson will start one hour from now. I will tell you when half the time for the ride is gone so that you know when to return. Your lessons will not be cut short. If you're late, you won't go to the play. Is that understood?"

"Yes," she said, rushing out of the study.

*Had* she understood? Not likely. But she would.

He sighed and rubbed the ache that was building at his temples. A minute later, Beale tapped on the study door, walked in, and placed a large mug of specially blended tea on the desk.

"Trouble?" Beale asked as Holt tapped on the door and walked in.

Daemon looked at the two men who were his consultants when it came to dealing with children. They not only had the benefit of observing how Saetan had dealt with Jaenelle Angelline and the coven; they had nieces and nephews as examples of "normal" behavior.

"Maybe I expect too much," he said. "She's still a child with a slippery concept of time."

"Yes, she's a child, but would you care to bet on whether or not the young Lady knows exactly how long it will take her to change into her outfit and get down to the village in order to have time to chatter with her friends before taking their seats for the play?" Holt asked.

Phrased that way, it was a sucker's bet, and he knew it. "How much?"

"Five gold marks."

Daemon looked at Beale. "And you?"

"The same."

Definitely a sucker's bet. "Fine."

Holt walked out, whistling.

Beale hesitated, then said quietly, "Under similar circumstances, if your father had already yielded once to accommodate a youngster's request to reschedule lessons, he would not have given up one minute of lesson time, even if it meant a youngster had to forfeit going to a play and spending time with friends."

"Thank you, Beale." Now Daemon hesitated. "I can't always be here for her."

"That is true, Prince, but you can't apologize for what you need to do for everyone's sake, including hers, by giving in and letting the young Lady have her way."

*Another hard truth,* Daemon thought as he drank the tea and read through some of the letters Holt had left on his desk that morning.

"Let's ride to the pond," Jaenelle Saetien said.

Mikal gave her a long look. "We could get back in time if we ride to the pond and turn right around."

"In time?"

"For your lessons. I asked the Prince if you needed to be back at a specific time, and he told me you had lessons this afternoon before you go to the play with your friends."

She gasped. "Why'd you ask him about that?"

"Because you were acting strange, and I wondered if you were trying to get out of your lessons for some reason. Because you said you wanted to talk, but you're not talking. And most of all, because I'm old enough now to be held accountable if I'm essentially standing escort."

"Well, you're not standing escort. We're just friends taking a ride."

"And more than anything else," Mikal continued, "the Prince gives *me* lessons in Craft and Protocol. He's your father, so you don't think anything about it, but it's a privilege to be trained by him, and I don't want to lose that privilege. So when he says the time is half gone, we're turning back."

"I don't have to turn back if I don't want to."

"Then you're walking home because the horses and I will turn back."

She pouted. "You're being mean, and this is *important.*"

*Then talk,* he said on a psychic thread.

This flavor of impatience with her was new, and she didn't like it. And she'd counted on being able to ride away from the Hall and then dismount and talk because she didn't want the horses to go back to the stables and blab to her father. And she didn't want to talk on a psychic thread because it didn't *feel* the same as saying words out loud. And they weren't even *riding*. They were just sitting on horses that were walking around.

But Mikal had stated his intentions, and she knew he wouldn't budge, so she took a deep breath and told him about going to the river with Daemonar and making a raft and riding it through the rapids and over the waterfall.

*Hell's fire,* Mikal said when she finished. *You did that and Lucivar saw you? And you can still sit on a horse today?* He whistled. *You're lucky he didn't get mad enough to make the river steam.*

*He couldn't get mad,* she replied with enough bitterness to have Mikal staring at her. *I heard Uncle Lucivar talking to Auntie Marian and Papa before Papa and I got in the Coach to come home. He couldn't get mad at Daemonar and me because he'd done the same thing with the *Queen*. I thought this was *my* idea, that this was a new adventure that nobody had done before, but *she* did it first! She always does things first!*

*I doubt the Lady and Prince Yaslana were the first people to have gone over a waterfall. Maybe not quite that way, but—*

*Everything I do, *she's* done first, but she was the Queen and important, so she did it better. Everyone thinks so.* *Even Papa,* she added silently, hoping it wasn't true.

Mikal was quiet for a too-long time. *Lady Angelline did a lot of things better than anyone else—did some things even better than the High Lord, and *he* was very powerful. She did some things no one else had ever done before or will ever do again. But that was Lady Angelline.*

*I can't be like her.*

*Nobody can.*

*Witch-child,* Papa said. His sudden presence on a psychic thread startled her so much, she almost fell out of the saddle. *You should be on your way back to the Hall if you want to get cleaned up and change clothes after your lessons and still reach the theater in time to meet your friends.*

Mikal gave her a sharp look. *Should we be turning back now?*

*There's time.*

They rode for another minute before Mikal turned his horse toward the Hall.

*Mikal! We're not finished talking!*

*Then talk fast.*

*I just . . . I'm not fanning around, okay?*

*Okay.*

*I want something that is mine, just mine. Something the Queen hadn't done before I thought of it, something she'd *never* done. I want to do something and not have people say they remember when *she* had done that same thing.*

Mikal looked thoughtful. *The High Lord once said everything a child does is a new discovery for the child and a familiar story for the adults. That's why children survive. There is a precedent for the young being courageous to the point of being stupid. Face it, Jaenelle Saetien. If Lucivar hadn't gone over that waterfall with Lady Angelline, he would have killed you and Daemonar flatter than dead.*

She thought maybe she would have preferred a fierce scolding for doing something that was just her own than acceptance because the Queen had done it.

Maybe she would have preferred that. Maybe.


Daemon knew Jaenelle Saetien had returned to the Hall with a few minutes to spare, not only because he had sensed the presence of Twilight's Dawn but because Mikal had poked his head into the study to confirm the time for his own lessons the following day and to ask permission to spend a day in Amdarh the following week in order to visit Beron, who had promised to take him around to a few places in the city.

Without asking what places the brothers would be visiting—Helton would be given an itinerary before the boys left the town house—Daemon confirmed the date. The family already had plans to be in Amdarh this week, so if he couldn't make another trip to the city that soon, he'd send Holt as an escort for Mikal.

That much decided, Daemon reviewed the next report—and waited. The clock ticked, ticked, ticked.

Jaenelle Saetien finally showed up, washed and dressed in the clothes she'd chosen for attending an afternoon play at the theater—and forty minutes late for her first lesson.

Offering no comment or criticism, Daemon came around the desk and indicated she should join him on the side of the study that was furnished for informal meetings, with its long sofa, comfortable chairs, and tables. He called in an hourglass that measured an hour and turned it to start the sand running in the glass. Setting it on the table in front of the sofa, he said pleasantly, "Shall we begin?"

She eyed the hourglass. "Maybe we should do the lessons this evening. There isn't time to do them now."

"There is plenty of time. One hour of basic Craft and one hour of Protocol."

"But . . ."

"I rearranged a meeting with a Province Queen to make this time available for your lessons. I'll be heading out for that meeting as soon as your mother gets home, so it isn't possible to do lessons this evening. Therefore, we will do them now, at the time you had requested." He waited a beat. "Shall we begin?"

The Craft lesson was more of a disaster than he'd anticipated. She pouted; she sulked; she became weepy and claimed she couldn't do what he wanted her to do. Since they were reviewing making a ball of witchlight—something he *knew* she could do—he persisted until the last grain of sand fell.

Before she could jump up and head for the door, he turned the hourglass and said pleasantly, "Now for the lesson in Protocol."


Surreal dropped from the Green Wind to the landing web in front of the Hall, then hesitated when she saw Beale standing in the open doorway.

"Should I assume you're just taking the air?" she asked as she crossed the gravel drive to stand with him.

"That assumption will do," he replied.

A shriek came from the direction of Daemon's study. Since it came from behind a closed door and she had the full length of the great hall between her and that closed door, the sound had to be uncomfortable for anyone inside the room.

"I thought Jaenelle Saetien was seeing a play with some of her friends in the village."

"After ignoring some agreed-upon rescheduling that she herself requested, the young Lady still thought her father would shorten the Craft and Protocol lessons in order for her to reach the village in time to see the play. I believe she has just realized that she will not reach the theater in time to see anything."

"Oh, Hell's fire." Surreal raked her fingers through her hair, then caught the decorative comb before it fell to the ground. "How long can we stand out here taking the air?"

The study door opened. Jaenelle Saetien stormed out, spun around, and screamed, "You're the meanest papa in the whole Realm! You ruined everything by making me do those stupid lessons! I never get to have fun!"

"This from the child who wasn't killed flatter than dead for going over a waterfall on a raft," Surreal murmured. She eyed the Hall's butler. "I guess you heard about that."

"We heard enough."

Using a light psychic probe, Surreal followed her daughter's vigorous journey to the family wing. The distance between the great hall and the family wing was such that she shouldn't have been able to hear a door slam. But she did.

"I guess that's one Craft lesson that took hold," she said cheerfully as she stepped inside. "I'd better check on the other participant of this to-do."

It unnerved her to walk into the study and see Daemon standing near his desk, a half-filled glass of brandy held in a hand that trembled.

"Sadi?" She kept her voice quiet—and she kept the study door open.

"I'm the meanest papa in the whole Realm."

He sounded hurt. She wanted to smack him for that, so she walked up to him, took the brandy, and swallowed down half of it. "That's today. Tomorrow it will be someone else's turn." She handed back the glass. "I take it the lessons went badly?"

"Oh, I think the lesson about being on time for lessons if one wants to go to a social activity made an impression," he replied. "I'm sorry to leave you with this, but I have an appointment with a Province Queen that I need to keep, and I won't be back in time for dinner."

Odd time for Daemon to make an appointment, unless . . .

Ah. If he'd inconvenienced someone besides himself in order to accommodate Jaenelle Saetien, that explained some of his hurt over being called mean because *she* hadn't lived up to her side of the agreement. "So what else have we learned from this?"

"Well, I don't know about you, but I've learned that there are days when I'm going to be wrong no matter what I do."

"Hmm. In that case, I'll postpone Jaenelle Saetien's crossbow lessons a while longer."

A huff of laughter before he said dryly, "Yes. Thank you for that." He hesitated, then gave her a light kiss. "I'll be back this evening."

*But you won't ask to spend the night with me,* she thought as he walked out of the study. After the fracas with Jaenelle Saetien, he wouldn't feel easy about sleeping with her in case his temper took on too much of an edge.

At least she'd been able to quiet some of his emotional storm. Now she'd see what she could do to settle her daughter's mood before the girl gave her father a reason to cancel the trip to Amdarh—and the ride in the park with Lady Zoela.

# SIX

Surreal broke open a warm biscuit and added generous portions of butter and berry jam, as well as a dollop of fresh whipped cream, before taking a bite.

She didn't know what had been said yesterday when Jaenelle Saetien had gone to Manny's cottage, no doubt to complain about having the meanest papa in the Realm, but the girl had come home chastened to the point of apologizing to Daemon for saying mean things to him when it was her own fault that she hadn't gone to the play with her friends. The apology had smoothed things over between man and girl, and the three of them had spent an enjoyable evening together after arriving in Amdarh.

Daemon finished his coffee, then pushed his chair away from the breakfast table. "Are you sure you don't want to come with us? It's a refreshing morning for a ride."

Surreal gave him a sharp smile. "It rained last night, so *refreshing* means riding under drippy leaves. No, thank you. Besides, Zhara invited me to join her for coffee and pastries, served with a hefty side of information exchange and a dollop of gossip. *That* is my idea of refreshing."

He laughed softly. "Well, aren't you sassy?"

"I'm not the one who will spend the morning with two giggling girls."

"That's a matter of opinion."

"Watch it, Sadi."

Daemon walked around to her side of the table and gave her an affectionate kiss—a kiss that might have become warmer if Jaenelle Saetien hadn't appeared in the doorway of the breakfast room and said, "Come on, Papa! We're going to be late!"

"I guess someone has developed a new appreciation for being on time," Surreal whispered.

"I guess someone has," he whispered back. He gave her another quick kiss before he and Jaenelle Saetien left the town house.

Surreal poured herself another cup of coffee, then let it go cold.

How could she tell Daemon that she wanted to be his second-in-command and his occasional lover but not his wife?

Maybe she was putting too much emphasis on the word "wife." Or the wrong emphasis. For a Warlord Prince, what was a wife, anyway? A buffer against the unwanted attention of other women. Oh, she could be other things as well, but a weapon that was always honed for war needed someone to keep bloody conflicts to a minimum. That buffer was usually a wife or a Queen—or both. Especially when the Warlord Prince wore a dark Jewel.

"Both," she whispered. At the time of Witch's return, she'd been so scared or angry, so desperately trying to survive the emotional storm caused by Daemon's growing instability combined with his increased sexual heat, that she hadn't appreciated what the Queen had meant about being a buffer between herself and Sadi. Hadn't appreciated that her partnership with Sadi wasn't her only partnership.

Leaving the breakfast room, she found Helton and requested a fresh pot of coffee, two mugs, and cream and sugar. An unusual request since she drank her coffee black, but Helton didn't ask who might be joining her. She couldn't have given him an answer even if he'd asked.

When he brought the tray to the morning room, where

she took care of correspondence whenever she was in Amdarh, she thanked him and locked the door behind him—then put a Gray shield around the room.

She wasn't sure how this worked, even though it had happened a few times. Wasn't sure it *would* work with her being at the town house. But she fixed the two mugs of coffee, then held them and closed her eyes as she descended into the abyss to the level of the Gray.

*Lady. Sister. Can we talk?*

That moment of biting cold. When Surreal opened her eyes, she stood in the Misty Place.

A moment later, Witch appeared, wearing a sleeveless sapphire dress that reached midthigh. "Hello, Surreal."

"Hello, sugar. It's been a while."

Witch smiled, but she looked puzzled. "You could come to the Keep if you want to talk. Most days, that would be safer."

"No time to travel today." *And I want to do this before I lose my nerve.* Surreal held out one mug. "I brought coffee." She hesitated. "Can you drink coffee now?"

"No, but I appreciate the thought." Witch took the mug. "What brings you here?"

"I don't want to be a proper wife."

"Well, thank the Darkness for that. I hope you smacked whoever said you needed to be."

Surreal blinked. Then she tried again to explain something she wasn't sure how to say. "Sadi needs a wife. We can agree on that."

"Yes, he does, and yes, we can."

"But I'm not suited to be a . . . a buffer. As a wife, Marian is a buffer between Lucivar and the rest of the Blood."

"Buffer" somehow sounded soft and comforting, which were words that suited Marian—when she wasn't riled.

"So tell me, my Dea al Mon Sister, what kind of wife are you?" Witch asked.

"Sword and shield." The moment she said the words, she knew they were true.

A warm smile. "So you've decided." Witch paused, as if

considering what to say. "You're not the first witch who chose to marry a Warlord Prince in order to be his sword and shield. That position, while not official since it isn't always connected to a court, is as valuable a service to the Realm as any other service to a Queen and has much in common with a Queen's Consort in its duties. Because those duties are intimate, one always hopes for at least affection between the two people if not some kind of love. The details of that arrangement are as individual as the people involved, and those details are no one else's business. But you have to tell him, Surreal. You have to tell Daemon what to expect from a wife who is a sword and shield."

"And if he won't accept it?" she asked softly.

"Why wouldn't he?" Witch asked just as softly. "It's what you were when you married him, even if you hadn't used those words."

"And then, that night . . ." She didn't have to be more specific about the night that had changed—and broken—so much. "I ran the next morning in order to survive. I can't be the Sadist's lover. I can't."

"No, you can't."

"But you could."

"Daemon and I suited each other in every way, including the darkest ways. If he hadn't survived what had been done to him in Terreille, if he hadn't managed to reach Kaeleer when he did, I would have never known that kind of love because he was the only one who was able to get past the scars I carry from Briarwood. And he was the only one who had the strength and courage to be a lover to everything I was."

"If he hadn't met you, he wouldn't have known anyone who could love and accept everything he is," Surreal said.

"As I said, we suited each other in every way."

*And you still do.*

"It's time for you to go. Even the Gray isn't safe in the Misty Place." Witch handed the mug back to Surreal. "Tell him where you're drawing the lines, Surreal. It will be easier for both of you if you do."

"Maybe I should start tucking my crossbow in bed with me, like Mrs. Beale does with her meat cleaver."

Witch stared at her, wide-eyed. "Do you *ever* want Daemon to sleep with you?"

"Well, Beale seems to manage with—"

"Good-bye, Surreal."

Biting cold.

Surreal blinked. Then she laughed and felt a part of herself begin to heal. Setting the mugs on the tray, she went up to her room to freshen up before her visit with Lady Zhara.

"Thank you for inviting me to ride with you," Zoey said. "Lord Weston and I ride in the park at least once a week, because I like riding and he's a good rider, but it's different riding with another girl. I mean, Weston *listens* to what I'm saying, but he's a grown-up male and doesn't *understand* what I'm saying half the time."

Jaenelle Saetien looked over her shoulder at the two men riding far enough behind them not to overhear her conversation with Zoey. That didn't mean they were unprotected. She knew Papa had light defensive shields ahead of them and on either side to keep them safe. "My papa understands what I'm saying most of the time. That's not as comfortable as you might think."

"I think it would be wonderful."

Zoey's wistful smile made Jaenelle Saetien feel a little guilty. Papa was supposed to be riding *with* them, not behind with Zoey's guard, but there had been something about the light in Zoey's eyes when she'd looked at Papa that made Jaenelle Saetien reluctant to share him with *another* person. That was the reason she had emphasized that Zoey was *her* guest. Papa had yielded—and had looked pleased—but she wondered if he'd known it was because she didn't want to share him with a Queen, who would be more important simply because she was a Queen.

"That's why I'm going to send Prince Sadi reports,"

Zoey continued. "I think it's important for Queens to keep the ruler of a Territory informed."

"What can you tell him? It will be years and years before you rule even a village."

"That doesn't mean I don't pay attention to the people who live in Amdarh or notice when someone needs help. I tell my grandmother about what I observe because that is part of my training as a Queen, but sending Prince Sadi a report would be . . . nice."

"Can't you tell your own papa?"

Zoey's lips quivered. "I don't have a father. I have a sire."

Jaenelle Saetien gasped. Her hands tightened on the reins, causing her horse—a kindred Warlord—to toss his head and snort. "Sorry," she murmured, patting his neck. "It's all right."

She'd never met anyone who wasn't one of the kindred who just had a sire instead of a father. "Why?" she asked—and then wondered if she was being too curious. After all, she and Zoey had just met, and this seemed like the kind of heart-deep stuff you only told a good friend.

Unless you didn't have any good friends?

"He told my grandmother he didn't want the weight of duty that came with raising a Queen, but he would be there for the Birthright Ceremony so that paternity could be acknowledged," Zoey said.

"What did your mother say?"

They rode in silence for a forever amount of time before Zoey said, "My mother wasn't a natural Black Widow, but the Hourglass's Craft called to her. She was near the end of her apprenticeship when she met my father and they fell in love. My grandmother says my father isn't a bad man, just a selfish one, but my grandfather said once that my father had been more in love with the status that came from being part of our family than with my mother. I was born while my mother was a journeymaid. One day, she wove a tangled web of dreams and visions, and something went wrong. She didn't fall into the Twisted Kingdom. She's not insane, exactly. She's just . . . gone. Lost in whatever she saw in the tangled web. Grandmother visits her once a week at the healing house that takes care of people whose minds are . . . not right. I only have to visit her for an afternoon every month. That's hard because I remember who she was, but she doesn't remember me. She's still connected to her body enough that she can feed and clothe herself and knows how to use the toilet, but my mother isn't there. Not really."

Jaenelle Saetien thought about her own grandmother. Tersa was a broken Black Widow who wandered the roads in the Twisted Kingdom, but she was able to live in Halaway, knew her family and talked to them, and participated in celebrations like Winsol. Mikal lived with Tersa, and Papa wouldn't have allowed that if Tersa wasn't a little bit able to look after a boy.

"I'm sorry," she said—and meant it.

"Me too."

She hesitated, but Zoey's life was so different from her own that curiosity won over what Papa might call good manners. "Is that why your papa doesn't live with you? Because he couldn't raise a Queen on his own with your mother being lost that way?"

Papa had been very, very ill for a while, but he was getting better, would continue to get better. But if he *hadn't* gotten better, would her life be more like Zoey's? Without either parent? No. Her mother would have stayed, would have protected her, loved her.

Zoey's smile was bitter and too old for someone their age. "He doesn't live with us for the same reason he didn't show up for the Birthright Ceremony, even though he promised he would—he expected to be paid. When he found out Grandmother wasn't going to provide him with an income, he moved to another Province in Dhemlan. So Grandmother had him listed as my sire in the official registers so that the bloodline would be recorded, but he doesn't have any say in my life. He's not a part of my life."

That was so sad. "But you have your grandfather."

Zoey's smile warmed. "Yes, I do. And my grandmother. And Weston."

Jaenelle Saetien hesitated, but only for a moment. "And my papa. He'll read your reports—and he'll help you if you need help."

The horses snorted.

"I think they're bored with walking." She gave Zoey a mischievous look. "We can—"

"Canter, not gallop," Papa said, his deep voice rolling over the distance between them.

Zoey's eyes widened. "How did he know?"

Jaenelle Saetien focused on the space between her horse's ears. "The horses are kindred. I think Papa was telling *them*, not us."

"Oh." Zoey looked at the mare she was riding. "Kindred? I didn't realize. How . . . ?"

That was as far as Zoey got before the horses lifted into a canter.


Daemon watched the two girls and resisted the temptation to ask the horses what they were discussing. If the mare and stallion he'd asked to be the girls' mounts had decided the human chatter wasn't interesting, he didn't want to give them a reason to pay attention. Keeping anything private in a household with Scelties was a near impossibility, but the dogs eventually learned that they didn't have to tell him *everything* that his daughter was doing or saying—just the things that might threaten her well-being in one way or another. Since he resisted crossing that line with the Scelties, he wasn't going to smudge the line with the horses.

"So serious," he murmured.

"Your invitation to ride this morning means a great deal to Lady Zoela," Weston said. "She was excited enough to enlist her maid, her grandmother's maid, and her grandmother into helping her select a riding outfit." A beat of silence. "She even asked for my opinion."

Daemon swallowed a laugh. "Hell's fire, man. It's just a ride in the park."

"To Zoey, it's more than that."

After a quick psychic probe to assure himself that nothing was amiss around them, he gave his attention to the other man.

"You know about Lady Zhara's family," Weston said.

"Some things," he replied. "I know her daughter is a Black Widow lost in a tangled web and, so far, even the most skilled Sisters of the Hourglass haven't been able to bring her back."

When he'd first heard about Zhara's daughter, he'd considered if his being a natural Black Widow who wore the Black could help their family. In the end, he admitted he didn't have the skill—and he couldn't risk his own fragile sanity. He could weave a tangled web and see the dreams and visions, but he was always careful not to look too deeply into a vision—or step too far into the Twisted Kingdom. He'd climbed out of madness once with Witch's help. And having a mother who always lived on the border of the Twisted Kingdom was a daily reminder of the price she'd chosen to pay in order to regain some of her Craft.

But times had changed. There were two skilled Black Widows residing at the Keep now. Their knowledge hadn't been available to him when Zoey's mother slipped into the visions. Maybe there was something he could do now.

At what price? Zoey's mother wasn't the only Black Widow to be trapped in a tangled web. If he convinced Karla and Witch to help one woman, how many more would want the same help?

Slippery choices. He was whole and sane because Witch had intervened to heal him when he needed her the most. She had come back for him. Not only for him, since she had maintained contact with Daemonar because she was the boy's Queen, but she had returned enough to be a presence at the Keep for him, Daemonar, and Lucivar—and for Karla, who had informed them all that she wasn't going to put up with dealing with so much wiggle-waggle unless she had someone sensible to talk to.

Since she was Lucivar's administrative second-in-command, no one had dared to argue.

"Even girls from aristo families will fawn over a girl who is a Queen," Weston said. "But when the girl's mother is . . . lost . . . and her father is something of a scandal . . . Children can be cruel. Maybe that was a reflection of what they picked up from the adults around them, but the end result was the same. Zoey had become more and more isolated living at Lady Zhara's country estate, even though there were a lot of things she enjoyed about country life. Bringing her here to live in Amdarh . . . I think Lady Zhara hoped to give Zoey a fresh start at a new school."

Daemon hadn't detected loneliness in the girl when he'd met her at the art supplies shop, but he'd been so much on edge, he'd responded to the Queen. Now he wondered how much her delight in assisting him had covered other feelings.

"Jaenelle Saetien faces similar challenges," Daemon said. "A girl with an unusual Jewel who comes from the family that has ruled Dhemlan for thousands of years. Sometimes it's hard for her to maintain her balance."

"But there are a few who accept the girl for who she is."

"A few." Most of them were either family or had fur, but he didn't tell Weston that part.

Then he had a thought. Zhara would try to skin him alive if he made *that* introduction, but the girl, as girl and Queen, might benefit from having a special friend.

Another quick check on the girls. Still so serious.

"Is this your assignment in Zhara's court? To be Zoey's primary guard?" he asked.

Weston nodded. "Zoey's paternal grandfather and mine are cousins. I was already serving in Lady Zhara's court when Zoey's father decided to stay in his current lover's bed instead of attending his daughter's Birthright Ceremony. The day after the ceremony, I asked to be assigned to Zoey."

"Family." That explained some things about the casual give-and-take between girl and guard.

*We are bored.* That from the Warlord who was Jaenelle Saetien's mount. *Our little humans are done talking about sad things and need to run to be happy.*

Daemon saw the look on his daughter's face and let his voice roll through the park. "Canter, not gallop."

The horses didn't wait. They lifted into a canter as the girls' delighted laughter floated back to the two men.

*We are not running. Why aren't we running?* The stallion carrying Daemon had recently made the Offering to the Darkness and was now a Sapphire-Jeweled Warlord Prince. Not a male who was inclined to put up with nonsense from his rider—no matter who was on his back.

Besides, the girls were getting a bit too far ahead of their escorts.

"Shall we join the girls?" he said.

"Is that your way of telling me our mounts will be joining the girls whether we're still on them or not?"

Daemon nodded a moment before both horses shot forward like they'd reached the starting line for a race. Once the men were riding alongside the girls, the horses slowed to a walk and headed back to the SaDiablo town house, where the riders were encouraged to dismount so that the horses could return to the stables and enjoy a snack.

Having never been encouraged to dismount in quite that way—having a horse use Craft to shove him out of the saddle when he didn't move quickly enough on his own—Weston looked a little dazed as he stood on the sidewalk and watched the horses trot away. Zoey, on the other hand . . .

Even at the risk of raising Zhara's ire, Daemon thought Zoey would benefit from some personal experience with the kindred.

After changing her clothes, Jaenelle Saetien chose a book from her current stack of reading material and went downstairs to find Papa. He wasn't in his study, which surprised her, since he always had business papers to read or letters to write to the managers of the family's various estates. He wasn't in the morning room or the sitting room either. Just when she became uneasy and wondered if he'd left without saying anything, she found him in the informal sitting room that looked out over the town house's back garden.

He wore casual black trousers and a deep green shirt that had a soft gray pattern, like wisps of smoke, and his feet were bare, the soft house shoes dropped near the sofa where he sat reading a letter from the stack in his lap. He looked amused by something in the letter. When he looked up and saw her, his smile warmed and deepened.

She sat on his right side, so close she could feel the heat from his body, could breathe in his scent—a scent that, today, meant safety. And love.

Zoey's story about her sire brought home the truth that, even when she felt cross with Papa, he still loved her and would be there if she really needed him, whatever the price.

She intended to read her book while he read his letters. She often cuddled next to him in the evening, reading her book while he read one of his, although, if she asked, he would read her a story like he'd done when she was younger. But she didn't feel content. Instead, a thought scratched at her, and she wasn't sure which would be worse—getting an answer or always wondering what the answer might be.

"Papa?" she asked after he put aside the first letter.

"Witch-child?" he replied as he broke the wax seal on the next letter.

"Should I write reports for you?"

She braced for him to tell her she was being foolish because she wouldn't have anything interesting to say, not like Zoey, who was a Queen. Not that Papa had ever made her feel foolish when she asked a question, but . . .

He stared out the window at the garden beyond. Quiet. Thoughtful. Then he said, "If something troubled you and you weren't comfortable talking about it directly, you could write it down for me to read. Otherwise, I would hope that you could sit down and tell me whatever was on your mind."

"Zoey is going to write reports to send to you."

"Zoey doesn't live with us, and she doesn't live near the Hall." He put an arm around her. "I receive reports from Dhemlan's Queens informing me about any concerns they have regarding things happening in their territories, but the Queen of Halaway comes up to the Hall once a month. We sit in my study and have coffee and whatever treats Mrs. Beale has made that day, and we talk about the village and the people. She rarely writes a report because she's just down the road, and I'm in the village several times a week to see Tersa and Manny, and I spend a few minutes chatting with her Steward or Master of the Guard. Those chats are just as valuable as the reports." He gave her a hug. "It's a question of distance."

Jaenelle Saetien leaned against Papa. "Zoey doesn't have a papa who listens to her."

"I know," he replied softly.

"And her mother . . . That's so sad."

"Yes, it is sad."

She looked up. "You'll read her reports?"

"I will read her reports."

"And we'll all be friends?"

"If you and Zoey like each other and want to spend time together, then, yes, we can all be friends."

She hesitated, then asked her final question. "Do you wish that I was a Queen?"

"Never."

His firm, and instant, answer surprised her.

"A Queen is bound by her caste. Everything in her pushes her to rule something, regardless of whether it's large or small. No matter what other talents she has, or what she might have wanted to be, she is first, and always, a Queen. There were boundaries around Zoey's life from the moment she was born. But you, my darling, can be anything you want to be, can follow your dreams to do whatever work gives you joy. I've always been happy that you have that choice."

"So many choices," she said quietly.

"We make our life out of choices. Do we like the color green better than blue? Or strawberries better than radishes? Small things or big things, eventually those choices shape who we are." He kissed the top of her head. "But you don't have to choose everything today. Except whether you want to eat strawberries or radishes, which taste very different but are both red."

She giggled. "That's silly."

Satisfied, she opened her book. Papa went back to reading his letters. When her mother came home, the three of them talked for a little while. Then Papa put on regular shoes and he and her mother went outside to walk around the back garden together. Jaenelle Saetien watched them, the way they talked—so serious!—and the way Papa held her mother's hand.

Sometimes her mother and Papa didn't get along. Sometimes Papa had to live apart from them even when he was still at the Hall. But today, as they walked back to the house, they looked happier with each other—and she had made a new friend.

# SEVEN

❖

———————

A month later, Daemon rode the Black Wind to Amdarh
for an early-morning meeting with his second-in-
command, whose terse summons made him a little wary.
Surreal had returned to the town house a couple of days ago
and Jaenelle Saetien was at the Hall, where he was supposed
to be the parent on duty for the next several days, since he'd
been away from home so much these past few weeks.

After being told Surreal was on her way downstairs to
meet him, he entered the breakfast room and sat down.
Then he looked at the two letters Helton placed next to his
plate with a care and precision that gave him a good idea
of how much trouble he was in.

"Couldn't those wait until I've had breakfast?" he asked.

"Lady Surreal also received a letter this morning," Helton replied. "Hers was marked *Urgent* and came from the
Queen of Amdarh. I thought you would want the letters
that were delivered at the same time—by the Queen's
Master of the Guard."

Hell's fire. Sending the Master out before dawn to deliver letters seemed a bit excessive.

Then Surreal strode into the breakfast room, a letter in
one hand. "Sadi, what in the name of Hell did you do?"

"Do?" He might have gotten away with sounding as if
no one should be concerned if Helton hadn't chosen to

make a hasty retreat from the room, almost slamming the door in his hurry to leave the field of this particular battle.

Not that there should be a battle.

Daemon broke a corn muffin in half and took his time buttering it. "You summoned me to Amdarh, remember?"

Surreal sat opposite him. "I requested your presence because yesterday two of the Ladies in Zhara's First Circle approached me and hinted that you were the cause of considerable agitation in the Queen's family. I thought it best to find out why. Then this letter arrived before any reasonable person should be awake." She dropped the letter on the table and leaned toward him. "You shoved a Prince into Zhara's court without consulting her?"

"I did no such thing. I merely introduced Zoey to a young Prince whose company I thought she would enjoy."

"A *Sceltie* Prince."

"But not a Warlord Prince. That would have been excessive."

Surreal narrowed her eyes and said nothing when he poured a cup of coffee and set it in front of her. Then, "Have I met this one?"

"No." And thank the Darkness for that. "He's been at the school in Scelt."

"Is he the reason you've spent so much time in Scelt these past few weeks?"

"One of the reasons." The main reason. Princes didn't have the aggression and volatile temper of a Warlord Prince, but Trace's driving desire to manage things, combined with a Sceltie's passion for herding, had had the instructors at the Sceltie school pleading with Daemon to find the youngster a place where all that energy could be put to use. And since the youngster had come away with an Opal Jewel after the Birthright Ceremony and had the potential to wear the Red when he matured, finding work for that Prince had been a priority.

It wasn't his fault that Trace and Zoey had adored each other at first sight.

Surreal folded Zhara's letter and vanished it. After filling her plate, she gave his unread letters a pointed look.

Probably best if he read them before they discussed anything.

Daemon picked up the letter from Lord Weston and broke the seal.

> *Prince Sadi,*
>
> *I am sure that Lady Zhara will appreciate your gesture after she's had a few more days to adjust to the new member of her household. Until then, may I suggest, man to man, that you absent yourself from the city to avoid a vigorous discussion with Amdarh's Queen. You should also be aware that the teachers at Zoey's school may want to have an equally vigorous chat with you. It seems Prince Trace has firm opinions about proper education, and he has named you as his source for the Right Thing to Do.*
>
> *Zoey meeting Trace is the best thing that has happened to her in quite some time, and you have my wholehearted thanks for bringing this about.*
>
> *Sincerely,*
> *Weston*
>
> *Postscript: Please burn this letter after you've read it.*

Daemon folded the letter, then called in a stone bowl. Holding the letter over the bowl, he created a tongue of witchfire and watched the paper swiftly burn to ash.

"What . . . ?" Surreal asked.

Daemon merely smiled and opened the next letter.

> *Dear Prince Sadi,*
>
> *Trace is so smart! When we went to school yesterday—Weston, too—my teacher said students weren't allowed to bring pets to school, and Trace*

*told her he was an escort just like Weston, only he was a Sceltie and a Prince, and he would wait for me in the room set aside for escorts. Except then he decided he should be learning, too, but my studies would be too hard for him right now. So he found the classroom for the younger students and sat in an empty chair in the front and participated in the reading lesson. And he did as well as the other students! He was also quick to snarl at a couple of boys who weren't paying attention to the teacher. At least, that's what Weston told me after school. The teacher had called him after Trace cornered the boys and put up a shield to keep them in the corner and told them bad sheep had to stay in the pen until they learned how to behave. I guess Weston had to negotiate with the teacher and Trace about how much time bad sheep had to stay penned.*

*I'm not sure if anything else happened because Weston didn't tell me, but there was a loud burst of laughter from the escorts' room a couple of times yesterday.*

*At recess, some of the girls came over to talk to me. They really wanted to meet Trace, but they were nice to me too.*

*I think Grandmother is a little miffed because Trace wanted to know what time I should wake up and go to bed and go outside and play. He said you had taught him how to read clocks, so he should know these things in case my human family forgets to tell me. I don't think Grandmother or Grandfather—or Weston—will forget, but it's so much fun to have a friend like Trace, and I don't feel so alone now.*

*Thank you, Prince. I'll take good care of Trace, and he'll take good care of me.*

*Sincerely,*
*Zoey (Lady Zoela)*

Daemon folded Zoey's letter and vanished it. Then he quietly cleared his throat. "If there's nothing else, I think I'll return to the Hall."

"You might not want to be that easy to find," Surreal suggested.

"It's one Sceltie." He had good reason to know that it was, at best, a feeble defense.

"Uh-huh. I seem to remember you lobbing that argument at Lucivar after a few of Jillian and Khary's adventures. And look what happened in Little Weeble."

He would rather not think about that. Really rather not.

Lucivar would forgive him for that misstep. Someday. Besides, Lucivar had agreed to the arrangement, so it wasn't all his fault.

Being the Warlord Prince of Dhemlan meant he couldn't tuck tail and run. At least, he couldn't be obvious about it.

"I'll return to the Hall," he said. "I don't want to leave Jaenelle Saetien on her own for too long."

"I'll stay here for a couple more days and provide a sympathetic ear."

"Thank you."

She laughed. "The sympathetic ear is not for you, Sadi."

"It's one Sceltie." He imagined that someone kicking the pebble that starts an avalanche said much the same thing.

# EIGHT

Tersa wandered the streets of Halaway, shivering. With effort, she focused on some of the people going in and out of shops. Coats. The significance of coats was . . . Couldn't remember. Didn't matter.

"Tersa."

Her boy glided toward her, smiling. But the look in his gold eyes? Concern. Yes.

Did he know? No, someone in the village must have told him she was wandering. Had someone asked her something? Had she answered in a way that had caused enough concern for them to summon him?

Couldn't remember. Couldn't hear past that *sound*.

"Darling, put this on. It's chilly today, and you're not dressed warmly enough." Her boy helped her into a coat. His coat by the scent rising from the material, warmed by his body and by warming spells that he must have added for her sake.

No amount of outside warmth could stop this shivering. Tersa turned and grabbed fistfuls of her boy's white silk shirt. "You must tell the Queen."

His hands closed over hers. "Tell her what?"

"I still hear them. The footsteps are getting closer."

When he tried to question her, she shook her head and allowed him to lead her back to her cottage. She had given the answer and had to trust that he would deliver it.

✦ ✦ ✦

Delora linked arms with Hespera as the two girls walked along the perimeter of the lawn where the afternoon party was taking place. She had dressed in her best party frock, not to impress her hosts—they were minor aristos who had recently moved to this part of Dhemlan and *embraced* country life—and certainly not to impress the girl who was the reason for this celebration. No, she'd worn it to please her father so that he could boast that she was the brightest and prettiest girl in the Province. She could do no wrong when he believed other men envied him for having such a daughter, and she liked to keep it that way.

"What do you think of Dahlia?" Hespera asked, indicating the girl who was talking to one of the older boys while cuddling the kitten that had been one of her gifts.

"She's . . . adequate," Delora replied. "But she has a selfish streak that I don't think will suit us for being friends."

"Selfish?"

"I admired the fancy comb in her hair and asked if I could borrow it. She said no."

"It *is* a gift she just received today," Hespera pointed out.

"So?"

"Is the comb going to fall out and go missing?"

"Oh, no," Delora said. "I've decided it isn't pretty enough for *me* to wear."

"I don't see Zoela here," Hespera said after a minute. "Don't tell me the little Queen wasn't invited. I think Dahlia's parents invited every aristo girl in the Province who is the same age as darling Dahlia."

"I heard Lady Zhara brought Zoela to the city and is going to have her live there now. Just as well. Zoela really isn't *our* kind of aristo. She's almost a *rube*." And not a girl who looked the other way when rules were bent, let alone broken. That was a shame. Having a Queen as a good friend would have been useful. But there were other girls, other Queens. It was just a matter of choosing the right kind of friends. Blood sings to Blood. Like calls to like.

And if a person didn't fit with her? Well, *someone* had to be the prey in the games she enjoyed the most.

She and Hespera split up as they reached the tables set out with platters of food. They moved in and around the adults, smiling and polite, as they selected a small amount of delicacies and were encouraged to take more. She looked away, blushingly shy, when complimented on her dress—and she laughed silently when she overheard a Warlord who was going flabby in middle age tell her father how delightful it was to see a girl her age who was so well-behaved.

An hour later, Dahlia began looking for her kitten, who wasn't in the shielded basket where she'd put it while she had something to eat.

Delora and Hespera rushed to help with the search.

"I'm sure we'll find him," Delora said, putting an arm around Dahlia. "A small thing like that couldn't have gone far." She stayed with the other girl as they looked for the kitten, staining her party frock by getting on her hands and knees to check under bushes.

No sign of the kitten. Nothing. Gone.

As Delora led weeping Dahlia toward the house, she said very quietly, "It's too bad about the kitten, but it could have been worse. If your baby brother had gone missing, that would have been a tragedy."

Dahlia stared at Delora. Delora patted the girl's shoulder and smiled sympathetically.

The party continued a while longer, mostly because one didn't invite this many aristos—and have a sufficient number deign to attend—and then ask them to leave before the usual time.

After receiving praise for their efforts to find the kitten, Delora and Hespera linked arms and made another circuit around the lawn.

"Do you think anyone will find the kitten?" Hespera asked.

Delora didn't even glance at the large tree or the roots that were lifted above the ground. Didn't need to look to know that no one would check around the trees carefully enough to spot any sign that the ground had been disturbed. She passed by the tree and imagined she could still hear faint, desperate mewing.

"Perhaps someone will someday." She gave her best friend a brilliant smile. "But not in time."

Lucivar slipped into the communal eyrie after dinner, not sure why Hallevar had acted so cagey about wanting to see him this evening. The crusty old arms master had been one of his own trainers in the Askavi Terreille hunting camps and was now teaching the Eyrien youngsters in Ebon Rih how to handle weapons—and was the sort of man who usually said whatever was on his mind.

When Lucivar saw Rothvar waiting with Hallevar, he hesitated. He didn't want to think Rothvar had turned on him or that Hallevar had betrayed him, but his previous second-in-command had not been an honorable man and had managed to hide that truth for several years.

"Figured you should both hear this," Hallevar said. "I didn't promise the boy I'd keep quiet about it, so I'm not breaking trust."

Lucivar approached slowly. "All right."

"It comes down to the traffic and trade between Kaeleer and Terreille," Rothvar said.

"Some people have always come through the Gates, and I guess there's always been some trading." Lucivar couldn't imagine wanting anything from Terreille, but that didn't mean other people felt the same way.

"Just because someone left Terreille doesn't mean there aren't ties," Rothvar said. "Some of the Eyriens living here have family that either stayed in Terreille by choice or didn't get to the service fairs before the purge that cleansed the Realms. News from family can have a powerful pull." He looked Lucivar in the eyes. "Not for me—I was glad to leave that pus-riddled Realm—but for some."

"Are we talking about anyone in particular?"

"Dorian," Hallevar said. "Alanar overheard Dorian and Endar arguing over some letters she received from family still living in Terreille. The boy doesn't know what the letters said, just that it sounded like Dorian had been sending and receiving letters for a while now and his father was upset about it."

"People in Terreille poisoning the well out of spite?" Rothvar suggested. "Or preparing the ground for a battle to help the family's Queen gain control of some territory?"

Hallevar snorted. "Endar brought his family to Kaeleer because it's obvious the girl has a bit of a short-lived race in her bloodline, and Eyriens in Terreille wouldn't have accepted her as a Queen they were willing to serve."

"That was before the purge," Lucivar said. "Now?" It was a possibility. Train the girl here and then return to Terreille to set up a court. Except anyone who thought Daemonar would follow Orian to Terreille was a fool. More likely, set up the daughter's court as the means of bringing the rest of the family to Kaeleer.

"Ask around," he said. "Find out what you can about Dorian's family. My impression was they weren't aristo, but they might have unrealistic expectations about what they can gain from having a Queen in the family— especially if they're looking to reconcile with Dorian for some kind of profit."

What sort of profit they thought to gain from Endar was anyone's guess. But it could explain Dorian's interest in setting a hook into the Yaslana family. He—or one of his children—had the kind of wealth that could support a Queen's court in style.

He'd send them to Hell—and to the High Lord—before he let that happen.

After thanking Hallevar for bringing this to his attention, Lucivar walked out with Rothvar.

"Might be nothing more than letters from home," Rothvar said. "Might not have anything to do with Dorian feeling sour about her life."

"Might not," Lucivar agreed. "But distance can make

some things look better, just like stories can gloss over a truth to make it less ugly."

"Or less frightening?"

"You don't think the stories about me are frightening?"

"They are." Rothvar lowered his voice. "They're still not close to the truth about you. I've worked alongside you enough years now to have figured that out. There may come a time when I can't stand with you, Lucivar, but I'll never stand on the other side of a line against you. You need to know that, here and now."

Lucivar stepped aside and spread his wings. "Then let's hope we never find that line."

Tomorrow he would go to the Keep and ask Geoffrey for whatever was available about Dorian's bloodlines. Now, as he flew home, he wondered if Marian had received any letters—and he wondered what he would do if she had.

Daemon waited until Jaenelle Saetien fell asleep before riding the Black Wind to the Keep, leaving his girl in the care of Beale and Holt. It was the same arrangement they had worked out for the times when Surreal wasn't at the Hall and he needed the solitude of staying in his father's old suite, with the layers of Black shields keeping everyone away from him while he regained his self-control and emotional balance.

As he waited in the sitting room across from the Queen's and Consort's suites, he thought about the change in Surreal since they had taken that walk in the town house's back garden. Not a change so much as a return of the woman he had known.

*"I tried to be something I wasn't, and it hurt both of us,"* she'd said. *"I thought I wanted to be a wife, but that night when you invited me to play and offered everything you were, when you showed me what it would be like to be with you without any barriers . . . I can't be a wife to that man, Sadi. It's taken me years to realize I felt safe enough to be with you because a part of you was still Jaenelle's husband.*

Witch's husband. Even when we didn't know she was here in some way, you were always going to be her husband."

"Is that your way of saying you want to leave?" he'd asked quietly.

"No, that's my way of saying I want to be a different kind of wife, the kind that suits my nature." A hesitation. "I'll be your sword and shield, Sadi. I'm the sword." She raised her left hand so that he could see her wedding ring. "This is your shield. As long as you have a wife and you wear a wedding ring, you'll have at least some of the companionship you need—and a reason to refuse any companionship you don't want."

"You want to be celibate?"

"Hell's fire, no." Another hesitation. "I want to be the Warlord Prince of Dhemlan's second-in-command. I want to be Daemon Sadi's lover. But I can't be lover to the Sadist or . . ."

"Or the High Lord of Hell?" he finished.

"Yes."

He nodded. Not so different from where they had started.

"And I know Sadi as a lover has a bit of an edge, so you can stop asking permission before you do every damn thing. It's annoying."

"How will I know if that edge is too much?"

"You'll feel my knife against your ribs."

"You could just tell me to stop."

"I like my way better."

He laughed softly and took her hand. "Of course you do."

"Daemon?" Witch said as she walked into the sitting room.

He turned to look at the Queen who was his life. "Thank you."

"For what?"

"For helping Surreal set the boundaries of what she wants to give as a wife and what she expects in return."

"Can you accept those boundaries?" she asked quietly.

"I can." He smiled dryly. "Actually, it's a relief to know

where the lines are drawn." *I can accept that from her. It would have destroyed me if you'd needed those lines.*

Not something he would say. Not something he needed to say. Not to her.

She stepped closer and studied him. "It doesn't feel like you need to drain the Black or need my help regaining your balance. And I don't think Surreal defining the terms of your marriage brought you here at this time of night. So I have to wonder what's really on your mind, Prince?"

"Tersa asked me to deliver a message. She said the footsteps are getting closer." Seeing the feral light that came into Witch's eyes, Daemon smiled a cold smile. "What does it mean?"

"The approach of a potential enemy."

"Who? Where?"

"I don't know. The only thing I see in the tangled webs I've woven is the need to prepare. Tersa is the one who has felt the approach of an enemy, one who is not yet on the horizon, let alone close enough to be seen and recognized."

"Have other Black Widows seen anything?"

Witch shook her head. "There have been no whispers, Prince. Nothing. But Tersa has always been more farseeing than most."

"An enemy that well hidden?" He stepped close and bent his head until his lips were a breath away from touching hers—if he could have felt her lips under his. "Use me," the Sadist crooned.

She placed a hand on his chest, over his heart, and pushed just enough to have him ease back.

"When the time comes," Witch said. "One of Saetan's regrets was that Mephis and Peyton had to live with the truth of what he was while they were still young, that they felt the weight of it before they were old enough to understand. Give your daughter as much time as you can before Kaeleer has to acknowledge the truth of all that you are."

"What will you do?"

She gave him a smile that held some regret. "I'll help forge a weapon to stand beside you in this fight."

# NINE

◈

———

Tersa wandered through rooms and corridors in the Keep, muttering, "Wrong place. Wrong place. Can't see what must be seen until I find the *right* place."

She'd stopped hearing the footsteps approaching when she wove a tangled web. Now she felt something that scratched at her bones and filled her dreams with figures made of shrouded mist and voices that screeched and screamed—and laughed. The laughter was the worst because it almost sounded familiar. But the tangled webs she'd woven lately told her nothing more than her dreams, except that she was in the wrong place because the *right* place held lethal cold and deadly heat that would ensnare—and then kill.

Tersa pushed open an ornate metal gate, took a few steps into that part of the Keep—and froze as something very male and predatory became aware of her presence.

Lethal cold. Deadly heat. Her boy—but not her boy. This was the predator who knew how to turn pleasure into a kind of fatal pain a person would beg to feel until it was no longer possible to beg for anything except to be allowed to die. And even that wouldn't free a person from his attention. Not anymore.

As the sexual heat washed over her, wrapped around her, she braced a hand against the wall. She should have been immune to that part of him, but that safety was now erased by the cold rage braided with the heat.

*Intruder.*

Yes, she was. And she wasn't the only one. Another male, familiar to her, had already scraped at the predator's control with his presence.

This threat, this bone-deep fear of someone she loved, was the element her tangled webs had been missing. She needed those things, needed to be here to spin the web that would let her see the visions clearly.

Tersa hurried into a sitting room closest to the gate and closed the door.

Tables. Chairs. Sofas. A gathering place for a First Circle.

Yes. It would do.

Choosing a table with an empty surface, she called in a wooden frame and her spools of spider silk and began to weave a tangled web of dreams and visions.

Lethal cold. Deadly heat. Voices that screeched and screamed. And one voice whose laughter was filled with joyful malevolence.

She had barely time to attach the last thread, hadn't even taken that one mental step to the side when the web revealed the visions the previous webs had kept hidden.

Tersa sucked in a breath. Much was still hidden and wouldn't be revealed until the enemy's shape—a shape that would be shrouded by deceit for many years—crossed paths with that lethal cold and deadly heat. And then . . .

*He is coming.*

A whisper of warning spoken in a midnight voice.

She hesitated. He was a Black Widow. He could—and would—read what was revealed in her tangled web.

As her trembling hand reached out to break the strands of spider silk, she felt that Black power moving swiftly toward her. Leaving the web intact, she fled from her son, running out of the room and past the metal gate, knowing he wouldn't follow her once she was no longer in the Queen's part of the Keep.

She found another sitting room and curled up on a sofa, shivering, to wait for Witch's summons.

◆ ◆ ◆

Daemon prowled the Consort's suite, stared at the un-locked door that would give him freedom, then turned away to pace to the windows and stare at the Queen's private garden. He had promised, had given his word he would remain in his suite when that other male came here for lessons.

Not just another male. Nephew. Daemonar. Not a rival. Just a boy the Queen wanted to train because the boy would become a strong man one day—if he could tolerate the boy's presence enough to let the boy live.

He paced and prowled, prowled and paced, in a room that seemed to be shrinking with every circuit he made from door to windows, windows to door.

Had to stay away. Had to stay here. He'd tolerated the arrangement the first few times he and the boy had been here at the same time, had even been able to join the boy, and two other Warlord Princes, in a sitting room beyond the Queen's part of the Keep to talk about the lesson.

This time it felt different. He didn't understand why, but it felt different.

Still unwilling to break his promise, Daemon turned away from the door leading into the corridor—and the small sitting room directly across from the Queen's suite—and tried the door that opened into Witch's bedroom. It was unlocked, which gave him some relief.

He walked into the room, walked over to the bed, and ran a hand over the covers, breathing in the various scents. A hint of scent, physical and psychic, from the witches who tended the Keep and kept these rooms clean drifted up from the sheets and bedcovers. Nothing else in Witch's room except her own psychic scent—and his. No indication that the other male was trying to stake a claim in *his* territory.

Nephew. Daemonar. Not a rival. A Brother in the court. So hard to remember that today because something was scratching at him. Had been scratching at him.

Returning to his own room, Daemon removed the cuff-links from his shirt and tossed them on the dresser, then undid the buttons one . . . by . . . one. He shrugged the material off his shoulders, letting the shirt fall to the floor. Today even silk abraded his skin.

He would stay in his room. He would keep his promise. The boy was no threat to him—or to her.

He shaped his Red Birthright power into a psychic probe that rippled through the Queen's part of the Keep. Rippled over the boy. Rippled over . . .

*Intruder.*

Smiling a cold, cruel smile, Daemon unleashed his sexual heat and sent it out to touch everyone in this part of the Keep—to ensnare everyone who foolishly entered his territory. And yet . . .

He recognized her tangled mind and her psychic scent. How could he not recognize her? But today even she was an intruder.

One person where there should be none besides himself and his Queen? That he could tolerate. Had to tolerate. He'd given her his word. But two? *Two?*

Standing in the corridor with no memory of choosing to leave his suite, Daemon stared at the sitting room door, then turned away. After wrapping a sight shield around himself, he located the intruder and headed for that room.

He was several man-lengths away when she bolted from the room and ran past the metal gate that marked the boundary of his territory.

Letting her go, he went into the sitting room to figure out what she had been doing in there—and spotted the tangled web.

Dropping the sight shield, he wrapped a tight Black shield around himself. Then he approached the table and carefully probed the wooden frame and the spools of spider silk. Nothing dangerous about those things. No spells or traps laid for the unwary. Which left the tangled web itself.

He braced one hand on the table, his long black-tinted

nails cutting into the wood, and took that mental step to the side to see what the tangled web revealed.

A minute later, he stepped back, stepped away, his rage so huge it rolled through the entire Keep and so cold that ice formed on the windows, looking like frozen streaks of lightning.

The enemy had no face. Not yet. But . . .

He turned away from the web and headed back to the small sitting room across from the Queen's suite.

. . . the male who had invaded his territory was part of it, and he would know why, even if it meant taking the boy's body and mind apart piece by piece in order to find out.

He opened the sitting room door and stared at the boy. Nephew, yes. Brother in the court, yes.

It didn't matter. What mattered—all that mattered—was the boy was somehow connected with a laugh filled with joyful malevolence, and that sound—*that sound*—had been laced through all the pain and fear and misery of his childhood until he became old enough and strong enough to fight back. To be the destroyer instead of the destroyed.

He stepped into the room. The boy looked up—and the Sadist smiled a sweetly murderous smile.

Sitting cross-legged on a padded bench near one of the large windows, Daemonar carefully opened the old book of scenarios to the page he had marked with a ribbon. The scenarios—exercises using actual experiences as examples of what to do or not do—were nothing like the books Lord Endar had acquired for the lessons he gave the Eyrien children. From what the Rihlander boys said about their lessons, Daemonar figured they didn't have a book like this either.

Why didn't anyone in Askavi have a book like this now? Protocol was important, and knowing what to do in a court was important, but *this* information was equally useful. Prince Chaosti admitted that teachers among the Dea al Mon had a book similar to this, but the scenarios were read aloud and then discussed because there wasn't one correct answer, since the answer changed depending on who was the dominant power at that moment.

The books he was using for his lessons with Auntie J. couldn't leave the Keep. Some were too old and fragile. Others were too valuable to be removed from the Keep's library. It was a concession made by Geoffrey as a favor to Auntie J. that Daemonar was allowed to keep the books in this room and read them here.

That was one of the reasons he always arrived early for his lessons. The other reason . . . Well, he wasn't sure if he was doing it for himself or for her, but he thought maybe Auntie J. wouldn't feel as lonely if there was someone in the part of the Keep where she stayed. He wasn't sure she *was* lonely, and he wasn't sure she *couldn't* leave or if her Self could leave but the shadow wouldn't take shape outside this part of the Keep or in the Misty Place. He knew his mother sometimes wanted to be alone—really, physically alone—but other times she enjoyed what she called quiet company, when she would be reading or doing some needlework and the rest of them, his father included, would be working on one of those puzzles that were broken into pieces and had to be put back together.

So he came early to be quiet company if Auntie J. wanted company, or just to read more of the scenarios— and to figure out who would be the best adult to approach for getting new copies of this kind of book made so that he could take one home.

His first choice would be Uncle Daemon because his uncle enjoyed books and appreciated the knowledge they held and might see the value of having more young men, especially Warlord Princes, learn lessons Daemonar was sure were important. But even when Prince Sadi joined him and his father and Prince Chaosti to talk about the scenarios and how they would have responded and the choices they actually had made in similar circumstances, Sadi felt . . . strange. Not sick. Just . . . strange. A little off.

The men noticed, but they didn't act differently toward the Prince. They were just . . . watchful. The Prince knew. Of course he knew. But, like Lucivar and Chaosti, he pretended not to notice, pretended that everything was the way it always was between them.

His father had said Uncle Daemon felt that way because he was still rising from the healing time, still fitting back into his skin. And that made sense, because Uncle Daemon often joined them for dinner on his last evening at the Keep, and Daemonar had never sensed that strangeness. A difference of a few hours, no more than that, but enough time for his uncle to be—

The door opened and someone walked into the sitting room. Daemonar looked up.

The Warlord Prince who looked at him, whose mouth curved in a sweetly murderous smile, wore his uncle's face but wasn't his uncle. He knew that with everything in him.

*Remember your lessons. Remember. Remember.*

Daemonar swallowed hard to keep fear, and his midday meal, from rising. "Good afternoon, Prince. I'm here for my lesson with the Lady."

No response. No reply. Just that smile and gold eyes that looked glazed and sleepy.

Hell's fire, Mother Night, and may the Darkness be merciful. The Prince was riding the killing edge—and *he* was the target.

He wanted to uncross his legs in order to have some chance of moving when the strike came. Because it was going to come. He had no doubts about that. But he knew it would come faster if he made any kind of move.

The Prince took another step into the room. Power— and something else, something more and just as deadly— washed over Daemonar. Sadi wore nothing above his waist except the pendant that held his Black Jewel. A solid body with defined muscles. Not bulky, more . . . sculpted.

Daemonar felt his face heat. Why would he think such a thing about his uncle? It was *true*, but why would he think it?

And the scars on the right biceps. Thin white ridges marking the golden brown skin.

He'd seen those white ridges plenty of times, but today, here and now, he understood that Witch's claws had given Sadi those scars.

The Prince—no, that was too tame a word for the man who glided across the room toward him—stared at him in a way that made his heart beat too fast, made fear threaten to swallow sense. He wanted to run, but if he moved now, he wouldn't survive long enough to take another breath, to feel his heart take one more beat.

"Prince." Witch's midnight voice was equal parts threat and command.

Sadi—or whoever lived inside that skin right now— stopped moving, but his eyes and rage remained focused on Daemonar.

Witch appeared beside Sadi. "You gave me your word, Daemon. *Your word.*"

The Prince turned his head just enough to focus those glazed eyes on her—and he snarled.

"He is mine, Prince, as you are mine."

Sadi snarled again. Louder.

Witch waved a hand as if to erase the words. "Not exactly as you are mine, but he is mine as his father is mine. You know this, Daemon. *You know this.*"

Silence. Daemonar held his breath. Whatever discussion was now going on between Sadi and Witch was taking place on a private psychic thread, but whatever was said had Sadi turning fully to face her, had Witch resting her hand over his heart, her claws barely pricking the skin.

Sadi breathed in. Breathed out. And said, "Your will is my life."

"Yes," Witch replied softly. "And I am asking you to obey my will."

Sadi hesitated, as if he wanted to turn once more to the

other male in the room. Then he walked out of the sitting room.

Moments later, Daemonar heard another door close.

"Come on, boyo, you have to go." Witch closed a hand around his arm and hauled him to his feet.

Daemonar almost dropped the book. Just managed to close it without tearing any pages. "But . . . our lesson."

"Not today." She pulled him toward the door.

"Auntie J.! The book!"

"Take it home with you."

The words shocked him enough that he stopped resisting and kept pace with her. Take the book out of the Keep? A book Geoffrey had barely allowed to leave the library?

"You can't be here today," Witch said. "Chaosti will stay with you until your father arrives to escort you home."

His father here at the Keep when Uncle Daemon was acting so strange? No.

"I can go home by myself," he said.

"Not today." She sounded grim—and worried.

Prince Chaosti stood on the other side of the metal gate that separated Witch's private area from the rest of the Keep.

"Do you know?" Chaosti asked softly.

"Not yet," she replied. She looked at the big sitting room that was closest to the gate. "But I will."

She gave Daemonar's arm a light squeeze. "Wait for your father, boyo."

Daemonar looked back in the direction of the Queen's and Consort's suites. "Will you be safe, Auntie J.?"

She smiled. "I'll be safe." She took a step back—and faded away.

"Come, little Brother," Chaosti said. "Give Sadi a chance to regain control."

As soon as Daemonar walked past the metal gate, he felt the other familiar presence. "What is Tersa doing here?"

"I think that is a question between Tersa and the Queen," Chaosti replied.

"What if Uncle Daemon . . . ?"

"Draca will look after Tersa." Chaosti tapped the top of the book. "What have you got there?"

"A book I was reading. Auntie J. said I could take it home." He was sure she meant he could borrow it, not keep it. He'd take extra care with it too. Maybe Geoffrey would let him borrow other books if he took extra care with this one.

Chaosti sat with him for an hour, discussing some of the scenarios, before his father arrived. Lucivar stared at him for a long moment. Just stared.

"Father?" Wondering if he *had* done something wrong, Daemonar waited.

"This was unusual," Chaosti said quietly. "Unforeseen."

"But it can happen again," Lucivar said.

"Yes, it can happen again. He is who, and what, he is."

Lucivar nodded. Then he held out a hand. "Time to go, boyo."

"Are we going home?" Daemonar asked. Something about the look on his father's face—a look that *might* be fear.

Lucivar didn't reply, just kept moving until they walked out of the Keep and stood in one of the open areas where Coaches carrying visitors and scholars could land.

"Are we going home?" Daemonar asked again.

Lucivar shook his head. "We'll go to the hunting eyrie for a little while. This is a private talk. Just you and me." He took a deep breath, let it out in a shuddering sigh. "There are things you need to know about your uncle Daemon."

Calm and once more in control, Daemon stood on the flag-stones outside of Lucivar's home and waited to see if the door would open. Lucivar knew he was there. If his brother chose to shut him out tonight, he would accept it.

*"He is part of it! I saw that much. I know that much!"*

*"Maybe," Witch had replied when his rage had been*

*purged enough that he could speak—and listen. "Or maybe he is part of it because he is a weapon that fits my hand. Like you, Prince."*

Queen's weapon. Like him. Like Lucivar. Power and temper shaped to do a Queen's will.

She said he hadn't hurt the boy. He wanted to believe that. Whether or not the door to the eyrie opened or remained closed would tell him if she was right.

The door opened. Lucivar stood there, watching him.

Breathing a sigh of relief, Daemon walked across the flagstones and stopped in front of his brother. "I'd like to speak to Daemonar, if you'll give your consent."

He recognized the wariness in Lucivar's eyes. He'd seen it enough times before when Yaslana had brushed against the Sadist. It stung to see that look now, even if it was deserved.

"Not alone," Lucivar finally said.

"Not alone," he agreed.

Lucivar didn't step out of the doorway to give him room to enter the eyrie. "I told him who, and what, you are. And some—enough—of the why."

He nodded. Lucivar's choice wasn't unexpected, but the boy's response? He had no way to gauge what Daemonar might think about him being the High Lord of Hell—or the Sadist.

Lucivar stepped back. "We'll talk in my study."

Daemon followed his brother. He could sense the presence of Marian and the children, but no one came out to greet him.

Once they were in the study, Daemon settled in one of the visitors' chairs. Lucivar leaned against the front of the blackwood desk, leaving the other chair for Daemonar.

A minute later, the boy joined them.

"Your uncle would like to talk to you," Lucivar said.

Daemonar nodded and took the other chair.

Daemon wondered what the boy was looking for in that careful study of his face.

Then Daemonar said, "You don't feel strange anymore. At the Keep today, you felt strange. Not like you."

"Not like you know me, but that is also who I am," Daemon replied. "Your father has told you who, and what, I am."

"Yes. But that's not always who you are."

"You're wrong, boyo. It's always who I am. It's just not the part of me that is usually seen."

The boy pressed his hands between his knees and seemed to be thinking hard. "Like Papa always being the Demon Prince now, but not always *being* the Demon Prince?"

"Like that, but . . . more."

"So that's why you stay with Auntie J. at the Keep? Not just for healing, but because you can be all that you are when you're with her?"

"Yes."

"And she isn't scared of you when you're all that you are because she can be even scarier?"

Daemon blinked, not sure how to answer that. "Well . . ."

"The scars on your arm. I didn't understand until today that Auntie J. gave them to you."

"Yes, well . . ."

Daemonar leaned forward. "How much stupid did you have to do to get her that mad at you?"

Lucivar coughed and looked away.

Daemon stared at the boy, speechless.

"It's just . . . I get a whack upside the head sometimes for being stupid, but it would be good to know how much stupid I'd have to do to get her *that* mad at me."

"Probably more than you would ever think to do," Daemon finally said, not daring to look at Lucivar. "I argued when I should have listened and got her very riled."

Daemonar nodded. "She gets That Look when you don't listen. Mother has that look, too, but not like Auntie J."

The boy was taking this better than he'd hoped, accepting so much that so many others couldn't—wouldn't—accept. "Is there anything you'd like to ask me?"

Daemonar didn't say anything for almost too long. Then the boy called in a book and held it out. "It's old and fragile, and I have to bring it back to the Keep's library."

Lucivar straightened. "You aren't supposed to take the books that belong to the Keep."

"Auntie J. told me to take it home."

Daemon opened the book to the page marked with a ribbon.

"These are the scenarios," Daemonar said, looking at both men. "The 'if you saw this happen, or if someone did this to you, what would you do?' exercises."

"Yes," Daemon replied. "We've talked about some of these."

"I go to the Keep before my lessons in order to read that book." Daemonar pointed to the book, in case everyone else couldn't figure out which book was under discussion. "And maybe my being there for extra time today bothered you. But if I had a copy of the book to keep at home, then I could read it here. It's a really good book, Uncle Daemon. And useful. And not just for me. Titian and Andulvar would learn from it too. And Jaenelle Saetien when she came to visit."

"You gave this some thought, didn't you, boyo?" Daemon murmured.

"Yes, sir."

Daemon carefully closed the book and gave it back to Daemonar. "Let me ask around and see if there are other books like this that might already be available in another Territory. If not, we'll see about getting copies of this one made."

"Okay."

"Anything else?"

"No, sir."

Lucivar tipped his head toward the door. "Go on."

Giving them a big smile, Daemonar left the study.

Daemon looked at Lucivar. Lucivar looked at him and said, "A Sceltie couldn't have boxed you in better. What are you going to do if that kind of book of lessons isn't available anymore?"

It probably wasn't. Or if there were similar books out there, they didn't have the exercises that Witch specifically wanted Daemonar to consider.

Daemon pushed out of the chair. "It looks like Marcus and Holt are going to investigate the availability of a publishing house that might be for sale or figure out what I'll need to do to create a new one."

"You feeling that guilty about this afternoon?"

"How is Titian getting on with the artist's primer?"

"She's excited about it, talks about what she's learned." Lucivar laughed. "I guess the boy isn't the only one who has boxed you in. I doubt there is a publisher in Dhemlan who wouldn't publish one book as a favor to the Warlord Prince of Dhemlan. But publishing art primers *and* long-forgotten books that won't make a profit?"

"Yeah." Daemon smiled wryly. "One way or another, I'm going to include a publishing house in the family holdings. Something small and eclectic, so Marcus doesn't shake his head and look mournful every quarter when we review the accounts or sigh too much if the endeavor doesn't at least pay for itself." He growled. "It's not like I can't afford to take a financial loss on *one* business when I'm adding it to the holdings to gain another kind of profit."

"Well, you have my total support, Bastard."

"But not your help."

"Hell's fire, no. Now, if you want to talk about establishing a shop for finely made weapons . . ."

"Take a piss in the wind, Prick."

Lucivar laughed again, then rested a hand on Daemon's shoulder. "You all right now? This afternoon . . . Hell's fire, Daemon. The cold rage in you . . . I thought we were preparing for war."

"We are. I am." Daemon looked into Lucivar's eyes. "I don't remember what I saw in a tangled web. Once I felt calmer, I wasn't permitted to go back into the sitting room and look again. But the Sadist's response to what had been seen . . ."

"When?" Lucivar asked.

"I don't know. But Daemonar will be part of it."

"On which side of the line?"

"Hopefully ours." Daemon rested his forehead against Lucivar's. "I'm sorry I frightened him this afternoon, but I'm glad you told him about me. He needs to know. More than the other children, he needs to know. As a young male, he needs to be careful around me, especially when he's at the Keep."

"Nothing we can do until the storm is on the horizon."

"Be vigilant."

"Yeah. We can do that." Lucivar eased back. "You staying at the Keep tonight?"

Daemon nodded. "I'll head home in the morning."

"Marian made a pie this afternoon."

"Oh? Her pies are usually not up for grabs."

"If we're caught helping ourselves, I'll just blame you."

Daemon laughed. "That's fair."

They found Marian in the kitchen. Half the pie was already divided into four pieces and on plates. The other half was divided in two and still in the dish. She put the plates on a serving tray, then gave Daemon a kiss on the cheek.

"You do realize that that old book isn't the only one in the Keep that Daemonar would like to have for his own?" She smiled at him. "He's making a list for you."

Daemon looked at the remaining half of the pie. "So I get a quarter of the pie as a reward for future endeavors?"

"Something like that." She picked up the tray and walked out of the kitchen.

Lucivar took two forks out of a drawer, put the pie dish on the table, and said, "Dig in."

Since Marian's pies were delicious, and Lucivar wasn't above taking more than his share from a common dish, Daemon did exactly that.

◆ ◆ ◆

The Seneschal had done something to the room where Tersa hid to keep her presence undetected until her boy had left the Keep.

Cautious—a feeling she'd never experienced before because of her boy—Tersa returned to the sitting room closest to the metal gate. The door stood open. The tangled web on the table was still intact. And studying that web . . .

Witch turned to look at her. "I know what I see in this web. Tell me what you see."

Tersa walked up to the table and stood near the Queen. She felt anger burning under ice. Contained. Controlled. For now.

"Malevolence and rot, hidden by youth and a mask of innocence," Tersa replied. "Choices that will ripple through the Shadow Realm and leave Dhemlan bloody. And a sharp price that will have to be paid."

"Have you and I ever paid any other kind of price, Sister?" Witch asked.

"No," Tersa whispered. Then she hesitated before adding, "What the boy saw in the web . . . He will not remember what called to his rage, but he will recognize it when the malevolence begins to crack through the mask of innocence. And then—"

"I will hold him back long enough for him to make a clear choice, to recognize and accept what will come from his actions and what price will have to be paid," Witch said.

Those sapphire eyes looked beyond the madness of a tangled mind, looked deep and acknowledged all the choices Tersa had already made.

A secret between them, forever contained in the Twisted Kingdom—and in the Misty Place—beyond the reach of anyone else.

"Say the words that are at the core of this tangled web. Speak the truth of what the visions revealed," Witch said softly.

"If the High Lord hesitates, if he does not shape his rage into a blade for slaughter, a witch like Dorothea Sa-Diablo will rise in Dhemlan and spread her particular kind of poison, will sink her roots into the hearts of Dhemlan's people. Another like Dorothea will gain enough power and support to corrupt and then destroy."

"She is coming?" Witch asked.

Tersa looked at the tangled web. Shaking her head, she reached out and swiped a hand through the strands of spider silk, destroying the vision. "She is already here."

# PART TWO

---

## Weapons Unleashed

# TEN

❖

*Centuries Later*

Daemonar stood on the canyon's edge, looking down at the Blood Run in Askavi Kaeleer. For generations, the Eyrien males in Askavi Terreille had gone to the Blood Run to test their strength and skill, a rite of passage to prove they were ready to be warriors, ready to be *men*.

The Rihlander friends who were near his equivalent age and on the cusp of reaching their majority thought it was an insane way to prove you had balls enough to be an adult, with adult privileges and responsibilities. Even Beron, who was part of the SaDiablo family, questioned the merits of a custom that required young men to fly the length of a canyon where winds and Winds collided in a dangerous, grueling test of mental and physical strength.

Daemonar understood the reason the custom was questioned. The Blood Run, as the lesser run, held the threads of the lighter Winds, from White to Opal. You had to be able to ride those Winds—or at least the ones that were your Jewel strength or less—while being buffeted by fierce winds that could push you off course enough to have a wing strike the canyon walls or the spears of stone you had to weave through as you dropped from one Wind and caught another.

A grueling test that had been required of every Eyrien male in Terreille.

Some hadn't survived it. Some had survived but were

maimed and lived on the edges of Eyrien society, dregs who were considered useless and had little future—and often went back to the Blood Run to be smashed to pieces and die.

The Blood Run was hard enough. The Khaldharon Run was the ultimate test of the strongest warriors, since the Winds that ran through the Khaldharon were the darker Winds, from Green to Black.

Lucivar was the only Eyrien living in Kaeleer who had made the Khaldharon Run. Had, in fact, made the Khaldharon more than once, which was something no other warrior could say.

Someday, after he made the Offering to the Darkness and wore the Jewel that was the reservoir for his mature power, Daemonar would test himself in the Khaldharon. But today, he faced the Blood Run.

Lucivar left the group of Eyrien warriors who had gathered as witnesses and walked over to Daemonar. Still a strong man and still in his prime, but there were some mornings when it was obvious to anyone who noticed—anyone Lucivar allowed to notice—that the damage that had been done when he was younger bothered him more as the years passed, might cost him more when he stepped onto a killing field. It would be a lot of years before anyone could stand against him and survive, but that day would come.

And that was the main reason Daemonar Yaslana was standing at the edge of this canyon, preparing himself for this particular rite of passage. Because when that day came and he took his place at his father's side, he needed to be acknowledged as a warrior by the rest of the Eyriens living in Kaeleer.

"You don't have to do this," Lucivar said.

Daemonar gave his father a crooked smile and looked him in the eyes. "Yes, I do."

It still surprised him that they were the same height now. Oh, he had the leanness of youth and didn't have the breadth of shoulders or the muscle of an adult male, but he no longer looked up at his father.

Lucivar huffed out a laugh. "Yeah, you do. And better to do it the traditional way than having you leap into the run unprepared." A brutal reminder of a recent death.

Daemonar had been preparing for decades, training with the warriors who worked for Lucivar—and training with Lucivar. Learning the aerial dances that were beautiful to watch and damn hard to perform. Spending hours doing precision flying with Lucivar, Rothvar, and Zaranar. More hours practicing with Tamnar and Alanar, since the three of them were the only Eyrien males of a comparable age living around Riada.

Tamnar had successfully made the Blood Run some time ago. Alanar had made the Run a couple of months ago. An Eyrien youth who lived around Doun was supposed to make the Run on the same day, but Lucivar had refused to give his permission. He said, and Rothvar had agreed, that the youth needed more practice and seasoning. The youth hotly insisted that he was ready—and just as hotly denied that he was showing up late for his training because he preferred the lessons he was receiving from some of the older Rihlander girls.

A week later, angry and defiant, the youth dove into the canyon to make the Blood Run on his own.

Daemonar had watched with Alanar and Tamnar as Lucivar and his men walked the canyon floor to find what they could. He saw the look of sorrow and anger on Lucivar's face as the Warlord Prince of Ebon Rih took the grisly remains to the Keep, where the High Lord of Hell waited to escort the youth to the Dark Realm—and send him to the final death once the Eyrien made the transition to demon-dead.

"I'm ready for this," he said.

Lucivar nodded. "I know you are."

Daemonar glanced at the group of Eyrien men. Women were not permitted to stand witness. They would attend the celebration later. But there was someone missing among the witnesses. "Uncle Daemon isn't coming?"

"He'll be here." Lucivar brushed a hand over Daemonar's hair. "Sun's in the best position now, so whenever you're ready."

As Lucivar walked away, Daemonar saw Rothvar, Zaranar, and Tamnar spread their wings and fly to the other side of the canyon. Hallevar, Endar, and Alanar stayed on this side. And Lucivar would be flying above the canyon and behind him to avoid casting a distracting shadow. But if he got in trouble, his father would be there to pull him out, just as Lucivar had been there to watch over Tamnar's and Alanar's Runs.

Staring at the canyon below, Daemonar opened his wings their full span, then closed them softly. He'd warmed up his muscles earlier. There was nothing more to do except leap toward his future.

No fear. Just the thrill of the challenge.

He took a deep breath. Then he dove into the canyon, caught the Tiger Eye Wind, and began the Blood Run.

Wings open to catch air currents. Wings tight and body turned as he followed the Tiger Eye between two stone spears before switching to the Purple Dusk and running on that thread. Hell's fire, the difference in speed! Up. Down. Catching the Opal, then dropping back to Summer-sky to keep as close to the center of the canyon as he could while weaving between obstacles. It was a hundred times better than riding the rapids on that raft he and Jaenelle Saetien made all those years ago.

Back to Purple Dusk, and there was the end of the canyon—a wall of stone. Time to head for the sky, pumping his wings. Pumping and pumping to get himself above that stone wall.

Up. Out. He kept heading for the sky and then turned to circle back to the land above the canyon—where Daemon Sadi waited for him.

He backwinged and landed as the other Eyriens flew toward that spot to meet him. He had fulfilled the rite of passage. He was a man now.

He let out a whoop and leaped into his uncle's arms.

Laughing, Daemon swung him around once before setting him on his feet. "Well done, boyo. Well done."

Grinning, Daemonar stepped away from his uncle and looked at his father when Lucivar landed nearby.

"So," Rothvar said. "We've got another Eyrien man among us."

"Now you're old enough to stay out as long as you please," Zaranar said.

Lucivar made a rude noise. "The first time his mother worries, he'll find his bed on the flagstones outside the eyrie."

"And you're old enough to walk into any tavern and drink yourself stupid," Hallevar said. "Just don't expect any of us to hold your head while you puke up your balls."

"So I've just spent decades training to do something that will allow me to get drunk and sleep outside?" Daemonar asked.

"Sounds like it," Daemon said dryly.

Daemonar looked at all the men who watched him. He was the Demon Prince's firstborn son and, by Eyrien tradition, he was a man. Everything he did from now on would matter.

"Do we get anything to eat?" he asked.

The men laughed.

"There's a feast waiting for you at the eyrie," Lucivar said. "Your mother's part of the celebration, as well as edible tributes from Manny and Mrs. Beale."

Daemonar's mouth watered, and he didn't even know what was going to be served.

"Why don't the rest of you head up to the eyrie?" Lucivar said. "We'll be along in a few minutes."

Daemonar felt the ripple of concern that passed from man to man, and shrugged in response to the questioning looks Tamnar and Alanar gave him. His own concern heightened when Uncle Daemon put a hand on his shoulder and led him farther away from the canyon's edge.

"There is another Eyrien tradition that is part of this rite of passage," Lucivar said.

Pretty sure what was coming, Daemonar tried to take a step back, but Uncle Daemon's hand was now between his shoulder blades, holding him in place.

"I can't say my experience was a good one, and I'd like yours to be better," Lucivar continued. "Being a man in this family can be a delicate, and difficult, position. And somewhere, somehow, you need to learn how to be a lover."

*No,* Daemonar thought, pressing against his uncle's hand. *I'm not ready for that.*

Oh, he was plenty interested in what he and a girl could do together, but when you were Blood and male, it wasn't that easy—and the price for pleasure could be terribly high.

"Which is why, with your parents' permission, your aunt Surreal and I are giving you this as our gift." Daemon called in a thick envelope and held it out.

Not seeing a choice, Daemonar took the envelope and opened it.

Hell's fire, Mother Night, and may the Darkness be merciful. His stomach flipped and his knees went weak. He enjoyed kissing girls. He really did. But . . .

"Lessons?" His voice cracked.

"While there aren't Red Moon houses in Kaeleer as there were in Terreille, there are establishments where young men can receive instruction on how to be a lover," Daemon said. "It's required for consorts, and recommended for any man who wants to be a husband who is welcome in his wife's bed."

Leaping back into the Blood Run was sounding like a good idea right now.

He looked at his uncle. "Couldn't I just keep talking to you about . . . stuff?"

"Of course you can," Daemon soothed. "And those conversations can be as basic or explicit as you want them to be. But you will need some experience in areas that I will not teach you."

*And that line has been drawn at my request,* Lucivar said on a psychic thread directed at him.

"This place is very exclusive and discreet," Daemon said. "Among its clientele are the sons of Queens because those are young men who, otherwise, could be vulnerable when they are first learning about the pleasures of the flesh. It's located in Amdarh, so it will be easy to arrange for a lesson when you come to visit." A beat of silence before he added, "Beron received his instruction at the same establishment. You could talk to him before making a decision."

Instructions away from Ebon Rih. Private. Discreet. Nothing the girls in Riada needed to know about— especially girls who might be having their Virgin Nights soon and would be free to indulge in having lovers.

"If you're worried about being cornered by a girl who expects you to be accommodating now that you've made the Blood Run, you can tell her your father and uncle are being pricks and holding you to the no-sex-without-permission rule," Lucivar said. "We'll back you."

"Against anyone," Daemon purred.

"Thank you." Not sure what else to say, Daemonar vanished the envelope. "Can we go eat now before all the food is gone?"

Father and uncle laughed and said, "Sure."

Daemonar just shrugged as they all caught the Green Wind and headed for the Yaslana eyrie.

Sex was all well and good, but a man had to set his priorities.


Later that evening, Lucivar and Daemon dropped from the Winds and walked toward the southern-facing Sleeping Dragon. Some stories said the Sleeping Dragons were actual dragons from the legendary race that had created the Blood. Other stories said some ancient hand sculpted stone into the shape of two dragons, one facing north and the other south. Didn't matter which story might be true. What mattered was the northern-facing dragon was at the end of the Khaldharon Run—and between the stone teeth in its gaping mouth was the entrance to a Gate between the Realms.

A person couldn't climb past those teeth without making at least part of the run—or so Lucivar had been told—so only the desperate or foolhardy would try to use that Gate instead of one of the others.

He'd been that desperate after he'd escaped from the salt mines of Pruul. Running from all the warriors who were intent on bringing him down, and already dying, he'd made his choice to die in the Khaldharon as a free man. He'd made the Run and flown between those stone teeth—and had ended up in Kaeleer. Had ended up being saved by Prothvar Yaslana and healed by Jaenelle Angelline.

But the Sleeping Dragon that faced to the south? No winds or Winds to slam a man against the stone teeth, and yet no one used the cavernous mouth as a hiding place. No one among the living, anyway.

"Did we have to do this tonight?" he asked. He would have preferred being at home, keeping an eye on his firstborn.

"Yes," Daemon replied. "I'm not sure if this is coincidence or if the timing is significant, but you need to see this."

Shit. Choosing to think about something else until they had to step past those teeth, he said, "Do you think Daemonar will use those lessons?"

Daemon smiled. "Eventually. He and I have had a number of frank discussions about . . . technique . . . over the past few years. And I know, because they've snarled at me for it, that he's asked Surreal and his auntie J. for confirmation that women actually like those techniques."

"Sweet Darkness," Lucivar breathed. "The boy's got more balls than sense."

"Oh, I don't know, Prick. I suggested to Beron that he talk to Surreal when he first showed a rising interest in women."

Lucivar snorted a laugh.

"Talking to Jaenelle about sex is a bit more adventurous than talking to Surreal, and I can tell when he's had one of those talks with his auntie J. by the way Daemonar looks at me." Daemon waited for Lucivar to stop laughing. "Just wait until he works up the nerve to ask you if you like doing the things he's thinking about doing because you'd both have to acknowledge that you're doing those things with *his* mother."

Lucivar swore. "She was my wife before she was his mother."

"That, old son, is an insignificant detail."

"Well, there have been whispers of Alanar and Tamnar setting up a bachelor eyrie, so I expect Daemonar will be looking to join them."

"No," Daemon said as the air around them turned cold. "You're going to keep him on a tight leash. Or you'll send him to me, and I'll do it."

Lucivar studied the man walking beside him. "So who wants to show me whatever is inside the Sleeping Dragon? My brother or the High Lord?"

"Not your brother."

Mother Night.

They didn't speak until they eased past the teeth. Daemon created a ball of witchlight that floated above them as they walked toward the end of the cavern.

Something was out there, watching them.

Lucivar formed an Ebon-gray shield around himself and called in his war blade.

Daemon didn't react to shield or blade, and he didn't react to whatever watched them.

"Dark Altars were built around every Gate," Daemon said. "Except this one. Here, you don't light the black candles in a certain order to open the Gate to a specific Realm."

"There are tunnels," Lucivar said quietly. "Two tunnels, one for each of the other two Realms."

"That's true, but access is no longer a simple choice."

The witchlight above them expanded, revealing more.

Two tunnels, as Lucivar had expected. The light that filled one tunnel was the forever-twilight of Hell. The other tunnel, which should have led to Terreille . . .

Lucivar sucked in a breath as he stared at the tangled webs that filled that tunnel. Some were broken, as if something desperate had managed to escape after being ensnared— or had been collected and carried away.

"There are Arachnians in the tunnels now?" Lucivar asked. Black Widows also spun tangled webs, and it was possible that demon-dead Sisters of the Hourglass had made the webs at Daemon's request, but he didn't think these webs had been made by anything human.

"Beware the golden spider that spins a tangled web," Daemon said softly. "From what I've been told by the demon-dead who guard this Gate, the webs appeared a few weeks ago. They cover the tunnel's exit into Kaeleer from the northern-facing Dragon and this southern tunnel that leads out of Kaeleer. Because the golden spiders' tangled webs ensnare a person's mind, letting the body fail on its own before they begin to feast, anyone who reaches the Shadow Realm and meets up with someone on this side isn't going to have the mental ability to return to Terreille. He either stumbles into the webs in that tunnel or stumbles into Hell, where he is considered fresh meat and blood for the taking."

Movement in the twilight tunnel. Three demon-dead Eyriens stepped out. Lucivar didn't recognize them, but they had been his age and they had died hard.

"Prince," one of them said, nodding to Lucivar. "High Lord." He laid a large sack at Daemon's feet and retreated. "We didn't open the bag to see what the last fool carried."

"My thanks for holding on to it," Daemon said, his smile cold and knowing. "Go enjoy your share of the feast. You've earned it."

With another bow, the three Eyriens retreated.

A few hours ago, the feast had been a living man. The body might be kept among the living until all the fresh blood had been consumed and the heart stopped beating.

What was left, after the High Lord finished the kill and the person's Self became a whisper in the Darkness, would feed Hell's flora and fauna.

Lucivar wondered if Saetan had ever flinched from such brutal practicality. He knew Daemon never would.

"There has always been some trade between Terreille and Kaeleer," Daemon said. "There is more now as every generation of the short-lived races becomes farther removed from the purge that cleansed the Realms."

"You have businesses in Dena Nehele and Shalador Nehele, so you've traded with those Territories for centuries."

"I have. I've also drawn lines about what I'll allow to come into Dhemlan from Terreille, and I extract a heavy price from anyone who crosses those lines. But I can't watch everyone, and things have slipped in." Daemon stared at the tunnel filled with tangled webs. "Surreal caught the first whispers about a year ago of items being smuggled into Dhemlan, but she couldn't find anything tangible to support the whispers. It seems that there is a growing nostalgia for Hayll and the way it was ruled."

Lucivar swore fiercely. "Have people lost their minds? Have they forgotten how many died because of that bitch Dorothea?"

"It is the romance of believing power can be had without a price." Daemon shrugged. "Apparently some people collect Hayllian memorabilia—especially anything that can be connected to Dorothea's court—and are willing to pay enough for those items to make bringing them in worth the risk."

"She was a High Priestess, not a Queen. She didn't *have* a court." That wasn't true. The bitch had had a court because she *said* she had a court and no one had dared challenge her. And the ones who did challenge her? Well, they ended up dead . . . or worse.

"Are you telling me this shit is being brought in through this Gate in Askavi?" He felt his temper burn hot and fierce as he rose to the killing edge.

"Some of it," Daemon said. "It's likely coming in through

other Territories that have a Gate, but there's nothing I can do about that except inform the Queens."

"Why didn't you tell me until now?"

"I had no way to confirm it." A quiet laugh, cutting and cold. "Oh, I knew from having chats with fools who didn't survive the attempt to return to Terreille that items were being smuggled in because any goods coming into Dhemlan are inspected, and these items weren't something anyone wanted me to know about. But the smugglers didn't know what they were bringing into Kaeleer, just that the money was worth the risk."

"Inspectors can be bribed to let goods in."

"Not after they are required to witness a slow execution of someone who had betrayed my trust."

The murderously sweet smile. The glazed eyes.

*Hell's fire, Bastard. You won't be able to hide who, and what, you are for much longer.*

Lucivar looked at the sack. "I gather this smuggler didn't live long enough to deliver the goods. So what's inside?"

Daemon raised a hand. Using Craft, he opened the sack.

Lucivar's breath caught. His stomach rolled. And everything in him screamed that he needed to fight.

"Coincidence?" Daemon asked. "Or was this shipment timed for a particular event?"

He stared at the gold rings lying on top of other items. He didn't need to touch one to feel the malevolence crawling through the metal.

"A Ring of Obedience is the only way to control a Warlord Prince if he doesn't choose to serve." Daemon waited a beat, then said, "Orian?"

"She's ignored Daemonar since that collision when they were children. She resents him for the training she was required to have with the Queens in Ebon Rih." The girl was especially resentful for the apprenticeships she'd had to serve in the courts of the Queens ruling Agio and Doun since she'd had to live away from home and those Queens had insisted that fun was a reward for good work and good behavior.

For a while, it had seemed the time away had helped Orian settle back into the girl she had been before her mother had embraced a warped idea of what a Queen was entitled to claim.

"She was at the eyrie tonight," Daemon pointed out.

"Every Eyrien youngster within the appropriate age was invited to the eyrie. And Daemonar's Rihlander friends as well, both male and female, aristo and not aristo."

"If your boy is old enough to make the Blood Run, Orian is old enough to have her Virgin Night. And once that happens, she won't continue to ignore him, Prick. He is a handsome young man who comes from a wealthy, powerful aristo family. He is also the only available Eyrien Warlord Prince in Kaeleer. And in case you hadn't noticed, he's entered the first stage of his sexual heat."

Lucivar vanished his war blade, then scrubbed his hands over his face. "I noticed. And I noticed how all the females in Riada have noticed. He and I have talked about why some people respond differently to him now."

"Which of us is going to tell him about the Ring of Obedience and what it can do—and why he needs to be vigilant from now on?"

"I'll tell him, and I'll let him know he can talk to you as well."

"Don't soften it, Lucivar. Give him the worst truth you know about being Ringed."

"His first lesson as a man?"

"At least he's learning it when he's old enough to be considered a man."

Lucivar shivered at the reminder that, in so many ways, Daemon was what he was because of what had been done to him as a child. "Let's get out of here. We've been gone long enough."

Daemon vanished the sack. "I'll look through what's here and let you know if anything else poses a threat."

Nodding, Lucivar led the way out of the Sleeping Dragon. Before they caught the Winds back to the eyrie, he said, "Who is going to tell Witch?"

"I will," Daemon replied.

"I guess it's time to prepare for war."

"We don't know the enemy yet."

"But we know one of the weapons the enemy will bring to the fight." As soon as he said the words, Lucivar felt the change in his brother's temper.

"Yes," the Sadist whispered. "We know that much."

# ELEVEN

---

After a few days of Daemonar's silence and sharp looks, Lucivar was delighted to see Titian when she walked into his study. He understood his boy's need for distance after being told—after being shown—what a Ring of Obedience could do, but he wondered if he'd made a mistake sharing one memory of how the Ring was used to punish a man.

Pushing that worry aside, he smiled at Titian. His smile faded when she closed the door, perched on the edge of one of the chairs in front of his blackwood desk, and gave him a smile that held a lot of nerves and a dollop of courage.

He knew what that meant. His sweet little witchling was about to stab him in the heart.

"Father . . ." She hesitated.

Father, not Papa. Another sign that she was shedding—or shredding—childhood. And that meant he had to strap some steel to his spine and help her.

"Titian . . . ?"

"I want to go to school. To study art. It's time, Papa."

It *was* time. Titian had been drawing and painting for centuries now, developing her own artistic style. During all those years, she'd retreated from every suggestion he or Daemon had made about taking lessons. Now, it seemed, she was ready to take that step.

And now, it seemed, he wasn't quite as ready to let her go.

*Show some balls, old son.* "All right. We can look into . . ."

"In Amdarh," Titian added hurriedly. "There's a private school in Amdarh that has an art course. Zoey is going to be there. Lady Zhara has already reviewed the school's credentials and given her approval. But . . ." She winced. "It's expensive, but I could use my allowance to help pay for it."

Lucivar sat back and eyed his daughter. Did she think the *cost* was the issue? He might live simply for a man who came from an aristo bloodline, but that didn't mean he wasn't wealthy. Taken as a whole, the SaDiablo family was *the* wealthiest family in the entire Realm of Kaeleer. Daemon had seen to that, as had their father before him.

In Amdarh, Titian would be under Daemon's hand, even if she boarded at the school. He could count on his brother to know what was happening in his daughter's life—or at least know as much as any man could know about a daughter.

He pushed back from the desk and headed for the door. "Come with me."

She followed him through the eyrie's corridors until they reached the large front room. He kept going, using Craft to open the glass doors to the yard where the children played and practiced their fighting skills in good weather. As he walked into the yard, he called in two sparring sticks and held one out to her.

"Papa . . ."

She seemed to wilt in front of his eyes, reminding him how easily this child's heart could bruise, how easily she could be damaged by harsh or cutting words.

"Papa, I don't want to learn to fight."

*But you have to learn, witchling, even if it's not the same kind of fighting your brothers embrace.* "This isn't about learning to fight. This is about proving you can defend."

She met his eyes. As timid as she was so much of the

time, she always had the courage to meet his eyes—something even her brothers didn't do.

He rested a hand on her shoulder, a connection. "You want to go to this school and study art? Then show me that you can defend my precious daughter. Show me that you can shape protective shields fast enough to block an attack and strong enough to hold you safe until someone who does know how to fight can reach you. When you show me you can do that, then I will see about getting you enrolled in the school and whatever else is required." His hand tightened on her shoulder, just a little, just enough to warn her he was serious. "There will be rules, witchling, lines that will be drawn about what you can and cannot do. Your uncle Daemon and aunt Surreal will know the conditions I'm setting for you attending the school, and your uncle will have the same authority over you when you're in his Territory as I do here. If you cross any of those lines, one of us will haul you back here before you have time to spin. You understand me?"

"Yes, Papa." The smile, shy and slow in coming, became bright enough to dazzle. "I won't break the rules."

"There will be people who will try to convince you—or force you—to break them. Maybe they'll do it just to see if they can push you hard enough to give in. Maybe they'll do it just to be mean and hurtful."

"Zoey wouldn't do that."

He wasn't sure if he wanted to hug Daemon or smack him for introducing the two girls. The threesome—Titian, Zoey, and Jaenelle Saetien—made so many plans when they were together in Amdarh, he didn't know how Daemon got any sleep during those days.

Well, he did know, actually. Daemon, quite sensibly, assigned Scelties to be chaperones and escorts, since the dogs could doze through late-night giggles and innocent foolishness.

"No," he replied, "I don't think Lady Zoela would do that, but others will. Don't let them win, Titian. You hold to who you are."

"Yes, Papa." She raised her sparring stick.

Lucivar suppressed a sigh. "All right, witchling. Let's see what you can do and what still needs some work before you leave home."

Wondering if Alanar had set him up for an "accidental" meeting with Orian, Daemonar shaped a tight Green shield around himself, then let his awareness flow through what Uncle Daemon called a psychic web, using a touch of power to identify the position of everyone around him within a block of where he stood on Riada's main street. He couldn't identify the psychic scent of all of the individuals, but he knew the Eyriens who lived around this village.

Alanar and Tamnar weren't within the radius of his psychic web, but Orian was. Ever since he'd made the Blood Run, he'd had the uneasy feeling of being hunted whenever he crossed her path, and they seemed to be crossing paths a lot more lately. They were courteous whenever they saw each other on the street or at some event, but they hadn't been friends for a long time now. He didn't want anything to do with her physically, and as sure as the sun didn't shine in Hell, he did not want to serve in any court she formed. Ever.

Besides, he already served a Queen, even if the memory of her was fading among the short-lived races, turning an extraordinary woman and Queen into a story, a legend. She wasn't a memory or a legend. Not to him. No longer flesh, but Auntie J. was still extraordinary—and powerful.

Abandoning the spot where he was supposed to meet his friends, Daemonar strode to the bakery and went in. Since he'd been coming down to the village anyway, he'd offered to pick up the bread, greens, and other foods the family needed during the three days when his mother stayed home and quiet. His father had priority when it came to fussing over Marian during her moontime, but taking care of errands like this was a subtle way of fussing that appeased his own need to take care of her. He'd already placed an order at The Tavern for two steak-and-ale pies, figuring he could run the rest of his errands and talk to Alanar and Tamnar in the time it would take for the pies to cook.

He'd decided on a loaf of cinnamon swirl to have with tomorrow's breakfast and was chatting with the baker's son about which herb-flavored bread Marian would like with the pie and greens when Orian and her latest Rihlander coven of followers walked into the bakery.

"Ladies." Daemonar gave the young women a nod carefully balanced to indicate respect and also remind them—especially Orian—that he outranked all of them. "If you'd like to place an order . . ." He gestured toward the racks of bread and rolls behind the counter.

"I know what Lady Orian would like to order," one of the women said, running the tip of her tongue over her upper lip.

The baker's son blushed, but the female's blatant crudeness filled Daemonar with hot anger. He was still feeling raw over what he'd learned about the Ring of Obedience, and he responded to the tone and action as a call to battle, not an invitation to the bed.

Adding a little more power to his shield, he turned his back on the women, made his selections, and vanished the loaves after the baker's son tallied up the purchases and gave him the ledger to initial. Then he turned again and said quietly to Orian, "You want to get out of the way."

"I'm going to have my Virgin Night soon," she said.

"That doesn't have anything to do with me."

Her skin whitened around her tightly pressed lips. "It could."

"No. It won't." He expanded the Green shield to keep everyone from getting closer than a forearm's distance from his body. Then he took a step, knowing Orian would brush up against the shield. He gave her a moment to step aside; then he moved toward the door, knocking against the girls who foolishly didn't get out of his way.

"Daemonar!" Orian shouted. "You shame your mother with that behavior."

To say that to a man, especially a young man, was a serious insult.

He stopped at the door and looked at her. "Considering *your* behavior recently, I wouldn't talk about someone else shaming their family, *Lady* Orian. I really wouldn't."

He walked out of the bakery and spotted Alanar and Tamnar hurrying toward him.

"Do all girls go through a stage when they're completely out of their minds?" he demanded.

Alanar looked toward the bakery. "Ah, Hell's fire. Has she started on you again? I thought she'd gotten over that."

"So did I." He walked away from the bakery, the other Eyrien males falling in beside him.

"It's because you're the only Eyrien aristo Warlord Prince in Kaeleer," Tamnar said. "I think Orian sees seducing you as a point of honor. Or something."

"Well, thank the Darkness she isn't foolish enough to make a play for my father," Daemonar snapped. "We'd need buckets and shovels to pick up what was left of her after *his* temper exploded." He glanced at Alanar's gray face and stopped walking. "Please tell me your mother hasn't become so unhinged that she's thinking in that direction."

"I don't know what she's thinking anymore," Alanar said bitterly. "Father left, moved someplace around Doun. She didn't want him around anymore. Said he shamed her, not being a real Eyrien warrior."

Endar had never been a skilled warrior and would have been among the first to fall on a killing field. When their children were small, Dorian had been pleased that her husband had been hired to teach the Eyrien children instead of being carelessly spent in a fight. Now Dorian was even more obsessed with what a Queen would be entitled to have when she came of age and could form her own court, and every attempt to curb the sense of privilege Dorian encouraged in her daughter had failed.

And no one, not even Lucivar, knew what had shaped the whip that was driving Dorian toward a battle she couldn't win.

"I've heard talk—whispers not quite behind the hand—that Eyrien men aren't suited to live with women and children," Tamnar said. "That Eyrien men living with their families is unnatural, just like having male children remain at home instead of being fostered at a hunting camp isn't natural."

Daemonar snorted. "Tell that to Rothvar or my father. Tell that to any of the men who have started families and live with those families. That's Terreillean thinking, and it has no place in Kaeleer." He thought about what Lucivar and Daemon had found at the Sleeping Dragons, then looked at his friends. "Someone is stirring up trouble, and I may not be the only target. You need to be careful."

"Tamnar and I are going ahead to establish a bachelor eyrie," Alanar said.

"Are you going to join us?" Tamnar asked.

They had talked about it before he'd made the Blood Run. But this encounter with Orian showed him why he shouldn't leave the protection of living under his father's roof. He'd be battling her every damn day, and eventually she would end up bloody because he wasn't going to let her corner him into any kind of commitment.

"No," he said. "Not yet, anyway."

They kept him company while he went to another shop and selected greens for the salad before heading to The Tavern to pick up the steak-and-ale pies.

"You'll be all right?" Alanar asked when they reached The Tavern.

That was as close as any of them came to acknowledging the way Orian and her coven had followed them from place to place.

What in the name of Hell was wrong with that girl?

"I'll be fine."

Tamnar and Alanar spread their wings and leaped for the sky. He went into The Tavern.

The current owner of the tavern and inn could trace his line back to Merry and Briggs, who had run the place when Lucivar first came to Ebon Rih. It was still one of his father's favorite places to stop for a glass of ale or a meal, and the steak-and-ale pies were a recipe that had been handed down through the generations.

He felt Orian's presence the moment she entered The Tavern, felt his temper flash hot as he began rising to the killing edge. And then . . .

"Hey, boyo. Why aren't you out kissing sky?"

Daemonar turned and let out a whoop as anger vanished, conquered by delight. "Jillian!"

Dropping the Green shield, he grabbed her and spun them around so many times they had to hold on to each other for balance when he finally set her on her feet.

"You've gotten tall," Jillian complained.

"Nah, you just stopped growing—at least upward."

She narrowed her eyes. "Watch it."

He grinned, unrepentant. She wasn't boyishly lean anymore. Then again, she wasn't a girl anymore, and while she wasn't soft, her body said woman now.

"Are you here for a visit?"

"Going to stay a while."

"We'll see about that," Orian muttered.

Daemonar swung around to challenge—and hit the fist Jillian thrust in front of his chest. He started to protest, then saw her give Orian a smile so sharp, it could have cut leather.

"Yes, I guess we'll see about a lot of things, won't we?" Jillian said. "But if people start dumping shit on my doorstep, I'll know *exactly* where to find the buckets—and I know *exactly* what to do about it."

Daemonar collected the pies and hustled Jillian out of The Tavern.

"That girl is going to be trouble," Jillian said.

"Yeah, I know." And now Orian had Jillian in her sights. "Maybe you should stay with us while you're here. We've got plenty of room."

She hooted. "Not a chance." She linked arms with him. "I appreciate the offer. I do. But you're a man now, and being around the sexual heat of *two* Warlord Princes?" She shook her head. "You might want to consider that Orian's reaction to you isn't all her doing. Your heat isn't overpowering, but it is noticeable."

If Jillian was right, then living in Ebon Rih was going to become intolerable. "Where are you staying? With Nurian and Rothvar?"

"Not exactly. Nurian kept the Healer's eyrie, and my room is still available there. So I'll stay there, visit with my niece and nephew, and have my own space when I don't want company."

"Alone? You're going to stay on your own?" His voice rose loud enough to draw attention to them from people on the street.

"I've been on my own for quite a while."

"You've always had someone with you, a companion." He felt the tension in her, the grief. "Ah, Jillian."

"Kindred don't usually become demon-dead. Did you know that?" she asked softly. "I don't know why that's so; it just is. But Khary made the transition and stayed with me for a long time after his body died of old age. Their lives are so short compared to ours. A few decades at most. But he stayed with me while I learned so much."

"When did your . . ." What word could he use? Current companion?

"A couple of weeks ago." Jillian sniffed, blinked, looked away from him. "I finished a project I'd been working on, and when he became a whisper in the Darkness, I knew it was time to come home for a while. Lady Perzha and the current Queen of Little Weeble agreed." She sniffed again. "That's something I need to discuss with Lucivar."

"You might have to get in line," Daemonar said. "Titian didn't come to the village with me today because she wanted to have a private talk with Father."

"Oh, no," Jillian breathed. "She's reached that age, hasn't she? Poor Lucivar."

Well, that didn't sound good. "Come on. I'll escort you home—and if you don't make a fuss about it, I'll give you a share of one of the pies and part of a loaf of bread so you'll have something to eat while you get settled in."

She studied him. "You're bossy—you can't help that—but you're clever about it. All right. Escort me home and then let your father know I'd like to talk to him at his earliest convenience."

Once they'd reached the eyrie Jillian had once shared with her sister, Daemonar gave her a third of a pie and half a loaf of the herb-flavored bread.

"Do you need anything else?" he asked.

"I did pick up a few supplies before I spotted you going into The Tavern," she said with a smile. "I won't starve."

So she probably didn't need the steak-and-ale pie. Which wasn't the point. She was family, and Warlord Princes took care of family.

"Be careful who you let in when you're on your own," he said.

"If I need help, I'll holler. I promise." She gave him a hug and pushed him out the door.

When he arrived home and walked through the big front room on his way to the kitchen, he glanced toward the glass doors that opened onto the yard and stopped, frozen by the sight of Titian kneeling in the grass, looking miserable as tears ran down her face.

A few minutes later, after he'd coaxed her to tell him why she was upset, he stormed into his father's study, ready—hoping—for a fight.

Lucivar tossed a report on his desk and leaned back in his chair. "I take it you've talked to your sister."

"Talked to her?" Daemonar snarled. "She's out in the yard crying her heart out because you're putting her through exercises she can't possibly do."

Lucivar's eyes glazed, a warning of temper being held on a tight leash. He rose slowly and opened his dark membranous wings their full span before closing them again.

Daemonar opened his wings halfway for balance and

settled his feet in a fighting stance. If they were really going to fight, he would end up bloody, but he wasn't backing down. Not after seeing his sister hurting so much.

"What I'm asking of her is what I need from her in order to let her go," Lucivar said. "She has to be able to build shields fast enough and strong enough to withstand an attack—and she has to hold those shields until help arrives."

"So you're going to keep testing her?"

"Yeah, I am. And you're going to help her hone those skills so that she passes the test and can go to school in Amdarh for her art."

Daemonar felt his jaw drop. He'd thought this was some kind of trick to *keep* Titian home—and that made him feel ashamed of himself because Lucivar wouldn't stoop to a ruse for any reason.

"You're really going to let her go to school in Amdarh?"

Lucivar huffed. "It's not the other side of the Realm, boyo. It's in your uncle's Territory. In fact, it's the capital of your uncle's Territory."

"But Uncle Daemon doesn't live in Amdarh."

"Not all the time, no, but he's there often enough."

He felt panic rising at the thought of Titian being out of reach if she needed help. "But he's not there all the time. What if he's staying at Ebon Askavi when she needs help? What if he's in Scelt? That *is* on the other side of the Realm."

"If Daemon is away from Dhemlan, then Surreal will be in residence, either at the Hall or the town house in Amdarh," Lucivar replied. "If neither of them are close by, Titian can ask for help from Lady Zhara or anyone in her court."

Daemonar paced, feeling the room closing in around him.

"This is important to her, Daemonar," Lucivar said quietly. "Important enough that she came to me and asked for my permission. If she meets the terms I set, I will not refuse to let her go. And neither can you."

"She's not strong." He heard the plea in his voice—*protect her.*

"She's not a fighter like you—or me. That doesn't make her weak. That just means she has a different kind of strength. All we can do is help her prepare to meet the challenges she'll face and to let her know we will always have her back. Always." Lucivar came around the desk until they stood barely an arm's length apart. "Can't clip her wings, boyo. I won't do that to her."

"She's vulnerable." He meant sex, meant the risks a young witch faced on her Virgin Night, but wasn't going to say that. Titian was *way* too young for *that*.

"You're vulnerable too," Lucivar said quietly.

"That's beside the point," Daemonar snapped. "I'm older than Titian, and I can take care of myself."

"Well, your mother and I made sure you know how to cook. Now all you have to do is remember that underwear doesn't walk itself to the laundry tubs."

"You're just twisting my balls because you're worried about Titian."

"And worried about you."

Daemonar saw that truth in his father's eyes. "You don't have to worry about me. I've been trained by the best."

Lucivar smiled. "Yes, you have. And what did she say?"

Daemonar shrugged. "I just found out about Titian wanting to go to school, didn't I?" He'd have to think about how to present his concerns to Auntie J. to avoid getting a whack upside the head if he sounded like he wouldn't support his sister. He *would* support her. He just needed time to get used to the idea of her being gone.

"Ice on a cliff's edge and a long drop to the river if you lose your footing."

Meaning his father had a really good idea of how Witch would react if he didn't support Titian—or sounded like he didn't support her.

"What about you?" Lucivar asked. "I have concerns about you joining Alanar and Tamnar, but if you felt strongly about it . . ."

Daemonar shook his head. "I don't like being hunted."

Would he ever think of the Ring of Obedience without a kick of fear?

Lucivar leaned against the front of the blackwood desk. "Well, Alanar couldn't refuse to let his sister in if she came for a visit, just as he couldn't say much if that sister, who is also a Queen, decided to take a nap in his friend's bed."

"You think I'm a coward for not wanting that fight?"

"Never that. It's not cowardly to want to feel safe in your own home."

Daemonar looked into his father's eyes and felt chilled by what he saw there.

"Orian is a cat trying to play with a mouse, refusing to recognize that the mouse is a wolf who can snap her in half," Lucivar said softly. "Witches tried to play those kinds of games with me. The ones who survived didn't walk away unscathed. Hopefully Orian will outgrow this latest bitch phase and show some potential to be a good Queen. But if she starts playing cat and mouse with other young men who aren't so well able to defend themselves, I will break her, Daemonar. I will strip her back to basic Craft. If that isn't enough to stop her from causing harm, then I will bury her. You understand me?"

"Yes, sir."

Lucivar seemed to shake off the edge of temper. "Well . . ."

"Jillian is back. She wants to talk to you." He should leave it at that. He should. "She's staying at the Healer's eyrie. On her own."

Lucivar stared at him, then made a twirling motion with one finger. "Turn around."

"What?"

"Turn around."

Not sure what was about to happen, he turned around.

"Hmm," Lucivar said. "Since I'm not seeing a dent in your ass the shape of Jillian's boot, I'm guessing you didn't say outright that she couldn't take care of herself and stay on her own."

He chose not to confirm or deny.

Lucivar laughed. "While you were busy evading one female and trying to boss around another, did you remember to pick up the food?"

Turning, he narrowed his eyes at his father. "Yes, I picked up the food—but I gave some to Jillian when I escorted her to her eyrie."

"Of course you did. She's family."

In harmony with each other, they went to the kitchen to put together the midday meal.

Titian sat by the pool that was fed by a mountain stream. A small defiance, refusing to hear her father's call to come in and eat. Maybe not the best defiance, since Daemonar told her he'd bought steak-and-ale pies from The Tavern, and she really was hungry. But it was a way to get back at her father for setting this impossible test that she had to pass in order to go to school and study art. Her refusing to eat would upset him. A lot. Not that she *wanted* him to be upset. Not for long, anyway. But . . .

A plate with a piece of pie, lightly dressed greens, and bread generously spread with butter appeared before her.

"You going hungry will make Lucivar crazy, but it won't make him back down," Jillian said as she settled on the grass beside Titian. She held out a fork. "So you might as well eat."

"He's not being fair," Titian said. She took the fork, her resolve wavering as she breathed in the pie's delicious smell.

Jillian smiled. "Actually, he's being very fair. And I say this as someone who fought a few battles with him when I was your age."

She didn't remember a lot about that time, just that Papa and Jillian seemed to wrangle a lot over some boy, but this wasn't about a *boy*. This was about her *life*.

"I want to go to school in Amdarh," she said.

"And he wants you to be able to defend yourself. If you and a good friend were out walking and you were suddenly attacked by a . . . by a crazed dog as big as a pony, wouldn't you want to be able to form shields around yourself and your friend to avoid being savaged? Wouldn't you want those shields to hold until the city's guards could reach you and deal with the dog?"

"Well . . . sure."

"Your father wants that too. He wants those shields to hold. And if you're pushed to it, he wants you to have some skill with a weapon so that you can whack the crap out of that dog while you're waiting for the guards."

*"Jillian!"*

"What? You live with three Warlord Princes. You've never heard any of them say 'crap'?"

Uncertain of the ground, Titian ate the pie. While she was chewing over Jillian's words, she somehow polished off the greens and the bread as well.

"Papa doesn't want me to go."

"Of course not. You're his little girl. Hell's fire, Lucivar was miserable when he escorted me to Little Weeble for my first apprenticeship in a court, and I wasn't that far out of reach that he couldn't check on me every day. He didn't, and I think it cost him, but he could have."

"The school is in Amdarh. Uncle Daemon will be there."

"You think your uncle will be any less strict?"

"No." But Uncle Daemon wouldn't beat on the shields she could create until they failed. Would he?

"Daemonar will help you work on building stronger shields," Jillian said. "So will I. I'll be around for a while."

"But the paperwork has to be turned in soon if I'm going to start school in the fall with the other students."

Jillian bumped arms. "I bet that if you work on those shields and show your father that you can protect yourself, you'll find that all the arrangements have been made and all the papers signed. Your father didn't set up this test so that you would fail. He expects you to succeed, and then he'll have to let you go. But I'll tell you what Prince Sadi told me. After you're gone, send a letter home once a week to let your parents know how you're doing."

"Papa doesn't like to read."

"I said that, too, but I wrote the letters, and I realized long after that first apprenticeship ended that Lucivar had read those letters often enough to remember every detail." Jillian smiled. "Write the letters for your mother and father, but include a sketch or two with each letter, something especially for him."

"You'll really help me work on the shields?" Titian asked.

"Of course I will. I've got some time now if you want to get a little more practice in today."

She smiled. "Okay."

Sighing, Lucivar backed away from the glass doors and dropped the sight shield. He'd chucked Daemonar and Andulvar out the door right after the meal, giving them permission to fly a couple of circuits around Riada on their own. Nothing new for his firstborn, but a heady freedom for his youngest.

Marian wasn't in her workroom, reading or doing needlework. She wasn't in the bedroom napping. He went out the door in the laundry room and found her in her garden, weeding.

"Are you sure you feel up to doing this?" he asked as he knelt beside her.

She just looked at him.

He sighed, ripped a weed out of the ground, and tossed it in the basket.

"Did Jillian convince Titian to eat?" Marian asked.

"Yeah, she did. And now they're out there practicing shields."

She smiled. "You're teaching your daughter how to leave us. That's your job."

"I don't like my job."

"Yes, you do. Not today, but you do."

Couldn't argue with that.

He watched his darling hearth witch weed the flower

bed. He wanted to smash boulders into gravel, not daintily pluck weeds from among the flowers.

"Have you heard from your brother lately?" Marian asked.

"Not since Daemonar made the Blood Run." He'd have to talk to Daemon soon, get his assessment of the school and the teachers and . . . "Why?"

Marian gave him a kiss that held some sympathy swirled with amusement. "I'm just wondering what sort of argument Jaenelle Saetien is presenting to Daemon to convince him to let her go to the same school. After all, if Titian and Zoey will be attending . . ."

Lucivar sat back on his heels. "Oh, Hell's fire."

"What's that saying about misery and company?"

He snorted. "Like that, is it? Well, get in the boat with the rest of us while I tell you about Jillian's scheme."

She was not astonished. She wasn't even all that surprised when he told her. Instead she looked thoughtful and said, "I hadn't realized she'd gotten this far."

Lucivar blinked. "You *knew* about this?"

"Jillian had mentioned it the last time she was home."

"And you didn't tell me?"

"She wanted to surprise you." Marian smiled. "I think she didn't want you to ask Daemon until . . ."

"Never. She wants to do this on her own, without his help or mine. Otherwise, how will she know that her work has merit?"

"Oh, dear." She burst out laughing. "Your daughters are being difficult, aren't they?"

Difficult? Hell's fire, yes. Which meant they were growing into the women he'd hoped they would be.

# TWELVE

Daemon walked through Tersa's cottage, giving the downstairs rooms a quick inspection. Manny lived next door and still did the day-to-day tidying, but she had reached the late autumn of her years and her eyesight was fading. Not so much that she couldn't cook or bake or get around on her own, but he noticed that she needed more help these days with some tasks, which was why Helene, the Hall's housekeeper, sent some of her younger staff to the two cottages each week to "help with the heavy lifting."

The arrangement worked for everyone, mostly because Helene's argument for providing the help was that it gave *him* peace of mind. Which was true. Knowing that his mother and the woman who had been his caretaker during the violent and painful childhood he'd endured with Dorothea SaDiablo were looked after helped quiet the cold, deep rage that could rise in him with little warning.

Tersa wasn't in the cottage, but her psychic scent and the feel of her fragmented mind told him she was nearby. He went out the back door and headed for the herb beds in the garden. She'd been weeding, but now she sat back on her heels, staring at the plants.

He angled his approach so that she would see him— assuming she was seeing anything in the world around her. He crouched beside her, balancing on the balls of his feet to avoid getting dirt or grass stains on his black trousers.

"The plants are growing well," he said, wondering if they were going to talk about the herb bed in front of them or something else. With Tersa, he could never tell.

"They are growing well," she agreed. "So are the weeds." She pointed to one plant, then another. "Hard to tell which is which."

"Not so hard if you recognize one."

"Can you tell one from the other?" She brushed a hand over the two plants. Now they looked the same.

A chill ran down his spine, twanging the leash that held his temper.

Tersa scooped up a double handful of soil. "Good soil, rich with tradition, nurtured by the power that rules. But some gardens have imported Terreillean soil. Weeds like that soil. They grow fast and thick. The roots aren't so deep yet that they can't be plucked from the garden. They aren't so widespread that they can't be purged."

No, they weren't talking about plants. Centuries ago, Tersa had spun a tangled web and had seen the first warning of trouble in Kaeleer. He'd seen that web, had read the warning—and had become dangerous to everyone in that part of the Keep. When the rage had quieted, he couldn't remember what he'd seen and neither Tersa nor Witch would tell him. All his Queen would say was he would recognize the danger that the web had revealed.

That was why one of his visits to Tersa each week began with an innocuous question about the everyday world. Sometimes she answered the question; sometimes she plucked an answer from the fragments of her mind that he couldn't translate into something that made sense. But he came every week and asked a question, waiting for this day.

This day, when she would give the second warning, and he would know that the threat had grown to the point where he would recognize it.

"What can get rid of the weeds?" he asked quietly. "What can cleanse the Terreillean soil out of Kaeleer's ground?"

"Ice. And fire."

Cold and heat? Or his icy rage and Lucivar's hot temper?

She rose, a smooth movement—and a sharp reminder that his mother, with her tangled hair and tangled mind, was just approaching her autumn years. Then she handed him the basket of weeds and said, "Put those in the compost bin."

He emptied the basket into the bin before returning to the kitchen and setting the basket by the door.

She turned toward him, her face brightening with a delighted smile. "It's the boy. It's my boy."

She said the words as if he'd just arrived.

"Hello, darling." He walked up to her and gave her a kiss on the cheek.

"Have you come to visit?"

"I have." He waited until she went to the sink to wash her hands before asking, so casually, "Who were you talking to out in the garden?"

The clarity in her gold eyes had nothing to do with sanity and everything to do with who he suspected she had been before she'd been broken, before she'd sacrificed her sanity to regain some of the Hourglass's Craft.

"Tersa? Who were you talking to?"

"The Queen's weapon."


Surreal called in the two trunks she used when traveling to the SaDiablo estates and left them where the senior maid assigned to look after her room and wardrobe at the Hall would be able to sort the clothes that needed washing from those that just needed airing.

She wasn't looking forward to meeting with Sadi to discuss the events she was sure were going to break a District Queen's court and divide a village between two aristo families who claimed grievous harm had been done to their children. Grievous harm *had* been done to both children, but it was the boy who had died just hours before she'd arrived. And it was the boy she'd personally escorted to the Keep to be confined while he made the transition to demon-dead—and to await the High Lord's pleasure.

She had a feeling the prick-ass's time in Hell would be short and painful since he had dosed the girl with *safframate*—a drug that, in very small doses, would enhance a lover's staying power and was mostly used within a court under specific circumstances. In Kaeleer, anyway. In Terreille, it had been used to create a sexual need beyond sanity, making the person a desperate participant in what amounted to prolonged rape, whether that person was male or female.

Sometimes the sexual need erupted as violence. Lucivar had torn women apart under the influence of *safframate*, had left courts choking on the carnage his rage had produced. Daemon had never experienced an erection or arousal under the influence of *safframate*, but Surreal wondered if the Sadist had been born in the pain produced by the drug when that pain had no outlet.

Whether the boy had given the girl too much or whether the girl was one of the individuals who reacted with rage instead of arousal didn't matter at this point. Surreal hadn't been able to tell what the girl had used to strike the first blow that put the boy on the ground because she'd ripped through skin and muscle and had managed to pull out the boy's entrails with her hands.

There was no law against murder among the Blood, but rape was punished by slow execution, so while she had a little sympathy for the boy's shocked parents, she sided with the girl's family, especially after a quick search of the boy's pockets uncovered a vial with a second dose of *safframate*.

Now she had to tell the Warlord Prince of Dhemlan that a drug he hated was being used in his Territory in the same way it had been used in Terreille. And she had to tell him that she suspected that the boy's father had supplied his son with the drug. Which meant they would be studying the ebb and flow of sexual activity in and around that village, from the District Queen's court on down, because a man who gave *safframate* to his son probably used it himself to "persuade" women who didn't want his attention.

Having a good idea how Daemon would react, she wasn't sure if she wanted him to stay with her tonight, just for company, or if she hoped he would choose to sleep alone—or sleep in the High Lord's suite, away from the family wing.

Well, she would decide about the sleeping arrangements after she had a chance to measure his mood and temper. A quick psychic probe when she'd first arrived home told her he was in Halaway, probably visiting Tersa. That, too, would determine what she needed to ask of him for her own safety, as well as the safety of everyone else at the Hall.

No point waiting inside when her own skin felt itchy from the need to move. She'd go out to the back lawn and work with the Dea al Mon fighting knives, going through the warm-ups and exercises that kept her skills as sharp as the blades she used.

She'd changed clothes and was lacing up the ankle boots she used for these exercises when Jaenelle Saetien knocked on her bedroom door and walked in before she had a chance to answer.

"It's courteous to wait to be invited," Surreal said, struggling to keep her tone mild. "Especially when you get so upset about anyone entering your room before you give permission."

Jaenelle Saetien just shrugged, as if she couldn't make the connection between her intense desire for privacy and respecting someone else's privacy.

Some days Surreal dealt with the girl who had grown up in this house—a girl who was usually full of curiosity, intelligence, courage, kindness, and enough sass to stand up for herself without forgetting courtesy and manners. Other days she wrangled with a pissy, bitchy stranger who wore her daughter's face. Couldn't tell day by day—or even hour by hour—which one it would be.

She might have enjoyed being pissy and bitchy at the same age if she'd grown up in a different way and could have indulged in such emotions. Or maybe she'd just channeled those feelings into the way she'd used a knife for some contracts.

"I'm going outside to work with the Dea al Mon knives. You're welcome to join me."

Jaenelle Saetien wrinkled her nose. "Who wants to get sweaty?"

*Someone who wants to survive. And the girl I saw today got a lot more than sweaty.* "Suit yourself. If you have anything to discuss with your father, you should do it before I sit down with him."

"Why?" That habitual hint of annoyance changed to a concern that might be genuine. "Did something happen on your trip?"

"Yes, it did."

Hesitation. "Do you have to tell him today?"

"Since this will produce a storm that will roll through every village and court in Dhemlan, yes, I have to tell him."

Jaenelle Saetien looked alarmed. "What happened?"

"A boy died, but it was the way he died and why he died that will produce the storm."

"What did he do?" She sounded so much younger than she had a minute ago.

Surreal weighed her answer against the painful truth: the girl who had been drugged was the same age as Jaenelle Saetien—a girl nowhere near old enough to have her Virgin Night and come away from the experience with her Jewels and power intact. "He used a drug that should have made it easy for him to rape a girl. She fought back. She survived. He's dead."

When Jaenelle Saetien didn't respond, Surreal walked out of her bedroom. She really needed the feel of those knives, really needed to remember that she was no longer a child struggling under the first man who had raped her. She had to let the movements and her muscles help her remember that she was very, very good with a knife.

"I want to go away to school," Jaenelle Saetien said, following her down the corridor.

Surreal stopped and stared at her daughter. Go away? When the smell of blood and shit was still so fresh she wondered if she'd brought it home with her, her daughter wanted to go away? "Where?"

"It's a private school in Amdarh," Jaenelle Saetien said eagerly. "It's very exclusive—and has excellent teachers."

Exclusive obviously mattered to the girl. Excellent teachers would matter to Daemon—if he was even willing to entertain the idea.

"Zoey and Titian are going to be there." A beat of effort at restraint before the next words burst out. "All my friends are going to be at that school."

"I don't think all of them will be there. What about your friends in Halaway?"

Jaenelle Saetien shrugged. "They're all right, but they're . . ."

When she hesitated, Surreal filled in the rest. "No longer special enough to deserve your attention? No longer exclusive enough, aristo enough?" She kept her voice mild while she struggled with the furious desire to force open her daughter's first inner barrier and show the girl what she had seen in that village.

"You don't understand!" Jaenelle Saetien wailed.

"I understand more than you think." Titian and Zoey being in attendance might tip the balance in favor of Jaenelle Saetien going to that school. "You won't convince your father to give his permission by using posturing and a snotty attitude. Write a report explaining why you want to go to the school. Make a list of the educational—and social—benefits that being there will provide. Then you'll have to wait for his decision."

"Can't you talk to him?" Wheedling now.

"No. If you want this, you need to ask him yourself."

"Why won't you do this for me? You never do anything for me!" Back to bitchy.

Little girl one moment, defiant adolescent the next,

wanting to believe—maybe even believing—that she could call herself a woman.

Little fool.

Telling herself that she should make some attempt at understanding, or at least tolerating, the girl's mood swings, Surreal took a step closer and raised a hand to touch her daughter's hair.

Jaenelle Saetien took a step back and tossed her head.

So be it. Understanding had to work both ways.

There was nothing warm about Surreal's smile. "Why won't I talk Daemon into letting you go away to school? First, because I don't do favors for a bitch. Never have, never will. And second, sugar, because I don't want you to be another girl who rips out a boy's guts with her bare hands because he tried to rape her. But I do hope, if you were in that position, that you've inherited enough spine from me to be able to do exactly that."

Daemon walked through the front door of the Hall and let his power quietly flow through the immense structure, picking up the emotions of everyone in and around his home. Raising an eyebrow, he looked at Beale as his butler stepped into the great hall, holding a silver tray with a single piece of folded paper.

"High drama, low drama, or farce?" he asked as he weighed the female emotions that seemed to swirl through the Hall. When Beale didn't answer, he sighed. "How is it possible that one woman and one adolescent girl can't manage to live in a place this size without clashing over *everything*?"

"Your father once said that drama had no purpose without an audience," Beale replied.

"So the performer seeks out the intended audience?"

Beale inclined his head and held out the tray. "This arrived from Ebon Rih."

He didn't see it often, but he recognized Lucivar's labored writing.

Taking the letter, he turned over the carefully folded paper and looked at the seal. Personal seal, not the official seal of the Warlord Prince of Ebon Rih—or the Demon Prince's seal. He wasn't sure personal was better than official, but he broke the seal and unfolded the paper.

> *Bastard,*
> *We need to talk about that damn school.*
> *L*

"What school?" Daemon muttered.

"That I don't know," Beale replied. "However, after the latest drama between the Ladies, the young Lady SaDiablo informed me that she would have her meal in her room this evening."

"Did Jaenelle Saetien try to dictate the menu for her solitary dinner?"

"She tried." Beale held out a neatly written menu. "This is what Mrs. Beale had planned for the evening meal. The checked items are what will be on the dishes for the tray meal."

No checkmark next to the sweet. That would go over *so* well.

*Everything has a price,* Daemon thought. "And Lady Surreal? Where is she dining this evening?"

"She said that would depend on whether you were home for dinner." A beat of silence. "I think there was trouble in one of the villages. She has been outside working with the Dea al Mon knives for over an hour. The house drama occurred between the time she returned home and her going outside."

High emotions and household drama. "I need to talk to you and Holt."

"The young Lady gave orders that she wanted to see you as soon as you returned."

Daemon's smile had a cold edge. He called in a book of basic Protocol, which would be perceived as the slap he intended, since basic Protocol—the first level of phrases that were used in courts and were also used to protect the weaker

Blood from the stronger—was on a level with the basic manners any child should have learned by the time she received her Birthright Jewel. He handed it to Beale. "Please deliver this to the young Lady with my compliments and convey the message that the Warlord Prince of Dhemlan will see her at his convenience."

A sparkle in Beale's eyes. "My pleasure, Prince."

"I'll check on Surreal and meet you and Holt in the butler's pantry."

"Prince?" A moment's alarm before Beale regained control.

"This needs to be a private—and discreet—conversation."

Surreal was still in the backyard, but she'd put aside the elegant fighting knives of her mother's people. Now she held an Eyrien hunting knife, which she rammed into a straw figure over and over and over.

Daemon stood on the edge of the terrace and watched her, a woman full of raw fury. He knew the moment his psychic scent, and the leashed sexual heat that was still too potent for her comfort most days, reached her. She turned toward him, the knife raised and ready.

"I understand you had some trouble," he said, keeping his voice courteous.

"Not me, sugar. But I don't think the High Lord is going to have a pleasant evening."

Too many warnings today. "Want to tell me why?"

Surreal nodded. "But your daughter wants to see you first."

"My wife has first claim." They both knew that wasn't true. Witch had first claim on him—body, mind, and heart. And power. After all, a Warlord Prince was a Queen's weapon, and he was hers. Always hers.

Surreal vanished the knife and called in a small towel to wipe the sweat off her face as she walked toward him.

He watched her. Was his wife approaching him, or Surreal the assassin?

"You should talk to her first," Surreal said. "Just don't agree to anything yet."

He held out Lucivar's note. "Does this have anything to do with a school?"

She read the note and snorted a laugh. "Well, he sounds thrilled."

"He does manage to say 'I'm the prick with the biggest balls' even when he doesn't use any of those words."

"Jaenelle Saetien made it sound like Titian going to the school was all settled."

"Titian?"

She shook her head. "Talk to your daughter."

Seemed Jaenelle Saetien was *his* daughter a lot lately. "I need to have a chat with Beale and Holt first." A hesitation. "It's you and me for dinner tonight. Or just you, if you prefer."

"As a punishment, depriving children of food is frowned upon, Sadi. Even when they're trying to act like the dominant bitch."

"The child declared she is having a tray in her room."

"Hmm. Then you and I can have a quiet meal in the dining room."

Daemon smiled. "I'll convey that to Beale."

They walked into the Hall together, then headed in different directions.

He walked into the butler's pantry, crammed with two rolltop desks, file cabinets, and a wine rack that held the selections for a few days' worth of meals. Holt and Beale were already there.

The butler gave him a sour look and said, "I gave the young Lady the book. High drama."

Not unexpected. "I need your help." He tucked his hands in his trouser pockets and leaned against the door. "Dealing with adolescent girls is unfamiliar to me. I don't know where to draw the lines for Jaenelle Saetien when she acts like drawing any boundaries is the equivalent of me killing her Self and yet seems relieved to have boundaries. You were both here when Jaenelle Angelline and the coven lived with my father. He dealt with the Territory Queens when they were this age. He dealt with Witch when she was this age. How did he do it?"

Holt tipped his head. "You were never around adolescent girls?"

"When I was a pleasure slave in Terreille?" Daemon knew by the way the two men tensed that his smile had turned cold—and cruel. "When they wanted to practice their social manners, I could oblige and respond with courtesy. When they wanted to practice playing the bitch or touched me without my consent . . ." He watched them shudder as they realized they were trapped in a room with the Sadist. He said too softly, "I gave them reasons to stay away from me."

Beale cleared his throat. "Those years with your father were not without high drama and unpredictable emotions."

"But all the males who became part of the First Circle were also in residence, so dealing with the drama and emotions was spread out among all of them," Holt said.

"It was my impression that the High Lord had little or no previous experience dealing with girls that age, but after Lady Angelline came to live with him, it seemed to us that he quickly decided where he could yield and which lines he would hold," Beale said. "And once he drew a line, no one could shift it. Not even his daughter."

Daemon frowned. "Where were the lines?"

"Where it would make a difference in a young woman choosing good over bad, right over wrong. Good Queen or bad Queen. The High Lord once told the coven after some disagreement, 'These are not the actions of a good Queen, and I will not stand by and let you become the destruction of your own people. The only way you are going to do this thing is by going through me, and you'd better be sure there is nothing left of me to stand against you. Because I will stand—and I will fight.'"

*Mother Night.* "Jaenelle Angelline could have gone through him. Could have ripped him apart with one moment's loss of control."

Beale nodded. "But he meant it, and they all knew he meant it. Especially the Lady. I don't remember what that argument was about, but after that, the coven always knew when they brushed too close to one of his lines—and they were the ones who stepped back to avoid a fight."

"He did support the adolescent drama in other ways. Even encouraged it by ignoring it," Holt said.

Encouraged it? Damn man had more balls than sense.

Holt added, "He also seemed to convey without actually saying anything that these dramatics held no interest to an adult male, and if the coven wanted his time and attention to discuss whatever they wanted to discuss, they had to act like intelligent, talented young women—at least while they were around him."

Beale smiled. "Of course, once Prince Lucivar joined the household, he constantly stirred up and shut down trouble in that way he has, leaving the High Lord to act as arbitrator between Ebon-gray Eyrien temper and adolescent female sensibilities."

"Sweet Darkness," Daemon muttered. "And they all survived."

Holt laughed. Beale chuckled.

"Some days there was a fair amount of roaring and screeching," Holt said. "Depending on the tone of the roaring and screeching, the staff either found things to do elsewhere or we drew straws to determine who had first-row seats to the dramatics."

He really didn't need to know that. "So. Allow for some victories without giving up any of the important lines."

"I would say that is accurate," Beale agreed.

He eyed his butler. "Would one of those lines I'm supposed to hold be the courtesy that is shown to the staff?"

The sparkle returned to Beale's eyes. "Yes, Prince, it would."


Surreal had just slipped on the calf-length green dress when Daemon knocked on the door between their bedrooms. She hesitated, studying the dress in the mirror. It was a favorite of hers, but it was old enough that she usually wore it when she was on her own. Still, she thought Daemon would understand that her choice of dress indicated that she would welcome his company as a friend tonight but not as a lover.

"Come in."

He looked as elegant as he always did. In some ways, the mature beauty of his face, with the thick black hair turning silver at the temples, was more devastating than when he'd been young.

"Want some help?" he asked.

"Sure, sugar." She turned and lifted her hair to give him access to the zipper.

His movements weren't careless, but they also weren't the sensual movements of a man looking for an invitation. Apparently, he wasn't looking for a lover tonight either.

"You should wear a shawl over that, at least in the corridors," he said. "I've added power to the warming spells in this wing, but it has started to rain, and everything feels damp and chilly."

"Pick one out for me."

He chose a shawl with a gold-and-green pattern that complemented the dress—and was soft, thick, and warm.

He was right about the corridors. They were damp and chilly, the first touch of autumn. "Did you add any power to the warming spells in Jaenelle Saetien's suite?"

"She's not a child and doesn't want to be treated like a child." He smiled. "So she's old enough to take care of the temperature in her rooms. She knows the Craft required for a warming spell and has the power to create and maintain that spell. She also knows how to add power to an existing warming spell. I doubt the staff working at a school will drain the reservoirs in their Jewels to keep the buildings at a temperature that will match a girl's idea of comfy."

"Maintain your own place?"

"Mmm."

Surreal waited until they were seated in the dining room and Beale had served the first course—a hot, hearty soup she suspected was part of the staff's dinner since she didn't remember seeing it on the menu that had been presented to her.

"Are you going to let Jaenelle Saetien go to school in Amdarh?"

"Don't you mean are *we* going to let her go to that school?" Daemon countered.

"What I think doesn't matter."

He lowered the soupspoon. "Surreal." A warning.

"It matters to you," she amended. "It doesn't matter to Jaenelle Saetien. So this negotiation is between the two of you. Frankly, Sadi? Physically, she's ready for this independence she wants to claim, but I'm not sure she's emotionally mature enough to live away from home. However, I understand the storms in her right now, at least to some degree, and lately I've wondered if I would have quarreled with Titian in the same way if my mother had still been alive when I reached that age. Because of the Dea al Mon part of her heritage, Jaenelle Saetien is growing up a little faster than the children in Halaway who are her friends. Her body has matured a little quicker, and the need to assert her independence. . . . "

Surreal took a roll from the basket and tore it into unappetizing pieces before she realized what she was doing. She pushed the bread plate aside. It vanished, and a clean plate appeared.

"I didn't appreciate how young I was," she said softly. "I was already a whore working in Red Moon houses that were almost the best, and I was a well-paid assassin. I was good at both kinds of work, but I was also still a girl trying on attitudes to figure out who I was beyond those two things. I made mistakes during those years. I made a big mistake with you during those years."

"That's the past," he replied just as softly.

The past, yes, but that night had changed things between them for a lot of years. Even now it was one of the dark notes in their complicated relationship. "Jaenelle Saetien will make her own mistakes. She'll acquire her own regrets. She . . ." Surreal swallowed hard. Did the girl in that village regret killing the boy who had drugged her? Or was she just relieved that she had survived?

"Tell me what happened, Surreal."

She couldn't look at him, but she told him about the boy, the girl, the *safframate* the father had given to his son. When she was done, he told her about Tersa's warning.

"Terreillean soil." She spat the words. "Will we ever be free of that corruption, that taint?"

"Power without price will always be a seductive idea," Daemon replied. "Those who rule the Shadow Realm now have to make sure there is always a price—and that the price is high."

"The bastard wasn't expecting to have his son die," Surreal said. "That's a fairly high price."

"Do you think that will be the only price?" Daemon asked too softly.

Her breath hitched as the room turned icy for just a moment before he regained control of that formidable temper. What other price would that father pay for giving his son that drug?

She didn't have to wonder long because Daemon added, "The son is beyond any benefit of a lesson, but do you think that man has ever experienced the effect of a dose of *safframate* that was equal to what the girl received?"

She had been an assassin. Was still an assassin. And right now, looking at his glazed gold eyes, she didn't dare speak.

"I think it's best if I go to the Keep this evening and stay for a day or two."

She nodded. If he was descending into a cold rage, it was better for all of them if he was in the one place where there was someone who could hold the leash on the Prince of the Darkness, the High Lord of Hell—and the Sadist.

They both gave up on the now-cold soup. Daemon requested the next course, and Beale came in and removed the soup dishes.

"So," Daemon said when they were alone again and he

felt like Sadi and not some other aspect of his temper. "Do we keep Jaenelle Saetien with us at the Hall and put up with all this high drama, or do we allow her to board at this school in Amdarh, which she seems set on attending?"

"And pay her a weekly visit that will leave her snarling and embarrassed because her parents are watching her so closely?"

"You wear Gray. I wear Black. If we're sight-shielded, I doubt anyone will know we took a prowl around the school."

She nodded. "With Titian there, we'll have another reason to check up on the children. Three reasons, if you want to include Zoey."

"Zoey will be there too?" His eyes glazed again. "She's just the kind of young Queen who was at risk in Terreille."

High Lord or Sadist? Surreal wasn't sure who sat across from her now, but for Jaenelle Saetien's sake, she needed to coax Daemon back into thinking like a father—and the current employer at the Hall. Picking up her knife and fork, she cut into her steak. "Who do you think will be more sulky this evening? Jaenelle Saetien because she's eating whatever Mrs. Beale dumped on her plate, or Mrs. Beale because we aren't doing justice to the meal she carefully prepared for us?"

Daemon choked out a laugh. "Mother Night, what a choice." Then he began to eat.


Jaenelle Saetien tried not to fidget while her father read her report a second time. When he turned back to the first page for a *third* time, she jumped up and paced around the sitting area in her room.

"Everyone who is anyone is going to that school." She heard the whine in her voice and tried to modulate her tone to something that sounded more mature and less . . . provincial. She couldn't tell him that the girls she desperately wanted as friends thought she wasn't sophisticated enough to belong to their exclusive aristo circle, that they'd been polite when she had seen them at social gatherings in Amdarh or when she'd participated in a country outing near one of the family estates, but their surprise that *she* was the daughter of the elegant and sophisticated Warlord Prince of Dhemlan had stung.

*"Who is the country mouse?" one of the boys had asked Delora, not even checking to see if Jaenelle Saetien was close enough to overhear them.*

*"Oh, that's Jaenelle Saetien, Prince Sadi's daughter," Delora had replied.*

*"She can't be!"*

*"Poor thing," Hespera had added. "You'd think her father would want her to dress with a little style and have some social polish, even if her mother is so gauche."*

She didn't want to be pitied by the girls who came from Dhemlan's aristo families. She didn't want the boys laughing at her clothes. Zoey wasn't any help in that way. The exclusive circle of girls laughed at her, too, because of her dress and manners, and she was a Queen!

Delora wasn't a Queen, but all the girls wanted to copy the way she dressed, and all the boys wanted a bit of her attention. And more than that—the best thing of all—Delora didn't think Jaenelle Angelline was anything special.

"Not everyone who is anyone goes to that school," Daemon said mildly. "Let's just say that the individuals you feel are important social contacts attend that school."

"Yes, let's say that." Did she sound snarky? She wasn't trying to sound snarky. "Father, this is so important."

He set aside her report and studied her. What did he see? What was he looking for? How could she be whatever he was looking for long enough for him to agree to let her go to the school?

"Sit down, witch-child," he said quietly.

She sat at the other end of the sofa, barely able to breathe.

"Your mother and I will allow you to attend this school, and we will allow you to board at the school instead of living at the town house."

216 ✦ ANNE BISHOP

She squealed with happiness. Couldn't help it.

He gave her a sharp, amused look. "I'll go to Amdarh in a couple of days and make the arrangements."

"Couldn't you go tomorrow?" Sometimes girls had private rooms and sometimes they had to share. When Delora and Hespera had told her about the school, they'd explained that it was social death if you ended up sharing with a girl no one wanted to befriend.

The look was still sharp but no longer amused. There was something cold in his eyes that was struggling to rise to the surface, and that cold made her nervous.

"I'll go to Amdarh in a couple of days," he said too softly.

"Okay."

He hadn't moved, hadn't tried to hug her like he would have done when she was little, but the man sitting on the other end of the sofa was no longer quite her father.

"There are conditions to this agreement, and there are rules," he said. "The conditions are fairly simple, I think. I will pay for the school, which includes the books and any other supplies required for your classes. I'll take care of the room and board. I will also provide a clothing allowance that will cover the basics you will need for school itself, and I will entertain paying for an outfit for a special occasion. You will pay for any other expenses out of your spending money, whether it's clothes or books or paying for a social outing."

She almost asked if he would increase her spending money, but Zoey's and Titian's jaws had dropped when they'd learned what she already received as spending money, so she didn't think she should ask for more, even though Delora and Hespera had given her a pitying look that made it clear they thought her father was being stingy—especially since he was so wealthy and could afford to give her more. But once he spoke to the school administrators and learned about all the incidental things a girl would need, she was certain he would increase her quarterly spending money without her having to ask.

"You might be tempted to ignore the rules," he said. "After all, you're going to be on your own, making your own decisions and having the exciting experience of living among your peers with limited supervision. But I strongly urge you to listen carefully and listen well, Jaenelle Sae-tien, because these are lines I will hold with everything in me, and the consequences for breaking the rules will be severe."

Her stomach churned, and she felt a little sick. "What rules?"

"Nothing you haven't heard before, but it's what a basic rule encompasses now." His smile had an edge. "Permission before action. A simple enough thing to remember."

Was that all?

"You look very like your mother, and that means you're a lovely young woman. There will be young men at that school who will want to become friends, companions. Lovers. As friends and companions, that choice is yours. Lovers?"

She rolled her eyes. "I already know about sex. Mother explained things years ago."

"Good. Then you can't claim ignorance of how things work as an excuse if you defy me and cross a line that is being drawn here and now. You're too young to have your Virgin Night and come through it with your Jewels and your power intact, so your choices will have consequences beyond the risk to yourself."

She wasn't talking to her father anymore. Maybe this was how he sounded when, as the Warlord Prince of Dhemlan, he summoned someone to account for something they had done. Or maybe this was something—someone—else, a side effect of the healing treatment he still had done at the Keep. Whatever this was, she wished her mother was here to shield her from the man whose mouth curved in a cold, cruel smile.

"Knowing you as I do, I am granting you, here and now, my permission to engage in the first stage of romance. That means holding hands. Hugging. Kissing. But the sexual encounter, which is touching and kissing, stays between collarbone and crown of head, between elbow and fingertips. If you're interested in doing more, you will both come to me for permission. Anything that involves your vagina or his cock requires my consent. And that includes kissing."

Her face flamed with the heat of embarrassment.

He leaned toward her. Just a little. Just enough to have her lean back to maintain the distance between them.

"My darling," he purred, "should you be so unwise as to let one of those young studs talk you into letting him see you through your Virgin Night, it won't matter if you come through it undamaged or not. His execution will be slow, it will be painful, it will be messy, and it will be very public. And I will leave no doubt in anyone's mind that the reason he died that way was because he had dared lay a hand on my daughter without my consent." He waited a moment. "Is there anything about that line that you don't understand?"

"No," she whispered. "No, sir."

"I'm delighted." He rose. "In that case, I'll bid you good night. I imagine you and your mother will want to do some shopping before classes begin."

He walked out of her room.

She raised one hand and watched it shake. But a minute later . . .

"He said yes. He said I can go to the school."

She leaped up and danced around the room.

Her father had said yes! And he'd said more. He'd said she could go shopping for clothes before she started school. Sure, she'd have to go with her mother, and that would be embarrassing, but maybe she could talk Surreal into letting her buy some *stylish* clothes.

# THIRTEEN

Lucivar walked toward the Queen's private area of the Keep. He'd hoped this day would never come, but even before the door to the Consort's suite opened, even before he saw the man who looked at him with glazed eyes and a sweetly murderous smile, he knew he'd been summoned to the Keep because he'd insisted on a promise. Now he'd have to fulfill his side of that promise.

Black shields formed a Craft-made wall across the corridor, blocking any retreat. He stood his ground and waited while the Sadist glided toward him, while one hand with its slender fingers and long black-tinted nails curled around the back of his neck.

"You told me once that if I needed to play, I should come to you," the Sadist crooned. "Do you remember?"

"I remember." He could survive this. No matter what was done, he could—and would—survive this.

Wrapping a hand around Lucivar's right wrist, the Sadist led him to another room in this part of the Keep. Another bedroom.

*May the Darkness have mercy on me,* Lucivar thought as he heard the snick of the lock, as he felt the Black shields surround the room, cutting off all hope of escape.

"Strip," the Sadist said.

Everything in him wanted to fight, wanted to challenge, wanted to refuse any kind of submission. But whatever was driving his brother tonight would turn totally merciless if challenged. Besides, he had agreed to this to keep everyone else safe.

He turned his back to the Sadist and faced the bed as he undressed. Oh, they'd seen each other naked plenty of times, spent hours talking some evenings while they'd soaked in the heated pool in his eyrie.

This was different.

As he tossed the clothes to one side, the covers on the bed rolled back, leaving nothing but the bottom sheet.

The Sadist said, "On the bed. On your belly."

He obeyed. Raising his arms over his head, Lucivar locked his left hand over his right wrist, a self-inflicted manacle, as he listened to the Sadist undress.

A weight on the bed near his thigh, a knee carefully placed to avoid catching his wing. Another weight on the other side.

Straddled.

He flinched when the Sadist's hands touched his back— a light but firm touch that seemed to be exploring. For what? Weaknesses?

"What have you been doing lately?" the Sadist murmured as he raised his hands.

A scent in the air. Not unpleasant. The sound of skin rubbing skin. Then . . .

Hands rubbing warm oil over his back. Long strokes and shorter ones, moving over tight muscles.

Lucivar kept his eyes closed. The Sadist blended intense sexual pleasure with exquisitely vicious pain. So what in the name of Hell was the man doing? He didn't want to be lulled into not being prepared for the first shock of pain.

"I miss this," the Sadist said quietly. "I can't be around Surreal when I need . . . I miss touching someone." His hands moved over skin and muscle. "Sometimes when I needed to play, Jaenelle would let me do this for hours, touching her and coaxing the muscles to relax, coaxing her to let go of the day's burdens." He chuckled. "I got around to relaxing her in other ways, too, but that was a quiet swelling, a gentle rise and fall. I loved those nights, loved that this part of me could pleasure her so much that everything else disappeared and there was nothing but her and me in that bed."

The hands kept moving, kept coaxing knotted muscles to relax.

Was that what this was? A simple need for the most brutal side of Daemon's nature to touch someone else?

*He's enjoying this. Just this.*

He tensed when the Sadist's hands rested on his ass. Couldn't help it.

The fingers digging into muscle weren't as gentle in response to his unintentional resistance.

"What have you been doing to get knots in your ass?" the Sadist muttered.

"Same thing I did to get all the other knots," Lucivar grumbled. "Testing my children's shields and pulling the blows against the shields just enough that the children don't get discouraged without *looking* like I'm pulling the blows."

"Huh."

More oil. More heat in the warming spells in the oil and on the hands.

Lucivar groaned as the Sadist worked on the backs of his thighs and down to the calves.

"All right, roll over."

"How am I supposed to do that? My muscles have melted."

A soft laugh as hands slid under his thighs and the Craft used to float objects lifted him high enough to be turned and settled back on the bed.

Keeping his hands above his head and shackled, Lucivar opened his eyes and studied the Sadist as those hands worked on his feet and began moving up his legs.

There were places he would rather not go with his brother, and he knew all too well that the Sadist could make him beg to go to those places, so he said, "Jillian is home."

The hands stroked his thighs from knees to hips. "Oh?" A smile Lucivar couldn't interpret. "A descendant of Lord Dillon is now working as one of Mrs. Beale's apprentice cooks. She calls him Dharo Boy."

"Hell's fire." He was not going to be the one to tell Jillian that a however-many-generations-in-between descendant of the boy who had been her first romantic encounter worked at the Hall.

But in a verbal pissing contest, whatever worked was fair. Right?

"She's written a book. For children. And not just human children. At least, that's how she explained it."

"Oh?" Another smile. "I happen to own a publishing house, so . . ."

"She wants to get it published on her own. Without help from us."

"Why?"

"Damned if I know. Something about the story being published on its own merit."

"Phhht," Daemon said.

"Yeah. But your publishing house is on Jillian's list, and she's made an appointment next week to see the acquisitions editor. Marian is going with her."

A pause as the muscles along the side of one thigh were persuaded to relax. "Have you read the book?"

"No, but Marian did and said it's a good story. It's based on some of the adventures Jillian and Khary had during their apprenticeship in Lady Perzha's court."

"Well, then . . ."

"It's called *A Dog and His Weeble*."

Daemon's hands spasmed, and his fingers dug into Lucivar's thighs hard enough to hurt.

"It's about a Sceltie who has adventures and solves problems with the help of his pet weeble and his human female companion," Lucivar continued.

"But how Little Weeble got its name has been a secret since the village was founded."

"Well, the former Queen, in her position as court consultant, and the current Queen have given permission for that secret to be revealed. Their reasoning is that since so many other things are dressed up to suit the story, everyone will think Jillian made that up too." He waited a beat. "This is your fault, you know."

"How is this my fault?" Daemon sounded miffed.

*And the Sadist has been knocked right out of the room.* "You gave permission for Khary to go to Little Weeble with Jillian. If you hadn't done that, Khary wouldn't have been digging on the beach and wouldn't have found the diamond that indicated it was time for a new Queen. If Khary hadn't been the one to find the diamond, the Queen who fit the village and its people's needs wouldn't have been a Sceltie, and I wouldn't have ended up dealing with generations of Sceltie Queens ruling an eccentric village in Askavi."

"Kiss my ass."

"Tch."

Daemon shifted to one side and growled, "Move over."

Before Lucivar could move, he was floating on air—and shoved with enough force that he would have ended up across the room if he hadn't used Craft to stop himself and land on the mattress.

Daemon flopped down beside him.

They stared at the ceiling.

"Are you sure we can't help with publishing the book?" Daemon asked. "She's family. We take care of family."

"We will be allowed to host, and pay for, the party when the book is published."

"Well, good for us."

They looked at each other and sighed before going back to staring at the ceiling.

"Are you going to let Titian go to that school?" Daemon asked.

"Yeah. She really wants to study art there. I told her if she could build the defensive shields I require for her to be on her own, she could go. She's working hard, which makes me proud and guts me. Another day or two she'll have the shields solid, and I can't say no. Daemonar isn't taking this well, but he's working with her on the shields." A pause. "Jaenelle Saetien?"

"I'll make the arrangements when I return to Dhemlan. I'm not easy about it, and I'll talk to Lady Zhara and confirm that Zoey is attending before I make a final decision."

"If Titian is in Amdarh, you'll be the one who has to draw the lines about behavior and hold them."

"I know. And I will."

Lucivar blew out a breath. "You think there's anything to eat around here?"

"It's the Keep. There's bound to be." Daemon rolled off the bed, scooped up Lucivar's leather trousers, and tossed them on the bed before stepping into his own black trousers.

They didn't bother with shirts or shoes before wandering out and following the scent of coffee to the small sitting room across from the Queen's suite. Plates of cold meats and cheeses, sliced fruits, different kinds of breads with a variety of flavored butters. Coffee, wine, brandy, ale.

They ate, drank, and grumbled about Jillian not wanting their help. Then they ate some more and drank some more as they decided where the lines would be drawn once their daughters went to that damn school.

When they were down to crumbs and empty glasses, Daemon retired to the Consort's suite. Lucivar retrieved the rest of his clothes and walked to the part of the Keep that contained the office of his administrative second-in-command.

"Kiss kiss," Karla said, a wicked twinkle in her ice-blue eyes. "Since you did well tonight, I won't torment you with reports."

"Did I do well?" Lucivar asked.

"Jaenelle thinks so. She would have intervened if you'd been in danger but thought it best to let the two of you work it out on your own."

He'd wondered why she hadn't appeared. He and Daemon had been in the part of the Keep where Witch's Self could take on form. Not substance. They could see her, talk to her, feel her touch but not be able to touch her. That much presence was enough for him, who had been her brother. He wondered if, sometimes, that inability to touch her was a torment for Daemon.

Torment or pleasure didn't matter. Daemon needed Witch's hand on the leash to stay whole and sane, and Sadi would cherish every moment he had with any part of her.

The sky started to lighten by the time Lucivar flew home to catch a couple hours of sleep before facing the day's work—and to begin preparing himself for his daughter going to school in Amdarh.

# FOURTEEN

Enemies didn't announce their presence, didn't give any warning before an attack, but Daemonar couldn't make a surprise attack that much of a surprise. Not with Titian. So he scuffed his boot to make a sound before he sprang at her, a wooden club raised to strike.

Titian yelped, dropped her drawings and the wooden box Uncle Daemon had given her to carry her supplies, and formed a Summer-sky shield before his club could touch her. As he beat on one shield and felt it start to break, she formed another one a finger length beneath the first and another one behind that.

He yelled. She shrieked. Instead of moving and trying to maneuver, she foolishly held her ground to protect her drawings.

He broke her second shield and raised the club to strike the third when a hand closed on the club, stopping his swing. His father dropped the sight shield that had kept him hidden and gently pulled the club out of Daemonar's hand.

"Enough," Lucivar said. "Titian, you can lower the shield now."

She gulped air and looked so distressed, Daemonar felt like a knife had been slipped into his gut and twisted.

"Titian?" he said, glancing at Lucivar. "It's okay now."

Two Warlord Princes waited for her to regain enough

control to drop the last shield. Then Daemonar scrambled to collect her drawings, hoping the box, which was one of her prized possessions, hadn't been damaged when she dropped it.

"Three shields correctly made that held long enough for someone to reach you," Lucivar said quietly. He called in one of those large envelopes that usually contained official documents and held it out to Titian.

"What's that?" she asked, sniffling and rubbing tears off her cheeks.

Daemonar hoped they were angry tears. He could deal with angry tears.

"The paperwork for your enrollment in the school. Information about your lodgings. You like your quiet time, so I arranged for you to have a private room. And there are the lists of books and supplies we'll need to purchase before classes begin." Lucivar cleared his throat. "Your mother and Jillian are going to Amdarh on business in a few days, so we'll all go and stay at the town house with your uncle while you gather your supplies. Then we'll take a look at the school and help you and Jaenelle Saetien get settled."

Titian blinked at her father. "I can go?"

"You can go."

To Daemonar's eyes, Lucivar's smile looked forced, but he doubted Titian noticed as she threw herself into her father's arms.

"Thank you, Papa. Thank you." She stepped back. "Does Mother know?"

Lucivar shook his head. "I thought you should tell her."

She turned to gather her drawings, but Daemonar said, "I'll put these in your room."

She rushed into the eyrie, shouting for Marian.

Daemonar picked up the box and the drawings and then looked Lucivar in the eyes. "Knowing how to shield isn't enough."

"You think I don't know that?" Lucivar snapped. Then he shook his head, blew out a breath, and stared at the land beyond their home. "We have to let her go—and hope."

*Maybe there is a way to do more than hope,* Daemonar thought as he took the drawings and art supplies to Titian's room.

He found Lucivar in the weapons room, honing his Eyrien war blade.

"I'm going out for a while."

Lucivar gave him a long look. "Be back for dinner."

No demand to know where he was going. Maybe Lucivar didn't need to ask.

He slipped past the kitchen, where the female voices sounded tearful and happy. As soon as he was outside, he spread his wings and flew to the Keep. It wasn't his afternoon for a lesson, but that didn't matter. Couldn't matter when he needed to talk to Witch.

He landed in a garden close to the Queen's private area of the Keep, then strode through the corridors until he walked past the ornate metal gate that was the boundary. When he reached the sitting room where he usually had his lessons, he said, "Auntie J.? Auntie J.! I need to talk to you!" He waited, feeling his heart thump against his chest. Seven, eight, nine, ten. "Lady?"

"What's wrong, boyo?"

He turned, shaking with relief. "It's Titian."

It poured out of him—Titian's art, which she'd been working on for years now; her desire to go to the private school in Amdarh; her finally creating shields that Lucivar deemed sufficient to allow her to leave the safety of her family.

He paced, unable to sit still. His throat hurt with his effort to tell Witch everything without shouting at her. When there was nothing more to say, all he could do was stare at her.

"What, exactly, do you want, Prince Yaslana?" Witch asked.

"Shields won't be enough if no one comes to help. I'd like some way for Titian to let me know she's in trouble and needs my help."

"Just your help?"

Something that would be a call to battle for his uncle and father would be better, but they would kick his ass if they knew he was asking Witch to become a little more entangled with the living. "Just mine." If necessary, *he* would give the call to battle.

"When does your sister leave?"

"We're going to Amdarh in a few days. The whole family."

"I'll consider your request. Come back in two days."

A plain white mug appeared on a table beside him.

"A tonic," Witch said, "with honey and lemon. It will help the soreness in your throat. Drink it before you go."

"Yes, Auntie. Thank you."

She vanished.

Daemonar drank the tonic slowly.

Had he asked for too much? That Witch still existed in some way was a closely guarded secret held by his father, his uncle, and him—and Lady Karla. The Keep's Seneschal and historian/librarian knew, of course, but they knew so many secrets. He suspected they were, in their way, secrets themselves.

He finished the tonic, then left the mug on the tray where he usually left dishes when he'd been given something to eat during his lessons.

Then he flew home and spent an hour sparring with his little brother to keep his and Andulvar's attention away from their sister.


Karla entered the Queen's suite and waited.

She'd observed the boy as he grew into a young man who showed promise of being a powerful Warlord Prince with a hot temper like his father's but more control. Even now there was more control—because someone he trusted held the leash. The man Daemonar Yaslana had become knew that if the person who held the leash threw him into a fight, it was for a reason, and he would step onto that killing field without hesitation.

That kind of trust had to be nurtured carefully.

"You know what he's asking?" Witch asked as the shadow of her Self took shape.

"Easy enough to guess," Karla replied. "Are you going to do it?"

"Yes." She smiled dryly. "It won't keep him home long, but maybe long enough not to be obvious—at least as far as his sister is concerned."

A small ornate box appeared, floating on air. The lid opened, revealing a special kind of gold coin.

"What do you need?" Karla asked.

"A discreet jeweler."

"Well, then. I think I should go to Amdarh this evening and pay a call on Banard. His daughter runs the shop now and designs most of the jewelry, but he still creates a few pieces for select customers."

Two days later, Daemonar slipped into Titian's room without knocking, then kept his eyes focused on the door when he realized she wasn't dressed.

"You could have knocked," she said, sounding snappish as she hurriedly pulled on the rest of her clothes.

He did a quick count and wondered if Lucivar had figured out when Titian's moontime would start before he decided on when the family would go to Amdarh. She would be done with the vulnerable first three days before they left home, which would make it easier for everyone.

"Hurry up," he said, wanting this done before his father got home.

"Okay. Now, what . . ."

He rushed to her side. Calling in Witch's gift, he placed the gold pendant in Titian's hand.

She studied what looked like a gold coin, except no one had seen a coin like this in centuries. It had a unicorn's horn over a simplified etching of Ebon Askavi on one side and a stylized *A* on the other side. It was held within a simple gold ring attached to a gold chain.

"Daemonar . . ."

"It's a mark of safe passage," he said quickly. "It's a protection. And it has to be our secret. We have to blood it on the back. Then, if you're in trouble and need my help, you use this and I'll know. Even if you can't get word to me any other way, I'll know."

"Where did you get this?"

"Wear it under your clothes. Better yet, keep a sight shield on it. No one can know you have this, Titian. *No one.* Not even Father."

She studied him. "Will you get in trouble if someone finds out?"

"Maybe. But that's not important. What's important is that someone will reach you before your shields fail."

"Is Jaenelle Saetien going to have one of these?"

"I don't know. I just . . . Please, Titian. Please wear this, always, and keep it a secret unless you need to use it. If you do, nothing else will matter."

She hesitated, probably thought he was being bossy and overprotective. He might have thought it, too, if Witch hadn't honored his request.

Girls talked about things, told one another things. He knew that much from the times when Jaenelle Saetien stayed here or Titian went to the Hall or to Amdarh for a visit. But his sister wasn't going to take this seriously if he didn't tell her something, so he had to take that chance.

"How many sides does a triangle have?" he asked.

Titian frowned. "A triangle has three sides."

"No. A Blood triangle has four sides. Steward, Consort, Master of the Guard. And the fourth side is the one who rules all three."

She gave him a long look, struggling to understand what he didn't dare say in words, didn't dare say even on a psychic thread. Then she looked at the mark of safe passage and rubbed the etching on the front. "That's Ebon Askavi."

"Yes."

"And that's a unicorn's horn."

"Yes."

"Father has one of these. He fiddles with it when he's at his desk thinking about something that bothers him. He told me once that he got it from the . . ." She looked up, stunned, and Daemonar knew she understood what he was telling her. "You . . . She . . ."

He pressed a finger against her lips. "Never spoken. Ever. To anyone." A pause. "The triangle isn't always made up of Consort, Master, and Steward."

He didn't think her eyes could get any bigger, but they did.

Three men. Three Warlord Princes. Yes, they were family, but they were also a triangle that served an extraordinary Lady.

"She's always been my Queen," he whispered. "She'll always be my Queen."

"She gave this to you? For me?"

"Yes."

"What do we . . . ? How do we . . . ?"

He removed his working knife from its sheath on his belt, pricked his left thumb deep enough to get a good bead of blood, then pressed it against the back of the mark. When Titian held out her left hand, he pricked her with the knife and watched as she added her blood to his. Then they watched as the blood disappeared, leaving no sign that the mark was more than an odd pendant.

But they felt a connection to each other that was more and different from family as the spells Witch had woven into the mark absorbed the blood.

Titian slipped the chain over her head and tucked the pendant under her clothes before adding a sight shield.

"Is she wonderful?" she asked.

Daemonar smiled. "Yeah. She's wonderful." He blew out a breath. "But she's probably going to give me a whack upside the head for telling you as much as I did."

She rose on tiptoe and kissed his cheek. "Our secret, brother. I promise."

"Having that doesn't mean you should get careless about the shields."

"Don't spoil the gift by being bossy."

Daemonar slipped out of Titian's room and went to his own to study. He'd done what he could to keep Titian safe. He just hoped he'd done the right thing.

# FIFTEEN

"They're letting rubes in now?" Hespera said. "This school is supposed to be *exclusive*."

Delora watched the group of adults and youngsters stroll toward the dormitories. It wasn't unusual for parents to escort their children to a new school and get them settled in before classes started. After all, aristo families wanted to make sure everyone knew how important their own darlings were, even if they failed to understand that the pecking order changed the moment those parents walked away. And most of them never knew who was really in control of the students the moment the instructors were out of sight—who had gained control step by careful step since her first year at this school.

Helpful Delora. Kind Delora, who, with her closest friends, guided the newcomers through the first days at the school. Instructive Delora, secretly disciplining students who failed to understand who *should* claim their loyalty and obedience. There were some she couldn't touch—not yet, anyway—some who had enough clout and influence of their own that they wouldn't keep quiet, keep things secret, regardless of the punishment that would follow.

She wasn't sure if the Eyrien girl would be useful or not, but the other girl, with some delicate coaching, could have enough clout and influence to help her undermine the Queen who was her primary adversary. Jaenelle Saetien

SaDiablo had such a need to rebel against the burden of her powerful family, and that made her malleable—made her vulnerable to someone who offered sympathy, thoughts, and opinions that fed that rebellion.

Delora allowed herself a little smile as she watched that particular group of adults and newcomers. She'd been preparing this ground since the first time she'd met Jaenelle Saetien at some children's party years ago. That the girl had convinced her parents to let her attend this school was confirmation that Jaenelle Saetien would be guided by *her* instead of listening to anyone else.

And wasn't that delicious?

She'd never seen Lucivar Yaslana before, but she knew who he was. Everyone who was anyone knew who wore the Ebon-gray. He had no official influence in Dhemlan, so it wasn't likely he would be useful, even if the winged girl turned out to be malleable. But Daemon Sadi! Beautiful, even at this distance. Certainly desirable. And the way he moved, all power and grace. There was no way to get control over *him*. Not directly.

Delora looked at Jaenelle Saetien—and smiled. Even powerful men could be trained to make the preferred choice in order to quiet rebellion and have some peace in their home. He might be powerful and dangerous, but the Warlord Prince of Dhemlan was still a man and a father. In her experience, very few fathers had enough spine to resist becoming putty in a daughter's skillful hands.

As for Yaslana, he might be a rube, but he had a savage reputation as a warrior and, therefore, couldn't be completely dismissed as insignificant to her ambitions—especially when there was a connection between those two men.

What they needed was a little test.

Delora gave Hespera the slightest nudge to make sure she'd be watching. "Leena, walk across the green like you're heading for the book exchange. Wave at Jaenelle Saetien and keep going."

"Why?" Leena asked.

Delora gave Leena the smile other girls recognized—and feared. "Because I want you to."

While the other girls and the three boys who were the core of their male companions stepped back into the shadows, Leena hurried across the green. When she came abreast of Prince Sadi and his pack of coattail relatives, she looked over and waved.

Jaenelle Saetien waved back, looking desperately embarrassed to be seen with her family, such as it was.

But every damn male in that group, including the younger boy, focused on Leena with a predator's interest. So did the woman Delora assumed was Jaenelle Saetien's mother.

No wonder the girl was so desperate to get away from all of them!

Well, she could help with that. She certainly could.

Delora studied the adult males. One Warlord Prince paying attention was dangerous. Two?

They were going to have to scatter that focus, crack that unity.

Time enough to do that once the adults had gone home.

Jaenelle Saetien wanted to sink into the ground, embarrassed beyond words that Leena, one of the girls who was in Delora and Hespera's exclusive group of friends, had seen her parents taking her to her room. How humiliating was that?

"I'm not a baby," she said. "I can find my own room."

"Humor me," her father said. "And if you don't want to humor your father, humor the Warlord Prince of Dhemlan—who outranks you."

She bristled at the reminder that a condition of her being at this school was following the rules with regard to caste and Jewel rank. At home, she could argue with her father. In public, she now had to address him as the Warlord Prince of Dhemlan—and a man who wore Black Jewels.

"Go on, then, if that's what you need to do," he said

quietly. "I won't call you to task for a lack of manners." He turned away from whatever had held his attention and looked her in the eyes. "This time."

She heard the warning, and she wanted to say it wasn't him, not really him, that she wanted to get away from. But couldn't Uncle Lucivar have dressed a little better? Couldn't Daemonar? Did they have to look like they'd just come in from a patrol? And did they have to look around like they'd never seen a school or a real building?

She reined in the desire to bolt. "Thank you, Father. I appreciate your understanding."

His smile held sharp amusement, but all he said was, "Lady," which was permission for her to leave.

She walked quickly, tempted to run, but running would have raised questions. Or not.

She didn't want them asking questions, so why did it make her heart hurt to think they might not ask?

She found her room. The bed was made; the clothes were hung or neatly placed in drawers. The desk was empty except for the long list of books and materials she needed to purchase and a piece of paper—a note from her father with the amount of credit available for her use at the book exchange so that she wouldn't have to worry about buying her books or other school supplies.

It was a generous amount, but it was restricted to whatever could be purchased at the book exchange. It wasn't the open credit line the other girls had that could be used in *all* the shops in Amdarh.

It didn't matter that her father put spending money into an account every quarter and let her use the money for anything she pleased. Restricting *this* credit line to the book exchange was just another way of him telling her she was still a little girl playing at being a grown-up.

When they had talked during an afternoon picnic this summer, Delora had expressed a concern that Jaenelle Saetien's father was refusing to see his daughter as an emerging adult, as a woman coming into her own. They had discussed the school and the best way to convince her

parents to let her attend, and what she needed to have in
order to fit in. They'd talked about rules and parents and
all kinds of things. In a moment that was part bitchy and
part worried embarrassment that the other students would
find out, she'd told Delora about her father having "mental
days" and how, even after years and years, he still required
special healing and isolation.

Delora had sworn not to tell *anyone*, had even suggested referring to it as his having a funny turn because
there was someone in *every* family who had a funny turn
now and then, and no one would think it was *serious*. And
no one would wonder what was involved in this "special
healing."

Jaenelle Saetien looked around her room and sighed.
She'd have to go down to the book exchange all by herself
and pick up all those books and supplies. It didn't matter
that she could use Craft to vanish the books and call them
back in when she returned to her room. Someone should
have offered to help her. They would be helping Titian
settle in and buy her supplies.

*But you didn't want their help.*

Which wasn't the point. Or was it the point?

She felt like she couldn't breathe at the Hall. It was too
big—and not big enough. Her father was so important but
rarely acted important. And her mother! Mannish in her
manners and dress. That was what Hespera and Borsala
told her people said about Surreal. Was it any wonder that
her father slept alone so many nights or went to Ebon Rih
for the "special healing"?

Oh, he still had times when it was obvious that he
wasn't quite right, but he was always more relaxed after
spending a couple of days in Ebon Rih, and now that her
sophisticated friends had made a few observations about
what men and women did together, she wondered if they
were right when they hinted about what sort of healing
could make him relax that way.

It certainly wasn't anything her mother was doing.

But it was more than that. It was her *name* that had begun to chafe because it was a constant reminder of the most important woman in her father's life—a witch who was all things wonderful and never ever did *anything* wrong and was so perfect, it made her want to puke.

Not that anyone at the Hall or in Halaway said anything about the Queen who had been her father's first wife. Not to her, anyway. But because of the name, they made the comparison—and found her wanting. As long as she lived where the Queen had lived, she would be found wanting.

Maybe she didn't know who she was or who she wanted to be. But the one thing she did know, and the biggest reason why she wanted to get away from the family and attend this school and be with these new friends, was she was sick and tired of being compared to Jaenelle Angelline.

"Where is Jaenelle Saetien going?" Daemonar asked.

"She wants to get settled on her own," Daemon replied.

Lucivar eyed his brother, not fooled by the mild tone. *You teach them to be independent. Then when they are, it's a kick in the balls.*

Daemon laughed softly. *Yeah.* Then the amusement faded. *But independence shouldn't eliminate good manners.*

Picking up a bit of ice at the level of the Black, Lucivar brushed against Marian's first inner barrier. *Can you and Surreal find something to do? Go look at something?*

"I'd like to see Titian's room," Marian said, turning to Surreal. "Come with me?"

Surreal glanced at Lucivar and then at Daemon—and went off with Marian.

Now he focused on the boys and his daughter. "Witchling, you have a stack of books and supplies to haul up to your room, and you have two pack mules available today. Make use of them."

"Pack mules?" Andulvar asked. "Where . . . ?"

"Father means us," Daemonar said. "Come on, Titian. We'll help you get settled in."

"She's happy and excited and didn't realize that you've cleared the field," Daemon said quietly.

"Yeah, she and Andulvar haven't figured that out."

"What do you think?"

"A cluster of males and females keeping to the shadows. No dark Jewels among them—yet. They send out a scout and measure the response."

"And Jaenelle Saetien took the bait."

"Or she waved at a girl she had met at a social gathering but never mentioned to you, and we're reacting to a pricking on our skin caused by a memory, like an itch on a missing limb." Lucivar scanned the area around the green. That cluster of youngsters was gone now. Would have been smarter to have shown themselves and just gone about their business. That choice to stay hidden gave him a reason to pay attention. "What's wrong with your girl? Aren't we good enough for her anymore?"

"Well, Surreal and I are on the wrong side of some line most days, and damned if we can figure out why—except that Jaenelle Saetien has me for a father, and that's . . . difficult."

Lucivar gave his brother his full attention. "Why?" Not that he didn't think it was true. His being who and what he was wasn't easy on his children either.

"I'm damaged and always will be."

"Dangerous, yes. Damaged? Not so much anymore. Not from where I'm standing."

Daemon studied him. "You can say that after . . . ?"

"Yeah, I can. I want everything you are keeping my daughter safe. *Everything.* Understand me?"

"Yes, I understand."

"As for your girl, just keep an eye on my firstborn. If Jaenelle Saetien is heading for any real trouble, Daemonar won't stand aside and let her fall. He never has."

"And maybe some things will be easier to swallow if they come from him instead of me."

*And she'll tell the boy things she won't tell either of us.*

"Prince!"

The girl running up to them wore a short-sleeve shirt and the bib overalls he associated with farmers and gardeners, but she was definitely a Queen and wore Opal as her Birthright. A light Opal, but that still gave her considerable power.

The last time he saw a Queen dressed like that was when Jaenelle Angelline and the coven were around the same age.

*May the Darkness have mercy on whoever is trying to hold the leash on this one.*

"Lady Zoela," Daemon said. "I don't believe you've met my brother, Prince Lucivar Yaslana."

He'd heard her name for years and had wondered why a formal introduction had never quite happened—or why Titian had never asked to have this friend stay with them in Ebon Rih. Now Zoela beamed so much excitement and goodwill toward him, he felt wary.

"Is Titian here yet?" she asked.

"She's gone to the book exchange with her pack mule brothers," Daemon replied. "Have you picked up your supplies?"

"Weston helped me this morning."

"My sympathies," Daemon murmured.

She laughed. "Grandmother said he isn't going to stay with me when I'm on school grounds, but he will stand as escort whenever I'm out and about in the city."

"That's reasonable."

"Weston wasn't happy about that. About not staying with me at the school, not about standing escort the other times."

"You're a Queen. He's your escort as well as being family. You can't expect him to be happy about you being on your own."

"That's what Grandfather said." Zoela let out a sigh, then beamed more goodwill at both of them. "I'll go help Titian pick out the art supplies. We have a pottery class together."

And off she went, a running bundle of energy.

Lucivar looked at Daemon.

"Lady Zhara's granddaughter," Daemon confirmed.

"So that's Zoey." When she wasn't at the SaDiablo town house visiting Jaenelle Saetien and going on excursions Daemon had arranged for the three girls, Titian had waited for letters from her friend Zoey. He frowned. "Pottery. That's making misshapen things out of mud?"

"Expensive mud, and the end result will be admired."

"Of course." Admiring it wouldn't make it any less misshapen.

Daemon bumped shoulders. "Let's take a look at the rest of this place."

By the time they circled back to the green and met up with the girls and took some of the load the boys were lugging, Lucivar knew the position of every building and every piece of open ground. If this place became a killing field, the Demon Prince knew exactly where and what to strike in order to destroy the enemy.

# SIXTEEN

"he first dance is *so* important," Delora said. "Espe-cially for the new students."

"Making the right friends is critical," Hespera added. "And not just for the time in school."

"The friends you have now will be your friends for-ever."

Jaenelle Saetien drank in this wisdom, flattered that Delora and Hespera would take the time to tell her these things. They were just enough older to have been at this school for a few years. They knew so much about how to go about in aristo society and who should be cultivated and who should be avoided. She didn't understand why Zoey was so dismissive of the things Delora and Hespera had to say. Shouldn't a Queen want to cultivate the people who would serve in her court? And Titian . . .

*She's delightfully rustic.* That was how several girls had described her cousin. They said it kindly and with a smile, but inviting Titian to join Delora's circle for girl talk was always an afterthought. After the first couple of times, when it became clear that Titian didn't know anything about anything aristo, she declined to join them—to ev-eryone's relief.

"You'll want a new gown, of course." Delora held out a piece of paper. "Something exquisite since you come from such an aristo bloodline. Here are the names of two shops that cater to girls our age. They do custom-made clothes, of course, but they also have designs that are already made and just require the alterations for a perfect fit."

Jaenelle Saetien looked at the names on the paper. "I don't know. My mother prefers . . ."

Delora rolled her eyes. "Whose mother *doesn't* prefer? But who is going to make the right impression wearing fusty clothes suitable for older women?"

"Well . . ." Surreal might kick about her going to another dressmaker, but if she could get her father to agree, her mother couldn't say anything, could she?

She smiled at her friends. "Yes. A new gown to signal a new chapter in my life."

"Actually," Hespera said, "you'll need two gowns."

"And you'll have to buy them soon," Delora added. "The dance is only a few days away."


"Lord Beron was here last evening," Helton said as he helped Surreal remove her coat.

"Was he?" Daemon said mildly. "I trust he left a crumb or two in the pantry?"

Helton looked a trifle defensive. "We are always ready to receive the family or their guests, Prince. But Lord Beron is rehearsing for a new play and is working very hard. That doesn't give him time to prepare proper meals."

Surreal swallowed a laugh and didn't dare look at Daemon. Helton and the rest of the town house's staff doted on Beron.

"You provided him with enough meals to sustain him until his next visit?" Daemon asked.

"Just some leftovers."

Daemon laughed. "I hope you gave him more than that, but we'll invite Beron to join us for dinner while we're in town. You should tell Cora to overestimate the amount of food needed for that meal to assure that there will be leftovers." He winked at Helton, who dropped his professional demeanor long enough to smile in return.

Surreal felt Daemon's hand lightly touch her back as he escorted her into the sitting room. His sexual heat swirled around her, a seductive blanket that wrapped around a woman tightly enough to ensnare.

She kept reminding herself that it wasn't his fault. He kept the heat leashed as much as he could, but being around him for more than a day or two felt like being imprisoned by sexual need.

Unfortunately, the heat didn't influence *his* interest in sex—or lack of interest. Would he sleep with her tonight, or was his current preoccupation going to consume his desire to be a lover?

"Sadi, you're as bad as a Sceltie with a single sheep," she said as she picked up the mail that had been left for her review.

"I'm not *that* bad," he replied. "Besides, I have two sheep."

She laughed. "Well, one of your sheep sent you a letter."

"Which one?"

*Not the daughter.* She held out the envelope.

He opened the envelope, unfolded the paper, and let out a whoop of laughter. Then he handed the paper to her.

"Oh, Hell's fire. He's not even at the school." She laughed with him.

Titian's drawing showed two fluffy sheep on the school's green. One had Titian's face; the other had Zoey's. And the Sceltie busily trying to herd them . . .

"Titian captured Daemonar's likeness very well," she said.

"Hmm."

Suddenly he turned toward the door, an alert predator. A moment later, she picked up the psychic scent of her daughter. Agitated.

"What's she doing here?" Surreal said, feeling a pang of concern.

Jaenelle Saetien rushed into the sitting room, barely giving Helton time to open the door. Then she stopped so fast, she almost lost her balance.

"You're here." The girl sounded surprised—and not pleased—to see her father.

"We're often here," Daemon replied.

*I am,* Surreal thought. *You're not.* Was the girl in some kind of trouble that would provoke a lethal response from Daemon and end with some idiot being executed? Was that why Jaenelle Saetien had hoped to find her alone?

Since Daemon seemed willing to wait for hours for an explanation, Surreal didn't break the silence. Lately, she and Jaenelle Saetien couldn't seem to agree on the sky being blue, let alone anything else, so the girl had to be desperate if she was coming here for help.

"There's going to be an important dance at the school, and I need a new gown," Jaenelle Saetien said in a rush.

Feeling a little weak with relief, Surreal nodded. A new gown for a special dance made sense. She just wished the girl had shown more sense and control after realizing that Daemon was in residence. Being happily excited was one thing; rushing in like the city was under siege usually meant a Warlord Prince needed to sort out the problem in some bloody and permanent way. "All right, we can—"

"I don't want some fusty old thing from *your* dressmaker."

The room chilled at the discourteous tone. Surreal didn't think Jaenelle Saetien even noticed.

*Foolish girl.*

"The young Ladies at the school have some preferred dressmakers?" Surreal said. Then to Daemon on a psychic thread, *You agreed to this, Sadi.*

"Very well," Daemon said, sounding cool. "One dress made by the dressmaker of your choice, whatever the cost."

Hell's fire. She wasn't sure she wanted him to agree *that* much.

"However," he continued, "your mother has to approve the dress before I pay for it."

"But . . . ," Jaenelle Saetien began.

"My wallet, my terms."

"But . . ."

*Sugar, if you really want this dress, stop arguing with him,* Surreal said on a psychic thread. *His temper is sharp enough right now.*

"Very well." The words weren't graciously said, but they were said. "We can go to the shops tomorrow morning—"

"You have classes in the morning," Daemon said, "and you're not going to ignore your education in order to buy a dress when you can shop in the afternoon."

"But this is so important!"

Daemon said nothing.

"I'll pick you up tomorrow after your classes," Surreal said. "Will Titian and Zoey be coming with us? I imagine they'll want new dresses too."

"How should I know?"

The room went bone-chilling cold, finally knocking the girl out of her self-absorption.

*Sadi, leave the room. Please. Let me handle this.*

His eyes were glazed when he looked at her, but he said, "If you will excuse me?"

"Of course."

He walked out of the sitting room.

Surreal let out a shaky breath and looked at the girl, who had already shrugged off her father's displeasure. "You cannot win a pissing contest with him."

"Don't be vulgar, Mother."

"Don't be a bitch, Daughter. I don't do favors for bitches. Ever. Remember?"

Jaenelle Saetien looked surprised, then a bit uneasy, as if she'd been testing how far she could push and hadn't expected this reaction. And that made no sense.

"You are standing on dangerous ground with him," Surreal warned.

Jaenelle Saetien tossed her head in a practiced move. "He wouldn't hurt *me*."

Thinking of when she'd been a brash, foolish girl who had broken Daemon Sadi's trust, she looked her daughter in the eyes and said, "Don't count on it."

Daemon studied the drawing Surreal had left on his desk and didn't turn around when she walked into his study after taking Jaenelle Saetien back to the school.

"Maybe this drawing is more telling than I thought," he said. "For years, it was the three girls whenever they could get together here in Amdarh. Now there are two of them and no sign of the third." He looked at Surreal. "Jaenelle Saetien hasn't been at that school for a full month yet, and she doesn't know if her cousin and a girl who has been a friend since they were children are going to this important dance?"

"It's easy to become dazzled by something new. New place, new friends."

"Maybe." He set the drawing on his desk. "Did you get things settled?"

"Dress and dressmaker of her choice, and I won't approve of anything that will have you bouncing off the ceiling."

He smiled because she needed him to. He'd stay long enough to support her through the purchase of this special gown that Jaenelle Saetien wanted for the dance. Then he'd return to the Hall. Or go to the Keep and get the help he needed to settle a temper that was now too sharp to deal with this childish performance that ignored everything his daughter had known since childhood about how to behave around a Warlord Prince.

"We really should invite Beron over for dinner soon," Surreal said. "At least we know how to deal with his kind of drama."

# SEVENTEEN

Surreal had thought the shopping trip was going well until Jaenelle Saetien spotted another girl who was looking for a dress. When that girl loudly announced that the gowns weren't good enough for her to blow her nose on, let alone wear to a special dance, Jaenelle Saetien looked mortified that she'd been seen in that shop—and suddenly there was nothing that was good enough for her to try on, so they got in the carriage and went to the next shop on the list.

Things should have gone well there. Jaenelle Saetien found a dress that cost more than a District Queen's quarterly income, but the girl loved it and looked wonderful in it. And then . . .

Weary of drama, Surreal walked into the town house behind Jaenelle Saetien, who turned on her and screamed, "Why are you trying to ruin my life? Why are you being so mean? I hate you!"

*Right now, the feeling is mutual, sugar.*

"Ladies."

Shit shit shit. *That* was the voice of the Warlord Prince of Dhemlan. She just hoped Daemon wasn't in a meeting with one of the Province Queens.

"If you have something to discuss, we'll do it in my

study," Daemon said. "If you want to stand there and scream, then do it outside so that everyone in the square can hear why you're in your current snit."

A dismissive word for such a storm of emotion. A cutting word coming from him.

"You don't know!" Jaenelle Saetien wailed.

"And I won't know until you're ready to discuss the problem." He walked back into his study but left the door open.

Tearful and resentful, Jaenelle Saetien stomped into Daemon's study.

"Young Ladies feel so much about so many things," Helton offered as he eased into the entryway from the sitting room.

"Yeah," Surreal replied.

"Perhaps a restorative tea?"

"For her or me?"

Tiny smile.

"I'll let you know." She walked into the study, determined not to participate any further in a battle that made no sense.

Apparently Jaenelle Saetien had given her father a condensed version of the afternoon.

Daemon gave Surreal a baffled look. "You told her she couldn't buy a second dress?"

"Yes!" Jaenelle Saetien looked triumphant. "That's what she said."

"No, that's not what I said." Not exactly.

Daemon turned his attention back to his daughter. "Jaenelle Saetien, if you want another dress, you can certainly buy another dress."

"I can?"

"Of course." Daemon continued to look baffled. "As long as you have enough money in your account to cover the cost, you can buy as many dresses as you like."

"But you're supposed to buy it for me!"

*Shit shit shit. Now he finally understands,* Surreal thought as a chill came into those gold eyes.

"I agreed to buy one dress for this dance, and from what you told me, you found a wonderful dress," Daemon said.

"But I need two! Everyone who is anyone will have two!"

"Why?" Surreal couldn't hold back her own frustration. "Do you really think these girls are going to change into another dress in the middle of a school dance?"

Jaenelle Saetien turned on her. "You don't understand anything!"

"I understand you're being played by someone who is, at best, misinformed and, more likely, unkind."

*"Enough."* Daemon's voice rolled through the town house like soft thunder, but that thunder was the prelude to a potentially violent storm. "You have the dress for the dance."

"I can't go to the dance. I can't. Titian is going to Ebon Rih instead of going to the dance. I want to go too. I can't be seen in that rag Mother made me buy."

The girl ran out of the room.

"Well," Surreal said, "I hope you don't choke on the bill for that rag."

Daemon settled in the chair behind his desk. She sank into a chair on the other side.

"Tell me what happened," he said too quietly.

She told him about the shop and Jaenelle Saetien's response to the other girl's comment about the gowns, and ended with Jaenelle Saetien choosing a second gown after they had purchased the first and announcing loudly that her father would buy that one too. The drama exploded when Surreal informed her that Daemon wouldn't buy the second dress but she was welcome to do so with her own money. Apparently the loud comment was meant to impress some of the other girls in the shop, and Surreal's quieter correction was humiliating and vicious.

"Did you sense any power?" he asked, his voice still too quiet, too close to lethal. "Any spell or use of Craft that might have spurred this bizarre reaction?"

Surreal blinked. "You think . . . ?"

"Jillian's behavior became erratic because of that 'if you loved me' spell. Is it possible someone at the school has wrapped a spell around our daughter, and the other girls in the shop provided the key to releasing it?"

A spell that couldn't be detected by someone wearing the Gray or the Black?

She thought about it, then shook her head. "The truth, Sadi? Peers are more important than parents right now, and even you couldn't have competed with the opinion of that bitch in the first shop."

"What about putting Jaenelle Saetien in a different school?"

"And have her hating us for the next few decades—or more—because we ruined her life? No, thank you." Surreal hooked her hair behind her delicately pointed ears. "Those girls all come from aristo families. I'm sure they all go to that school, and that means they come from families with money. Jaenelle Saetien will be dealing with them for the rest of her life. If you don't let her make her own choice about these girls, she'll never forgive you. Not all the way forgive you."

"Would you have, when you were her age?"

"If you had forced me to follow the choice you knew was better for me instead of accepting the path that had been *my* choice?" She sighed. "I would have hated you, especially once I realized you were right. That's the truth of it."

Now he sighed.

*Best to tell him now.* "I bought an estate a few months ago."

One eyebrow rose in query. "I haven't seen any paperwork about it."

"It's not a family holding. It's mine."

He didn't move. She wasn't sure he even breathed. "And you want me to stay away."

She nodded. "But if I call for help, it's because things

are going to get very bloody, and I need your particular skills."

He leaned back, folded his hands, and rested his forefingers against his chin. "Explain."

"I purchased a run-down estate that had been owned by an aristo family who slunk away instead of paying their tithes to the District Queen—and who, as their fortunes declined and the whispers began, weren't comfortable about being on the other side of a village that caters to one of the SaDiablo estates. Seems too many pointed questions were being asked by people of consequence in the village about how they were spending their fortune that they couldn't afford to take care of the estate."

"Hayllian memorabilia?" Daemon asked.

"Don't know." She called in a folded sheet of paper and set it on the desk. "That's their name and what your estate manager knew about them. Or Lucivar's manager, since Yaslana owns the deed to that Dhemlan estate."

"Are you going to live there?"

"No. I'll stay at the family estate when I'm visiting. I bought this place as a sanctuary for girls who were broken on their Virgin Night and need a safe place to heal and learn who they are now." She felt the air turn cold. "It's always tragic when a witch is broken, but the breaking isn't always deliberate."

"Something compelled you to set up this place now," Daemon pointed out.

"Maybe it's as simple as feeling like I can't help my own daughter because she doesn't want my help, but maybe I can do some good for other girls."

Daemon took a deep breath and let it out slowly. "What can we do for our own girl?"

"I don't know, Sadi. Let her go to Ebon Rih. Let Lucivar deal with her for a couple of days."

"If she's like this with him, he'll drop her in a cold mountain lake."

She shrugged. "It might do her some good."

# EIGHTEEN

Daemonar sat on the riverbank, staring at a familiar waterfall and fighting to keep a rein on his tongue and his temper as he listened to Jaenelle Saetien's tearful . . . rant . . . about a dress. She'd needed someone to listen, and she'd needed to say things away from the adults, and had asked him to bring her here.

Now he knew why.

When there was silence for a full minute—he counted—he finally looked at her. "Your father bought you a dress that cost more than Tamnar earns *in a year*, and you're pissed at him because he wouldn't buy another dress when you already knew he would only buy one?"

"He was supposed to buy me another dress! Everyone else's father—"

"Whose father?"

"Everyone—"

"Everyone is no one. Who, exactly, was going to have a second dress for this dance? Give me names, Jaenelle Saetien. If someone told you this, then that person knows the names of the girls whose fathers are so indulgent or so spineless that they buckle under a girl's petty whining. So who is going to have a second dress for a school dance?"

"You don't understand!"

"I understand that your father drew a line and held it, just like he's always done. Just like my father does. You were testing him to see if he would give in to your hysterics about a dress, as if that would prove he loves you. But if he'd given in after he'd set the terms, you would have lost respect for him. He held the line because he does love you, and if you stopped being a whiny, selfish brat for a minute, you'd realize that."

She leaped to her feet, her hands clenched into fists. "You take that back, Daemonar. You just take that back."

He rose to his feet slowly enough to be insulting. "No." He gave her a lazy, arrogant smile. "If you throw a punch at me, I'll hit back. Do you really want to explain to my father why we're fighting?"

She hesitated, as he'd known she would. Then she came back swinging—verbally. "Everyone—"

"I don't want to hear about everyone. But let's say there were a few girls who brought a second dress to the dance, intending to change halfway through. I've seen how long it takes you and Titian to get ready to see an amateur musical evening in Riada. If you'd brought a second dress, the dance would have been over by the time you left the changing room."

"That's not true!"

He'd had enough. "Come on. I'll take you back to the eyrie."

"I want to stay here a while longer."

"I'm not leaving you here alone, and I want to go home."

"Are you afraid I'll throw myself in the river?"

"A few months ago, I would have said you wouldn't do something that stupid. Now? Yeah, I think you would do it for the drama, to prove how unhappy you are about not getting your way about some damn dress."

She stared at him, clearly insulted—and hurt. "You said you had my back. You've always said that."

"And I do. But having your back doesn't mean agreeing with you all the time or giving in to whatever you want to do. Sometimes having your back means fighting you into the ground if I think you're wrong."

"I bet if precious Jaenelle Angelline had wanted something Lucivar had considered stupid, he would have gone along with it."

Scalding fury flooded through him before he tightened the leash on his temper and regained control. "Based on the stories my father has told me about his dealings with the witch who was his sister and Queen, you would have lost that bet."

He took a step toward her. She took a step back.

"Do you hear yourself, Jaenelle Saetien? Do you think acting like some petty bitch is going to impress anyone?"

"I'm not! Why is everyone against me?"

He had one more thing to say to her. "Titian was excited about this dance. Instead of being at the school, she's home. Did you wonder why? Did you ask her? Or are you so self-absorbed that you don't care about anyone else anymore?"

He grabbed her and caught the Green Wind, taking them back to the eyrie. He dropped from the Wind when they were close to home, glided in low until he was over the flagstone courtyard, and then dropped Jaenelle Saetien almost on top of his father.

He didn't stop, didn't land. He made a tight turn and flew to the communal eyrie, where he hoped to find someone who was in the mood to spar. He really needed to work off some temper. If he couldn't find anyone at the communal eyrie, well, he was pretty sure Lucivar soon would be in the mood to oblige.

Jaenelle Saetien straightened her clothes and raised her chin—and tried not to shiver at the way Uncle Lucivar's eyes traveled down her body.

"Well," he finally said, "since neither of you are bloody, I guess I don't need to know what you were wrangling about. This time."

She heard the warning.

"Besides," he continued, "I already have enough testing the leash on my temper."

"Why?" she asked.

That lazy, arrogant smile. Daemonar had that smile too.

"The next bitch who uses words to hurt my daughter is going to lose her tongue. And I don't give a damn who she is." He turned and walked into the eyrie, leaving the door open.

Jaenelle Saetien stood outside until she was fairly sure he was somewhere deep in the eyrie. She started to rush to Titian's room, then stopped and looked out the glass doors that opened to the yard. Spotting Titian at the far end, she ran across the yard.

Her cousin sat cross-legged on air, her drawing board and box of pastels also balanced on air. She didn't look distraught or weepy or . . . anything.

Since her trousers already felt damp from sitting on the riverbank, Jaenelle Saetien also used Craft to sit on air. "Why didn't you stay at school and go to the dance?"

Titian carefully put one pastel back in the box and carefully—too carefully?—selected another. "Some of the girls said the boys wouldn't want to be seen dancing with a fat bat. Why would I want to spend an evening standing against the wall, watching everyone else have fun? Or pretend they're having fun."

Calling an Eyrien a bat was a serious insult. Not as bad as calling an Eyrien a Jhinka, but close.

"You're not fat." An uneasiness went through her. "Which girls?"

"Doesn't matter who said it. It doesn't matter if the aristo girls think I'm an Eyrien rube. The art classes are good. Really good. I'm learning so much, and that's mostly why I wanted to go to that school."

"Maybe I could talk to those girls. If you told me . . ."

"Leave it alone. It doesn't matter."

Titian gave her a long look filled with warning, and Jaenelle Saetien suddenly wondered if Uncle Lucivar was in his study taking care of the business of ruling Askavi—or if he was in the weapons room sharpening his knives.

# NINETEEN

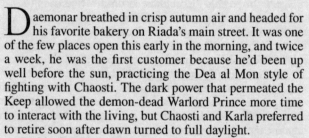

Daemonar breathed in crisp autumn air and headed for his favorite bakery on Riada's main street. It was one of the few places open this early in the morning, and twice a week, he was the first customer because he'd been up well before the sun, practicing the Dea al Mon style of fighting with Chaosti. The dark power that permeated the Keep allowed the demon-dead Warlord Prince more time to interact with the living, but Chaosti and Karla preferred to retire soon after dawn turned to full daylight.

So his fighting and strategy lessons were finished by daybreak, and because he was a young man and a Warlord Prince, breakfast became his next priority. A fruit pastry and a folded bread filled with cheese and spicy meat would go down well with a large mug of coffee. And after that? He wasn't required to report to Hallevar and do any sparring with the other Eyriens on these days, but he still felt edgy and could do with a little more physical work before going home to sort the mail and spend a couple of hours with his father learning the "desk" side of ruling a territory like Ebon Rih—or a Territory like Askavi.

His mother still handled the social invitations, but after being reassured that her firstborn wasn't being given too much to handle on top of his studies, she'd handed over the business tasks connected with Ebon Rih without a backward glance. Oh, she still met with the women who pre-

THE QUEEN'S WEAPONS ✦ 259

ferred telling her their concerns, and she still paid all the monthly bills submitted by Riada's merchants, but the time she no longer gave her husband for paperwork was spent at her loom, where she created pieces that were as artistically beautiful as they were practical.

She'd even been invited to contribute some of her work for an exhibit in Dharo, the Territory famed for its carpets and fabrics.

His mother was happy with her home and her family and her work, and he didn't want to spoil that. But he had to think about—

"Daemonar!"

*Hell's fire, what's she doing up at this hour?* he thought as Orian rushed toward him, then stopped and covered the rest of the distance with a suggestive hip-swaying walk that made him embarrassed on her behalf. A Queen shouldn't act like that. Not in public.

*Something off about this.*

As she came toward him, Daemonar created a tight Green shield around himself that would prevent her from touching him. Then he formed a defensive shield a finger length above that—a shield that included a bit of Craft Auntie J. called a kiss of lightning.

Orian wasn't alone, but the two Rihlander girls who were part of her current unofficial court remained on the other side of the street, watching.

"Orian," he said when she reached him.

She clearly expected him to invite her to join him for breakfast. Since he wasn't interested in spending an hour with her while she tried to make plans for *his* future, he just stood there, waiting for her to say something.

"I need to get to work." He'd learned not to ask if there was something she wanted, since she usually wanted something he didn't want to give.

Angry? Petulant? Desperate? He couldn't name the feeling he saw on her face, and he didn't care. She'd ignored him for years, which had been a relief, but lately she'd been trying to renew their "friendship" and seemed determined to put him in a compromising position that would create some obligation to her.

She stepped closer. He didn't step back, wouldn't yield even that much since he was protected by Green shields.

She reached for his arm, then shrieked when the Green defensive shield sizzled, inflicting enough pain to hurt like a wicked bitch without doing permanent damage.

*Thank you, Auntie J.*

"Don't touch me," he said quietly.

Fury filled her eyes, but her words were quietly spoken, and the sound of her voice became enticing, persuasive. "I have a device that can make a man feel all kinds of things when it's slipped around his cock. If I put it on you, you wouldn't dare turn down an invitation from a Queen."

For a moment, all he could hear was his heart pounding. All he could feel . . .

*Lucivar set a shielded gold ring on the edge of the blackwood desk.*

*Daemonar leaned forward to get a better look. Too big for anyone's finger, so . . .*

*"It's called a Ring of Obedience," Lucivar said. "It's put on a man's cock."*

*"Like a Ring of Honor?"*

*"The difference in what they're called should tell you something about how they're used. Some of . . . the High Lord's men retrieved a sack of goods from a smuggler who didn't survive the journey through the Sleeping Dragons. A few of those Rings were in the sack."*

*Lucivar gave him a long look, as if trying to force himself to step up to a line. "I can share a memory of what it's like to wear a Ring of Obedience, of what it feels like to be punished. A few seconds. No more. But only if you want to know."*

*His father didn't want him to know. That much was clear. And that was why he said, "Show me."*

*A memory of something that had been done to Lucivar long ago. But as soon as mind touched mind to share that memory, it felt like his nerves were on fire, and he thought his cock and balls would explode from the pain. Terrible. Terrifying.*

*Done.*

As he struggled to catch his breath and wipe the tears from his face, he watched Lucivar's hands tremble as his father poured two large whiskeys and held one out—then had to help him hold the glass.

"That's what the Queens in Terreille did to you?" he asked when he could draw a full breath.

"That's what they did."

"More than once." Not a question.

"More than once," Lucivar confirmed. "For centuries, boyo. Every time I defied them, and that was often."

"How old . . . ?"

"A little older than you. I'd made the Blood Run. I wasn't close to making the Offering to the Darkness, but I was getting too strong to be controlled any other way, too good in a fight."

"How did you survive?"

Lucivar smiled. "For a long time, I was just too angry to give up and watch the bitches hurt anyone else. Then I held on and kept fighting because I was told the Queen was coming. In the end, it took almost dying to find her again after our first brief meeting."

*To hold on so long for a dream.* "Uncle Daemon?"

Lucivar swallowed hard. "He was Ringed soon after his Birthright Ceremony."

Daemonar met his father's eyes. *To be a boy and feel that pain, to be punished with that pain again and again and again. To shape yourself into a weapon that could strike back in retaliation. To become someone who could wrap pain in desire and need so intense, it would ensnare an enemy and crush them. Crush every part of them.*

*Now he had some idea of the pain that had birthed the Sadist.*

"You need to be careful," Lucivar said. "Some of those Rings might already be in Askavi. Trust your instincts before you trust anyone else."

Daemonar took a step back. Then he smiled a lazy, arrogant smile while his heart pounded and pounded. "Orian, this much I promise you. If you ever touch my younger brother for any reason, I will drag you into the middle of the street and gut you."

She looked shocked—and afraid. Did she really think he wouldn't hear her words as a call to battle?

He strode down the street just far enough to give himself wing room. Then he launched himself skyward and flew home.

Ever since Jaenelle Saetien's last visit, he'd been thinking about spending time in Amdarh to support Titian. But he hadn't figured out how to tell his father that he wanted to attend the same school when he wasn't sure they had any studies of interest to him. Now . . .

As he walked into the eyrie's big front room, he heard the rise and fall of his mother's voice coming from the kitchen and his father's quiet, husky laugh.

Shit. Not a good time to interrupt them. Maybe he should go to the communal eyrie and work off some of this rage before talking to his father.

As Daemonar hesitated, Lucivar stepped out of the kitchen, his gold eyes filled with a lustful heat. Then the look in those eyes changed, sharpened.

"What's wrong?" Lucivar asked.

Marian stood in the archway. "Daemonar, what happened? You're shaking!" She started to rush toward him, then stopped, blocked by Lucivar's hand.

Was he shaking? He felt his heart pounding and pounding, felt a memory of pain that he was sure would never quite go away—and fury erased caution.

"If Orian tries to put a Ring on my little brother, I will kill her."

*"What?"* Marian said.

Lucivar gave her hand a gentle squeeze, then focused on Daemonar. "In my study. Now."

He strode to the study. In the minute he had alone, he thought of friends at risk. The moment Lucivar walked into the study, he said, "Tamnar. Alanar. They need to be warned."

"They're at the communal eyrie sparring with Rothvar and Zaranar," Lucivar said. "They'll be safe until I get there. Now tell me what happened."

He took a moment to gather his thoughts, to recall every detail he could. The Demon Prince would expect that from a warrior who served him. Witch would expect that from a Warlord Prince who served her.

Then he told Lucivar about his encounter with Orian.

"Is that exactly what she said?" Lucivar asked. "That she had a Ring or that she could get one?"

"She didn't call it a Ring of Obedience. She said she had a device that could make a man feel all kinds of things when it was slipped around his cock. What else could it be?"

The Demon Prince said nothing. Then, "Pack your trunks. I want you gone in an hour."

"Sir, this is my fight."

"Not anymore. This is about the safety of the Eyrien people under my hand. This is about the safety of every man in Kaeleer. If Orian wasn't bluffing and really does have a Ring, I will execute her, and I do not want you in Askavi when that decision is made. You understand me?"

"Yes, sir." It wasn't exactly how he'd intended to approach receiving permission, but there was no point wasting the opportunity. "I could go to Amdarh for a few days. See Uncle Daemon. Visit with Titian."

Lucivar gave him a long look. "And maybe inquire about attending that school?"

Hell's fire. Did his father have to know *everything* before he did? "Maybe."

"Get packed, boyo. I'll let Daemon know you're on your way."

"What should I tell Mother?"

"That you're going to Amdarh to talk to your uncle about enrolling in that school. It won't come as a surprise. She thought you'd make this request before now."

He packed in a hurry, filling one trunk with everyday clothes and weapons, and the other trunk with his better clothes and the books he valued most. His little brother was still asleep when he stood on the flagstones in front of the eyrie and hugged his mother—and said good-bye to his father.

And wondered what was going to happen in Ebon Rih after he was gone.

*Bastard, I'm sending Daemonar to you for a few days.*

Daemon stood in front of the door of Lady Zhara's home, responding to a request for an urgent meeting. It sounded like he would need to deal with something urgent within his own family too. *What's wrong?*

The door opened. Zhara's butler stepped aside to let him enter, but it was Zhara's husband, Garek, who waited for him just beyond the door.

Daemon held up a hand, indicating that he was occupied.

*I need the boy out of Ebon Rih while I take care of a problem. He might talk to you about going to that school.*

*Should I encourage or dissuade?*

*If he really wants to study there, help him enroll in the school. If he just wants to pester Titian by being a protective brother, keep him for a few days and then kick his ass back to Ebon Rih.*

*Done. When is he coming?*

*He's on his way.*

*Do you need help?*

*Not yet. But I'll need to talk to the High Lord and the Queen about the smuggled goods you're holding.*

Daemon knew that Lucivar, being Lucivar, could handle any problem caused by anyone living in Askavi. He wanted to press for more information, but he needed to deal with Zhara before Daemonar arrived.

"Thank you for coming so early, Prince," Garek said when Daemon crossed the threshold.

"There's some trouble?" Daemon asked as they headed for the room that overlooked the back garden—a room Zhara used for personal discussions with visitors, which meant he wasn't dealing with the Queen of Amdarh.

"Not trouble, no. Something . . . extraordinary. Zhara will tell you."

The way Zhara clutched his hands when he held them out to her, the look on her face, in her eyes, as she struggled to control her emotions . . .

"Zhara . . . ," he began.

"Sheela," she said, her voice breaking. "My daughter. Zoey's mother. After all these years, after *centuries* of being lost, she found her way out of the tangled web. She's been ensnared since she was a journeymaid Black Widow, but she found her way out."

"Darling, sit down." Daemon led her to a sofa and sat with her since she hadn't released his hands. He glanced at Garek, who brought over a straight-backed chair and sat nearby, tears running down his face as he smiled. "That's wonderful news."

Extraordinary news. Learning to see the dreams and visions in a tangled web was part of a Black Widow's training, but every year the minds of some of the witches became trapped in those webs. It was the potential price that was paid for being a Sister of the Hourglass.

"Does Zoey know?" he asked.

"She knows, but hasn't seen her mother yet," Garek replied. "We'd like Sheela to have some time to adjust to living in the world again before we talk to her about how much time she's been away. Zoey was just a young girl when Sheela was lost."

He remembered that, just as he remembered his first encounter with Lady Zoela.

"Song in the Darkness," Zhara said suddenly. "Sheela said there was a song in the Darkness. Sometimes it sounded far away. Sometimes, when she thought it was nearby, a thread seemed to shine and she would follow it for a while, would see things, understand things. And then she would lose her way. Over and over, losing her way and finding it again when she heard the song. Until she found her way out."

Daemon said nothing. Didn't dare say anything. He'd mentioned Zoey's mother to Witch and Karla once, just once, centuries ago. He hadn't asked either of them to intervene. Wasn't even sure there was anything to be done. Witch had led Tersa to the border of the Twisted Kingdom and helped the broken Black Widow build a life that could mesh with the day-to-day rhythm of a small village. But his Queen had been among the living when she'd done that extraordinary bit of healing.

He'd only mentioned Zoey's mother once, and neither Witch nor Karla had responded at the time. Or maybe he hadn't read the signs correctly.

"Sheela isn't the only one," Zhara continued. "The Sisters who tend the witches who are mentally damaged said other Black Widows are more aware of the world than they've been in a long time, and all of them mention a song."

He squeezed her hands in warning. "Zhara."

"I heard that phrase once. It was at your daughter's Birthright Ceremony. A song in the Darkness." Zhara sniffed and looked him in the eyes. "It's best, I think, not to ask about some things. Or call too much attention to some things. I also think you have a connection to Ebon Askavi that few others can claim."

"Be careful," he said too softly.

"What is said here today will not leave this room or be mentioned again." Zhara nodded toward Garek, who quickly agreed. "I think that song in the Darkness healed you, too, when you fell ill shortly after your daughter's Birthright Ceremony. And I think that song, somehow, still holds the leash of the most powerful men in Kaeleer."

"Is that what you think?"

"If a song can hear as well as be heard, please thank her for helping my daughter come home."

"Thank who?"

Zhara smiled. "Perhaps it's all just a dream."

Daemon studied the Queen of Amdarh and knew Zhara would keep her word and never speak of this again. Returning her smile, he said, "Perhaps it is."

Releasing her hands, he stood. "If you'll excuse me, I have a nephew who will be landing on my doorstep in a few hours."

"Trouble?" Garek asked.

Daemon raised one eyebrow and said dryly, "He's Eyrien. Of course there's trouble."

Lucivar didn't knock, didn't give any warning. He just used Craft to blow the front door of Dorian's eyrie off its hinges. As he walked in, he put an Ebon-gray shield around the eyrie. Then he called in a round-headed club— a useful weapon if a man wanted to break a lot of bones and turn a person into a bloody mess.

Dorian and Orian rushed into the front room that was decorated like a Queen's waiting room. They both appeared upset, but Orian had a look in her eyes that made him think she knew exactly why he was there.

"Your son just threatened my daughter!" Dorian's voice was filled with wrath.

Ignoring Dorian, he turned to Orian and snarled, "Where is the Ring of Obedience?"

"I don't know what you're talking about," Orian stammered. She tried to look haughty. She stank of fear.

"You told a Warlord Prince that you have a Ring of Obedience. You threatened to use it on him. For that alone, I could drag you out of here and skin you alive. This is your only chance, Orian. Hand over the Ring or die."

"Orian said no such thing!" Dorian protested.

"Were you there? Did you hear the words?" Lucivar demanded.

"It's his word against hers."

"Then let's bring them both before a tribunal of Queens and have them open their inner barriers to reveal the truth."

Orian swayed. Dorian put her arms around her daughter.

"I was just teasing," Orian said. "I didn't think Daemonar would take it *seriously*."

"Liar."

"How dare you! Orian is a Queen!" Dorian snapped.

"Doesn't make her any less of a liar." Lucivar stared at Dorian. "You want your daughter to live? Tell me where you've hidden the Ring."

"I want you to leave," Dorian said. "Right now!"

He spun, swung the club—and turned a table into kindling.

Orian let out a scream that was more like a squeak. Dorian stumbled away from him, pulling Orian with her.

"Where is it?" he snarled.

"I don't know what you're talking about."

"Lie to me again, and I'll use this club on your girl, and there won't be much left of her when I'm done."

"You wouldn't dare!"

He bared his teeth. "Tell that to all the Queens I killed."

Dorian glanced at a small round cabinet with a locked door.

He'd seen that cabinet listed in a delivery of goods when it arrived in Ebon Rih. A year ago? Maybe two? Dorian had said it had come from her family home and had been patched up with Craft so many times it had no worth beyond sentimental value. Rothvar had inspected it carefully and hadn't sensed anything that didn't match Dorian's claim—had, in fact, thought sending it to Dorian was her relatives' way of pissing on her.

But a man who had been exposed to the brilliance of Jaenelle Angelline and the coven would pay particular attention to the spells around the lock and the door. A man who had spent some time being tutored by Saetan would know that malicious spells could be hidden under benign ones.

What he was sensing now wasn't Dorian's work. She didn't have the power or the skill. But someone did. Was that someone here or still in Terreille?

Wrapping Ebon-gray power around the club, he threw it at the cabinet. His power collided with the power in the various spells with enough force that, if he'd been holding the club, he could have lost the use of part of his arm—for good.

Nothing benign about *that*.

Lying in the cabinet's ruins was a wooden box. No spells on it. No lock. Considering what had been around the cabinet, Dorian hadn't needed anything else to protect whatever the box held. Still, he used Craft to float the box out of the debris, lift the lid, and riffle through the contents.

No Ring of Obedience. Just letters. Lots of letters. Years' worth of letters. Written in Eyrien.

Dorian had shown him one of these letters from her family. The content was banal and made him wonder why someone would go to the trouble of paying the expense of sending it to Kaeleer. And he'd wondered why her smile had been so sly and satisfied when he'd shown no more than polite interest in her correspondence. Now he knew why.

It looked like his power had smashed more than the spells on the cabinet and had revealed the real messages beneath the other ones.

Lucivar swore silently. Most formal correspondence and business contracts were written in the common tongue used by every race in Kaeleer, and with Marian's and Daemonar's help, he'd gotten pretty good at reading such things. But this?

He wouldn't ask Marian to read these, and until he knew the contents, he didn't dare go to Ebon Askavi and ask the Lady there who was fluent in Eyrien. The Darkness only knew how Jaenelle would respond when she found out about this. He wanted to have an answer—and a decision—before he told her.

There was one person.

He wrapped an Ebon-gray shield around the box, in case he'd missed a trap. Then he looked at the woman and girl, who looked back with defiance.

"When I know what these letters say, I'll decide if the two of you are going to be exiled back to Terreille or executed and sent to Hell."

"You can't do that," Dorian said, her voice rising in panic. "Orian has no future in Terreille."

"I was just teasing," Orian pleaded. "I didn't know it was such a bad thing!"

*You knew,* Lucivar thought, feeling a pang for the young family who had come to Kaeleer centuries ago to escape the very thing Orian now threatened to bring into his Territory.

"Pack up your personal belongings," he said. "Only what the two of you can carry using Craft. One way or another, I'll be back at sunrise."

He walked out of Dorian's eyrie, made sure his Ebongray shield was in place, and flew to the Healer's eyrie.

Still early enough in the morning that Jillian wasn't quite ready to greet the day, but she let him in, then hurried to the kitchen to start a pot of coffee.

"Help yourself to the coffee when it's ready," Jillian said. "I'll just finish getting dressed."

"Take your time." He waited until she dashed for her room before going into the kitchen.

She was young, but he couldn't talk to any of his men. Not yet. He knew how Rothvar, Zaranar, and the rest of them would respond to what might be in those letters—especially since they knew of the attempt to smuggle Rings of Obedience into Askavi. Jillian was young, but she was intelligent, she was family, and she could read the Eyrien language.

She returned, fully dressed, with her hair up in a kind of messy knot that he found oddly appealing.

He poured two mugs of coffee, filled her mug a third of the way with cream, then indicated the chairs at the kitchen table. "I need your help."

"Of course."

Not a daughter of his loins, but a daughter of his heart. She never called him Father, but she acted like a daughter—

and anyone who tangled with Jillian swiftly learned how he felt about her.

"It's delicate," he said once they were seated. He called in the box he'd taken from Dorian and set it on the table. "I need you to read these letters to me."

He huffed out a laugh at the look on her face. "Relax, witchling. They aren't letters Marian has received from a secret lover." All amusement fled. "If they are what I think they are, they're much worse."

She looked alarmed. "Maybe Rothvar . . . ?"

He shook his head. "I can't talk to any of the men until I know what is in these letters."

Before he could say anything, she put a tight shield around herself, then a second shield on her hands and forearms. As she riffled through the letters, she said, "You would have kicked my ass if I didn't shield before I picked up a potentially dangerous object that came from an unknown place."

"It's good you learned the lesson," he replied mildly.

"Hell's fire," Jillian muttered a minute later. "Based on the dates, the letters in this box go back years. One or two a year in the beginning, then more frequent until it's one a month now."

Did these letters from Terreille go back far enough to explain the change in Dorian and her ambitions for her daughter? Or had the earliest letters already been destroyed? The ones Jillian pulled out of the box had nothing more than an initial for the signature, but not all the letters were written by the same hand or signed with the same initial.

"Read the past two years."

She pulled those letters out, put them in order from oldest to most recent, and then began to read them out loud. She tried to read them without her own feelings showing through, but with each letter her voice became sharper; her temper rose closer to the surface.

One writer was sharp and critical of Dorian not doing more to help other members of the family settle in

Kaeleer—and even more critical about the lack of money available to support those family members when they finally arrived. What was the point of having a Queen—of sorts—in the family if she couldn't bring wealth to heel?

The other writer sympathized with Dorian's frustration over her daughter being an impoverished Queen. Wasn't there some way to bring that young Warlord Prince to heel and gain access to his family's fortune? Orian would never be able to achieve her full potential and rule a substantial part of Askavi without that kind of wealth.

The first writer again—and a veiled reference to Dorian soon having access to a Ring of Obedience so that Orian could control the defiant cock and persuade him to give her everything she desired.

Jillian dropped the last letter, drank the cold coffee, then thumped the mug on the table. Her eyes were so hot with anger, Lucivar tightened the leash on his own temper so that she could vent her feelings here and now.

"Your thoughts?" he asked.

"This is obscene," Jillian snarled. She snatched up a letter and shook it at him. "This is what all of us left Terreille to escape. How dare that bitch threaten Daemonar with a Ring of Obedience? *How dare she?*"

*Well, Orian didn't remember that he has an older sister with a sharp temper and a wicked roundhouse punch.*

"Where is she?"

Oh, no. Unlike Titian, Jillian had wanted to learn how to fight and use Eyrien weapons—and she had learned well. After she and Khary went to Little Weeble the first time, she decided she didn't want to be a guard or a warrior as such, but she trained hard during her visits home and wanted him and Rothvar to teach her more. She didn't explain why she wanted that training and neither man had asked. But they gave her the training—and they gave her an Eyrien war blade made by Kohlvar, the weapons maker, that was specially balanced for her hand.

He wasn't letting Jillian anywhere near Orian and her mother.

"She's mine to deal with," he said.

She stared at him. "You're going to let her live?"

That question was exactly why he hadn't wanted any of the men to know about the letters before he knew the contents.

"How can you let her live?" she demanded in a tone that warned him that he'd damn well better be thinking of something else.

Shit. If Jillian was this riled, Marian was going to . . .

How long would his hearth witch refuse to sleep with him if he locked her in their eyrie to keep her from going after Dorian?

"If I had found a Ring of Obedience, neither of them would be among the living right now," he said carefully. "But—"

"Did you search the whole eyrie?"

No, he hadn't. He wouldn't have had the option of exile for those two if he'd found a Ring, so he wouldn't do a thorough search until they were gone. That was as much mercy as he could give them.

"The choice of punishment is mine, Lady Jillian."

"None of the other Eyrien men would let her live once they knew she'd threatened one of them with that obscenity."

"They have that luxury. As the ruler of Askavi, I don't." The truth was, if he'd still been in Terreille, he wouldn't have hesitated to kill Orian for the threat. "Orian no longer has a future here. Exile will give her a second chance. If she shakes off these corrupt ideas, she has the potential to be a good Queen."

"And if she doesn't shake off these ideas? Or more to the point, if Dorian and her *family* keep pushing these ideas?"

"Then I doubt Orian will survive a year in Terreille."

"A stay of execution, then."

Would the Eyrien warriors who worked for him see it that way?

He put the letters back in the box and vanished it. "Jillian . . ."

"Yours to do. I know." She sighed. "I won't say anything. But that doesn't mean I don't feel exercised about the whole thing."

"Really? I hadn't noticed."

At least that made her smile. When he pushed away from the table, she rose up on her toes and kissed his cheek. And then was cheeky enough to say, "Was I a dress rehearsal?"

"For . . . ?"

"Explaining this to your son's mother."

Jillian wasn't wrong about that. After the first minutes of horrified silence, Marian raged—first at Dorian and then at him for, among other things, letting the bitch continue to draw breath when it was obvious that she had fully intended for Orian to use a Ring on *their son*.

When she showed no sign of winding down, he ordered Andulvar to remain in his room, put an Ebon-gray shield around the front room, and handed Marian one of the sparring sticks to let her vent some of that temper by using him as an opponent.

Rage seemed to sharpen her skill because she almost managed to hit him a couple of times. Under other circumstances, he would have been pleased about that and praised the skill. Now he just let her whack at him until the muscles in her arms shook so much she couldn't lift the sparring stick.

Not being a fool, he wasn't careless about approaching her—and didn't breathe easy until he pulled the sparring stick out of her hands and vanished both.

He could deal with rage, but it ripped him when she started to cry.

"Shh, sweetheart, shh. It will be all right." He wrapped his arms around her.

"Our boy, Lucivar. She threatened to do that to our boy."

"Daemonar is smart and he's trained."

"So were you at his age, and Prythian and her bitches still managed to put one of those things on you."

Nothing he could say to that, so he just held her and

waited for the storm to pass. Once she'd stopped crying and quieted enough to sniffle into a handkerchief, he said, "I think I understand now why Andulvar, the previous Demon Prince, stayed as long as he did after he became demon-dead."

Marian wiped the tears off her face and tucked the handkerchief into the pocket of her skirt. "He stayed to keep Saetan company, to help him maintain his balance."

"That was part of it." Lucivar ran a hand down her long black hair, noticing there were a few strands of silver now. "But I think he stayed because someone needed to remember why the war between Terreille and Kaeleer had been fought, and why so many died.

"When I first came to the Shadow Realm and met the boyos who were living at the Hall, none of them had heard of a Ring of Obedience. A Ring of Honor, yes. That was a prize only worn by a man who served in a Queen's First Circle. Yes, she could use it to control every aspect of their lives, but why would she? And any Queen who did want that much control didn't have a court for long. What they couldn't see was how the use of a Ring of Honor might have been corrupted, step by step, until it was turned into a Ring of Obedience. None of them knew that, had considered that, until I came to Kaeleer and told them about what was done in Terreillean courts.

"For the short-lived races, the purge that removed Dorothea and Hekatah SaDiablo's taint from the Realms was something that happened long ago. It's history, a story. But we remember. For us it's the past, yes, but not history, not something that happened to someone else in another time. We knew the court; we knew the Queen. And while none of us knew all the choices Jaenelle had made, our children have grown up safe because of those choices."

"If you send Orian back to Terreille, aren't you making her someone else's problem?"

"Maybe, as Jillian put it, it's just a stay of execution. Or maybe Orian will find a way to be a good Queen."

"What are you going to say to Endar and Alanar?"

"The truth. I'll give them a choice of going with Dorian and Orian. I doubt they will, but I'll give them that choice. And then I'll talk to the Eyriens who live around Riada. Rothvar and Zaranar will take my decision to the rest of them."

"Do you want something to eat?"

Lucivar gave her a light kiss. "Not right now."

He dropped the Ebon-gray shield around the room and used a psychic thread to tap his younger son, giving the boy permission to leave his room.

Then he sent a summons to Endar and Alanar to meet him in the communal eyrie.

He wasn't surprised to find Rothvar waiting for him. And he wasn't surprised to find Nurian, the Eyrien Healer and Jillian's sister, waiting with his second-in-command. After all, Rothvar was her husband and the father of her children, so she would have guessed that a Healer might be needed for . . . whatever.

Rothvar shrugged. "The Ebon-gray thunders through the valley, and there's an Ebon-gray shield around Dorian's eyrie, locking everyone in—and keeping everyone out. And your boy is nowhere to be found in Ebon Rih. Smells like trouble to me."

Lucivar sighed. "Yeah."

Marian had felt the Ebon-gray too. That was one of the reasons she'd been pissed off at him for making her wait to find out what was going on.

He watched Endar and Alanar hesitate in the doorway before walking into the communal eyrie. "Let's get this done."

Daemonar dropped from the Winds at one of Amdarh's official landing webs and informed the guards on duty that he was in the city to visit his uncle. He could have dropped from the Winds anywhere a Green thread ran over the city, but it was a necessary courtesy to use an official landing web and inform the Queen's guards when a Warlord Prince arrived in a city that wasn't his own. When a male of his caste ignored that courtesy, the guards tended to respond with weapons drawn.

As soon as the guards waved him on, he flew to the family's town house and landed lightly on the sidewalk. He'd spent the journey from Ebon Rih to Amdarh wondering how to explain enough to get the permission he wanted to go to that school without explaining too much.

He had a feeling that the sun would shine in Hell before Uncle Daemon let him get away with not explaining everything.

So be it.

He bounded up the steps and knocked on the door, then smiled at the butler. "Good morning, Helton."

"Prince Yaslana." Standing aside to let him enter, Helton closed the front door too carefully.

Daemonar felt his shoulders tighten and itched to call in his war blade.

"Prince Sadi told us to expect you, but he didn't give any instructions to have a room made up for you," Helton said quietly.

That wasn't good. "Maybe he hasn't decided which side of the town house I'll be staying in."

"Perhaps." Helton didn't look convinced. "The Prince is waiting for you in his study."

He wasn't in trouble. He hadn't done anything wrong. Then again, his father and uncle were strong enough to communicate over long distances using Ebon-gray and Black psychic threads, so the Darkness only knew what Uncle Daemon already knew. Which made leaving out anything in his explanation even more precarious.

When he entered the study, he found his uncle sitting in the chair behind the blackwood desk, hands loosely folded with the forefingers lightly resting against his chin.

"So," Daemon said. "You're thinking of attending the same private school as Titian."

"I'd like to further my education, which is something I've been thinking about for a while."

"Not getting enough instruction at the Keep?"

"Different instructors bring different things to the table. You've told me that more than once. And spending time with men my own age who are also from a long-lived race would be another kind of seasoning."

This was going well. His arguments were sound. And there had been no mention of why his father had shoved him out of Ebon Rih so fast. Daemonar felt a trickle of relief—until Uncle Daemon rose, came around the desk, and settled gracefully in the other visitors' chair.

"Now," the Prince said in a voice that wrapped sensuality around threat. "You can tell me the real reason you want to go to that school, or we can have a pleasant visit for a few days before I escort you back to Ebon Rih."

Shit. Everything he'd said was the truth, and *he* wasn't going to be the one to tell Daemon Sadi about Orian's threat to use a Ring of Obedience. But . . .

"There is something wrong with Jaenelle Saetien." He'd meant to ease into his concern about his cousin, not club his uncle with words.

"Oh?"

Bland word, bland voice. But nothing bland in the gold eyes that watched him, assessing. This wasn't the most terrifying aspect of Daemon Sadi. He'd only seen *that* once, but he'd never forgotten the feel of being in a room with the Sadist. This was more than his uncle, more like . . .

*Prince of the Darkness. High Lord of Hell.*

Somehow he'd plucked that thread, and now he had to dance on that knife's edge.

"She's been different since she started going to that school," Daemonar said.

"I've been told adolescence is a difficult time for girls."

"Fine. It's difficult. Why should that erase reason? It's like expecting grass to grow on clouds, even though you know it can't, and then getting pissy because it doesn't."

"Well . . ."

"And that damn dress. She comes to Ebon Rih pissing and moaning because she bought this dress for an important dance, a dress that cost—" He took a breath and *tried* to hold in his criticism. He really did try, but . . . "Hell's fire, Uncle Daemon, what were you thinking to allow her to buy a dress that costs that much? And then—*then*—she gets angry because you won't buy her a *second* dress when you'd already told her you would only buy one? She knows you. She's lived with you all her life. She *knows* you don't move a line once it's drawn. And if she'd wanted another dress so much, she could have bought it with her own money! But no, she's wailing that *everyone else's* father is buying a second dress. Who is everyone? She couldn't name one girl who was going to have a second dress for the same dance."

"If you're done scolding me and storming around the room, perhaps I could explain."

He hadn't noticed he'd sprung out of the chair to pace and "storm" around the room. And he hadn't *intended* to scold his uncle.

Daemonar blew out a breath and returned to the chair.

"Perhaps I thought that not putting a limit on how much could be spent for a dress would eliminate a source of contention and allow Jaenelle Saetien and Surreal to have an enjoyable time shopping together."

He considered that for a moment, then nodded. "Good thought. Didn't work, but it was a good thought."

"I'm glad you agree." Dry humor—and something else beneath it. "I don't have experience with adolescent girls. Not the kind that is useful here. From time to time I discuss things with Beale and Holt, since they were both working at the Hall when your auntie J. and the coven lived with your grandfather."

Daemonar leaned closer. He loved hearing stories about Auntie J. and the coven and the boyos.

"Saetan had some difficulties dealing with the girls when they were the equivalent of this age," Daemon continued. "And he was often . . . compelled . . . to negotiate along the lines of 'I will pay for the new saddle you want if you also buy three new dresses.' He didn't get much support from Lady Sylvia about what constituted feminine dress; hence the negotiations. When your aunt and the coven went along with his terms, Saetan was often dismayed to discover that the saddle cost more than the three dresses combined. And just as often the negotiations failed because the girls would simply buy the desired item with their own money and ignore the dresses altogether.

"And then, seemingly overnight, they all became interested in clothes that left no doubt in anyone's mind that they were women—clothes that were both warning and temptation. Which created a different set of challenges for the men who were committed to keeping them safe."

"Father and Prince Chaosti would have made sure all of them knew how to use a knife," Daemonar said.

"Oh, yes, all of the Ladies who lived at the Hall were skilled with a knife," Daemon agreed. "Some more than others." He sighed. "But you think this . . . trouble . . . with Jaenelle Saetien is more."

"Yes, sir. It feels wrong somehow, like she's imitating what someone else would say instead of being herself. Like she wants to shed who she was—but someone has to be convincing her that being a bitch is desirable."

"What about Titian?"

Daemonar huffed. "I don't think Titian notices much beyond her art classes. That's all she writes about—and singing in a group and learning to play music. I don't think she's made many friends, but she *seems* happy."

"If you're right about something being wrong, even if it's just a group of students who have infatuated Jaenelle Saetien, your presence could stir up trouble that could swing back at you."

He was counting on it. "I can protect myself, Uncle Daemon."

"Boyo, even the strongest warrior can make a mistake and let his guard down at the wrong moment. As much as I'm concerned about my daughter, I don't want anything to happen to you."

"Father would walk into it, even knowing there was trouble. So would you."

"Yes, we would. Of course, most of the time, we were already in the middle of that kind of fight. Made the choice easier." Daemon smiled dryly. "And if anything happens to you, your auntie J. . . ."

"Mother Night," Daemonar breathed.

"And may the Darkness be merciful."

"I'll be careful," he promised.

"Do that—for all our sakes." Daemon stood. "Why don't we stretch our legs and walk around the square a couple of times while we discuss what subjects would be of interest to you? Then, in the morning, we'll go to the school and see about getting you enrolled."


When Lucivar told Endar and Alanar about his decision to exile Dorian and Orian—and why—Endar's only response was to request that Lucivar, as the ruler of Ebon Rih, grant him an immediate divorce in order to sever all connection with Dorian. Then he walked out of the communal eyrie.

Alanar drew in a shuddering breath. "Sir, if I'd known Orian was thinking about doing that to Daemonar . . . to *anyone* . . . and actually had a Ring, I would have told you."

"I know," Lucivar replied.

None of the other Eyriens who lived in Ebon Rih had endured wearing a Ring of Obedience, but every man among them had seen what it did, had listened to the screams of strong men crawling to the Queen who controlled them and begging for the pain to stop. The stories about why men like Rothvar and Zaranar had left Terreille had been softened somewhat when the boys were young. But since they were considered men who were approaching their mature strength, the Eyrien warriors had told the stories about the brutality in the courts in Askavi Terreille and why they had left everything they'd known for a chance at a different kind of life.

"Are you settled into the bachelor eyrie?" he asked.

"Yes, sir. Tamnar and I have everything we need," Alanar replied.

He'd check with Hallevar, the arms master who gave all the young warriors their basic training, to make sure that was true. Alanar might be happy sleeping on a stone floor wrapped in a thin blanket if that got him away from his mother and sister.

After considering what might be helpful to the youngsters without pinching their feeling of independence, he said, "There's a laundry service in Riada. The women who run it won't deal with leathers, so you'll have to clean those yourself, but they'll handle other clothing and towels and bed linens. You and Tamnar can take your things there to get washed. I'll pay for it."

"Thank you, sir."

"The two of you have enough to eat?"

"Yes, sir." Alanar looked around. "Are we going to have any training today?"

"You are," Lucivar replied. He nodded to Hallevar, Tamnar, and the others as they entered the communal eyrie. Then he tipped his head to indicate that Rothvar and Nurian should follow him outside.

Rothvar must have tapped Zaranar because the other warrior turned and went out with them.

"Zaranar should stick with Endar today," Rothvar said.

"You think he's going to try the Khaldharon as a suicide run?" Zaranar asked.

"I guess we're all thinking the same thing," Lucivar said. He blew out a breath. "If it looks like he's heading in that direction, we'll stop him."

Zaranar flew off to find Endar.

"I think Alanar will miss the mother Dorian had been when he was young," Nurian said. "But I also think he'll be relieved not to have her as a shadow hanging over his life or his choices."

The boy would do all right. For Lucivar, the question was whether Endar, who had once taken pride in being a teacher for the Eyrien children, would find that pride again after years of Dorian's disappointment scraping away his feeling that he was of value to the Eyrien community.

"I'll be at the Keep for a while," Lucivar said. "I need to find out how to sever a marriage contract. I'd like to give Endar that much peace of mind before I send Dorian and Orian back to Terreille."

He spread his wings, glanced at Nurian, then folded them again. "You going to the Healer's eyrie?"

"Yes," she replied. "I have some tonics to make and a couple of patients who are coming in."

He nodded. "Your sister is a bit exercised over this."

Nurian looked at him with wide eyes. "Jillian knows that Orian threatened Daemonar?"

"Yeah."

Rothvar swore. "You left that girl alone when she's feeling exercised?"

"There's an Ebon-gray shield around Dorian's eyrie. Jillian can't get to either of them."

"I seem to recall an Arcerian cat who could get through any shield, including the Black."

"Jillian deals with Scelties, not Arcerian cats." Besides, Kaelas was the only cat who had managed that particular bit of Craft. On the other hand, Scelties still had a bond with the Arcerian cats, so he couldn't be sure what skills Jillian might have picked up. "Hell's fire."

"If she's not at the Healer's eyrie, I'll let you know," Nurian said before she flew off.

"Sun's barely up, and we've already had a full day," Rothvar said.

Lucivar snorted. "Wait until your two are a little older. This will be normal."

"May the Darkness have mercy on me."

*Prick.*

Lucivar sighed as Daemon tapped him with a psychic communication thread. *Well, that didn't take long.* *Bastard? Is the boy going to that school?*

*He is.*

*At least he'll be a pain in your ass for a while instead of mine.*

*Thank you very much.* A beat of silence. *Are things settled in Ebon Rih?*

*They will be.*

*I'll be at the Keep tomorrow evening. We need to talk.*

*About all kinds of things.*

But who would be more dangerous once he told them who had been expecting to receive one of the smuggled Rings of Obedience? The Sadist—or Witch?

# TWENTY

———— ✦ ————

Daemon listened to Lady Fharra, the school's administrator, and wondered what it was about the woman
now that had him quietly rising to the killing edge when
she hadn't provoked his temper during their other meetings. She struck him as being ambitious, but there was
nothing wrong with that. She and the senior instructors
made sure the school catered to the wealthiest and most
influential aristo families in Dhemlan, and there was nothing wrong with that either. But there was a faint echo to
everything she was saying—not the words themselves, but
the *way* she said the words. It was an unsettling sensation,
like a cobweb brushing against his face—a wisp of memory there and gone. Something he'd seen? Something he'd
known long ago? Something to do with Lucivar and
schooling?

Or was something scratching at him now because of the
boy sitting beside him?

Yes. Daemonar, not Lucivar, was part of that wisp of
memory, was part of something . . . dangerous.

Odd that Fharra was putting up barriers about Daemonar attending the school when she'd shown no resistance to having Titian among the students. Did she have a
reason for not wanting a Warlord Prince studying at the
school? He hadn't sensed any others within the school
grounds, so she might not be comfortable with dealing

with a male of that caste. Or was she worried about having a young man with all the arrogance of a trained Eyrien warrior living at the school and observing the instructors and other students?

And wasn't that exactly why he was helping Daemonar attend this school? To have a warrior who was family walking among the other students and stirring things up enough to discover if Jaenelle Saetien's behavior was adolescent female drama or something that would require his own kind of savagery?

He would have listened to Fharra for hours, letting her resistance and excuses reveal more and more of what might require his attention, but the boy was getting restless and, being Eyrien, was more inclined to meet a challenge head-on.

"Lady Fharra." Daemon smiled and watched the woman try to suppress a shiver. "I'm aware that classes started a few weeks ago. I'm aware that my nephew might not have the same foundation of education that your other students enjoyed. That doesn't mean he is without education. He has studied with several individuals to advance his knowledge of subjects that are of interest to him. And the time he has spent with his father and with me as we've gone about our duties as rulers of our respective Territories means he has as good a grounding in the workings of a court as any other student here. Probably more."

"My concern is that Prince Yaslana will have difficulty catching up with the classwork at this point and might benefit from starting next year," Fharra said.

"When my daughter and my niece were enrolled a few weeks ago, you assured me that the instructors here were willing to tutor students one-on-one or with two or three other students in order to help them keep up with the classwork. I would think those instructors would be willing to work with a student to create an individual plan of study."

"That would create more work for the instructors," Fharra protested.

Daemon's smile turned colder and sharper—and Daemonar watched him closely now, a warrior alerted to a potential battle.

"Accommodate me," he said too softly. "Not as the uncle of a new student but as the Warlord Prince of Dhemlan."

*Uncle Daemon . . . ,* Daemonar began.

*Later.* He stared at Fharra, giving her time to realize he was no longer making a request—and that defying a command from Dhemlan's ruler would carry a high price. What he found interesting was the change in her psychic scent. That told him she often faced the necessity of accommodating aristos who had wealth and influence and wanted some special consideration. He had the impression she didn't object to making those accommodations as long as the person hinted there would be some personal benefit for her.

He gave no hints. He simply smiled—and waited.

"Very well." Fharra's voice carried brisk annoyance, but her hands shook as she reached for a pen and filled out the admission form. "All students live in the dormitories. In the male dormitory, there is only one room available. It's a private room."

"I'm taking care of the cost of my nephew attending the school as well as room and board. So the extra cost of a private room is not a concern."

"Yes. Well. It's only available because the fine young Warlord who was supposed to attend this year met with a tragic accident."

"Would that be the fine young Warlord who had his guts ripped out by the girl he tried to rape?" Daemon asked, his voice so pleasantly sharp, it could make air bleed.

Fharra dropped her pen. "I wasn't aware . . . I was given to understand . . ." She swallowed hard. "I assure you, Prince, that nothing like that has ever happened at the school. No witch has ever been broken on school grounds."

That wasn't the same thing as saying the Blood males attending this school hadn't persuaded—or forced—girls to have a premature Virgin Night that stripped those girls of their power.

Not something the school could do anything about if it took place off of school grounds. Fharra was right about that.

But there was that wisp of memory.

May the Darkness have mercy on everyone once he caught that wisp and saw all that the memory revealed.


It wasn't that Daemon Sadi *changed*. He just became *more* of what he was. It was like watching an already sharp blade being honed, stroke by stroke, until it had the edge required for a killing field. It was like watching a mask melt away, revealing the truth underneath.

His father's temper ran hot. Uncle Daemon's ran cold, and listening to Sadi explain things to Lady Fharra, Daemonar wasn't sure the cold was all that accurate a measure of the depth of temper—or what a Black-Jeweled Warlord Prince in a cold rage could, or would, do.

"Why do you think she set her heels down about me being here?" Daemonar asked as he and Daemon walked to the book exchange to pick up the books for his classes.

"An excellent question," Daemon replied, sounding more like his uncle than like the someone *more*.

"She seemed genuinely surprised about that Warlord and why he died."

"She did."

*And that is why she is still alive.*

The words weren't said. Didn't have to be said.

He felt a lift in his uncle's mood and temper when they reached the book exchange and perused the books. Daemon's lips twitched when he noticed two of the books on the required reading list were books he'd arranged to have published because Daemonar had found them at the Keep and wanted his own copies.

Daemonar had been nervous about attending classes here, although he wouldn't have admitted that to either his father or uncle. There were bound to be holes in his education, things the other students had read. But in some subjects, he'd already been taught by the strongest and the best.

The room in the dormitory was more spacious than he'd expected and looked out over the green. Each floor of the dorm had its own hygiene facilities, with several toilets contained in narrow stalls and a shower room that had plenty of space but offered no privacy. He was used to the lack of privacy since the communal eyrie had the same kind of shower arrangement. The toilet stalls could be an easy way to trap someone, but putting a Green shield with a little added sizzle around a stall would stop anyone who wanted to cause trouble. Not that he expected anyone here to cause trouble. Shielding when he was vulnerable would be done to soothe his father's and uncle's tempers.

He called in the two trunks and unpacked while Daemon watched him. Some clothes in the small dresser, some hung up in the closet. Didn't take him long. One of the sparring sticks he'd brought with him rested in a corner of the room. The rest of the weapons that were small enough to fit into a trunk and the special books he'd brought were arranged in one trunk, which he vanished. He put the novels he'd bought for fun reading in the other trunk, along with a spare blanket. That trunk he placed against one wall—in plain sight. The books for classes went in the narrow bookcase next to the desk.

Daemon watched him—and said nothing. Then he smiled, a smile that held warmth and amusement. "Helton informed me that you should bring your laundry to the town house the evening before washday."

"I can wash my own clothes," Daemonar said, although he wasn't sure where students could do that. "And Helton wouldn't *inform* you of anything, Uncle Daemon." Unlike Beale, the butler at the Hall, who was a Red-Jeweled Warlord and informed Prince Sadi of a great many things.

"It was worded as a suggestion but didn't leave much room for interpretation. Neither did the *suggestion* that you could have a decent dinner at the town house that evening. He mentioned that Beron often had dinner at the town house the evening before washday and sometimes stayed the night to get a decent breakfast in the morning."

"Uh-huh. Are Titian and Jaenelle Saetien also coming for dinner one night a week so they don't expire from eating whatever slop is served at the school?"

"It was suggested that the young Ladies could come to dinner on another night."

"So they have a different washday than the men in the family?"

"Apparently."

There was a reading chair in the room. It looked comfortable, but it wasn't built to accommodate Eyrien wings. Still, it would work for visitors. Did work for visitors, since Daemon was sitting in it.

Daemonar straddled the wooden desk chair. "Are all servants this pushy, or do the pushy ones end up working for you because they know you'll put up with it?"

"Because they think I'm weak?" Daemon asked too softly.

"Because they know you're strong and you're not intimidated by them showing their own strength."

Daemon stared at him. Daemonar shrugged. Neither of them mentioned Mrs. Beale and her meat cleaver and how *everyone* in the family, except Marian, was intimidated by the Hall's cook.

A knock on the door.

As Daemonar went to open it, he noticed how Daemon sat with his legs crossed at the knees, his fingers with those long black-tinted nails steepled and lightly resting against his chin. Would anyone outside the family recognize the danger in that pose?

The visitor turned out to be Prince Raine, a young instructor from Dharo who had just started at the school that year and had been assigned to be Daemonar's tutor in three areas of study.

Had Prince Raine volunteered for the extra work or, because he was the newcomer, had the work no one else wanted been piled on him?

"Picked up your books, I see," Raine said. He handed Daemonar a piece of heavy paper with a neatly written list. "These are the times for your classes and tutorials." A glance at Daemon, whose glazed eyes were fixed on the man. "I understand that you wanted the tutorials to be free study, but it might be beneficial to use one of our study times to answer any questions you might have from your other classes."

"That sounds like a good idea," Daemonar replied. "Thank you, sir."

Prince Raine hesitated, then gave Daemonar a strained smile. "I'll see you tomorrow."

"Yes, sir." Daemonar saw the man out of the room, then turned to his uncle. "Problem?"

"Not for me." Daemon rose. "Do you want to find out what slop is served in the dining hall or come with me to a steak house for a decent meal?"

"What happens if the food here is very good?"

Daemon laughed. "If that's the case, I hope you, at least, are smart enough not to mention that within hearing of anyone who works at the town house or at the Hall."

The laughter faded. Daemon stepped close to him and wrapped a hand around the back of his neck, a gesture his uncle had in common with his father.

"If there is trouble here, I want to know about it," Daemon said. "I don't care if you think you can, or should, handle it yourself. I don't care if you *do* handle it yourself. If there is trouble, you will tell me."

"Because it's not just about me."

"That's correct."

As they walked to the steak house, Daemonar observed how people reacted to the man beside him. Some people were wary, but most of the people were unafraid and smiled at the two of them or gave a nod of greeting that didn't ask for attention. Uncle Daemon might not notice all the people who had no reason to be wary of him, but Daemonar was certain Prince Sadi made note of the people who might have a reason to fear his temper.

Daemon Sadi and Lucivar Yaslana maintained a veneer of civilized behavior, but they didn't hide the first layer of truth about what they were, even when they walked down a street. They were Warlord Princes born to stand on killing fields. They were predators. They were dangerous.

And ever since he'd made the Blood Run, they had quietly acknowledged that he was ready to stand on those fields with them.

"What's the rube doing back here?" Dhuran said. "Isn't having one of those bats at the school bad enough?"

Delora wanted to slap Dhuran for calling attention to the Eyrien because Jaenelle Saetien turned around and said, "That's my cousin Daemonar." Then she muttered, "Why *is* he back here?"

"Probably visiting his sister," Delora said.

"Maybe." And off Jaenelle Saetien went across the green to talk to the Eyrien.

"He's not visiting," Leena said. "I heard he's attending classes here and Prince Raine has been assigned as his special tutor."

"Going to try to teach the bat how to read?" Clayton said, sniggering.

"Hold your tongue," Delora said sharply. "We don't want Jaenelle Saetien to feel obliged to defend her lesser relations."

"He was given Silas's room," Krellis said, coming up to stand beside Delora. "My source in Lady Fharra's office said she's concerned that he isn't going to fit in with the rest of us and might cause trouble when he finally figures that out, but she wasn't able to persuade Prince Sadi to send the Eyrien to another school."

Borsala sniffed. "Fharra shouldn't have let the first bat attend our school. I wrote to my mother and told her *all about it.* She was quite appalled that Fharra is lowering standards."

"Titian might prove useful," Delora replied. She turned to Krellis. "Why didn't Silas come back to school?"

Krellis looked grim. "He's dead. The girl he'd picked for some fun killed him. He must have given her the wrong dose of the party favor and she turned savage."

"Hell's fire," Clayton muttered.

"Silas was from an aristo family," Hespera said. "That girl was insignificant. She's been punished, hasn't she?"

Krellis shook his head. "*Lady* SaDiablo investigated and decided Silas was at fault. Besides, among the Blood, there is no law against murder—especially when the killing is considered self-defense."

Delora felt a rising fury burn through her as she watched Jaenelle Saetien and the Eyrien boy. Nothing malleable about the boy, and he could ruin all the careful work she'd already done grooming Jaenelle Saetien to be one of *her* kind of aristo. "Blaming aristos for having a bit of fun won't do. It won't do at all."

"We can't change that," Hespera said.

"Oh, I don't know." Delora smiled as she continued to watch Jaenelle Saetien and the Eyrien. "We just need to find the right tool to rupture some family bonds."

Now Krellis smiled. "I might have found the right tool for that."


"Daemonar?" Jaenelle Saetien ran up to her cousin. "What are you doing here?"

"Getting a feel for the school grounds and the location of everything," he replied, smiling.

"Why? Are you looking for Titian?" *Or are you checking up on me to report to Papa?*

"Titian is in the potting shed. Pottery barn?" He shrugged and pointed. "She's that way, apparently up to her elbows in mud, so I'm heading over to see her and let her know where I'll be."

"Where you'll be?"

"I'm taking some classes here. I have a room in the male dormitory." Daemonar studied her. "Is that a problem?"

"No, I'm just surprised." Because it still stung that he'd criticized *her* about wanting a second dress for the dance, she added, "I didn't think you were interested in attending classes with other people."

"I figured I'd expand my education, in more ways than just books."

In other words, he'd expect her to introduce him to her friends even though she already knew those friends had no interest in being around him.

She felt a twinge of disloyalty. Daemonar had always been her best ally, her partner in mischief—and the one who pulled her back before she got into *too* much trouble with Papa and Uncle Lucivar. But status among the Blood was three-pronged—Jewel rank, caste, and social influence. Daemonar respected Jewel rank and caste, but he shrugged off the social aspect as insignificant. The girls and boys who were at this school soon would be the social power of Dhemlan. He didn't care about that, but she did. She wanted to dazzle. She wanted to shine. She wanted so much sophisticated gloss that she was beyond comparison with anyone else.

She wanted to be like Delora, commanding the social stage and setting the standard for what was interesting and fashionable. Deciding what behavior was acceptable and what was not. They'd had long discussions already about why aristos shouldn't be bound to the same rules as the rest of the Blood. Some rules didn't apply to Warlord Princes because of their nature. Why shouldn't aristos enjoy the same kind of leniency?

She was tired of rules. She wanted to make her *own* decisions, not be hemmed in by rules that were only there to get in the way of her being who she wanted to be.

Daemonar would interfere with all her dreams of social prominence. She could see it so clearly, but she knew him.

He'd decided to go to this school, and nothing she said would change his mind.

She would just have to be too busy to spend much time with him. That shouldn't be hard to do. She and Titian and Zoey had been friends for years, spending days at the town house laughing and talking. She barely saw them now that they'd started school. She felt bad that the other girls had made fun of Titian and called her a fat bat, but Titian and Zoey could be such *rubes*, despite their bloodlines. They went to classes and did their schoolwork and thought pottery class was great fun. And, Mother Night, the embarrassment when she'd seen them doing the Eyrien warm-up exercises with the sparring sticks!

Daemonar would be out there with them for the warmups. Maybe even sparring with them. If they did that where they could be seen, she would just curl up and die!

"Jaenelle Saetien?"

Had he been talking all this time? "What?"

Something in his eyes, like he'd seen something that shouldn't be there. "I'm meeting up with Titian and her friend. Do you want to join us?"

"No. Thank you."

"Suit yourself."

"I will."

He started to walk away, then stopped. "Be careful you don't suit yourself too much."

What did *that* mean?

Jaenelle Saetien watched him walk away. She was glad he hadn't insisted that she join him and Titian and Zoey.

Wasn't she?


An hour before dawn, Lucivar stood in front of Dorian's eyrie. She'd raised the door he'd blown off its hinges and rested it against the Ebon-gray shield that covered the doorway, as well as the rest of the eyrie.

The repair was done in a way to elicit sympathy. By itself, the door didn't keep out the cold, but it did keep anyone from easily seeing the front room. By itself, the door's position was intended to be a message that this was the best the two women could do in the face of his unjust decision.

It was too bad for Dorian that not a single Eyrien had come to the eyrie and seen the message.

He created an opening in the shield the size and shape of the doorway.

The door, which had been leaning on the shield, fell with a crash.

When Dorian and Orian rushed into the front room, all he said was, "It's time."

"No!" Dorian protested. "We haven't finished packing."

He'd given them sufficient time to gather what they valued the most and could carry by using Craft. He wasn't interested in delaying tactics or any other kind of game.

Ignoring their increasingly shrill protests, he wrapped Dorian and Orian in Ebon-gray shields that he tethered to himself. Then he flew to Ebon Askavi.

No sign of Endar or Alanar when he arrived at the Keep with his burden. He'd wondered if man and youth would come to say good-bye to wife and sister, but it seemed they already felt enough hurt.

All the way to the Dark Altar, the two women protested their innocence and screamed at his mistreatment of them over something that couldn't be proved and had been nothing more than foolish words.

Lucivar stopped at the door leading to the Dark Altar, one of the thirteen Gates between the Realms. Nothing he could do for Dorian, but there was one brutal lesson he could give the girl, who was a Queen, one chance to help her understand what she had threatened to do to Daemonar.

Daemon was so much better at this subtle kind of Craft, but . . .

He hit both of them with power shaped into pain—the kind of excruciating, nerve-burning pain inflicted by a Ring of Obedience. He counted off the seconds as the women screamed.

Just a few seconds. So little time compared to what men had endured, but enough, he hoped, for this warning and lesson.

He ended the spell and the pain. Then he walked up to Orian. No defiance there now. Just fear.

"That's what a Ring of Obedience does," he said quietly. "That's what you threatened to do to my son."

"I didn't," she whimpered. "I didn't."

"Yes, you did. And now you know how it feels. There are plenty of Eyrien men living in Terreille Askavi who had worn a Ring of Obedience. There are plenty more who witnessed what those men suffered. Orian, the day you so much as hint that you have a device that can be used to control men and force them to be accommodating, all those warriors will sharpen their knives and come for you, and you will not survive to see another sunrise. You could still be a good Queen. . . ."

"I could," she said. "I will."

"But not here. I am a weapon that stands against anyone who tries to bring Terreille's poison into Kaeleer. If you stay, I can't allow you to survive. Once you get settled in Terreille, don't let whatever is twisting up your mother destroy you too."

Lucivar used Craft to open the door and guide his burdens to the Dark Altar. Karla and Chaosti—and Draca—waited for him as witnesses.

"The reassonss for banishment have been recorded in the regissterss," Draca said. "A ssmall taint on the bloodline that will grow or be forgotten, depending on what the young Queen doess from now on."

Karla lit the black candles in the four-branched candelabrum, lighting them in the sequence that would open the Gate between Kaeleer and Terreille.

Lucivar walked through the Gate, bringing Dorian and Orian with him—and was followed by Chaosti.

"I'll wait for you here," Chaosti said when they reached the Dark Altar in the Keep in Terreille.

So few steps for such a significant journey.

Lucivar nodded and began the long walk through the corridors of the Keep, finally reaching the outer door that opened to a courtyard and the gates where . . .

Memories crowded him, even now.

He used Craft to open the tall wrought-iron gates and float the two women to the other side. Then he closed the gates and put an Ebon-gray lock on them. Finally, he released the shields he'd wrapped around Dorian and Orian.

"You're standing on the spot where Hekatah SaDiablo was destroyed when the Realms were finally purged of her taint," he said, swallowing bile. "If you choose to become like her, may the Darkness have mercy on you because the living, and the demon-dead, will have none." He called in a pouch, vanished it, then called it back in on the other side of the gates. "Twenty thousand gold marks."

Dorian grabbed the pouch, then caught herself and sniffed. "That's not a sufficient annual allowance for a Queen."

"That's not an annual allowance, Dorian. That's a one-time resettlement gift, given in memory of the woman and girl who came to Kaeleer looking for a better life. It's more than enough to pay for food and lodgings until you find work." He raised his voice to override Dorian's protest that *she*, the mother of a Queen, should not be required to work. "You'll receive nothing else from me . . . except this." The document floated in front of her. "Endar's request for an immediate divorce was granted and has been recorded in the registers at the Keep in Kaeleer. He is no longer bound to you in any way—or you to him."

He walked away from their screams and cries and curses.

That camp in Hayll during those awful hours before the purge. Dorothea and Hekatah so sure they were going to have control of the Realms. Marian and Daemonar—and the Sadist—in that place.

He hadn't set foot in Terreille since that time. He hoped with everything in him that he wouldn't have to again.

When he returned to the Dark Altar, Chaosti held out a

flask. He didn't ask what it contained, didn't really care at that moment. He just drank—and then wished he'd asked because his throat burned, his stomach melted, his lungs crisped, and the room did one slow spin before his body burned off enough of the stuff for him not to be staggeringly drunk. Which should have been impossible.

"Too strong?" Chaosti asked.

"Hell's fire, what *is* that?" All right, throat and lungs were working, and his stomach was intact—he hoped. His voice was raspy, but he had one.

"It's been a while, but I attempted to re-create Lord Khardeen's home brew. I thought you might find it beneficial."

"Mother Night." Lucivar handed back the flask. "It's been a long time since something came close to knocking me on my ass."

"This Realm holds bad memories for you."

"Terrible memories."

"Leave them here, Lucivar, and go home to what you've built since then."

Lucivar nodded. Chaosti lit the candles and opened the Gate, and the two of them returned to the Keep in the Shadow Realm.

# TWENTY-ONE

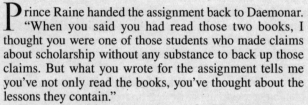

P rince Raine handed the assignment back to Daemonar.
"When you said you had read those two books, I
thought you were one of those students who made claims
about scholarship without any substance to back up those
claims. But what you wrote for the assignment tells me
you've not only read the books, you've thought about the
lessons they contain."

Daemonar felt the question in the pause that followed.
He thought for a moment about how to answer without revealing too much. "My family has a strong connection to
the Keep. Before he became a whisper in the Darkness,
my grandfather had been the assistant historian/librarian.
Once I was old enough to appreciate the library, I was allowed to read anything an adult felt I could understand.
And when I had questions or got myself into trouble, as
Eyrien boys tend to do, I was given things to read that
would address the trouble or teach me the lessons I needed
for the next stage of my training."

Raine had an odd smile. "It's not just book learning to
you, is it?"

"A Warlord Prince's training starts early," Daemonar
replied. "It has to."

Raine leaned back against his desk. "You've been here
a week now. Any problems with your classes?"

"No, sir. A bit different in the rhythm of things, and I've

wondered about the amount of reading each instructor as-
signs since it seems like half the males in the classes don't
even try to read the assignments and the other half can't
finish all of it—including me. But it's the half that tries
and doesn't finish who are criticized, and the ones who are
too busy with social prancing to do any work receive no
reprimand at all." He shrugged. "Not the Eyrien way of
teaching. Then again, the consequences of not learning
how to handle a war blade properly are more severe than
not reading a couple of chapters."

Raine coughed. "I can see the difference."

Daemonar sensed a curiosity in this man, who came
from one of the short-lived races. Living among the Dhemlan race was a new experience, and maybe that allowed
Raine to be less prejudiced about "uneducated warriors"
who settled everything with a fight.

"Would you like to feel the difference?" he asked.

Raine looked alarmed. "What?"

"Titian, Zoey, and I work out with the Eyrien sparring
sticks in the morning before getting ready for classes."

"I couldn't spar."

Daemonar laughed. "No, sir, you couldn't. Not right off,
anyway. But that's not where someone starts. You could
join us for the warm-up moves and observe the sparring."

Raine hesitated. "Instructors aren't supposed to social-
ize with students."

"I've noticed instructors joining students for a ride in
the park or participating in some kind of sport. This
wouldn't be any different."

A smile. "Early, you said? Does that explain your attire
for this tutorial?"

He returned the smile. "It does. Herding girls who want
to try just one more move is a job for a Sceltie, not a brother
who's ignored because he's not allowed to nip."

Raine choked back a laugh. "Then you'd better get
yourself washed and properly attired for your classes.
And . . . I might join you tomorrow morning, just to observe."

Daemonar vanished his assignment and the books, then headed for the dormitory to take a shower and get ready for the more pompous instructors he had to deal with that day.

"The bat is in the shower," Clayton said, hurrying back to where Krellis and Dhuran waited.

Krellis felt his guts rumble. Felt a need that was becoming urgent.

Perfect.

The three of them slipped into the bat's room. One trunk with a few novels and spare clothes. Clayton and Dhuran moved the trunk away from the wall while Krellis pulled all the clothes out of the dresser. The clothes in the closet followed, along with the books in the bookcase.

"Make sure everything is watered down," he told the other two.

After Clayton and Dhuran emptied their bladders, Krellis dropped his pants, squatted over the trunk, and smiled. "Let's give Prince Daemonar a proper welcome."

Securing the loin wrap around his hips, Daemonar left the men's facilities and headed back to his room—and noticed how Krellis, Dhuran, and Clayton hovered nearby, as if waiting for something.

The smell hit him as soon as he walked into his room.

He hurried to the trunk and lifted the lid, then took a step back.

Urine soaked his books and clothes, and in the center of the trunk was a stinking pile of shit.

His temper didn't snap the leash. His lessons with Auntie J. had given him control of a volatile temper that would one day match his father's, but the burning clarity of fury shaped the choice of what he needed to do. Because this wasn't just about him. He recognized that the moment he swung into the hallway and saw the look on Krellis's face. And in that look, he also saw the faces of the younger boys who had been cowed by the school's bullies—younger boys who would be taught to participate in cruelty in order to escape being a victim.

The sun would shine in Hell before a prick-ass like Krellis turned him into a victim.

Daemonar gave no warning when he walked out of his room. He wrapped himself in a Green shield a heartbeat before he grabbed Krellis by the arm and neck and dragged the prick-ass into his room—and shoved Krellis's face into the still-warm shit.

Krellis struggled as Daemonar dragged him back across the room and threw him into the hallway. He used Craft to close the trunk and vanish it, then left his room, not bothering to close the door, and strode through the hallway and out of the dormitory, wearing nothing but the loin wrap.

*Prince Sadi, you're needed at the school,* he called on a Green psychic thread as he headed for the building that held most of the classrooms as well as Lady Fharra's office.

It didn't matter if the Black showed up. Daemonar could, and would, deal with this problem the Eyrien way.

He marched past Lady Fharra's assistant, shoved open the office door, and kept going until he reached the desk. Lady Fharra stood behind the desk and two of the more priggish instructors stood to one side.

He called in the trunk so that it hovered over the desk—and let it fall, smashing the bits and pieces that had been on the desk's surface. Using Craft, he flipped the trunk's lid, revealing the soiled contents.

Lady Fharra stumbled back. The instructors called in handkerchiefs to hold over their noses and mouths.

"What is the meaning of this?" Lady Fharra demanded.

"I'm wondering the same thing," a deep voice crooned from the doorway.

He knew even before he turned and saw the glazed sleepy eyes—saw the sweetly murderous smile. Daemon Sadi was a heartbeat away from the killing edge.

No. It wasn't his uncle or the Warlord Prince of Dhemlan or even the High Lord of Hell who had risen to the killing edge in response to his call.

Daemonar shivered—and hoped the Sadist thought it was from being inadequately dressed.

Sadi glided into the room and looked into the trunk.

"I've just been informed that this Eyrien assaulted another student," one of the instructors said. "A fine boy from a good family. He's been taken to the school's Healer."

"Is that what you did?" Sadi asked too mildly. "Assaulted another boy?"

"The shit belongs to Lord Krellis," Daemonar replied. "I just returned it."

"And the piss?"

*Be careful. Be careful. The Sadist is capable of doing anything.* "I can't say for sure." And he wasn't about to guess right now.

"Well, there are ways to find out."

Sadi called in two glass straws about the length of his hand. Using Craft, he cut out a section of urine-soaked cloth from each end of the trunk's contents, then wrapped the cloth around the straws. Then he slipped witchfire into each straw—and waited as the witchfire burned.

Screams in the corridor. Had to be Dhuran and Clayton coming to find out what would happen to him and report back to Krellis.

*Sir,* Daemonar said, knowing he was dancing on the knife's edge by calling attention to himself. *Uncle, that's enough. Please.*

The Sadist looked at him. Just looked at him. But the witchfire disappeared—and the screaming changed to cries and loud whimpers.

"The pain is quite real, but there is no actual physical damage," Sadi said in a terrifyingly pleasant tone of voice. "This time. Should it become necessary to discipline those two again . . ."

No one was foolish enough to speak.

"This is what is going to happen," Sadi said. "Effective

immediately, my nephew will reside at the family town house and be what you call a day student. You implied that all the students reside at the school. I have since learned that is not the case. So Daemonar will reside with the family and attend classes during the day. You will adjust his schedule to accommodate that." He looked at Fharra and his smile became colder—and crueler. "Should my daughter or niece experience this kind of teasing, you and I and all the instructors will have a little chat, and I expect the survivors to be more vigilant about curbing pranks in the future."

Daemonar felt his knees grow weak. He'd seen a glimpse of this side of his uncle now and then since that day at the Keep when he'd encountered the Sadist, but this was the first time he'd seen the kind of punishment that side of Daemon's temper could, and would, inflict on someone.

"The school will absorb the cost of replacing all the damaged books," Sadi continued. "I will take care of replacing the clothes."

Lady Fharra nodded, too frightened to do anything else.

"Prince Yaslana, with me." Sadi walked out of the office and kept going.

Daemonar matched his stride as they headed for the men's dormitory.

After a minute, he felt the difference in the man as Uncle Daemon huffed out a laugh and said, "I know about Eyrien pride, but at least put a warming spell around yourself so you don't freeze your balls."

He hadn't wanted to do anything that might cause the Sadist to slip the leash. Now he gladly wrapped a warming spell around himself.

"*Do* you have anything to wear besides that loin wrap?"

Such a commonplace question. "Nothing clean, but I have the clothes I was wearing when I was sparring with Titian and Zoey this morning. And I do have a couple changes of clothes in my room at the town house."

The SaDiablo town house was actually two residences with a common wall and connecting doors in the servants' areas to make it easy for the staff to take care of both halves of the building. His grandfather had used one side for guests while the family resided in the other side. Now the Yaslana line of the family used one side and the SaDiablo branch used the other—and guests were tucked into rooms on either side.

"You might be on your own there at times," Daemon said.

"I'll be fine." And "on his own" still meant under Helton's watchful eyes.

"If that Warlord, Krellis, had done that to Titian's things . . ."

"I would have killed him."

Daemon said nothing until they reached Daemonar's room in the dormitory. "Then I accept the line you drew in terms of punishment." He looked around. "Come on, boyo. Let's gather the rest of your things and get you settled in the town house. Then we'll come back and deal with the rest."

Daemonar pulled on the clothes he'd worn for sparring and quickly gathered the belongings that hadn't been damaged. He felt a shaky relief that Uncle Daemon had stepped away from the place where the Sadist dwelled, but he wondered if there was a way to gently suggest that his uncle needed to spend a day at the Keep.


Daemon felt Surreal's presence as the horse-drawn cab stopped in front of the town house. He downed the brandy in the snifter, then poured himself another drink.

He'd been spending too much time in Amdarh, being available if the children needed help. He didn't have the private suite of rooms here where he could siphon off the sexual heat that constantly threatened to overwhelm his staff. He didn't have a place where he could relax the leashes for a day or two in order to fully be what he was.

The constriction had begun to chafe, but he hadn't

wanted to be that far away. And today had proved that he needed to be here. Daemonar had handled things in typical Eyrien fashion—and that had to be a shock to the pricks who had thought he'd submit to their brand of "teasing." The boy had handled his contemporaries, but he'd needed someone at his back to deal with the adults at the school.

Surreal walked into the sitting room, where Daemon waited, and stopped a step away from the door Helton closed behind her.

"Sadi?" She sounded wary.

"There was an incident at the school."

"Jaenelle Saetien?"

"The girls are fine, but Daemonar will be residing at the town house from now on and going to the school for his classes."

"What happened?"

He told her about the trunk and the soiled clothes and books. He told her Daemonar's response to having his things ruined. He told her about the line he'd drawn with Lady Fharra. Then he said, "Lucivar is on his way here. When he arrives I'll go to the Keep. I might not be back for a day or two."

Surreal took one step toward him, then stopped again, clearly unwilling to get any closer. "Why is Lucivar coming here?"

"I scared the boy. He needs to talk to his father." Daemon watched the muscles in her throat as she swallowed.

"Did you hurt him?" she asked.

It stung that she would ask the question, but she needed to ask, both as the wife who was his sword and shield and as his second-in-command. "No. Not him."

"Mother Night." She gathered herself, then walked up to him, took the snifter, and drank the rest of the brandy. "You don't need to wait. I'll keep an eye on things until Lucivar arrives."

"I appreciate that, but I do need to wait for him." Because he needed to tell his brother everything that happened today—including the things he hadn't told Surreal.

He saw the change in her eyes, in her breathing. He was aware of the change in her body's scent—aroused and wet and ready to be claimed. But that was her physical response to his sexual heat, not true desire for the man. Right now she felt more fear than lust. He knew how much courage it took for her to approach him when the Sadist was so close to the surface.

Surreal shuddered. "I'm sorry, Sadi."

"No need to be." Right now even a kiss on the cheek from him would feel more like a threat than a comfort, so he stepped back. "I'll be in my study until Lucivar arrives."

He went to his study and put Black shields around the room and a Red lock on the door. Some protection for Surreal and the staff. Not enough protection, but some. He could, and would, do that much for them.

Surreal used one of the passageways in the back part of the town house to enter the other half. Her legs shook as she climbed the stairs to the bedrooms. With no one else on this side except a footman, the Green wasn't hard to find.

She tapped on the open bedroom door. Daemonar looked up from the books he was arranging and smiled.

"Your father is on his way," she said.

He sprang to his feet. "Hell's fire, I didn't think I was in *that* much trouble."

She laughed out of sheer relief. Whatever Daemon had done that had scared Daemonar hadn't gone bone deep. "I'm guessing you have something to discuss with Lucivar about the change in living arrangements."

Wariness, which she hadn't expected.

"Uncle Daemon said we're going to keep the room in the dormitory as a place where I can go between classes. He's going to put protection spells in the walls that will weave into a Green shield that I will control. I'll have to do my own housekeeping since the school's staff won't be able to come in when I'm not there, but I can borrow a carpet broom and some . . ."

She whooped, and that made him scowl.

"Five silver marks," she said.

His scowl deepened. "What?"

"I bet you five silver marks that you can't 'borrow' a carpet broom from the town house without also 'borrowing' the maid who has her hands wrapped around the handle."

"My mother is a hearth witch. I know how to clean."

"Dream on, boyo."

"Fine. I'll take the bet."

"In that case, I'll see you at dinner."

She'd made the bet to help Daemonar shake off whatever fear he still had about whatever had happened at the school. As she returned to the SaDiablo side of the town house, Surreal wondered if the boy had taken the bet in order to help her shake off her own fear.

The Ebon-gray arrived at the town house. An hour later, the Black departed.

Daemonar stared at a chapter he was supposed to read for tomorrow's class and waited for a summons that didn't come until Lucivar gave him a psychic tap and told him it was time for dinner.

Uncomfortable subjects were set aside, which meant no one asked about the school. Instead, Lucivar and Surreal talked about the SaDiablo vineyards and the book Jillian had written, which had been purchased by Uncle Daemon's publishing house. Talking and teasing to cover the fact that Aunt Surreal felt uneasy about the most lethal side of Uncle Daemon's temper coming to the surface at the school.

As soon as dinner was over, Surreal excused herself and went to her room. He and Lucivar walked over to the sitting room in the other side of the town house.

Lucivar poured two fingers of whiskey into two glasses, then handed one to him before settling into a chair designed for Eyriens. "Tell me what happened today. All of it."

"Didn't Uncle Daemon tell you?"

"He did. Now I want to hear it from you."

He told his father all of it, starting with the warm-up and sparring with Titian and Zoey, his meeting with Prince Raine, and his reaction when he returned to his room after his shower and realized what Krellis and the other two boys had done. He tried to be matter-of-fact about his decision to summon the Warlord Prince of Dhemlan because Uncle Daemon had told him to report any trouble at the school and how that wasn't the side of his uncle's temper that had responded to his summons. Finally, he told Lucivar what the Sadist had said—and done.

He sipped the whiskey. A far better blend than the stuff Tamnar had purchased. "Before I walked into the dining room, I heard Aunt Surreal tell you that I might have danced with the Sadist." He'd heard the phrase before, but now he had some idea of what it meant.

"Have you left anything out?" Lucivar asked.

"No, sir."

"Then you didn't dance with the Sadist. You brushed against that side of Daemon's temper, saw a little of what he can do, but his attention and his rage weren't aimed at you."

That attention had been aimed at him once when he'd been in the Queen's part of the Keep. Auntie J. had stopped whatever might have happened, but he remembered how it had felt when the Sadist had focused on him and seen rival or adversary or enemy.

A pause. Then Lucivar said, "What you also saw was that the Sadist trusted your judgment when you asked him to stop. He trusted that the punishment and pain he'd inflicted sufficiently balanced the offense because you told him it was enough. He doesn't offer that trust to many people."

"Did Aunt Surreal ever dance with the Sadist?" He knew that Daemon and Surreal had a different kind of marriage from his parents. If Aunt Surreal couldn't cope with being around the Sadist, that would explain a lot about their living arrangements.

"The Sadist as lover is playful, terrifying, and magnificent," Lucivar replied. "And he's focused on giving pleasure rather than pain. But even at his mildest, he can be overwhelming. Surreal has brushed against those same edges that you did today, and she experienced the Sadist as lover—once—but she's never really danced with the Sadist."

Daemonar studied his father. "But you have."

Lucivar downed the whiskey, then poured himself another glass. "Yeah, I have. And I am one of the few who have danced with him and survived."

"Why did the Sadist show up at the school instead of the Warlord Prince of Dhemlan? I thought Uncle Daemon would come in an official capacity, but not . . ." He didn't know how to explain.

"That's the question, isn't it?" Lucivar hesitated. "That day at the Keep when you saw the Sadist for the first time? Daemon saw something in a tangled web. He doesn't remember what he saw, just that you're somehow connected. He's been preparing for war ever since. *We've* been preparing for war, and that trouble with Orian makes me think that war is on the horizon." He blew out a breath. "I also think you're the reason the Sadist walked into Fharra's office. Something about you being at the school calls to that side of him because whatever was in that web connects the two of you. But that means you and the girls need to be careful."

"We will."

Lucivar set his glass on a marble coaster. "You spar with Titian and Zoey. What about Jaenelle Saetien?"

Daemonar hesitated. "She's made new friends since she's been at school. They think sparring is a rube activity, so she doesn't want to join us and have them make fun of her."

"Do they make fun of you?"

Hearing that matter-of-fact tone of voice, and recognizing it as a warning sign that Lucivar's temper was straining the leash, Daemonar hesitated again. "It's hard to feel insulted when I don't think any better of them. There are some boys who would be interested in learning to spar, but they're intimidated by Krellis and his pack, as well as by the coven of malice."

Damn. He hadn't intended to say the name he'd given Jaenelle Saetien's new friends.

"Coven of malice," Lucivar said softly. "Did you mention that to Daemon?"

"No." And he wasn't going to.

Lucivar said nothing for a moment. Then, "Anything you want to do with the rest of the evening?"

Daemonar smiled. "Spar with someone who's better than me. I'm getting soft with no one but Titian as a partner, although Zoey is becoming more of a challenge."

Laughing, Lucivar pushed out of the chair. "That suits me."

Sweating and working against a man who was brilliant when he put his hand to any weapon—Daemonar couldn't think of a better way to spend an evening.

Daemon slowly unbuttoned his shirt and let it slide off his shoulders. He'd enjoyed a simple meal of soup, bread, and cheese, along with a bottle of wine from the SaDiablo vineyards. As he ate, he'd let the leashes loosen and slip away from his power, his temper, and his sexual heat. Now he let the last leash slip away—and the Sadist drew in a full breath, reveled in the feel of cool air against his skin as he finished undressing, and looked forward to slipping into a warm bed.

Something at the school. Every time he brushed against the boy at the school, he brushed against . . . something.

As his fingers traced the thin raised scars on his right biceps, he felt comforted by this tangible promise that, even at his darkest and most lethal, he wasn't alone.

Getting into bed, he settled on his belly with his arms folded under his pillow—and waited. He must have dozed off because he came back to wakefulness when he felt a weight on his ass and two hooves planted on either side of his spine.

Daemon smiled and murmured, "I wondered when you would show up."

"Sometimes solitude serves a mood better than company," Witch replied.

"But it doesn't always supply answers. You know, but you won't tell me."

"What I know is that you're the one who will recognize the danger."

"The boy seems to call to the Sadist, seems to call a wisp of memory closer to the surface." A huff of laughter. "He stirred up the school's pricks right and proper."

"Did you ever doubt he was Lucivar's son?" she asked.

"Never. And today he proved it."

"Oh, dear." She waited a beat. "Aren't you going to tell me?"

He thought for a moment. "No."

He could feel her sapphire-eyed stare focused on the back of his neck.

He rolled over slowly enough for her shadow to float to one side and settle next to him. When he was modestly covered up to his chest, he touched the candle-light on the table next to the bed, adjusting the illumination to softly light the room.

"Daemonar will tell you if he feels inclined," Daemon said.

She stared at him.

"No. I'm not giving in. But if you want to be entertained, I can recite a very long nonsense poem that was written by a pack of Scelties."

Witch blinked. "Why would you memorize something like that?"

"You say that like I had a choice." He raised his hand and wiggled his fingers. "Fingers hold a pencil better than paws, and I got cornered into being the scribe on my last visit to the Sceltie school. Are you sure you don't want to hear it?"

"More than sure."

The Black power he needed to drain from his Jewels in

order to keep his mind and sanity intact, the sharp edge of temper, and the sexual heat were quietly absorbed by a power far darker and deeper than his own. Knowing he was loved and accepted by his Queen if by no one else, the Sadist extinguished the candle-light and slept.

# TWENTY-TWO

Surreal rapped on the study door and walked in, her attention on the gloves she was pulling on. "Sadi, I'm heading out to . . ." She looked up and stopped talking, stopped moving—and wondered what had put that look of baffled concern on his face. "What's wrong?"

He held up a note. "Titian needs to see me at my earliest convenience, which is apparently this evening. She's already informed the school that she'll be having dinner here with us."

"With you," Surreal corrected. "I'm heading out to check on the girl who gutted that prick-ass with her bare hands. I won't be back until tomorrow at the earliest since I'll stop by a couple of the family's estates." And there were some other things she wanted to check out before voicing her suspicions to the Warlord Prince of Dhemlan—or whatever side of Daemon's temper responded to what she said.

"You're the one who is standing in for Lucivar when it comes to rules and decisions," she added cheerfully—and then added silently, *Thank the Darkness I'm not involved in that. Dealing with one adolescent girl is quite enough.*

"Daemonar is having dinner with Beron and a handful of friends from the theater company, so he won't be here either," Daemon said.

"Maybe that's why your earliest convenience is this

evening. Titian must have dashed off that note and had it delivered as soon as she'd heard about her brother's plans."

Daemon stared at her, then muttered, "Sweet Darkness."

Since his sexual heat was still down to a sensual warmth after his visit to the Keep, Surreal walked up to him and gave him a wifely kiss on the lips. "You can tell me all about it when I get back. Are you going to be here or at the Hall?"

He gave her a dry smile. "That will depend on Titian."

A flutter of anticipation swept through the town house's staff.

Since he'd let his awareness spread out beyond the town house to pick up the emotional currents and psychic scents of the people coming and going within the square where his family resided, Daemon knew the moment Titian paid the driver of the street-coach and walked up the steps to knock on the door. He tidied the papers on his desk, capped his pen, and tried to convince himself—again—that it couldn't be *that* serious. Maybe some art supplies that weren't within the budget she'd been given or . . . something else that was urgent for a girl her age but would seem trivial to an adult.

He'd come to expect moodiness from Jaenelle Saetien, but he hadn't seen those swings in temper from Titian, so he didn't know what to expect.

He didn't like not knowing what to expect.

A quick knock on the study door before Helton opened it and Titian walked in.

"Hello, witchling." Daemon came around the desk to accept the hands she held out to him and give her a kiss on the cheek. "You're looking well." He glanced at Helton. "Dinner in an hour?"

"Yes, Prince."

The door closed, leaving him alone with his quiet, talented niece . . . who looked well, yes, but also looked a little different. She'd put up her hair, and her dress, while demure, had more style than what he was used to seeing on Titian. It wasn't quite *her* style, but he was definitely looking at a girl growing into a woman.

"Should we . . . ?" he began, thinking they could sit in the social area of the room, where he visited with people or read for pleasure.

Titian perched on the edge of a chair in front of his desk and looked at him expectantly.

Whatever she wanted to talk about was more official than social. Damn.

Resigned, Daemon took the other seat. "What's on your mind?"

She stared at him for much too long before blurting out, "Permission before action."

Hell's fire, Mother Night, and may the Darkness be merciful.

It was going to happen. Of course it was going to happen. But why in the name of Hell did it have to happen on *his* watch?

"Who?" He was pleased that he sounded interested yet calm.

"Zoey." Titian gave him a wobbly smile. "Lady Zoela."

Daemon blinked. *Not* what he expected.

"Uncle Daemon . . ."

Realizing he had to say something before she took his silence as a negative answer, he delicately cleared his throat. "I know what you're going to say. You're going to tell me that since you both have breasts, it's not like you'd be seeing anything you haven't seen before."

Although, since she had brothers, the same could be said for her knowing about the male body.

He leaned toward her and closed her trembling hands in his. "But, my darling, the same rules for the first stage of romance are going to apply. That means kissing and touching are permitted from collarbone to crown of head and from elbows to fingertips. If any other body parts start to connect, you and I are going to have trouble." He released her hands and sat back. "However, since you and Zoey are responsible young women, I will extend the touching to include assistance with buttons and zippers and clothing that laces up or ties—as long as you're careful about where you put your hands. Understood?"

"Understood." Her eyes were tear-bright and her face seemed flooded with too much emotion. "Thank you, Uncle Daemon. Thank you!"

He was halfway out of the chair when she leaped on him with enough force to knock him back in the chair and lift the front legs off the floor. If he hadn't used Craft to hold the chair upright, they would have gone over backward and landed in a heap.

After getting everything and everyone upright and the correct number of feet solidly on the floor, Daemon took a step back. "Why didn't Zoey come with you to ask permission?" His father had always required both people's presence when making a request of a sexual nature. Saetan had done it simply to be sure that both people were willing participants. So it bothered him that Zoey hadn't been with Titian for such a significant moment.

"She's talking to her grandparents and getting their permission," Titian replied. "And . . ." She hesitated, then added in a rush, "And Zoey respects you so much and your opinion matters so much, it would have crushed her if you were upset or angry or disappointed in her. In us."

"Well, she doesn't have to worry about that." He smiled. "Your hair looks lovely that way, but I think a couple of pins have come loose. Why don't you go upstairs and freshen up? I expect Helton will be announcing dinner very soon."

When she didn't follow him to the door, he returned to where she stood staring at him. Apparently there was more.

"Uncle Daemon?"

"Yes?" He slipped his hands in his trouser pockets and waited.

"Mother says you have a very good eye for women's clothes."

"I like to think so."

"The thing is . . . I'm good with colors, but I don't know . . . And some of the girls at the school have started wearing all this lace and so many ruffles . . . Who wants to wear rows of ruffles around their hips?"

"No one with taste," he murmured, wondering what might be in Jaenelle Saetien's closet at school.

"Exactly! I don't want to look ridiculously girlie, but I don't want to look like a little girl either. And neither does Zoey." Expectant, hopeful stare.

It had been a long time since Surreal had felt comfortable receiving clothing of any kind from him. Maybe that would change when his sexual heat diminished with age, but that would take centuries. And Jaenelle Saetien didn't want his help with anything right now.

He missed accompanying a woman to a dressmaker's and playing with styles and fabrics to help her look her best. But here was his niece, asking for exactly that kind of help.

"When used correctly, ruffles and lace can be effective accents," he said. He waged a tiny battle with himself before adding, "Seductive accents."

"Really?"

Lucivar was going to kill him flatter than dead. Ah, well. Everything had a price.

"Really. If you like, I would be happy to escort you and Zoey to a dressmaker who created a lot of outfits for Lady Angelline. She didn't like excessively girlie clothes either."

Titian beamed at him.

He walked her to the study door, then handed her over to Helton . . . who had been hovering nearby. Which made Daemon wonder exactly what his staff knew that he didn't.

Something to find out later. Right now . . .

He wrote a quick note to Lady Zhara, informing the Queen of Amdarh that he had no objection to this budding romance. He barely waited for the ink to dry before he folded the paper and secured it with red wax and his personal seal. Then he left the study to look for someone to deliver the message.

Helton once more hovered in the entrance hall.

Daemon held up the note. "I need to get this to Lady Zhara as quickly as possible."

"As soon as you and Lady Titian are seated for dinner, I'll take it myself," Helton replied.

Before he could comment about that, someone knocked on the door. Vigorously.

Helton hurried to open it. Lord Weston strode in, then stopped when he saw Daemon.

"Do you object?" Weston asked brusquely.

"Are you asking for yourself or for Lady Zhara?" Daemon countered.

"Both."

He held out the note. "I have no objections. There are discussions that need to be had tonight within the family, but I can meet with Lady Zhara in the morning if that's convenient."

Weston took Daemon's note and held out the one he'd brought. "I believe that will suit the Lady."

*Did you suspect anything?* Daemon asked on a psychic spear thread.

*Art and Titian have been part of Zoey's conversation for decades, so her talking about either one wasn't unusual,* Weston replied. *The only thing I've noticed is that Jaenelle Saetien is mentioned less since the three of them started school.* He shrugged. *Girls grow up, and some friendships fade for lack of common ground.*

Why was there no longer common ground? Or was it as simple as Zoey and Titian growing closer in a way that excluded others, at least for a while?

"What about you?" Daemon turned to Helton as soon as Weston left. "Did you suspect anything? Something that maybe you should have mentioned?"

Helton hesitated. *Hesitated.* "Lady Titian told the maid

who looks after Lady Surreal's clothes that she'd like to get a couple of new outfits and asked what material might suit her figure and Eyrien wings and which dressmaker made Lady Surreal's clothes. And she asked about suggestions for new hairstyles. But young Ladies do those things, don't they, even if there is no hint of romantic interest?"

Daemon suppressed a sigh. It seemed that not only did his staff have opinions; they all had a romantic streak. "If anything the children asked about might be a cause of concern . . ."

"I would tell you at once."

"Thank you, Helton." He had to be satisfied with that. "I'm going to have some things to deal with after dinner, so I'd like you to escort Titian back to the school."

"With pleasure, Prince."

As Daemon went upstairs to freshen up before dinner, he thought about how much Helton doted on the females in the family. Surreal had been the butler's favorite for centuries, and she allowed Helton to fuss over her and pamper her in ways she didn't tolerate from anyone else. Marian, too, received a large share of attention when she visited Amdarh.

Judging by the dishes that were presented at dinner that evening—all of them among Titian's favorites—Daemon realized that, according to some measure by the town house's staff, Lucivar's quiet daughter had ascended to the level of care given to a woman rather than the permitted indulgences given to a girl.


Daemonar reviewed his evening as he knocked on the front door of the SaDiablo side of the town house. While he was closer to Mikal in age, he'd always liked Beron, who had settled into the role of older cousin after becoming Uncle Daemon's legal ward. Tonight he discovered that he also liked Beron's friends a lot more than most of the boys he'd met at the school. They were funny and opinionated and passionate about the theater, whether they worked in the theater or were training in some other profession. They were full of noisy enthusiasm, and at one point three of the young men stood and sang an impromptu song about the dishes the chef had made that evening.

It became clear that patrons of this particular dining house were used to being serenaded about the joys of a properly cooked steak or delicately spiced potatoes—or being entertained by a snippet from a play in rehearsal.

What made them stand out in comparison to the boys at the school was their interest in him. What was he studying? Had he ever seen the dragons who lived on the Fyreborn Islands? Beron used the Eyrien sparring stick he'd been given years ago as a way to exercise and stay fit for the more demanding and active roles. Several of them had also acquired sparring sticks and had learned the exercises, but that wasn't the same as actually sparring with someone who had been doing it since he could stand on his own feet. Would he be willing to work with them when they all had a free day?

Some of those young men came from aristo families. Some did not. A couple of them wore darker Jewels. Most did not.

If there were bullies in the theater like there were at the school, they weren't among Beron's friends.

Daemonar smiled at Helton when the butler opened the door. "My uncle asked to see me when I got home."

"He's in his study."

Of course he was. The town house was more Aunt Surreal's residence, so Uncle Daemon tried to keep his presence contained to his study and his bedroom.

He walked into the study and spotted his uncle in one of the comfy reading chairs.

Daemon closed the book and set it on the round table beside the chair. "Did you and Beron have a good dinner?"

"We did. An entertaining one with some of his friends from the theater." He studied Daemon Sadi and felt his stomach sink. "Sir? Is there a problem?" The request to see him wouldn't have been casual if there had been an accident or serious illness within the family. But *something* had happened.

"No, there's no problem—and you are not going to make a fuss about this."

That didn't sound good. "About what?"

"Titian had dinner with me tonight, and we talked about permission before action."

"Per— *What?*" He stared at Daemon. "You said no, of course."

Daemon slowly rose from his chair. "As a matter of fact, I did give my permission."

He wanted to punch his uncle. He really, really did. But challenging a Black-Jeweled Warlord Prince was just plain stupid. "Which one of those aristo curs—"

"Lady Zoela."

He could have sworn that his brain spun a couple of times. "What?"

"Zoey," Daemon said patiently.

"Zoey is a girl."

"We've noticed that."

"But . . ." This study had an annoying lack of room to pace, so he circled the open floor space as he tried to regain his balance. "Is this our fault?"

Daemon blinked. "I beg your pardon?"

"Is Titian attracted to a girl because of us, because of the way we are?"

Daemon delicately scratched an eyebrow with one long black-tinted nail. "Boyo, even for a man in our family, that is an arrogant statement."

"You know what I mean."

"No, I don't."

"We're bossy and volatile and there's the sexual heat everyone else has to deal with, and we're born to stand on killing fields, and that makes us different from other men. That's a lot for a girl to live with."

It was Daemon's smile that warned him he was close to getting a whack upside the head.

"Titian adores her father, and she's fond of you most of

the time," Daemon said. "So if I were you, I would not voice those reasons to anyone else."

Daemonar spun around and headed for the door. He felt the Black lock even before his hand closed on the knob—and he felt the chill in the room warning him that he had provoked Daemon's temper. "I need some air. I need to think. Please."

The room chilled a little more. Then the Black lock vanished.

He opened the door and rushed out of the town house.

Needed to think. Needed to talk to someone who might understand.

He spread his wings and flew to another part of the city. A few minutes later, he knocked on the door of Beron's flat.


"Well, that was disappointing," Daemon muttered as he poured himself a brandy. He'd expected surprise, certainly. Hell's fire, *he'd* been surprised. But he hadn't expected the boy's total refusal to accept Titian's choice.

He could keep Daemonar leashed to some degree. But Lucivar . . .

He swallowed the brandy, then reached for his brother on an Ebon-gray psychic thread. *Prick?*

*Bastard?*

*Am I interrupting something?* Considering the lateness of the hour, he could be interrupting something.

Amusement. *Nothing that will earn you a fist in the ribs.*

Would that be true after this conversation? *We need to talk.*

*About?*

*Permission before action.*

A pause. *Daemonar is interested in someone?*

*Not Daemonar. Titian.*

A long pause. Even the distance between Amdarh and Ebon Rih couldn't mask the heat of rising temper. *Who?*

Daemon sighed and prepared to fight. *Zoey.*

A *long* pause. Then Lucivar said, *Huh. You drew the lines?*

*I did.*

*I'll be there in a couple of days.*

*Luci—*

Lucivar had already broken the link between them.

Daemon returned to his chair and picked up the book. Instead of reading, he sat for a long time and thought about the many flavors of love—and thought about what it would mean to someone like Titian if her family wouldn't accept her feelings.

Beron didn't immediately agree with him, but he listened while Daemonar told him about Titian and poured out all his concerns about her reasons for choosing Zoey.

"I could use something stronger than that," he said as he watched Beron prepare some kind of tea.

"Maybe you could, but you're getting a cup of the Lady's blend of tea," Beron replied with a smile. "What do you think Jaenelle Angelline would say about your . . . opinions?"

"Thank the Darkness, she is never going to find out." At least, *he* wasn't going to tell her.

Beron poured the tea into two large mugs and set one in front of Daemonar before taking a seat on the opposite side of the table. "Jaenelle and I were good friends for most of her life. When she was fifteen, we were in school together for a short while. When my mother was killed, I was still a youth too young to live on my own, and Jaenelle was thirty-five. She and Daemon stood against my grandfather and became legal guardians for Mikal and me, assuring that we could follow our dreams. She was the reason I was able to come to Amdarh and study at the school for dramatic arts.

"My grandfather isn't a bad man. He loved my mother, but he didn't want *her* son on the stage. She was a Queen after all, and he had been fiercely proud of her. He would arrange to meet me in the city or summon me to have dinner with him, but every meeting was a heavy-handed attempt to get me to come live with him so that he could shape me into what *he* thought I should be. Eventually, I stopped meeting him, but I sent him tickets to every opening night and looked for him, hoping he'd come just once to see me perform and understand how much I love acting. But he never came. Not once. Jaenelle and Daemon came to every opening night."

Beron drank some of his tea. "While I was in school, and all the years after, I would come to the town house once a week for dinner. Sometimes both of them were in residence, sometimes one or the other. Jaenelle always knew when I'd wrangled with my grandfather, and she would make up this blend of tea to quiet the mind and soothe the heart. Sometimes we'd talk. Sometimes we just sat and drank this tea—and I would feel better.

"When I got out of school and rented my first flat, proclaiming my independence, or as much independence as one can have in this family, Jaenelle took me to the tea broker—a small shop crammed with jars of teas and herbs. It's still in business. I can show you where to find it if you're interested. Anyway, she asked the teaman to make up two jars of the Lady's blend." Beron smiled. "Jaenelle's special blend that she had created from the teas in his shop. It didn't taste quite the same when I made it for myself. Her handling the tea added something extra, something that was just her."

Dangerous ground because he heard a yearning beneath the words. "Do you miss her?" Daemonar asked.

"I do. But when I'm feeling heartsore for some reason, I make a cup of this tea, and it's like she's here again, listening to what my heart can't put into words."

"What do you think she would say about Titian?"

Beron gave him a long look. "Your sister is quiet and she's sensitive—and she has the lesson of your father's reaction to Jillian's first romance."

"*Everyone* remembers my father's reaction to seeing Lord Dillon put a hand on Jillian's breast."

"Exactly. Titian isn't the kind of girl who would take a chance of upsetting her father—or her uncle. Daemonar, you don't know if the girls are thinking of hot petting and kisses that involve tongues . . ."

He choked.

". . . or if they don't want to get into trouble for holding hands and brushing each other's hair. I think Jaenelle would tell you that this is the moment when you could lose your sister's trust, and you have to decide if this is so important to you that you'll step away from Titian."

"I'm not stepping away," Daemonar snarled. "But she'll know that I'm not easy about this. Not yet, anyway."

Beron called in two ticket-sized pieces of heavy paper and set them on the table. "An art exhibit that is showcasing new work but also is displaying some very old, very rare paintings. Each ticket is for one person and an escort. If you want to let Titian know you're standing with her, even if you don't understand her choices—yet—you'll invite her and Zoey to attend this exclusive preview."

"Me go to an art show? I'd rather be stabbed with a fork."

"I know. So does Titian. That's why the invitation will mean a lot."

Daemonar drank his tea. He could go up to the Keep and ask Auntie J. what she thought. He could do that. But he figured her advice wouldn't differ from Beron's.

Then he looked at the tickets. Had to be expensive if they were for an exclusive preview. "Who were you going to take to this preview? You wouldn't have bought the tickets on the chance that you'd need them."

"Who doesn't matter," Beron replied with a trace of bitterness. "It turned out she had targeted me as a way to get close enough to rub up against other members of the family."

For a moment, Daemonar forgot to breathe. "Hell's fire, Uncle Daemon would have killed her."

Beron nodded. "Best if we keep that between us, all right?"

"All right." He sighed. "I'll invite Titian and Zoey, but . . ." He wasn't going to beg. He wasn't.

Beron laughed softly. "I do want to see that exhibit, so I will stand as the other escort."

"Thank the Darkness."

Beron vanished the tickets and took the mugs to the sink. "Go home, cousin. Make peace with your uncle and get some sleep."

Good advice. He hoped Uncle Daemon would be in the mood for peace.


Daemonar returned before Helton locked up for the night. At least the boy had that much sense.

What surprised Daemon was the tentative rap on the study door. "Come in."

Daemonar stepped inside and closed the door, but kept the room's length between them.

*Not drunk,* Daemon decided, *and not in a fighting mood.*

"Zoey's a Queen," Daemonar said.

"She is," Daemon agreed.

"A Queen's triangle is made up of three males to balance the power between genders—Steward, Master of the Guard, and Consort."

"Or First Escort. But yes, that is the structure of a court, and it does not, cannot, change."

"What happens to Titian when Zoey sets up her court?"

Daemon closed his book and set it aside. "There are a lot of years between now and the day when Zoey forms an official court. Some Queens have a Consort and a husband who are not the same man. Some Queens have a First Escort whose duty ends at the bedroom door, and a husband whose relationship with her is personal and outside of the court." He sighed. "I don't know what will happen, boyo. They're very young. First love doesn't always mean forever love."

Daemonar's wings opened and closed, slight movements that usually meant he was agitated about something. "Beron and I are going to take Titian and Zoey to an exclusive art exhibit."

Daemon smiled—and saw his nephew shiver. "Beron finally realized the bitch was using him to get her feet under the SaDiablo table?"

"It wasn't her feet she wanted under something," Daemonar muttered.

"I see," Daemon said too softly.

"I didn't mean . . ."

The men in the family needed to be able to talk to one another, needed to be able to confide in one another. He wouldn't damage the strength of the bond between Daemonar and Beron by going after the bitch.

But the High Lord of Hell wouldn't forget about her either, and someday she and he would have a little chat.

"Lucivar will be here in a couple of days."

"Did you tell him?" Daemonar asked.

"I told him. He didn't sound impressed."

Daemonar laughed reluctantly. "Since he can't promise to rip off a cock and shove it down the offender's throat, what do you suppose he'll use as a threat?"

Daemon pushed out of the chair and walked to the door, then waited for Daemonar to open it before saying, "Knowing your father, I'm sure he'll think of something."

# TWENTY-THREE

———◈———

Surreal turned her cup so that the handle faced her left hand. She lowered her right hand to her lap and called in her sight-shielded stiletto. Whoever was approaching her table at this coffee shop was making considerable effort to avoid attracting attention.

In her experience, sneaky usually equaled enemy.

She created a tight Gray shield around herself, sipped her coffee, and waited.

The person who slipped into the chair opposite hers was female, felt like an Opal Jewel—and was sight-shielded.

An Opal aural shield went up around the table, keeping anything that was said private.

"I heard you've been asking about girls who were broken on their Virgin Night," the woman said.

The voice had a husky, sexual allure, but Surreal had the impression the speaker was young enough not to have made the Offering to the Darkness. Which made the Opal the speaker's Birthright Jewel. And that made her unknown visitor a potentially powerful witch when she reached her mature strength.

"You have a problem with that, sugar?" Surreal kept her face turned away from the rest of the room. The Blood in the coffee shop would detect the aural shield and might already know the identity of the sight-shielded witch, but there was no reason to draw more attention to this chat than necessary.

"I've made some discreet inquiries and heard that you established a place, a sanctuary, where young women—witches—can go after their lives have been . . . damaged."

The inquiries must have been very discreet if the people who worked at the sanctuary or on the nearby SaDiablo estate hadn't realized someone was sniffing around.

"I repeat," Surreal said. "You have a problem with that?"

"No. I have someone I'd like you to consider if there is room for another person."

"I'm listening."

"She's a friend of mine. She's not aristo or a Sister of the Hourglass . . ."

That told Surreal the speaker was both.

". . . but she would have been a strong witch—and she was, and is, a person with a strong moral code."

*Mother Night.* "She was deliberately broken?"

"Yes. 'The girl lusted for a cock. What was the boy to do?'"

"Did she lust for that particular cock?"

The speaker made a disparaging sound. "The first time he suggested she have some fun under him, she said no, thank you. Then she said no, loudly and in front of witnesses. And then . . ."

A flash of anger rattled the dishes on the table before the speaker regained control. "And then several of us were invited to an outdoor party, hosted by the aristo family whose son didn't want to keep his cock behind his zipper. My friend didn't want to go—there was something odd about her being invited in the first place—but her father insisted."

Surreal felt cold. She'd heard this story before. But not in Kaeleer. Not in Dhemlan. "Your friend ate or drank something and began to feel strange. Then someone, probably not the cock, helped her to someplace a bit private where she could rest."

"She doesn't remember much after that. Images. Then she was tied down and gagged, and a hood was pulled over her head. Then he came. I think he hit her with a belt, judging by the welts I saw. Hit her buttocks, her legs. He put a hand over her face, blocking her ability to breathe. Just a few seconds at a time, but over and over. She tried to use Craft, she tried to use raw power to strike back, but she said she couldn't find it—and he was just a little bit stronger. Just enough. And when she was too frightened to think, that's when he did the rest . . . and broke into her body and broke her power. Shattered her ability to wear her Birthright Jewel, and destroyed the potential of whoever she could have been."

"She went home and told her parents?"

"No. She came to my home, and my parents and I took her to the District Queen to have the Queen's Healer make a record of the damage. She couldn't name the boy. She hadn't *seen* him, and all his friends swore he hadn't gone near her that afternoon."

"What did her father say?"

"He said she'd been acting the slut, and it wasn't the boy's fault if she'd ended up broken," the speaker said bitterly. "Of course, his wife was wearing new, expensive clothes shortly after that, and he had plenty of money to toss around on wagers. For a while. Then that aristo family left the village, and the wife was no longer able to buy expensive clothes and he was struggling to pay off his bets. Lately, he's been making cutting remarks about how a girl who only had one chance of getting pregnant and having a child didn't have much to offer a husband who could help out the family."

Surreal pushed the tea aside, her stomach too queasy to tolerate food or drink. "Anything else?"

Silence. Then, "When he was . . . pounding . . . himself inside her, he said the descendants of Hayll's Hundred Families would rule Dhemlan one day, and he was helping to bring that day about a little sooner."

Hell's fire, Mother Night, and may the Darkness be

merciful. This was a connection to the secret acquisition of Hayllian memorabilia and the other obscenities that were being smuggled into Kaeleer. This was confirmation that at least some of the girls had been broken deliberately, like they'd been broken in Terreille.

But who was the bitch who fancied herself to be the next Dorothea SaDiablo?

"How fast can your friend be ready to leave?"

"Anytime. She'll be running with the clothes on her back and whatever is in her hands."

"She has to be sure, because there's no going back," Surreal said. "Every person who comes to live at the sanctuary . . . A record is made at the Keep as to why the person is there and if her relatives are a danger to her. Or him. There are a few boys there as well."

"I think her father knew," the speaker whispered. "I think the aristo paid him to make sure she would be at the party."

"Have your friend meet me at the edge of the village in an hour. We're running."

"Her father may try to stop you if he realizes she's leaving."

Surreal smiled. "It's been a while since I skinned a man alive, but I haven't forgotten what my mother taught me."


*SADI!*

Daemon surged to his feet, dropping the stack of invitations he'd been reviewing with Holt—an instinctive response to the fury in Surreal's voice.

*Surreal?*

*Where are you?*

*The Hall.*

*Stay there. We need to talk.* She broke the communication thread.

Daemon looked at Holt, who looked at him, wary and wide-eyed.

"Problem?" Holt asked.

"Surreal is heading home, and she is pissed." Daemon resumed his seat. "I don't know if I'm the cause, but she hasn't sounded this angry in a long time. You may want to make yourself scarce until I know what this is about."

"Should I inform Beale to keep the staff away from this part of the Hall?"

"Yes."

Holt stood and gathered his notes. "I guess there's no point deciding on invitations."

"Oh, I'll look at them and make some preliminary decisions."

Once Holt was gone, Daemon leaned back in his chair, crossed his legs at the knees, and steepled his fingers, resting the index fingers against his chin—and wondered if Surreal would walk into his study and aim a crossbow at him to make sure she had his undivided attention.


Daemonar hesitated on the town house's steps, surprised to feel the tug of that fragmented mind.

What was Tersa doing in Amdarh?

The front door of the SaDiablo side of the town house opened. Helton looked at him, then looked toward the park that made up the center of the square. "I think she's been waiting for you."

"For me? Are you sure?" More likely, Tersa would be looking for Uncle Daemon, *her* boy.

"The winged boy's son. I told her you would be home soon. She walked into the park."

Daemonar nodded, then crossed the street. The park had a small fountain that provided drinking water for birds and small animals—and children who couldn't be bothered to go inside when they were thirsty. There were flower beds and benches, stands of trees at either end, and a grassy, open center that had been great for sparring and playing with Scelties or other children.

When he reached the open center, he stood still and

opened his first inner barrier just enough to feel that tug again.

There. Beneath the trees.

He strode to that end of the park, then slowed down. Tersa rarely ventured out of Halaway. The familiar village provided touchstones for her broken mind. Amdarh was too busy, too noisy. If she was here . . .

"Tersa?" he called. "Tersa? It's Daemonar. You wanted to talk to me?"

He waited. He'd learned a long time ago that you couldn't rush Tersa, especially if she was trying to find a path back to the borders of the Twisted Kingdom.

"How many sides does a triangle have?" She stepped from behind a tree and walked up to him, holding out her hand.

How many times over the years had she asked him this question?

Cupping one hand under hers, he used the forefinger of his other hand to draw three lines on the palm of her hand. Over and over and over.

"A triangle has three sides," he said. Before she could contradict him, he added, "But a *Blood* triangle has four sides." As he traced the shape on her palm, he named the sides. "Steward, Master of the Guard, and Consort—and the one who rules all three." He pressed his finger in the center of the triangle to indicate the Queen.

"That is not your triangle," Tersa said. She slipped her hand under his and began tracing lines on his palm. "Father, uncle, nephew. Father, uncle, nephew. Queen's weapons, all. Dangerous. Deadly. Necessary." Her finger kept tracing the lines. "Don't die, young Prince. She will be very displeased if you get careless and die."

Mother Night. "Have you seen me standing on a killing field, Tersa?"

"Love will bring you to that field. Love . . . and betrayal."

She released his hand and stepped back. She looked

around, suddenly shivering as she wrapped her arms around herself. "Is this Draega?"

Draega? A familiar word from a history lesson? Draega was . . . Ah! The capital city of Hayll, in the Realm of Terreille.

Daemonar felt as if the sun had faded without warning.

"No, Tersa." He gently put an arm around her shoulders, hoping he wouldn't frighten her into running. "This is Amdarh, the capital of Dhemlan, in Kaeleer. Your boy's house is right over there." He pointed. "I'm pretty sure there are nutcakes today."

"Nutcakes? I like nutcakes."

"Me too."

"You will share?"

"I will share."

He coaxed her to the town house. After one startled glance, Helton performed all his duties and more, providing the nutcakes and milk—and then contacting Beale on a psychic thread so that the Hall's butler could inform Prince Sadi that his mother was in Amdarh.

Daemonar could have reached his uncle on a Green communication thread, and probably should have. But what he'd been told about Daemon's life in Terreille made him certain that he didn't want to be connected to that formidable mind in any way when Daemon Sadi heard the word "Draega."

Surreal stared into Sadi's glazed, sleepy eyes and felt more fury than fear.

"That's what that obscenity said?" he asked too softly. "The descendants of Hayll's Hundred Families would rule Dhemlan one day, and he was helping to bring that day about a little sooner?"

"That's what the girl remembered. But she was drugged and terrified."

"You think she made it up?"

"No."

"Is the girl safe?"

"She's safe."

"And the witch who sought help for her friend?"

"All the other customers in that coffee shop may have guessed who sat at my table—and why—but if questioned by her family or the District Queen, no one can say they *saw* her talking to me."

"Have the Queens in that Province been negligent?"

She shook her head. "I think the . . . prey . . . is carefully chosen. That girl. She would have been a strong witch. Now all that potential is gone. If she hadn't had a friend with enough steel in her spine to bring the girl to the District Queen *and* approach me, we wouldn't have known about drugs being used at parties to subdue at least some of the girls."

"You found more like this?"

"I don't think the staff at the sanctuary specifically asked the girls if they'd started feeling odd at a party before they were broken, but I'll find out. Until now, there was no reason to connect those girls being broken with families that might want to embrace Hayll's corruption and bring it here. Whoever is behind breaking these girls has been careful not to draw the attention of the Province Queens—or you—but when you start looking at the potential power that is being snuffed out in a handful of girls each year, it stops feeling like accidents of youthful lust and starts feeling calculated." She gripped the arms of the chair hard enough to hurt the muscles in her hands. "We have to stop this, Sadi."

"We will." He smiled a cold, cruel smile. "Newcomers to the games are so predictable. They always think no one has seen their plots and ploys before. But if they want to play, with Dhemlan and its people as the prize, then I am willing to play."

For the first time since she'd seen the truth about the man she had married, Surreal looked forward to the moment when the High Lord of Hell—and the Sadist—revealed himself in all his terrible glory.

# TWENTY-FOUR

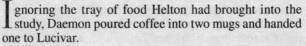

Ignoring the tray of food Helton had brought into the study, Daemon poured coffee into two mugs and handed one to Lucivar.

Yesterday he'd escorted Tersa back to Halaway, then checked on Manny and Mikal. Manny was still spry for a woman her age, but the toll of living as a servant in Hayll for all those centuries was starting to show. And Mikal wasn't a boy anymore but a young man who should be thinking of living on his own. Oh, there were decades yet before he'd make the Offering to the Darkness, but he'd finished the formal education available at the Halaway school and needed to think beyond that—maybe beyond the village—to what sort of work he wanted to do.

Mikal was content where he was—at least for now. His brother, Beron, was immersed in the acting profession he loved. Jillian was writing another story about the Sceltie who had a pet weeble and a human companion, and hinting that she'd like to live in the village of Maghre on the Isle of Scelt for a year to observe instructors and students at the Sceltie school located there. Young Andulvar was still too young to cause any kind of trouble beyond what the adults expected from an Eyrien boy.

Which left the other three children in the family: Jaenelle Saetien, who was becoming more of a moody stranger every time he saw her; Titian, who might become the most challenging of their children as she followed her heart to unexpected choices; and Daemonar, who was intelligent and loyal and committed to serving a Queen few people knew existed—and was born to stand on killing fields. Like him. Like Lucivar.

The Queen's triangle, weapons all.

"Was Tersa right?" Lucivar asked after Daemon recounted Daemonar's meeting with Tersa. "Is Amdarh starting to feel like Draega?"

"No," Daemon replied. *But it could. That was her warning, because the first time she had asked me the question about the sides of a triangle we had been in a park in Draega.*

"Not even a full generation later, and the taint is starting to show again? Hell's fire, Bastard. The children like Orian, who were babes or toddlers at the time of the purge . . . This is all the breathing room we get? A few centuries? Our children fighting the same battles we fought?"

"Not the same battles. Your sons may have to fight to hold the Blood in Kaeleer to the Old Ways, but they aren't slaves who are also fighting to survive."

"They could have been," Lucivar said grimly.

He couldn't disagree with that. If Orian had acquired a Ring of Obedience and had targeted any boy except Daemonar, she might have gotten away with using it—until Lucivar found out what she'd done and killed her for it.

"We see the threat that could cast a shadow on our children, but for all the short-lived races, there have been generations who have been free of that taint," Daemon said. He hoped that was true, but he was going to meet with the Queens in other Territories very soon to let them know what he and Lucivar were seeing in Dhemlan and Askavi. "Unfortunately, I'm getting the impression that the aristo Hayllian way of life has been romanticized to the point of seeming desirable, certainly gratifying for those who have power. Corruption without cost. Dorothea achieved that for centuries."

Lucivar looked at him, memories creating deep shadows in those gold eyes. "If that corruption is in Kaeleer, there will be a cost. I'll make sure of it. I will drown cities in corpses and blood if that's what it takes."

Daemon smiled. "So will I." He stood. "Shall we slip away to the school before Helton comes in and gives us a nonverbal scold for not eating the food?"

Lucivar looked at the tray of food and sighed. "Why do you have so many bossy servants?"

Daemon shrugged. "Someone has to hire them."


From her favorite place in the shadows, Delora watched the two men walk across the green. No, that wasn't right. One of them walked; the other glided.

"Don't they have something else to do?" Jaenelle Saetien sounded mortally embarrassed when she spotted her father and uncle on school grounds.

Good.

"They must have found out Titian is . . . you know," Hespera said. "I can't imagine *that* has been easy to swallow."

Clayton and Dhuran sniggered. Krellis just smiled, which was somehow more condemning—and was the reason Delora liked him the best.

"And you never had any hint that Titian and Zoey . . . ?" Leena opened her mouth just enough to let the tip of her tongue lick her upper lip. "The three of you used to be *so* close."

"They weren't like that," Jaenelle Saetien snapped. "Titian isn't like that."

Defensive. Wasn't that lovely?

Amara gave Delora a nod as she joined the group. She'd taken a few of the second-tier girls who wanted to prove they should be among the chosen rather than the chosen's prey and had created a surprise in the pottery shed.

"Come on," Delora said. "We mustn't be late for class."

"We mustn't?" Krellis asked.

"Not today."

She led her companions around the green, keeping to the shadows until they were behind the men who were almost at the other end of the green. Then her group stepped out, laughing and chatting, not so loudly to be obvious that they were calling attention to themselves, but not hiding either.

Delora snorted softly as the men focused on Zoey and Titian running toward them. Those two Warlord Princes were supposed to be such great warriors, but they hadn't even noticed the group of students at their backs?

They'd gotten soft—and soft men tended to be careless about a great many things.


Having picked up Jaenelle Saetien's psychic scent the moment he stepped onto the green, Lucivar tracked the group who were making an effort to remain unseen. Not too much of an effort, which made him suspect that most of the children, and at least some of the adults, had stopped noticing this group of males and females, giving them a kind of invisibility without needing to use a sight shield.

That told him none of those youngsters had enough experience with Warlord Princes to understand that Warlord Princes always knew who was around them, always assessed the strength of a potential enemy. Always knew what was needed to destroy that enemy.

Jaenelle Saetien would have known that, and that made him wonder, given the pissing contest she seemed to be having with Surreal lately, why she wasn't taking the opportunity to introduce her friends to her father. Smarter to do it before introductions were required—unless there was a reason those friends didn't want to come to Daemon's notice.

Then again, Titian had held this particular secret close to the chest, so maybe girls this age needed to draw a line between their parents and their personal life and feelings. Maybe this show of independence was as much a rite of passage as Daemonar making the Blood Run—and potentially just as dangerous if the girl hit the emotional equivalent of bad air. He'd tolerate standing on the other side of the line—up to a point—but it was time to make it clear that he would have more tolerance for the things he knew about his daughter's personal life than the things that were kept a secret.

As Titian and Zoey ran toward them, Lucivar created a Red perimeter shield halfway down the green, curving it round so that he would have warning if someone tried to attack from a blind spot.

*Problem?* Daemon asked on a spear thread.

*No.*

Pretty young girls who were changing into women, bright-eyed and a little breathless as they came to an abrupt stop in front of him and Daemon.

"Hello, Father," Titian said, twisting her fingers together but looking him in the eyes.

Nerves and a little fear. And hope.

He brushed a streak of mud off her cheek. Or was that clay?

"Prince Sadi," Zoey said. Then she nodded at Lucivar. "Sir."

Lucivar gave her a slow look from head to toe. Bib overalls and a man's shirt underneath. He said to Daemon, *I thought you took them to buy clothes.*

*That's tomorrow's outing.*

*Huh. So whose closet did the little Queen visit to snitch that shirt?*

*Since it wasn't my closet, I do not care.*

"Lady Zoela." Lucivar gave the young Queen a lazy, arrogant smile.

Titian, recognizing that smile, gulped audibly.

"Sir?" Zoey said.

"Since you and Titian are particular friends, the next time you're invited to the town house to join the family for dinner, I don't expect you to make up some piss-ass excuse. You want to spend time with my daughter? You deal with all of us."

"Yes, sir." Zoey sounded wary.

Good. Even a Queen should be wary of provoking a Warlord Prince like him. "And if you cross any of the lines Prince Sadi has drawn, you'd better hope he gets to you first, because if I get to you . . . Your ass, my hand. Understood?"

She beamed at him. "Yes, sir!"

*Why is she so happy about that?* he asked Daemon.

*Her father didn't care enough about her to show up for her Birthright Ceremony. You, on the other hand, are going to hold her to the same rules that you set for Titian.*

*So we're going to end up informally adopting stray witchlings like our father did?*

*She's a Queen, Prick. Do you want anyone else to influence her?*

Good point.

"We want to show you what we've been working on in pottery class," Zoey said. "I'm making a piece for my mother, and Titian is making one for Lady Marian."

Titian studied him, still unsure. "Daemonar and Beron are escorting Zoey and me to an art exhibit at the end of the week."

"That sounds like something you'll enjoy." Lucivar swallowed a laugh. Since Daemonar would rather be stabbed with a fork than go to an art exhibit, he hoped Titian recognized that her brother might not understand her choice—yet—but he had her back. "All right, witchling. Let's see what kind of art the two of you have created." He just hoped he could recognize what it was supposed to be and say something positive.

Titian and Zoey led the way, their hands meeting in fluttering touches.

*Did we give our permission because they wanted to do *that*?* he asked, a lift of his chin indicating the hands. *That?*

*Titian has always been the more cautious child—at least on the surface,* Daemon replied. *And *that* might be *more* during a private moment.*

*Tch. You had to spoil—*

As the girls walked into the pottery shed, their happiness changed to shock and an angry grief that had him striding forward a step ahead of Daemon.

"Someone destroyed our work," Titian wailed. "Why would someone be so mean and destroy the gifts we were making?"

He had a good idea why someone would—and he was looking forward to inflicting some pain in return.

"Bitches," Zoey muttered.

Lucivar felt a phantom hand on his chest, stopping him just inside the door as Daemon moved forward swiftly and grabbed the girls before they could touch the ruined pieces. Hustling them to the door, Daemon pushed the girls at Lucivar, forcing all of them outside.

"Bastard . . ."

Daemon looked at him with sleepy, glazed eyes before whispering, "Wood and stone remember." Then Sadi stepped back into the pottery shed, closed the door, and locked it.

Black Widows could draw memories out of wood and stone, could replay something that had happened. And Daemon, a Black Widow who had been trained in the Hourglass's Craft by his father and by Witch, would know how to draw out those memories and put faces on those responsible for hurting Titian and Zoey.

Lucivar led the girls away from the pottery shed.

Titian cried silently, which ripped his heart. Zoey blinked back tears but looked like she wanted to use a sparring stick on someone.

"What's Prince Sadi doing?" Zoey asked.

"What needs to be done," he replied. Someday she would understand what that meant, but he wasn't going to explain it now. Besides, he was focused on letting his own power flow beneath all the minds in the school, picking up what wasn't contained by inner barriers—like emotions.

Most of those emotions felt like the usual mix of daily life. But at the other end of the green, back among the shadows, he detected malice and glee. Satisfaction. Then there was Jaenelle Saetien, who was close enough to realize her cousin was upset but didn't come over to offer help. Embarrassment. That was what he picked up from her. It grieved him that she would choose these new friends over family. The girl she had been never would have done that.

Daemonar, on the other hand, hurried to reach them. "What's wrong?" He gave a hard look at the group at the other end of the green.

"Someone broke Titian's and Zoey's pottery," Lucivar replied.

Daemonar snarled and took one step.

Keeping his hand at his side, Lucivar snapped his fingers once, a command for the boy to stay put. His father had controlled a room full of Warlord Princes rising to the killing edge with a single snap of his fingers. And like the others in that room, Lucivar had stopped and waited for the next command from the dominant male in the Dark Court.

Titian called in a handkerchief and wiped her eyes and nose. "It wasn't just our work. I don't know how many things were broken, but I saw it wasn't just our work."

"You can make the pieces again," he said.

"They won't be the same," Zoey said, a deep sorrow coming through the words. She looked at the group watching from the other end of the green.

"No, the next pieces will be better because you learned from the first." If he was going to take this young Queen under his wing at least part of the time, she was going to learn the same control that he demanded of his own children—and that meant knowing when to obey without question. "Stay out of this, Zoey. This is no longer your fight."

Her hands curled into fists as she turned to face him. "It damn well is my fight."

Titian gasped at her friend's show of defiance.

Daemonar said, "Zoey." A clear warning for her to back off.

Lucivar looked into her eyes and knew she wouldn't back off because she was a Queen in every way—and because she didn't understand *why* she needed to back off. "Not your fight anymore. You focus on remaking whatever you had made for your mother." He gave her that lazy, arrogant smile. "Witchling, I will tell you this only once. The only way you are going to defy me and get into this particular fight is by going through me—and you aren't strong enough to go through me."

Zoey bared her teeth. "You'd protect them?"

"Not them. You. I'm going to keep you from getting in between them and the storm that's coming."

Zoey's eyes widened. She allowed herself a swift glance at the pottery shed before focusing on him again. "Should we report this to Lady Fharra?"

"Will any of the other girls report the destruction of their work?"

"Not likely," Titian said, vanishing the handkerchief. "They'd be afraid to draw the coven of malice's attention."

Lucivar looked at Daemonar, who said, "Yeah. Them."

Shit. Did that mean Jaenelle Saetien had had some part of that meanness?

Daemon walked out of the pottery shed.

"Stay with them," Lucivar told his son.

"Yes, sir."

He covered the short distance between him and his brother. "Did you find out who did this?"

"I did," Daemon replied.

"What are we going to do about it?"

"You're going to pay a visit to Lady Zhara and inform her that I would like Lord Weston and two of Zhara's guards on duty here at the school to discourage any further mischief. They can make use of Daemonar's room in the male dormitory for resting periods, although he'll have to let them in since the room has shields and a Green lock on the door." Daemon smiled a cold, cruel smile. "I'm going to the Keep. I need a little assistance on a project." A pause. "This is a punishment, Prick, not an execution."

*This time.* That was the part that didn't need to be said. Not between them.

"I'll stay at the town house tonight, but I'll be heading back to Ebon Rih at first light. My men need to know there might be trouble ahead."

"Can our young Brother keep Zoey contained?"

An acknowledgment that Daemonar was one side of the triangle ruled by Witch. "He'll keep her contained."

"Good."

Their shoulders brushed as Daemon walked past him—and then faded away.

Lucivar returned to the children and looked at Daemonar. "You're standing escort until Lord Weston and the guards arrive."

"Yes, sir," Daemonar replied.

"Weston wasn't needed on school grounds," Zoey protested.

"He wasn't needed," Lucivar agreed. "Now he is."

"But . . ."

He turned to her, spreading his wings and curving them to separate Zoey from his children. Then he said quietly, "If Lord Weston isn't willing to teach you how to use a knife, I will."

She stared at him, then whispered, "It was just some broken pottery."

"This time. What about next time?"

She swallowed hard. "Daemonar is here every day. Could he start teaching me the basics?"

"I'll talk to him about that." The girl was not a fool, and he could see why Daemon wanted to nurture her potential as a Queen. "I'll inform the authority here about the broken pottery. You and Titian should get to your classes."

"We had a free afternoon, but Daemonar is supposed to be at one of his tutorials soon. We'll sit with him so he doesn't miss out."

That consideration confirmed that she had the potential to be a good Queen.

Folding his wings, he informed Daemonar and Titian of

the new plans for the afternoon, then followed his son when the boy stepped away from the girls.

"Prince Sadi is taking care of this?" Daemonar tipped his head toward the pottery shed.

"He is. And may the Darkness have mercy on whoever was responsible."

He just hoped that Jaenelle Saetien wasn't going to be among the ones who needed that mercy.

Arriving at the Keep, Daemon made his formal requests through the Seneschal, alerting the two Black Widow Queens in residence that his need to see them came from duty. Then he began setting up his tools and supplies on a table in the sitting room across from the Queen's suite. Wooden frame, spider silk . . . and seven pieces of broken pottery.

"Kiss kiss," Karla said as she and Witch walked into the sitting room.

"I need your assistance in shaping a punishment." He looked at Witch. "With your permission, Lady?"

She nodded.

He reached for both their minds, then opened his first inner barrier and showed them the images—and emotions— he had drawn from the pottery shed.

More than petty cruelty, although there had been enough of that laced with fear. There also had been a kind of malice that had a familiar feel. Harm for the pleasure of doing harm. An almost lustful glee in forcing others to rape their own honor because they weren't strong enough to stand up for themselves—or were too afraid of what would happen if they did.

If he hadn't been at the school that day, Lady Fharra could have dismissed the incident as malicious mischief and either searched for those responsible or pretended it wasn't significant enough to bother with. But he had been there that day, and he'd drawn the images out of wood and stone.

Taking their age into account, he would give the girls a warning and lesson.

The room turned very cold. Since Witch had no physical body and Karla was demon-dead, he wondered if he was the only one who felt this manifestation of his rage.

He closed his inner barrier and waited as they approached the table and studied the pieces of pottery.

"What did you have in mind?" Karla asked.

He told them.

"This is permanent?" Witch asked.

"No. If it was permanent, I could do it on my own." And he wouldn't need to work with a tangled web to extract the price owed for the destruction. "I would like this to be temporary and for a very specific amount of time. I don't have the delicacy of skill to do that."

Karla smiled at him, then looked at Witch. "He's become quite terrifying when he's pissed off."

"He always was." Witch returned Karla's smile, but the icy rage Daemon saw in her sapphire eyes reminded him that he was not the most terrifying individual in the room.

The smile he gave them in return was equally sharp, equally cold—and it delighted him to be in their presence. "Shall we begin?"

# TWENTY-FIVE

---❖---

J aenelle Saetien fell halfway out of bed as she tried to
kick off the covers and turn on the bedside lamp. For a
moment, she thought it had been a bad dream. Then she
heard more screams.

She ran out of her room in the dormitory, then stopped.
Girls were hovering in the hallway like little animals that
were reluctant to move too far from their burrows.

More screams.

Not knowing what else to do, Jaenelle Saetien headed
for Delora and Hespera, who stood in front of Amara's
door, looking frightened and furious.

"What happened?" she asked as a scream changed to a
wail behind the door. "Is Amara hurt? Should I fetch the
school Healer?"

The door opened. Borsala and Leena guided Amara out
of the room.

Jaenelle Saetien stared at Amara's hands. Not only were
the hands clenched so tightly the fingernails were cutting
into the palms; they were curled inward to such a degree it
was a wonder that something in Amara's wrists didn't tear
from the strain.

Tacita came out of another room, leading Dahlia, a girl
who had been on the periphery of their little group. Her
hands were fisted and curled like Amara's.

Other girls were led from their rooms, their hands useless.

Someone must have alerted the school's Healer because now there were shocked adult voices mingling with the cries and wails.

Once the afflicted girls were taken to the healing rooms and the dormitory settled into a wary quietness, Jaenelle Saetien felt the fury pumping out of Delora and followed the other girl's line of sight—to Titian, who looked shocked, and Zoey, who looked stunned and yet not completely surprised.

"What did you do?" Delora snarled, taking a step closer to Zoey.

"Nothing." Zoey faced Delora. "But *they* must have done something."

"Couldn't keep your mouth shut, could you, fat bat?" Hespera said, spitting the words at Titian. "Had to go whining about a little teasing."

Jaenelle Saetien looked at her friends, then at her cousin. Titian had been upset about something that had happened at the pottery shed yesterday, and Papa and Uncle Lucivar had been quite angry about it. But Delora and Hespera said it wasn't anything significant and asking Titian about it would give the girl notions of being important beyond her scope. So she hadn't crossed the green to where her cousins and Zoey had stood. She hadn't asked what happened. She couldn't be blamed if she didn't know.

And she wasn't going to ask who had shaped the punishment for whatever had happened in the pottery shed.

Not wanting to be pulled into taking sides between Zoey and Delora, Jaenelle Saetien hurried back to her room—and wondered whether things would have been different this morning if her father and uncle hadn't been at the school yesterday.


Daemon hadn't gotten more than a couple of hours of sleep between finishing the tangled web that held the punishment spell and returning to Amdarh—and the school.

After he activated the spell, there was nothing more for

him to do except wait for Lady Zhara's request for an audience.

Helton was startled to find him walking into the town house shortly after dawn, but there was coffee available since Lucivar had left for Ebon Rih barely a quarter of an hour earlier. Apparently, Daemonar had chosen to remain at the school last night to give Lord Weston a hand at squelching any trouble, should any arise.

That told him Zhara had taken her little chat with Lucivar seriously.

He had his first cup of coffee while reviewing the correspondence that had been left on his desk. He enjoyed the second cup in the dining room while he tucked into a hearty breakfast.

The urgent knocking on the town house's front door came as he finished the last bite. A message from Lady Zhara.

He didn't rush—he was the Warlord Prince of Dhemlan, after all—but he didn't make the Queen of Amdarh wait long before he arrived at her home and was escorted into the morning room, where Zhara and the court Healer waited for him.

"Ladies," he said pleasantly.

"There has been a troubling occurrence at the school," Zhara said. "Zoey was shaken by it and wasn't making a lot of sense when she contacted me on a psychic thread, but from the report Lord Weston provided, I gathered some girls were mysteriously injured."

"Ah." Daemon took a seat and crossed his legs at the knees. "Guilt can manifest itself in odd ways. Physical ways. Perhaps the girls who are afflicted were involved in some intended cruelty and are now paying the price. Perhaps your Healer could suggest to the school's Healer that such an affliction in girls that age is temporary, although restoring the hands to their full use will probably be painful."

He watched the muscles in Zhara's throat work.

"This affliction *is* temporary?" she asked.

He smiled. "This time."

A clock in the room *tick*ed, *tick*ed, *tick*ed while he waited.

"If it's temporary . . ." The Healer stopped, then seemed to gather her courage. "Do you know how long this affliction lasts?"

"About seven days," he replied, his voice still brutally pleasant.

*Tick, tick, tick.*

"Thank you for the information, Prince," Zhara finally said. "We'll make sure it's passed on to the school."

He rose and bowed to Queen and Healer. "Ladies."

He'd almost reached the morning room's door when Zhara said, "Prince? Zoey sent a note yesterday afternoon, telling me that the gift she'd been making for her mother had been among the work that had been destroyed in the pottery shed. Including Zoey and Titian, how many girls had their work damaged?"

He looked back at her and said too softly, "Seven."

# TWENTY-SIX

For seven days, Amara and the other girls afflicted with Curling Hands had needed help getting dressed. They'd needed help being fed, blowing their noses, wiping their asses.

Disgusting.

Delora knew the source of that spell. Oh, yes, she knew. No one in the school, instructors included, had the skill to do something like what was done to Amara and the other afflicted girls, so that left two possibilities. One, really, since the girls hadn't had their hands chopped off.

Prince Sadi's interference had cost her the loyalty of her second-tier followers. Girls like Dahlia, whom she'd been breaking down bit by bit since they were girls—since the day they'd searched for the missing kitten. Now, on the eighth day, as the muscles and tendons in their hands started to relax, she saw the moment the girls who had been in the pottery shed with Amara realized this had been a specific punishment for a specific bit of mischief—and fear of another round of punishment from someone brutal enough to do *this* to *them* would remain stronger than fear of whatever she might inflict on them for losing her favor.

She blamed Zoey the Insipid and the fat bat for boo-hooing to the grown-ups about a little bit of fun. Now there were *guards* patrolling the school, maintaining enough distance around those two girls to give the illusion they were on their own but never letting them out of their sight. Hell's fire, that Lord Weston even stood guard outside the facilities in the girls' dorm. When she and several other girls complained to Lady Fharra about it, they'd been told the order came from the Queen of Amdarh herself, so the girls should make sure their robes were sufficiently modest when they left their rooms to take a shower.

The first time they spotted Weston on guard, Leena and Tacita had worn attire that was less than modest to test the possibility of providing a distraction. They had returned to their rooms thoroughly withered by a disinterest that bordered on contempt.

It wasn't Weston or the guards they needed to distract. It wasn't *those* men she needed to punish for the sudden cracks in her careful plans that could spoil all her lovely dreams of power—the kind of power that had once controlled the Territory of Hayll and then had brought the whole Realm of Terreille to its knees. She wanted that. She could *do* that.

But she needed to start weakening a particular adversary or two.

Delora summoned Hespera, Borsala, and Krellis. They stood in plain sight on the green, where other students and the instructors could see them.

"Krellis found out something delicious, and now it's time to put it to use," Delora said. "This is what I want you to do."

*This* would teach Prince Sadi to keep his nose out of her business.


Jaenelle Saetien didn't understand the odd looks she'd received throughout the morning or the way so many of the students scattered when she went in for the midday meal. Delora and her other friends weren't in the dining room, and when she sat down at a table, Delora's and Hespera's wannabe friends picked up their plates and found somewhere else to sit.

Her table filled up with what Hespera called the school dregs—the girls who were barely qualified to be with girls from *real* aristo families. The last two places at the table were taken by Zoey and Titian.

"Did something happen?" Jaenelle Saetien asked. She glanced toward the door. Sure enough, one of the guards had taken up a position where he could keep Zoey in sight.

No sign of Daemonar. She wondered if that was good or bad. He'd been a little testy lately, and it was annoying.

"The coven of malice has been whispering about something all morning, but I don't know what it's about," Zoey replied.

"I think some of the instructors know," Titian said. "One of them told me I shouldn't believe everything I hear." She hesitated. "I think the instructors *do* believe it, but they're afraid."

"Of what?" She suddenly wondered if they were afraid of a *what* or a *who*.

Jaenelle Saetien ate because she was hungry, but the food filled her stomach with a sour, churning burn, so she abandoned the meal, said good-bye to Zoey and Titian, and went looking for Delora.

Tacita, Leena, Borsala, and Hespera gave her pitying looks but slipped away before she got too close. Only Delora waited for her on the edge of the green.

"You're being so brave," Delora said. "I'm sure I couldn't be so brave and go to classes with *everyone* talking about how your mother . . ." She pressed her lips together. "No. We're friends, so I'm not going to say."

"Say what? Delora, what is it everyone else knows?"

"*I* only found out this morning, or I would have told you so that it wouldn't be so much of a shock." Delora sighed. "Someone heard the adults talking at a party a couple of days ago and told a friend who told a friend—and now *everyone* knows. I'm surprised Titian didn't tell you, her being family and all. Then again, maybe she's ashamed and didn't want to talk about it."

"Talk about what?" Jaenelle Saetien made a huge effort

to rein in her impatience. "What do you know about my mother?"

Jaenelle Saetien dropped from the Purple Dusk Wind to the landing web in front of SaDiablo Hall. Maybe she would have taken a moment to gather her thoughts and leash her feelings so that she could discuss this with her father like an adult and let him know she would stand by him if he chose to divorce *that woman*, but *that woman* stood in the open doorway of *her home*, wearing one of those long coat-and-trouser outfits that she often wore when she went to the village or was "working" as her father's second-in-command.

At least, that was the kind of "work" her father believed was being done.

But seeing *that woman* snapped her control.

"YOU!" she screamed.

Surreal gave her a long look, then turned and walked into the Hall. Into *her father's* home.

Jaenelle Saetien rushed after Surreal, almost knocking over the footman at the door. Ignoring the footman and Beale, who was talking to *that woman*, she screamed, "You vile, disgusting creature! You filthy *whore*! You *tricked* my father into marrying you. He never would have touched something like you if he'd known what you are!"

She heard a door open, felt the cold dark power, but she stayed focused on her quarry.

Surreal hooked her long black hair behind one delicately pointed ear. "First off, sugar, I bathe regularly, so I'm not filthy. And I've never tricked your father into anything."

"That's enough," Daemon said too softly as he approached from the direction of his study.

Wasn't enough. Would never be enough. "She's a whore and she tricked you into marrying her."

"Was a whore," Surreal said. "I retired before I came to Kaeleer."

*Mother Night,* Jaenelle Saetien thought. *She just admitted it in front of him.* "Well, everyone knows your secret now."

"It was hardly a secret. There were plenty of people from Terreille who came to Kaeleer around the same time I did, plenty who knew part of what I did for a living."

"You're disgusting!"

"And you can take a piss in the wind."

"I wish you were dead! You are *not* my mother. I could never come from something like you!"

*"Enough,"* Daemon snarled.

Grabbing Jaenelle Saetien's arm, he hauled her into his study and locked the door.

Deprived of her desired target, ashamed that her father had been duped so badly and had now lost all credibility with the aristos and Queens in Dhemlan—maybe even the whole Realm—she turned on him.

"How can you stand letting her touch you, letting her live here? She's a *whore*, Father. Everyone is laughing at you because of her!"

He slipped his hands in his trouser pockets. The smile he gave her was cold and oddly cruel—and made her shiver.

"I know far better than you ever will who and what Surreal is," he said with a savage pleasantness.

"You couldn't have known she did *that.*"

"Since I paid for her education in the best Red Moon houses, I was well aware of what she did—and could do."

Stunned, Jaenelle Saetien stared at him. "You knew?"

He took a step toward her. She took a step back. He had a look in his eyes that he usually had when he was about to take one of his funny turns and needed "quiet time," but that look had never been focused on *her.* Until now.

She turned and tried to open the door—and felt the heat of his body at her back as his left hand gently pressed against the door next to her head.

"You want to twist a verbal knife?" he crooned. "All right, then. Here's another truth about your family. I was a pleasure slave for centuries before your mother was born and for a lot of years after that. I was on my knees pleasuring hundreds, maybe thousands, of bitches over the years. I was very good at providing pleasure. I was even better at turning pleasure into pain. One way or another, I destroyed every bitch that used me—including the ones who were barely older than you. Anything you want to say about that?"

She shook her head. She didn't want anything except to get out of that room and get back to the school.

"Now," he continued, "who told you about Surreal in a way guaranteed to have you come home hurling accusations instead of talking to your mother?"

Jaenelle Saetien shook her head. Considering what had happened to Amara and those other girls, she wasn't going to give him names.

He leaned closer, his breath warm against her cheek. "You'll have dinner on a tray in your room. In the morning, I'll escort you back to the school, and you will introduce me to your new friends. And just in case you're considering slipping out in the middle of the night . . ."

Soft thunder rolled through the Hall, and she felt the Black shields and locks that effectively turned the Hall into a prison.

"Either I escort you in the morning and you introduce me to your friends, especially the one who was so helpful in telling you about Surreal, or you don't go back at all."

"I have to go back to school!"

"No, you don't. I am in no way obliged to permit you to return to that school, especially if this bitch behavior is what you're learning from the other students."

He was so angry right now, he wasn't going to listen. Well, she'd swallow her disgust and make nice. "I don't need a tray in my room."

"If you don't want dinner, that's your choice, but you're not sitting at a table with my wife tonight." He reached down and closed his hand over the doorknob. "One other thing you should know. Surreal was a very talented and very expensive whore, and she earned a good living doing it. But she was, and still is, even better as an assassin—and you've just given her a reason to sharpen her knives. Something to think about this evening." He opened the door and stepped back. "We'll leave early enough for you to be at school for your first class. Don't procrastinate getting ready tomorrow morning. We leave when I'm ready, and I will deliver you in whatever you are, or aren't, wearing."

"Why are you being so mean?" she whimpered.

"If you don't know, that will give you something else to think about this evening."

The look in his eyes, that smile . . . She came close to wetting herself out of fear.

She'd never been afraid of her father, even when he was starting to take one of his funny turns. But the man standing in the study wasn't really her father, and she wanted to get away from him as fast as she could.


Daemon walked into Surreal's bedroom without waiting for permission since he didn't think she would grant it right now.

He'd expected fury, was prepared to listen to her rage about the girl acting like a snippy bitch. He didn't expect to walk into the room and find Surreal staring out a window and crying.

"Surreal." He came up behind her, wrapped his arms around her waist. "Sweetheart, don't cry. This isn't worth your tears."

"Hell's fire, Sadi. How did you stand me when I was her age?"

He kissed her temple. "You weren't like that."

"Yes, I was. So full of myself and needing to prove . . . something. I looked like an adult. I looked like a woman with an exotic heritage. But inside . . ." She sniffed. "Whenever you went to one of those flats or secret places you owned, you slipped away from the Queen who owned you and her court in order to get away from the bitches and their demands. And then I would show up, and you were so patient, so tolerant of this girl who wanted your attention just like everyone else."

"I enjoyed your company."

"Until the night I asked you to show me what it was like to be in bed with Hayll's Whore."

His arms tightened around her. "Stop."

"Snippy little bitch thinking of no one but herself, never considering how that might hurt you. And then you gave me a taste of what it was like to be with Hayll's Whore."

"Surreal, stop."

"I'm so sorry for what I said that night, and you were right to do what you did."

"It was a long time ago."

"I was afraid of you after that. Until I met Jaenelle Angelline all those years later, I was afraid of you."

"I know." He sighed. "You're still afraid of me."

"Some days," she agreed. "Some aspects of you."

He called in a handkerchief and handed it to her.

Surreal wiped her nose. Then she sighed and leaned against him. "Daemon? Could Jaenelle Saetien just be your daughter for a little while?"

"Why? She had no right to speak to you that way about your former profession, but—"

"It's not that." She hesitated, and he felt her brace for his reaction to what she would tell him. "When she said I wasn't her mother and that she wished I was dead, I felt something inside me break, and I don't know if I can fix it. I don't know if anyone can fix it. But I'd like to not deal with her for a few days."

"I'll take care of it." He kissed her temple again. "Talk to Tersa."

She laughed, a reluctant sound. "I don't think Tersa knows much about adolescent girls."

"She knows about being broken."

"Yeah, I guess she does."

They stood quietly for several minutes.

"Why don't you rest for a while?" Daemon said. "Then you and I will go down and have dinner."

"Your daughter doesn't want to dine with us?"

She tried to sound amusing, but he heard pain under the words. "She hurt my wife, my friend, my partner. I don't want her dining with us tonight."

Surreal turned in his arms. "She needs you, Sadi."

"And in the morning she'll have all my attention." He kissed her mouth softly. "But you need me tonight."

# TWENTY-SEVEN

---

The following morning, Daemon met Beale and Holt in the butler's pantry. The third time Beale offered the plate of shredded-beef-and-cheese sandwich triangles, Daemon conceded that he wasn't going to be offered the coffee sitting on Beale's desk until he took a sandwich.

He accepted a sandwich, received a mug of coffee, and waited. He didn't need to ask; he could tell by the look in their eyes that the whole staff knew about Jaenelle Saetien's emotional firestorm as well as what was said.

"It is difficult to know what to do with a girl that age," Beale said. "Your father had less trouble, despite the number of Ladies living here, because the coven was united by a single purpose—to be here with Lady Angelline. And while there were . . . eruptions . . . on occasion, it was the opinion of the senior staff that those moments were caused by an excess of feelings."

"Once Prince Yaslana came to live here, he simplified things," Holt said. "He'd haul whoever was erupting outside, hand her a sparring stick, and wouldn't let her go back inside until she'd worked off enough of the energy behind those feelings. She could yell about anything while they were sparring, but the moment there was any meanness in the words, he'd put her in the dirt—and he didn't care who she was."

"I don't have that kind of fighting skill," Daemon said dryly.

"You have your father's skill for cold disapproval," Beale pointed out. "That is just as effective, if more subtle."

"There was intentional meanness in what Jaenelle Saetien said yesterday." The words had wounded Surreal so deeply, he wasn't sure she would fully recover. Now he wanted to know what the other men thought.

Beale and Holt exchanged a look before Beale said, "What the young Lady said about Lady Surreal's former profession was driven by embarrassment coupled with a sense of drama. She had been mortified in front of friends and wanted to make a scene."

"Or was encouraged to make a scene?" Daemon asked.

"Possibly," Holt said after a moment.

"The young Lady is displaying an attitude of entitlement with the staff that wasn't there before she began attending that school," Beale said.

It kept coming back to that school, where many aristo families sent their children because it was supposed to have the finest education—and also provided those children with a way to meet their equals. When he'd considered the school as the place for the next stage of his daughter's education, he'd seen no cause for concern. But Jaenelle Saetien's presence at the school seemed to be cracking the veneer of polite behavior, giving him a whiff of some kind of rot underneath.

"I suggest assigning the more seasoned members of the staff to take care of any requests coming from Jaenelle Saetien," Daemon said. "I'm sure they know how to respond to an attitude of entitlement."

Beale's eyes sparkled with sharp amusement and understanding. "Very well, Prince. I will adjust the assignments whenever the young Lady is at the Hall."

Daemon handed the empty mug to Beale. "The eruptions that follow will be educational for the younger staff."

"Indeed they will be."

"What are you going to do about Jaenelle Saetien's behavior?" Holt asked.

"That will depend on what I see when I escort my daughter back to the school."


Jaenelle Saetien sat in the seat next to her father as he caught the Red Wind and guided the small Coach toward Amdarh. She wished he'd chosen to ride the Black, which would have gotten them to the city so much faster. As it was, they wouldn't reach the school much before the first class.

She'd had plenty of time to think last night. She'd been horrified to learn her father had been a pleasure slave and didn't want to think of him doing some of the things the men did in an erotic romance she'd recently borrowed from Borsala. It wasn't his fault that he'd been *forced* into doing those things, at least until he became powerful enough to refuse. But *that woman* had *chosen* to sleep with who knew how many men—for *money*.

"I suppose you want me to apologize to her," she said when the silence had dragged on so long she couldn't stand another minute of it.

"It wouldn't be sincere, and I'm sure you'd phrase it in a way that the words would add salt to an open wound," he replied coolly. "So, no, I don't want you to apologize. In fact, I don't want you to say anything to my wife that isn't courteous."

"Your *wife*? How can you—"

"And to help you remember this warning, since I will not say it again, every time you are discourteous to Lady Surreal, whether by word or deed, you will forfeit half of your spending money for the next quarter of the year."

Jaenelle Saetien stared at him. "You'd punish me for having opinions?"

"There is a difference between opinions and deliberate cruelty. You were cruel. You will not be again without paying a price."

"And you're never cruel?"

"I am. Often. I can rip the heart out of someone with a few well-chosen words. That's why I know that sometimes wounds made by words never fully heal." He finally looked at her. "That's why I know you caused more damage than you realize, although I suspect it was exactly what you and your little friends intended. Now you have to live with the consequences."

She swallowed hard. "What consequences?"

"That's something we'll all have to find out."

They didn't speak for the rest of the trip. Then Daemon dropped from the Winds and guided the Coach to . . .

"Father!" she yelled. "You can't set a Coach down on the school green!"

Ignoring her, he did exactly that. It caused a commotion. Of course it did. Then, as he escorted her out of the Coach and onto the green, she felt something flow from him, undiluted and unrestrained. *That woman* had explained it was the sexual heat that was part of a Warlord Prince's nature, but immediate family members—like the man's children—had a little protection from that heat. But this was more than what she felt at home.

This was dangerous.

She saw her friends hurrying toward them. She saw Zoey and Titian head toward them before Daemonar grabbed them, turned them around, and shoved them in the opposite direction. Then she saw Daemonar and that instructor Prince Raine walking toward them—and everything about the way Daemonar moved screamed the need for caution.

When her friends were gathered in front of them, her father crooned, "Introduce me." It wasn't a request.

"This is my father, Prince Daemon Sadi," Jaenelle Saetien said, trembling.

"You never told us he was so handsome," Hespera cooed.

"Father, these are Ladies Amara, Borsala, Leena, Tacita, and Hespera. Lords Dhuran, Clayton, and Krellis. And this is Lady Delora."

He smiled a cold, cruel smile and purred, "Dorothea."

She took his arm, mortally embarrassed that he was about to have one of his funny turns in front of *everyone.* "No, Father. You must have misheard me. This is *Delora.*"

The smile didn't change, but the look in his eyes when he focused on her . . .

*Daemonar,* she called as she released her father's arm and took a step back. *Help me.*

"May the Darkness have mercy," Daemonar muttered as he lengthened his stride. He knew what the Black felt like when Sadi went cold. And he knew what it felt like to be near the Sadist.

"What's wrong?" Raine asked, matching his stride.

"You should get out of here."

"I'm an instructor, and there is clearly a problem."

"You notice no one else is rushing out to meet the problem?"

"You think this has something to do with the rumors that were sweeping the school yesterday?"

"Yeah." More likely, the Sadist had come there today to find the source of those rumors.

"Good morning, sir," Daemonar called when he was a few strides away from the group. Knowing he was about to dance on the knife's edge, he took the last steps toward the man he always loved and sometimes feared.

Today was a day it was prudent to fear.

"May I be of service?" he asked.

Those gold eyes, glazed and sleepy, stared at Prince Raine for much too long before the Sadist said, "Who is this?"

"Prince Raine. My tutor. You met when I started classes." He waited a moment. "Sir?"

"Escort Lady SaDiablo to her class."

"It will be my pleasure." Wrapping a hand around Jaenelle Saetien's arm, he eased her away from the group—and the man—before escorting her across the green. He felt relieved when Raine hurried to join him.

"What . . . ?" Raine began.

"Not now," Daemonar said quietly.

"You have to do something," Jaenelle Saetien said. "He's having one of his funny turns."

Daemonar almost jerked her off her feet when he stopped moving. "Funny turns? What's wrong with you? You never used to make light of something so serious. And Prince Sadi is not having a 'funny turn,' cousin. He's in a cold rage, and the coven of malice is the reason for it."

"Don't call them that," she snapped. "It makes them sound—"

"Like what they are."

She tried to pull away from him, but he tightened his grip on her arm, maybe hard enough to bruise. Right now he didn't care. She was being willfully blind, and he was desperately afraid of what was coming.

"He is having one of his . . . fits," she insisted. "Moments after I introduced Delora, he called her Dorothea."

A shiver went down Daemonar's spine. "The name Dorothea means nothing to you?"

"Maybe I heard it in some dull history lesson." She shrugged, but he suspected that she remembered enough from stories shared within the family and just didn't want to think about why her father looked at her new best friend and saw his most hated enemy.

He didn't say anything else, just delivered her to her first class and walked away.

Raine continued to stay with him, and he wondered where the instructor was supposed to be.

"What does that name mean to you?" Raine asked.

"Death and destruction. War." When Raine stopped walking, Daemonar turned to face him. "Family history—and the price that was paid to save the Blood in Kaeleer. That's what that name means to me."

"Prince Sadi didn't make a mistake, did he?"

He shook his head.

"What are you going to do?"

"Send a message to my father." *And to Witch.*

✦ ✦ ✦

Surreal found Tersa in the cottage's kitchen, standing next to the table and staring at a broken vase, a dozen red roses, and a dozen flowers that looked like daisies but were the same color as the roses. She wasn't sure what advice Tersa could give her about this latest collision with Jaenelle Saetien, but Daemon's mother did know about being broken. He was right about that. Besides, she and Tersa had been looking after each other, on and off, for most of her life. Who else could she talk to?

"It's getting colder," she said as she removed her outer coat and scarf, placing both over the back of one kitchen chair. "We might have our first snow tonight." She let her psychic senses flow through the cottage. Just the two of them here. "Where is Mikal?"

"He's out doing boy things." Tersa paused. "Or talking to a girl. Maybe kissing, although it's early in the day for kissing."

Not in her experience, but that wasn't the reason for concern. "He asked Daemon for permission?"

Tersa frowned at her. "The Mikal boy lives with me, so he asked me."

She'd better talk to Mikal soon and find out what rules Tersa had laid down before the boy found himself in trouble with the patriarch of the family—especially right now when Daemon's temper would be sharper and colder than usual.

Tersa reached out and tapped Surreal's chest. "What's broken can't be mended. Put the pieces back together, they won't be the same. Can't be the same."

"What can't be mended?"

"The girl broke the bond. Can't mend it."

"I have to mend it. She's my daughter."

"Not anymore." Tersa stroked Surreal's hair, an odd gesture since Tersa's hair was always as tangled as her mind. "She is Daemon's daughter. You are Daemon's wife. That is your connection now. You build new feelings or you don't, but what the girl broke in you can't be mended."

She knew the truth of that, had grieved for it last night. "I tried to keep her safe."

"You did that. Now it's time to let go. Soon it will be time to be a guide—if she chooses to listen."

Tersa stepped back and picked up two flowers. "What is this?" She held out the flower in her left hand.

"A rose," Surreal replied, relieved to have a distraction.

"And this?" She held out the flower in her right hand.

"A red daisy."

"Are you sure?"

Surreal shivered. Broken Black Widow. Mad Black Widow always living near the borders of the Twisted Kingdom but never fully sane. And that meant Tersa had seen some things that only one other Black Widow had seen. If she went to the Keep and asked, would Witch also tell her a part of her heart had broken beyond mending?

Tersa set those flowers down and picked up two more, both roses.

"A daisy travels, calls itself a rose, blends in. Changes itself in order to become one of the land's roses, while others . . ." Both flowers bloomed. One remained a rose while the other unfurled its petals to reveal itself as a daisy with needle-thin thorns filling its center. ". . . hold on to what they were and wait to reveal their true nature. The trusting, the unwary, are fooled by daisies that claim to be roses. You can't afford to be a fool."

Surreal pressed her hands against the table. Daisies and roses. Hayllians and Dhemlans. The mingling of blood-lines. Why not? Sadi had Hayllian and Dhemlan blood-lines. He couldn't be the only one. Hayllians could have come to Kaeleer over the centuries, married into Dhemlan families, and adopted those family names. Honorable men and women who had been drawn to the Shadow Realm.

But what about the ones who were less than honorable? What about twigs from the family trees of Hayll's Hundred Families who had slipped into Kaeleer shortly before or after Witch had purged the Realms of Dorothea's taint and now were biding their time, fostering the corruption that had eventually destroyed Terreille?

Or was the interest in Hayllian memorabilia a sign that the corruption already had taken root again? Were the girls who were being broken another sign? And what about the disruptions within the Realm's most powerful family caused by a girl's rebellion?

An orchestrated rebellion?

"Jaenelle Saetien," she whispered. She shouldn't have consented to let the girl go to that damn school.

"You can't save her," Tersa said. "Not this time."

Jaenelle Saetien skipped one of her classes—it was a class that *everyone* found boring and useless, anyway—and waited for Daemonar to leave his afternoon tutorial. She'd wanted to meet him sooner, but he'd been a prick and had refused to give up a lesson. So *she* had to give up one of *her* classes instead.

He walked out of the building, gave her a slashing look, and kept going.

She hurried after him. "We have to talk about this morning!"

"Do we? Seemed pretty clear to me."

She tried to grab his arm and jerked back when she met a defensive Green shield that had some snap to it that hurt. "Why are you pissed off at me?"

"You want me to pat your head and say 'There, there, no one minds you turning into an insufferable bitch,' or do you want the truth?"

"You're being mean!"

"Just giving back what you're dishing out, darling." Daemonar finally stopped walking. "Tell me this: Did you tell Delora about Prince Sadi's need for solitude? Did she come up with calling it his funny turns, or did you belittle what he does to protect all of us as a way to impress her?"

"I needed to talk to someone, and it makes those times

sound . . ." She trailed off as she saw his eyes fill with hot anger.

"Tame? Amusing? Harmless? He isn't tame and he isn't harmless, and you're damn lucky his temper didn't snap the leash this morning because he would have splattered the coven of malice all over the green."

Her father had been scary and strange because he was pissed off about what she'd said about *that woman*, but he wouldn't have *killed* anyone at the school. Would he?

"Did you know my father was a pleasure slave?" She wanted to shock him.

He didn't look impressed. "Yeah, I did. He told me. Not all of it, certainly not the worst of what he'd endured, but we've talked about it."

"He never told me!"

"Well, he probably figured you weren't mature enough to understand."

It burned that he would say that, that he believed that. It burned enough to douse the anger and make her lower lip quiver. "You said you'd always have my back."

He didn't even try to give her a hug, and that shield around him made it impossible for her to touch him.

Daemonar sighed, a sound of impatience. "I don't like the girl you've become, Jaenelle Saetien. I don't like that girl at all. But you're still my cousin, and I will still have your back—up to a point. If I have to choose between you and Titian, I will choose my sister every time."

He walked away.

When she turned to head toward the dormitory, she saw Krellis. He stood far enough away that he wouldn't have heard what was said, but he must have realized it wasn't a friendly discussion.

He fell into step beside her. "Having trouble with the bat?"

She should have told him not to insult her cousin. Instead, she said, "Yeah. He's being a prick."

Krellis tucked her arm into his. "What can you expect from a rube?"

*Some* people didn't think she was an insufferable bitch. "Yeah. What can you expect?"

SaDiablo Hall was an immense structure, and yet there was nowhere to run. Not for her.

As the frigid warning of Sadi's return rippled through the Hall, Surreal stepped into the great hall, looked at Beale and Holt, and said, "Get the rest of the staff out of this part of the Hall."

She had the best chance against the Black. Not because she wore Gray. She had no chance against the Black if it came to a fight, but as Sadi's wife, she could offer a distraction that might keep everyone else safe.

She retreated to the sitting room and waited for him to walk through the front door. She didn't know where he'd been after he escorted Jaenelle Saetien to school, but if this was as much as his temper had thawed, they were all in trouble.

He walked into the sitting room—and she struggled to control bowels and bladder.

The Sadist, unleashed.

Lucivar had told her years ago that she had never really danced with the Sadist, that she had never seen that aspect of Daemon's temper without him showing some restraint. Well, she was seeing it now, and there was nothing she could do to stop whatever he was going to do to her.

When he walked up to her, the room turned so cold, she could see her breath. His hand, with its lethally sharp black-tinted nails, curled around the back of her neck, drawing her closer. As the sexual heat wrapped around her, his lips settled over hers, making her shake with lust and fear. And when his tongue demanded entry and he gave her a brutally gentle kiss, she knew there was nothing of the lover in him. Not now. And yet . . .

He ended the kiss, smiled at her, and crooned, "Surreal, darling, we're going hunting."

# TWENTY-EIGHT

───────◈───────

Lucivar walked into the Keep and hesitated. When he'd left his eyrie to fly here, the Black had been inside the Keep. Now he had no sense of Daemon being anywhere in Ebon Rih. Of course, that could mean Sadi had gone into the Queen's part of the Keep. Once a person walked through the metal gate that separated that part of the mountain from the rest, Witch's vast power cloaked everyone else within those rooms.

He couldn't find the Black, but he felt the presence of two Gray Jewels.

He went to the rooms that had been converted into the official office of the Warlord Prince of Askavi. That was Karla's domain within Ebon Askavi, but the demon-dead Black Widow Queen who was his administrative second-in-command wasn't there.

*Karla?* he called on a psychic thread.

*In the library with Surreal.*

That confirmed the identity of the second Gray Jewel.

He strode to that part of the Keep and found both women in the private section of the library, standing around a large blackwood table filled with the registers that held the information for generations of bloodlines and Jewels.

Karla glanced at him, said, "Kiss kiss," and went back to making notes about whatever she was reading in the registers.

Surreal, on the other hand, stopped and straightened. Her gold-green eyes still held residual fear and she looked shaken. Easy enough to guess why after receiving Daemonar's terse message yesterday about the collision at the school. But she didn't appear to be physically hurt. In fact, despite the fear and shakiness, she looked more like a predator who had caught the scent of prey.

"Chaosti showed up a little while ago," Surreal said. "Sadi was needed in the Dark Realm. He'll be back after he takes care of business there."

Lucivar nodded. "What are you two doing?"

"Looking up bloodlines and family connections."

Surreal held out a list. Recognizing Daemon's blend of printed script—a form he'd developed because it was easier for his brother to read than regular handwriting—Lucivar took the paper and read the list. He knew some of the names from things Daemonar had said and from letters Titian had written to Marian.

"Daemonar refers to this group as the coven of malice," Surreal said. "I'm tracing the bloodlines to find out if the families originally came from Dhemlan or Hayll—and how long those families have been in Kaeleer."

"You think some of them slipped in during the service fairs?" he asked.

"Or before that. A minor aristo family with enough money to purchase a small estate could have slipped into Kaeleer and settled in a village easily enough—as long as they followed the Old Ways of the Blood and didn't give anyone a reason to wonder where they had been before that. And it's not like there is an obvious difference between the Hayllian and Dhemlan races."

Unlike Eyriens, whose wings made them distinctive among the long-lived races.

"I'm checking out a different list," Karla said. "Apparently, Daemon went back to the school and had a little chat with Lady Zoela to obtain the names of the girls *she* considers friends. Most have some claim to an aristo bloodline, which seems a requirement for being accepted at that school, but otherwise, what I'm looking at is the beginning of an unofficial court. One girl is a natural Black Widow and should be leaving that school soon to begin an apprenticeship in the Hourglass. One seems to be a natural Healer who, like the Black Widow, will need to begin a different kind of training within the next year or so. The rest of this group has the potential to wear dark Jewels when they mature." She smiled grimly. "Just the kind of young witches that a rival group would not want coming into power around a strong Queen."

"Mother Night," he muttered.

"One other name was on my list," Karla said. "An instructor named Raine, a Prince from Dharo. This is his first year at the school."

"He's tutoring Daemonar. I haven't heard any reason to think ill of him."

"I don't think you will." Karla looked at Surreal. "I followed his line back to one of Rainier's brothers."

Surreal sank into a chair. "Rainier? He's kin to Rainier?"

Surreal and Rainier had been friends for decades, had shared a house for decades. Never lovers, as far as Lucivar knew, since Rainier preferred men when it came to the pleasures of the bed, but they had loved each other in their own way.

Karla nodded. "I wonder if that's why he came to Amdarh to teach at a school here. From what I can see, Rainier was the only Warlord Prince in the family who wore dark Jewels, and that caste has been rare in this bloodline, regardless of what Jewels were worn."

"Rainier's family liked him better when he kept his distance," Surreal said. "That's why he rarely went back to Dharo to visit—and why he never went back to live there."

"Anyway," Karla said. "Everything points to him being an honorable man who can be trusted."

"Daemonar likes him," Lucivar said. He felt the Black approaching and turned toward the library door.

Daemon opened the door and took one step inside. "Prince Yaslana, we need to talk."

Not his brother standing there. Not the Warlord Prince of Dhemlan. And not the Sadist. Which left the High Lord of Hell.

He followed Daemon to one of the sitting rooms situated not far from the library. Daemon walked over to a table that held a tray with several cut-crystal decanters and glasses, filled two glasses, and held one out.

He took the glass but didn't drink.

"I'm sorry, Lucivar."

He studied Daemon's eyes. This wasn't . . . personal. This wasn't about his wife or children. But Daemon thought it would hurt him and wanted to tell him in private.

"Who?" he asked.

"Orian and Dorian."

Lucivar sighed. "Hell's fire, that didn't take long."

Daemon took a long swallow of whiskey. "The demon-dead Eyriens who keep watch over Askavi Terreille brought them to Hell. When the two women made the transition to demon-dead, more or less, Chaosti came to get me."

"More or less?" A fine tremor went through his hand, almost sloshing whiskey over the rim of the glass. He drank half of it, letting the burn steady him.

"I don't know what they did or said, but the rage behind those executions . . ." Daemon hesitated. "I drained what was left of their power and finished the kill. They're whispers in the Darkness now."

"You gave them mercy."

"That was part of it. Another part was wondering if Orian would become a malevolence like Hekatah became if she was allowed to remain in Hell, hiding until her presence was forgotten."

He didn't want to think that about someone he'd watched grow from toddler to young woman. But he also didn't want to think about the significance of those lists Daemon had made.

He *had* to think about that. "You're going after the children."

"Yes."

"Because one of them reminds you of Dorothea."

"Because there was a warning in a tangled web that another like Dorothea was going to rise, cloaked in youth and innocence. Well, she's come, Prick. Our Queen said I would remember when I needed to remember. Your boy being at that school kept chipping away at the lock on that memory, and seeing that girl . . ." Daemon released a breath in a way that was too controlled, too careful. "That people are collecting Hayllian memorabilia troubles me. That people are romanticizing Dorothea's cruelty to make it more palatable to those who had never been on the receiving end of that cruelty enrages me. But there is no indication of some widespread conspiracy to start a war here, no threats being made toward the rest of the people in Dhemlan. At least, not by the adults. However, there is a group of youngsters who seem to be actively following the kind of viciousness that Dorothea relished. Maybe their families are the ones who want to remake Dhemlan into another Hayll, or maybe the adults just like to talk about it and it's the youngsters who have gathered around someone who has the right blend of malevolence and charisma to make it a reality. Either way, I've seen the faces of these particular enemies and have to deal with them, no matter the cost."

A burning in his gut. "If you do this . . ."

"I will be known throughout the Realm as the High Lord of Hell, monstrous and feared." Daemon smiled bitterly. "It was coming. Had to come. And I would rather it come saving Queens like Zoey and all the other strong young witches than for some lesser reason. I can live with destroying some in order to save the best."

Lucivar huffed out a breath. "All right. What do we—"

"Me. Not you."

"Piss on that," he snapped. "You don't walk into this alone."

Daemon drained his glass and refilled it. "I need to be sure they deserve . . . When I destroyed bitches in Terreille, regardless of their age, I was always sure because of what they'd done to me or what I witnessed them do to someone else."

"Okay. How can we be sure?" The thought of executing girls Titian's age made him sick. "You think this is why Dorothea managed to grow up to become what she was, to do what she did? Because the Warlord Princes who saw the warning signs didn't have the balls to carry the weight of those executions?"

"And she had Hekatah whispering in the shadows, nurturing that malevolent side of her nature," Daemon said. "Be sure you want to carry the weight of this particular war, Lucivar."

He held out his glass and waited for Daemon to refill it—and wished the whiskey decanter was filled with Chaosti's home brew. That, at least, would knock him on his ass for a little while.

"If you're going to do this, I have to carry part of that weight." He stared into his glass. "My body still carries some of the scars from the beatings, the whippings, the torture. Inside me, I carry other kinds of scars. I still dream about it sometimes. Still feel the burning rage from the drugs they used to try to breed me. Still wake up some nights because I feel my skin part beneath the whip." He looked at his brother. "You?"

"Sometimes."

"My boys have seen some of the scars; I tell them stories so they have some understanding about the scars that can't be seen. And I will stand on a killing field and meet whatever I need to meet in order to prevent them from knowing those things firsthand."

"Agreed." Daemon sighed. "Surreal and I are going to look at every girl who was broken in the towns or villages where one of the coven of malice resided. We're going to find out who did the breaking. The Province Queens know me well enough to know how I'll react if I find a pattern, so I have to think that there was nothing obvious enough to draw their attention."

"Wouldn't have drawn our attention right now if our children weren't at that school too," Lucivar said.

"Surreal set up a sanctuary for broken witches where they can receive training and rebuild their lives. She would have noticed eventually that specific kinds of girls were being 'accidentally' broken."

"And she would have honed her knives." But how many strong witches would have been lost before that?

Daemon smiled. "Of course."

Lucivar drank the whiskey, then used Craft to float the glass back to the tray. "I'll have a word with the Province Queens in Askavi, have them look to see if there is a pattern to the girls who aren't surviving their Virgin Nights with their power and Jewels intact."

"I'll set up meetings with the other Territory Queens, give them warning that things could get messy in Dhemlan."

"Winsol is coming soon."

"I know. I won't have enough information to act before then."

"A last celebration."

Daemon stepped close and rested his forehead against Lucivar's. "Let's hope it's not the last." He stepped back. "I've asked Chaosti to bring a fist of his men and take the night watch at the school. Weston and Zhara's guards can take the day watch. We'll keep the children safe, at least while they're there."

"Appreciate that." He hesitated. "You have any objections to me paying my respects?"

"She's your Queen too."

She was, but entering Witch's area of the Keep tended to prick Daemon's temper.

They parted ways when Daemon headed for the library and he headed for the part of the Keep very few people knew was still occupied—in a way.

She no longer had a physical body, and he suspected that her choice to appear as Witch, the dream that had been clothed in flesh—the dream that hadn't been fully human—was as much a kindness to Daemon as it was an acknowledgment of who she had always been. This form wasn't the body Daemon had worshipped with his own as husband and lover. This shadow, this illusion, was the Queen powerful enough to crush the Realms and everything in them.

He walked into the sitting room across from the Queen's suite and waited.

He didn't wait long.

"Daemonar sent a note telling me about the Sadist's visit to the school," Witch said, seeming to take shape out of the air.

"He's the third side of the triangle and one of your weapons," Lucivar replied. "Did you think he wouldn't?"

"You'll all do what needs to be done."

"Yeah, we will." He wasn't sure how to ask. "Jaenelle . . ."

She shook her head and huffed. "Your boy was quicker off the mark this time. Inform young Prince Yaslana that he should tell you about the charm he gave his sister before she went to school. The Queen commands."

He studied her. "A charm?"

"A protection. Blood sings to Blood. If Titian is in danger, she can call him."

"If he's within her reach."

"No, Lucivar. If he's within *my* reach." She shrugged. "It was a reasonable request from a member of the triangle."

"If it's more than he can handle?"

Oh, he remembered that look in her eyes. "Then I will summon the Demon Prince—and the High Lord of Hell."

He looked around the room, not sure what to say to her. That he was grateful she was still here? He was. More than he could say. That he had some inkling of what it must cost her to stay in this form, interacting with the people she had loved when she'd walked among the living—and still

382 * ANNE BISHOP

loved enough to do this? That he felt relieved that she was teaching Daemonar what a Queen *should* want from a Warlord Prince? That he felt even more relief that Daemon was still sane because he was under her hand? She already knew those things.

Instead, he said, "I haven't heard about any explosions lately, so I guess you and Karla have been too busy to experiment with spells."

"You haven't heard about any? Oh, good."

She gave him a smile that turned the bones in his legs to water.

She could have been teasing. Maybe.

He'd ask Draca. The Seneschal would know if any part of the Keep had turned to rubble.

Lucivar walked out of the Keep, smiling. The Queen's weapons would carry the weight of killing. They would pay the price. But today he would remember a sister and her coven—and mischief that had never contained any trace of malice.

# TWENTY-NINE

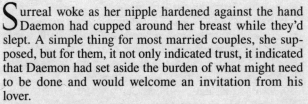

Surreal woke as her nipple hardened against the hand Daemon had cupped around her breast while they'd slept. A simple thing for most married couples, she supposed, but for them, it not only indicated trust, it indicated that Daemon had set aside the burden of what might need to be done and would welcome an invitation from his lover.

The first few days of Winsol had been . . . fraught. They had attended the parties and public celebrations as required by the Warlord Prince of Dhemlan and his wife. They had quietly taken aside the Province Queens and the District Queens who ruled the larger cities in Dhemlan and told them to put together lists of the young witches who had been broken during the Virgin Night—and they told the Queens why they wanted those lists, told them what they suspected without naming the youngsters they believed were responsible. They didn't want the Warlord Princes living in Dhemlan to turn on youngsters who had been stupid rather than malicious.

But the demands of those days had been felt by both of them. Some nights, after a day full of meetings and an evening full of parties, they had slept in the same bed but as far from each other as they could get. Some nights she woke and realized Daemon had gone to his own room to sleep alone, his temper too sharp and cold to stay with anyone.

Titian and Daemonar had asked to have parties at the town house in Amdarh to celebrate with friends before the whole family went to the Hall to celebrate Winsol Eve and Winsol. Jaenelle Saetien had thrown a hissy fit at first when she found out Titian hadn't invited any of *her* friends to the party, and Daemon wouldn't allow her to add those friends since it was Titian's party and the girl wasn't comfortable being around what Daemonar called the coven of malice.

The boys had their party on the Yaslana side of the town house, and the girls took over the SaDiablo side of the town house. Casually chaperoned by the adults, each group had seemed to have a good time, if the laughter and giggling had been the measuring stick.

Winsol Eve and Winsol Day at the Hall had been pleasant. She and Jaenelle Saetien had maintained a stilted formality, but Marian and Lucivar didn't ask what had brought about that change in their relationship. For that, she was grateful. At first, she had hoped that Tersa had been wrong, that the bond between her and Jaenelle Saetien hadn't been broken beyond repair. But the girl's words had severed that connection between them, and she felt the jagged break those words had made inside her. She needed to figure out how to accept that and move beyond it.

No longer a mother. Maybe a guide.

Maybe that was just as well, considering how much blood she would have on her hands soon.

But this morning, they had reached the quiet side of the Winsol celebrations, the days that Daemon and Jaenelle Angelline had established as time just for themselves. For family. No work, no meetings, no parties. Quiet days to rest and read, or go out for a gallop over fresh snow, or walk down to the village. Days she and Daemon spent together as friends and lovers.

This year, those days would also be used to prepare body and mind for a vicious kind of war that most of the people in Dhemlan would never know had been waged—if they were lucky.

She didn't think they would be that lucky.

Daemon's hand flexed around her breast. His thumb stroked her nipple.

She reached back and between them, and her hand closed around the part of him that was standing at attention, begging to be stroked.

The sound he made was part sigh, part dark chuckle.

She smiled. "What would you like to do today?"

"Is staying in bed an option?" he asked.

Releasing him, she vanished her nightgown and turned toward him, reclaiming the part of him that was exclusively hers. Guiding his cock into her, she said, "If you put a Black shield around the room, we can stay long enough to combine breakfast with the midday meal."

"You won't get too hungry?" he asked as he moved inside her.

*Not for food.* She kissed him—and his response was to give her an edgy sweetness they hadn't shared in a long time.

"Ease up now," Jaenelle Saetien said, putting a little pressure on the reins attached to the mare's halter.

The kindred mare—a witch who wore a Tiger Eye Jewel—slowed to a walk. *I am not tired. We can run some more.*

"I'd like to go down to the village and visit Manny."

*We can run?*

"Sure." The snow was deep enough she didn't think the mare would want to run for long.

The mare gave a funny hop that almost tossed her out of the saddle. When she regained her balance and looked around to see what the mare had reacted to, she realized the hooves were standing on air just above the snow.

*Now we can run.*

That was all the warning she got before the mare took off in the direction of Halaway. They galloped, they cantered, they wove around trees, they jumped over shadows on the snow just because the mare wanted to jump.

"We can go over the bridge," she said when they reached the creek and the bridge that separated the land belonging to the SaDiablo family seat from the village.

The mare just snorted, bunched her hindquarters, and used Craft to help her fly over the creek and land lightly on the other side.

Jaenelle Saetien laughed and shouted, "Well done!"

Pleased with herself, the mare slowed to a walk when they reached the edge of the village.

Jaenelle Saetien dismounted and the two of them walked side by side for a minute before she stopped. She unclipped the reins from the halter, carefully looped them as she'd been taught, then attached them to a ring on the saddle.

"I'm going to be visiting a while. Why don't you go back to the Hall so you don't stand out here in the cold?"

*No more running?* the mare asked.

"Not today."

The mare trotted off, heading toward the Hall. She would get there eventually, when she was ready for a rub-down and a meal.

Jaenelle Saetien walked into the village.

There were paddocks at the Hall's stables like you would expect to see around any place that had horses, but they weren't used in the same way. Each stallion in residence had his own paddock, where he romanced his chosen mares, and there was a paddock for the youngsters. That was more like a large playpen than anything else to keep them out of trouble—and out of Mrs. Beale's kitchen garden. But the kindred horses roamed the estate, usually returning to the stables in the evening.

In the same way that Beale and Helene assigned chores to the staff working in the Hall, the stable master assigned horses to stay nearby for any human who wanted to go out riding. So you never knew who would go riding with you, although the horses did have their favorite humans. The stallion who was an Opal-Jeweled Warlord Prince preferred her father and often refused to consider anyone else for his rider.

That was fine with her. Warlord Princes were bossy at the best of times. One that didn't have hands tended to use his teeth to grab and tug you where he wanted you to go, and arguing with something that outweighed you by that much was futile most of the time.

Halaway was a pretty village. Being so close to the Hall and under her father's watchful eye, it couldn't be anything else. Delora had made disparaging comments about her being stuck in a little village for days and days and days, and Jaenelle Saetien hadn't disagreed with her because she didn't want Delora and Hespera to think she was a rube. But Halaway was a comfortable place. It didn't bustle like the city, and maybe it didn't have the best of the best shops, but it had everything people needed.

She'd been tired of the village children she had grown up with, had played with and gone to school with. She'd wanted—*needed*—something exciting, something different. She'd wanted—*needed*—to be around people who had never met, let alone known, that Queen she couldn't begin to compete with. From the moment she'd met Delora at a party when they were still children, she'd wanted to be part of the dazzle the other girl made happen so effortlessly. Wasn't that what aristos did? Dazzle everyone else?

Except . . .

Daemonar's comment that he didn't like her anymore had hurt. A lot. But, somehow, hearing that comment had made her hear other things that she had ignored—or made excuses for. Like Hespera calling Titian a fat bat all the time. Titian wasn't fat. Her bones weren't showing through her skin and she didn't have a caved-in belly that looked like someone had scooped out her insides, but she wasn't fat.

They *said* they were only teasing, and if a girl's feelings were hurt, it was her own fault. But meanness was meanness. Wasn't it? She wasn't sure she would ever be sophisticated enough to participate in that kind of teasing. But if you weren't doing the teasing, then you were on the receiving end. Weren't you?

She could admit to herself that she'd been upset—all right, she'd been bitchy—when Papa wouldn't let her add *her* friends to the girls invited to the party at the town house. Then Titian had said, "Why would I want people who call me a fat bat to come to my Winsol party?"

Words that hurt. Meanness disguised as teasing.

But Delora wasn't like that. She *cared* about people. And she'd be hurt if she knew what other people called *her* group of friends.

The truth was, the girls who had come to the party, the girls Titian and Zoey had befriended at school, weren't rubes or dregs or the ballast the school needed to stay afloat financially. They were interesting. They didn't make snide comments about how someone dressed or said someone wasn't aristo enough to deserve notice. They were just . . . happy. They were from aristo families, but they were happy. They talked about horses; they talked about books; they talked about art. Titian and Zoey had found several copies of an old play or drama or something no one had heard of, carefully preserved in a trunk in the attic.

They had drawn names out of a hat to decide who would play the characters and who would be the audience. They had giggled and moaned and thrown themselves into the parts—and sometimes had to stop for several minutes because they were all laughing too hard to read the next lines.

They'd had fun. And if a few of the girls had been a little wistful about the boys' party being out-of-bounds, it wasn't because they wanted to spy on the boys as Hespera had wanted her to do; it was because they wanted a minute to talk to Beron, who was very handsome and a rising star in the theater.

It just seemed that everything had spun out of control at home since she'd been included in Delora's select group of friends. When she was around Delora, she felt justified in feeling angry about not being given a second dress for a dance. Wincing at the cutting remarks Delora's friends made about everyone they deemed inferior, she'd felt mortified by the behavior of some members of her family—and humiliated by the truth about . . . that woman. She couldn't even say the word "mother" anymore, and she thought there might be something wrong with that. Maybe.

She blinked and sucked in a breath when she realized someone was walking beside her.

"You were doing some hard thinking," Mikal said.

She shrugged. "It was nothing."

He cocked his head and kept looking at her. "You sure?"

She wanted to ask if he knew about *that woman*, but she wasn't sure she could stand the shame if he did know. And if he didn't, he'd figure it out from her questions. "I'm sure."

"You going someplace in particular?"

"I'm going to visit Manny."

"Stop by Tersa's cottage when you're done. We've got two puppies in residence." His grin came and went. "One is Uncle Daemon's new special friend. For Breen, it was love at first sight, and the Sceltie Queens said she had to come here to live because she was barely weaned and she kept trying to run away in order to find him. The other pup also requires extra attention. He's friendly enough, but he's . . . sad. So they're staying with Tersa and me until Uncle Daemon sorts out whatever needs to be sorted out and can stay home for a while."

"What needs to be sorted out?" she asked.

"I don't know. But Uncle Daemon said if any of the girls who were fluttering around me wanted more than first-stage romancing, he wanted to know—especially if any of them indicated that I could somehow be persuaded to break the rules. And he said if *I* overstepped the lines that were drawn, he'd have my skin—and he meant that. So I figure something is going on. The Halaway Queen's court is . . . watchful . . . in a sharp kind of way." He rolled his shoulders, as if shaking off a weight. "Anyway, come see the puppies."

"I will." She hesitated. She didn't want to put his back

up, but she really wanted to know. "Mikal? Do you ever want more than just living in Halaway?"

"I don't know. Maybe. So many skilled people live in this village or have a connection to the Hall, I could study a dozen different kinds of work right here. And I've been thinking of doing a kind of apprenticeship rotation, working with someone for a season to see if I fit the work."

"You're aristo. You don't have to work."

Mikal smiled. "Everyone has to work in one way or another, Jaenelle Saetien. An idle life gives nothing to anyone. And even if it doesn't appear that they're doing much, a Queen works the hardest of anyone in a village because the health of the village is in her hands."

Krellis, Dhuran, and Clayton would sneer at such talk. Aristo families provided the means for others to have work and food and that was more than enough—and anyone who wasn't grateful for that should be taught how to be grateful.

She couldn't think of a single person in her family who would agree with that.

Manny's and Tersa's cottages were next to each other, so Jaenelle Saetien parted with Mikal at Manny's front walk. The old woman invited her in with smiles and a hug.

"Quiet days after the big Winsol celebration," Manny said. "The cold box is full of food, and the pantry shelves are bending under the weight of all the treats I prepared or was given, so there's nothing for me to cook. I've got my feet up this afternoon, and I'm reading a book the boys would be embarrassed to see me reading—especially since I'm old enough that I can point to something in the story and ask them flat out if they do that with their wives." She laughed. "Last time I did that, Lucivar blushed."

So tempting to ask for the title of that book, but there were other answers she wanted today. "Could we talk in the kitchen?"

Manny's good humor remained, but it was tempered by concern. "Sure we can. Do you want some tea?"

"Thanks." Because she knew it would make things less

grim, she added, "And maybe I could help reduce the weight on one of those groaning pantry shelves?"

Manny put the kettle on for the tea, then handed Jaenelle Saetien a plate and sent her into the pantry to select some treats. They worked without small talk. Jaenelle Saetien hadn't come for small talk.

"What's on your mind?" Manny asked when the tea had been poured and they'd each selected a couple of treats.

"Did you know my . . ." She choked, unable to say the word. "Did you know Surreal was a whore?"

Manny nodded. "I wasn't comfortable with how she made her living, wasn't always comfortable being around her when we were in Terreille. But she was a good friend to Daemon, and when he was lost in the Twisted Kingdom and finding his way back, she found a place where he would be safe and hidden from everyone who was hunting for him. She asked me to go with her to help look after him, and I did. He and I stayed hidden, and she went out and did what she had to do to keep us safe until he finally walked out of the Twisted Kingdom."

Shocked, Jaenelle Saetien bobbled the tea cup. She set it on the saucer. "My father had been insane?" Was that different from whatever had made him ill when she was young? Was it different from the funny turns he still experienced?

"He was for a while. Unlike Tersa, he was able to cross the border and come all the way out. He had a reason to come out."

"When he was my age . . ." She wasn't sure what she wanted to know.

"He suffered." Manny breathed in, an angry sound. "That evil woman put a Ring of Obedience on him and started training him to be her whore within hours of him making the Birthright Ceremony and her arranging for his father to be denied paternity."

"What woman?" She grabbed the old woman's hand. "Manny? What woman?"

"The High Priestess of Hayll. Dorothea." Manny seemed to struggle to breathe. "Just saying that name makes me want to spit. A foul woman. She used him and abused him and raped him and tortured him until he became old enough and strong enough—and lethal enough—to be a danger to her and her coven. Then she sold him to Queens and aristo witches who curried favor with her, trying to break him down. But he didn't break the way she wanted. He became cold and cruel and deadly, and in the end, she had to keep him away from Hayll because she'd known that if he got close enough for long enough, he would have ripped her to pieces with his bare hands, regardless of what happened to him afterward."

*Dorothea.*

Remembering the sound of his voice and the look in his eyes when he met Delora and called her by another name, Jaenelle Saetien shivered.

Manny sighed. "That bitch hurt him so much, he didn't remember that Tersa was his mother, but once they met again, he loved her and looked after her. He didn't remember his father, but he was too much his father's son for Dorothea to be able to control him or shape him into a weapon she could use. Daemon was never truly happy after he was taken from his father. Not until he met Jaenelle Angelline. She saved the best that was in him—and she loved the side of him that everyone else feared. Without her, he would have become death on the killing fields. Death . . . and nothing more. Lucivar too." She sat back. "I don't want to talk about this anymore. Too much pain."

"I'm sorry I brought up bad memories."

"There wasn't much else in Terreille. Not for those boys, or for Surreal either. Not for any of them." Manny blew out a breath. "Enough of looking back."

She nodded. She'd heard more than enough. For now, anyway. "Mikal says there are puppies next door."

"That there are." Manny pushed to her feet. "Let me wrap up those treats. You can take them next door."

Figuring the puppies would be in the kitchen area, she went out the back door of Manny's cottage, entered through the back door of Tersa's, and turned toward the basket and the puppy who looked into her eyes, then struggled to get away from Mikal and reach her.

Love at first sight. For him. For her.

She almost dropped the plate in her haste to set it on the table before rushing to the basket, sinking to her knees, and cradling the pup in her arms.

"Oh, you adorable boy!" she cooed. "Aren't you a lovely boy?"

The adorable, lovely boy was beyond excited to see her. She put him down on the diaper Mikal dropped in front of her, but she had to hold on to him until he piddled to keep him from wetting her lap.

"That's Shelby," Mikal said. "He's a direct descendant of Ladvarian. Breen comes from Morghann's line."

A Warlord. A strong-willed one. He was too young for her to get a sense of his power, but may the Darkness have mercy on anyone trying to deal with him if that strong will was combined with a darker Jewel.

Mikal had his hands full with the little female, who was focused on something in the front of the cottage and cried in a way to break a person's heart.

"Breen," Mikal soothed. "Hush now, Breen. Daemon isn't here."

"Yes, he is." Daemon stepped into the kitchen behind Tersa, shrugged out of the short winter coat, and sank to his knees beside the basket. He picked up the puppy and cradled her against his chest, a brown-and-white ball of fur against the bright red sweater.

The sweater was a signal that her father was home and off duty, his obligations as the Warlord Prince of Dhemlan put aside—at least for the day.

She wasn't sure what he'd intended, but he moved his hands and the puppy sank her sharp little teeth into the sweater, anchoring herself to him. From his quick intake of breath, she suspected Breen's teeth had caught more than the sweater.

When she picked up the Warlord again to cuddle him, she realized he was focused on Breen. Before he could follow the other pup's example, she lifted him away from her chest and said firmly, "No. We don't claim humans by biting their clothes." *Or the body part under the clothes.*

Shelby hadn't learned to talk to humans yet on a psychic thread, but she could feel his frustrated objection. *But Breen is doing it.*

Mikal snorted a laugh, then tried to look innocent.

Yes, these two pups needed extra attention and someone to love—and herd. She wasn't foolish enough to think there wouldn't be extra herding as well. She'd lived around Scelties all her life, but after she'd made a mistake with Morghann and told her to do a wrong thing, the Scelties who lived at the Hall would play with her, but none of them would let her teach them anything. They learned what was proper from her father and Beale and Holt—and Mikal.

She wanted that connection again, wanted to be teacher as well as playmate. Wanted someone to think she was special.

Quiet murmurs from her father in his deep, soothing voice finally convinced Breen to release the sweater. He petted and praised. They all played with the two pups until exhausted bundles of fur were tucked back into the basket for a nap.

As she and her father rose to take their leave, Jaenelle Saetien realized Tersa had been sitting at the kitchen table all that time, watching them. Just watching.

Tersa followed them to the front door, then grabbed her wrist, holding her back with one hand while giving Daemon a push to indicate she wanted him out.

He gave his mother a puzzled look but stepped outside and closed the door.

Sometimes Tersa just seemed eccentric. Other times she was strange in a frightening sort of way—like now.

"Everything has a price," Tersa said. "You will pay what you owe. He will ask, and she will answer—and she will do what needs to be done. For him. For you. When the time comes, you should remember that."

"I'll remember." She had no idea what Tersa was talking about, but it was better to agree with her.

"Yes," Tersa whispered, "you will." She released Jaenelle Saetien's wrist.

As Jaenelle Saetien opened the door, Tersa added, "Not all scars are visible. You put a scar on the girl that will never fully heal. You both have to live with that now."

She wasn't going to think about that. She wasn't.

Her father waited for her at the end of the walkway.

"Everything all right?" he asked.

"Everything is fine." Nothing was fine, so she focused on the one thing she wanted to think about.

"Papa? Could I help you and Mikal teach Shelby?"

He said nothing. As they walked up the main street, he nodded to the people who were going in and out of the village shops, but they all seemed to sense that he didn't want to stop and chat. Finally, he said, "I think it would break that pup's heart if he couldn't be with you at least some of the time, but you will be going back to school in a few days. Won't you?"

"Yes." It hadn't occurred to her that she *wouldn't* go back to school. "But when he's a little older, Shelby could come to the town house on the study days. I could stay home then, and we could take walks around the square. It wouldn't be good for him to come to the school. Too many people who might accidentally tell him a wrong thing without appreciating the damage they could do." Like she'd done. But she'd been a child then. She wouldn't want any of the boys at the school to spend time around Shelby when he was so young and impressionable.

None of the boys except Daemonar.

That uncomfortable truth was something else she didn't want to think about.

"I agree," he said. "When it comes to Scelties, all the teachers have to agree on the rules—and uphold them."

Pretty much the way it worked in the family. Her father and uncle decided on the rules and where the lines were drawn—and they both upheld those rules, regardless of place and whose child was being called to task.

But she was almost an adult, and she had to make her own choices, her own decisions. Didn't she?

And yet, today felt comfortable. She knew the boundaries of acceptable behavior as well as she knew the boundaries of the family seat. Delora and Hespera kept saying she was *afraid* to step beyond the rules, that she would never prove to anyone that she was a strong woman unless she showed everyone that she could make up her own mind about things—something her parents, her *father*, clearly would never allow her to do.

They always *sounded* right when she was with them. She wasn't allowed to do half of what they were allowed to do, and doing those things with them gave her a taste of defiant freedom.

But Titian and Zoey had stepped outside all expected lines, and no one had made a fuss. Her father and Uncle Lucivar had listened to Titian—and then had drawn new lines. No fights, no defiance.

It wasn't that they *never* moved the lines. They just couldn't seem to understand when *she* needed the lines moved. Maybe because *she* didn't know where she wanted them to draw those lines?

"Witch-child?"

She linked her arm in his and remembered something that was sure to distract him. "What was the title of the book Manny was reading that made Uncle Lucivar blush?"

He choked. "It doesn't matter since it will be a few more decades before you're allowed to read it."

Maybe tomorrow she would chafe at his deciding she wasn't old enough to read a particular book, but for the rest of the way home, they talked about puppies and made plans to go out riding together in the morning.

# THIRTY

Delora watched from the shadows as Jaenelle Saetien stopped to talk with Insipid Zoey and Fat Bat Titian, as well as the group of girls—and boys—who were infatuated with Daemonar's fighting skills.

Something had changed during the thirteen days of Winsol, when Jaenelle Saetien had been away from school—and away from her influence. When the girl had arrived at the school that fall, she'd been ripe for rebellion, craving an escape from her stodgy little village and the rules her parents used to constrict her choices.

She'd been ripe to embrace some of the Hayllian traditions that Delora found so fascinating because you had to read between the lines of what was written in history books and listen for what wasn't quite said in the stories her family told when they acquired a new object that had come from Hayll.

It had been such a thrill when Jaenelle Saetien's father had misheard her name and called her Dorothea, like he already acknowledged her ambition and destiny.

But something had changed in Jaenelle Saetien during her time away from school. Instead of being embarrassed or laughing with the rest of Delora's followers when the boys used their cutting wit to demean the girls unworthy of their notice except as prey of one sort or another, Jaenelle Saetien had looked uncomfortable and actually told Krellis yesterday that he was being unkind to one of the school dregs.

That would not do. It wouldn't do at all. Where was the anger, the need to embrace what only Delora could offer? Who had reinforced that rube morality? Someone in that village, no doubt. Jaenelle Saetien should be avoiding her cousins—both of them—and the girls and boys who formed the core of Insipid Zoey's friends. Instead, she was *talking* to them where everyone could see her—and might wonder if she'd changed allegiance.

Well, there were ways to bring her to heel and make sure that a good bitch stayed a good bitch.

"We have a problem," Krellis said as he joined her.

"More than one," Delora replied, continuing to watch as Jaenelle Saetien, Insipid, and Fat Bat led the group toward the classrooms.

"Prince Sadi and his bitch wife have been asking questions about girls who were broken on their Virgin Nights. They want a list of names from each Province Queen, which means the Province Queens are asking questions of the District Queens, and that means the District Queens are looking hard at everyone in their territories, especially the aristo families. And Sadi wants the name of every male responsible for breaking the power of a witch when the girl's virginity was taken."

Delora turned to look at him. "You said you were all careful and only had fun with the girls I told you would cause us trouble later."

"We *were* careful, and we sometimes did nothing more than help some boy enjoy what he couldn't have had otherwise—and witness the taking to encourage him to be accommodating when we wanted his assistance for some other entertainment." Krellis stared at Jaenelle Saetien. "If Sadi and his whore put all the pieces together, they'll find me and Dhuran and Clayton—and they'll find you right at the heart of all those 'accidental' breakings."

"Well," Delora said, "we'll have to give him a reason to back off."

✦  ✦  ✦

Daemonar wasn't as good at reading people as his father or uncle, who could glance at a person and know what he was thinking, feeling, planning. But it didn't take that much skill to recognize Prince Raine's discomfort—or figure out the reason.

He'd invited Raine to the Winsol party, in part because he liked the man and partly because Raine hadn't planned to visit his family in Dharo until Winsol Eve. It was hard for a man to be alone during the Blood's most important celebration, and since Raine lived at the school, Daemonar didn't think the instructor had made many, if any, friends.

And he'd wanted Uncle Daemon to become acquainted with a man Daemonar thought was being wasted trying to teach the prick-asses at the school.

Until the party, he hadn't known that Raine, who was in his mid-twenties, came from the same family as Rainier, the Dharo Warlord Prince who had served in Witch's Second Circle. Curiosity about Rainier had been the spark that had had Raine applying for an instructor's position at a school in Dhemlan, where he would live among people who came from one of the long-lived races, just as Rainier had.

He had observed Raine's shock and delight at learning that Rainier had taught Beron the dance moves the young actor still practiced and used on the stage. He'd watched Raine stumble over the easy way Beron and his theater friends chatted with Uncle Daemon, how the conversation bounced from one subject to the next, as if they weren't talking to the most powerful man in the Realm.

And he studied Raine's discomfort now that the Winsol celebration was over and they had returned to school. He figured the reason for that discomfort was that Raine hadn't served in a court or otherwise been exposed to the flow of power and titles that he saw as natural.

"I invited you to the Winsol party as a friend," Daemonar said, setting his books on the table.

Raine turned away from the window. "I appreciate that, but . . ."

Daemonar raised a hand to stop the words. "But now you're concerned that you won't be seen as an instructor with any authority."

"That sums it up."

He smiled. "At home, in our eyrie, my father is my father—most of the time. I address him as Father, and we argue about things as family, although his decisions are final—unless my mother overrules him. She doesn't do it often, but when she does, he yields. The Warlord Prince of Ebon Rih rules the valley where I live. His second-in-command can argue with him in private. So can the most trusted Eyrien warriors who work for him. But his word is law, and those men are careful about how they phrase their disagreements. So am I. And then there is the Demon Prince who rules all of Askavi. His word is also law, but when *he* shows up in a city or village in Askavi, he is there to stand on a killing field as the Queen's weapon. He is there for slaughter, and everyone knows it. Same man, different titles. You could call it different aspects of the same man, since Father can change to Demon Prince in a heartbeat when he senses a threat of any kind."

"Your point?" Raine asked. "Besides a very interesting lesson about your family."

"At the town house, you're a friend. Here you're my tutor. I don't have any trouble making the distinction or understanding that different rules apply to each aspect. Courts work the same way. A fluid dance of power." Daemonar waited a beat. "Rainier understood that."

Raine narrowed his eyes. "I can understand Beron knowing Rainier, but you . . . ?"

It was as if the difference between the long-lived and short-lived races became real, and Raine finally realized the adolescents he was teaching had already lived centuries compared to his twenty-some years.

"I don't remember a lot about him," Daemonar said,

"but I know from family stories that he was one of my aunt Surreal's closest friends."

"Perhaps we can meet up for dinner one night. I'd like to hear the stories." Raine smiled. "Should we get on with this lesson?"

"One more thing." Daemonar didn't return the smile. "If Prince Sadi asks anything of you, don't ask questions and don't argue. Just do it."

Raine's smile faded. "Why would he ask anything of me?"

*Your instincts are good, boyo. Your Dharo friend has potential.*

Daemonar shrugged. "I don't know. But if he does, consider it a command, not a request, regardless of how it's phrased."


*Would I want Shelby to learn anything from Dhuran or Clayton or Krellis? A Sceltie puppy will trust what humans tell him—until he stops trusting anything most humans tell him.*

Funny how asking that question kept changing things. Where she'd previously heard biting wit when those boys targeted another student, now she heard cruelty.

*"You seem different, Jaenelle Saetien,"* Delora had said a couple of days after they'd come back to school. *"Did you meet someone over Winsol, enjoy a little romance?"*

*"Maybe she learned how to enjoy some petting,"* Dhuran said, giving her a look that made her uneasy.

*"Don't be crude,"* Hespera scolded. Then she looked at Jaenelle Saetien from head to toe. *"Although, if you want to keep his interest, you should pay more attention to your clothes, darling. You don't want people to think you're following your cousin's example and have started tonguing other girls."*

*"Now you're being crude,"* Delora said. *"Jaenelle Sae-*

402 ◆ ANNE BISHOP

*tien just hasn't had time to switch back to the city style of dressing. I imagine your father doesn't allow you to look like a sophisticated woman when you're home. Nothing he can do about your mother's reputation, but he probably wants you to look like a little girl for as long as possible."*

She'd worn this outfit on the last day of school before they all went home for Winsol, and Delora had said it was a sleek look for a powerful woman. Now it was childish and only something a rube would wear?

She had a feeling she was being punished for failing to get Delora and Hespera invited to the party at the town house. But all those two had talked about since they'd returned to school was how many parties they *had* attended and how exhausting it was to be so much in demand, so it was just as well they hadn't been invited to Fat Bat's little party.

Zoey didn't like Delora. Not at all.

Jaenelle Saetien might have put it down to jealousy because Zoey was a Queen who was barely noticed, while Delora had a way of dazzling students and instructors alike. But there was that word. *Dorothea.* It bothered her that her father had looked at one of her best friends and had been reminded of a witch who had tortured him. Had done more than torture him.

She'd been rushing to her last morning class, had intended to meet up with Zoey and Titian for a few minutes beforehand since they were the only girls at the school who could appreciate the excitement and craziness that came with dealing with a kindred Sceltie, especially during puppyhood. She'd received a terse note from Mikal telling her to stop pestering him. Shelby was fine. Breen was fine. They were all working hard on understanding the rules for "pee here, don't pee there." Unless she wanted to come home and help him clean up the accidents, there was nothing to say, and when there was, he'd tell her.

She'd written only five notes in the past few days, asking him for reports on Shelby's progress. That could hardly be considered pestering.

"Trouble at home or trouble in love?" Hespera said, suddenly coming up along one side of her.

"Neither," she replied, noticing how Delora now walked on her other side, with Leena, Amara, Borsala, and Tacita forming a little pack just behind them.

"You looked . . . anxious," Delora said. "We were concerned."

Friends cared about friends. Of course they were concerned. And yet she hadn't told Delora about Shelby, hadn't even mentioned the puppies, let alone acknowledged how much it mattered to her to have a Sceltie want to be her special friend.

She hadn't said anything because she was afraid they would make fun of her for caring about something so *rube*—and because of that word: *Dorothea*.

"We wanted to warn you about him." Delora made a subtle gesture to indicate one of the boys walking toward the classrooms.

She recognized him as one of the young Warlords who attended the morning workouts with Daemonar. "Warn me about Nelson? Why?"

"He's a slut," Hespera said. "And a mean one at that. Not only will he give anyone a ride, he tried to use some forceful persuasion on a couple of girls when they said they weren't interested."

A boy who was a slut and also leaned toward rape? Was that possible?

"Does Zoey know? He's one of her friends." Did Daemonar know? Probably not. He wouldn't have anything to do with a slut. And definitely not a boy who danced on the line of being accused of rape.

"We thought you should know so you can be careful when you're around him," Delora said.

"Thanks." Jaenelle Saetien gave Delora a strained smile. "There's something I need to do. Do you want to meet up for lunch?"

"Of course."

She hurried toward Zoey and Titian. She had to warn

them that a boy they considered a friend might not be as honorable as they thought.

"You think she'll spread the rumor?" Hespera asked as they continued walking to their next boring class.

"She'll spread it. And being the daughter of the Warlord Prince of Dhemlan, her concern will carry more weight."

"Serves Nelson right for refusing to go down on his knees to make you happy."

Delora smiled. "Yes. It serves him right."

# THIRTY-ONE

※

Daemonar ignored the churning in his gut that had started when he'd come upon Jaenelle Saetien, Titian, and Zoey just in time to overhear Jaenelle Saetien sharing a rumor about Nelson and clearly intending to tell the other girls who were in Zoey and Titian's group of friends. Promising himself that he'd release some of his anger by sending his uncle a blistering letter informing Prince Sadi of this serious hole in his cousin's education, he had aimed enough of that anger at the girls to silence their nattering and get an I-will-hurt-you-if-you-break-this promise from each of them that *nothing* would be said to anyone else until that evening when they would all talk about what Jaenelle Saetien had heard.

They'd all been shocked by the depth of his anger, which made him a little less pissed off with Uncle Daemon since his anger now stretched to include his father and Lady Zhara for also being negligent. Then a nugget of common sense helped him consider that the difference in his age and the girls' could account for his deeper level of understanding about the consequences of that particular rumor. Telling a lie about *something* had always brought out the sharp side of Lucivar's temper—and Daemon's, too, for that matter—but telling a lie about *someone* . . . The price for that kind of lie was always steep—and not a price Lucivar or Daemon would have required a daughter

to witness. And when he was the girls' age, Lucivar hadn't
allowed him to stand witness either. But just a few years
ago, he'd been permitted to stand witness and had watched
the Warlord Prince of Ebon Rih use an Eyrien club to
break a man to pieces for spreading lies that had resulted
in another man killing his wife.

The execution had been brutal and merciless. Since there
was no law against murder among the Blood, the man who
had killed his wife received no official punishment, but less
than a month later, he made arrangements for his children to
visit his wife's family and he disappeared. A few days after
that, the High Lord informed the Demon Prince of a man,
newly transformed to demon-dead, who had arrived in Hell
searching for his wife, hoping that she, too, had made the
transition and was somewhere in the Dark Realm.

So he knew, as the girls did not, that Jaenelle Saetien
could be in serious trouble.


He wanted a place that was neutral ground, so Daemonar
didn't hesitate to pull rank on Prince Raine and get the instructor's reluctant permission to use the room that served as
Raine's office and tutorial space. Lady Fharra wasn't happy
about Lord Weston and his men standing guard over Zoey
even in the girls' dormitory. She would have screamed the
roof off the building if she'd known about Prince Chaosti and
the fist of demon-dead Dea al Mon warriors who were guarding Zoey, Titian, and Jaenelle Saetien at night. And considering the subject they were here to discuss, it was better for a
man of Daemonar's age not to be seen in the girls' dormitory.

Raine had insisted on being present, and Daemonar had
agreed—mostly because he wanted the Dharo Prince to see
firsthand that courts, and families, had a dangerous side usually only seen by those involved—or those who were killed.

Jaenelle Saetien, Zoey, and Titian had slipped out of
their rooms, wrapped in sight shields to avoid detection.
None of the girls was happy about seeing the men in the
room, but Zoey looked more resigned than surprised to

find Raine and Weston at this meeting. Judging by her squirming, Jaenelle Saetien hadn't realized this would be more than a family discussion and that she would have to explain things to adults who had some authority.

Everyone in the room except him looked stunned—and frightened—when Chaosti walked in and put a Gray shield around the room and a Gray lock on the door.

"Prince Yaslana," Chaosti said.

Daemonar stood and gave the other Warlord Prince the small bow that indicated respect as well as acknowledged Chaosti's darker Jewel. He introduced everyone else in the room, including Titian. He'd known the High Lord's second-in-command his whole life, but he didn't think his sister had ever met the Dea al Mon Warlord Prince. He was certain Jaenelle Saetien had not, although he knew Aunt Surreal had taken her to visit the Dea al Mon who came from the same clan as Surreal's mother.

Zoey's reaction was the most interesting. After the initial shock, he could see her thinking hard about why this particular man was in the room—and what it might mean.

He'd bet a hundred gold marks that she would write a report tonight and send it to Uncle Daemon by special messenger in the morning. He wasn't willing to bet on how his uncle would reply.

Chaosti tipped his head to the three witches, then focused those large forest-blue eyes on Jaenelle Saetien. "Now, little Sister, tell us about this boy you claim has not only abandoned his honor but has also threatened the well-being of young witches."

"It's not true," Zoey growled. She sat on the edge of her chair, her hands curled into fists.

Chaosti simply looked at her. She met his look for ten heartbeats before she lowered her eyes and yielded.

"Lady SaDiablo?" Chaosti said. "Tell us the names of the girls who have used this boy—and the names of the girls he attempted to violate."

"I don't know," Jaenelle Saetien said hurriedly, "but that's not important. Everyone knows—"

"The names are everything, little Sister." Chaosti stared
at her. "These are serious accusations. You told two others
and would have told more if Prince Yaslana hadn't insisted
that you curb your tongue until we could meet tonight. If
you were going to tell others, then you must know the
names of the girls who used this boy and the names of the
girls he tried to use."

"I—"

"Jaenelle Saetien, this is an official inquiry being con-
ducted by a Gray-Jeweled Warlord Prince," Daemonar interrupted. "'Forceful persuasion' means attempted rape.
This will be reported to the Queen of Amdarh and the
Warlord Prince of Dhemlan. If any of what you told Zoey
and Titian is true, Nelson will be castrated for the offense,
if not executed outright. In telling other people what you
heard, you were willing to smear Nelson's honor and possibly be the voice that was instrumental in his forfeiting
his life. You *have* to know the names, and you have to tell
Prince Chaosti *now*."

She looked frightened, shocked. Daemonar wanted to
smack her for being so obtuse. But Titian looked equally
shocked, which reminded him how much the years between them meant in terms of maturity. She might not
have repeated the rumors because they were unkind, but
she wouldn't have equated something said at the school
being worth an official inquiry.

Only Zoey seemed to have some appreciation of the se-
verity of what was happening in this room tonight.

"I don't know," Jaenelle Saetien admitted. "A friend
told me about him because she'd heard the rumors and was
concerned for Zoey's safety."

Zoey snorted. "The coven of malice doesn't care about
anyone but themselves. It was one of them who told you,
wasn't it? I bet they spread the rumor as punishment because Nelson didn't capitulate to one of them." She stared
at Chaosti. "Do you want *their* names?"

"We are already aware of the coven of malice," Chaosti
replied.

"Don't call them that," Jaenelle Saetien snapped. "It's mean."

"It's accurate, little Sister."

"Why do you keep calling me that?"

"Surreal is kin to me. Therefore, you are kin to me."

She looked like she'd been kicked by a draft horse.

Zoey, however, stood and raised her chin. "I'll be sending a report to Prince Sadi about this."

Weston groaned. Raine made a sound that might have been a whimper. Daemonar sighed.

Chaosti laughed softly. "That is a Queen's privilege. I, too, will be sharing my observations about this evening with Prince Sadi." He looked at everyone in the room. "It is my judgment that the rumors and accusations about this boy, Lord Nelson, were falsely made. Therefore, no one in this room will repeat those rumors and accusations or discuss the content of this meeting with anyone except if officially required by the Queen of Amdarh or the Warlord Prince of Dhemlan. Prince Yaslana, what is the penalty for ignoring or defying my judgment?"

"Anyone who repeats the accusations that were made about Lord Nelson or repeats what was said in this room will forfeit his or her tongue," Daemonar replied.

Zoey flopped back into her chair, clearly not expecting so harsh a penalty.

Chaosti studied her. "Lady Zoela, having stated your intention before I passed judgment, you have my consent to write an official report to Prince Sadi. You must have *his* consent before you write any other report or discuss this with anyone else." He looked at Weston. "You may report to the Queen of Amdarh."

Weston bowed. "If you require nothing else of me, I'll escort the Ladies back to their rooms."

"We are done." Chaosti released the Gray lock on the door and vanished the Gray shield around the room.

When the girls and Weston had left, Daemonar blew out a breath, scrubbed his hands over his face, and muttered, "Mother Night."

"Under the circumstances, I would recommend a large glass of whiskey—for both of you," Chaosti said.

"I have a bottle here," Raine said.

"Then I'll take my leave."

"Chaosti . . ." Daemonar wasn't sure what he wanted to ask. He didn't need to be sure. Not with a Warlord Prince who had helped train him to fight.

"My knives are very sharp, and I will not falter to extract the price if that is required—no matter who must pay," Chaosti said.

Daemonar hadn't expected any other answer, so he'd corner the girls in the morning and make sure they didn't dismiss what had been said because the sun was shining and things might not sound as serious in the light of day.

Chaosti would not falter in his duty, and he didn't want any of the girls to learn that lesson the hard way.

Once Chaosti left, Raine poured two large whiskeys and handed one to Daemonar.

"Why did you let me stay?" Raine looked pale.

"I didn't think you would have witnessed one of these inquiries and judgments before," Daemonar replied. He took a long swallow of whiskey. "Chaosti is family, too, and he works with my uncle. That's one reason why his judgment will stand in a Territory that's not his own."

"But he's demon-dead. I picked up that much."

"He is. When he walked among the living, he was the Warlord Prince of the Dea al Mon, the Children of the Wood. He not only served the Queen of the Dea al Mon, he was also in the Queen of Ebon Askavi's First Circle."

"He's dangerous."

Daemonar studied his tutor and wondered if he'd shown the man too much. "So are all of the men in my family."

Jaenelle Saetien sat on Zoey's bed, her arms wrapped tight around her legs, a soft winter shawl tucked around her. Her aunt Marian's work—a Winsol gift given to Zoey.

Zoey called in a silver flask, unscrewed the top, and offered it to Jaenelle Saetien. "Weston slipped it to me. I have to give it back in the morning."

She took a sip, made a face, then handed the flask to Titian, who took a sip and handed it to Zoey.

That first sip of brandy warmed the kernel of ice inside her that had formed when she'd realized that meeting was *official*, with consequences, and had more to do with who was spreading the rumor than the rumor itself. The second time the flask went round, she gathered the courage to speak.

"Why would Daemonar tell someone like that Warlord Prince?" It bothered her that he had turned this into something official.

"You were accusing Nelson of attempted rape," Zoey said. "He had to report it to someone. I think he chose Prince Chaosti because the connection with Prince Sadi meant Chaosti had the authority to pass judgment but wasn't your father or my grandmother." She capped the flask and vanished it. "They're going to want the names, Jaenelle Saetien."

"I don't have names!"

"Do you think that Warlord Prince already knew the rumors were false?" Titian asked.

"Maybe," Zoey replied. "Probably. I didn't see Nelson in class today after Daemonar . . . avalanched . . . on us, so I'm guessing Nelson was quietly removed to have a chat with someone who could command him to open his inner barriers so that he—or she—could look into Nelson's mind and see everything he's done."

Jaenelle Saetien shivered. No thoughts or feelings that were private? Wasn't that a kind of rape too? Or was it done because that invasion was part of the punishment?

"It's something I'm going to have to learn how to do," Zoey said quietly. "As a Queen, that will be one of my duties when required."

"If someone is falsely accused, that person can ask to stand before a tribunal of Queens, or even the Territory Queen, and have her look into his mind to see the truth," Titian said. "Before my parents were married, my father was accused of something bad and my mother said the witch accusing him was lying. My mother offered to open her mind to the Queen of Ebon Askavi and reveal the truth, but the witch who made the accusation wasn't willing to do that and have everyone know she'd been lying, since she would have been broken back to basic Craft. I think." She made an apologetic face at Jaenelle Saetien. "I know you don't like hearing stories about the Queen, even when the story isn't really about her."

"It's hard to hear about someone who was beyond wonderful when everyone expects you to be like her." Wasn't that one of the things she liked about Delora? That the other girl hadn't met the Queen and *couldn't* make comparisons?

Zoey looked concerned. "Jaenelle Saetien, if my grandmother or your father wants to know who told you about Nelson, you have to tell them."

She shook her head. "I'm not getting anyone else in trouble."

"That's the point. Someone is going to ask, and you'll have to answer. My guess is Delora or Hespera told you about Nelson. They will be required to reveal who told them about the accusations, and that person will be asked, and the next person will be asked until the source is found. Someone will hunt for the original source because Daemonar stopped you from spreading the rumor and becoming the source that a lot of students could point to."

"They were just trying to be a friend, trying to warn you," Jaenelle Saetien insisted. "If they didn't believe the rumors, why would they try to get Nelson in trouble?"

Zoey laid a hand on her arm. "Maybe Nelson wasn't the person they were trying to get into trouble."

# THIRTY-TWO

It made no sense. The rumor should have run through the school like fire. But there wasn't so much as a whisper. Jaenelle Saetien had tangled with Fat Bat's brother and had been subdued all day yesterday—and looked cowed today.

Krellis had reported that Nelson hadn't been in any of his classes yesterday afternoon and had returned to the dorm late in the evening, looking stunned and frightened—and had looked at all the boys with suspicion except for the handful who did morning workouts with the Eyrien. But even they didn't know what had happened.

No one was talking, and that was not right.

Wondering if she was going to have to break her own rule of having her underlings come to her, Delora almost stepped out of the shadows where she habitually kept watch on the comings and goings on the green when she saw Jaenelle Saetien hurrying toward her.

"You seem out of sorts this morning," Delora said. "Did something happen?"

"Yes." Jaenelle Saetien sounded agitated. "I know you meant well. I truly believe you did. But the accusations that were made against Nelson were false, and you shouldn't repeat them to anyone else or you'll get into trouble."

"Oh, I doubt that."

"You will. An official inquiry was made and judgment was passed." Jaenelle Saetien hesitated. "You may be summoned to reveal who told you the rumors in the first place. Just tell the truth, and you'll be all right."

What in the name of Hell . . . ? "What are you talking about?"

Jaenelle Saetien shook her head. "I've already told you more than I should have. I'll get in big trouble if I say anything more, but I had to warn you that there will be serious consequences for whoever even whispers that rumor now." She turned away and looked ready to bolt.

"You have to tell me—"

"I can't! I have to go."

Shaken, Delora stared after the other girl until she disappeared into the building that held the classrooms. An official inquiry? A *judgment* was passed? In all the years when she'd played her little dramas to amuse herself or punish someone for not doing what she wanted, no one had made a formal complaint. No one would have dared—and no one would have believed someone who accused thoughtful, charming Delora of some wrongdoing when she was among the first to help search for a lost kitten or to bring a basket of treats to a girl who had been beaten and broken by an ardent lover who lost control.

Who would have even *thought* to turn a *rumor* into an official inquiry? Insipid Zoey, that was who. She might have more backbone than Delora had given her credit for, and that was a problem.

How was she supposed to shape things in Dhemlan to her liking if there were *official inquiries* about every little thing? Zoey could claim the attention of the Warlord Prince of Dhemlan, something that was Delora's fondest ambition. She'd find a way to wrap Daemon Sadi around her little finger. Yes, she would. She just had to wait until she was old enough to supply the proper incentive, which meant not showing him until then what could be achieved if he had the right partner.

It looked like she would have to . . . diminish . . . Zoey's influence sooner than she'd planned. That was all right. She had an idea of how to do that and assure that Jacnclle Saetien's loyalty would never waver again.

# THIRTY-THREE

———————— ✦ ————————

Daemon opened a bottle of red wine. He and Surreal were meeting with Lucivar at one of the family's vineyard estates, so it was appropriate to sample and savor the wine that was produced there. Besides, the bottle he'd opened had been a very good year—a sop for what he expected would be a bitter truth for the three of them.

Surreal walked into the sitting room, looking tired and tense. "I know I'm late," she snapped. "I had things to do."

"Actually, you're not late," Daemon replied. "Lucivar hasn't . . . Ah."

Lucivar walked in behind Surreal and said, "What things?"

She moved to avoid being between them, which made Daemon very interested in—and wary about—what had made her late.

"A respected Warlord in a village," she said. "Served as a Consort for several Queens when he was younger. Served in several more courts as an escort. In the past few decades, he's performed the service of seeing witches through their Virgin Nights. He attends only three or four girls a year, accepting the commission if there is enough attraction between him and the girl that she would be receptive to him as her first lover. He has never left a girl feeling disappointed in her first experience, and he has never broken a witch's power."

"Until?" Daemon prompted when she didn't continue.

"Until a couple of months ago. A witch, a natural Black Widow. Someone who could have worn a dark Jewel when she reached maturity. 'Gifted' is how her mother described her. She'd been gifted with her understanding of the Hourglass's Craft." Surreal prowled the room. "The mother came to this Warlord. Her daughter was a bit young to have her Virgin Night, but there were concerns she didn't want to discuss that made it imperative to protect her daughter's power and potential."

"Shit," Lucivar said softly. He took the glass of wine Daemon offered and drank half of it.

"Yeah," Surreal agreed. "I couldn't find the Warlord. No one has seen him since that night. Speculation, based on his reputation, is that he prepared the girl for her Virgin Night, giving her what he believed was the proper dose of the aphrodisiac brew called Night of Fire. Then he told the girl he would be right back and he left the room, which he'd never done before, so it could be that something—or someone—gave him a reason to step out. The next thing the girl knew, the room was moving in strange ways and a creature with a misshapen face and reeking of evil tied her to the bed . . ."

"And broke her," Daemon finished.

"What she saw could have been an illusion spell designed to terrify her, or it could have been her reaction to whatever had been added to that Night of Fire. But it didn't disguise the voice of her father's cousin—the man whose salacious interest in the girl was the reason for the mother's concern. Yes, he broke her. Viciously. Then he slipped away, leaving the missing Warlord to take the blame."

"Did the girl tell anyone about recognizing the man's voice?" Lucivar asked.

"The girl was half mad by the time she was taken from that bed, and the Healer explained that the girl had latched on to a recognized voice because the cousin was in the house, consoling her father." Surreal stared at Daemon. "But her mother believed her—and her mother told me."

Daemon studied his second-in-command. "Where is the father's cousin now?" He knew by the look in her eyes, but the formality between them when she went hunting in Dhemlan required that he ask.

Surreal bared her teeth in a smile. "Did you know the Hall in the Dark Realm has a dungeon of sorts?"

"I did, yes." He didn't use those chambers often, but some executions required extreme privacy.

"Well, he's there. I expect he'll have made the transition to demon-dead by the time you get around to having a chat with him."

He'd have to make inquiries into Dhemlan Warlords who had arrived in Hell a couple of months ago to see if he could locate the missing Warlord. And the first person he would ask about that missing Warlord was the fool waiting for him in Hell's dungeon.

"The cousin who broke the girl," Lucivar said. "Does he have any bloodlines in common with anyone connected to the coven of malice? Was this girl targeted by a man's lust or because some bitch wanted to eliminate a rival?"

Surreal shrugged, as if uninterested in the question.

That seeming lack of interest was telling—and suspect. Either she was still looking for an answer or she was sharpening her knives for a particular person and didn't want to tell him.

Lucivar gave her a lazy, arrogant smile. "Did you manage to slip the knife in clean, or did you nick bone and damage the blade?"

She rounded on him, clearly insulted that he challenged her professional skills. "You arrogant prick."

He raised his glass in a salute. "Now she's feeling better." He glanced at Daemon. "Although I could knock her on her ass a couple of times if you think that will help."

The only way Daemon could describe the sound she made was a squeal with fangs.

He really hoped she wanted to sleep alone tonight.

"Let's sit down." He refilled wineglasses, then led them to a round table at one end of the sitting room where adults sometimes played cards or children put together puzzles. The clean wood surface and straight wooden chairs seemed more suitable for a grim discussion.

When they were seated, Daemon didn't waste time. "We don't have enough evidence to prove that Delora and her coven of malice are behind the breakings that have happened over the past few years. Either this is just beginning, or these girls—and the boys who are consenting to be their instruments—already know they have to be careful and selective, and they know how to hide their true intentions. They have time. Eliminate a handful of rivals every year, and decades from now, when that coven reaches maturity . . ."

"There won't be many left to oppose their vision of the Blood," Lucivar finished.

"And that fits in with the current infatuation with Hayllian memorabilia that might have some connection with Dorothea and her followers, and the whispers that a few aristo families want to bring Hayllian traditions to Dhemlan," Surreal said.

"Every instinct I have, every minute of pain I experienced, tells me that Delora will be the next Dorothea if she isn't stopped," Daemon said. "If she was an adult, I wouldn't hesitate to bury her in a deep grave, but there's not enough proof to connect her to girls her age being broken."

"As the ruler of Dhemlan, you can't execute a child without that proof," Lucivar said, sighing. "I've informed the Province Queens in Askavi that I'm holding them accountable for the safety of every young Queen, Black Widow, and Healer in their territories, as well as any witch who has the potential to wear a dark Jewel."

Daemon nodded. "We've done the same. What Surreal and I have found is that witches who don't have the potential to be rivals aren't being targeted."

"Are we pissing in the wind because we don't like a group of snotty bitches, or should we believe what our instincts tell us, despite the lack of proof?" Lucivar asked.

"No way to know—yet."

Surreal stared at her wineglass. "We know someone who might be able to confirm that the coven of malice is a real threat because she saw Dorothea's rise to power."

Daemon looked at Lucivar. "Tersa."

Lucivar's wings fanned out and resettled. "We're tangled up in so much of what Dorothea did, do you think Tersa could tell us anything without confusing that rise to power with what came after?"

"Can't be either of you," Surreal said. "Can't be me either for the same reason. We have too much history with Tersa." She looked at Lucivar. "But Daemonar could tell her he's worried about the attention some girls at school are giving his sister, and he needs to know the warning signs that Titian might be in danger. He won't be asking about what happened to Tersa, not directly, so she might tell him something that will help us decide."

"It might work," Lucivar said. "But he'll need another reason to go to the cottage in order to ease into talking to Tersa."

Daemon smiled. "I know the perfect excuse."

# THIRTY-FOUR

Daemonar knocked on the front door of Tersa's cottage and considered, again, how he should ask her about warning signs in order to get the information Lucivar and Daemon needed. Tersa rarely answered a question with an answer that seemed related to the question. You usually got a direct answer to "Do you want butter or jam on your toast?" but asking her about this? If she'd seen the warning signs, wouldn't she have done something to protect herself from being broken?

Except . . . Tersa got her power back. Not in any usual way, and not in a way that enabled her to wear a Jewel. She had paid for regaining the Hourglass's Craft with her sanity. The Darkness only knew what price she and the rest of the family would have to pay in order to receive the answer to his questions.

The door opened. Mikal scowled at him and said, "Hell's fire. Now she's sent *you* to pester me about the puppy?"

"The puppy is the excuse for me being here today," Daemonar said quietly. "But give me something I can take back so that Jaenelle Saetien doesn't pester *me*."

Mikal continued to block the doorway. "Tersa is having some trouble holding on to the threads of daily life, and over the past couple of days, she's been spending a lot of time in the attic. Something's wrong. Don't make it worse."

"I'll try not to, but Prince Sadi needs some answers."

Mikal finally stepped back and muttered, "Good luck with getting those." In a louder voice he added, "Well, come on back and meet them. Actually, it's good you're here. They haven't seen an Eyrien."

He followed Mikal to the kitchen. The puppies were in their basket. Two cute little bundles of fur who stared at this two-legged creature who was strange and might be frightening. Then . . .

Bark, bark, bark. Yap, yap, yap.

"This is Lord Shelby and Lady Breen," Mikal said, raising his voice to be heard over the yapping. "Hush, you. This is Prince Daemonar."

Nope. Not hushing.

He slowly spread his wings, knowing he would suddenly look different from any human they had seen.

They both cringed away from him, and there was silence for one, two, three . . .

Bark, bark, bark. Yap, yap, yap.

He wasn't sure how they could have gotten louder. Remembering what Uncle Daemon had dryly referred to as a bribe for the female puppy, Daemonar folded his wings and crouched. Calling in the square of neatly folded linen with the initial *S* embroidered in one corner, he held it out to Breen.

Bark, bark . . . She stopped. Sniffed. Moved closer. Sniffed again. Moved closer.

All right. Odd way to make friends, but . . .

Breen latched her teeth into the handkerchief and tried to pull it out of his hand.

Mikal sighed and said on a psychic spear thread, *Let her have it.*

Daemonar moved his hand forward to loosen the tension on the cloth, then released it.

Having her prize, Breen sat in the basket with the handkerchief under her front paws. She growled at him, as if daring him to try to take it back.

Shelby sniffed his hand, but since he wasn't carrying a

scent the fuzzy Warlord found sufficiently interesting, Shelby settled down with the chew treat Mikal handed out to both pups.

He and Mikal retreated to the cottage's sitting room.

"Is she going to let me take it back?" Daemonar asked. Uncle Daemon hadn't said anything about letting the puppy keep the handkerchief.

Mikal laughed. "You want to find out just how possessive a Sceltie puppy who's a witch can be, go ahead and try. At least a handkerchief is easier to replace than shirts and not as embarrassing as other things."

Daemonar perched on the arm of a chair. "Oh?"

"Oh. I've heard stories. Morghann, the first Sceltie who was a special friend for Uncle Daemon, used to 'acquire' his shirt before Jazen could remove the used clothing. When Uncle Daemon's scent faded, she'd go digging in the clothes for another shirt. Another of his special friends had a passion for socks, which made Jazen crazy because that Sceltie figured out how to stuff more socks into a sock and turn it into a sniff-and-chew toy."

He. Would. Not. Laugh.

"The most difficult one was the Sceltie who developed a passion for Uncle Daemon's underwear."

His jaw was clenched so hard, he was going to break a tooth if he didn't laugh.

"That one trotted into the study one afternoon when Uncle Daemon was meeting with some aristo Ladies. Let's just say the underwear the pup retrieved from the clothes hamper wasn't the sort to provide what could be called modest coverage."

Daemonar snorted.

"No one had the spine to ask, but the Ladies wondering what kind of underwear Uncle Daemon had on that afternoon added some zing to the meeting."

Daemonar burst out laughing. "You're making that up."

"Hand on heart," Mikal said. "I heard this from a reliable source. More than one, actually. So you might mention to Jaenelle Saetien that when a Sceltie becomes someone's special friend, he likes to keep something that belongs to her that holds her scent. Something that can be washed is a good idea."

"I'll tell her." He felt a change in the air, the approach of fractured power. Keeping his movements casual, he stood and turned toward the door—and wondered if he should call in his war blade.

Mikal sucked in a breath.

Daemonar stared at Tersa, who looked back at him, at them, with no recognition.

*She's gone deep into the Twisted Kingdom. How do we get her back?*

Then, belatedly, he realized the wet patches on her green dress came from her bleeding wrists. "Tersa!"

"No." Her voice was guttural, feral. Mad. She moved toward a rectangular table that was positioned against the sitting room's back wall.

*Fetch the Healer,* Daemonar told Mikal. *And tell Beale that Prince Sadi needs to come home now.*

Mikal hurried out of the sitting room. Daemonar moved toward Tersa. Carefully. Cautiously. Until she remembered who he was, he couldn't help her—and even broken, she was formidable enough that he didn't dare touch her.

Tersa pointed to the table's empty surface, her blood dripping on the wood.

"Tersa, you hurt yourself. Will you let me put something on those wounds?"

"How many sides does a triangle have?"

"If I answer, will you let me help you?" How much blood had she lost before coming downstairs? How much time did they have before she lost too much?

"How many sides does a triangle have?"

*Not an idle question,* he realized. He placed his forefinger lightly on the wood. As he traced a triangle, he said, "Father, uncle, nephew." He set his finger in the center of the triangle. "And the one who rules all three."

She nodded. Then she pointed to the bottom side, the nephew side, of the triangle. "This one stands between, stands for the other two. They will be feared, but he is still young, still approachable. He will be the first blade in this fight. Not the deadliest, but his heart will make him the fiercest."

He watched the blood drip, drip, drip from her wrists. "Tersa . . ."

"The boy must wait for the knife that will nick his heart. Then he will have the answer."

The boy. Uncle Daemon. "All right. I'll tell him."

"You want to know about the girl who is gone."

Daemonar hesitated, chilled by the warning she'd already given him.

She held out her arms. Daemonar breathed a sigh of relief and called in two clean handkerchiefs to bind the wounds.

"You want to know about the girl Tersa had been before she was Tersa."

"Sure, but first . . ."

She stepped back, drew her arms out of reach. "The Tersa who is now can't survive the telling. The boy must promise she won't be forced to survive." A beat of silence. "Choose."

He stared at her. Choose what?

He knew. The knowledge made him sick, but he knew. If he let her bleed out and die, here and now, she would make the transition to demon-dead and be able to hold on to what was left of her sanity long enough to tell Daemon Sadi about two young witches named Tersa and Dorothea before one was broken because of the machinations of the other. And then Daemon Sadi, the High Lord of Hell, would be required to give his mother mercy and send that completely shattered witch to the final death so that she could become a whisper in the Darkness.

He could have an answer, or he could save the woman.

"There's nothing more to talk about." He took a step toward her. "Let me see your arms." Between his father's lessons and instructions from Nurian, the Eyrien Healer in Ebon Rih, he knew enough basic healing Craft to stanch the wounds and had them wrapped by the time the Healer arrived to do the full healing.

He helped the Healer escort Tersa up to her bedroom. Leaving them, he climbed the stairs to the attic and followed the blood trail to a worktable. His gorge rose as he looked at multiple tangled webs saturated with her blood.

This wasn't normal. He knew enough about Black Widows and their Craft to know that much. What had she needed to see that had driven her to do this?

The spider silk hung from the wooden frames, the threads of the tangled webs of dreams and visions broken to keep other Black Widows from seeing what she had seen.

He wanted to clean the blood off the floor, off the stairs, off the table in the sitting room. He didn't feel qualified to clear away the remnants of her tangled webs, and he admitted, with sorrow, that it would be better for Uncle Daemon to see everything before the cleanup.

Manny, who had been out and about the village, returned flustered and scared by this turn in Tersa's mental instability. She sent Mikal next door for the pot of soup she'd made the previous day, and then went about making rolls to go with the soup. Then she sent him to the butcher's for a roast she could cook and then slice wafer thin. Tersa preferred her meat in very thin slices.

While Manny agreed that they needed to leave the blood trail on the attic stairs and in the attic until Daemon saw it, she set Daemonar to work on cleaning up the blood in the sitting room. Helene, the housekeeper at the Hall, arrived with two of the footmen. They used Craft to lift the furniture so that she could take the bloodstained carpet back to the Hall to clean it.

When the puppies tried to climb the stairs to the bedrooms, he and Mikal took them up to Tersa's room for a brief visit. She looked docile—and ill—but the puppies made her smile. The Healer assured them she would be all right, but she'd lost a lot of blood and needed to stay quiet for a few days.

When she fell asleep, they returned the puppies to the basket in the kitchen. Mikal went back upstairs to take the first watch.

Daemonar sat in the kitchen with Manny and waited for his uncle to arrive.

It took Daemon an hour to remove the tangled webs from their wooden frames and burn the blood-saturated threads with witchfire. He made note of the spools of spider silk that were on the table and had been contaminated by blood, and burned those too. He would replace them in a few days.

He cleaned the wooden frames and scrubbed the blood off the worktable and the floor, using muscle until muscle alone wouldn't remove the final stains. Then he used Craft to pull the blood from the wood in the table and floor.

She'd done this before Daemonar arrived at the cottage. Had she seen something in one of those webs that had told her why the boy was there? What else had she seen that she would require Daemonar to make such a terrible choice?

Once the room was clean and all the supplies needed for the Hourglass's Craft were neatly put away, Daemon shrugged into his black tailored jacket, straightened the cuffs of his silk shirt, and went downstairs to hear the full accounting of what had happened.

He listened without interrupting. Daemonar's shaking hands were a reminder that the boy might be a man and a warrior, but he was still young. He'd held until it was safe to let go, to let someone else shoulder the burden.

"Did I make the right choice?" Daemonar asked.

Daemon stood and pulled his nephew into his arms. "There was no other choice to make, boyo." *And her warning about a knife in my heart is enough of an answer. We will hunt and we will fight, regardless of the cost.*

The boy held on hard, his cheek pressed against Daemon's shoulder. Then he whispered, "She scared me. Not just because she was bleeding that way. She didn't sound like Tersa."

*Or maybe she did,* Daemon thought. *Maybe this was the Black Widow she would have been, the one who, even broken, had had the power and courage to look into a tangled web and see Witch being shaped by dreams and needs, rising out of the abyss. A feral intelligence. A midnight, sepulchral voice. It must have taken a certain kind of strength and madness to look at what was coming, all of what was coming. She'd done her best for me and Lucivar. She still did. And whoever she had been before she became what she is now? I'll let that forgotten girl sleep. I must.*

He held on to Daemonar, using a light soothing spell to comfort and help the boy relax.

"Do you want to stay at the Hall tonight?" Daemon asked.

The boy hesitated. "I'd like to go to Ebon Askavi, unless you need to be there."

He needed to talk to Witch and Karla about what Tersa had done, but not tonight when his mother needed him here—and not when the boy needed to talk to his auntie J. "You go. And let your father know when you arrive." Lucivar would know the moment Daemonar returned to Ebon Rih, but there was no reason to get sloppy about courtesy.

"Yes, sir." Daemonar loosened his hold and eased back enough to look at Daemon. "The knife that's supposed to nick your heart. Do you think that was an image to represent an emotional wound or did she see an actual blade?"

Daemon brushed the boy's hair away from his face and kissed his forehead before saying softly, "It doesn't matter, does it? We will do what needs to be done."

# THIRTY-FIVE

He used to sprawl like that when he was little, but you'd think he'd learn to sleep more neatly at his age," Karla said as she watched Daemonar. "The way those limp wings fan out, there will never be enough room for anyone else in his bed."

"I slept with a grown man, an eight-hundred-pound Arcerian cat, and a Sceltie," Witch replied. "I managed."

"But they were all rather neat packages, despite the various sizes. He's . . ." She waved a hand.

"I can hear you," Daemonar mumbled.

Karla eyed the boy. She'd used a light hand with the sedative she'd put in the witch's brew, but when he finally stopped talking and moving last night, he went down like a felled tree. And just as sprawled, with his limbs flopping every which way once he stretched out on the padded bench in the sitting room across from the Queen's suite.

"Can you?" she asked doubtfully. "Your eyes aren't open."

"Funny thing about Eyriens. We don't hear with our eyes."

"Hmm."

He rubbed his eyes and got them open. "Aren't Healers supposed to know the difference between eyes and ears?"

"Same number of letters," Witch said cheerfully. "And

both words start with *e*. Not that hard to confuse one with
the other."

He groaned. "Please, Auntie J. It's too early for you
both to be playful."

Karla looked at Witch. "I think he's awake." She leaned
over to bring her face in line with the boy's and smiled
brightly. "Kiss kiss."

"Only if there's coffee."

She laughed. "I'll see about getting you some before we
throw you off the mountain."

"I can fly, you know," he called as she left the room.

She didn't know what Witch had said to him in her ab-
sence, but Daemonar looked a little less hollow by the time
she returned with the large tray that had appeared at the
metal gate that marked the Queen's part of the Keep.

She warmed and drank a glass of yarbarah while she
and Witch watched Daemonar consume a staggering
amount of food. When he couldn't find a single thing left
to eat, he let out a sigh, sounding content. Not full, but
content.

"What?" he said when they stared at him. "I was hungry."

"And now it's time for you to go, boyo," Witch said,
putting a hand on his shoulder.

Daemonar wasn't the only person who needed to feel
that hand made out of illusions and Craft, and Karla wondered how soon Daemon Sadi would be arriving at the
Keep, equally raw from what Tersa had done and the price
she had demanded that neither man had been willing to
pay.

Karla escorted Daemonar to one of the courtyards that
had a stone landing web and watched him leave before she
returned to the Queen's part of the Keep.

"Tersa broke the tangled webs to prevent anyone else
from seeing the visions," Karla said. "She did it so that
Sadi won't know what's coming, won't know the shape of
the knife that is going to nick his heart." She studied the
Queen who had been her friend since they were children.
"But you know what's coming."

"Tersa doesn't walk any roads in the Twisted Kingdom that I haven't seen."

"Sadi won't thank you for not telling him and giving him time to prepare."

Witch's sapphire eyes were filled with sorrow and icy determination. "Yes, he will."


Daemon pressed a hand over his heart and studied the tangled web he'd spun in an attempt to find some answers.

It was impossible to re-create a tangled web. If even the smallest thread was missing or out of place, it wouldn't be the same web, wouldn't reveal the same vision. He'd hoped that, using the warning Tersa had distilled from her webs as his starting point, this web would show him some of what his mother had seen.

This web had shown him entirely different truths about his heart.

The first truth, a bitter one, was that he couldn't save his daughter from whatever was coming because of choices she had made. The only thing he could do now was shake her willful blindness to the consequences of her own actions by responding to her in the same way he would to any witch who continuously undermined his trust until there was no trust at all.

The second truth confirmed something Witch had told him centuries ago. Most men probably would feel sorrow or regret. All he felt was relief.


Jaenelle Saetien vanished her books and marched toward the exercise field where Daemonar usually held the morning workouts for a dozen girls and a handful of boys, plus Prince Raine. Everyone thought a tutor joining the workout was a little weird and was bound to get Raine in trouble with Lady Fharra sooner or later. Since the participants all worked up a sweat—her cousin didn't think a workout was successful unless you sweated—they all had to rush to take showers and put on fresh clothes before hurrying to their first class.

Fine for the boys, with their short hair, but what about the girls? Did Daemonar even consider how long it took to dry and style long hair, especially in the winter, even if you used Craft to help with the drying and styling?

That wasn't the point. Not today. The point was he'd missed a day of classes, and when he'd returned early this morning, the only thing he'd told her was to expect Shelby to confiscate something of hers that the puppy could smell when she wasn't around. But when she'd pushed, because *something* about the visit to the Hall and Halaway had upset her cousin a lot and had kept him away from Amdarh overnight, he'd just said Tersa wasn't well and needed some quiet time to recover.

Puppies at the cottage wouldn't help Tersa have quiet time. Which made her wonder if the puppies—Shelby at least—should be relocated to the town house, where she could play with him and work with him every day after her classes. It sounded reasonable, didn't it? Of course, that would leave the staff at the town house to deal with the puppy's potty training since she wouldn't be around that much—and she wouldn't be around at night, although Daemonar was living at the town house, so he might be talked around to taking care of the middle-of-the-night piddle if she . . .

"Are you avoiding me?" Delora asked.

She spun around, surprised to find the girl just a couple of steps behind her. "No."

"I called your name half a dozen times. I thought I'd done something to upset you and you were ignoring me."

She didn't recall hearing Delora say her name—or say anything else for that matter. Had she been *that* lost in thought? "My grandmother isn't well. It's worrying." That was true enough, but she felt a bit guilty, as she always did, about not mentioning Shelby. Delora might really enjoy hearing about the puppy's progress. Except then she might want to see the puppy, and Shelby was still too impression-able to be exposed to too many humans.

Yes, that was it. She wasn't keeping *Delora* away from Shelby. She was keeping *everyone* away from the puppy. Even Zoey and Titian, who knew about the puppy.

"Oh, I'm sorry," Delora said. "Any illness is a concern when someone is elderly, but she's not *too* ill, is she?"

During their late-night talks, had she given Delora the impression that Tersa was elderly? She didn't think so. And not being well wasn't the same as being ill.

"No, she'll be fine in a day or two. She just needs rest."

Delora looked relieved. "That's good, because I wanted to talk to you about something important."

Wondering why Hespera and the other girls weren't with Delora as usual, Jaenelle Saetien followed her friend to one of those shadowy places that Delora preferred when she watched the comings and goings on the green.

"I've been thinking about Zoey and Titian and the other girls, and I feel awful," Delora said. "The boys go too far sometimes, but Hespera and I were just *teasing* with the nicknames. We didn't realize Zoey and Titian were taking the words *seriously* and were hurt by them."

"They were hurt enough that I wasn't allowed to invite you to the Winsol party," Jaenelle Saetien pointed out.

"Exactly! And your calling Krellis and the other boys to task about some of the things they said made me see that we've really been unkind and need to make amends."

"That's a good idea."

"Calling me and my friends the coven of malice isn't kind either, but I guess it was meant as retaliation, only I didn't understand that." Delora's smile looked . . . too big. "So now I need your help."

Jaenelle Saetien blinked. "With what?" Delora should be able to work out what she wanted to say as an apology.

"With getting Zoey's friends and my friends together so that we can do something away from school and maybe start over."

"You want to have an afternoon party at the town house?" She'd definitely need her father's permission to have more than a couple of friends spending an afternoon at the town house, but maybe he'd warm to Delora if he had a chance to talk to her and see that she wasn't anything like that Dorothea woman who had hurt him when he was young.

"Not at the town house. That's so close to the school, all the students would be trying to get in to see the place and devour the food." Delora looked so earnest. "I was thinking of an overnight house party at the Hall. You keep saying how big the place is, and no one except those who were invited would know where the gathering was being held, and even if other students found out, they're unlikely to come all that way. Oh, please say you'll talk your father into letting us have a house party. I really want a chance to settle things with Zoey, and I can't do that around the school."

There was Zoey's group of friends and Delora's group of friends, and everyone else at the school avoided both so they wouldn't be forced to take sides. She was the only one who had tried to be friends with people in both groups. If she could help Zoey and Delora settle their differences . . . Well, she didn't think they would ever be best friends, but they could show each other the courtesy of two leaders who didn't want their differences to turn the school into a battleground. Almost like they were both Queens ruling neighboring villages.

Of course, talking her father into letting Delora stay overnight at the Hall would be much harder than getting him to agree to having her as a guest at an afternoon party at the town house.

As if anticipating the problem, Delora rushed to explain. "I know your father had that funny turn when he met me at the school. I don't know why he took such a dislike to me. Maybe I reminded him of someone else?"

*Dorothea.* Jaenelle Saetien swallowed the compulsion to explain her father's reaction. No one would want to be compared to such a terrible person. "I don't know. But his reaction will make it harder to invite you and Hespera and some of the others to an overnight party."

"Well, you don't have to be specific about *who* is coming to the party. *Everyone* just invites friends, and *no one's* father asks for names. Not when girls reach our age and come from aristo families. Parents *know* the guest list is . . . fluid. But definitely mention Zoey and your cousin, since your father knows them."

Jaenelle Saetien hesitated. She couldn't remember there *ever* being a casual overnight party at the Hall. Family gatherings, yes. There were also formal gatherings where the invited Queens brought some family members along with a handful of people who served in their First Circles. Gatherings that included Queens *required* a detailed guest list.

Official Queens with official courts. Surely her father wouldn't require so much formality for a party just because Zoey would be there. Would he?

"Just get him to agree to the party," Delora said. "It's *so* important, and it would be splendid to have it at the Hall."

And everyone wanted to see an end to this feud between Zoey and Delora.

"Don't say anything to the other girls until I talk to my father, but I'll see what I can do," Jaenelle Saetien said.

"This week?" Delora looked pained. "The more time goes by, the more this misunderstanding with Zoey will fester. It will be awful to go through the rest of the school year this way."

"I'll discuss this with my father as soon as I can, but we'll have to settle for having the house party whenever he says we can have it."

"Of course," Delora said brightly. "But . . . soon?"

Jaenelle Saetien smiled. "Soon."

"Do you think she believed you?" Krellis asked once Jaenelle Saetien hurried off to her class. "You're not at all convincing when you act contrite."

Delora gave him a sharp smile. "You don't think so? She's so eager to have everyone be friends and be the person who brings it about so that she doesn't have to choose sides. I'll be surprised if she doesn't have us for an overnight visit by the school's next study day."

"Have you, you mean. She's not likely to invite the boys."

"Then your showing up will be a surprise."

# THIRTY-SIX

---

The letters and visiting cards had been neatly stacked on the salver Helton held out to him, but Daemon noticed the town house's butler had placed one letter across both stacks as if to emphasize its importance.

Recognizing his daughter's handwriting, he noted the blend of impatience and neatness that was typical when she wanted something and needed his answer an hour ago but knew an indecipherable scribble wouldn't get any kind of answer from him. Most of the time, it amused him. They'd been having this push and pull since she was a little girl and was too excited about some adventure to remember that permission wasn't granted if he was asked ten minutes before she wanted to dash out the door. They would go for months with her making requests in a timely manner, and then she'd . . . forget . . . for a few weeks before resigning herself to the fact that *he* didn't forget his own rules and also didn't break them.

He hadn't seen much of her since she'd started attending that private school, and she hadn't bothered with even a quick note to let him know how she was doing—unless she wanted something. Beale and Holt had confirmed that this wasn't unusual behavior for an adolescent, but this communication, coming on the heels of a couple of heart-tearing days . . .

"When did this arrive?" he asked Helton.

"A short while ago," Helton replied. "I was about to send it to the Hall since it was marked *urgent*."

"Does anything else in that stack look to be of importance?"

"Messages from Ladies Titian and Zoey, as well as a letter from the Queen of Amdarh." Helton indicated the three letters under Jaenelle Saetien's missive.

"I'll take those to the study now. Hold the rest." He hadn't intended to do more than stop at the town house on his way to the Keep, but it looked like he might be staying overnight—depending on the content of the letters.

"Have you eaten, Prince?" Helton asked. "I could have sandwiches brought to the study. Maybe a pot of coffee or a soothing mug of tea?"

Food. Had he eaten today? "Did Prince Daemonar return to the town house last night?"

Helton looked grim. "No. But Lord Weston informed the house that Prince Daemonar returned to the school early this morning. He seemed . . . emotionally raw . . . but otherwise unharmed. He led the morning workout and then cleaned up and went to his tutorial." He hesitated. "Lady Tersa?"

Of course Beale would have informed Helton that Tersa must have walked some dangerous roads in the Twisted Kingdom and that Daemonar had been the first to see the result and sound the alarm.

"She'll be fine," Daemon replied. "She's . . . regaining . . . the rhythm of her life. And she has some helpers now." He wasn't sure *who* had sent a message to Scelt, if any human had, but he'd been willing to agree to anything that would help Mikal cope with living with Tersa. He'd floated the idea of Mikal moving into a suite at the Hall. The boy had slapped the idea down, but had embraced the new helpers without hesitation.

"Another Black Widow?" Helton asked.

He nodded. "A journeymaid." Of sorts. No, not *of sorts*. Having four feet and a tail, and practicing the Hourglass's

Craft a little differently, did not make that young witch any less a Black Widow. "A sandwich and coffee would be welcome. And I'll need someone to deliver messages once I've found out what everyone wants."

Daemon retreated to his study and opened his daughter's letter.

Jaenelle Saetien needed to talk to him *urgently*. No hint of why, which reminded him of Titian's request a few months ago when she wanted permission before action.

*Sweet Darkness, let it be that simple.*

No mention of her grandmother, which made him wonder if Daemonar had seen her yet.

He wrote a quick reply, informing her that he was in Amdarh and would be available to talk later in the afternoon when she was done with her classes. He folded the paper and applied his personal seal in red wax before opening Titian's and Zoey's notes—and felt a stone of sorrow press on his heart.

*They* had heard about Tersa, and the brief notes expressed concern for Tersa and the hope of a swift recovery. Zoey's note included a restrained sympathy for him and the hope that his mother would find her way back to him just as Zoey's mother had found the way home to her own family.

It was possible that Jaenelle Saetien had spoken to Daemonar and now wanted to speak to him about Tersa, but somehow he didn't think so. The girl she'd been before she'd entered this difficult transitional age would have cared. The girl she was now? He wasn't sure.

The letter from Lady Zhara requested a meeting at his earliest convenience and, in a postscript, expressed concern for Tersa and an offer to him of any assistance she could provide. Clearly she'd been just about to seal her letter when the news had arrived.

He invited Zhara to join him for dinner and have time afterward to discuss her concerns. He hesitated, then added that his daughter might need his attention that evening. If so, he would reschedule the meeting as soon as he returned to Amdarh.

One way or another, he needed a night at the Keep.

Jaenelle Saetien tried to consider all her father's possible responses to her request, but realized everything depended on the degree of Tersa being "not well." Her last encounter with her grandmother had made her uneasy. Tersa didn't live at the Hall, but if she was slipping into a mental decline, Father might not want to deal with overnight guests. Of course, *he* wouldn't have to do anything. She'd make the arrangements with Beale and Helene for the guest rooms that would be needed and present suggestions to Mrs. Beale for the food to be served.

Better if she took care of the arrangements. Then she could put off telling him that Delora was one of the guests until the girls showed up on his doorstep. He wouldn't mortally embarrass his daughter by refusing to allow some of her guests to enter the Hall.

If he was too preoccupied with Tersa, would Father want *that woman* to chaperone the party like she'd done at Titian's Winsol party? That would be humiliating, especially when everyone knew what she'd been. Well, Jaenelle Saetien would warn everyone to be civil to Father's wife or they'd all be returned to the school before they could take the next breath.

With luck, *that woman* . . . No, the other girls would follow her lead there, so better to think of Father's wife as Lady Surreal than slip up and call her something that might spark Father's anger.

When the horse-drawn cab pulled up in front of the town house, a footman was waiting at the curb to assist her from the cab. She paid the driver—and gave the man a generous tip, knowing her father would hear about the amount and that might influence his decision for the party in her favor, especially since she'd used her own money for the cab fare as well as the tip.

Her father was in his study, as usual, reading reports and making notes on correspondence of things Lord Holt or Lord Marcus would need to deal with. As she entered the room, he capped his pen and came around the desk to greet her.

He'd never done anything to make her uneasy, not in *that* way. In fact, the sexual heat all the girls couldn't stop talking about didn't seem to affect her most of the time. Zoey had speculated that being directly related to Prince Sadi, his daughter might somehow be protected from the heat. Even if she noticed it to some degree, it wouldn't create the same response as it did in other women.

No, he'd never done anything, but girls her age did not hug and kiss their fathers. She wasn't sure why, but everyone knew they didn't. So when her father approached her, she braced for the hug she didn't want—and resented that he didn't even try. He just kissed her cheek in the same way he kissed Titian or Aunt Marian or any other female he considered family.

"Do you want anything to eat?" he asked. "Or a cup of hot chocolate?"

*That* was tempting, but then they would sit in the social area of the study, and she'd prefer having the desk between them.

"No, that's all right." Ignoring his light attempt to guide her, she headed for one of the chairs in front of his desk—and heard him sigh.

He resumed his seat behind the desk. "What's on your mind, witch-child?"

"How is Tersa?"

His surprise that she would think to ask stung a little. Stung a lot.

"She's recovering," he replied. "We have some help looking after her, including a journeymaid Black Widow."

"That's good."

"We'll adjust."

An odd thing to say, but since it sounded like Tersa would be all right, she leaped into her own agenda. "It's about Zoey and Titian and some of the other girls at school." She'd decided on the way here that Delora was right and being vague about who else was coming to the party would be best.

The room chilled. "Is someone causing trouble for them?" he asked too softly.

"No! Not at all. But there are some girls who would like to get to know them better but feel awkward about doing that at the school." She waited a moment. Thank the Darkness, he didn't ask *why* the girls would feel awkward. "So I thought we could have a house party at the Hall. Everyone could stay overnight, so we could go riding or maybe skate on the pond if the ice is thick enough."

He gave her a dry smile. "I can make sure the ice is thick enough."

Of course he could. Using Craft, he could freeze the water to make ice as thick as a man's leg was long—and smooth out the surface for good measure.

She smiled at him. "And maybe we could put on that play again—the one Titian and Zoey found in the trunks in the attic here."

"There are probably more plays like that stored at the Hall, along with props," he said, his mouth curving in a warm smile. "The coven used to create what they called fragmented plays. They'd choose a type of story—romance, mystery, something else—and each of them would select a piece from that genre. Then they selected a handful of characters from those stories and lifted the dialogue without changing anything, added a narrator to fill in bits, and then reassembled the whole thing as a play.

"My father was always the narrator because he was the only one who managed to keep a straight face and read his part as if it made sense. Lucivar was always assigned a special guest role. He had one line, which was what he said in response to every interaction with the other characters. Everyone else who was at the Hall to celebrate Winsol had to pick from a hat to see if they were playing a part. We had an afternoon to read through the play and select whatever props or costumes we wanted for our character."

"That would be a fun activity if it turned out to be too cold or snowy to do things outside," Jaenelle Saetien said. A part of her burned with resentment. She'd *liked* doing that play at the Winsol party, but she *didn't* like knowing the Queen had done it first.

Another comparison. Another thing that wasn't really her own.

She ignored the fact that there wouldn't be any of those plays if the Queen and her coven hadn't done them first.

"All right," he said, taking a fresh piece of paper from the stack on his desk. "You can have an overnight house party at the Hall for a maximum of twenty girls."

"Well, there are some . . ."

"Girls, witch-child," he said as he uncapped a pen. "If you want to invite some of the young men from the school, you can have an afternoon gathering here at the town house. If you want an overnight house party at the Hall, the invitation is only for girls."

She'd expected that, so she nodded. Delora would be disappointed that he'd limited it to twenty girls, but they could accommodate Delora's and Zoey's closest friends in that number. "Twenty girls at the Hall." She nodded, then smiled brightly. "The guest rooms near my room—"

"No, they will not be in the family wing. We'll use the square of guest rooms nearest the sitting rooms at the front of the Hall. Easier for everyone that way." His smile was warm, but there was a slight chill in his gold eyes. "The names of your guests and where their families are located?"

She felt a shiver of alarm. "Why do you need to know that? It's just a party for some girls at the school."

"I need to inform each girl's parents or legal guardian that she will be attending a house party and staying here overnight. Therefore, I need the information."

*Or the house party doesn't happen.* That was what he didn't say but meant.

Guests were housed by degree of trust. The most trusted were given rooms in the family wing, which also meant having access to more of the Hall as people navigated the corridors to public rooms like the dining room or the sitting rooms or one of the libraries. Guests who were an unknown were usually housed nearest the public rooms, and wandering around was discouraged by the number of footmen stationed in the corridors to "help" guests find their way around—and to report guests who were where they had no business being.

She didn't know where Delora's family resided, but she was certain the idea of the house party would end the moment she said the other girl's name. Just like Delora had said it would.

"Zoey and Titian, of course." She wanted to be snippy and ask if he needed to know where *their* families resided, but snippy would crush the house party and it would be months, if ever, before she could bring up the request again.

She told him the names of the girls who had been at Titian's Winsol party and were among Zoey's group of friends but admitted she didn't know them well enough to give him the location of their families.

"That's all right," he said as he wrote the names in that beautiful script that was ornate and yet perfectly readable. "I believe I have that information for most of the girls, and the school can oblige me by providing the information I don't have." He looked up. "Anyone else?"

It would be harder to sneak Delora and Hespera in if no one from her group was on the list. "Leena and Tacita. They usually spend time with another group of girls, but I'm certain they would like to get to know Titian and Zoey better. My apologies, Father, but I don't know their home villages."

"Anyone else?" he asked.

She wondered if a mouse felt like this when the cat's claws were on its back. *Just tell him! If he gets upset about the guests, Delora can find another time and place to talk to Zoey.* "No, no one else."

"All right," he said after a moment. "When would you like to do this?"

"At the end of the week?"

Silence. Then a whispered, "That soon?"

She wasn't sure he was talking about the house party.

He sighed. "Very well, witch-child. Lady Zhara is coming for dinner tonight. Would you like to join us?"

"Thank you, but I should get back to the school. There's a lot to do before the party, and I didn't want to say anything to the other girls until I had your permission." She sprang out of her chair, came around the desk, and gave him a quick peck on the cheek. "Thank you, Father."

"You're welcome. Don't worry about the arrangements. I'll take care of that part."

She hurried out of the study, then had to wait for Helton to send a footman for a driver and one of the small Craft-powered coaches her father often used in the city.

Delora wasn't going to be happy about Father knowing Leena and Tacita would be at the party, but they would have to work around that in order for the two groups to come together on neutral ground.

Daemon stared at the list of names. He'd given Jaenelle Saetien every opportunity to ask if she could invite Delora and that coven to the house party. She'd been so pissy when she hadn't been allowed to invite the bitches to Titian's party, but when she was making up the guest list, she hadn't even asked.

Half-truths and lies of omission.

Well, he could play the game of half-truths and lies of omission too. He knew how to contact the families of most of the girls because Titian and Zoey had supplied the information when Titian had hosted her Winsol party. The rest of them? He would ask Lady Fharra to supply the contact information for the other girls Jaenelle Saetien had named since that would be expected. As for the girls he anticipated his daughter would include as last-minute guests? Well, he couldn't contact their parents, could he?

At the bottom of the list, he wrote the names Delora, Hespera, Amara, Borsala.

Besides, he didn't need to ask anyone about their contact information. He already knew where to find their families.

"Only twenty?" Delora let her stare convey her sharp disappointment in Jaenelle Saetien, let it say without words that the girl had failed to meet the standards of a true aristo witch. "But the Hall is so big! Surely it can accommodate more than twenty guests?"

"That's enough invitations for your core of friends and Zoey's to spend time together," Jaenelle Saetien said defensively. "My father set the limit. If I had pressed for more girls to stay overnight, he would have said no to all of it."

Well, they would have to work with that. As long as Insipid Zoey was there, the boys would have some fun.

"I had to tell my father that Leena and Tacita were invited."

"*What?* Why did you do that?"

"I had to give him the names of the girls I was inviting so that he could contact their families."

Hell's fire! No, that might be better. No one could deny where the "accidents" took place if Prince Sadi informed everyone's parents that the girls would be at his home.

She would just have to make sure he and his whore wife were summoned away from SaDiablo Hall while the party was going on. Hespera might have ideas about how to achieve that, and hadn't Krellis mentioned something about a school hidden away on a SaDiablo estate?

Delora pitched her voice to sound uncertain. "Did you tell your father about me or Hespera? Did you tell him we'd like to come to make amends to Zoey and Titian?"

Jaenelle Saetien shook her head. "But if you come in

with Leena and Tacita and the rest of the girls, he won't shame me or you by telling you to leave."

"And you'll have room for Amara and Borsala too?"

"Yes."

"And we can have the house party at the end of the week?"

Jaenelle Saetien nodded.

Delora looked around as if just noticing the empty green. "Oh! We'd better get to the dining hall or we'll be late for dinner."

After dinner, Delora, Hespera, and the rest of her coven slipped away to meet up with Krellis and the other boys who would help provide the sharp entertainment at the house party.

Daemon appreciated Zhara's effort to keep the conversation at dinner light. They talked about the latest plays and which ones they had enjoyed. They talked about books, including Jillian's story.

Zhara frowned and cut a small piece of beef into smaller pieces. "Let me see if I understand this. Lady Jillian submitted her story to the publishing house you own. She was accompanied by Lady Marian Yaslana, your sister by marriage, when she met with the acquisitions editor. But *you* haven't been allowed to read the story or express an opinion about whether or not your editor should publish the book because that might unduly influence her decision?"

"Exactly."

"Prince, that makes no sense."

"Thank the Darkness for that." Daemon raised his wineglass in a salute. "If this sounded reasonable to you, I was going to have to concede that it was male thinking that was getting in the way of my understanding, but if you don't understand it either . . ."

"So no input at all?" she asked.

"Lucivar and I get to host and pay for the party that will

be held when the book is published. That is our contribution." He growled the last words. He couldn't help it.

"This frustration at not being allowed to help is very . . . Sceltie . . . of you," Zhara observed, fighting not to smile.

"It is a trait Warlord Princes share with that race of the Blood." He drained his wineglass and set it aside. "But if you want to observe the pinnacle of being insistently helpful in the face of refusal, try to deal with a Sceltie who is a Warlord Prince. He doesn't allow anything to get in his way—including the opinions of the foolish human he's decided to help."

Zhara eyed him. "Is this a long-standing observation, or have you been cornered recently?"

"Both. Would you like coffee in the sitting room?" When she hesitated, Daemon added, "Or my study?"

"The study," Zhara replied. "This discussion is both a personal favor and an official request that I am relaying."

Unlike Jaenelle Saetien, Zhara recognized the balance between the personal and official and settled into one of the comfortable chairs on the social side of his study. Daemon waited until Helton brought in the tray with coffee and a plate of desserts. He handed Zhara a cup of coffee fixed the way she liked it, then poured a cup for himself and waited.

"The Hourglass has always taken care of the Black Widows who become lost in the tangled webs of dreams and visions," Zhara began. "Now they have a concern, and they asked me to speak with you because my daughter is one of those they are concerned about."

Daemon set his cup and saucer back on the tray. "I thought she was recovering."

"She is, along with a handful of others. But it's difficult for Sheela to see the Sisters who are still lost and be reminded right now that she'd been one of them. It's difficult not to feel some guilt that she found her way out and they have not."

"She couldn't do anything about that. Your daughter followed a song in the Darkness. It led her back to the bor-

der of the Twisted Kingdom. Led her out of the Twisted
Kingdom." He knew what that felt like. He'd regained his
sanity by following the path Jaenelle Angelline had laid
out for him when he'd been lost in madness.

"Feelings are not always rational," Zhara said. "The
Sisters of the Hourglass who run that home for the lost all
agree that the witches who have recently returned need to
live somewhere else, a place where they can relearn the
routines of day-to-day living and participate in a village in
some way."

"And they think Halaway is the place for those women
to regain that balance?" Daemon asked. He couldn't think
of another reason why Zhara would be talking to him
about this.

"The strongest Black Widow Healers among the care-
takers looked into tangled webs for the answer, so the Sisters *know* those women should be in Halaway. They said
that village will be the most dangerous place in Dhemlan,
and that will make it the safest place to live. Because of
you."

Daemon sighed. Apparently the Black Widows in
Dhemlan weren't the only ones who had seen something
coming.

He selected one of the miniature desserts. "Surreal
owns a house in the village. She's rented it to a number of
people over the years. I'll talk to her about turning it into a
home for a small number of Black Widows who need some
time readjusting to daily life." Better if he was the one to
discuss this with Surreal. She strongly objected to being
nipped into giving the desired answer, and the decision had
already been made—without any help from the humans.

He suspected Zhara would find his next comment
amusing. Then again, she hadn't been the one who'd been
cornered. "A handful of Scelties showed up soon after
Tersa reacted badly to a vision." That was as far as he was
willing to explain to anyone about what had been said and
seen. "Two of them are going to live with Tersa and Mikal.
The Warlord will help Mikal teach the puppies. The witch

is a journeymaid Black Widow who is going to help—and learn from—Tersa."

"Oh, my." Zhara looked at her hands. "Do they . . . ?"

"Have a snake tooth and venom sac like human Black Widows? I do not know. I asked, and my answer was bright eyes and a wagging tail." He'd found it unsettling to realize that, until she had shown up, he'd never seen a Black Widow Sceltie. He knew they existed, but if any of them had gone to the Sceltie school, they'd either left before their caste was apparent or they had learned to hide what they were very, very well.

"Oh, dear. Does anyone know about kindred Black Widows who could tell you?"

Daemon gave her a sour look. "Does anyone know about them? Oh, yes, I'm sure of that. Will those Ladies share that information? That is a different question."

"But you're . . ." Zhara looked at him. Considered. "Yes. Of course. Can't exactly pull rank on anyone at the Keep, can you?"

"No, I can't." Daemon selected another dessert and popped it in his mouth. He'd have to mention to Helton that these were delicious—and remember to ask Mrs. Beale about providing sweets this size for the girls' house party. "Anyway, the other three Scelties who arrived at the same time—one of them being a Warlord Prince—informed me that they would help the rest of the village until I brought the humans who needed them to their new house. Which is, or was, Surreal's house, since that is where they've taken up residence—an unexpected event that has encouraged the current tenants to leave as soon as possible."

"Sweet Darkness." Zhara put her cup down with a clatter. "They knew about Sheela and the other women who needed a new place to live."

"Well, someone knew." And he hoped his Queen was in the mood to chat when he arrived at the Keep tonight.

After promising to make the arrangements for the Black Widows' residence in Halaway, he escorted Zhara to her carriage, made sure there was nothing Helton needed from him, and left the town house.

He stood on the sidewalk, studying the unoccupied side of the town house, then gave in to the need to know the boy's state of mind. *Prince Yaslana.*

*Sir?* Daemonar replied instantly.

The boy didn't sound unsettled, so the visit to the Keep had done him good.

*Where are you?* Daemon asked.

*With Beron. We spar a couple of times a week.*

*Not much room in his flat for sparring.*

*Close-quarters work. More Dea al Mon than Eyrien in style.* A beat of silence. *Uncle Daemon? Is there something I can do for you?*

*Not for me, but I had dinner with Lady Zhara this evening, and the cook was a bit too enthusiastic in the number of dishes she prepared, not to mention some excellent desserts that will go to waste if they aren't eaten tonight.*

*Oh.* Another beat of silence. *Beron and I were just talking about going out for something to eat before I returned to the town house. It would be a shame to waste good food—or excellent desserts.*

*I'll let Helton know to keep the food warm for you. I'm heading to the Keep now and will be returning to the Hall in the morning.*

*Good night, Uncle Daemon.*

*Good night, boyo.*

After informing Helton that two good appetites would be arriving soon, Daemon caught the Black Wind and headed for the Keep.


Karla looked at Witch. Witch looked at Karla. Then they looked at him.

If they had tails to wag, their expressions wouldn't be much different from the damn Scelties.

Come to think of it . . .

Daemon took a step to one side to see if Witch's fawn tail was twitching in the equivalent of a wag.

"Prince?" Witch asked too sweetly. "Looking for something?"

"Besides answers?" he replied with equal sweetness.

Karla held out a hand. "Give me the list of names for this party. I'll help Geoffrey identify the families and home villages of the ones you don't already know." She took the list and left the Queen's part of the Keep.

Daemon studied the Queen whose will was his life—and whose continued love made it possible for him to remain among the living.

"How did Tersa end up with a journeymaid Black Widow who is a Sceltie?" he asked.

Witch looked at him.

"All right. How about the three Scelties, one of whom is a Warlord Prince, who are going to help the Black Widows who will apparently live in Halaway while they readjust to daily life?"

Witch looked at him.

"Hmm. Any thoughts about whether kindred Black Widows have a snake tooth and venom sac?" He felt his temper sharpen, felt his anger turn cold and jagged. "A simpler question. Do you know what my mother saw in those tangled webs? The webs she'd soaked in her own blood?"

"I didn't see them," Witch replied softly.

"Do you need to see them, Lady? You and Tersa have a connection. You always did."

"You're the connection, Daemon."

She walked up to him and placed a hand on his chest. He felt the weight of it, the warmth of it through the silk shirt.

"You need to rest," she said. "And you need to drain some of the reservoir of power in your Black Jewel. You have a headache—the kind that is dangerous for you."

He shook his head. "I'm going to need the power. It's going to happen soon."

"You won't need all of that power, but you will need a strong body—and a strong heart." She touched his face. "There is nothing else you need to know because you already know the most important thing."

"What is that?" he whispered as his left hand moved of its own accord to touch his right biceps and the scars she'd given him.

Witch noticed the gesture and smiled. "You won't go into this fight alone."

# THIRTY-SEVEN

The timing of the house party bothered Titian because it didn't make sense. For an adult party? Maybe. But not for a gathering of girls who wanted to skate on the pond or go out riding. Not in winter, when the sun set so early. They should have arrived in the afternoon, right after the midday meal, gotten settled in their rooms, and then headed outside for an activity, returning to the Hall in time to freshen up and change for dinner. Then they would have the evening for playing cards or games or putting on a silly play. The following morning, there would be time for another ride or a walk to the village or leisurely indoor activities. Then they would be on their way home after the midday meal.

That was how it was done. That was how she'd expected it to be done because Jaenelle Saetien knew how and when guests arrived for this kind of party, same as she did. But after talking to Delora and Hespera, Jaenelle Saetien had rescheduled the time when the Coach would take them to SaDiablo Hall. They'd reach the Hall around sunset. No time for riding or skating or anything fun.

It felt wrong, and Zoey thought so too. They'd discussed backing out and staying at the school, but an overnight house party at the Hall felt so grown-up, so like the stories her father told about the Queen and her coven. Besides, Uncle Daemon would be there, and anyone who misbehaved would be stuffed into a Coach and sent back to the school. Or stuffed into one of the cells below the Hall, cells where people were kept while they waited for the Warlord Prince of Dhemlan—or the High Lord of Hell—to decide their fate. She'd never seen those cells and wasn't supposed to know about them, but Daemonar had found them once when he'd been exploring the Hall with the Scelties who were in residence at the time. He'd told her there was something cold and merciless about those cells, something that made him think they weren't used often—and weren't used unless one of the Blood did something horrific.

Titian shuddered. They were going to a house party. Why think of something scary?

Why indeed?

She knocked on the door of Jaenelle Saetien's room, then went in when her cousin used Craft to open the door.

"Are you packed?" Jaenelle Saetien asked. "Did you remember to bring a dress for the evening?"

"Yes, and yes. I also remembered warm clothes for skating or sledding." She could ride horses. Uncle Daemon had taught all of them to ride, and there were kindred horses at the Hall, which made riding more fun and exciting. But Eyriens did a kind of upright sledding that was also great fun—almost like sailing on snow. There were Eyrien sleds at the Hall, and she really wanted to teach Zoey how to sled. "I came to tell you that Jhett and Arlene won't be coming to the party because their moon's blood started a little while ago."

"What?" Jaenelle Saetien looked put out. "But they have to come. It's all arranged."

Titian stared at her cousin. Witches were in isolation during the first three days of their moontime and only interacted with family or close friends. Trusted friends. Since it was only girls at the party, it might be all right, but Uncle Daemon's temper would have a lethal edge the moment he scented moon's blood—and he would be paying sharp attention to every guest in his house. Besides, the girls would decline to participate in the more vigorous activities and be on their own in an unfamiliar house, being looked after by servants they didn't know. At least at the school, they could tuck into their rooms to read and sleep.

Alone.

"Well, they aren't coming," Titian said.

"Can't you talk them into it?"

"No." Titian's uneasiness increased. Why would Jaenelle Saetien be so insistent about them coming to the party when the girls wouldn't feel well enough to have fun? "Surely enough other girls will be attending the party for whatever you and Delora have in mind."

Hell's fire. That came out pure bitch.

Jaenelle Saetien looked as if she'd been slapped. "Delora and Hespera just want to get to know Zoey better. Start over without everyone watching. Two groups of friends sharing some fun activities and hopefully finding some common ground. That's what we have in mind."

*But Delora and Hespera aren't on the guest list. Neither are Amara and Borsala. And yet all four of them are coming to this party.* She knew that because Lord Weston had shown Zoey the list of guests. Prince Sadi had sent him a copy because he needed to know which girls he would be escorting to the Coach that would take them to the Hall before returning to the school to stand guard.

She wondered if that Dea al Mon Warlord Prince who worked with Uncle Daemon had also been given the guest list and knew who was, and wasn't, supposed to be at the school tonight.

Jaenelle Saetien sounded sincere, but Delora had been able to push and pinch Titian's cousin into reacting and lashing out and defying rules instead of setting her heels down and holding the lines their parents had drawn. And not holding the lines their *fathers* had drawn . . . That was just out-and-out dangerous.

"Well, it's their loss." Jaenelle Saetien sounded as if the party was ruined because Jhett and Arlene couldn't attend.

Unable to think of anything to say, Titian shrugged. "We'll meet you at the school gate to ride to the landing web."

Jaenelle Saetien nodded. "Don't be late, all right?"

Titian returned to her room, thought a moment, then put on her winter cape and went out to find Lord Weston. It turned out that while she'd been talking to Jaenelle Saetien, Zoey had talked to Weston about the two friends who would be staying at the school. He, in turn, had informed Daemonar and had also sent a guard to SaDiablo Hall with a note from Zoey to let Prince Sadi know the change in the guest list.

She hoped Jaenelle Saetien remembered to do the same thing. She hoped Jaenelle Saetien had already sent a message to Uncle Daemon telling him about the change in their arrival time. When dealing with Warlord Princes, informing them about a schedule change wasn't just courtesy, especially when a Queen was among the travelers. It was the only way to keep them from reacting as if being late was a declaration of war.

Jaenelle Saetien knew that as well as she did, so her cousin *had* to have informed Uncle Daemon about the girls arriving later than expected.

It wasn't until she was back in her room, selecting a book to take with her in case there wasn't time to look through any of the Hall's libraries for a book to borrow, that she wondered if all this sharp attention on a girls' house party was because Zoey was a Queen and this was what it would always be like for a Queen, or if the men, warriors all, had another reason for that attention.

"We've prepared twenty guest rooms, as requested," Beale said. "Mrs. Beale has prepared finger foods for the afternoon and a buffet to be served in the dining room for the evening meal. While Lady Jaenelle Saetien requested a couple of dishes that are favorites of Lady Zoela and Lady Titian, she didn't indicate if the evening meal was to be formal or informal. When Lady Angelline and the coven dined without male company, they preferred a buffet, so Mrs. Beale made the same kind of plans for this dinner."

"Very good." Daemon stepped away from his desk and accepted the note a footman brought on a salver.

"There aren't twenty guests on the list you provided."

"I know. I expect there will be four last-minute additions." Recognizing Zoey's handwriting, he opened the note. "Ah. Two of the girls on the original list are 'feeling too delicate to attend the party,' but would be much improved in three days." He smiled. "An interesting way to describe a girl's moontime, don't you think?"

"Perhaps she didn't want you to blush," Beale said, returning the smile.

Daemon huffed out a laugh. "Zoey will eventually have a moontime when she's around Lucivar, and then she'll learn in a hurry that nothing about dealing with a female body makes him blush." He paused. "Of course, being a Queen, she's probably never had anyone pick her up and toss her on a bed because he's decided she needs a nap."

"With Prince Yaslana, his sister, and her coven, it was a bit like watching sheepherding contests at the harvest fair," Beale observed. "Especially when the Ladies tried to bolt and the Scelties jumped in to help him with the herding."

Daemon choked.

"Quite entertaining for the staff," Beale finished.

"I'm sure it was." His amusement faded as he considered the two girls who would not be attending the house party. Jhett was a natural Black Widow; Arlene was a natural Healer. Strong assets for a Queen's court. Assets Dhemlan couldn't afford to lose.

Using Craft, Daemon turned the small clock on his desk so that he could see it from where he stood. "Beale, why would Lady Zoela write to tell me two guests won't be attending?"

"Courtesy?"

"That, yes. But the girls should be arriving on the heels of my receiving this. Knowing now won't change preparations." His temper sharpened and turned cold. "Unless the girls aren't going to arrive until much later today."

"There was no other note," Beale said, anticipating the question.

They heard the knock on the front door. A minute later, a footman hurried into the study with another message.

Daemon read that one and felt his temper become a little sharper, a little colder. "The Coach driver says Jaenelle Saetien rescheduled the time of departure. The girls won't be arriving until around sunset."

"Should I tell Mrs. Beale to delay the evening meal? Otherwise, the Ladies won't have time to do more than get settled in their rooms and change for dinner."

"No. My daughter did not inform me of any change in the girls' arrival, so dinner will be served as planned. Confirm the time with Mrs. Beale, then return here. I need to talk to you, Holt, and Surreal."

When Beale left to tell Holt he was needed and to confirm the time the buffet would be served, Daemon gave Surreal a light psychic tap. *We need to talk. Now.*

*Problem?* she asked.

He didn't reply because the need to deny what every instinct told him was going to happen tonight was so strong, he felt ill. And the possibility that his daughter had knowingly participated in planning tonight's vicious game was a knife twisting in his gut.

He considered going to Amdarh now and personally escorting Zoey, Titian, and their group of friends to the Hall to destroy any possibility of them being attacked on their way to the Coach. He considered cornering Jaenelle Saetien and demanding an explanation for this game she was playing.

Then he considered the girls who had been broken, considered what even he couldn't do without sufficient proof of who was responsible.

And then he considered how many more years Zoey and other strong young witches would be vulnerable to this particular kind of attack, and how the enemy might choose another time and place when Zoey had far less protection.

So they would all play the game tonight.

May the Darkness have mercy on the survivors.

While he waited for them, he reached for Daemonar, using a Green psychic thread. *Prince Yaslana.*

*Sir?*

*Have the Ladies coming to the house party left the school yet?*

*No. Titian said the departure was rescheduled, and they're now going to arrive at the Hall around sunset.* A pause. *Jaenelle Saetien didn't tell you?*

*No, she didn't.* Changing travel plans without telling him when one of the travelers was a Queen? Even if it was forgetfulness caused by excitement, it was also an insolence that could not be tolerated. *I want you at the town house tonight. I want Lord Beron there as well.*

*I was going to stay at the school. A couple of Zoey's friends—*

*I know about them. Prince Chaosti and his fist of men will guard the girls. Your presence at the school tonight might alert someone and cause a change of plans. I will let this game play out here so that we aren't blindsided at another time when the girls are more vulnerable. You will give Chaosti the names of the boys who Zoey considers friends. They will be kept under watch in case they, too, need protection. Also, tell Prince Raine to stay at the school and stay available. His services may be required tonight.*

*Sir? Are we preparing for a fight?*

*I'm not going to give the enemy a chance to fight.* *Possibly.*

Daemon broke the link with Daemonar when Surreal walked into the study, followed by Holt and Beale.

Daemon handed her both notes.

Surreal read them and hissed out a breath. "No word from Jaenelle Saetien?"

"None."

She frowned. "This is a girls' party. Where is the cock and balls who will oblige Delora and claim Zoey wanted him too desperately to wait for a proper Virgin Night?"

Daemon looked at Holt. "You reviewed the credentials and background of all the new servants? Including the ones here for training?"

Holt nodded. "Nothing to link anyone here with Delora or her group of friends, male or female." He turned toward Beale. "Just in case one of the youngsters can be flattered or bribed to look the other way for just a minute, we should have teams of experienced footmen assigned to the public rooms and to serve as escorts."

"Already done," Beale said.

"Then the cocks will slip in somehow." Surreal met Daemon's eyes. "But Delora will have to get you out of the Hall first. Can't have the Black ripping apart her prize studs before they eliminate her rival."

"If anyone has told Delora about your skill with a knife, she won't want you here either." Daemon looked at Beale and smiled a cold, cruel smile. "I expect the bait will be something Surreal and I can't ignore. If that happens, the protection of Lady Zoela and the other girls will fall to you until we return."

"Understood, Prince."

"I'll show you some extra defenses that I created to help you with that."


Surreal reviewed the guest rooms around the interior courtyard. Only two of the rooms had a bathroom en suite. Those were usually assigned to the most important guests in the party. Like a Queen, for instance. The remaining guests, usually the Lady's companions and escorts, had to share the available bathrooms within this two-story square.

She and Helene had agreed that Lady Zoela would have one of the en suite rooms, with Titian assigned to the connecting bedroom that would normally be occupied by a companion or escort. She expected the girls would share the bathroom but would have enough sense to sleep in their own beds in order to follow Sadi's rules of romance.

It set her teeth on edge to do it, but she assigned the other primary guest room to Delora. She didn't like implying that Delora deserved the same status as a Queen. She knew what the bitch had done, even if she and Sadi didn't have enough proof to bring the girl to the official attention of Dhemlan's Queens. But Jaenelle Saetien would likely claim that her friend was being slighted if she wasn't given the other suite—even though they weren't supposed to know that friend was going to show up.

"The family wing has been locked down with a Red shield," Surreal said. "Prince Sadi's private suite and that square of rooms have a Black shield. The maids understand that they're not to answer any summons alone?"

Helene nodded. "Feels strange to have hostile guests at the Hall, but we've had them before and the staff knows what to do. I've already paired off the maids to make sure that at least one of them has had some lessons in defending herself. Same with the footmen who are on duty to look after the guests. You think this girl and her friends will be so foolish to start something here?"

"She isn't foolish, but she's arrogant enough," Surreal replied.

"It's all girls at the party."

"Yeah." And every time she'd thought about that and why the girls should be safe, she had honed another knife.

"I'll be bunking in the staff's room across from those guest rooms. Sadi is planning to stay in his study to keep an eye on things until the girls retire." And he would still be there in the morning. Watchful. Ready.

"Are you going downstairs to greet the girls?" Helene asked.

"Oh, I'll be down there, but not exactly to greet them." She gave the Hall's housekeeper a sharp smile. "I intend to shove the truth of what I am right down the little bitches' throats." And hoped that would be another layer of protection for Zoey and Titian.

"Everything's set?" Delora asked.

"It's set," Krellis replied. "You sure she'll convince her father to let us stay?"

"I'll convince her. She'll convince him." Delora smiled. "It's a big place. Plenty of dark corners. And Jaenelle Saetien's papa won't even be there. Just make sure you take care of Insipid Zoey before he realizes his mistake and returns."

"With pleasure." His eyes gleamed. "I've given a couple of our secondary cocks a chance to prove themselves with a blooding and breaking."

"Proving themselves on Jhett and Arlene?"

Krellis nodded. "Not much of a test, since the bitches won't be able to use their own power to defend themselves, but the boys will get it done."

Jaenelle Saetien felt exhilarated as the girls finally piled into the Coach and the driver caught the Winds and headed for SaDiablo Hall. She'd had parties before, and she'd had friends stay overnight at the town house. But she'd never had a house party like this. And she'd never arbitrated a truce between two quarreling groups of strong women.

She heard Hespera laugh at something Delora whispered.

Something about the sound made her a little uneasy, felt just a little wrong, so she hoped Mikal had received her last message and kept the puppies at the cottage tonight.

Four Scelties arrived at the Hall. The fifth dog, the journeymaid Black Widow, would remain with Tersa, Mikal, and the puppies. She would also stay alert for any trouble in or around Manny's cottage.

Two of the Scelties would stay near Beale, lending whatever assistance he needed; the other two would roam the corridors near the guest rooms to encourage humans to behave.

Daemon leaned back in his desk chair and rubbed his temples as he waited for the girls to arrive. But it wasn't his head giving him trouble tonight; it was his heart.

Lucivar stood on the flagstone courtyard outside his eyrie. Below him, he could see the lights in Riada's houses and businesses. In the mountains, he saw the lights glowing from the windows of other eyries. Everything as it should be.

But there were no lights shining anywhere on Ebon Askavi. At least, none that he could see. A knife-sharp coldness that had nothing to do with a winter's night was coming from that direction. It wasn't a coldness that touched his skin. It was a cold rising up from somewhere deep in the abyss.

*Rothvar?* he called. *Anything I should know about tonight?*

*We made a last sweep before sunset,* his second-in-command replied. *It's quiet everywhere in Ebon Rih.*

*Not everywhere,* Lucivar thought, staring in the direction of the Black Mountain.

He turned and went inside to have dinner with his wife and younger son. All he could do now was wait—and be ready for whatever his Queen required.

Zoey was being a bitch.

To keep things equal, Jaenelle Saetien had wanted Zoey and Delora to walk in right behind her, leading the rest of the girls. As the daughter of the house, she *had* to enter first so that the rest of the girls would be acknowledged as her guests, but when Zoey realized she and Delora were supposed to be considered of equal status, she stepped aside and suggested that Delora and her friends go first.

That instantly divided the girls into Zoey's friends and Delora's friends, and that was *exactly* the line Jaenelle Saetien had wanted to erase with this party.

It also put Delora, Hespera, Amara, Borsala, Leena, and Tacita in her father's sights the moment they walked into the Hall. Maybe, hopefully, he would be in his study working and she could get everyone to their rooms and settled before he found out about the unexpected guests.

"Good evening, Beale," she said when the butler opened the door and stepped aside for them to enter.

Her steps faltered, almost causing Delora and Hespera to run into her. Her father stood in the great hall, his hands tucked into his trouser pockets. He didn't smile in greeting. He didn't step forward. He didn't say a word. He just looked at her with a chill in his eyes that felt like he was slipping needles of ice under her skin.

"Father," she said. "Some friends couldn't make it, but other friends were available at the last minute to round out the house party."

"Ladies Delora, Hespera, Amara, and Borsala weren't on the guest list you provided, but they were expected," he said with cold civility that was worse than a shout. "Lord Beale, please escort our guests to their rooms. Ladies, a buffet will be served in the dining room in one hour. Lady SaDiablo, your presence is required in my study *now*."

He turned and walked away, expecting her to follow meekly.

"How rude," Hespera said in a loud whisper. "*My* father would never treat guests that way."

"I think the message is he is treating the guests as they deserve to be treated," Zoey said. She looked at Jaenelle Saetien and added on a psychic thread, *Be careful. Don't let Delora and Hespera push you into doing or saying something you'll regret.*

Jaenelle Saetien lifted her chin and stomped into her father's study, ready to do battle.

He stood in front of the desk, just as he'd stood in the great hall.

"Since you were so pissy about Delora and her friends not being invited to Titian's Winsol party, I had to wonder why you didn't invite them to a party where you controlled the guest list." His voice had become silk over burning ice. "I didn't like the conclusion I reached about your honesty, but we'll table that for now. Right now I want you to know that if you ever again change travel plans that involve a Queen and don't inform her host and her escorts, I will assume your intentions are to cause her harm, and I will summon every warrior at my disposal to go to her aid and to hunt you down."

Jaenelle Saetien stared at him, shocked. "We just changed plans."

"Someone changed plans. I'll agree with that. Exactly why? Well, that's what we'll find out, won't we? It's clear that Delora has you wrapped around her little finger, and you will do whatever she wants you to do." His lips curved in a cold, cruel smile. He took a step toward her. "But here is what I'm wondering, my darling. How much of your honor have you whored for her? How far will you go to please that bitch?"

His words crushed her ability to speak.

He walked up to her, his arm brushing hers as he walked past her. Then he stopped and whispered, "Make sure none of the other guests come to harm, and make sure Lady Delora obeys the rules of this house. If she doesn't, she won't see another sunrise. I will bury that bitch in a grave so deep, she will never be found. That, by the way, is something I learned how to do by watching Dorothea, but I am a much better gravedigger. Even she couldn't find my graves. I wonder if Delora, whose psychic scent reminds me so much of Dorothea, has acquired that skill."

Jaenelle Saetien gasped and focused on the threat, ignoring what he'd said about Delora's skill. "You'd kill Delora just because someone has an accident while they're here?"

"Kill?" He laughed softly, and there was something dark and terrible in the sound. "I'm not feeling that merciful." He waited a moment, then added, "You're dismissed."

She stumbled out of the study.

"Shall I show you to your room?" Beale asked.

"I know where my room is," she snapped, too frightened to remember anything, even courtesy.

"The family wing is closed and shielded. You've been assigned a room with the other guests."

What in the name of Hell was going on? They'd arrived a little late. So what? Was her father being unreasonable just because Zoey was a Queen? She was in trouble because of *Zoey*?

As she followed Beale to the assigned guest rooms, she knew Zoey wasn't the reason she was in trouble. She should have sent a message to let her father know the change in arrival time. She should have told him she wanted to invite Delora and that group of friends—and told him why—instead of bringing them to the Hall and hoping he wouldn't make a fuss. But everyone else's father would have shrugged it off, would have been just a little bit indulgent.

She could almost hear Daemonar saying, *Who is everyone?*

But to have *her father* say she was whoring *her* honor when *he* was married to *that woman*? That made her so angry, she could scream.

She'd deal with her feelings later. Right now she had to impress on Delora the need to follow the rules of the house, the need for *everyone* to follow the rules of the house. Delora would want to dismiss his words as a bluff, but Daemon Sadi never bluffed when he talked about killing someone.


"This is a lovely room, Aunt Surreal," Titian said. She glanced at Zoey, who was leaning against the connecting doorway.

"We assumed you two wouldn't mind sharing a bathroom," Surreal said with a smile. "And no one will kick if the door between your rooms remains open. But Prince

Sadi's temper is cold and sharp tonight, so don't test him. Sleep in your own rooms and in your own beds."

"I should have informed him of the delay when I sent the note about Jhett and Arlene not coming with us," Zoey said.

"It wasn't your responsibility, and you had no reason to think that he *hadn't* been informed. But it seems Jaenelle Saetien needs to learn the consequences of ignoring basic rules and courtesies in order to appreciate the reason for those rules and courtesies."

Her aunt looked sad. Looked . . . wounded. And worried.

"Should we go back to the school, Aunt Surreal?" Titian asked. "Or go to the town house?" They'd have to take the friends who had come with her and Zoey, and she didn't know where they would all stay at the town house.

"It's better if we stay here," Zoey said.

"Yes, it is," Surreal agreed. "I'll be staying in the staff room on the other side of the corridor. If you need anything, or if anyone starts any mischief, you call me."

"We will."

"I'll make sure the other girls are settling in." Surreal left Titian's room.

Titian looked at Zoey. "I wish we'd never agreed to come to this party."

"We're safer here," Zoey insisted. "Delora has been leading Jaenelle Saetien into believing things that go against the Old Ways of the Blood, and your cousin refuses to see it—or can't see it." She hesitated. "Are you wearing the good-luck piece Daemonar gave you?"

Titian had never explained exactly what that mark of safe passage was or what it was intended to do—or who had given it to Daemonar to give to her—but Zoey wasn't a fool and had realized weeks ago it was a lot more than a good-luck charm.

She touched her chest and felt the coin hanging on its chain just below the pendant that held her Birthright Summer-sky Jewel. "I'm wearing it. I wish I could give it to you, but . . ." But the mark had been blooded and wouldn't work for anyone else.

Zoey gave her an odd smile. "I have my own luck charm." She called in a knife and slid the blade out of its finely tooled leather sheath.

Titian's mouth dropped open. "That's . . . that's Lord Kohlvar's work." Her father said that Kohlvar was the finest weapons maker he'd ever met.

Zoey nodded. "Your father gave it to me as a Winsol gift. A private gift." She gently slid the blade back into the sheath and vanished it.

"Is my father going to teach you how to fight with it?"

"Daemonar has started teaching me the basics with a wooden blade. Once I'm proficient, your father will add to the instruction."

Titian had never wanted to learn to fight or use weapons, and her father hadn't forced her to learn beyond a few basic moves that were more about defense than fighting. Now she wished she'd learned more. But Zoey wasn't aggressive, so this need to know how to fight puzzled her.

"Why?" she asked.

Zoey looked away, which wasn't like her since she usually met problems or questions head-on. "Since they share a name, I guess I understand why Jaenelle Saetien doesn't want to hear the stories about the Queen who was so powerful and so beloved, but I want to know everything I can about the Queen of Ebon Askavi and her court. I want to be strong enough to stand up for myself and my people. I love my grandmother, and I think she's a wonderful Queen, but the Dark Court is legendary. Every powerful man in the Realm had been connected to that court, your father and Prince Sadi the most powerful among them. I wish I knew what she had studied so that I could study those things too. Sometimes I wish there was a way to talk to her."

*Be careful what you wish for, Zoey,* Titian thought as she touched the charm again. She wouldn't say anything, wouldn't reveal what remained unspoken but known within her family, but she would ask Daemonar if it might be possible, just once, for one Queen to meet another.

Jaenelle Saetien's temper spiked when she saw Surreal standing at the railing outside one of the bedroom balconies. *Her* bedroom, which was away from the rest of the girls.

"Why was I assigned this room?" she demanded. Had Surreal *talked* to Delora and Hespera? How mortally embarrassing! This party was going from bad to worse and it hadn't even started.

"We weren't sure which camp you were in, so you have a room that straddles the line," Surreal replied.

"You make them sound like enemy forces about to do battle at dawn. They're two groups of friends who want to find a way to get along."

Surreal laughed. "Oh, sugar, if you really believe the coven of malice wants to get along with a Queen like Zoey, then you have not been paying attention." She gave Jaenelle Saetien a strange look. "But I've paid attention, and all of my knives are honed. Something for your little friends to think about before they start any trouble."

"They aren't going to . . ."

Surreal walked away, not even listening to her.

Her parents were going to spoil this house party!

She went into the bedroom to inspect the clothes that had been brought from her bedroom in the family wing. A couple of her favorite dresses, probably the ones she would have picked for the evening. But she hadn't been able to choose, had she?

One of Uncle Lucivar's sayings suddenly popped into her head: kick a pebble, start an avalanche.

If she'd been honest about the guest list, if she'd done the courteous thing and sent a message to her father about being delayed, would everything be different now?

# THIRTY-EIGHT

Responding to Beale's flash of anger, Daemon rose to the killing edge as he strode toward the Hall's open front door. A slower-burning anger came from Tarl, the head gardener, who stood in the doorway holding a short-handled scythe.

Then Daemon focused on the young Warlord dressed in a messenger's livery—and the Sadist instantly embraced cold rage.

Everything about the boy felt *wrong*, but . . . wrong in a way that made him hesitate.

*Saw him arrive, then keep low and quiet for a few minutes before coming to the door,* Tarl said on a psychic thread.

*He said the message was for you, personal and *urgent*, then tried to hand it to *me*,* Beale told Daemon. *No stationmaster would send an untrained boy with an urgent message.*

That was true. If there was no one else, the stationmaster would have brought the message himself instead of entrusting it to someone who would wait outside for several minutes before delivering an *urgent* message to the Warlord Prince of Dhemlan.

Until that moment, he had hoped he'd been wrong about some part—any part—of this sordid game that Jaenelle Saetien had brought into his home along with her *friends*.

Now he had to play his part in the game and hope the bloody and painful result would be worth the cost.

He heard female chatter and giggles as Jaenelle Saetien's friends came down the stairs to the informal sitting room. Since there was another staircase that provided a more direct route between the guest rooms assigned to the girls and the dining room, the only reason to be near the great hall was if someone knew something was about to happen.

*Perfect timing,* Daemon thought as some of the girls entered the great hall from the informal sitting room while others crowded the doorway. He indicated that Beale should accept the message. Then he looked at Tarl. *As soon as our little friend is out of sight of our guests, take him to the stables and lock him in. Full shields so he can't contact anyone. Can you handle that?*

*I can and will,* Tarl replied.

*When he bleats about needing to deliver other messages, which he will if he's been coached properly, offer to send a message to the stationmaster explaining the delay. But he stays here, isolated, until I know who sent him.*

Tarl stepped out of the way. The messenger bolted, his heels barely crossing the threshold before Beale closed the door, preventing anyone from seeing that the messenger never made it to the landing web to catch one of the Winds and escape.

"What's going on?" a girl asked loudly.

"Let me through," Surreal said, coming up behind the girls.

Daemon saw two of the girls look back, roll their eyes, and make no effort to move. He almost smiled when Surreal used an arrow-shaped shield to shove the girls out of her way.

Then he noticed his daughter, who looked horrified—not at the girls' insolence in refusing to yield to a Gray-Jeweled witch in her own home but at Surreal taking a direct approach to removing the obstacle. Remembering why he had to play his part, Daemon opened the sealed message.

"Sadi?" One side of Surreal's long skirt flashed open, revealing the sheathed knife strapped to her thigh.

He handed her the message. She read it and stared at him.

"The *special* school is under attack?" Fierce anger turned her face hard. "Those children have endured enough. If someone is trying to hurt anyone at the school, I will skin the bastards alive and feed them to the hounds of Hell."

He wondered if anyone realized Surreal could, and would, do exactly that—especially if he helped her.

When she turned toward the door, Daemon caught her wrist. "You go on ahead and sound the battle cry. Have the District Queens call up every guard under their hands and tell them to be ready to fight. And tell them every girl in their villages is at risk until we say otherwise, and it is their duty to keep those girls safe, no matter who they have to kill. I'll join you as soon as I take care of things here." As he let her go, he added on a psychic thread, *I'll check the school for half-Blood children. You check your sanctuary, just in case the message was real.*

"Lord Holt, have the large Coach brought to the landing web," Daemon said.

"At once," his secretary replied, stepping outside.

Since it wasn't necessary to leave the Hall in order to summon the Coach and driver, Daemon thought Holt's exit was a bit theatrical, but it gave the Warlord an excuse to scan the grounds around the front of the Hall.

That much done, he turned his attention to the girls.

They were all there. Jaenelle Saetien stood in front of the group. Zoey and Titian stood to one side, arms linked. It only took moments for the young Queen to make eye contact with each of her friends, and those friends all moved a little closer together, separating themselves from Delora and her coven of malice.

"Ladies, as you heard, there has been a reported attack on a special school that is run by the SaDiablo family. Lady Surreal and I have to investigate, which means I must return you to the school in Amdarh immediately.

There's no time for you to go back to your rooms. My staff will take care of packing your things and returning them to you. We leave now."

He watched Zoey nudge Titian, urging her toward the front door in order to obey him. He saw Delora give Jaenelle Saetien a nudge and a hard look. Did she really believe he wouldn't notice?

But his daughter leaped forward and said in a voice dangerously close to a whine, "Why can't we stay here and have our party? We'll be fine here."

"The girls can't stay here without Lady Surreal or me in attendance." The chill in his voice should have warned her, but that bitch gave her another nudge and was probably coaching her on a distaff thread in what to say to convince him.

"It's not like we'll be alone," Jaenelle Saetien wheedled. "Beale will be here, and he wears a Red Jewel."

*Oh, yes, he does, and in this, it is the Jewel that counts, my darling.* "You will follow any orders *Lord* Beale gives and accept any decisions he makes as if they were mine?" he asked.

She looked relieved. "Yes."

He scanned the girls' faces, noting the different expressions. Then he focused on his daughter as Holt returned.

"Lady Jaenelle Saetien SaDiablo, do you swear to me, the Warlord Prince of Dhemlan, that you will abide by all orders given and decisions made by Lord Beale on my behalf? Do you swear on your Jewels that you will keep this promise, regardless of anyone else's wishes?"

She looked startled and uneasy to be required to make a formal promise, but said, "Yes, I swear."

"Lady Zoela, do you stand witness?"

Zoey sucked in a breath. Then she nodded and said, "I stand witness."

"Lord Holt, do you stand witness?"

"I stand witness," Holt replied.

Daemon kept his eyes on his daughter and said softly,

"This isn't a game, and it isn't a bluff." He looked at Delora, then back at Jaenelle Saetien. "If there is any trouble here while I'm gone, you will not be the only one who will forfeit your power and your Jewel."

Before he walked out of the Hall, he touched Zoey's first inner barrier with the lightest psychic thread he could manage at that moment, but it didn't hide anything. He felt some regret that his touch revealed the full measure of who, and what, he was. *If you feel uneasy about anything or anyone, find Beale or Holt. They'll protect you.*

*I will.* She swallowed hard. *Good hunting, Prince.*

He admired the courage it took to say those words to him at that moment.

Leaving the Hall, Daemon glided toward the landing web that was circled by the gravel drive. Using Craft, he moved the large Coach to one side. Then he caught the Black Wind and headed for the school for half-Blood children.

Delora looked at Hespera, who shook her head to indicate she hadn't been able to slip into the dining room yet and add a little surprise to a couple of dishes.

Damn.

"Why don't we spend a few minutes in the sitting room?" she said brightly. "No one in *real* aristo houses goes directly from their rooms to dinner."

"But we were late getting here, and the food is ready," Jaenelle Saetien said.

"You said it was a buffet. If the cook is any good, the food will keep."

Jaenelle Saetien gave the butler a nervous glance but said, "I guess we could visit in the sitting room for a few minutes."

Delora felt a fizz of excitement as Hespera, covered by the movement of the other girls, wrapped herself in a sight shield and headed for the dining room, with Tacita, in plain sight, walking with her to act as a diversion. "A few minutes is all we'll need." *For a lot of things,* she added silently.

*Prince Chaosti.*

About to enter the girls' dormitory to check on Arlene and Jhett, the Healer and Black Widow who hadn't gone to the house party, Chaosti stepped back and waited for one of his demon-dead Warlords.

*The need to serve and protect doesn't always end with the physical death,* Chaosti thought. This fist of Dea al Mon men had been with him when he'd walked among the living. They were among the men who were still with him.

"Report," he said quietly when the Warlord reached him.

"I found that Dharo Prince challenging the gatekeeper, demanding to know which boys had left the school. The gatekeeper denied that any of the boys had left, but friends of Lady Zoela told Prince Raine that the males who serve the coven of malice slipped away from the school and forced two of Zoela's male friends to go with them."

"And the gatekeeper denied they had left school grounds?" Chaosti sent out Gray psychic threads, a web of power that would sweep under the power of the school's residents. He couldn't identify every individual, but he'd made a point of recognizing specific ones. And those males weren't here. Which meant the gatekeeper had lied to Raine. "Inform the gatekeeper that he can tell you the truth or he can explain himself to the High Lord of Hell."

"Already did that—and kissed the bastard's throat with my blade to make sure he understood. After that, he admitted that Krellis and the others who serve that bitch Delora, as well as two of Zoela's friends, left the school and didn't tell him where they were going. He'd been given a hefty sum of silver marks not to record their leaving so that everyone would think they were still at the school."

Which might have worked if he and his men hadn't been here tonight—and if Raine hadn't called attention to the gatekeeper letting those males slip away.

"Tell Prince Raine to pack a bag, enough for a couple of days. Then go to Zoela's male friends and help them pack. I'll fetch Ladies Jhett and Arlene, and we'll take all of them to the SaDiablo town house."

"Done," the Warlord said. He hurried toward the boys' dormitory, no doubt using a psychic thread to relay Chaosti's orders to the Dharo Prince.

Not bothering to sight-shield, Chaosti entered the girls' dormitory. A sudden spike of fear and anger—and something male and rancid—struck his senses and ignited his temper. He raced down the corridor and bounded up the stairs to the second-floor bedrooms.

His Gray power splintered the door of the Black Widow's room. She and the Healer were there, their teeth bared in fury and their faces filled with the pain of their moon-times as they used short-handled clubs to hold off the two males whose psychic scents were rank with twisted lust.

Chaosti called in his Dea al Mon fighting knives and shouted his battle cry as he strode into the room. The males spun around—and his knives, honed for killing fields, slid into their bodies and sliced through their hearts. He pulled out his knives, put shields around the bodies as they fell, then vanished the newly dead.

He almost pitied them because they would have to stand before the High Lord of Hell's cold and merciless rage.

"Ladies." He noted with approval that the girls hadn't relaxed their fighting stance. "I am Prince Chaosti. I served in the Queen of Ebon Askavi's First Circle, and I still serve in her name. I am known to the Warlord Prince of Dhemlan and have been assisting Lord Weston in guarding Lady Zoela." Credentials were everything in a situation like this, and lying about *these* credentials went beyond suicidal.

There were other things that needed to be done, but he waited.

"Does Prince Daemonar know you?" Lady Jhett finally asked.

He smiled. "In-close fighting with a short-handled club is something Daemonar learned from me."

Another excruciating moment while they considered his words. Then they nodded and lowered the clubs.

"You must pack a bag with enough clothes and supplies for a couple of days," he said. "I will escort you to the Sa-Diablo town house. You will be better protected there."

"Zoey," Arlene said.

"She'll be protected," he promised.

He stepped into the corridor and watched Arlene hurry to her own room to pack. Then he sent out a call on a psychic spear thread. Daemon Sadi didn't answer, so he sent out a summons to another of the Queen's weapons.

*Daemonar.*

*Chaosti?*

*Krellis and the other males who are known to serve Delora's coven have disappeared, but two males who associate with them just attacked the Black Widow and Healer who stayed behind.*

*Were the girls harmed?*

*No. You taught them well, Brother.* He paused. *I can't reach Daemon.*

*I'll go to the Hall. Beron is at the town house.*

*I'll bring the Ladies there, along with Prince Raine and the boys who may also be vulnerable to attack.*

*Weston,* Daemonar said.

*I'll tell him, and he'll inform Lady Zhara's Master of the Guard.* And within minutes of that message, every guard who served Zhara and every Warlord Prince who lived in the city would be on the move, ready to fight.

Everything had a price, and the price for whatever mischief the coven of malice was making tonight would be steep.

"Prince Chaosti is bringing students from the school. They need protection," Daemonar told Helton and Beron. "Prince Raine will also be staying here until things are settled. I'm going to the Hall to inform Prince Sadi that some of the boys have left the school without supplying a destination." And if Uncle Daemon wasn't there for some reason, *he* would be there to stand between his sister and the enemy.

"Go," Beron said. "We'll take care of things here."

Daemonar took a moment to check his weapons—fighting knife, Eyrien club, and his Eyrien war blade. He vanished all of them, then ran out of the town house, launched himself skyward, caught the nearest thread of a Green Web, and rode that Wind toward the Hall with all the skill he had.

Titian watched the way Delora and Hespera moved around the sitting room, making cutting remarks about the furniture and carpets being old-fashioned or how some of the decorations were beyond quaint. Jaenelle Saetien looked so embarrassed, Titian felt sorry for her cousin and wanted to point out that Delora and Hespera were probably saying those things because they couldn't recognize the quality of the Dharo carpets on the floor, and that beautiful crystal sculpture displayed on a hand-carved side table probably cost more than the income either of their families made in a year.

There was age and power in this place—and the weight of memories of someone who had lived here and been beloved. And was still beloved.

"We stay together," Zoey said quietly. "We'll ask Lord Beale to escort us to our rooms right after dinner. There is a common room in that square. We'll stay there, together, until Prince Sadi returns."

"But I need to . . . ," one of the girls began, then blushed.

"It's a buffet," Titian said. "We can go in and eat now. There will be plenty of footmen on duty to escort people to the nearest water closet."

Zoey sucked in air between her teeth as Delora moved in a kind of slithering dance toward the sitting room's large windows—and opened two of them, despite the cold winter air. Moments later, Krellis, Dhuran, Clayton, and several more of Delora's male friends climbed into the room. Krellis's eyes glittered as he looked at Delora and then focused on Zoey.

"This is a girls-only party," Jaenelle Saetien said, sounding alarmed. "You can't be here." She turned to Delora. "They can't be here."

"Of course they can," Delora purred. "They came all this way to have some fun with us."

"Delora, you don't understand—"

The sitting room door opened. Beale stepped in, his Red Jewel now worn over his pristine white shirt.

"There are no male guests at this party," Beale said, his voice rumbling through the room. "Leave. Now."

"They were invited, and they're staying," Delora said.

"They aren't guests; they're intruders." Beale took another step into the room.

At the doorway, Titian saw Holt and a handful of footmen. All of them held a hand at their sides in a way she recognized meant they were holding sight-shielded weapons.

Mother Night.

Jaenelle Saetien looked at Hespera, then at Beale, then at Delora.

*You gave your word,* Titian thought. *Don't break your word, not for her.*

Jaenelle Saetien turned back to Beale. "As the Lady of the house, I'm inviting the gentlemen to stay."

"As the one who is speaking for Prince Sadi, I say they go," Beale replied.

Titian saw her cousin hesitate, saw the look on Delora's face before Jaenelle Saetien shouted, "I don't take orders from a *servant*. They are *my* guests, and *I say they can stay.*"

Silence.

"Very well," Beale finally said. He looked at each boy. "Are these *all* of your guests?"

Jaenelle Saetien raised her chin. "Yes."

Beale took two steps back—and closed the sitting room door.

Zoey grabbed Titian's arm and turned her so her back was to the rest of the people in the room.

"Are you wearing the charm Daemonar gave you?" Zoey whispered.

"Yes," Titian replied. She always wore it. She'd promised Daemonar she would.

Zoey glanced past Titian and shivered. "Whatever that charm is supposed to do? Titian, it's time to use it. Please."

She drew the gold chain out from beneath her dress, then pressed the mark of safe passage between her thumb and forefinger.

*Daemonar, we're in trouble. We need help.* She waited a moment, not sure what was supposed to happen. *Daemonar? We really need help. Please.*

She waited a moment longer, then slipped the mark beneath her dress and looked at Zoey. "I don't know how it's supposed to work."

Zoey sighed. "Let's get something to eat. There should be footmen in the dining room to keep an eye on things."

Linking arms with Zoey, she led their group of friends to the door.

"Where are you going?" Delora called. "The party is just getting started."

"Some of us are hungry and prefer to be selective about who sits at our table," Zoey replied coldly.

Dhuran hooted. Clayton grabbed the hand of one of Zoey's friends as she walked by and began talking to her with quiet intensity. Krellis's eyes still glittered.

*We shield,* Titian thought. *We shield and we fight until help can reach us.*

She just hoped it wouldn't take long for that help to arrive.


Beale closed the sitting room door, then turned to face Holt and the footmen who had gathered in the great hall to assist in removing the intruders.

He swallowed his anger, let it burn away the affection that had existed since the moment that girl had been born.

The presence of those pricks confirmed the true nature of this party—and proved the threat against Lady Zoela tonight was very real. And the threat was in this house because a girl who had been loved and protected all her life had chosen to break her word and put other girls in danger.

"What do we do?" Holt asked quietly.

"I don't take orders from that *child*," Beale growled. "*I* serve the Prince of the Darkness, the High Lord of Hell."

Holt's eyes widened because he'd said the words aloud, and the newer footmen-in-training sucked in a breath. But Beale knew this . . . betrayal . . . would strip away the last illusion about the man who ruled Dhemlan and ruled this house—and ruled so much more.

"We lock the Hall," he said. "Those intruders got in, but they aren't getting out until the High Lord returns."

He moved toward the front door, his strides measured. He called in an old seal that bore the SaDiablo crest, fit it into a metal circle embedded in the door's wood, and turned the seal to the right. As seal and circle moved, the spells Daemon Sadi had woven into the Hall engaged, and Black shields flowed through all the outer walls of SaDiablo Hall—flowed through stone to prevent anyone from using Craft to pass through a wall; flowed over windows, whether they were open or closed, forming bars that were felt but not seen; locked every door that would allow anyone to leave the building; and wove power over the rooftops and inner courtyards, creating something like a steel mesh that would allow nothing to escape by going skyward.

People could still enter, but no one could leave now. Not even him.

"I'll put a Red shield on the staircase that's in the informal sitting room," he said. "And engage the shields in the interior walls of that sitting room and the room beyond it."

Holt called in another seal and held it up. "I'll slip around to the other side of the formal sitting room and engage the shields in those walls."

"It's possible some of *them* have already slipped out for whatever they intend to do here," Beale said. *Whatever* they intended? As if anyone now believed there were other intentions.

"You should wake the other security Prince Sadi left in your care," Holt replied.

Before he could give the footmen his orders, the sitting room door opened and Lady Zoela and Lady Titian walked out, followed by their friends. But not all the girls Beale had identified as belonging to Zoela's unofficial court were present.

Holt was right. It was time to wake the other security and have them capture the wandering guests.

"Ladies," Beale said quietly. "I think it best if I escort you to your rooms."

"Could we have something to eat first?" Zoela asked. "Or fix up some plates to take with us?" She glanced at one of her friends. "And use the nearest water closet?"

Two of the younger footmen had been posted at the dining room door and hadn't reported any trouble, so it should be safe for the Ladies to stay there long enough to eat. And one of the girls did look distressed. He assigned two of the senior footmen who had been in the great hall to escort that girl to the nearest necessary and then stand guard inside the dining room while the younger footmen remained at the door.

He escorted Lady Zoela and the other girls to the dining room. A psychic probe detected no one else in the room and nothing seemed to be amiss when he opened the door and scanned the serving dishes arranged on a long table. After telling the footmen not to allow anyone else in the dining room except the one girl who would be escorted by the senior footmen, Beale hurried to the informal sitting room, engaged the interior defenses that would keep the intruders confined, then headed for the butler's pantry to summon the Scelties—and release the cats.

When something more feral than cold rage shivered through the sitting room across from the Queen's suite,

Karla looked up from the story she'd been reading aloud. "What's wrong?"

Witch's sapphire eyes had that distant look of someone seeing something beyond the immediate room. She tilted her head as if trying to locate a sound.

"Blood sings to blood," she said softly. "Titian has engaged the gift Daemonar asked me to make so that he would hear her when she couldn't call for help any other way."

"But she's at a house party at the Hall, isn't she?" Karla rose and dropped the book on the chair. "Sadi should be there."

"And still Titian is calling her brother for help."

Which meant Sadi wasn't at the Hall for some reason—or Daemon's temper had snapped the leash and he was the danger.

"Daemonar isn't answering," Witch said. "I'd feel him if he answered."

"Maybe he's beyond her reach."

"But not mine, and as long as he's within my reach, he'll hear her call."

"Unless he's riding the Winds."

Witch nodded.

"Do we wait?" Karla asked.

"No," Witch said in that midnight, cavernous, sepulchral voice that seemed to rise from somewhere deep in the abyss. "I'll send the other weapons."

*I promised,* Jaenelle Saetien thought as rising panic made her stomach churn. *I made a promise before witnesses.* And she'd broken it. Why had she broken it? Why had she said that to Beale about him being a servant? He must be so angry with her. And when her father found out!

She shivered as she looked at Delora talking with Krellis as if nothing had happened, as if everything was going to be all right and they would receive nothing more than a slap on the wrist for being naughty.

*I'm in so much trouble.*

When she was around Delora, her father's rules didn't seem to matter. Seemed archaic. Moth and flame. That was what she and Delora were. Moth and flame. Delora was so compelling and exciting and knowledgeable about everything aristo and was so different from her own family, who were so hampered by duty they seemed stodgy in comparison. Not that she didn't love her father and uncle, but in some ways, they were such *rubes* who weren't interested in the excitement that could be found in the city and in things that were new.

Now she wondered if the boys really had come to the Hall uninvited or if Delora and Hespera had arranged for them to be there, and that was why Delora had pushed her to convince her father to let the party continue.

Now she wondered how the boys had known when to arrive, slipping into the Hall so soon after her father had left.

She walked up to Delora and Krellis at the same time Hespera joined them, smiling as if she knew a particularly delicious, and nasty, joke.

"Tacita is *such* a flirt," Hespera said. "She can turn *anyone's* head and have him standing at attention."

Jaenelle Saetien stared. Was Hespera saying that Tacita was trying to arouse someone who worked at the Hall? That she *had* aroused . . . ? "The boys have to leave. Now." *Before there is no way to fix this.*

"Don't be such a sniveling little girl," Hespera said. "Or does the butler still wipe your little nose—and other things?"

She turned on the other girl. "Shut up, Hespera."

Delora waved a hand in a dismissive gesture. "Stop being such a rube, Jaenelle Saetien. Your father isn't going to do anything because a few of the boys came to the party."

Had Delora really said that? Did she really think that? "I agreed that Beale would be in charge and would act on my father's behalf. I gave my word. And Beale told the boys to leave."

"The butler," Krellis sneered. "True aristos don't take

orders from *servants*. Then again, your mother is probably used to taking orders from all kinds of men."

"You're the one who foolishly gave your word," Delora said with a sniff. "If there's a problem—"

"I'll forfeit my Jewel—and so will you and all your friends," she snapped.

Delora looked startled—and, finally, just a little frightened. "He was bluffing. He wouldn't do that to his daughter because of a few extra people at a party."

"My father doesn't bluff." Jaenelle Saetien caught a glimpse of Clayton and one of Zoey's friends slipping out the door on the other side of the sitting room. She looked at Krellis. "And you should know that any male who has sex at the Hall without my father's permission will be skinned alive. He doesn't bluff about that either."

She hurried out of the sitting room. She'd been so stupid. Whatever Delora had in mind for this house party, it wasn't to mend any differences with Zoey.

And yet . . . If Delora came after her and apologized for dismissing her concerns and made the boys' arrival sound reasonable, would she be able to resist the glitter and excitement that was Delora and align herself with Zoey, who had such prosaic ideas of fun?

"Maybe this wasn't a good idea," Krellis said.

"There are too many guards at the school. This was the best chance of taking care of Insipid Zoey and some of her friends," Delora said. "And no one knows you left the school. You paid the gatekeeper enough to keep him quiet?"

Krellis nodded. "But I want to be gone before—"

"Hell's fire," one of the boys said, pushing against something that blocked the open window. "There are shields over the windows! We can't get out that way."

"Well, I guess I have to persuade my 'friend' that I've seen the error of my ways and get her to convince the butler to open the door and let you leave," Delora said.

Hespera shook her head. "Insipid went into the dining room. By now she'll be needing whatever Krellis wants to give her."

Delora smiled and gave Krellis an arch look. "How long does it really take for you to get the job done?"

Finding nothing amiss at the school for half-Bloods, Daemon still sent commands to the District Queens and their Masters of the Guard to be alert to any attempts to attack the girls in their villages.

As he strode toward the landing web, he felt Surreal tap his first inner barrier with a Gray psychic thread.

*Anything?* he asked.

*Nothing,* she replied. *It was a ruse.*

*We had to be sure.*

Then a midnight, sepulchral voice full of feral, icy rage filled his mind before he could break the link with Surreal. *Daemon, you're needed at the Hall. Now.*

*Mother Night,* Surreal whispered.

Daemon broke the link with Surreal as gently as he could. If something had provoked Witch's temper and she was giving him that command, he knew which aspect of his own temper needed to reply, and it wasn't the Warlord Prince of Dhemlan or the High Lord of Hell.

It was the Sadist.

Beale looked at the two shadows Prince Sadi had left with him, to be used if that kind of protection was needed. One was a shadow of Kaelas, the eight-hundred-pound Arcerian cat who had been a Red-Jeweled Warlord Prince. The other shadow was Jaal, who had been a Green-Jeweled Warlord Prince—and a six-hundred-pound tiger.

He opened his first inner barrier and offered the shadows and the four Scelties careful images of Ladies Zoela and Titian and the other girls he'd identified as their friends. "These witches need protection. Find them. Take them to Helene." He offered an image of the Hall's house-keeper so they would know her on sight. "Capture but don't kill any males who are with the girls and don't serve this house."

"We will find the human females," the Sceltie Warlord Prince said.

Dogs and cats left the servants' dining room, the only place in this part of the Hall that was large enough to hold cats that size—after Beale vanished the table and chairs.

He remembered the real Kaelas and Jaal and had no illusions about what he'd unleashed in the Hall. The Scelties would herd the girls to safety, and the shadows would capture any males they found wandering where they didn't belong. But if any of those girls showed fear of the boy who was with them . . .

Well, everything had a price.

*Lucivar, you're needed at the Hall. Now.*

Hearing that midnight voice, Lucivar abandoned the game of hawks and hares he'd been playing with young Andulvar, walked out of the family room in his eyrie, and headed for the front door. He wasn't surprised that the command had come, but the location troubled him.

"Lucivar?" Marian hurried after him.

Feeling an icy calm settle over him, Lucivar called in the double-buckle fighting belt that Eyriens wore in battle. He slipped the fighting knife in the sheath and then sheathed the palm-sized knife between the belt buckles. Two more knives went into sheaths in his boots.

"Lucivar . . . ?"

"Trouble at the Hall." Leather gauntlets closed over his wrists and forearms before he used Craft to fit the light leather vest and chain mail over the shirt he'd been wearing for an evening at home.

"But Titian's there," Marian said.

He looked at his wife, saw her coat a mother's fear with a woman's courage. "I know."

*Rothvar,* he called to his second-in-command. *There's trouble at SaDiablo Hall. Put the men on alert in case that trouble is meant to draw me away from here.*

*I'll bring Nurian and our children to your eyrie. Easier to defend all of them that way,* Rothvar replied.

"Bring Titian home, Lucivar," Marian said.

He nodded and walked out of the eyrie, still wrapped in an icy calm. That would crack soon enough, and when it did, his hot, volatile temper would be another weapon on a killing field.

Except . . .

*Won't get there in time. Not from here. Not even riding the Ebon-gray Winds will get me there in time to protect my girl.*

Then he saw it, felt it, the crack and sizzle of power that dwarfed his own.

Black lightning.

Only once had Jaenelle Angelline offered him the terrifying and thrilling experience of riding black lightning with her. It wasn't like the Winds, which were set out in webs with predictable tether lines and radial lines. Black lightning ran deeper than the Black Winds and was so much faster. But it was dangerous because there was no way to predict the shape of each bolt and no way to recover from a miscalculation. He could die making this run.

But it might get him to the Hall in time to save Titian.

*Thank you, Lady,* he said on an Ebon-gray thread.

He launched himself skyward and caught the Ebon-gray Wind. Then he deliberately flung himself off that Web and fell in the Darkness, just catching the edge of the next bolt of black lightning.

Using all his strength and skill, Lucivar rode the lightning to SaDiablo Hall.


Holt walked toward one of the Warlord intruders and the girl who was trying to free herself from the bastard's tight hold on one arm while he rubbed the knuckles of her hand.

"If you loved me," the boy began.

"Can I help?" Holt interrupted, not looking at the girl or breaking his stride.

The Warlord scowled at him. "Just go about your business."

"I will." Holt smiled as he took a last step, grabbed the Warlord's shirt, and turned his fist so that the Jewel in his ring pressed against the bastard's chest. Then he unleashed a jolt of power from his Opal Jewel. That small amount of power, used on someone who wore a Jewel lighter than the spell's wielder, wouldn't pulp the heart or sear the lungs, but it would seize all the muscles in a person's chest and hurt so much it would bring a person to his knees.

Jaenelle Angelline had taught him that defensive spell, and he'd used it over the years when a visiting guest or servant at the Hall tried to cross a line that shouldn't be crossed.

As the Warlord's legs buckled, Holt used Craft to float him on air. Then he turned to the girl. One of Lady Zoela's friends. "Come with me. I'll get you to a safe place, and the housekeeper will look after you."

He headed for the nearest servants' staircase, summoning two footmen who would take over and escort the girl the rest of the way while he took the Warlord to the austere accommodations that were deep beneath the Hall.

It was winter and the corridors in the Hall tended to be chilly, despite the warming spells Prince Sadi replenished regularly. Since the girl was wearing long sleeves, he couldn't tell if she carried any bruises from the Warlord's rough handling. Helene would find out and make a careful record of every one.

The number and placement of the bruises would matter to Prince Sadi when it came time for this bastard's execution.

It was like having excessively large mousers roaming the corridors as they hunted for vermin, Beale thought as the

Sceltie trotted toward him, her teeth in the sleeve of the male's coat as the dog used Craft to float the body.

Wouldn't have been possible for something the Sceltie's size to lug the deadweight of an adolescent male without knowing that bit of Craft. And that male was definitely dead. Judging by the way the head bounced and flopped, it had taken one swat from an angry cat to snap the neck.

Kaelas, the shadow cat in question, also moved toward him, with one of Lady Zoela's friends clinging to him, a bruise already forming on her face from cheek to jaw. In fact, the girl was holding on so tight, if this had been the real cat, she would have been choking him.

"Can you help me?" she asked, her voice breathy.

He recognized the significance of that breathy voice. He wasn't a coward, but he wanted to get her into someone else's hands before the hysterical weeping began. "Yes," he said. "We have a safe place for all of you."

"Can he stay with me?" Her hands, buried in all that white fur, must have tightened a little more since the cat actually grunted in response.

"Of course," Beale said. Then to the Sceltie, *Take the carrion downstairs. Holt will show you where we are keeping them for the High Lord.*

The Sceltie stopped, thought for a moment, then used Craft to pass through an interior wall, taking the body with her.

Except for one foot and a shoe.

Well, the dog *was* young, and passing through a solid wall was a practiced skill.

Setting aside his task of locking down various wings of the Hall, Beale escorted girl and cat to the guest rooms where Helene and the maids were waiting.


Zoey dropped her fork, startling the other girls at the table.

The senior footmen inside the dining room snapped to attention.

"What's wrong?" Titian asked.

"I don't feel good. I think there's something in the food."

"But it's one of your favorite dishes. Maybe Mrs. Beale uses different spices?"

Zoey shook her head. Beads of sweat sprang up on her forehead. "Something bad in the food. Take that dish so no one discards it. Black Widows should test . . ."

Titian stared at her friend. Black Widows should test it? That meant . . .

Mother Night. Poisoned?

Zoey swallowed hard. She looked scared. "Titian, I'm sick."

Titian put a shield around Zoey's plate and vanished it. Then she rushed to the buffet table, put shields around the serving dishes that held every food Zoey had taken, and vanished those too.

"Lady Titian?" one of the footmen said.

The other girls were huddled around Zoey, who was panting and saying, "I can't, I won't, I *need* . . ." She started to cry.

Titian put her arms around Zoey and hauled her friend away from the table. "Zoey's sick," she told the footmen. "We need Beale. And we need a Healer. And maybe a Black Widow."

"This way," one footman said, escorting them out of the dining room.

The other senior footman turned toward the front of the Hall, then hesitated and said, "No way out."

"What does that mean?" Titian asked, alarmed. "Zoey needs help *right now*."

"We'll find Beale," the footman assured her. "He'll find a way to get a message to someone in Halaway."

The other footman eyed the two younger footmen, who looked nervous and guilty. "And I'll find out how this happened."

"Bedroom . . . too far," Zoey whimpered. "Don't want . . . bed. No bed."

What had been put in the food to make her sweat like

that—and make Zoey's psychic scent have the tang it held when they were kissing but was twisted up somehow?

"Come on," Titian said. "The sitting room is closer."

*Daemonar? Where are you? We need help!*

"I don't need protecting, Dharo Boy," Mrs. Beale said as she put an extra shield around the larder and pantry. Her Yellow Jewel wouldn't keep anyone out for long, but it would tell her there was an intruder trying to mess with her supplies.

"I know that," he replied, keeping up with her. "But even a strong witch should have someone watching her back when there are enemies in the house."

Huh. Couldn't argue the point, but whoever would have thought that a descendant of Lord Dillon would be the one standing with her to defend guests in this house?

Sounds of a struggle. *In her kitchen!*

She strode into the big room and saw a boy pinned to her worktable. He struggled against the phantom restraints as the girl grabbed his hair and tried to pour something into his mouth.

"You'll like it," the girl said, smiling viciously.

"No! I don't want . . ." He choked as some of the liquid went down his throat.

Nothing but fear in the boy's psychic scent, and something ugly in the girl's.

Mrs. Beale was a big woman, and it took only moments for her to cover the distance between the storerooms and the table.

The Dharo Boy made some sound of angry protest and leaped toward the table.

The girl looked up, her face twisted with malicious glee.

Mrs. Beale called in her meat cleaver.

*Whack! Thwack!*

She had the girl off the boy and shielded before the body voided one drop onto her clean kitchen floor.

The boy scrambled away from the body with its almost severed neck and spine. The Dharo Boy grabbed him and got him to the sink before he began to vomit.

The Dharo Boy looked at her, his face drained of all color. But he nodded, and that nod told her he was worthy of her time to train him—and worthy of serving in this house.

Maybe it was time for her to learn his name.


As Jaenelle Saetien left the sitting room, she saw Titian and the other girls clustered around Zoey.

She ran to meet them. "What happened?"

"Zoey's sick," Titian said fiercely. "Someone put something in the food to make Zoey sick."

*Someone* meaning Delora or one of her friends.

"Don't be—" The dismissive remark had become automatic when Zoey or Titian criticized Delora. Then Jaenelle Saetien remembered the look on Hespera's face when the girl walked up to them.

A prank taken too far? Or something more serious, more sinister?

Hell's fire, now *she* was suspicious of everything Delora or Hespera did.

*You should be,* some long-ignored part of her whispered.

"We'll find Beale. He'll summon the Healer in the village," she said. "Let's get Zoey to bed."

"No!" Zoey cried. "No bed! No . . ." She collapsed, almost pulling Titian down with her.

"Zoey not feeling well?" Krellis asked as he, Delora, Hespera, and Dhuran strolled into the great hall, followed by most of the other boys and girls who obeyed every snap of Delora's fingers. "I know what ails her, and I have just the thing that will fix her up, right and proper."

Zoey gave Krellis a look of lust mixed with disgust and fear. "Stay away from me."

"That won't help." Krellis gave her a sharp smile and took a step closer.

"Krellis," Jaenelle Saetien said. "Leave her alone. She's not well. She needs a Healer."

"That's not what she needs."

"Hurry up," Delora said.

Krellis pushed aside the other girls and made a grab for Zoey.

Jaenelle Saetien made a grab for Krellis and was shoved out of the way by Delora.

Titian called in a sparring stick and jabbed him in the gut. When he stumbled back, she formed a Summer-sky shield around herself and Zoey, then formed another one. With her hands tight on the sparring stick, she spread her wings partway, settled her feet in a fighting stance, and faced Krellis.

"Stay out of this," Delora hissed at Jaenelle Saetien.

Finally having some idea of what this friendship was going to cost, Jaenelle Saetien bared her teeth and said, "Go to Hell."

*Hell's fire,* Daemonar thought as he stepped off the landing web and strode to the Hall's front door, probing warily at the power he felt around the massive building. Black shields around the entire Hall? Not good.

He called in his Eyrien club. He'd rather lose that weapon than his war blade—or his hand—if Uncle Daemon had shaped an aggressive shield that would strike at any power that struck at it. A passive shield would be better, safer for sure, but would keep him out just as easily.

Wrapping himself in a tight Green shield, Daemonar used Craft to open the door just to see if he could. Then he used the club to push the door open a little more.

Nothing happened. Except he couldn't withdraw the part of the club that had passed through the shield.

Shit. The shield wasn't shaped to keep people out; it had

been made to keep people—and everything else—in. It wasn't a fancy shield, unless you considered the size of the building it covered, but anyone inside was nothing more than a mouse trapped in a maze.

The prudent thing to do was try to reach Uncle Daemon. If Sadi was inside, then he should contact Halaway's Master of the Guard and leave a message for his father. If Sadi wasn't there, then . . .

Titian screamed. In fear? In warning? He couldn't tell—and it didn't matter.

Daemonar shoved the door open, passed through the shield, and raised the club, prepared to beat the shit out of whoever was scaring his sister.

He saw Krellis, Dhuran, and a handful of other boys from the school.

"Now!" Krellis shouted.

Several blasts of power hit his Green shield before he took another step into the great hall. He struck back with a bolt of Green, blowing out the knees of one of the boys.

Screams from the girls and the sizzle of power against shields.

*Deal with the fight in front of you, or you won't get to the fight you need to reach.*

Ignoring the strikes against his shield, he swung the club, taking out another of the boys by shattering the prick-ass's hip.

A moment when everything seemed to stop. Then Krellis, Dhuran, and the remaining boys all sent blasts of power against his left side. He tried to counter, tried to bolster his shield, but he had committed to another strike against a boy standing on his right and couldn't adjust fast enough. He felt a bone in his left forearm break, felt ribs break before he formed another shield.

Not just a fight with the odds against him. Whatever was happening here, Krellis wanted him dead. And that left him no choice.

Vanishing the Eyrien club, Daemonar called in his war blade—and stepped onto a killing field.

# THIRTY-NINE

Go to Hell," Jaenelle Saetien said.

"You'll go with me," Delora replied, "so you might as well have some fun."

That was all the warning she had before Delora, Hespera, Leena, and Tacita unleashed their power against Titian's Summer-sky shield.

Titian screamed out of fear or defiance as her first shield broke. She quickly shaped another one behind the shield that still held.

"We don't want you, Fat Bat," Hespera said. "Get out of the way, and we'll let you go. This time."

"But Zoey is a problem and will always be a problem," Delora said. "Since Krellis can't deal with her in his way, I'll deal with her in mine. It makes no difference if she's broken or dead; she'll no longer be a rival."

"The bat has arrived," Dhuran said, staring at the front door. "Can't mistake *that* psychic stink."

"Then we'll deal with him once and for all," Krellis snarled. He pointed here and there, arranging the other boys to attack whoever opened the door.

"Stop this," Jaenelle Saetien said as Delora and the other girls struck Titian's shield again, breaking another one and weakening the one behind it.

"When I'm finished," Delora replied.

Then Daemonar walked into the great hall—and Krellis and the other boys attacked, unleashing the power in their Jewels against Daemonar's Green shield.

"No!" she screamed. Daemonar was fighting like a warrior dealing with untrained bullies instead of boys who wanted to kill him.

His Green shield broke, just for a moment, and strikes on his left side . . .

She saw the pain in his face—and she heard Titian scream as the last shield her cousin could shape with the Summer-sky's reservoir of power broke, leaving Titian and Zoey vulnerable.

Then a midnight voice rose up from somewhere deep in the abyss.

*Choose.*

Daemonar called in his war blade and turned the great hall into a killing field.

Delora and Hespera gathered their power for the strike that would permanently damage or even kill Titian and Zoey.

Jaenelle Saetien stepped between her cousin and the girls she'd thought were friends and formed a defensive shield that flickered wildly with all the colors in her Twilight's Dawn Jewel as Delora's and Hespera's power hit the shield.

Seeing Leena and Tacita sidling toward the other girls who were clustered near Zoey, Jaenelle Saetien extended her shield to protect the rest of Zoey's friends.

"Bitch," Delora said, her fury fixed on Jaenelle Saetien. "I should have known you didn't have the spine to be a true aristo."

Then dark power flooded the Hall, and with it, a sexual heat that slammed into Jaenelle Saetien, shattering some protective barrier and producing a flash flood of excruciating arousal unlike anything she'd felt before—and never wanted to feel again.

Titian gasped. Zoey wailed. Daemonar, closest to the front door, almost fell to his knees before he regained some balance.

Jaenelle Saetien stood there, caught by the heat like everyone else, while hope warred with terror.

Her father—some part of her father—had returned.

Daemon stepped off the landing web and glided toward the open front door, his gold eyes glazed and sleepy, his lips curved in a sweetly murderous smile as the screams and sounds of fighting reached him.

His sexual heat, free of all restraint, rolled through the Hall, ensnaring everyone, making them all desperately pliable to whatever game he wanted to play—even if the game killed them.

His sexual heat wasn't the only aspect that was free of all restraint.

As the Sadist stepped into the great hall, he cataloged the people, the power, the invaders who had soiled his home. With each step, the air around him grew colder. The pond of blood on the floor froze as he surveyed everyone within sight and let Black psychic threads locate everyone else.

The Green-Jeweled Warlord Prince. He knew that psychic scent, knew the Sadist was not permitted to touch the boy who met his eyes briefly before making a small bow to acknowledge dominance. He noted the face made older by pain and the way the boy held himself. Injured. Well, that would require some discipline, but not from him.

The other males who were still among the living were swiftly wrapped in phantom chains of Black power. So were the girls who were his enemies. The girls who stood behind a shield that flickered with the Rose through Green of Twilight's Dawn? They would be gently confined until he was ready to step away from the killing edge and deal with them.

The Red-Jeweled Warlord he'd left in charge appeared at the far end of the great hall, along with an Opal-Jeweled Warlord. He knew these men. He'd still kill them with the slightest provocation, but he knew them.

Power sizzled behind him. The Sadist pivoted toward the open door to meet this new enemy.

A bolt of lightning, blacker than the night, struck the landing web—and the Demon Prince strode across the gravel drive and walked into the Hall. His eyes were wild, but the hand holding his war blade was steady.

Their eyes met. Held. Before the Sadist could decide if this required a dance, a midnight voice rose from the abyss.

*How many sides does a triangle have?*

The tone was conversational, as if they were in her sitting room at the Keep.

He heard the words. So did the Demon Prince. So did the Green-Jeweled Warlord Prince, the third side of this triangle that served Witch.

They served as he served. They could be trusted because she trusted them.

The Demon Prince walked around him and looked toward the girl on the floor who was gasping with the effort not to draw their attention. The Demon Prince bared his teeth in a snarl, and his gold eyes went molten with fury. Then he leashed his temper, vanished the war blade, and said, "I'll deal with her. You can have the bitches."

One flick of the Demon Prince's fingers shattered the Twilight's Dawn shield. He grabbed the girl on the floor and half carried, half dragged her toward the front door. The Sadist obligingly released the shield on the door, and the Demon Prince went out with the struggling, screaming girl.

Zoela. The girl's name was Zoela.

A winged girl took a step toward the door, catching his attention. She stopped moving, her wings flaring in an effort to keep her balance on a floor that was now slick as ice.

"Please," she said.

"No," he replied, turning again to meet the Gray power that rushed through the open door.

The Assassin. His second-in-command. Not his wife.

She wasn't the Sadist's wife. Sometimes she was wife and lover and friend. But not tonight.

"Hell's fire," Surreal said, taking in the blood and the bodies. Then she looked at him, wary.

"Surreal," he crooned. "Escort Lady SaDiablo to her suite—and then seal those rooms with a Gray lock and shields."

Surreal tipped her head in acknowledgment of her orders, stepped out of the shoes now stuck in the frozen gore, and used Craft to stand on air. She walked over to the girl who looked so like her, grabbed an arm, and pulled the girl to the back of the great hall and the servants' staircase that would eventually take them to the family wing.

"Lord Beale."

Beale bowed. "High Lord."

"Escort the invited guests to their rooms."

"Some of the young Ladies should be seen by a Healer," Beale said.

The Sadist looked over his shoulder at the young Warlord Prince, then back at Beale. His smile made the Red-Jeweled butler shudder. "The Ladies are not the only ones who require the Healer. Summon her."

Beale hesitated. "There was an attack in the kitchen. There has not been time to remove that body."

Meaning Beale had been dealing with other bodies. How interesting.

"Leave it there until I come down."

"Very well."

Beale collected the witches who were guests the Warlord Prince of Dhemlan had allowed in his home and shouldn't be harmed without sufficient cause.

"Lord Holt."

"High Lord," the Opal-Jeweled Warlord answered.

"Do you know where to take these intruders?"

"I do. Some of them are already occupying those accommodations."

The Black chains he'd put around his enemies would drain their Jewels if they tried to use their power or any kind of Craft. Holt should be safe. But he didn't underestimate an enemy, so he wrapped them all in bubble shields, including the dead, and connected the shields so that Holt could take them all, like beads threaded through a single cord.

Finally, he turned to the Eyrien boy, who vanished the war blade and watched him in silent wariness.

"You're injured," he said silkily as he approached the boy and used a psychic tendril to make his own assessment of the damage. "The Queen will not be pleased."

"Couldn't you scold me instead?"

The question surprised him, amused him enough for the Sadist to take a step back.

"Oh, boyo," Daemon said. "I will not deprive the Queen of the pleasure of hearing you explain, in person, why you were so careless with someone she values." He leaned in, almost close enough for his lips to brush the boy's. "But better to explain this lapse to the Queen than to have to explain it to your auntie J."

Lucivar dragged Zoey to the snow-covered grass beyond the gravel drive. It was a cold night and the girl wasn't dressed warmly enough to be outside. Wasn't dressed for what was coming either, but he couldn't let that matter. Not right now. One look at her, collapsed on the floor of the great hall, had told him what had been done.

He created a domed Ebon-gray shield around them, large enough for the area inside the shield to be a sparring ring. He added warming spells to bring the air from freezing to chilly. And he added an aural shield so that whatever was said would not be overheard.

The moment he released her, Zoey rushed to get away, slammed into the shield, and turned to face him. A cornered little animal hating herself for her own need and desperation.

"Sex or violence," he said. "Those are the only ways to burn out the drug they gave you."

"I'm not having sex with you," she rasped.

"Damn right you're not."

He called in two Eyrien sparring sticks. One was his personal stick. The other was smaller and lighter—and an appropriate size and weight for a female Zoey's size and age. He tossed it to her. She caught it and bared her teeth.

"So that leaves violence," Lucivar finished. The next words came out as both order and challenge. "Come on, witchling. If you don't want to end up under someone tonight, show me you've got enough spine to fight."

She screamed and launched herself at him. At first her moves were frenzied, mindless, desperate. He countered them with enough force that she would know he was neither playing with her nor mocking her attempts to defend herself. When she began to understand that he would let her fight, she settled into actual sparring, unleashing anger and unwanted sexual arousal as she beat at him and beat at him and beat at him.

Daemonar had done a good job of teaching Zoey how to spar. Too bad he was going to have to knock the boy on his ass for getting hurt.

Surreal solved the problem of Jaenelle Saetien struggling to get away by creating a Gray shield around the two of them that allowed the girl to walk beside her or get knocked down by the moving Gray wall and dragged. The girl needed to get knocked down only once to realize there were no other options.

*Beale,* Surreal called. *What happened after I left to check on the sanctuary?*

His report chilled her, especially the part about Jaenelle Saetien giving her word before witnesses and then breaking her word when Beale stepped in to do his duty, insisting that he back down because he was the *butler.*

Hell's fire, Mother Night, and may the Darkness be merciful.

She used Craft to open the door of Jaenelle Saetien's

bedroom, then let the Gray shield pull the girl into the room with her. She closed the door and dropped the Gray shield around the two of them before she pressed her hand against the wall and created a Gray shield that followed the outer walls of the suite, carefully wrapping the shield around the pipes and plumbing in the bathroom to avoid cutting off the water. Then she leaned against the door and studied the girl, who tried to look defiant but was, in truth, very frightened.

"You don't have to lock me in," Jaenelle Saetien said. "I'll stay here."

"The High Lord gave me a direct order." Actually, the *Sadist* had given her that order, which was far worse. "I'm not going to disobey him or challenge him tonight. Not for anyone."

"I can explain."

"I hope so, sugar, because based on the little I saw when I walked in, the best you and the rest of the coven of malice can hope for is being broken back to basic Craft. I suspect some of you will be executed along with the prick-asses who survived the fight with Daemonar."

Jaenelle Saetien's eyes widened with shock. "My father would never—"

"You're not dealing with your father anymore," Surreal said coldly. "You have to answer to the High Lord of Hell for breaking the promise you made *before witnesses*."

"High Lord?" The girl's voice rose to the point of shrillness. "I didn't—"

"Prince of the Darkness, High Lord of Hell, Warlord Prince of Dhemlan. Daemon Sadi has held all of those titles since before you were born, but until tonight, very few knew he was the High Lord, that he'd assumed that title when his father became a whisper in the Darkness. Now everyone will know because he will ram that title down everyone's throat when he starts hunting for the rest of his enemies."

Jaenelle Saetien stood there, saying nothing.

"We should thank you for this little game," Surreal

said. "We didn't have enough proof against Krellis, Dhuran, and the other males to convince the Dhemlan Queens that those boys had been breaking young witches deliberately at Delora's behest. Because of their age, the Prince felt we needed sufficient proof before he executed Krellis and the others. And now he has the proof. The enemy came inside the walls of his home and drugged a young Queen with the intention of raping her body and violating her mind to the point where her inner web would break along with her power."

"You don't know that," the girl said, sounding desperate. "Father doesn't know that."

"He will. He will take those boys apart piece by piece, layer by layer, until he knows everything they have done, everyone they have hurt. Every girl each of them has raped. He will find every male connected to Delora, whether that male was here tonight or not, and have them taken to Hell to be questioned. Some will be released. Others will feed the demon-dead, as well as the Dark Realm's flora and fauna." Surreal didn't want to look at the girl anymore, but as Sadi's second-in-command, she had to fulfill her duties. "You will remain in this room until the High Lord is ready to deal with you."

"How long will that take?"

"That will depend on the injuries that were sustained by the girls you brought into this house as guests—the ones who were on the list you provided. But you need to understand something, Lady SaDiablo. Daemon and Lucivar have a long and complicated relationship, and Daemon needs his brother more than he needs me or you. If Titian was hurt tonight because you betrayed the family and commanded Beale to allow an enemy into this house, Lucivar will come for you—and Daemon will not stop him. He will grieve the loss of you, but he will not stop the Demon Prince from calling in the debt you owe Titian's father."

The girl started to cry. "It was *nothing*. *Everyone* lets the boys slip into their parties."

"Maybe that was true. Maybe that's why it's been hard to prove whose cock was used in the rapes that were meant to look like an accident that happened at a party because two youngsters let lust rule instead of their heads. But now that we know *everyone* connected to Delora and her coven did this little trick, it will be easier to hunt down—and eliminate— the cocks who were responsible for the breaking." Surreal turned to leave.

"Mother . . ."

"You didn't want me to be your mother. Didn't want to be associated with a whore. You made that very clear. You don't get to change your mind now, just because you want me to stand in front of you." Surreal looked at the girl she had loved so fiercely from the moment she felt that presence in her womb. "I hope you survive this, Jaenelle Saetien. I truly do. But if you find someone like Delora so compelling that you would betray your family, betray your *father*, in order to please her, then maybe I stood in front of you too often, trying to keep you safe. That's all your father and I wanted to do, keep you safe and give you time to grow up. But we failed somehow, and you grew up to be the enemy."

She walked out of the room and put a Gray lock on the door. She'd arrange for food and water to be brought soon. Right now she needed to help Sadi make a list of the dead.

"Enough," Lucivar said, vanishing his sparring stick.

"No." Zoey tried to raise her stick—and couldn't.

He walked up to Zoey, vanished her sparring stick, and hauled her to her feet. "Witchling, you can't even stand up by yourself. You've had enough for now."

"It still . . ." She looked up but didn't meet his eyes. "It still burns inside me."

"Yeah, it will for a while longer. We'll get you through it."

She was exhausted, but with the *safframate* burning inside her and making her want something her mind and heart didn't want, she'd still fight his help. He made things simple by dropping the Ebon-gray shield—and the warming spell with it. He created a warming spell around himself, gave her a moment to get hit with the bitter cold air, then picked her up and strode toward the still-open front door of the Hall.

Zoey burrowed into the only warmth available, pressing her face against the chain mail he still wore, trying to work her fingers into the chain in order to hold on.

Wondering why no one had shut the door, he automatically used Craft to step up and walk on air when he crossed the threshold—and hit a cold so savage, the outside air couldn't compete.

He closed the door. The Black shield snapped back into place.

Well, that explained why no one had shut the door.

It didn't explain why no one was in the great hall cleaning up the mess.

A quick psychic probe told him Daemonar was in the family wing, in the room he usually occupied when he visited. It told him that Titian was in another area of the Hall—an area crowded with other minds. Female minds.

He headed in that direction. *Helene?*

*Prince Yaslana?*

*I'm bringing Zoey up to her room.*

*I'll run a hot bath. The young Lady will be chilled to the bone by now.*

*Do that. The Healer needs to examine her, and*—may the Darkness have mercy on him—*it would be good to have one of the Scelties stay with her tonight.*

*Four of them are here with the girls, along with the two shadow cats Prince Sadi left with Beale.*

Shadow cats? Shit. He wondered if Witch had helped Daemon shape those spells, then decided he'd rather not know. The shadows Witch used to create had been able to do a little too much independent thinking, and even if the cats couldn't eat what they caught, they still enjoyed tearing it into pieces and then playing fierce games of tug with the limbs.

Not any different from what the real Kaelas and Jaal had done a few times when someone unwelcome had come too close to Jaenelle Angelline when she had walked among the living.

When he walked into the bedroom that had been assigned to Zoey, he found Titian waiting for him. He stopped, gave his girl a swift, assessing look. Scared, mussed, and her Summer-sky Jewel was drained almost to the last drop of power.

"Papa . . ."

"You hurt?" he asked. No point asking if she was okay. She wasn't. But he'd start by dealing with the body and work from there.

"No." She thought for a moment. "Sore."

"Give me a minute to help Zoey, and then we'll talk."

"Can I . . ."

He shook his head and went into the adjoining bathroom.

Helene had started running the bath. The water had a fragrance. Pleasant enough if you were female.

He set Zoey on her feet and turned off the water taps. It would be easier to simply tear the dress down the back—he didn't think she'd ever wear it again—but she was shivering now and not because she was cold. So he turned her around and began dealing with the small buttons that ran down the back of a wet dress.

"You can't do that," Zoey protested weakly.

"Sure I can. I have a daughter. I've had practice with buttons. Besides, you can't raise your arms right now to do this by yourself."

While she pondered his matter-of-fact response, he finished undoing the buttons so that it would be easy for her to slide the dress off. He helped her sit on the wide rim of the bathtub and knelt to tackle the shoes. He tossed those aside, hesitated a moment, then reached under the dress to find the tops of the stockings, figuring they'd be similar to what Titian had started wearing and were secured with ribbons and Craft a finger length above the knee.

"As soon as you're undressed, you can get in the bathtub and soak the chill out of your bones and the soreness out of your muscles." He stripped off one stocking and swore silently when he saw the blisters on her foot. Party shoes and stockings weren't the proper footwear for sparring.

He was looking at her foot when he felt a flash of Craft. When he looked up, Zoey pushed a sodden wad of material at him. Her clothes. All of her clothes, except for the other stocking. Her eyes were so dull from exhaustion, he doubted she knew what she'd done. She wanted to get in the water, so she took off her clothes.

He stripped off the other stocking, laid one of the towels on the floor, then tossed all the clothes on that.

"Okay, witchling. In you go."

She just leaned back and would have cracked her head on the other side of the tub if he hadn't caught her and gently settled her in the water.

A scratching at the bathroom door before a Sceltie entered. A young witch who wore a Rose Jewel.

*I am Allis,* the Sceltie said. She glanced at him before focusing on Zoey.

"You watch over Lady Zoey," he told her. "Make sure her head doesn't go under the water."

*I will watch.*

Lucivar collected the clothes and ruined shoes and left Zoey and Allis to become acquainted.

Helene and a maid waited for him in the bedroom.

"The Healer is almost done examining the other girls," Helene said. "She was going to heal Prince Daemonar's broken bones next, but he insisted that she see to Lady Zoela first. She and her husband's sister will be up in a few minutes."

Of course the boy had insisted. Daemonar was a Warlord Prince. Zoey was not only a Queen but his sister's romantic friend. Which made her family. As long as he wasn't bleeding out and wasn't given a direct order to submit to the Healer, he would wait until the females in the family were seen.

The moment Helene and the maid walked out of the room, Titian flung herself into his arms.

"My shields broke," she cried. "They broke and I couldn't protect Zoey. If Jaenelle Saetien hadn't put up a shield, Delora would have . . ."

"You held until your brother could reach you," he said, holding her against him and hoping she wouldn't realize that he was the one who was shaking. "You held, witchling. You did what you were supposed to do."

She eased back, and he saw the pattern of his chain mail pressed into her cheek.

"I have the food," she said. "Zoey told me to take the food so that Uncle Daemon could have it tested. Papa, they put something in the food. It made Zoey sick."

He led her to a small table in the room's sitting area. "Show me."

She called in a plate of food, then the serving dishes.

A knock on the door. A swift psychic probe confirmed that he didn't know either witch, so he formed an Ebon-gray shield around Titian before using Craft to open the door.

The Healer and Black Widow walked into the room.

"Prince," the Healer said. "Lady Zoela . . . ?"

"In the bath," he replied. Reading the concern in her eyes, he added, "She's not alone."

No chance that the girl might harm herself in a desperate, misguided attempt to relieve whatever the drug was doing to her. Not with a Sceltie watching—and questioning—every move she made.

The Healer disappeared into the bathroom. The Black Widow stayed near the door.

"You are Tersa's winged boy?" she asked.

"I am."

She relaxed but stayed near the door.

"I'd like your opinion." He pointed to the food, then reached for Titian and placed her on his other side, putting himself between his daughter and an unfamiliar Black Widow.

In the time it took the Black Widow to walk from the door to the table, he'd probed the food, confirming what he'd expected to find—and thankful for what he *didn't* find. He just wanted the Black Widow to confirm that before he went searching for Daemon.

She held her right hand over the plate, then over each serving dish, the look in her eyes distant but thoughtful.

"I detect no poisons, if that was your concern," she finally said. "But . . ." She frowned. Then she stepped back and anger flashed in her eyes. *"Safframate?"*

"Yes."

"But so much? That's not an aphrodisiac. That's . . . *beyond cruelty.*"

"Yes."

She looked at him with sudden understanding. She flicked a glance at Titian and said, "I don't know if any of my skills will help her, but if there is anything I, or any Sister of the Hourglass, can do, please call on us." Then she added on a psychic thread, *And not just for Lady Zoela.*

He nodded. He waited until the Black Widow left before dropping the Ebon-gray shield and turning to his daughter.

"Did you eat any of the food that Zoey ate?" he asked.

Titian shook her head. "I put a little on my plate because she likes that dish so much, but she started feeling sick after two bites, so I never had a chance to eat anything."

"What about the other girls?"

"I don't know, Papa."

"All right." That one dish had so much powdered *safframate* dumped over it, he wasn't surprised that it had taken just two bites to hit Zoey that hard. If the other girls had taken the tiniest taste, they'd be showing some reaction to the drug by now. Wild rage or inappropriate—and desperate—amorous feelings. Something the servants—and the Scelties—would have to watch for tonight.

The Healer gave him a timid psychic tap.

"Witchling, what does Zoey sleep in?" When she gave him a wary look, he huffed out a breath. "I'm not saying you broke your uncle's rules, but I don't believe for a minute that you keep your preference of nightclothes a secret from each other. So find what she would wear so the Healer can help her get dressed."

"Oh." Titian hurried to the small chest of drawers, opened the second drawer without hesitation, and pulled out a long fleece top and matching long pants. She closed that drawer, then opened another one and pulled out a pair of thick socks. "The room feels cold."

"I'll increase the warming spell in this room," he said mildly. "In yours too."

She looked relieved.

He would talk to Beale about getting some food for Titian and the other girls. They all needed something hot to warm up their insides and something sweet to help them deal with the shock of the attack.

He took the nightclothes and handed them to the Healer, who waited at the bathroom door.

"She's in bad shape," the Healer whispered.

"I know." The muscle pains and strains would be the least of it and, for Zoey, the most understandable. But what that much *safframate* was doing to her? Hell's fire, he'd slaughtered entire courts and exploded the buildings that held those courts, trying to burn out an equivalent dose of *safframate*. He'd pushed Zoey as hard as her body could stand to help her get rid of some of it, but she was going to suffer tonight because of Delora and her coven of bitches.

It was tempting to suggest that every one of them be given the same dose, then locked up and left to scream. They wanted to embrace Hayll? Let them embrace it.

But he didn't think Daemon would agree because of one of Delora's friends. Daemon knew the pain caused by excessive doses of *safframate*, so Lucivar didn't think Sadi could be persuaded to pour a dose down Jaenelle Saetien's throat.

✦ ✦ ✦

He had other duties, but Beale waited in the kitchen with his wife. She had killed a guest—a hostile guest who was attacking another person, but still a guest and there would be a price for that choice. Prince Sadi could be reasoned with, even when he was angry, but *this* High Lord, who was a lethal blend of sex and death, was a dangerous unknown because Sadi had been so careful, so considerate, to keep himself away from the staff when this side of his temper was dominant.

No more. High Lord and Sadist would walk together from now on. Beale hoped that, once things calmed down, Daemon Sadi, rather than the High Lord, would reside at the Hall most of the time, just as he'd done before tonight.

The High Lord stepped into the kitchen, his gold eyes glazed and cold, his face a beautiful mask that revealed nothing. He glanced at the girl still hanging in the bubble shield Mrs. Beale had created.

Mrs. Beale stood by her worktable, her hand white-knuckle tight around the handle of her meat cleaver.

The High Lord walked up to her, lifted that fisted hand—and pressed a kiss on the back of it. Then he turned his head slightly and pressed his lips to the side of the meat cleaver. He looked Mrs. Beale in the eyes and stepped back, stepped away. Turned and walked out of the kitchen.

He didn't say a word, but a moment after he left, the dead girl vanished.

Beale stared at his wife, not knowing what to say. She stared at the meat cleaver—and the impression of a kiss now engraved on the side of the blade.

*Beale,* Daemon called when he reached the dining room. *Please attend.*

While he waited, he let psychic tendrils flow through the Hall, cataloging the location of everyone inside.

When his butler approached, he saw wariness and regret—and resignation.

"I failed in my duty," Beale said.

"Did you?" Daemon asked gently.

"If I had ignored the order given by a . . . *child* . . . Lady Zoela would not have been harmed."

"If I had ignored the plea to let the party continue instead of hauling all the girls back to the school . . ." He sighed. "Were any of the girls raped?"

Beale's shock crashed against his inner barriers.

"*No*, High Lord."

"No," Daemon agreed. "You chose to cherish and protect the Ladies who were left in your charge instead of obeying a command that was an insult to both of us. And you contained the enemy until I returned."

Beale hesitated. "Two of the boys, friends of Lady Zoela's, were not taken to the cells beneath the Hall. One is the boy who was attacked in the kitchen. The other was shielding another Lady from a hostile guest with a knife. The boys are currently in the staff room across from the square of guest rooms occupied by the young Ladies."

"Where is the hostile guest? In the cells?"

"She will be making the transition to demon-dead," Beale said. "The shadow Jaal was given the order to capture, not kill . . ."

"Even a shadow of Jaal would never obey that order when a young female was being attacked."

"No."

"Very well." Daemon thought for a moment. "The young Ladies are going to need some food. Regretfully, nothing that is in the dining room can be trusted. All of it should be taken out and burned."

"I'll see to that at once." Beale pursed his lips. "Mrs. Beale had made a beef soup for the staff. Would that do?"

Daemon nodded. "I'll be in my study, if Lucivar and Surreal have trouble finding me." He doubted they would, but all the Black shields might mask his location in the Hall.

"Tarl wants to know if he should continue to hold the messenger he has locked in the stables."

"Yes, I still want to have a chat with that messenger before I take the dead to Hell."

"I will inform him." Beale hesitated for a moment. "Tarl said the boy seemed grateful to be captured, that he wasn't trying very hard to reach the landing web and leave. And the boy keeps asking if you're going to hurt his younger brothers because he brought the message."

"Is that why he brought the message?" Daemon asked too softly. "Because someone had threatened to harm his brothers if he didn't obey?"

"Tarl thinks so."

How many times had he done something that had violated everything he was because Dorothea had threatened to harm Lucivar if he didn't comply? How could he blame this messenger for doing what he would have done in order to save someone he loved?

"Make sure the boy is fed, and have Tarl find out whatever he can about where the boy's family lives and who made the threat against the brothers."

Daemon walked to his study, feeling the leashes that usually controlled temper, power, sexual heat, and the Sadist slip back into place. Loose, yes, but he felt them again. Which meant he was no longer riding the killing edge.

Which meant he had to consider what was going to happen next—and the price that would have to be paid for the lies and betrayal that had provided an opportunity to damage a young Queen.


Lucivar returned to the great hall and found Surreal hovering there. She looked like she was watching several footmen and maids scrape up the gore and partially melted blood near the front door, but it didn't take him more than a moment to understand that she had been waiting for him, unwilling to walk into the study and face Sadi—or whatever side of his temper was behind the study door—alone.

"Come on, witchling," he said. "Let's get it done."

He walked into the study without knocking.

Daemon turned away from the desk and held out a brandy snifter filled almost to the brim.

Lucivar took it and swallowed down half, grateful for the heat. It had been a bitch of a night and it wasn't going to be over until the sun rose, if it ended there.

Surreal joined them, accepting another snifter that wasn't filled quite so full.

Daemon poured a third and took a long swallow before asking, "Zoey?"

"Not good," Lucivar replied. "Hell's fire, there was enough *safframate* in that food to have felled both of us, let alone a girl her size. I figure she'll go down for an hour and then the arousal and pain will drive her into something physical."

"Like what?" Surreal asked, looking drawn.

"I'll walk her tonight. Inside the Hall to keep her from getting chilled. We'll walk until she goes down again. Then I'll tuck her into the nearest sitting room and let her sleep until the drug drives her up again." He drained the snifter. "If her body doesn't give out, the drug's hold on her should ease in another day . . . or two."

"Shit," Surreal whispered. "That long?"

"Unless you want to hand her a knife and let her rage on the bodies in the cells, walking and letting her fight against me are the only ways to give her some relief." There was sex, but he wouldn't consider it and Daemon wouldn't allow it.

"Even if she tore into the dead, she wouldn't be able to live with that once her mind cleared of the drug," Daemon said.

*Unlike us,* Lucivar thought. *We relished the destruction of our enemies, and painted the walls with blood.*

"Is there nothing a Healer can do for Zoey?" Surreal asked.

Not any of the Healers living in Kaeleer. There were two who might be able to help the girl, but one was no longer flesh and the other was demon-dead. Still . . .

*I'll ask,* Daemon said on an Ebon-gray spear thread.

"I'll be taking the dead and all the male intruders to Hell," Daemon said. "We're all going to have a chat. Except the messenger. Tarl thinks the boy is another victim, so I'll talk to him before I leave."

"When?" Surreal asked.

"Within the hour. I may be gone for several days. Can you manage here?"

Slow executions took three days, so Daemon would be gone that long.

Lucivar glanced at Surreal. She was sweating from the effort to ignore Daemon's leashed sexual heat, and her eyes were glassy with need. Knowing what he'd be facing, he'd put a shield on the inside of his trousers to hide his own aroused response. Right now Daemon's control would be shaky at best. Hell's fire, *his* control of his temper and heat weren't much better. In other circumstances, they might tear into each other for some relief, but that wasn't going to happen because neither of them could afford to be wounded and bloody tonight.

Daemon's choice to go to the Dark Realm was the only way to protect everyone else right now.

"We'll manage," he said. "I'll stay until Zoey can go home. Surreal and I will arrange for the other girls to be sent home if they're fit enough to leave."

"Not back to the school," Daemon said. "None of them go back to that school."

"Agreed. I'll send that message."

Daemon nodded.

"Beale's probably arranging for some food for the girls," Surreal said, using Craft to float the barely touched snifter of brandy back to the desk. "I'll see how that's coming along."

After she left, Daemon said, "Titian?"

"Scared. Shaken. She almost drained her Jewel to the breaking point trying to maintain a shield around herself and Zoey." He hesitated, but it had to be said. "If Zoey is permanently damaged, I don't think Titian will ever forgive Jaenelle Saetien."

"I know. Neither will Lady Zhara." Daemon set his glass on the desk. "They might not be the only ones who won't be able, or willing, to forgive my daughter for what happened tonight."

*Can you? Will I?*

"It might help both of us if we remember that, in the end, Jaenelle Saetien stood for Titian and Zoey, shielding them from Delora and that other bitch," Lucivar said.

"It might help," Daemon agreed softly, sadly. "It might."

A quiet knock on the study door before Holt opened it just enough to lean into the room.

"Prince Daemonar would like to see you at your earliest convenience," Holt said.

"Did the Healer take care of those broken bones?" Lucivar asked.

Holt nodded. "He wouldn't let me in the room, but I had the impression the Healer isn't the only one who has seen your son."

Holt looked wide-eyed and a little pale, as if he'd caught a whiff of something—someone—who shouldn't exist.

"Mother Night," Lucivar said, setting his glass aside.

"And may the Darkness be merciful," Daemon added.

He and Daemon left the study to find out what his son had done now.

Daemonar paced around his room, hurting and angry. So angry.

He'd drunk the healing brew and submitted to having the bone in his forearm set and the broken ribs adjusted and sealed within a shield to keep them stable while the bones knit, but he'd refused the tonic that would have made him groggy enough to sleep. He didn't want to sleep. He wanted to be awake—and angry—when he faced his father and uncle.

And more than that, he wanted—

Before he finished the thought, intense cold seared the

broken bones. He gritted his teeth and grunted to hold back a scream.

Then he was in the Misty Place, standing almost within reach of Witch, who stared at him with those ancient sapphire eyes while the claw on one finger tap, tap, tapped against the stone altar.

"I don't want to forgive her," he burst out, his breath creating a momentary fog between them. "I know she's my cousin and she's younger and she's been so stupidly infatuated with that bitch Delora that she wouldn't listen to anyone else, and I know she's family, but Titian could have been raped because of her. *My sister* could have been raped and broken because Jaenelle Saetien was being so damn *stupid*, and *I don't want to forgive her.*"

"Then don't," Witch said calmly.

He stopped raging. Blinked. Wondered if he'd heard her correctly. "What?"

"If you can't forgive her, then don't."

"It will put a strain on the family. More of a strain."

"Daemon and Lucivar have plenty of experience dealing with their tempers colliding. They'll find their way through this. So will you." She moved toward him and placed a gentle hand on his right shoulder. "I know a bit about waiting to forgive, boyo. Give yourself time. Let the idea of forgiving float on the wind and return to you when you're ready."

He felt some measure of tension ease. "Okay. Thanks, Auntie J."

The hand on his shoulder tightened. The claws pierced his shirt and just pricked his skin, a warning that he needed to stay still if he didn't want to bleed.

"Now," Witch said too sweetly, "explain why you were so careless with someone who belongs to me."

Daemon walked into Daemonar's room ahead of Lucivar, took one look at the agitated boy storming around the room and waving his arms, and stopped. Just stopped. And closed his eyes against the visual assault.

He stopped so fast, Lucivar walked into him, shoving him another step into the room before slamming to a stop.

"Hell's fire," Lucivar said.

"Look at this!" Daemonar said indignantly. "Look!"

Daemon opened his eyes, but looked away from the boy. "Stand still," he ordered.

"All I did—"

"*Stand. Still.* And stop moving your arms."

Lucivar snapped out an order in Eyrien that finally pinned the boy's feet to the floor. Although it was possible that Lucivar had used Craft to actually pin the boy's boots to the floor.

Still feeling a bit queasy, Daemon cautiously approached his nephew, with Lucivar walking beside him.

"Well," Daemon said, "it's not blue."

"Mother Night, boy, what did you do to get your auntie J. *that* pissed off at you?"

"I didn't—" Daemonar started to wave his arms.

"Don't move!" they shouted.

When Daemonar was young, he'd broken his arm in a fight, and Daemon had put a bright blue shield around the arm to keep it safe while the bone healed—and to be a constant, annoying reminder to his nephew that there were penalties for getting hurt.

Witch's penalty was also coloring the shield around the boy's forearm and ribs, but the multiple colors were beyond garish and they kept swirling around the shield, and whenever Daemonar waved his arm, the movement created an afterimage of color in the air that followed every up-and-down and side-to-side move. And on top of all of that, the damn shield *sparkled.*

Their Queen could not have picked a better punishment for a Warlord Prince Daemonar's age.

"When you were young, you asked me what I had done to piss off Witch so much that she gave me the scars on my arm, because you didn't want to make her that angry with you." Daemon shook his head slowly. "Boyo, that shield is as close as you could come to that level of pissing her off *without* earning scars."

"She was using her too-sweet voice." Daemonar looked at the swirly, sparkly shield. "You know?"

"Oh, yeah," Lucivar said. "We know. The only thing worse than too sweet is ice."

The boy nodded. "Didn't get to ice."

"Lucky for you."

"Aren't you supposed to wear a sling?" Daemon asked.

"Yeah, but . . ." Daemonar looked toward a chair.

The sling was solid black. Thank the Darkness for that.

Daemon fetched it, braced himself to come that close to all that color, and gently arranged the arm into the sling. "Wear it. It hides the colors." He kissed his nephew's forehead, then stepped back as Lucivar stepped forward—and the boy braced for whatever discipline would come.

"You know why the Queen did that, don't you?" Lucivar asked.

Daemonar swallowed hard. "She said you'd explain it to me."

"You knew there was trouble here—"

"But I didn't!"

Lucivar stared at his son. "I beg your pardon? Titian called for help and—"

"I didn't hear it," Daemonar said hurriedly. "Two of Zoey's friends were attacked at the school. Chaosti dealt with the attackers and told me he was bringing the girls to the town house, along with Prince Raine and some of the other boys and girls who might be in danger. And he confirmed that Krellis, Dhuran, and some of the others connected to the coven of malice had left the school. So I left Beron to help guard the town house and came here to warn Uncle Daemon that the boys had left the school, in case they were going to cause trouble."

"But the prick-asses were already here, and you . . . what? Strolled in to see what they were doing?"

"I didn't stroll in," Daemonar said indignantly. "I came in shielded."

"A single Green shield? With what weapon?"

The boy was starting to look a little gray. Daemon wasn't sure if it was pain and fatigue or the realization that he was in trouble with his father.

"An Eyrien club."

Lucivar nodded. "There were . . . what? Six? Seven of them? And you figured if you smacked a couple of them, the rest would back off?"

"Not exactly."

Lucivar moved so fast, the boy had no time to evade. And the hand now gripping the back of the boy's neck closed tight enough to make Daemonar flinch.

"Listen to me," Lucivar said quietly. "Are you listening?"

"Yes, sir."

"Don't you ever again walk into a fight without shielding as if you're going into battle. If you'd done that, you'd have bruises instead of broken bones. And when the odds are against you, don't you ever again assume a few punches will settle things. You're a Warlord Prince. You knew there was trouble before you walked through that door. You should have been armed and shielded and ready to step onto a killing field. And you should never have raised a weapon or engaged in that fight unless you were willing to be the only one who walked away from that field."

"They weren't trained warriors," Daemonar said softly. "I didn't think I would have to kill them."

"They were trained well enough to hurt you before you recognized you were in a real fight. If I had been the first one through the door, I would have given the prick-asses one hit against my outer shield, just to be able to say they started the fight. And then I would have slaughtered them, regardless of their training or age, because my daughter needed me to reach her."

"Titian?" Daemonar asked, his voice and eyes full of fear.

"She'll be all right. She held on for as long as she could, but her shields finally broke, and she could have been killed." Lucivar released Daemonar's neck and stroked a hand over the boy's hair. "In a situation like that, you do not have time for mercy." He sighed and lightly tapped Daemonar's left hand. "And that's part of the reason your auntie J. gave you that . . . reminder."

"Are you hungry?" Daemon asked.

Daemonar thought for a moment, then nodded. "Yeah. I could eat."

Not surprising. The boy could *always* eat.

"I'll have Beale bring a tray up for you." He glanced at the small glass sitting on the table near a chair already nested with blankets and pillows. The Healer must have decided that would be a better place to rest while the boy's ribs knit. "You didn't drink the tonic to help with the pain."

"Figured I should be awake when I got my ass kicked."

Lucivar snorted a laugh. "Well, at least you've learned that much."

Daemon sent the request for food to Beale. Then he and Lucivar got the boy settled in the chair, tucked in with blankets and warming spells.

The food arrived with a speed that made Daemon wonder if Beale—and Mrs. Beale—had anticipated the request. Either way, they left the boy busily consuming a variety of dishes that didn't require the use of two hands.

"Witch couldn't reach him, so she summoned us," Lucivar said as they made their way back to the great hall.

"Sounds that way," Daemon agreed. And if they hadn't arrived when they did . . . "How did you get here from Ebon Rih so fast?"

"Rode black lightning."

Daemon raised an eyebrow.

"It's not something you want to know about when we're completely sober."

"Another time, then."

Lucivar nodded. "Another time."

# FORTY

❖

Daemon glided past the row of arrogant young Warlords who were tethered with phantom Black chains to
the stone wall. He had said nothing since he'd taken them,
both the living and the dead, from the Hall in Dhemlan.

"My parents are going to hear about this," Krellis said,
trying to sound sneeringly brave.

"They will," Daemon agreed as he glided past. "Eventually. But according to the gatekeeper's logs and as far as
anyone else knows, you never left the school. Your instructors will, no doubt, think you're ignoring your classes
since you often do in favor of something more exciting and
malevolent. No one is going to look for you, Lord Krellis.
Certainly not here."

The males who had experienced the physical death
hadn't made the transition to demon-dead yet, and it hadn't
taken more than a tiny flick of power to knock out the living long enough to open the Gate that was next to the Hall
and bring them to this place, to this room.

How many executions had been performed here? How
much blood had been collected as sustenance for the
demon-dead? How many bodies had been left out on the
land to be consumed by the Dark Realm's flora and fauna?

He imagined Saetan would have felt a measure of sickness along with the cold rage when *he'd* been required to
perform an execution. Unfortunately for these fools, the

humanity that would have felt that measure of sickness had been burned out of Daemon Sadi by torture and drugs like *safframate* long before he had reached the same age as these boys.

"Where are we?" Dhuran asked.

"SaDiablo Hall," Daemon replied. "In Hell."

"You can't keep us here," Krellis said, no longer sounding sneering or brave.

"I don't intend to keep you here. I don't want you with me any longer than I'm required to endure your presence." Daemon stopped in front of Krellis. "A slow execution takes three days. During that time, I am going to take you apart, body and mind. I will extract every moment of pain you've inflicted on someone else. I will know the name of every girl you raped or broke for your own pleasure or at Delora's request. I will know everything you have said and done—and once I have everything, I will collect the debt you owe for the lives you've damaged. When it's done, I will give you the mercy of the final death, and you will become a whisper in the Darkness."

He smiled a viciously gentle smile as his sexual heat flowed through the room, both a torture and a snare. He leaned closer to the Warlord, pleased by the mix of lust and fear that filled the enemy's eyes and psychic scent.

The Sadist whispered, "It's time to dance, Krellis."


Lucivar figured he and Zoey had walked every corridor in the entire Hall over the past two days—and judging by the color of her socks, some of those corridors hadn't seen a dust mop in years. That would change once Helene saw those socks. Then again, the Hall was a massive structure, and it wasn't surprising that some parts of it weren't being used or kept up to Helene's standard of clean. Those sections of the Hall and the connecting corridors hadn't been used when Saetan lived here either—at least, not used in any expected way. Jaenelle Angelline and the coven had found all kinds of things to do with corridors that weren't used.

As he walked with Zoey, he looked around for any sign that some part of the structure needed repair, but he didn't see anything. Amazing, really, since Jaenelle's coven had, with fair regularity, miscalculated the ingredients in a new spell, and that had ended with the damn thing blowing up. Or maybe not so amazing since they had also learned how to create some of the best shields he'd ever seen in order to avoid Saetan's ten-minute stare.

The agreement had been that Saetan would turn a ten-minute hourglass, and while the sand ran down in the glass, he could voice his opinion about whatever transgression had been made. At the end of that ten minutes, the subject was closed.

Sometimes, when he was truly angry about something, he would turn the hourglass and just stare at the witch or witches who had committed the offense. It was an impressive way to express anger and disappointment because no one could argue with that stare—and no one, not even Witch, had dared to break the silence.

Maybe he should mention that to Daemon when his brother returned to the Hall. In the meantime, there was Zoey.

She was so exhausted she couldn't hold up a stick well enough to spar, so he and Zoey and Allis walked and walked and walked. When Zoey went down, sometimes he created a mattress of air large enough for dog and girl. There was always a footman nearby with blankets and a pillow, so he'd cover them up and leave them to sleep while he checked on Daemonar, who, bored and restless, spent most of his time with Holt, sorting through the correspondence that was flooding into the Hall. Titian didn't want to go home until she knew Zoey would be all right, but she wanted to help her friend and kept getting her heart bruised by Zoey's screaming at her to stay away. Every time he checked on her, he told his girl that Zoey didn't want to connect her feelings for Titian with what the drug was still doing to her, and that was why she wanted Titian to stay away.

While Zoey slept, he checked on Surreal, who had been

sending the other guests home with a firm message to the parents that those girls were not to go back to the school until Prince Sadi gave his consent. He read the reports from Chaosti, who still had several students and Prince Raine staying at the town house under guard for their protection, and from Lady Zhara's Master of the Guard, whose men were keeping the instructors and other students contained at the school while Zhara's First Circle ferreted out the other youngsters who had assisted in the coven of malice's vicious games.

*We war against children,* he thought bitterly as he, Zoey, and Allis returned to familiar corridors in the Hall. *But what choice is there? To stand back and let Delora become another Dorothea? To let her followers destroy the strongest and best young women and men of that generation . . . and beyond? Can't do that. Can't. We know too much, have seen too much. If Daemon and I don't shoulder the burden now, don't pay the price now, then who will?*

Zoey stopped walking. She sniffed, then wrinkled her nose. "I smell bad."

*You are stinky,* Allis agreed. *But you do not smell sick anymore.*

Huh. Instead of wondering about the level of Zoey's recovery, he should have asked the damn Sceltie.

"Shower?" Zoey asked hopefully.

"Sure," he said. "We're close to your room. You can go there and get cleaned up. You want some food?"

She wobbled when she started walking again, so he wrapped a hand around her arm to keep her steady. "Not broth. I think . . . Did I eat broth?"

He nodded. "Broth, water, a slice of fruit or a bite of a sandwich when I could get it down you."

"I yelled at Titian." Her voice spiked. "Why did I yell at Titian? She saved me."

"You didn't want your feelings muddled by the lust caused by the drug. You needed her to stay away."

"Is she all right?"

"Yeah, she's fine. She'll be better once she knows you're feeling better."

She looked up at him, her eyes older and shadowed now. "You know how this feels."

"Yeah, I do."

"This . . . changed me."

"It did. But you survived it. Many don't."

They had reached her bedroom. "Do you think, if she doesn't touch me—I don't think it would be good to have someone touch me—that Titian could sit with me and have something to eat?"

He didn't point out that he had a hand on her arm to keep her from falling down. Not the same kind of touch. "She'd like that."

They walked into the bedroom. Titian rushed to the doorway between their rooms. Lucivar raised a hand to stop her.

*Zoey is stinky and needs a bath,* Allis said. *Then we will have food, and then we will sleep.*

"I forgot how bossy they are," Zoey whispered when Lucivar helped her reach the bathroom.

"Well, I hope you're resigned to having Allis around, because I think she's decided you're going to be her human to love and herd."

Zoey let out a small laugh, a sound that eased the tightness around his heart.

Leaving Zoey in the bathroom, watched by Allis, Lucivar dealt with Titian, who hugged him hard enough to constrict his ribs.

"She'll be all right, witchling," he said, stroking one hand down her hair. "She came out the other end of it, so she'll be all right. But she needs you to be patient about . . ." How to say it?

"Touching?"

"Yeah." He kissed the top of her head and eased back. "I'll have Beale bring up a meal for the two of you. And some food for Allis."

"Zoey will be going home soon, won't she?"

"Tomorrow or the day after."

"Will we go home too? I want to go home, Papa."

"We'll go home. Daemonar too." He wanted his children out of Dhemlan and away from the storm that was coming.


"You sure about this?" Surreal asked.

Daemonar nodded. "We're heading home, and I don't know when Titian and I will be back to visit. There are things I want to say."

"Don't expect her to listen." She opened the bedroom door. "Five minutes, boyo."

"Thanks, Aunt Surreal."

Daemonar walked into Jaenelle Saetien's bedroom and felt the Gray lock on the door reengage. Jaenelle Saetien sprang up from the reading chair, her face lighting up when she saw him.

"I came to say good-bye," he said.

The pleasure at seeing him faded. "Good-bye?"

"We're heading home. Don't know when we'll be back." *If ever.*

That possibility troubled him. There were people at the Hall and in Halaway who meant a lot to him, and he didn't want to stay away from them.

"My father hasn't come to see me," Jaenelle Saetien said.

*Is he that angry?* That was what Daemonar heard under the words that were spoken.

"He's not here." He studied his cousin. Did she really not understand, or did she hope if she kept downplaying her part in what had happened, her father would make all the unpleasantness go away and everything would go back to the way it had been?

"Where is he?" she asked.

"I don't know." Since he understood some things about Uncle Daemon, he had a good idea of where Sadi was—and why he was there.

"You're still angry with me." She sounded subdued.

"I am. I expect I will be for a while."

"Why? All I did—"

"Was open your arms and let the enemy walk in," he snapped.

She rallied enough to push back. "Well, *you* killed some of the guests!"

"Intruders. Enemies. And I didn't kill enough of them!"

They glared at each other. She looked away first.

"I really believed Delora wanted to mend her differences with Zoey," she finally said. "I made a mistake."

"You did, and I hope you're prepared for whatever price you have to pay."

Awkward silence. He took a step back, more than ready to leave.

"You're not going to forgive me, are you?"

He hesitated. "You're my cousin, and I love you. So I guess I will. But not today. Not tomorrow. Maybe once these bones fully heal and Titian stops crying in her sleep, maybe then I can forgive you because, when it really counted, you remembered who you used to be and protected Titian and Zoey. If you hadn't, Delora and Hespera would have killed them."

The door opened. He walked out, flinching when Jaenelle Saetien started to cry.

He and Surreal walked to the great hall in silence. When he saw the grim expression on his father's face, he wondered what else had happened.

"Titian?" he asked.

"She and Zoey are in the informal sitting room. We'll take Zoey to Amdarh on our way home."

Which would give the two girls a little more time together.

"Problem?" Surreal asked.

Lucivar handed her a stack of papers, professionally bound, but it looked like the printer had been in a hurry.

Or very, very frightened.

Lucivar handed him the second stack. "You are old enough, and you need to know."

The heading on the top page read: *The following individuals were executed in accordance with Blood law. The debts they owed were paid in full.*

*Mother Night!* Daemonar thought as he began to read.

Krellis. Dhuran. Clayton. Every male connected with the coven of malice who had come to the Hall during the house party, along with a couple more names he knew from school.

That was chilling enough. What he was sure was going to shake Dhemlan, to say nothing of the rest of the Realm, was the signature.

Daemon Sadi. Warlord Prince of Dhemlan. High Lord of Hell.

The rest of the pages listed each boy, and the girls he had raped, the girls he had broken, the where and when and how and why and his accomplices, both male and female, as well as the drugs that had been used. It listed each girl's Birthright Jewel—if she'd been old enough to have gone through the Birthright Ceremony. A few of the girls . . . So young!

"Well," Surreal said, her voice shaking, "Sadi isn't hiding his claws anymore, is he?"

"No," Lucivar agreed. He gave Surreal a long look. "Having heard Saetan's stories about how being the High Lord of Hell had made things difficult for Mephis and Peyton when they were growing up, Daemon gave you and Jaenelle Saetien as much time as he could before publicly acknowledging that title. More time than he should have, considering . . . this." He tipped his head to indicate the great hall.

Daemonar thought for a minute, then silently agreed. Delora might have targeted the daughter of the Warlord Prince of Dhemlan, somehow ignoring the fury of a Black-Jeweled Warlord Prince, but would she have been foolish enough to target the daughter of the High Lord of Hell? Maybe.

"Will you be all right?" Lucivar asked, still watching Surreal.

She nodded.

Lucivar took the bound pages from Daemonar and vanished them. "Collect your sister and Zoey, boyo. It's time to go."

Daemonar did as he was told, getting the girls in the Coach while his father and aunt talked quietly.

Everything had a price, and the debts that would be owed because of that house party would be steep. But he had a feeling Uncle Daemon was going to be the one who paid the highest price of all.

Surreal hesitated at Jaenelle Saetien's door.

A copy of the crimes printed and bound? Stood to reason more than two copies had been made. Which meant, by now, all of Dhemlan's Province Queens and District Queens had a list of who belonged to Delora's coven of malice, as well as who had acted as accomplices and secondary players. Most would be at the school and easy to find. As for the rest?

Had Lucivar and Daemonar read the last page, the list of girls targeted for elimination because Delora and Hespera had decided those girls would never be brought to heel and would interfere with their ambitions to be the dominant influence in Dhemlan—an influence that eventually could corrupt the Blood in Dhemlan until they resembled Hayll's depraved society?

The Queens would be out for blood, and rightly so. Everyone who ruled in Dhemlan remembered the purge of Dorothea's taint, remembered the power darker than the Black that had screamed through the Realms to stop a war that would have destroyed Kaeleer as well as Terreille.

She blew out a breath and walked in.

The girl had been crying. But she looked at Surreal with a mix of hope and defiance. "What now?"

Surreal dropped the bound pages on the table in front of the sofa. "Something for you to read while you wait for your father's return."

Jaenelle Saetien glanced at the top page, then gasped and stared. "High Lord of Hell?"

"I told you he was."

"But . . . now *everyone* will know!"

"They will. And they will fear him." *They have reason to fear him.*

A beat of silence. "Where is everyone?"

"The male intruders were taken to Hell and executed, as you will see in that report. Amara and Borsala were also taken to Hell. They were killed during the house party while attacking other guests. I imagine that, once they made the transition to demon-dead, they had a very unpleasant chat with the High Lord. Delora, Hespera, Leena, and Tacita are still here, confined in the lower cells. All the other girls, and the two boys who were also victims, have been escorted home."

Holt and Tarl had escorted the messenger home, but Surreal didn't think Jaenelle Saetien would care about an incidental player in this game—who might have suffered if he had refused to perform his role.

Another silence before Jaenelle Saetien asked, "What's going to happen now?"

"That will depend on Dhemlan's Queens." She ignored the ache in her chest, an ache that had begun when she received Zhara's warning of what was coming. "I've been told the Queens are going to make a formal demand to the Warlord Prince of Dhemlan that all the girls who belong to the coven of malice be executed. Unfortunately, sugar, because you were instrumental in putting a young Queen at risk, they consider you a part of that coven, which means Daemon will have to execute you too."

Unable to stay in that room a moment longer, Surreal paused only long enough to make sure she'd secured the Gray lock on the door before she ran to her own suite and made it to the toilet before being sick. Then she lay on the bathroom floor and wept for herself and for Daemon and for the daughter they were going to lose—and she wept for the woman Jaenelle Saetien could have been.

# FORTY-ONE

Hearing his daughter's cries, Lucivar rushed into Titian's room and held on when she flung herself into his arms.

"It's all right, witchling. It's all right," he murmured.

"My shields broke, Papa. They broke! I wasn't strong enough to protect Zoey, and *they killed her*."

He shifted around until he could sit on the edge of the bed and hold her in his arms while he rocked her.

"Your shields held long enough." He'd said the same words every night for the past week after she screamed herself out of the same nightmare. "You're safe now, and Zoey is safe."

"I want to learn to fight." Fierce desperation.

"All right, baby. All right. I'll teach you. Daemonar and I will teach you."

Marian came in, tears running down her face. She handed him the small cup of tonic Nurian had made after the first night of broken sleep filled with nightmares.

He took the cup and held it to Titian's lips. "Drink this. It will banish the bad dreams."

She drank. When she'd drained the cup and he had her tucked back in bed, she said, "You'll teach me?"

"I'll teach you anything you want to know," he promised. "We'll start tomorrow."

He escorted Marian back to their room and held her while she cried.

"Daemonar?" he asked when she sounded calmer.

"He's with Andulvar."

Of course he was. He wouldn't leave his younger brother alone when Titian's nightmares woke everyone in the eyrie.

"She's strong," Marian said. "She'll heal."

Lucivar smiled. "Yes, she will. She's your daughter."

"And yours."

He kissed her gently. "I'll come to bed in a few minutes."

Her eyes asked a question she didn't voice.

After she tucked into bed with a book, he walked to the front of the eyrie. Walked outside, ignoring the biting cold against his bare skin, and looked toward Ebon Askavi.

He'd felt the Black when Daemon arrived at the Keep, but there had been no request for a meeting, no contact of any kind. Now there was nothing, which meant Daemon was in the Queen's private part of the Keep.

He knew what the Dhemlan Queens had demanded after they'd seen the list of girls whom the coven of malice had targeted. A whole generation of Queens, Black Widows, and Healers—the strongest in power and will—eliminated in order to clear the way for that bitch Delora? Not again. Not while he could stand and fight.

But, sweet Darkness, he didn't know how Daemon would survive if he did what needed to be done.

# FORTY-TWO

Daemon stared out the window of the Consort's suite. He'd been staring out that window for the past two hours, turning everything over in his mind—and coming to the same bitter conclusion.

When he felt Witch's presence, he said, "All the Queens in Dhemlan signed a demand that everyone in the coven of malice be executed. Physical death and final death. They want nothing left of the bitches who wanted to turn Dhemlan into another Hayll. They are willing to allow the girls who were accomplices to be broken back to basic Craft so that they will never have the power or influence to be a threat, but that is as far as they will yield."

"They've included your daughter as part of the coven, rather than an accomplice?" Witch asked.

"Yes. If the Queens hadn't seen the list of targets, they might have settled for Delora and Hespera being executed and the other girls being broken, as their victims had been broken—forfeiting their Jewels as well as the possibility of becoming pregnant more than once." A broken witch had one chance to have a child of her own. Long, long ago, it had been a kind of defense against males who would have broken strong witches they couldn't control in order to breed them and have offspring from the witches' bloodlines that the males *could* control. Now it was part of the price that was paid. Only one chance, whether that chance ended in a miscarriage, a stillbirth, or a healthy baby.

"You are your father's son and his true heir, Daemon. You weren't going to lie to the Queens, and not telling them about the targets and all that had been at stake would have been a lie." She said nothing else for a minute. Then, "If you keep your bargain with the Queens, as the ruler of Dhemlan must do, but don't execute your daughter with the rest of the coven, what will happen?"

"She'll have no life outside the walls of SaDiablo Hall," he replied. "She'll have no friends. She'll be isolated from everyone because she'll be trusted by no one. And if she manages to slip beyond the walls of the Hall, every Warlord Prince in Dhemlan will be waiting for the chance to kill her, the last member of the coven of malice."

His darling girl, who had entertained his mind and delighted his heart. His little witch, who had loved the Scelties and had terrified him the first time she had ridden a horsey all by herself. His girl, who had been fearless when she'd engaged in adventures with her cousins.

And under the bitch she had become when she fell in with Delora, she was still his witch-child.

His throat worked. He tried to say the words that duty demanded, but instead he cried, "I can't do it. She's my little girl, my baby. I can't be her executioner."

Daemon turned away from the window and looked at the woman, the Queen, who meant more to him than anyone else ever could or would. Even his daughter. If Witch gave the command . . .

"Jaenelle," he whispered. "Help me. Please."

Those sapphire eyes stared right through him, and he felt the feather touch of a psychic thread rising out of the abyss beneath the level of the Black. He stood still, willing to give her anything she wanted from him.

"There is a way," she finally said. "But it is brutal, and I can't promise that she will survive. That will depend on how much of a debt she owes."

"It gives her a chance."

"A chance," Witch agreed. "But there will be a price, Daemon. Even if she lives, you will most likely lose her."

"I'll pay whatever price needs to be paid." His gold eyes met her sapphire ones. "What do you need from me?"

"The males who were part of this coven of malice. Where are they?"

"I executed them and made sure each of them paid what he owed."

"Then you have their memories. You know what they said and what they did. I will need all of it."

"It's . . . ugly. And familiar." Did she, in this form that was not flesh, still have nightmares about the things that had been done to her and other girls when she was young?

"I am the Queen, Prince. I am Witch. My justice will be brutal, but it also must be exact. Each must endure the harm he caused. For that, I need those memories."

"Then I offer them, Lady." He opened his inner barriers and sank to his knees, offering everything.

He felt her mind touch his, taking all the information he had extracted from Krellis, Dhuran, and the other boys. Intent on her task, she wasn't as careful as she would have been with anyone else, and he saw a truth she'd kept hidden from him for all the centuries since she'd returned to the Keep in this form in order to help him heal his shattering mind.

So simple—and so obvious. And something they would deal with very soon.

"Now," Witch said briskly as she retreated from his mind, "you will collect a thimbleful of blood from each member of the coven of malice, including any of the witches who died and made the transition to demon-dead, as well as all the girls who were listed as accomplices and are still confined at the school. Then you and some of Lady Zhara's guards will escort each girl to the District Queen who rules the village where her family lives and, with the Queen and her First Circle standing witness, you will deliver the girl to her parents."

Daemon rose and said dryly, "Delora and her closest friends have been in the cells beneath the Hall for the past week. Not the severest ones. The girls who are still living were moved to the cells that have a toilet and sink, as well as a narrow bed. They won't look pristine."

"But they will be alive. You've already informed the Queens of the girls who died at the house party when they attacked other guests?"

"I did." He waited, but she said nothing more. "Once I deliver all the girls?"

"You will remain in Amdarh at the town house, conspicuously in sight, until you receive word that the debts have been paid."

"What am I supposed to do in the meantime?"

She gave him a look that made him feel like an idiot. Holt would welcome the chance to bury him in reports and correspondence and all the other things he'd neglected since the house party.

Then the look in Witch's eyes turned feral, and she said in her midnight voice, "Why don't you find something to do with all that rage?"

"Do you want help?" Karla asked Witch once Daemon left the Keep to fulfill his tasks and the Queen had returned to her own bedroom.

"No." Witch looked away. "This is going to be . . ." She trailed off.

"Does Daemon know what you're going to do?"

Witch shook her head. "He wouldn't agree to it if he knew."

*He wouldn't agree because of what this will cost you?* "Then I'll ask again. Do you *need* help?"

A hesitation. "Afterward, yes."

"Before you slip into the abyss to wherever you're going to go to call in these debts, there is something you should see." Karla called in a shielded tangled web and set the frame on a round wooden table. "Take a look."

Witch bent over to be eye level with the web. She studied it, then looked at Karla in surprise.

"He really is his father's son," Karla said. She pointed at the web of dreams and visions. "Maybe Jaenelle Saetien can't thrive within the core of the SaDiablo family and needs to follow another road. But this one . . ."

"Not a daughter of his loins, but a daughter of his heart," Witch said softly. "We should send Daemon an appropriate gift."

"After I saw this, I placed an order for two extra-stout locks for his study door."

Witch laughed. Then she sighed. "He's not the only one who will need a gift. So there is something you can do while I'm gone. Two things, actually."

"Easily done," Karla said when Witch explained what she wanted.

A bitter smile, Witch's only acknowledgment of what sparing Daemon from these executions would cost. "I'll see you in a few days."

Karla watched her friend fade away and whispered, "May the Darkness have mercy on all of us."

Then she vanished the tangled web and left the Queen's part of the Keep. She had work to do, and . . .

Temper and Ebon-gray power rolled through the Keep.

. . . the first thing she had to do was tell Lucivar that he wasn't going to be able to talk to his Queen for the next few days. But she wasn't going to be the one to tell him why. He'd figure that out on his own soon enough.

# FORTY-THREE

As soon as he delivered the last girl to a District Queen's court, Daemon returned to the town house in Amdarh. Holt was waiting for him, already looking frazzled.

"Which do you want to look at first?" Holt asked. "The sternly worded letters from the Dhemlan Queens condemning your refusal to do your duty for the people in this Territory, or the irate letters from the parents of the girls who were at the house party because you released the coven of malice after a punishment that was no more than making them stay in a less-than-comfy room? Or maybe the report from Lady Zhara, who has been inundated with complaints from the parents who weren't allowed to remove their darling offspring until you'd taken some blood from said offspring without explaining why?"

"What makes you think I want to look at any of them?" Daemon asked.

"Well, then, how about this one?" Holt thrust a folded piece of paper at him.

Recognizing the seal, Daemon took the paper, broke the wax seal, and read.

> *What in the name of Hell are you doing?*
> —*Lucivar*

*Waiting,* Daemon thought. So was everyone else, but they didn't know it yet.

Helton entered the study with a pot of hot water and a plain white mug. He cast a worried look at Holt but said nothing.

Once the butler returned to his other duties, Daemon filled a tea ball with a mix of herbs, set it in the mug, and poured hot water over it—and watched all the blood drain out of Holt's face.

"You have a headache?" Holt asked.

"Yes." No point denying it. He hadn't had one this bad in decades—and having one now could mean his control, or his mind, was starting to crack again.

*"Why don't you find something to do with all that rage?"*

He'd walked into the Hall, collected the thimble of blood from Jaenelle Saetien, collected the blood from Delora and the other "guests" before delivering all the girls as his Queen had commanded. He hadn't discussed anything with Surreal, hadn't talked to anyone. What was he supposed to say? That he'd allowed the Queen who was his life to take this burden because he didn't have the balls to do what needed to be done?

The headache seemed a fitting punishment, but if he damaged himself and was no longer fit to serve his Queen . . .

*"Why don't you find something to do with all that rage?"*

What was he supposed to do? What compensation could he offer the Queens until they saw proof that the debts had been paid?

When the healing brew had steeped for the proper amount of time, he set the tray aside and settled in the chair behind the desk. Then he looked at Holt. "Let's start with the letters from the Queens."

Surreal looked at the tray and wondered when Mrs. Beale would relinquish her anger. Not that the food wasn't good, but there weren't any of the extras that had been included with her own meal.

The Queens were enraged—and they had a right to be. But until she could get Sadi to sit down and explain things to his second-in-command, she couldn't do anything that might interfere with whatever he had set in motion. She didn't doubt for a minute that he had set *something* in motion.

She released the Gray lock on Jaenelle Saetien's bedroom door and walked in. "Listen, sugar, you can piss and moan all you want about the meal but . . ."

She dropped the tray and rushed across the room to where Jaenelle Saetien lay on the floor. The girl was breathing and her heart beat, but there was a chilling blankness in those gold eyes.

Surreal reached for the girl's mind—and found that same terrible blankness.

*Beale!* she called. *Beale! We need the Healer and the Black Widow here right now.*

"Hang on," she whispered as she picked up the girl and laid her on the bed. She heard someone running moments before Beale appeared at the door.

"They're on their way," he said. "What happened?"

"I don't know." Surreal pulled off Jaenelle Saetien's shoes and covered the girl with a quilt. "But we may need the Black Widow more than we need the Healer."

Jaenelle Saetien opened her eyes and studied the plain ceiling. She pushed herself into a sitting position and looked around.

A room with a narrow bed that had leather straps at the top and bottom of the frame. The door was strange, with its knob set up high, as if only adults could reach it.

She remembered feeling intensely cold for a moment, and then . . . Nothing. Where was she?

Then a midnight, cavernous, ancient, raging voice that

held a whisper of madness seemed to rise out of the floor and the walls, out of the air that suddenly burned her lungs, out of her very blood and bones. And that sepulchral voice whispered, *Briarwood is the pretty poison. There is no cure for Briarwood.*

# FORTY-FOUR

*H*ave to get out of here. Have to get out.

Jaenelle Saetien reached for the knob set high on the door. Her fingers closed over it, turned it.

When she tried to use Craft to open the door, nothing happened. Locked? No. Stuck. As if no one had been here for a long time and the knob had rusted.

She tried again, felt some give. She pulled on the door. Pulled and pulled, desperate to get out of that room and find her father or . . . someone. The door's swollen wood resisted, then gave way just a little, then a little more. She pulled and pulled until she could squeeze through the opening.

Free of that horrid room, she found herself in a short, empty corridor. Nowhere to go behind her, so she moved toward the other end of the corridor, step by cautious step. A left-hand turn . . . and another door.

*To each is given what she gave,* the midnight voice said.

"Who are you?" Jaenelle Saetien shouted. "What do you want?"

Was there something familiar about that voice?

*Each of you must pay the debt you owe to those who were harmed by the coven of malice. Their pain will become your pain. What they experienced, you will experience. Everything that came from you will come back to* *you. You have seventy-two hours to find the way out and pay your debt. The sand is running in the glass. If you don't leave before the last grain falls, the link between your body and your Self will be gone. Your body will die, and your Self will stay here for as long as it takes for your power to fade.\**

Find the way out. Yes!

She shaped a Green shield around herself, protection against whatever was behind that door. At least the knob was properly positioned. For a moment, it felt insubstantial. Then she felt the smooth metal. She turned the knob and walked into the room, prepared for anything.

Except a girl swinging from a noose tied to a tree's perfect branch. Blood stained the girl's cheeks from the empty eye sockets down to her chin. Blood stained the dress.

Jaenelle Saetien whirled around to run away, to escape.

The door was gone.

"You don't get out until you stand witness or a tally is made of the debt you owe to whoever is in the room," a voice said.

She spun around. Another girl—a girl who hadn't been in the room a moment ago—stood almost within reach. She wore a blood-soaked dress, and her throat was slit.

Jaenelle Saetien put her hands over her eyes. She wouldn't look. She wouldn't.

"Are you only brave when you're hurting someone else? Don't have enough spine to look at what was done, to look at what you and your friends wanted to do?"

She dropped her hands and bared her teeth. "This *isn't* what my friends wanted to do!"

The girl laughed. "The sand is running in the glass. There are a lot of rooms between you and the way out. Or you can stay here with Marjane and become another of Briarwood's ghosts. Or memories, if you prefer. We've been gone a long time, but *she* remembers us. She can tell you the names of all the ones who died in this place."

"Who is *she*?"

The girl just smiled.

Feeling sick, Jaenelle Saetien looked at the girl hanging from the tree. Marjane. "Why did she end up that way?"

"She told an uncle she couldn't stand the sight of him, so they smeared honey on her eyes and hung her there for the crows." The girl tipped her head, considering. "Do you know what an uncle is?"

"My father's brother. A close relation."

"Not here. In Briarwood, an uncle is a man who likes to play with little girls. Sometimes boys, but mostly girls. Rape is more fun when a girl is too young to fight back. Or when they're given 'medicine' that makes them unable to think clearly enough to get away. You helped make a girl sick with that kind of medicine."

"I didn't!"

The girl shrugged. "Then you'll have nothing to fear when you reach that room."

She felt queasy. "What's your name?"

"My name is Rose. I wouldn't lick an uncle's lollipop so . . ." She drew a finger across her throat.

Jaenelle Saetien wasn't sure what the girl meant about the lollipop, but she wasn't going to ask.

"There's the door," Rose said. "Stay or go?"

"What's in that room?"

"Don't know. This is your debt to pay."

A last look at Marjane, then Jaenelle Saetien opened the next door.

"I've never seen anything like this," the Healer said.

"It's like your daughter is caught in a tangled web of dreams and visions," the Black Widow said, standing at the foot of the bed. "But this is more. Lady Surreal, you wear Gray. Your daughter's Jewel has some measure of Green. You should be able to feel her in the abyss."

"There's nothing," Surreal whispered. She stepped away from the bed where Jaenelle Saetien lay. *Think, damn you, think!*

An extraordinary healing, centuries ago. Marian falling

into a kind of healing sleep that Nurian couldn't recognize. But Tersa . . .

"I warned the girl," Tersa said, walking into the room. "I told the girl that if he asked, *she* would answer. He asked—and this is her answer."

The Healer frowned. "Who asked? Who answered?"

Surreal stared at Tersa. Mad, broken Black Widow whose mind, like her power, did not follow paths the rest of them could see, let alone reach. "Do you know where Jaenelle Saetien is?"

"A dark place," Tersa replied. "A place where she will pay her debt. Then what is left of her can return."

"That doesn't answer the question of who asked and who answered," the Black Widow said, but her voice was careful and respectful.

"My boy asked. His Queen answered."

Fear and fury burned through Surreal. *Sadi!* she called on a Gray thread. *SADI!*

*Surreal.* He sounded cold in a way that told Surreal she wasn't talking to Daemon Sadi.

*You asked *Witch* to punish our daughter?*

*It was Jaenelle Saetien's only chance to stay alive.* Before she could protest, he snarled, *Would you rather have me come to the Hall and perform the execution? That's what the Dhemlan Queens want.*

She knew that. She had seen the letter demanding the executions. It had made her sick to see Zhara's signature among the rest. She'd expected him to find a way around the executions, but she hadn't expected *this.*

*You need to come home. Now.*

*I can't.*

*Can't or won't?*

*Until I have the Queen's permission to return to the Hall, I am required to stay away.*

Surreal blinked away tears before they could fall. *You'll always choose her over the rest of us, won't you?*

A beat of silence before he said gently, *You've always known I would.*

He broke the link between them.

She turned to the other women. "There's nothing you can do now. There's nothing any of us can do now except wait."

The Healer looked puzzled. The Black Widow stared at her, all the color drained from her face.

"He asked," the Black Widow said. "And his *Queen* answered? Prince Sadi's *Queen*?"

"Yes," Tersa said. "My boy is one of her weapons."

"I thought . . ." The Black Widow swallowed hard. "We all thought . . ."

"It is best not to ask too much of someone who stands so deep in the abyss." Tersa's voice held a quiet warning. "The Queen no longer sees the living Realms in the same way." She looked at Surreal. "There is no cure for the pretty poison."

Surreal's legs went out from under her. She knew that place, had *seen* that place. But it didn't exist anymore. Hadn't existed for centuries.

Except in the memory of someone who had been haunted by that place all her life.

Briarwood. Somehow, Witch had sent Jaenelle Saetien to Briarwood—and the Darkness only knew what the girl would be like when she returned.

The next room held two redheaded girls who sat side by side in a patch of turned earth, wearing blood-soaked dresses.

"Myrol and Rebecca," Rose said. "This is the carrot patch where the uncles buried the redheads."

"You *ate* the carrots after . . ."

Rose pointed to another girl at the end of the garden. "That's Dannie. They served her leg for dinner one night."

Jaenelle Saetien retched.

"This is what happened after a witch like Delora gained power," Rose said, viciously cheerful. "Sand is running in the glass. Ready to see the rest?"

She had to get out of this place. And that meant seeing what was in each room until she found the way out.

"Let's go," she said. "It can't get any worse."

Rose laughed.


*"Why don't you find something to do with all that rage?"*

Daemon reviewed the notes Lord Marcus, his man of business, had given him. "You're sure about this?"

Marcus nodded. "Lady Fharra and a handful of the senior instructors own the school. They receive salaries for their work there, but they also receive the profits from the hefty fees. It *is* a private school, so there is nothing unethical about how they've structured the return on their investment."

"But they looked away from trouble that might take a bite out of those profits," Daemon said. "They ignored the bullying and abuse—and worse—that a group of aristo children inflicted on so many other children at that school."

"I couldn't find any indication that Lady Fharra or those instructors had any affinity for Hayll or for the way Dorothea SaDiablo's cruelty had eventually twisted the Blood in the whole Realm of Terreille."

"They still provided the fertile ground for a girl like Delora to prosper and gather a following while eliminating anyone she considered to be a rival."

"What are you going to do?" Marcus asked.

Daemon created a tongue of witchfire. He held one corner of the paper to the fire and watched it burn until he dropped the last scrap into a marble bowl on his desk. Then he smiled a cold, cruel smile as he finally knew exactly what to do with all the rage that had been building inside him. "I'm going to call in a debt."


Jaenelle Saetien didn't recognize the bedroom or the girl on the bed who was flailing weakly and begging for it to stop. But she recognized Clayton—and she realized he and the girl were having sex.

No, not sex. Not when the girl was begging him to stop and he seemed triumphant when the girl screamed and . . . became less.

Rose studied her. "Nothing? You didn't feel him pounding between your legs, driving you down to your inner web, using pain and fear to make you fall and shatter that inner web? That's how it's done, you know. That's how witches are broken on their Virgin Night."

Jaenelle Saetien stared at Rose, horrified. "But that's . . ." *Clayton. One of Delora's friends. A boy I thought was also my friend.*

"If you didn't feel the rape, then you didn't have a hand in that girl ending up under him. Some of your friends won't be so lucky." Rose paused. "You might want to take a good look at her face. She comes from a minor aristo family. You might see her again. Or what's left of her after he was done."

See that girl and remember this? No. Never.

"There's the door," Rose said. "Time to move on."

"Can't we find a room where we can rest for a while?" Jaenelle Saetien asked.

"You have no body here, nothing that requires rest."

*What about a heart, a mind?*

"You want to stay here?" Rose demanded.

And watch Clayton doing . . . that? "Let's go on."


Daemon walked onto the school grounds and let his Black power flow beneath all the minds still in residence.

He'd met Lady Fharra and knew what her mind felt like. She wasn't at the school. He'd bet the other instructors who owned a percentage of the school weren't there either. But there were still plenty of other people within the grounds. Students and instructors. The grooms who took care of the horses—and the horses.

He had given Lady Fharra the courtesy of informing her that the school would burn at midnight. Instead of using the time to evacuate the students and instructors, she had fled.

That made one decision simple.

He reached for two minds. One he knew well; the other was just learning what it meant to serve someone like the High Lord of Hell. *Prince Chaosti. Prince Raine. Your presence is required.*

News had traveled through Dhemlan about the unnatural sleep that had struck Delora and every member of her coven, as well as the youngsters who had been the coven's accomplices. No Healer could wake them. A few strong Black Widows had found enough of an answer to run from the bedrooms in terror. And he had remained in Amdarh, conspicuously in sight.

Chaosti strode toward him, the movement easy and confident. Raine came on the run from the direction of the instructors' rooms.

"At midnight, witchfire will consume the school," Daemon said. "Raine, inform the boys who are still in residence to pack what they don't want to lose and be ready to leave. Then pack your own belongings."

"A few of Lady Zhara's guards are still here," Chaosti said. "Not Lord Weston, unfortunately, since the other men are unnerved when approached by the demon-dead. They can rouse the grooms and any other staff who are still here."

"What about Lady Fharra?" Raine asked.

"She was informed about the fire earlier today," Daemon replied. "*She* isn't here."

Raine stared at him. "She knew *and said nothing*?"

"Don't concern yourself, Prince," Daemon crooned. "She'll pay her debts."

"My men and I will rouse the girls," Chaosti said. "Where should we take them? The town house can't hold all the people who are still here."

"Take them to Lady Zhara's court. She'll have rooms

large enough to accommodate them. Prince Raine, you may stay in one of the town house's guest rooms if you choose."

"Thank you, sir."

Daemon met Chaosti's eyes, then focused on Raine. "Witchfire burns," he said too softly. "Make sure you're off the school grounds by midnight."

He turned and walked away.

During the hours before midnight, he visited the homes of Lady Fharra and all the instructors who were partners at the school—and the death spells the Sadist wove around each of those fools were exquisite.

# FORTY-FIVE

Lucivar stared at the mounds of still-smoking gravel and ash that had been a school the day before. The ground looked more like clay fired in a kiln than soil capable of growing anything.

The taste of ash and the heat of witchfire still hung in the air.

So did the taste of merciless, cold rage.

Lord Weston walked toward him, trying to move within his sight without setting so much as the side of a boot on that barren ground.

"He gave everyone time to get out," Weston said, standing beside Lucivar. "From what I heard, some of the youngsters were pissing and moaning about packing up and leaving—until the witchfire started burning the outbuildings. The grooms didn't take as much persuading and removed all the horses from the school's stables. A couple instructors grabbed the last youngsters who were still dragging their feet and tossed them into the street. They were only a few steps beyond the school when the fire flashed from one end of the school grounds to the other, burning as tall as the buildings but contained within the school's boundaries."

"Where are they?" Lucivar lifted his chin to indicate the school's former residents.

"Boys are camped out in Lady Zhara's ballroom. I

think the girls were bedded down in a couple of the reception rooms."

"You were guarding Zoey?"

"Yes."

"Good." Lucivar gave the school grounds one last, long look. It wasn't the first time the city of Amdarh had experienced the Sadist's temper. Wasn't the first time his witch-fire had burned a building. At least this time . . . "No bodies as warning and lesson."

"Not here."

Lucivar looked at the Warlord who was Lady Zoela's primary escort.

"Lady Fharra and a handful of senior instructors were executed last night." Weston swallowed hard. "I didn't see the bodies, but Lady Zhara's Master of the Guard is a strong man who will stand in a fight to defend his Queen. He saw what was done, and he was . . . frightened."

Easy enough to guess what Weston felt too nervous to ask. "Sadi isn't in Amdarh. I'm not sure where he is." And he wasn't looking forward to finding out. "Tell Zhara if she needs help, let me know. I'd say my brother was settling the debts that were owed to his family and the people of Dhemlan. I don't think she needs to worry about him showing up to have a little chat."

Weston looked relieved. Then he called in a pale rose envelope and held it out. "Zoey asked me to take this, in case I ran into you."

Lucivar took the envelope, read Titian's name on the front, and vanished it. "How is Zoey doing?"

"She's not sleeping, and when she does sleep, she wakes up frightened. She wants to go back to the Hall. She says it's safer there."

"That's where she was attacked."

"I know, but she says—and I agree—that if she'd been at any other house and the same thing had been done, she wouldn't have survived. Krellis would have gotten to her and Titian and . . ." Weston stopped. "She says the people who serve Prince Sadi are strong, and even when he can't be at the Hall, they will still protect the people who live there."

"Nothing can be done until the coven of malice rises from wherever they are in the abyss," Lucivar said. He'd stopped at the town house before coming to the school and had heard all about the girls falling into a sleep and somehow escaping the Queens' demand for execution. "If you need any help with Zoey, Helton will know where to find me."

"Thank you, Prince." Weston bowed and walked away.

*Bastard?* Lucivar called on an Ebon-gray spear thread. *Daemon, where are you?*

*Unless you want to dance, stay away from me.*

Even that connection on a psychic thread was enough to wrap around him, making him painfully aroused—and frightened. He had danced with the Sadist before, and he was certain they would dance again. But not today. He didn't want to die that way.

*Is there anything I can do for you?*

*Do what you can for Surreal. I am not permitted to be at the Hall. Not yet.*

Thank the Darkness for that. *I'll go there now.*

Sadi withdrew from the link with a gentleness that almost felt like a blow.

Lucivar took a deep breath and blew it out, hoping to clear his head. Then he launched himself skyward and caught the closest Wind—the Red—and headed for SaDiablo Hall.

Jaenelle Saetien watched Delora and Krellis pick up rocks and beat a boy's face into an unrecognizable mess before they smashed his hands to pulp. And all the while, Delora kept saying, "Going to tattle on us again? Are you? Are you?"

"What happened to the boy?" she asked Rose.

"They didn't care, so that isn't part of what was remembered," Rose replied.

They didn't care.

She'd watched Krellis rape a girl, with Delora and Hespera urging him on. She'd watched Dhuran telling some of the other boys from the school that using the girl he'd selected was their initiation into the group.

She'd passed through rooms where other boys who were part of Delora and Krellis's pack of males beat and bullied younger boys to prove they were worthy of being . . . what? The predators instead of the prey?

At each room, Rose watched her and waited, but she felt no pain that matched what was being done. No pain beyond a growing misery as she looked at what the people whom she'd thought were her friends had done to other children.

And then, as she put her hand on the knob of the next door, she heard a familiar voice shout, "Jaenelle!"

She rushed into the room, then froze at the sight of a girl with golden hair and blue eyes tied to a bed and a man with maimed hands . . .

Surreal appeared out of the wall and whirled to face the man who kept thrusting into the girl's too-still body. She grabbed the man's hair in one hand and slashed a knife across his throat—and the walls turned red.

With her teeth bared, Surreal drove a knife into his heart, lifting him off the bed. Lifting him off the girl. As she pulled out her knife and raised her hand for the final strike, another Rose, more transparent than the one standing beside Jaenelle Saetien, moaned and Surreal glanced at the bed and the blood. So much blood. Too much blood.

"Jaenelle," Surreal said.

Jaenelle Saetien's stomach rolled as she watched Surreal, who looked more like one of her older schoolmates than her mother, cut the cords that bound the girl to the bed, wrap that body in the bloody sheet, and pass through the wall, shouting for Daemon Sadi.

Jaenelle Saetien backed out of the room and slumped to the floor.

Rose closed the door and crouched beside her. "Not much farther to go."

She pushed her hair away from her tear-dampened face

and climbed to her feet. Walking to the end of the corridor, she opened the next door.

Surreal pushed out of the chair by the bed when Lucivar walked into Jaenelle Saetien's bedroom.

"Sadi?" she asked.

Lucivar didn't reply, just opened his arms and wrapped them around her when she fell against him. She couldn't cry anymore. Maybe when this was over. Maybe when she knew . . . What?

"How long can she survive this way?" she asked.

"Slow executions usually take three days," he replied. When she jerked back to look at his face, he added, "I don't expect this to take longer."

"She didn't *do* . . ." She bit back the rest of the words. Most likely every parent of a girl who had belonged to the coven of malice was saying the same thing. *Their* daughter hadn't done anything wrong.

"Didn't she? From where I'm standing, she did enough to deserve some punishment."

She pushed away from him. She should have realized his anger was still close to the surface and might never go away. "Why are you here?"

"To help you."

"Jaenelle Saetien's father should be here. He's the one who got her into this by letting her go to that school." She hurt, and she needed to blame someone for the pain—and right now she couldn't blame the girl lying in bed.

"She got herself into this, Surreal. She made the choice to be one of Delora's followers."

"How could she know what that bitch could do?" Surreal cried. "We kept her *safe*, Lucivar. We kept her protected and safe so she wouldn't end up on some bed, torn and bloody and broken!"

"Yeah," Lucivar said. "You did keep her safe. Maybe she needed some scars in order to appreciate that being safe was a gift not everyone receives."

Surreal raked her fingers through her hair. "Witch sent her to Briarwood."

He said nothing.

"And her father—"

"Needed help to find a way to call in the debts without having to kill his daughter."

"But . . . *Briarwood*."

"I know what was there. I listened to enough of Jaenelle's nightmares over the years."

As she'd sat here hour after hour, watching an empty shell—*guarding* an empty shell—a question had formed. Now she faced the Demon Prince and asked, "If Witch, your Queen, told you to walk away from your wife and children to be with her and only her, would you do it?"

"She never asked that of the men who served her when she walked among the living. She wouldn't ask it now," he replied.

"But if she did?"

"I would miss Marian and the children every day for the rest of my life and beyond, but if that was my Queen's command, I would walk away and not look back."

So. It wasn't just Daemon's loyalty to Witch that ran that deep.

"What did you expect?" Lucivar asked. "We waited seventeen hundred years for her. We actively searched for her for seven hundred years because Tersa told us she was coming. We fought to stay alive in order to find her. She was, and is, *everything* that matters. And she always will be. And one reason why that's true is she will never ask for a sacrifice from us if she can pay the price herself." He smiled sadly. "You loved her as friend and sister, and you served the Queen. But you weren't one of the dreamers, Surreal. You weren't one of the yearning, desperate hearts that shaped dreams into flesh. I was one of them. So was Saetan. So was Daemon. She is vital to his survival. And his being with her is vital to the survival of the rest of us."

She knew that. Had known it for decades, centuries.

Witch was the only one who could control the Sadist. Without her . . .

"He destroyed the school," Lucivar said. "There's nothing left. And he executed the administrator and several senior instructors. The Queens are frozen in fear, waiting for his next move."

"Where is he?"

"I don't know. But you don't want the Sadist here. Not now."

*Not ever.* She wouldn't be that lucky. Everything had a price.

She looked at Jaenelle Saetien lying so still and frowned as Lucivar's words settled into her mind. "What sort of price is Witch paying in order to help Daemon save some part of Jaenelle Saetien?"

"Well," Lucivar said, "that's an interesting question, isn't it?"

# FORTY-SIX

Jaenelle Saetien pressed a fist to her chest and struggled
to breathe as excruciating pain ripped through her,
making it impossible to move, impossible to think, impossible to feel anything except that perfectly aimed blow.
Then the pain faded, leaving a cold, empty spot in her
chest where something had been scooped out. Had died.

"Well done!" Rose said, clapping. "Fatal blow to the
heart. How does it feel to make your first kill?"

Jaenelle Saetien stared at this frozen image of Surreal,
standing there with a deep, jagged wound in her chest, exposing everything beneath. And the handle of a knife
sticking out of her heart.

"I didn't do that." She rubbed her chest, feeling the
echo of pain.

"'I didn't, I didn't,'" Rose mocked. "That's how you
justify everything, isn't it? *Everyone* kills her mother, so
why shouldn't you?"

"I didn't do that!" she shouted. "Surreal SaDiablo is
still alive!"

Rose nodded. "Surreal is. But *Mother* . . ." She looked
at the knife's bone handle and then at the oddly shaped
blade—and pointed. "The blade is made from the words
'not my mother' and it sliced right through the piece of
Surreal's heart that's labeled *mother.* There's a piece labeled *wife, friend, sister, protector.* No damage to those

bits. But *mother*?" She shook her head. "You killed that part of her so well, there's nothing left. Must have hurt when you said those words."

"I didn't mean it."

Rose just looked at her.

"Okay, yes, I meant it. I'd just found out she'd been a whore. What would you have done?"

Rose shrugged.

"I meant to hurt her, but . . ."

"Yes, yes, adolescent drama. Big, big feelings that can't consider someone else's struggle because yours are the only feelings that count. You said things you knew would hurt, but you expected her to get over them as soon as it was convenient for you." Rose stared at her. "It doesn't always work that way. Maybe it does most of the time, but sometimes wounds go too deep, and you can't fix the harm you've done. When that happens, you have to accept the consequences. She'll always be your mother in terms of bloodline, and she'll probably always try to protect you to make up for the ones she couldn't save—she still dreams about them sometimes. Did you know that? But *Mother* is gone. Look. There's the next door."

A corridor in the Hall. Was she home? But . . . Why was she with Clayton and why was he saying . . . No. No! She didn't want to go with him, but if she loved him . . .

And then Holt walking up to them. A flash of power and Clayton unable to move. And the next door revealed . . .

. . . another corridor at the Hall, another boy from school, backhanding her for not letting him do . . . A snarl, a white paw, the crack of bone as the boy's neck snapped beneath that angry blow. Fur and strength and *safety*. She held on to the big white cat, held on until she stumbled through the next doorway and . . .

Her breasts were painfully swollen from a strange arousal, and her nipples were so tight, they *hurt*, and the wild throbbing she felt between her legs . . .

*Titian, I'm sick!*

Not excitement like the way girls felt in romantic stories. This was painful need that burned through her. Burned and burned.

*I'll help you to your room.* Krellis. No, not Krellis. He was the enemy, and he would . . . And there was Delora, her eyes glittering with the anticipation of destroying another rival.

She was on the floor. Had to get up. Had to run. Had to help Titian. *Titian!*

Would this pain, this need, never end? *Would it never end?*

"You reached the doorway, but there's not much sand left in the glass," Rose said. "If you don't leave before the last grain falls, you never will."

Jaenelle Saetien pushed herself to a sitting position. Not a proper doorway, just an opening in the wall.

An opening filled with a tangled web.

"We're surprised you only had to take back the harm done to Surreal and the girls at your party," Rose said. "*Everyone* thought you'd been thoroughly corrupted by the coven of malice. That's why the Queens wanted you executed along with the rest of Delora's friends. That's why you ended up here." She began to fade. "Sand is running in the glass. You'd better hurry if you want to get out."

"Rose?" Jaenelle Saetien cried. "Rose! What am I supposed to do?"

"Pay the debt," a midnight voice said.

On the other side of that tangled web stood . . .

She scrambled to her feet and approached the web. "I remember you."

"Do you? Not well enough."

She hadn't forgotten this strange female who had golden hair that looked more like fur, delicately pointed ears, a tiny spiral horn growing out of her forehead. A human female's body, but the human hands had cat's claws and the legs below the knees belonged to a horse and ended with delicate hooves.

"You gave me Twilight's Dawn," Jaenelle Saetien said, feeling hopeful for the first time since she'd awakened in this place.

"I gave you that Jewel because you had the potential to wear it," was the cold reply. "You had the *heart* to wear it. And then you no longer wanted to be the person who could wear it. Choice by choice, you turned away from who you had been until you became an enemy of everyone who had fought against what you now embraced, until you became an insult to everyone who sacrificed themselves to cleanse the Realms of Dorothea's and Hekatah's taint." She looked over her shoulder at the large hourglass floating on air. "It's time to pay the debt."

"I just did that!" Jaenelle Saetien said. "I paid!"

The creature she'd once thought of as her special friend laughed, a terrible sound that contained no mercy. "No. *That* was to tally up the debt and help you appreciate the pain you caused—and to show you what your friends had done to other people. By going through the web, you will pay what you owe to the Dhemlan Queens. Or you can stay here among the ghosts until your power fades. Your body will wither and die within a week so that your family won't be chained to caring for a husk, but *you* will be here for a long time. That, too, would be considered payment in full." A beat of silence. "Pay the price and, hopefully, live. Or stay here and let your body die. Choose."

Caught in the strands of the tangled web were Jewel chips. Rose, Summer-sky, Purple Dusk, Opal, Green. All the colors that made up her Twilight's Dawn.

The creature looked pointedly at the hourglass.

Jaenelle Saetien studied the web. Try to go through on one side or the other? No, the web seemed thicker there. Through the middle.

May the Darkness have mercy on her.

She rushed the web, flinging up her arms and tucking her head to protect her face. The strands of the web caught her, tangled her, bit and tore out pieces of her as she struggled to move forward, to get out.

A crack of power. A moment of feeling hollowed out, so terribly empty. Where was her inner web? Where was she in the abyss?

Nowhere.

She fell through that tangled web, landing on hands and knees beside the creature. She looked back and sucked in a breath. The tangled web across the doorway was in tatters, the strands turning to black ash.

She'd gotten out. She was free. And furious.

Scrambling to her feet, she shouted, "Who *are* you?" Had she ever asked? This creature had been her special friend, and she'd been dazzled when she was young.

"I am Witch, the living myth. Dreams made flesh." An odd smile. "As you can see, not all the dreamers were human."

She was who? What? That meant . . . "*You're* the Queen? My *father's* Queen?"

"I was. I am. I always will be."

But that meant . . . "*You're* Jaenelle Angelline?"

"I was when I walked among the living."

Too much, too much. "Do you know why I wanted to be Delora's friend? Because *I didn't want to be like you*! I was tired of being compared to you!"

Something feral and beyond ice filled those sapphire eyes. "Didn't want to be like me? That was *exactly* what you wanted when you were young. Or maybe it's more accurate to say that, before your Birthright Ceremony, you were who I might have been if I'd had your childhood instead of mine." A terrible smile. "Did you enjoy your tour of Briarwood?"

"It's an awful place."

"I was five years old the first time I was put in there."

Moments? Minutes? Jaenelle Saetien didn't know how long she stared into those sapphire eyes as she remembered Myrol and Rebecca, Dannie and Marjane. Rose. "Why?"

"Because I told the truth about meeting unicorns and dragons. Because I told the truth about the men who came to that place and what they did to the girls. Truth was in-convenient for the Queen of Chaillot, so it was decided that I was unbalanced and needed to be in Briarwood. I was in and out of that place until I was twelve and was raped by a man named Greer."

Jaenelle Saetien shivered. The girl on the bed, with golden hair and blue eyes. The girl Surreal . . .

"You grew up at the Hall, loved and protected by two of the strongest people in the Realm. Daemon and Surreal let you explore, they let you learn—and they always kept you safe. That was *your* childhood. Briarwood was mine." Witch stared through Jaenelle Saetien. "How dare you use me as the excuse for choosing corruption over honor?"

Black lightning flashed across the sky, its silence more terrible than the loudest thunder would have been.

"You didn't want to be like me?" Witch said. "You could *never* be like me. By keeping you safe, Daemon and Surreal made sure of that."

Jaenelle Saetien felt odd, hollow, not whole. She looked at the Jewel in the pendant that hung from her neck. "Something's wrong! My Jewel . . ."

Witch studied the Jewel. "Purple Dusk. You kept that much. The rest of what was Twilight's Dawn is gone. That was the price for the harm you have done."

"No."

"The girls—and boys—who were accomplices but didn't actively participate in breaking the girls Delora con-sidered rivals didn't lose their Jewels completely. Not this time. But, like you, their power is diminished, and if any of you stray toward someone like Delora again, you will lose a great deal more than your Jewels. After all, there is no cure for Briarwood. It will be inside all of you forever, as remembrance. As a reminder."

Jaenelle Saetien shivered. "But when I make the Offer-ing to the Darkness . . ."

"You might regain the Green. Maybe even Sapphire. But the Gray you might have worn is gone."

"You're cruel."

"If you mistake mercy for cruelty, then you have not learned enough." Plants suddenly grew all around them, bloodred flowers, with black throats and black-tipped petals. "This is witchblood. It grows where a witch's blood was spilled violently or where a witch who had met a violent death was buried. Witchblood is deadly, but if you sing to it correctly, it will tell you the names of the ones who are gone."

The look in Witch's eyes had Jaenelle Saetien backing away, but her feet got tangled in the plants and she ended up on the ground.

Witch pointed to the Purple Dusk Jewel. "That paid the debt you owed the Dhemlan Queens for what you did on behalf of the coven of malice. Now let's discuss the debt you owe *me* for hurting Daemon and Surreal."


A slight movement. The faintest moan.

Surreal sprang out of the chair next to Jaenelle Saetien's bed and grabbed the girl's hand.

"Wake up now, Jaenelle Saetien. Wake up!"

Glazed, dazed gold eyes focused on her.

"Wake up now," Surreal said.

"Am I home?"

"You're home."

The girl clung to her hand and cried.


No one asked any questions. Except for breathing and a slowly beating heart, it seemed her body hadn't worked at all while she'd been gone. Now needs returned with a vengeance.

Surreal helped her to the toilet, then helped her into the shower and back out. Helene and some maids changed the linens on the bed and opened the windows to let in fresh cold air. By the time Jaenelle Saetien was helped into clean clothes and returned to the bed, the warming spells had returned the room to a comfortable temperature and Beale brought up a tray with water, beef broth, and chunks of bread she could dip into the broth.

She looked at the Hall's butler, but she saw no relief that she had returned, no welcome or warmth in his eyes. The message was clear: from now on, she was just a daughter of the house—and not one he felt any liking toward.

She drank some water, swallowed a few spoonfuls of broth.

When Surreal set the tray on the table and sat on the side of the bed, Jaenelle Saetien dared to talk. She wanted to ask where her father was, but that might make her seem ungrateful for Surreal's help.

"My body was here?"

"Yes," Surreal replied.

"But I felt . . ." Wanton, desperate burning between her legs and fear when she realized what Krellis was going to do. "I thought I was in a place. A terrible place." Hard to breathe. Why was it hard to breathe? "Briarwood is the pretty poison."

"There is no cure for Briarwood." Surreal touched Jaenelle Saetien's knee, the covers separating them.

"You've seen that place." Not a question.

Surreal nodded. "Myrol and Rebecca. Dannie. Rose." Her eyes filled with tears. "Marjane was the daughter of a friend of mine. I didn't even know Deje had had a daughter until I was shown Briarwood."

"I saw them too." Jaenelle Saetien hesitated. "And I saw you when you saved Jaenelle Angelline."

Surreal shook her head. "I was too late to save her. But I did slit that bastard's throat—just like he slit my mother's throat. She died when I was twelve. I was raped a few days later and became a whore soon after that in order to survive."

Jaenelle Saetien plucked at the covers, not sure what to say. "Where's Father?"

"I don't know. He destroyed the school. There's nothing left of it. He executed Lady Fharra and several instructors for the part they played in allowing Delora to attack other students. And he executed all the boys who came to the house party uninvited."

Her stomach flipped. She swallowed hard. "*All* of them?"

"The two boys who were Zoey's friends were spared. The rest . . ."

"What about the rest?" Krellis, Dhuran, and Clayton were dead?

"They danced with the Sadist, and he ripped them apart, body and mind."

"Because they were here when boys weren't supposed to be at the party."

"Well, their being at the Hall to rape and break Zoey and some of the other girls certainly fueled his rage, but those boys died hard for what they'd already done."

She couldn't think about the boys, couldn't imagine what had been done to them. "Zoey. She was sick."

"She was drugged," Surreal corrected sharply. Then she softened her voice. "She'll be fine. Lucivar helped her while the drug was burning through her. She's still recovering, has some trouble with anyone touching her. Hopefully that will fade in time. Titian is having nightmares, wakes up crying." She shook her head. "I know you just woke up, but you should rest. You want me to fetch a couple of books, put them on the bedside table?"

"Yes. Thank you." She told Surreal which ones she wanted. "You haven't said anything about my Jewel."

"It's Purple Dusk now."

"The rest of Twilight's Dawn was taken from me."

"To pay the debt you owed." Surreal made an impatient sound. "Sugar, you weren't broken back to basic Craft, and you're not dead. By my figuring, you're way ahead of anyone else who was identified as part of the coven of malice. The problem now, for your father, is convincing the Dhemlan Queens and Warlord Princes that your debt was paid in full." She walked to the door, adding, "Get some rest."

No sympathy for what she'd lost. No understanding about the price she still had to pay.

She slid out of bed, bracing herself on the mattress until she trusted her legs to hold her. Then she tottered to the table where she'd left the printed-and-bound information about the girls who had been harmed by Delora and her friends.

*"There is a list. Choose seven of the girls. You will take the time to learn who they were, who they might have been. You will understand what they lost and what Dhemlan lost because they were stripped of their power, their potential. Until you can feel the weight of them on your heart, you will walk through Briarwood every night. You will become a kind of memento mori for those seven girls. They will become your scars. That is the price you will pay to me for hurting Surreal—and for hurting Daemon and forcing him to choose between giving you to me or killing you himself."*

Jaenelle Saetien picked up the printed list and shuffled back to bed. She shoved the list under one of the pillows and remembered the last thing Witch had said to her.

*"If it's the name that's getting in your way, then change your name to something that won't remind people of me. Daemon won't care. I doubt he chose that name in the first place."*

# FORTY-SEVEN

*D*aemon. The debt is paid. Go home.*

Daemon rushed through the open front door and into the great hall, where Beale waited for him.

"Any problems here?" he asked.

"No, High Lord." Beale studied him. "Would you prefer I use a different title?"

"No," he said softly. For most of the Blood, he would never be Prince Daemon Sadi again. He wondered if Saetan had felt the extra weight of being the High Lord once it became known throughout the Realms. No stepping back from it now. For any of them. "Where is Surreal?"

"In her suite. We persuaded her to get some rest now that the young Lady woke up and was bathed and had a bite to eat."

He couldn't think about the young Lady yet, wasn't ready to face what was left of Jaenelle Saetien. He moved swiftly through the corridors, acknowledging the footmen and maids with just a look. When he reached Surreal's suite, he knocked on her sitting room door and then entered before being given permission. But as he crossed the threshold, he leashed every part of himself as tightly as he could.

"Surreal?" He said her name softly, unwilling to disturb her if she was asleep—and unwilling to walk into her bedroom without her permission in order to check on her. That room was her sanctuary, and he spent time with her there as an invited guest.

She appeared in the doorway between the rooms, looking exhausted and fragile. "Sadi?" She ran across the room and threw herself into his arms.

He held her, his hands moving over her head and back to caress and reassure. "I'm sorry I couldn't be here to help you. I am sorry for that."

"Did that bitch Fharra get everything she deserved?" Her words were muffled, spoken against his chest.

"She did. They all did." He couldn't ease her back enough to get a good look at her, so he settled her more comfortably against him. "Sweetheart, did you get any rest?"

She shook her head. "I couldn't. . . . It was easier to keep watch." She finally leaned back and looked at him. "Have you seen her?"

"Not yet. I wanted to see you first, make sure you were all right." He kissed her lips. A gentle kiss, for comfort.

Surreal clung to him for a moment. "You need to see her." A hesitation. "Will you stay with me tonight?"

"Yes." He gave her another kiss, one with a little more heat. A promise.

Then he walked to his daughter's suite to find out how much of a debt she had owed.

When her father walked into her bedroom, Jaenelle Saetien almost tumbled out of bed in her haste to reach him. Her legs still wobbled, so she stopped halfway and waited for him.

He stared at her face, at her eyes. Finally at the Purple Dusk.

Then he crossed the room, pulled her into his arms, pressed his face against her head—and began to cry.

It was the most terrible sound she'd ever heard because it was coming from *him*.

"Papa," she soothed, patting his back. "Don't cry, Papa. Please don't cry."

As his emotions swamped her, she began to cry, too, when she realized he wasn't crying because of what she had lost; he was crying out of relief that she hadn't been so corrupted by Delora and the coven of malice to have earned being executed.

# FORTY-EIGHT

---

*A* re you sure about this?"
        "*Everything has a price.*"

Personally, Karla thought Witch had paid more than enough, lifetimes of enough. And this price would shake the Realm.

She knocked on the door, handed her card to the butler, who handed it to Lady Zhara's Steward, who wasn't able to hide his fear as he hurried to ascertain if the Queen of Amdarh would grant this audience—and would subject her granddaughter to this requested meeting.

There was no real question about Zhara granting this audience or about Zoey being there—only a fool would defy a Gray-Jeweled Black Widow Queen—but Karla appreciated the Steward having enough balls to go through the formalities.

Dhemlan was in turmoil since the girls who had fallen into that unnatural sleep rose from wherever they had been in the abyss. Delora and Hespera woke up, their Birthright Jewels looking like a thinned transparent eggshell filled with ash. That kind of destruction of a Jewel and its reservoir of power was something no one had seen before—and no one wanted to see again. The two girls had screamed for two days, occasionally babbling about pretty poison and feeling Krellis and Dhuran raping them over and over while they wore different bodies.

On the third day, their hearts stopped beating; their lungs refused to take another breath. Their bodies became a different kind of shell while their Selves went to the final death and became whispers in the Darkness.

Leena and Tacita had returned with their Jewels empty, their power broken back to basic Craft. They, too, whimpered about a pretty poison. On the same day that Delora and Hespera died, both girls slipped away from their family homes and wandered through the woods. Leena went to a nearby farm, and Tacita went to a cottage on the outskirts of the village. They'd been to those places before, watched Dhuran and Clayton break a girl from each of those families before giving the girls to some of the village rough boys, minor aristos who had ended up killing those girls for the fun of it.

The rough boys had mysteriously disappeared a few days after the news about the execution of the young men who had done the coven of malice's bidding. An elderly Warlord reported to his District Queen that he'd heard a tree crying and begging for forgiveness. But it hadn't been the first time that this man had claimed to hear a peculiar sound. The Queen and the Black Widow who served in her First Circle heard nothing when they went to investigate, and her men could find no indication that the soil around the tree had been disturbed.

Not that anyone would ever find those rough boys. The Sadist was a very good gravedigger, and he'd been busy cleaning up a few problems.

Leena and Tacita had wandered until they found the exact spots where the girls had died. Found the plant with the bloodred, black-throated flowers. Before their families located them, the girls had eaten a few of the petals—and the witchblood slowly bloomed in their bellies, giving unrelenting pain that was finally relieved by death.

What made the District Queens and Province Queens uneasy was the way Leena and Tacita kept asking if the debt was finally paid. Apparently it was, since both girls looked relieved when they took that final breath.

Most of the accomplices who had assisted Delora and her friends had been broken back to basic Craft. Those who had retained their Birthright Jewels discovered the Jewels were weirdly diminished. Instead of holding a reservoir of power, the power seemed to drain . . . *somewhere*. No one had seen a Jewel behave this way, and queries sent to the Keep had received no reply. And knowing how often Daemon Sadi visited the Keep—and had done so for centuries—no one was willing to go to Ebon Askavi to make direct inquiries and cross paths with *him*.

The only person who seemed to come away with negligible cost was Jaenelle Saetien SaDiablo. Some change in her Jewel, yes. The same unnatural sleep as the other girls, yes. But she hadn't *suffered* in the same way, and some of the Queens suspected the girl deserved far more than she'd received. So did the families of the girls who had been harmed.

Well, all that was about to change—and may the Darkness have mercy on Kaeleer.

Karla followed the Steward to a sitting room. Not the formal sitting room where Amdarh's Queen attended to some of the business of her court and not the sitting room where family and close friends gathered. This was a room in between, and Karla suspected it had been chosen for Zoey's sake.

The girl still looked ill, jumpy. Karla wasn't surprised to find Zhara's husband in the room. As Consort, he was the official witness. As husband and grandfather, he was a furious man barely controlling his anger.

Karla didn't bother with the niceties. She simply called in a folded document and held it out to Zhara. "This is for you. By tomorrow, the rest of the District and Province Queens in Dhemlan will have received a copy."

The document had no wax seal to hold it closed. Good paper, with a black border. Very little was printed on the paper. A list naming the girls who were, in one way or another, part of the coven of malice. Below the names were the words *To each was given what she gave. Each experi-*

*enced the harm she caused. The debts have been paid in full.*

Below the words, pressed into black wax, was a seal that hadn't been seen in centuries. An unmistakable command—and warning.

Zhara dropped the document, sucked in a breath, and stared at Karla. "She's . . . But . . . *how*? *When*?"

"For centuries," Karla replied. "Kaeleer needs Daemon Sadi, and she is the only one who could heal him and hold the leash. She found a way to be anchored to the Keep. But make no mistake, Zhara. She might stay at the Keep, but she has a very long reach, and when provoked, she is more . . . feral . . . than she used to be."

Zhara looked stunned. Then she whispered, "Song in the Darkness. But more than that? For some?"

"For a few," Karla agreed. She called in a velvet pouch and held it out to Zoey, who had been staring at the document. Mostly at the seal in the black wax. "These are for you."

Zoey took the pouch, opened it, and poured six gold coins into her hand. "These look like Titian's good-luck charm."

"Marks of safe passage. Each of those represents a two-hour audience with the Queen. You may discuss anything you want with her, whether it's about Craft or being a Queen or dealing with Warlord Princes or about the weight of scars. You should select a few dates for each audience, since the trip there and back, along with the audience, will take up a full day, and no one will be granted an audience when the High Lord is in residence. He requires solitary time with his Queen."

"I would be traveling . . . ?" Zoey said the words as if she were feeling each careful step on shaky ground.

"To Ebon Askavi." Karla saw excitement leap into the girl's eyes.

"And I would have lessons with . . . ?"

"The Queen of Ebon Askavi. Witch."

Watching Zoey stare at the coins, Karla felt the crackle

of possibilities in the air. She turned her attention back to Zhara, whose face was wet with tears.

"I'll bid you good night," Karla said.

"I'll walk you out." Zhara called in a handkerchief and wiped her face. She waited until they were away from the sitting room. "The Lady doesn't have to do this. Whatever she is now, it must be hard for her to deal with the living. Easier perhaps with the demon-dead who were old friends?"

"When did Jaenelle Angelline back away from anything because it was hard?"

"True. Still." Zhara slowed her steps and gave her butler a tiny signal to retreat so that they would continue to speak privately.

Karla didn't point out that psychic communication was possible with the demon-dead. Zhara knew that, but was cautious enough not to attempt it. This time.

"Zoey will appreciate the lessons," Zhara said. "She still needs schooling and careful study of Craft and a number of other things in order to become a good Queen, but she's afraid to go to another school. She believes Prince Sadi eliminated the current threat, but other girls might have managed to hide that same kind of malice and haven't come to his attention yet."

*Hell's fire, Jaenelle. You were right about this too.*

"A traditional school, even a private school, isn't the only place where a young Queen could receive an education," Karla said casually. "It is possible for certain young witches and exceptional males to receive an exclusive education that would cover a broad range of subjects. You, meaning the Dhemlan Queens, would need to be careful about who you presented to receive this education, but if you kept the numbers to something reasonable for long-term guests in a private house, and if a Queen who had a girl in need of such an education were to present the idea, I think the patriarch of the house could be persuaded to accommodate you."

"Is that how you did it?" Zhara asked, keeping her voice just as casual.

"Oh, Hell's fire, no. We just piled in on Uncle Saetan and never gave him a chance to refuse. We were settled in with our trunks unpacked before he knew what hit him. That won't work with Sadi, but I'm sure mentioning Zoey and Titian would undermine his resistance to the idea."

"There would be a problem with Zoey being there."

"The Lady knows that." Karla stopped at the front door, her ice-blue eyes taking in the measure of this other Queen. "Did you really think the loss of some of her power was the only price Jaenelle Saetien would have to pay?"

"The Prince's daughter won't be the only one who has to pay."

"No," Karla said regretfully. "She won't."

# FORTY-NINE

Daemon prowled the sitting room across from Witch's suite at the Keep while his Queen and Karla stood side by side and watched him pace back and forth, back and forth.

"Not a school, as such," he growled. "Zhara was quite specific about that, although I don't see how what she's proposing is different from a school."

"What is Zhara asking you to do?" Witch asked.

"Provide a place where the young Queens and Black Widows who are most at risk of being targeted by another coven of malice would receive an exclusive education, and where young men whose potential indicates they need a firm hand on the leash would receive the education and training they need."

"The Hall *is* a large place," Witch ventured.

"The first number that was suggested was *thirty-six girls and twenty-four boys.*" Daemon knew damn well the *Hall* could accommodate the number. That wasn't the point. "I told Zhara she was out of her mind, that I was *not* going to spend decades trying to herd sixty adolescents, with the boys thinking with their cocks and the girls thinking with whatever you think with during those years. I was *not* going to do that."

"He's more excitable than Uncle Saetan was," Karla said.

"Well, he is much younger," Witch replied.

Silence.

Then Karla asked sweetly, "So, how many are moving in with you?"

He glared at them as he glided past. They arranged their expressions to look dutifully sympathetic.

That look must have had his father bouncing off the ceilings. Assuming they used it on Saetan. And if they didn't, why use it on *him*?

Damned annoying. All of it. Especially since he had the feeling that Zhara had received a little coaching on how to corner him and get an agreement.

Karla cocked her head and lifted a hand to one ear, as if to help her hear something. "How many?"

"Thirty-six in total," Daemon grumbled. "Twenty-two girls and fourteen boys." May the Darkness have mercy on him. "Plus the instructors I'll have to hire, and the Scelties who have decided I need their help to herd the humans."

"Which you do," Karla said.

He paced. Back and forth, back and forth, back and forth. On his sixth pass, Witch said, "Have you discussed this with the staff? What did Beale say about this?"

Daemon stopped pacing and stared at her. "Oh, Beale is *thrilled*." Damn traitor. "Apparently, the Hall is considered one of the premier places where youngsters can receive training in domestic service. If your references say you were trained at SaDiablo Hall or worked at the family's town house to polish the training received elsewhere, you can find work in any aristo household in Dhemlan—or any other part of the Realm. Which is why Beale and Helene have not reduced the staff working at the Hall despite only having three family members in residence. Regrettably, Surreal and I don't provide enough for them to do in terms of personal service, so actual experience has been a bit . . . thin." That also explained why he'd seen new people working in the family wing every month. The youngsters were rotated in order to have something to do. "With thirty-six students plus instructors—"

"And Scelties," Karla added.

"—there will be plenty for maids and footmen to do. And *Mrs. Beale*! She informed me that the *main kitchen* is too far from where the young people will be residing and an auxiliary kitchen will need to be put in *at once* to her specifications. She will, of course, continue to make the meals for the family and those invited to dine at our table—she phrased it that way—but the youngsters can make do with hearty but simpler meals that the Dharo Boy and some of her other cooks-in-training can prepare after submitting those dishes for her approval."

"Who gets invited to your table?" Witch wondered.

"They've got that worked out." Daemon began pacing again. "Surreal and I will enjoy private dinners a couple of evenings each week. The rest of the time we're in residence, we'll share the table with any instructors who choose to join us, and a couple of times each week, some of the youngsters will join us to practice their social skills. And occasionally *all of them* will have their feet under the table."

Witch and Karla nodded. "That sounds reasonable," Witch said.

Daemon snorted. "Mikal has decided he's going to work for me in a revolving position. He's going to be the Scelties' teacher—reading, sums, Protocol, whatever it is he's doing. He's also going to be helping Holt with the secretarial work, specifically working with Beale on the engagement calendar to know who is dining where and when and accommodating actual guests. And he's going to work with Marcus, learning the first level of the business side of running estates or dealing with court finances, or husbanding the kind of family wealth that could buy entire villages and not feel pinched." Even though there was a firm of financial advisors who oversaw the day-to-day management of the finances that involved Dhemlan, Marcus, as his personal man of business, was thrilled to have additional help from a young member of the SaDiablo family. "I haven't been informed yet what salary I'm going to pay Mikal for the privilege of having him underfoot."

"Mikal's been underfoot for decades," Karla said, looking at Witch.

"Yes, but Daemon is finally noticing that, so it feels new."

Daemon made a rude sound.

The two Queens resumed their expressions of dutiful sympathy.

"Don't bother," he grumbled.

This wasn't what he'd planned to talk about, but he'd been ambushed by Zhara first thing that morning with her request that he use part of the Hall to provide a protected place for a few adolescent Queens and other young Blood to receive a full and proper education. She'd been politely ruthless about mentioning, more than once, how Zoey kept asking to return to the Hall because it was a safe place.

He didn't know who had let the idea slip, but by the time he sat down for the midday meal, Beale, Helene, and Mrs. Beale had everything planned for how this would work. Mikal's plan was independent of this schooling idea, but the boy had pointed out that he could explore several kinds of work and still be able to live with Tersa and the journeymaid Sceltie Black Widow, who had strong opinions, even for a Sceltie, and was devoted to looking after Tersa.

Since Surreal had agreed to rent her house in Halaway to the Hourglass as a residence for the Black Widows who were adjusting to daily life after being lost in dreams and visions for so long, and since Zoey's mother was one of the residents, having the girl living at the Hall and the mother living in the adjoining village would be a good way for them to connect again after so many years.

"We have a present for you," Witch said.

Karla called in a small packing box secured with red ribbon that ended with an elaborate Craft-shaped bow. She held it out.

He took the box and touched the bow to remove it.

The damn bow leaped like a crazed little animal, hit the carpet, and hopped across the room before it was stopped by the door.

"Hmm," Karla said.

Witch nodded. "That spell needs some adjusting."

Daemon opened the box and removed one of the two objects. Raising an eyebrow, he looked at the women.

"Stout locks," Witch said brightly.

"For your study door," Karla added. "Uncle Saetan had stout locks."

"Did they work?" Daemon asked. He didn't remember *ever* seeing multiple locks on the study door.

"When we remembered to pay attention to them," Witch said.

"Which wasn't often." Karla looked at Witch. "I think he stopped using them the third time you missed the signal that the locks were engaged and turned the study door into sawdust by channeling enough power from your Black Jewels to pass through the wood and all the shields."

Witch gave Daemon an unsure but game smile. "But the locks should work for you."

"I'm delighted," he said dryly.

He put the lock back in the box and vanished the present. He ignored the red bow that had resumed its hopping and looked like a puppy desperate to go outside.

"I'm going to my room to rest for a while." His eyes met his Queen's. "We need to talk later."

Her amusement faded. "Whenever you wish."

He returned to the Consort's suite and set the box on the desk. After removing his black jacket, he lay down on the bed and closed his eyes.

She probably thought he wanted to talk about Jaenelle Saetien. He didn't. *He* wanted to talk about Witch—and what he'd finally understood was possible for their future.

Standing beside Jillian, Lucivar studied the house and felt a weird little twinge in his chest when he accepted that this child really wasn't coming home in the foreseeable future—if ever.

"So you're looking to purchase this house?"

"Yes," Jillian said. "I've been talking to Lady Surreal about working at her sanctuary for broken girls. Since I'm close to the same age, Surreal thinks the girls would feel more comfortable talking to me about some things, and it would give me some wages while I work on my next book. And I wanted a place of my own," she finished softly. "I'm ready for a place of my own."

He remembered how it had felt to want a place of his own—and how it felt when he'd moved out of SaDiablo Hall and into the eyrie when he became the Warlord Prince of Ebon Rih. He couldn't fault her for that, but . . .

"One of the SaDiablo estates is next to the village, which is why Lady Surreal chose this location for the sanctuary," Jillian continued. "And the village isn't too big or too small. And this house has almost two acres of land. Plenty of space for me to put in a small garden and leave room for exercise and play."

"'Play' meaning a Sceltie will be living with you?" It took effort, but Lucivar kept his voice mild.

Jillian held up two fingers. "One from the Little Weeble pack and the other from Scelt. They wanted a new experience."

"Uh-huh." *Better with you than with me.*

"The owner's man of business assures me that, while some things could benefit from being updated, the house *can* be lived in right now. And I can have first consideration of the furniture the owner didn't take with her."

"Uh-huh."

"This is the price." Jillian hesitated, then thrust a folded half sheet of paper at him.

What in the name of Hell did he know about the price of houses in a Dhemlan village? He lived on a mountain in Ebon Rih, and the only time he focused on what should be considered a reasonable amount of money was when he set his children's quarterly allowances, reviewing them each year to make sure that what each child might want could be attained if spending choices were made wisely. The rest of it? The SaDiablo family's wealth was so vast, he refused to think about it.

He eyed the man of business Jillian had spoken to when she first viewed the house. The man had backed off after realizing who *he* was and what his being there with Jillian meant. Lucivar figured the price was going to be adjusted to avoid Daemon's sharp interest in this transaction. He also figured telling a young woman that the house could be lived in depended, again, on who was defining the terms.

A handful of men pulled up in a wagon, climbed down, and gave him a subtle bow.

"My witchling is interested in this house." Lucivar used Craft to make sure his voice carried to the man of business—who bleated in alarm at Lucivar's confirmation that Jillian was *his* witchling. "I'd like you, as skilled craftsmen, to go over the house and tell me what it would need to be livable."

The men eyed Jillian, gave him a long look—and nodded. He'd summoned them because they all had some connection to the vineyards, the winery, or the other pieces of this SaDiablo estate. They'd know whose standards, besides his, defined "livable."

"Don't you want to see it?" Jillian asked, sounding anxious.

"Let the men take a look on their own. Show me around the outside."

A low stone wall defined the boundaries of the property. Jillian pointed out a couple of places for gardens, both a kitchen garden and flowers. Plenty of room for sparring and for the Scelties to play.

"So what is it you're going to do at this sanctuary for broken girls?" he asked.

She met his eyes. "Teach them how to fight. Show them that, even without the power they once had, they can be strong in a different way."

Tension crackled between them.

"Anything you want to tell me?" he asked too softly.

"You taught me well. Now I want to teach them."

That didn't answer his question. Or maybe it did.

The men met them outside and gave their report. Good structure. No mold or damp. Chimneys were in good shape. Plumbing needed to be replaced from the pipes all the way up to the fixtures. And neither bathroom upstairs would comfortably accommodate an Eyrien. And the necessary on the main floor would need to be enlarged as well. Kitchen could use a new stove and cold box, new sink. Roof needed repairs in a couple of places before it started to leak. Give them the nod, they could pull in enough skilled labor to get the job done in a couple of weeks.

And every one of them, as he walked past Lucivar, mumbled that he wouldn't pay a hundred gold marks for all the furniture left in the place—just in case someone thought to sell it.

Jillian had gasped when they'd told her what the work would cost.

Once the men had climbed into the wagon and headed back to their day's work, Lucivar looked at the man of business and said, "Stay there." Then he led Jillian into the house to have a look around.

"There's no point," she said, sounding disappointed. "I've saved up some money, but nowhere near enough to pay for the house by itself. I certainly can't pay for the house and all these repairs."

"What were you going to do?"

She made a face. "Get a loan. Somehow."

"No." He wandered from room to room. Big enough for an Eyrien to live in comfortably. The men were right about the furniture. Most of it that had been left was barely worth the effort to turn it into kindling. "There's no need for you to take out a loan. I established accounts for all my children a long time ago. You would have had access to the money in a few years, anyway, and this is a good reason to let you use it now. The interest, at least."

"I have money?" Jillian frowned at him. "Enough to buy the house and make the repairs?"

He shrugged. "You'll have to talk to Daemon. He's been handling that for me. He won't let you touch the principal, so if the interest that has accumulated isn't enough for what you need, you'll have to talk to him about a loan." He'd be the one to fund it—quietly—but when it came to money and family, everyone talked to Daemon.

He looked at her. Nerves and excitement filled her gold eyes. "You sure about this, witchling?"

She nodded and gave him a brilliant smile. "The next adventure."

Lucivar tipped his head toward the man of business, who was still hovering nearby. "Then let's talk to him about what the house is really worth."

A quiet knock on the door between his bedroom and Witch's.

Daemon slipped back into his black jacket and said, "Come in."

The door opened and Witch walked into the room. *His* room. He allowed himself a moment to feel the bloom of possessive desire before he smothered it. Not here. Not yet.

In all the centuries since she'd healed his mind for the third time and made her bargain with him to help him remain sane and whole, she had never worn the illusion of clothing. She was Witch, and not all the dreamers had been human. The only times she'd made an exception to that was when Daemonar was present.

Now she stood before him in that same simple dress that left her arms bare and came to midthigh, but instead of the sapphire blue she usually wore when the boy was around, this dress was a shimmering black.

"Prince," Witch said.

He bowed. "Lady."

She looked troubled. Weary in mind and heart. "Daemon . . ."

He stepped up to her and raised his hands to rest just above her shoulders. If he tried to touch her right now, his hands would go through this shadow of her Self. "Take me to the Misty Place."

"What needs to be said can be said here."

"No, it can't." He leaned forward, letting his sexual heat uncoil as his lips almost brushed her delicately pointed ear, and whispered, "Take me to the Misty Place. Please."

A moment of brutal cold.

Daemon raised his head. Mist and stone. And a cavern that contained a spiraling web that still held so much power, it could engulf all the Blood.

He lowered his hands to his sides but didn't put any distance between himself and the Queen who was his life. Had always been his life. "I figured it out. It took me long enough, in part because I accepted at face value Daemonar's grumbles about not being able to hug you. Maybe some part of me knew that you needed me to accept instead of question. But the shadow cats changed that."

"You're not making sense," Witch said.

She sounded wary. She knew him better than anyone else ever could or would, so she had reason to be wary.

"There are different levels of these illusions you call shadows. The simplest are nothing more than a place marker—a stationary illusion that can fool the eye for a short time. Up a few levels from that is this kind of shadow." He nodded toward her. "Connected to the person who made it, this shadow is a shell for the mind and can move around. It can touch but it can't be touched. Useful when a person has to walk into a dangerous situation. Then there are the shadows that can touch—and be touched. Shadows that feel like a real animal—or a real person." He hesitated. "A shadow that could feel pleasure from a lover's touch."

She leaped out of his reach.

He nodded. Her response confirmed what he'd suspected. "The girls who were at the house party didn't want to let go of the shadow cats—hadn't even realized they *were* shadows—because they were big and furry, and hugging them made the girls feel safe. You taught me how to make a shadow that intricate so that the cats would be available if I needed them to protect the Hall. That exquisite piece of Craft takes a lot of power, especially if it needs to continue for several hours. You taught me because it was another safe way to drain some of the reservoir in my Black Jewel."

"Don't," she warned when he took a step toward her.

"When we made our bargain all those years ago, you told me I had to stay connected to the living. You told me to do what I could to fix my marriage. I did that, as much as I could. Surreal enjoys being my second-in-command and she enjoys my skills as a lover most of the time. I'm not the husband she imagined I would be, and she can't be a wife to all of who, and what, I am. But for the sake of the Realm, she'll stay married to me in order to be my sword and shield against unwanted female attention, and I'll stay with her because I'm grateful for her companionship." He gave her a moment to absorb what he'd said. "You warned me that I had done some damage to my heart and lungs by trying to leash what I am so tightly I almost destroyed myself. Do you remember that?"

She nodded slowly and watched him.

"You're not the only one who can spin a tangled web of dreams and visions," he said quietly. "I spun one a while back. Instead of showing me the answer to the question I had about a heart wound, the web showed me the end of my time among the living. It will come swiftly, with little warning—and I will not be an old man when my heart takes its last beat and my lungs draw their last breath. That much I know."

"Daemon . . ." She grabbed one arm, touched his face with her other hand.

"No." He covered her hand with his—and felt the truth. "You're not going to fix this. I will experience the physical death and make the transition to demon-dead. I will do as my father had done and continue to rule Dhemlan until there is someone who can succeed me. After that, I'll continue to look after the SaDiablo properties and wealth, and

I will rule Hell as its High Lord." He saw concern in her eyes. He saw sorrow. He also saw what he wanted—needed—to see. "I won't abandon Lucivar. I promise you, I won't do that. But I need a promise in return."

He lifted her hand from his face and pressed a kiss into her palm. She made a startled sound when she realized he had *felt* her palm.

"The first time I saw the Misty Place, the first time I saw you as Witch, as the dreams beneath the flesh, I could touch you. Hand to hand. I'd forgotten that. But I've had time to think about it, Jaenelle. I've had time to think about why you deliberately made a shadow that I couldn't touch."

"You needed to stay among the living," Witch said. "You needed to have a lover who was among the living. If not Surreal, then someone else."

"I couldn't have continued to be her lover if I'd known I could be yours again, even in a limited way. But my physical death will change everything. Even if she chooses to remain my second-in-command, Surreal will no longer feel obliged to be my wife. She'll be free to find a man who will adore her and whom she can love without fear." He rested his fingers lightly on her shoulders, thrilled to feel her skin. "It takes a lot of power to maintain a shadow that can pass as a living being, but you have plenty of power and could touch the world again, more than you're doing now. Could be held again."

"What, exactly, do you want, Daemon?"

"To be with you after I make the transition to demon-dead. To be your lover again. The body is not the only way to give pleasure, Lady. And in this place, where we are both Selves without flesh, there is no reason why we can't *feel.*"

Witch gave him a sharp yet sad smile. "Should I make that promise by swearing on my life?"

Daemon shook his head. "You don't value your own life enough. Make that promise by swearing on *my* life. Promise me that you will inhabit a shadow that is as tangible as my demon-dead body—or promise that you will burn out my power and send me to the final death. I don't want to be without you, Jaenelle. Not again."

Witch stared at him. Stared and stared. Finally she said, "The body that you knew and pleasured is gone. I will still look like this."

"I know."

She sighed. "I give you my word, and swear it on your life. But you will do everything you can not to hurry that day."

"Agreed." Taking her face in his hands, he kissed her. Slow. Deep. Another promise made to both of them. He stepped back because he needed to keep a promise to another woman for a while longer. He slipped his hands in his trouser pockets. "I won't make things difficult for you, but I'd like you to consider using that other shadow now. Daemonar may not have told you how he came by those injuries, but he stepped onto his first killing field when he came to the Hall to defend Titian and the other girls. That first time? A Warlord Prince truly begins to understand what he is—and why he'll be feared. It would help the boy to be able to hug his auntie J."

"I'm not sure I want to be that tangible until the colors on the shield protecting his arm have faded," she said dryly.

Daemon laughed. "You have a point. He is a bit exercised about that."

A moment of biting cold and they were back in his bedroom, facing each other.

"Tell Lucivar," Jaenelle said. "Even if the day you saw in the vision is still centuries away, tell your brother."

"I'll talk to him before I go back to the Hall and settle the rest of what is owed."

She walked back to her bedroom and closed the door.

Daemon turned and looked out the window. He'd waited seventeen hundred years for her the first time. He could wait a few more centuries to be with her again. In the meantime, he would do his best to take care of the living.

*Prick?* he called on an Ebon-gray thread.

*Bastard?*

*Do you have time to talk today?*

A sudden wariness, almost as if Lucivar had been expecting this request. *Sure. Now?*

*I'll meet you in one of the Keep's sitting rooms. You'll know which one.*

Daemon left the Queen's part of the Keep. After tracking down Draca and making a request for refreshments when Lucivar arrived and indicating the preferred room, he went to that room, then called in the latest letters Holt had shoved at him as he walked out of the Hall that afternoon. He flipped through the letters and pulled out one he hadn't expected.

Before he read the next round of concerns from the Province and District Queens, he would find out what Lucivar had needed to put in a letter.

"Are you sure?" Lucivar demanded. He'd thought that Daemon wanted to talk about the letter and his decision, not about *this*.

"I'm sure," Daemon replied.

"A Healer confirmed it?"

Exasperated, Daemon raked his fingers through his hair. "How can a Healer confirm it? I damaged my heart and lungs centuries ago and—"

Lucivar grabbed his brother, swung him around, and slammed Daemon's back against the wall.

"You've known for centuries?" he shouted. "*Centuries?* And you didn't tell me?"

"What was I supposed to tell you?" Daemon shouted back. "That I might only live another five or six centuries instead of twenty? Hell's fire, Lucivar. There's nothing yet for a Healer to detect, let alone heal. Which isn't possible, so stop snarling at me."

"Then how do you know?"

"Jaenelle told me," Daemon said quietly. "When she

healed the damage I'd done by trying to suppress the sexual heat too much. She told me then."

"And when did you find out that you were going to die young?" Lucivar gave Daemon a shake that thumped him against the wall again. *"When?"*

"I'm not going to die young. I'm past the age where someone could say I died *young.* I just won't be old." Daemon sighed. "I spun a tangled web after Daemonar conveyed Tersa's warning to me. The web didn't show me what I expected, but it made other things clear."

Lucivar relaxed his hold but didn't release Daemon.

"I won't leave you, Prick. 'Demon-dead' just means we don't meet in daylight. I'll still take care of the family wealth, and we'll still stand together and do whatever needs to be done for the family and for Kaeleer."

Lucivar felt his own heart returning to a less frantic beat. "Death ends your marriage to Surreal."

"It does."

"And Jaenelle?" It took him a moment to understand the look in Daemon's eyes. "There is a way for you and Witch to . . . ?"

"There's a way," Daemon confirmed. "But not until I'm no longer among the living."

Lucivar closed his eyes and rested his forehead against Daemon's. *I won't lose him. Not completely.*

"I love you," Daemon said softly.

"I love you too." He put his arms around his brother and held on for a long moment. Then he eased back and gave Daemon a lazy, arrogant smile. "But if you're going to be with my sister again, there is something you're going to do."

# FIFTY

Jaenelle Saetien closed the book she'd been trying to read and dropped it on the sofa.

Two days ago, the shields that kept her confined to her room had been extended to allow her to walk around the interior courtyard. Since each of those courtyards provided a private outdoor space, this one was for the immediate family. Her father and . . .

*"Well done! Fatal blow to the heart. How does it feel to make your first kill?"*

. . . Lady Surreal had suites on the opposite side from hers, an arrangement that blended privacy and closeness. Uncle Lucivar and Aunt Marian had a suite on another side of the square, and Daemonar and Andulvar were on the opposite side from them.

Titian's suite had been next to hers. It had been easy to slip into each other's rooms and talk and giggle half the night until one of their fathers showed up and tapped on the balcony doors—the signal that it was time to get some sleep.

She'd written to Titian to apologize for what happened at the house party, but Papa had looked sad when the letter had been returned, unopened. He'd looked sad when he'd told her that Titian didn't want to talk to her or receive any letters, didn't want to see her for a while. He'd looked sad when he'd told her that Uncle Lucivar had banned her from all of Askavi for two years, which meant she couldn't go to Ebon Rih to visit Daemonar either.

How could she have known there would be so many consequences to having a house party?

*"Maybe it's more accurate to say that, before your Birthright Ceremony, you were who I might have been if I'd had your childhood instead of mine."*

No, it hadn't been the house party by itself. All of this was happening because she didn't stand up for what she knew was right, didn't honor the promises she'd made to her father and to Beale. Now the penalties for the bad choices she had made continued to pile up, even though everyone had been told the debt had been paid in full.

Kick a pebble, start an avalanche. Uncle Lucivar was fond of that saying. Now she finally understood what it meant.

A knock on the door before Mikal walked in.

Jaenelle Saetien smiled, grateful to have someone to talk to—and then worried about what sort of trouble Mikal might get into for being there.

"Do you have my father's permission to be here?" she asked.

"Yeah, we do," he replied, smiling as he opened his coat.

*Saeti!* Shelby squirmed in Mikal's arms, trying to get down and reach her. *My Saeti!*

Mikal shrugged and set the puppy on the floor. Shelby raced over to her and tried to jump up on the sofa. She caught him before his failed jump ended with him hitting the table and getting hurt.

"Hello, Shelby," she cooed. "How's my boy?"

"He's missed you," Mikal said. "I brought Breen up to be with Uncle Daemon, and it was time for Shelby to be with you." He smiled. "But Helene said that if you ignore him in the middle of the night when he has to go out, you have to clean up the mess."

That explained why she'd been given access to the interior courtyard. She would need to take Shelby outside.

While Shelby settled himself in her lap, Mikal called in the puppy's things—a bed, toys, and treats—and used Craft to set them against one wall. *Make sure you keep those treats shielded,* he warned.

*All right.* She didn't want to admit that she was having trouble with Craft. Purple Dusk had been part of the power that had made up her Twilight's Dawn Jewel, but plain Purple Dusk didn't feel the same, and her ability to do even simple things didn't always work anymore.

Since she was pretty sure Shelby hadn't learned how to air walk yet, she'd just put the treats on a high shelf for now.

"I have to go," Mikal said. "The Scelties are arriving in a couple of days, and I have to help Beale, Helene, and Uncle Daemon work out where their suite will be located."

"They're getting a suite?"

"Yep." He grinned. "Complete with comfy furniture and a human bed for them to sleep on. I'm not sure what else was on their list of requirements, but since I'm going to be in charge of the Sceltie school here at the Hall, I'm about to find out." The grin faded. "You need anything?"

She shook her head. "Thanks for asking."

She thought he was going to say something else, but he smiled and walked out of the room.

A moment later, the Gray lock on the door was back in place.

Having something new to do, she was about to tell Shelby they were going outside to explore the courtyard, but the puppy was asleep in her lap.

Sighing, Jaenelle Saetien carefully retrieved her book and read until her little Brother woke up.

Momentarily speechless, Daemon stared at Jillian. Lucivar had told him the girl needed to see him but not why, so he'd been expecting her. But . . .

Jillian raised her eyebrows. "It's hair. It's short."

It was still black. Thank the Darkness for that. But the

spiky style was just like . . . "If you say 'kiss kiss,' I am tossing you out of my study."

Jillian laughed. "Fair enough." A flash of understanding in her eyes. "Is that why Lucivar and Daemonar got a bit exercised about my hair being short? Because it reminds them of Karla? That's actually a compliment."

"That depends on *how* you're dealing with Karla."

Her smile was a little bit wicked.

He would not whimper. "Something you wanted to discuss?"

Now she sat forward in her chair, looking a little nervous. "Surreal has that sanctuary for girls who have been broken, where they can be protected from anyone who might want to do them more harm and where they can learn how to use what power they have left—and how to do things physically that they used to do with Craft. I'm going to work there as an informal counselor, and also teach the girls how to fight and defend themselves. It's important to know that losing one part of yourself doesn't mean you have to lose everything. You're different afterward, and you need to learn to be who you are now. You need to fight instead of accepting."

She wasn't talking about herself. A delicate psychic probe confirmed that her power wasn't diminished in any way. But someone had given up. "Did the person who . . . surrendered . . . to the pain end up in the Dark Realm?" he asked gently.

"If she did?" Prickly response.

"I'll find her and do what I can to help."

She looked at him a long time, no longer the nervous young woman who walked into his study but a fighter. No wonder Surreal had hired her. She probably recognized a bit of herself at that age.

Jillian gave him three female names. And then she gave him four more—and his temper turned cold when he realized what those four male names meant. "Was that your first killing field?" he asked too softly.

She swallowed hard. "Yes."

"Did you tell Lucivar?"

"No."

"I'll give you two days. If you don't tell Lucivar, I will. You're not a Warlord Prince, Jillian. You don't walk off a killing field and just swallow the feelings. Even we don't do that the first time. I'm one of four Warlord Princes you can talk to who will understand how it felt and why you chose to step onto that field. Talk to one of us."

"Four?"

"Daemonar stepped onto his first killing field recently."

"Mother Night," she whispered.

"And may the Darkness be merciful." She looked distressed, ready to bolt, so he changed the subject. "You're going to work at the sanctuary and . . . ?"

Strong relief washed through the room. "I want to buy a house. It has enough room for me and the two Scelties who are going to live with me, and it has four bedrooms, so I can have guests."

"What kind of guests?" he asked sweetly.

"Not the kind that would put *that* look in your eyes. I was thinking more of friends from Little Weeble who might want to venture beyond their village or having Andulvar stay over for a couple of days. It must be hard for him to be considered too young to have adventures away from home, and this way . . ."

"Still with family but able to feel independent?"

"Yes." Her smile regained some of its brightness, but the nerves were back. "I talked to the owner's man of business on my own when I first saw the place, but Lucivar came with me the second time, and he had all these men from the SaDiablo estate come and inspect the house, and they came up with this list of things that would need to be done even though the man of business said the house could be lived in now."

Daemon kept his expression interested and encouraging— and said nothing about Lucivar being the one who held the deed to that particular SaDiablo estate. Jillian would figure that out soon enough when people from the estate began offering their time and skills to her because she was part of Lucivar's family.

"Anyway," Jillian continued, "I was going to try to take out a loan to pay for the house, but Lucivar said I should talk to you about having some of the interest released on the money he had set aside for me."

She looked baffled that there was money she hadn't known about, that Lucivar would have done that. Thinking of her as a daughter was one thing. Setting aside some of the family wealth said *daughter* in a different way. At least Jillian seemed to think so.

"Maybe the interest would offset the costs enough that I wouldn't have to take out that much of a loan?" she said hopefully.

Probably just as well that Jillian didn't know how much was in the account.

Daemon removed a sheet of paper from a tray on his desk and uncapped a pen. "Do you have any figures?"

Jillian called in a sheet of paper and used Craft to float it to the desk.

Daemon raised an eyebrow. "The man of business claimed the house was livable, and this is what the skilled craftsmen told you and Lucivar would be required to *make* it livable?"

"Livable by SaDiablo standards," Jillian said. "The asking price *was* reduced by the cost of the repairs."

Someone had thought they were dealing with a young woman excited about purchasing her first house and gullible enough to be persuaded to accept the asking price on a building that needed that much work. Someone had been smart enough to realize how pissed off Lucivar would be if—or when—he found out Jillian had been cheated. Which meant the girl really wasn't paying more than house and land were worth.

"There's no problem with providing you with the funds to pay for the house and the repairs," Daemon said. "However, before you sign the contract and hand over so much as a silver mark, Lord Marcus will read over the contract and answer any questions you may have about the language of a formal agreement, and he and I will be there to witness the signing." And that would guarantee that nothing was slipped into the agreement that would oblige Jillian to pay other costs.

"Okay," she said hesitantly.

He began making a list of expenses. "That takes care of the purchase of the house and repairs. What about your living expenses? Will you be making enough at the sanctuary to pay most or all of your bills? What about the income from your book?"

She laughed so hard, she had to catch herself before she fell out of the chair. When he just watched her, waiting, she settled herself and cleared her throat. "The people who work for you aren't fools, Prince. Yes, I stacked the odds in my favor by submitting my book to your publishing house . . ."

"And yet I still haven't read your book." His voice was less purr and more rumble of annoyance.

"Well, of course," she replied as if it should be obvious. "There is some envy among other writers who haven't been accepted, but I can look every single one of them in the eyes and say that you haven't seen the book yet, so publishing it wasn't your decision. Or done at your command."

It still rankled that he hadn't been allowed to help, at least not directly, but he understood her point. He'd just have to make sure she understood *his* point about this other bit of finance.

"And since your editor has to justify expenses to Lord Marcus *and* to you," Jillian continued, "she didn't offer one copper more than she would have offered any other writer for a first book. Which is one reason I needed to find work while I wrote the next book."

It made sense. All of it. And that was the most annoying part of all.

He continued making a list of expenses. "You'll have to pay the tithe each season like everyone else in the village."

"Tithe?" Jillian's voice faded a bit.

Obviously she hadn't equated owning property with needing to pay the tithe owed to the District Queen. Just as obvious, the man of business had neglected to mention the tithe and what she would be expected to pay each season.

He was definitely reading over that contract before he allowed her to sign it.

"You'll also need to figure on food for you and the Scelties, clothing, personal items," he continued.

She hesitated. "I do have some savings."

"Which you will not touch," he said crisply. "At least, not for these expenses."

He had a good idea of what the tithe would be and took a reasonable guess at what the rest would cost a young woman. He wrote in the numbers, tallied it per season, added a bit for unexpected expenses and household goods she would need to purchase, then handed it to her—and watched the color drain from her face as she realized the difference between her wages and her expenses as a property owner.

Then she noticed the final figure and looked at him.

"I will not release any of the principal. What you will receive each quarter is no different from what you would have started to receive a few years from now. The amount I've listed will help you pay the village tithe and your living expenses. You will do me and Lucivar the favor of not skimping on essentials. We are the wealthiest family in the Realm, and there are some things that will be done to help you get settled in a new home."

"Thank you." She took a deep breath and let it out slowly. "If I need advice about finances?"

"All you have to do is ask." Daemon smiled. "Well, I should get to these reports before Holt comes in and scolds me."

"There's something else." Not quite warrior, not quite young woman taking another leap into unknown territory.

He sat back.

"I heard about the . . . accommodation . . . you're mak-

ing to educate a select group of Queens and other youngsters."

"Beale assures me I can hide in his butler's pantry if I
feel the need to whimper. And I've been given extra-stout
locks for my study door."

"Have you told Jaenelle Saetien that she has to leave the
Hall as part of the price your family has to pay for her actions?"

He closed his eyes against the pain. "Not yet. Later today. The other children will be arriving in a couple of
days, and she needs to be gone by then."

"Where?" Jillian asked softly.

"I don't know. She can't stay at the town house. She's
been banned from entering Amdarh for two years. She's
also been banned from Askavi for two years. I guess she'll
stay at one of the family estates."

"Send her to the sanctuary," Jillian said. "Surreal will
have to give her approval, of course, since she set up the
place, but even though Jaenelle Saetien still wears a Jewel,
I'm betting she has to learn Craft all over again, just like
the other girls."

"Some of those girls are there because they were
harmed by the coven of malice."

Jillian nodded. "But the Scelties who are going to be
there will look after her, if for no other reason than to protect the puppy who is her special friend."

Was Jillian really the person making this suggestion, or
was she the messenger for a spiky-haired Black Widow
Queen?

"And I think Zoey and Titian and the friends who were
at the house party should be assigned rooms in the square
of suites that belonged to the Dark Court. Certain suites
will be out-of-bounds, of course, but . . ."

He stared at her. "You want young women to have
rooms across from the rooms I reside in when I need to
relinquish control and am too dangerous to be around anyone?"

She nodded again. "They are safe *because* you are dangerous, in the same way Jaenelle's coven was safe because Saetan was dangerous."

Jillian was a messenger. But so was Karla, who must have coached the girl in what to say.

*My Lady, your will is my life.*

"The suites that will be out-of-bounds," he said. "Those would be the Queen's and Consort's suites?" He couldn't tolerate anyone residing in the room that had belonged to Jaenelle Angelline. "And the suites that were set aside for Lady Karla and Prince Chaosti because they may start visiting again?"

"Yes." She looked relieved. Message delivered and understood.

Daemon eyed Jillian's spiky black hair and nodded. "You may say it. *Once.*"

Jillian gave him a brilliant smile. "Kiss kiss."

Surreal studied Daemon, who stood behind his desk, his hands tucked into his trouser pockets. The question of what to do with Jaenelle Saetien had been tearing at him from the moment he'd accepted that he'd have to send his daughter away—alone. His duty to the people of Dhemlan would keep him at the Hall much of the time because the point of all these young Queens taking up residence here was to have *him* here as well.

The girl couldn't live with Manny in the village— assuming Manny would agree to it—because the Province Queens didn't want Jaenelle Saetien to have contact with the girls who had been threatened at the house party. At least, not for a couple of years.

Being from long-lived races, the Queens—and Lucivar, too—could have banned the girl from entering specific places for two decades or two centuries. The two-year bans were a concession made for Daemon's sake, not for Jaenelle Saetien's. But this?

*Not his idea,* Surreal thought, *but a possibility that gave him hope.*

As she'd helped coordinate the arrangements for the girls who would be arriving, she'd seen the speculation in the eyes of the Province Queens and District Queens. The Queen of Ebon Askavi had returned—and everyone knew that whatever remained of Witch wouldn't have made her presence known, wouldn't have called in the debts owed by the coven of malice and personally extracted the payments for anyone but Daemon Sadi. And if the Queen had returned to *that* extent . . .

Surreal set those thoughts aside for the moment. "Does Witch know that some of the girls at the sanctuary are there because of the coven of malice and the males who ran with those bitches?"

Daemon flinched, since Jaenelle Saetien had been considered one of those bitches. "She knows," he said quietly. "I think that's why she suggested it."

"We both know a suggestion from Witch is tantamount to an order from any other Queen." She blew out a breath. "The other girls may not accept her, Sadi. If they don't, could she stay at the family estate near the village?"

"Only if Lucivar gives his consent, which is doubtful."

*Jaenelle, are you sure Jaenelle Saetien will be safe at the sanctuary? She may have rejected me as her mother, but I still care about her.*

She didn't have to wonder. She could go to the Keep and ask. Or she could trust the Queen who had been her friend—and still was. "All right. We need to have this done before the other girls arrive. Are you going to come with us as far as the estate? It would be better if you didn't come to the sanctuary." If Jaenelle Saetien was going to have any chance of being seen as just another girl who needed to repair her life, she didn't need anyone realizing that she was the High Lord's daughter. At least, not at first.

"I'd like that." He started to move around the desk. "Surreal . . ."

She raised a hand to stop him. "Ever since that black-bordered warning was presented to all the Dhemlan Queens—and let's not pretend it was anything less than Witch showing her claws and announcing that she had returned—I've been thinking about where that leaves you and me."

"It doesn't have to change anything between us."

He stood so quiet, so still.

"Mind and heart, you're Witch's husband. You always were. Am I correct in assuming that you can't be Witch's lover?"

"Not while I still walk among the living."

*"Sadi."*

He huffed out a breath. "You don't need to worry. I won't hurry that day."

"If you did, Witch would kick whatever was left of your ass."

Daemon laughed. "And Lucivar would stomp on whatever was left after that." Then he sobered. "But that day is on the horizon. Still distant, but it's there."

Mother Night.

"The Queen has no objections to me being your lover?"

"She has no objections. She expects me to honor my commitment to you."

"What about you? Can you accept having a lover?" She and Daemon didn't spend much time together, but he still needed the occasional relief of having sex and, more important, he needed someone physical to hold. So did she.

"I can accept it," he said quietly. A pause. "What do you want for yourself, Surreal?"

"I want to be who I am—a hunter who won't allow the debt owed a broken girl to go unpaid. Beyond that?" She shrugged. Then she smiled. "I don't think Jaenelle Angelline came back just for your sake."

Daemon put his arms around her. Held her as a friend and lover.

She eased back. "We'll get Jaenelle Saetien settled at the sanctuary tomorrow."

He gave her a gentle kiss, more friend than lover. "To-morrow."

Daemon sat behind his desk, a hard reminder to himself that it wasn't Jaenelle Saetien's father who had to hand down this decision but the Warlord Prince of Dhemlan—and the High Lord of Hell.

"Why do I have to leave?" His daughter's eyes were bright with tears—and shadowed with fear.

"It's part of the price for your involvement in the coven of malice," he explained again. "I'm sorry, Jaenelle Saetien, but it has to be this way."

"Couldn't I live in the village?"

"No," he said gently. "You've been banned from Amdarh and Askavi, so you can't live in those places either." His heart hurt, but he couldn't see any other way to help her now. "You'll be going to the sanctuary that Surreal created for girls who have been broken. It will be a good place for you to learn how to use the Purple Dusk Jewel. And Jillian is going to be working there, so you won't be all alone."

He'd been ignoring the scratching on the wood and the yips that had followed when he hadn't obligingly obeyed the demand to open the door. Now the yips became howls and the scratching became determined. To spare the door being refinished—again—Daemon used Craft to open the study door for Shelby.

The puppy raced across the room, then scratched at Jaenelle Saetien's legs until she picked him up.

*My Saeti,* Shelby announced.

"There will be other Scelties there who will help Shelby learn his own lessons," Daemon said.

Jaenelle Saetien cuddled the puppy. "Why did you name me after the Queen?" The question burst out of her, as if the need to ask had been building for days.

"I didn't choose your name." He sighed. "Surreal didn't have an easy time giving birth to you, and once you arrived, her need to keep you safe made her dangerous to everyone else for a little while. When she was rational again, she said she wanted to name you Jaenelle Saetien to honor two people we both loved. I agreed."

She wouldn't look at him. "So you wouldn't be angry if I changed my name so that people wouldn't compare me to the Queen?"

"No, I wouldn't be angry. My father gave me his name—Saetan Daemon SaDiablo—but Manny called me Daemon because, so she said, she wasn't about to stand at the back door and yell for Saetan to come wash up for dinner."

Jaenelle Saetien smiled.

*Saeti,* Shelby said. *My Saeti.*

Daemon raised an eyebrow.

"That's my Sceltie name," she mumbled.

"Easy enough to be Saetien for the humans. That would explain Shelby's choice of name. You could do what your grandfather did and use your initials to sign legal papers and be Saetien SaDiablo going forward."

"Saetien," she said softly, nodding. "Saetien." A hesitation. "Can I write to you?"

It took everything in him not to burden her with his own feelings of loss. "I'd like that."

"Would you write to me?"

"Yes." He would purchase a decorative seal that would only be used for her—a special communication between the two of them. "We'll leave tomorrow. A couple of the maids will help you pack."

When he stood, she grabbed the puppy and bolted for the door. Then she stopped and looked at him. "I understand some things now, and I'm sorry for all the trouble I've caused." She fumbled the door open and whispered, "Good-bye, Papa."

"Good-bye, witch-child."

Alone, Daemon locked the door. Then, finally, he allowed himself to feel the pain of letting her go this way—and felt his heart break.

# FIFTY-ONE

—————⊹—————

As the horse-drawn carriage took them from the Sa-Diablo estate to the sanctuary, Surreal wasn't sure what to say to someone who had come from her body and then had become the enemy. She didn't know what to say to this girl who had been protected her whole life and now was about to live among the broken.

*There is no cure for Briarwood. But you learn to live with the scars.*

Knowing that Witch had suggested the sanctuary as the place for Jaenelle Saetien, Surreal wondered what other price the girl still had to pay.

No, not Jaenelle Saetien. Just Saetien now.

"Jillian is going to be working at the home," she finally said. "If you run into trouble, you can ask her for help."

"All right." Saetien caught her lower lip between her teeth. "Is this like Briarwood?"

"No," Surreal replied sharply. She looked out the window. She supposed it was a reasonable question, but even the thought that one place might be mistaken for the other made her ill. "It's more like the school in Amdarh, only smaller." And more exclusive, considering who lived there.

The administrator, housekeeper, and Healer who ran the place came out to greet them. So did Jillian.

The pack of Scelties now in residence must have been

herding some other unfortunates who required their help. Thank the Darkness for that.

"This is Lady Saetien," Surreal said. "And this is Lord Shelby."

The women eyed the Purple Dusk Jewel and the girl's delicately pointed ears. Whatever conclusions the women made about why a girl who still wore a Jewel was being sheltered there went unspoken. This wasn't the first time Surreal had brought a girl to the sanctuary, and it wouldn't be the last.

"Why don't I take the luggage and show Lady Saetien to her room?" Jillian said. "Then I can show her around and help her collect the books and supplies for her classes."

"Thank you," Surreal said. She waited until the two girls went into the building, then turned to the women. "Questions?"

"Are you sure about her being here?" the administrator asked.

"No," she replied. "But the Queen of Ebon Askavi is sure, and that's all the young Lady's father and I need to know."

After promising to return in a week to review the women's observations about all the girls, Surreal returned to the family estate just long enough to collect her belongings. Then she caught the Gray Wind and headed for Dea al Mon to spend a couple of days with her mother's people. Among the Children of the Wood, she wasn't Sadi's wife or his second-in-command. She was the daughter of a young Black Widow Queen who had been taken from her people and broken by a Hayllian Warlord. She was Surreal, a hunter who was very good with a knife—and whose prey usually walked on two legs.

She spent the day wandering the land her mother had walked and thought about who she had been and who she was now—and who she might want to be.

Late that night, she brought two mugs of coffee to a tree she had chosen that afternoon for no particular reason. One mug held black coffee; the other held coffee mixed with a precise amount of sugar and cream. Holding out that mug, she said, "I brought coffee."

A biting cold. Mist and stone. And the living myth, the girl who had first shown her the pretty poison and then, later, become a great Queen despite her scars. Or, maybe, because of those scars.

"Saetien being at the sanctuary," she said. "Is that part of her price to pay?"

"It is," Witch said, accepting the coffee. "She needs to see what someone like Delora can do when there is no one to stop her. She needs to see that before you tell her about the maternal side of her bloodline."

"Tell her what?"

"That she's Dorothea's great-granddaughter. That Dorothea's son was your sire. That she is descended from one of Hayll's Hundred Families." Witch smiled. "That you took SaDiablo as your family name as a way to spit in Dorothea's eye."

"How was I supposed to know that the patriarch of the family was living in Dhemlan?" Surreal grumbled. Saetan's acceptance when she arrived in Kaeleer changed her life.

"This interest in Hayll has stirred up memories, and for the people who fled Terreille, most of those memories are painful. Don't let your daughter find out from someone else."

"You think some of the aristos will say Saetien was infatuated with Delora because she can trace her bloodline to Dorothea?"

"Better for both of you if she has an answer to that before the question is raised."

"My connection to Dorothea never bothered you, did it?"

"Why should it? You're Titian's daughter. You were always Dea al Mon. Kin of my kin."

"And that makes us kin." Surreal blinked away sentimental tears. Then she hooked her hair behind one delicately pointed ear. "I'm going to look for a place of my own. Something that doesn't belong to the SaDiablo family. I thought about living in Dea al Mon, but living among trees for more than a couple of days makes me itch. Besides, I like cities. Or maybe I could buy a cottage in a village like Halaway where I could walk to the shops but also have a choice of dining houses if I wanted to eat out."

"A first step in separating your life from Daemon's?" Witch asked.

Surreal hesitated. Then she nodded. "A life apart yet still connected to him and the rest of the family. I had that once, during the years I lived with Rainier, and I can have it again because a Warlord Prince belongs to his Queen before he belongs to anyone else, and Daemon Sadi's Queen is once more in residence at Ebon Askavi." She raised her mug in a salute. "Thank you for coming back to save all of us." *And for setting me free of a choice I made so many years ago.*

Witch smiled, handed the mug back, and disappeared.

Biting cold. Then Surreal felt the tree's bark against her back. Wiping a tear off her cheek, she walked back to the Dea al Mon equivalent of an inn.

# FIFTY-TWO

Y ou all right, witchling?" Lucivar asked.
"Uh-huh." In truth, even though she knew Jaenelle Saetien wasn't going to be there, Titian felt sick and
excited about being back at the Hall. She linked her arm
with her father's left arm, leaving his right hand free in
case he needed to call in his war blade. Not that she expected he would need to, but there were girls and boys
standing outside the Hall that she didn't know, and the unknown could be dangerous. Deadly.

Then she spotted Lord Weston, and excitement won out
over sickness. Zoey *had* come.

She pulled her father along as she wove through the
youngsters who were hesitating to approach the door, unsure, now that they were here, about the wisdom of this
choice. Then she caught sight of Zoey and stopped abruptly
as she noticed the face that looked drawn from the loss of
too much weight and the smudges under Zoey's eyes that
looked more like awful bruises.

"You look like shit, witchling," Lucivar said, eyeing
Zoey. Then he focused on the Sceltie pressed against Zoey's legs. "You need to persuade her to eat and do walkies."

*I am *trying*,* Allis complained. *But she is stubborn,
and I am not allowed to nip.*

"Says who?" Lucivar asked.

Lord Weston made an angry sound of warning.

"You have my permission to nip—"

"Hey!" Zoey protested.

"—and if Prince Sadi has a problem with that, he can talk to me." He gave Zoey, then Weston, a lazy, arrogant smile.

The door opened. Beale looked at them, then beyond them to the youngsters milling around the landing web.

"I'll fix it," Lucivar said. He untangled his arm from Titian's, then grabbed both girls by the backs of their tunics and toe-walked them across the threshold, first Zoey, then Titian. "Now, go say hello to your uncle while I deal with the rest of the youngsters."

Uncle Daemon stood in the great hall. His hands, tucked into his trouser pockets, made him look relaxed, but she saw the slightly glazed look in his eyes and realized he wasn't there to welcome them as much as he was there to inspect every person who walked through the door.

She didn't want to think about what would happen this time to anyone who didn't meet with his approval.

"Hello, Uncle Daemon."

His smile was warm when he leaned down to kiss her cheek. "I'm glad you're here. You too, Zoey."

When he gave Zoey a kiss as well, Titian wondered if he felt the flinch.

"Prince Sadi," Zoey said.

"You're safe," he said quietly. "You, Titian, and some of the other girls have been given suites that had belonged to the Queens in the Dark Court. No one can get to you without going through me—and no one will get through me, Zoey. You have my word on that."

"Thank you," Weston said quietly, coming up to stand behind Zoey as he kept an eye on the open front door.

Holt approached from the back of the great hall. "Should I show the Ladies to their suites?"

"Let's wait for a few more," Daemon replied. "Assuming they decide they're brave enough to enter."

A sharp whistle, followed by Lucivar's voice. "You can

enter the Hall on your own, or I can pick you up and toss you over the threshold. Your choice."

Weston looked alarmed. "He wouldn't do that, would he?"

"Care to bet on that?" Daemon asked dryly.

"But . . . there are Queens out there."

"That never stopped him before," Holt said. "Twenty marks says he tosses one of the Warlord Princes in first."

Daemon nodded. "I'll take that bet."

Titian stared at her uncle as if she'd never seen him before. He and Holt were *betting* on her father—

The first Warlord Prince came in low and horizontal, landing on his butt and skidding across the polished floor until he was stopped by Uncle Daemon's shoe.

"Hell's fire," Weston breathed. "He really did it."

Daemon stared at the young man for a moment before moving his shoe and allowing the Warlord Prince to stand up. Then he called in his wallet, removed a twenty-gold mark, and handed it to Holt.

Another whistle sounded outside, following by barking.

*Now they will listen,* Allis said happily.

Titian looked at her uncle, who looked back and shrugged. "It's always like this. Deal with it."

Titian had seen a sheepherding contest in Scelt once. The way the other boys and girls hurried into the great hall reminded her of that, especially when the Scelties came in behind them and fanned out to discourage any humans who might try to bolt.

Zoey snorted a laugh.

Lucivar entered the great hall. Beale shut the door. And Black-Jeweled power rolled through the Hall like soft thunder.

"Welcome to SaDiablo Hall." Uncle Daemon's voice held welcome and warning. "You're under my hand now. I strongly suggest you follow the rules."

Everyone looked at Uncle Daemon, then at her father, then at Beale, and finally at the Scelties. No matter where you turned, there would be someone nearby to make sure you followed the rules.

Titian breathed a sigh of relief.

Holt escorted the girls who were assigned to the Dark Court's square of rooms, while Helene took the other girls, and Beale escorted the boys to their assigned rooms.

On the way to their rooms, Titian brushed her hand against Zoey's and felt relief when her friend gripped her hand and held on.

"Uncle Daemon. Everyone calls him the High Lord now," she whispered.

Zoey thought for a moment and shook her head. "No, that was Prince Sadi in the great hall. I think the High Lord feels . . . different."

Different . . . and more dangerous. And that would keep them safe.

# FIFTY-THREE

---

S aetien turned toward the door of her room when Shelby made a funny sound, as if not sure if he should bark a welcome or a warning.

The girl who moved toward her had a vague look in her eyes, was partially dressed—and was holding a pair of scissors. Some of her hair had been cut close to the scalp and the rest was a tangled mess.

Saetien's breath caught as she recognized the vague look and the psychic scent of someone who had been shattered. Not just broken like the other girls she had met yesterday. This girl was a shattered chalice, a broken, mad Black Widow. Like Tersa.

*Jillian?* she called. *Jillian! I'm in my room. I need help!* Then to Shelby, *Stay on the bed and stay quiet.*

*But . . . ,* he began.

*Stay quiet.*

"Is there something I can do for you?" she asked. *Like take those scissors before you do more harm?*

"I saw you there, standing witness."

"I saw you too," Saetien said. She hadn't seen that much. She'd been too busy retching over what Krellis and Dhuran had done to this girl.

"We were in the pretty poison, where debts are paid." The girl grabbed a fistful of tangled hair and cut it off, dropping it on the floor.

"Maybe you should let someone help you with that." Saetien gestured to the scissors. "Otherwise, your hair will be uneven."

"Like the rest of me." She smiled, but the look in her eyes was strangely feral.

In order to pay her debt to Witch, she needed to become a living memento mori for seven girls who had been damaged by the coven of malice. This girl was one of them. "What's your name?"

"I am Tersa the Weaver, Tersa the Liar, Tersa the Fool." The girl cut off another hunk of hair and frowned. "No, she's the one who stopped me before I got lost following the twisting paths, told me I needed to stay close to the border, told me I needed to listen to the song in the Darkness. Have you heard it? The song is wonderful, so full of joy and pain, rage and celebration. It is beautiful and deadly, and it was the song that filled the place that was the pretty poison."

Saetien blinked back tears. "I know who you mean."

"She told me to stop doing this." The girl pushed up the baggy sleeves of a sweater she must have taken from someone else, revealing the still-healing slices in her arms.

*Jillian!* Saetien pleaded.

"She showed me how to find this place, said that parts of me could heal here." The girl stared at the scissors, then at her arm.

"Teresa," Jillian said quietly from the doorway. "What are you doing?"

It was like watching someone sort through pieces of a broken dish to find a specific part of the pattern.

*Delora did this, just like someone must have done it to Tersa,* Saetien thought.

"Krellis said my hair was beautiful," Teresa finally said, having found the answer to the question. "He said it was beautiful and made his lust burn, and that's why he . . ."

Her hands rose. Jillian rushed over and grabbed the scissors before Teresa drove the points into her own face.

Jillian vanished the scissors, then put an arm around Teresa's shoulders. "Come on," she said gently. "We'll go to your room and finish trimming your hair."

As they turned toward the door, Teresa stopped and looked back at Saetien. "Delora and Hespera didn't die."

"I think they did," Saetien replied, not sure if Teresa would find comfort in that.

"The flesh, yes, but not *them*. Not yet. They're still there, somewhere, and they'll be screaming in the dark, alone, for as long as any of us are screaming. The song carries too many memories of the ones who died in that place, and she is unforgiving because she was one of us. Rage and celebration." A tear rolled down Teresa's face. "I think I should try to be part of the celebration."

"I think she would like that," Jillian said. Then to Saetien, *Are you all right?*

Saetien nodded.

*First class starts in an hour. Eyrien sparring sticks.*

*I'll be there.*

As soon as Jillian led Teresa away and closed the door, Saetien sank on the bed and gathered Shelby in her arms.

*Saeti?* The puppy licked her chin. *She is like Tersa? We know Tersa. We can help her.*

"She needs to heal a bit before she'll be like Tersa. We need to be careful when we're around her, help her stay near the border." *And I will take the time to learn who she might have been.*

"Come on." She put Shelby on the floor, then nudged him aside when he became too interested in Teresa's hair. When her attempt to vanish it failed, she wrapped the hair in one of her towels and took it with her, stopping at the housekeeper's office to ask how to dispose of it.

Teresa wanted to be a part of the song's celebration. As Saetien walked outside to find the other Scelties and give Shelby some time to play, she wondered if she could ever pay the debt well enough to no longer be a note in the song's rage.

# FIFTY-FOUR

———◈———

Daemonar stepped into the large . . . ballroom? . . . and looked around. Either Uncle Daemon wasn't planning to do any formal entertaining for a while, or this was an auxiliary ballroom. He ran his boot over the wooden floor that was recently buffed but not polished to the equivalent of ice. He considered how the light coming in from the wall of windows could be used to teach someone to fight in sunlight or shadows. He eyed the various hooks and hangers in the walls. Bows would fit over there with quivers of arrows underneath. Eyrien sticks were already stored in that wall rack. If he asked, would Beale be able to uncover targets used for practice, tucked somewhere in the attic?

Maybe this room had been built for a kind of dance that wasn't social.

Calling in his own sparring stick, Daemonar rolled his shoulders. He still had light shields around the bones that were newly healed, but thank the Darkness, he no longer had the eye-throbbing shield Auntie J. had put around his arm. But, she had added sweetly when she removed that shield, if he didn't want to light up bright enough to wake up the folks in Halaway every time there was a twinge of pain in that bone, he would take care when he started practicing again with sticks and weapons.

He knew better than to call his auntie's bluff, so he put

a skintight shield over both forearms. Then he began to move through the warm-up while he waited to see who would show up. This was a beginner's class in fighting. Well, sparring. Fighting would come later. But this was offered to the instructors whom Uncle Daemon had hired, as well as the staff at the Hall.

He'd gone through the warm-up once when Prince Raine walked in. Not unexpected, since the instructor had been joining his little group for these exercises while they'd been at the Amdarh school.

"Sparring sticks are over there." Daemonar nodded to the stack. His father had sent twenty for the adults and boys and twenty-four that were a little shorter and lighter for the girls. Clearly Lucivar had indulged in a flight of optimism to think there would be that many who would get up this early in order to sweat and earn bruises.

Mikal was next, followed by a handful of Scelties.

"You all sit over there and watch," Mikal said. "And no chewing on sparring sticks or arrows. If you do that, you won't be allowed to herd anything for a whole day."

"Is that a serious punishment?" Raine asked Daemonar, coming up close enough to, he hoped, not be heard.

Daemonar nodded. "For a Sceltie? Oh, yeah. Just wait until the girls start spending too much time in the bathroom getting ready for class and get nipped in the shower."

Raine turned away and cleared his throat. Loudly.

Two of the younger instructors came in next. One had been at the Amdarh school. Daemonar didn't know where Uncle Daemon had found the other Warlord.

Weston and Holt came in together. At least with Weston present, there was one other man experienced in fighting, even if the sparring sticks were unfamiliar to the Dhemlan sword and shield, which was Weston's new position.

And then . . .

"Uncle Daemon?"

The black cotton trousers were loose and designed for movement. The sleeveless cotton shirt . . . Well, laborers wore shirts like that, and it wasn't that different from the clothing Mikal, Raine, and Holt were wearing, but on his uncle the simple clothes looked more like a uniform of battle—and they weren't new.

"I promised your father." The sound was more growl than words.

Oh, he would have loved to have eavesdropped on *that* discussion. And he wondered if the demanded promise, and Uncle Daemon's compliance, had to do with Witch now taking on a form tangible enough to touch—and hug.

*"Don't think for a moment that I don't need you, because I do,"* Lucivar had said the night before Daemonar left Ebon Rih. *"But right now Daemon needs you more."*

Daemonar acknowledged each man, then said, "Let's form a circle, and I'll show you the moves we use in the warm-up for sparring with Eyrien sticks."

The men found a place in the circle. Daemon took the place on Daemonar's left, a subtle acknowledgment that, in this room, his nephew was the dominant male.

The family had scattered and was coming back together in a different pattern. But the triangle around the Queen of Ebon Askavi would hold, and all of Kaeleer would have swords and shields—and strong young Queens—because of them.

Smiling, Daemonar looked at the other men. "Shall we begin?"

# ACKNOWLEDGMENTS

My thanks to Blair Boone for continuing to be my first reader and for providing encouragement and feedback in the story's roughest stage; to Debra Dixon for being second reader; to Doranna Durgin for maintaining the Web site; to Adrienne Roehrich for running the official fan page and Ashley Laxton for running the Anne Bishop Fan Group and Spoiler Fan Group pages on Facebook; to Jennifer Crow for being a sounding board and sharing so many interesting bits of information; to Anne Sowards and Jennifer Jackson for the feedback that helps me write a better story; to all the publicity and marketing folks at PRH who help get the book into readers' hands; and to Pat Feidner for always being supportive and encouraging.

And a special thanks to all the people who let me know how much my stories helped them through difficult times. You're the reason I kept showing up at the writing desk to do what I do.

In this engrossing and gripping
fantasy set in the world of Anne Bishop's
*New York Times* bestselling Others series,
an inn owner and her friends must find a killer—
before it's too late....

# CROWBONES

*Crowbones will gitcha if you don't watch out!*

Deep in the territory controlled by the Others—shape-shifters, vampires, and even deadlier paranormal beings—Vicki DeVine has made a new life for herself running The Jumble, a rustic resort. When she decides to host a gathering of friends and guests for Trickster Night, at first everything is going well between the humans and the Others.

But then someone arrives dressed as Crowbones, the Crowgard bogeyman. When the impostor is killed along with a shape-shifting Crow, and the deaths are clearly connected, everyone fears that the real Crowbones may have come to The Jumble—and that could mean serious trouble.

To "encourage" humans to help them find some answers, the Elders and Elementals close all the roads, locking in suspects and victims alike. Now Vicki, human police chief Grimshaw, vampire lawyer Ilya Sanguinati, and their friends have to figure out who is manipulating events designed to pit humans against Others—and who may have put Vicki DeVine in the crosshairs of a powerful hunter.

*Available March 2022 from Ace*